DOCTORS

BOOKS BY ERICH SEGAL

NOVELS

Love Story
Oliver's Story
Man, Woman and Child
The Class
Doctors

FOR CHILDREN

Fairy Tale

ACADEMIC BOOKS

Roman Laughter: The Comedy of Plautus
Euripides: A Collection of Critical Essays (Ed.)
Plautus: Three Comedies (Ed. and Trans.)
The Oxford Readings in Greek Tragedy (Ed.)
Caesar Augustus: Seven Aspects (Co-ed.)
Plato's Dialogues (Ed.)

ERICH SEGAL

DOCTORS

BANTAM BOOKS
TORONTO · NEW YORK · LONDON · SYDNEY · AUCKLAND

PUBLISHER'S NOTE

This is a novel about fictional members of a Harvard Medical School class. All of the characters and incidents in this novel are creations of the author's imagination. Any resemblance to actual events or real people, living or dead, is entirely coincidental.

DOCTORS
A Bantam Book / August 1988

Grateful acknowledgment is made for permission to reprint lyrics from: "Fly Me to the Moon—In Other Words," words and music by Bart Howard. TRO- © copyright 1954 (renewed 1982) by Hampshire House Publishing Corp. New York. "Everything is Coming Up Roses" by Stephen Sondheim and Jule Styne. Copyright © 1957 by Norbeth Productions Inc. and Stephen Sondheim. All rights administered by Chappell and Co. International copyright secured. All rights reserved. Used by permission.

Library of Congress Cataloging-in-Publication Data

Segal, Erich, 1937–
    Doctors / Erich Segal.
    p. cm.
    ISBN 0-553-05294-2
    I. Title.
    PS3569.E4D64 1988
    813'.54—dc19   88-14547
                                              CIP

Published simultaneously in the United States and Canada

PRINTED IN THE UNITED STATES OF AMERICA

FG 0 9 8 7 6 5 4 3 2 1

For Karen and Francesca

"The most fundamental principle of Medicine is love."
PARACELSUS (1493–1541)
The Great Art of Surgery

"We have turned doctors into gods and worship their deity by offering up our bodies and our souls—not to mention our worldly goods.

"And yet paradoxically, they are the most vulnerable of human beings. Their suicide rate is eight times the national average. Their percentage of drug addiction is *one hundred* times higher.

"And because they are painfully aware that they cannot live up to our expectations, their anguish is unquantifiably intense. They have aptly been called 'wounded healers.' "

BARNEY LIVINGSTON, M.D.
Doctors

". . . the United States loses the equivalent of seven medical-school graduating classes each year to drug addiction, alcoholism, and suicide."

DAVID HILFIKER, M.D.
Healing the Wounds

PROLOGUE

With a single exception they were all white. And with five exceptions all male.

Some were brilliant bordering on genius. Others, genius bordering on madness. One had played a cello recital at Carnegie Hall, another had played a year of professional basketball. Six had written novels, two of which had actually been published. One was a lapsed priest. One was a graduate of reform school. All were scared to death.

What had brought them together on this bright September morning in 1958 was their common status as first-year students at Harvard Medical School. They had gathered in Room D to hear a welcoming address by Dean Courtney Holmes.

His features could have come straight from a Roman coin. And his demeanor gave the impression that he had been born with a gold watch and chain instead of an umbilical cord.

He did not have to call for quiet. He merely smiled and the spectators hushed.

"Gentlemen," he began, "you are collectively embarking on a great voyage to the frontiers of medical knowledge—which is where you will begin your own individual explorations in the yet-uncharted territory of suffering and disease. Someone sitting in this room may find a cure for leukemia, diabetes, systemic lupus erythematosus and the deadly hydra-headed carcinomas . . ."

He took a perfectly timed dramatic pause. And with a sparkle in his pale blue eyes he added, "Perhaps even the common cold."

There was appreciative laughter.

Then the silver-haired dean lowered his head, perhaps to signify that he was deep in thought. The students waited in suspense.

When at last he looked up and began to speak again, his voice was softer, an octave lower.

"Let me conclude by disclosing a secret—as humbling for me to reveal as for you to hear."

He turned and wrote something on the blackboard behind him.

Two simple digits—the number twenty-six.

A buzz of bewilderment filled the room.

Holmes waited for quiet to return, drew breath, and then gazed straight into the spellbound auditorium.

"Gentlemen, I urge you to engrave this on the template of your memories: there are thousands of diseases in this world, but Medical Science only has an empirical cure for *twenty-six* of them. The rest is . . . guesswork."

And that was all.

With military posture and athletic grace, he strode off the podium and out of the room.

The crowd was too dazzled to applaud.

I

INNOCENCE

"They enter the new world naked,
cold, uncertain of all
save that they enter. . . .

"But now the stark dignity of
entrance— Still, the profound change
has come upon them: rooted, they
grip down and begin to awaken."

WILLIAM CARLOS WILLIAMS (1883–1963)
Pediatrician and poet

ONE

Barney Livingston was the first boy in Brooklyn to see Laura Castellano naked.

One August morning in the summer he turned five, he wandered into his backyard and was saluted by an unfamiliar voice.

"Hi."

He glanced toward the neighboring garden. Peering over the fence was a blond little girl who looked about his age. He felt a twinge of nostalgia for the previous occupants, who had included a terrific punchball player named Murray. And from what he'd heard, these new people didn't even have a *boy*.

Barney was therefore surprised when, after introducing herself, Laura suggested they play catch. He shrugged a sort of dubious okay, and went to get his Spauldeen.

When he returned a moment later clutching a small rubber ball, pink as Bazooka bubble gum, she was standing in the middle of his garden.

"How did you get here?" he asked.

"I climbed over the fence," she answered nonchalantly. "Okay, *vámonos,* throw me a high one."

Understandably, Barney was slightly off balance and bobbled the ball that Laura had deftly caught and vigorously tossed back. For he was still disconcerted by the fact that Murray had been *seven* years old and still had needed assistance to get over the fence, whereas this Laura had apparently vaulted it with ease.

After an energetic half hour, Barney decided that Laura had satisfactorily filled Murray's shoes (sneakers, actually). He reached into his pocket and produced a pack of cigarettes labeled "Lucky Stripe," and offered one to her.

"No, thanks," she responded, "my father says I have an allergy to chocolate."

"What's an allergy?"

"I'm not sure," she confessed. "We'd better ask my *papacito*. He's a doctor."

And then the inspiration struck her. "Hey, why don't we play Doctor and Patient."

"How does that go?"

"Well, first I 'esamen' you, then you 'esamen' me."

"Sounds kinda boring."

"We would have to take our clothes off—"

"Yeah?" Maybe this could be interesting after all.

Office hours were held beneath a venerable oak tree in the far corner of the Livingston garden. Laura instructed Barney to remove his striped polo shirt so she could establish that her patient's chest was sound. This was accomplished by means of an imaginary stethoscope.

"Now take off your pants."

"Why?"

"Come on, Barney, play the game!"

With some reluctance, he stepped out of his blue shorts and stood there in his underpants, beginning to feel silly.

"Take that off, too," the young physician ordered.

Barney glanced furtively over his shoulder to see if anyone might be watching from the house and then removed his final garment.

Laura looked him over carefully, giving special attention to the tiny pendant between his legs.

"That's my faucet," he explained with a touch of pride.

"It looks more like a penis," she replied with clinical detachment. "Anyhow, you're okay. You can get dressed."

As he eagerly obliged, Laura inquired, "Want to play something else now?"

"No fair—now it's *my* turn to be the doctor."

"Okay."

In an instant she had disrobed completely.

"Wow, Laura—what happened to your . . . you know . . ."

"I don't have one," she answered somewhat wistfully.

"Oh gee, why not?"

At this moment a strident voice interrupted the consultation.

"Baaar-ney! Where are you?"

It was his mother at the back door. He hastily excused himself and peered around the tree trunk. "I'm here, Mom."

"What are you doing?"

"Playing—with someone."

"Who?"

"A girl called Laura from next door."

"Oh, the new family. Ask her if she wants cookies and milk."

An impish face popped out from its arboreal concealment. "What kind of cookies?" Laura asked cheerfully.

"Oreos and Fig Newtons," Mrs. Livingston said, smiling. "My, aren't you a sweet little girl."

Theirs was a childhood paradise called Brooklyn, filled with joyous sounds: the clang of trolleys blending with the tinkle of the bells from the Good Humor Man's chariot of frozen fantasies. And most of all, the laughter of the children playing stickball, punchball—even hockey games on roller skates—right in the streets.

The Brooklyn Dodgers weren't just a baseball team, they were a cast of characters—a Duke, a Pee Wee, and a Preacher pitching on the mound. They even had a guy who could run faster than you said his name: Jack Robinson.

They gave their hearts for Brooklyn.

So who cared if they could never beat the New York Yankees?

It was 1942 and Americans were waging war on three fronts: in Europe against the Nazis, in the Pacific against the hordes of Tojo, and at home against the OPA. This was the body President Roosevelt established to ration the civilian supply of essential items to make sure the GIs had the best of everything.

Thus while Field Marshal Montgomery was engaging Rommel at El Alamein, and Major General Jimmy Doolittle was bombing Tokyo, back in Brooklyn Estelle Livingston was battling to get extra meat stamps to ensure the health and growth of her two sons.

Her husband, Harold, had been called up one year earlier. A high school Latin teacher, he was now at a military base in California learning Japanese. All he could tell his family was that he was in something called "Intelligence." That was very appropriate, Estelle explained to her two young sons, since their father was, in fact, very, very intelligent.

For some unexplained reason, Laura's father, Dr. Luis Castellano, had not been drafted at all.

"Is Laura nice, Barney?" Estelle asked as she tried to coax yet another forkful of Spam into her elder son's mouth.

"Yeah, she's okay for a girl. I mean, she can even catch a ball. Talks kinda funny, though."

"That's because the Castellanos are from Spain, dear. They had to run away."

"Why?"

"Because the bad people called Fascists didn't like them. That's why Daddy is in the Army. To fight the Fascists."

"Does Daddy have a gun?"

"I don't know. But I'm sure if he needs one, President Roosevelt will see that he gets it."

"Good—then he can shoot all the bad guys in the penis."

A librarian by profession, Estelle was all in favor of enriching her son's vocabulary. But she was taken aback by his newest verbal acquisition.

"Who told you about penises, dear?" she asked as matter-of-factly as she could.

"Laura. Her dad's a doctor. She doesn't have one, though."

"What, dear?"

"Laura doesn't have a penis. At first I didn't believe her, but she showed me."

Estelle was at a loss for words. She merely stirred young Warren's cereal and wondered how much *he* already knew.

With time, Barney and Laura went on to better games. Like Cowboys and Indians or GIs and Jerries (or Japs), democratically changing from goodies to baddies with each passing summer day.

A year went by. The Allied troops were now invading Italy and the Yanks in the Pacific were reconquering the Solomon Islands. Late one night Barney's brother, Warren, woke up screaming, with a fever of a hundred and three. Fearing the worst—the dreaded summer scourge, infantile paralysis—Estelle quickly wrapped the perspiring little boy in a bath towel and carried him down the front steps and over to Dr. Castellano. Barney, confused and frightened, followed a step behind.

Luis was still awake, reading a medical journal in his cluttered little study, and rushed to wash before beginning an examination. His big hairy hands were surprisingly swift and gentle. Barney watched in awe as the doctor looked down Warren's throat, then listened to his chest, all the while trying to calm the sick child.

"Is okay," he kept whispering, "just breathe in and out for me, yes *niño?*" Meanwhile, Inez Castellano hurried to fetch cold water and a sponge.

Estelle stood mute with terror, Barney clinging to the folds of her flowered bathrobe. She finally found the courage to ask, "Is it—you know . . . ?"

"*Cálmate,* Estella, is not polio. Look at the scarlatiniform eruption on his chest—and especially the enlarged red papillae on his tongue. Is called 'strawberry tongue.' The boy has scarlet fever."

"But that's still serious—"

"Yes, so we must get someone to prescribe a sulfa drug like Prontosil."

"Can't you—?"

Clenching his teeth, Luis replied, "I am not permitted to write prescriptions. I have no license to practice in this country. Anyway, *vámonos.* Barney will stay here while we take a taxi to the hospital."

During the cab ride, Luis held little Warren, dabbing his neck and forehead with a sponge. Estelle was reassured by his confident manner yet still puzzled by what he had told her.

"But Luis, I thought you *were* a doctor. I mean, you work at the hospital, don't you?"

"In the laboratory—doing blood and urine tests." He paused and then added, "In my country I *was* a physician—I think a good one. Five years ago when we first came, I studied English like a crazy man, reread all the textbooks, and passed the examinations. But still the State Board refused to license me. Apparently, to them I am a dangerous alien. I belonged to the wrong party in Spain."

"But you were fighting against the Fascists."

"Yes, but I was a Socialist—something also *sospechoso* in America."

"That's outrageous."

"*Bueno*—it could be worse."

"I don't see how."

"I could have been caught by Franco."

At the hospital, Luis's diagnosis was immediately confirmed and Warren given the medication he suggested. Nurses then bathed him with alcohol-soaked sponges to bring down his fever. By 5:30 A.M., he was pronounced well enough to go home. Luis escorted Estelle and the boy to a cab.

"Aren't you coming?" she asked.

"No. *No vale la pena.* I am due in the lab at seven. I will just stay
here and try to take a nap in an on-call room."

"How did I get in my own bed, Mom?"

"Well, darling, when we got home it was very late and you were
asleep on the Castellanos' couch, so Inez and I carried you and Warren
back."

"Is Warren okay?" Barney had not yet seen his brother.

Estelle nodded. "Thank God for Dr. Castellano. We're very lucky to
have him as our neighbor."

For a split second Barney felt a pang of envy. Laura's father was
home. Sometimes he missed his own dad so much it really hurt.

He vividly remembered the day his father had left. Harold had
picked him up and hugged him so closely he could smell the cigarette
smoke on his breath. Often now just watching someone light up a cigarette
made Barney feel lonely.

And yet there was one small source of consolation: A small rectangular flag bearing a blue star in a white field trimmed with red hung
proudly in the Livingstons' front window. This told every passerby that
their family had a member out there fighting for his country (some
households had banners with two, and even three stars).

Late one December afternoon, as the brothers were returning
from the candy store with a nickel's worth of Tootsie Rolls, Warren
noticed something surprising in Mr. and Mrs. Cahn's front window—a
flag that bore a star of gold.

"Mom, how come theirs is so fancy?" Warren complained as they
were having dinner.

Estelle hesitated for a moment, and then answered quietly, "Because
their son was . . . especially courageous."

"Do you think Dad will win a star like that one day?"

Though she could feel her face turn pale, Estelle endeavored to
answer matter-of-factly, "You never know about these things, darling.
Now come on, eat your broccoli."

After she had put the boys to bed, it suddenly struck her that Barney
had been silent through that entire conversation. Had he perhaps understood that Arthur, the Cahns' only son, had been killed in action?

Later, sitting alone at the kitchen table, doing her best to pretend
her cup of Postum was real Brazilian coffee, Estelle kept reminding
herself of Harold's frequent protestations that he would be in no danger.
("Translators don't get shot at, hon.") But then didn't security rules
forbid him from disclosing exactly where he was—and what he was doing?

A day never passed without some family in Brooklyn receiving one of those dreaded telegrams.

Then she heard her older son's voice. It was affectionate and reassuring.

"Please don't worry, Mom. He's gonna come back."

There he stood in his Mickey Mouse pajamas, all of six and a half years old, yet taking the initiative and trying to console his mother. She looked up with a smile.

"How could you tell what I was thinking?" she inquired.

"Everybody in school knows about Artie Cahn. I even saw one of the teachers crying. I didn't say anything because I thought it would've scared Warren. But Dad'll be all right, I promise."

"What makes you so certain?" she asked.

He shrugged and confessed, "I don't know. But worrying would make you sadder."

"You're right, Barney," she said, hugging him tightly.

At which point, her comforter suddenly changed the subject.

"Would it be okay if I had a cookie, Mom?"

1944 was a banner year. Rome and Paris were liberated, and FDR was elected to an unprecedented fourth term. Some time after the Americans retook Guam. Harold Livingston telephoned his family all the way from California to announce that he was being sent overseas. He couldn't specify where, only that it would be to help interrogate Japanese prisoners of war. His next communication would be by V-mail—those barely legible miniature letters, photographed on microfilm and printed on slimy gray paper.

The year was also a milestone for Luis Castellano. The State Medical Board reversed its decision and declared the Spanish refugee fit to practice medicine in the United States of America.

Though feeling pleased and vindicated, Luis knew they were moved not merely by the merits of his case, but by the fact that nearly every able-bodied doctor had been conscripted by the military. He and Inez quickly transformed their front ground-floor bedroom into an examination room. He received a loan from The Dime Savings Bank to buy a fluoroscope machine.

"What's that for, *Papacito*?" three-year-old Isobel asked her father as the quartet of young spectators watched the apparatus being installed.

"I know," Barney volunteered, "it's for looking inside of people, isn't it, Dr. Castellano?"

"You are right, my boy," he nodded, patting Barney on the head, "but good physicians have already a machine for looking at their patients' insides."

He then pointed to his temple. "The brain is still the greatest diagnostic tool a man can use."

Luis's reputation—and his practice—quickly grew. King's County offered him hospital privileges. Now he could send specimens to the laboratory where formerly he washed test tubes.

Sometimes, as a special treat, the children were allowed to visit his medical sanctum. Barney and Laura could touch some of the instruments and peer into their younger siblings' ears with the otoscope, provided *they* would then allow Warren and Isobel to listen to their chests with a stethoscope.

They had almost become a single family. Estelle Livingston was especially grateful. The only other relative she had was her mother, who—when other babysitters were not available—would take the subway from Queens to stay with Warren while Estelle worked in the library.

But she knew that boys needed a masculine figure in their lives and understood why Barney and Warren had grown to worship the rugged bearlike physician. For his part, Luis seemed to revel in the acquisition of two "sons."

Estelle and Inez grew to be good friends. They did air-raid warden duty together every Tuesday night, patrolling the silent, shadowy streets making sure every household had its lights out. And periodically glancing skyward for a trace of enemy bombers.

The soft darkness seemed to make Inez more comfortable—and freer with her thoughts.

Once when Estelle casually inquired whether Inez minded the lack of sleep, she was surprised to hear her respond, "No, it reminds me of the good old days. The only difference is that now I do not have my rifle."

"You actually fought?"

"Yes, *amiga,* and I wasn't the only woman. Because Franco had not only all his Spanish troops, but also *regulares*—mercenaries from Morocco that he paid to do his dirty work.

"Our only hope was to attack and run. There were so many of those butchers. And I am proud to say I hit a few of them."

She then realized that her friend was taken aback.

"Try to understand," Inez continued, "those bastards slaughtered children."

"Well, yes, I see your point. . . ." Estelle responded haltingly, while struggling to accept the reality that the gentle-voiced woman by her side had actually killed another human being.

Ironically, Inez's parents both had been staunch right-wing supporters not merely of Franco, but of Opus Dei—the church within a church—
which sided with the dictator. When their only daughter, fired with
socialist idealism, left to join a Republican militia unit, they had cursed
and disowned her.

"I had no one in the world—except my rifle and The Cause. So, in a
way, that bullet brought me luck."

What bullet? Estelle wondered to herself. But it soon became clear.

During the siege of Málaga, Inez and half a dozen other loyalists
were ambushed on their way to Puerta Real. When she regained consciousness, she was staring into the unshaven face of a heavyset young
doctor who introduced himself as "Comrade Luis."

"Even then he was a character. Of course we had no uniforms, but
Luis seemed to go out of his way to look like a peasant." She laughed.
"But I don't think he ever stopped working. There were so many wounded.
As soon as I could stand, I started helping him. Through all the long
hours, he never lost his sense of humor. In fact, that was about all we
could take with us when we fled. We barely got across before they closed
the French border."

When school started, Barney and Laura were in the same third
grade class at P.S. 148. Paradoxically, being thrown into a group
of thirty other children brought the two closer than ever. Laura
discovered what a valuable friend she had in Barney. For he could already
read.

In fact, what had originally drawn Estelle and Harold Livingston
together was their mutual love of books. And ever since his third birthday, each parent had taken turns giving Barney reading lessons. As a
reward they would read aloud to him stories from *Bullfinch's Mythology*
or poems from the *Child's Garden of Verses*. Their psychology worked.
Barney's appetite for books was almost as voracious as his craving for
Nabisco Vanilla Wafers.

As a result, he was now able to sit on their front stoop and conduct
Laura through the complexities of immortal classics like *See Spot Run*.

But in due course, Barney exacted reciprocity.

On his seventh birthday his mother gave him a basketball kit,
complete with backboard, rim, and a real net that went *swish* when you
sank a good one. The night before the gala day, Luis Castellano had
risked life and limb to nail it—at the official ten feet—to the Livingstons'
oak tree.

Barney let out a whoop of delight and proclaimed, "Laura, you gotta help me practice—you owe me."

Her assistance entailed acting as enemy defenseman and trying to block Barney's shots at the hoop. To his amazement, Laura was almost too good at it. She scored nearly as many baskets as Barney. And though he continued to grow tall, she continued to grow taller.

Germany capitulated on May seventh, 1945, and by the end of the summer Japan had surrendered as well. The joy was nowhere more intense than in the Livingston household on Lincoln Place where Barney, Warren, and Estelle paraded around the kitchen table singing, "When Daddy comes marching home again." It had been more than three years since they had seen him.

Harold Livingston came home. But not at a march. In fact, his gait was slow and at times uncertain.

Constantly pushed and jostled by noisy, excited crowds of other wives and children, Estelle and the two boys waited breathlessly as the train pulled in. Before it even stopped, some of the GIs leaped onto the platform and began to run full tilt toward their loved ones.

Barney stood on tiptoe. But he could not see a soldier who looked familiar enough to be the dad he had been seeing in his dreams.

Suddenly his mother gave a little shout, "Oh, there he is!" She waved at someone far down the platform. Barney looked where she had pointed but saw no one. That is, no one who corresponded to his memory of Harold Livingston.

He saw an ordinary man of ordinary size with hair receding from his forehead. Someone pallid, thin, and tired-looking.

She's wrong, he thought, this can't be Dad. It can't be.

Estelle no longer could contain herself. She cried out, "Harold!" and rushed forward to embrace him.

Barney stood there holding Warren's hand and watched, realizing that never before had Momma left them on their own like this.

"Is that our Daddy?" little Warren asked.

"It must be," Barney answered, still a bit confused.

"I thought you said that he was bigger than Dr. Castellano."

Barney almost said, *I* thought so too.

And now they were together, all four of them, Estelle still arm in arm with her husband.

"Barney, Warren, how you two have grown!" Harold Livingston

said with pride and put his arms around his older son. Barney recognized the once-familiar scent of cigarette smoke.

Somehow, despite the mob outside, they found a taxi—with a very patriotic driver.

"Welcome home, GI Joe," he proclaimed. "Hey—we really showed them Krauts, didn't we?" the cabbie crowed.

"My husband served in the Pacific," Estelle proudly corrected him.

"Oh, Nazis, Japs—what's the difference? They're all a bunch of lousy bums. Tell your husband he did good."

"Did you get to kill anybody?" Warren asked hopefully.

Harold answered slowly. "No, son. I just helped translate when we were interrogating prisoners. . . ." His voice trailed off.

"Don't be so modest, let your kids be proud. You obviously saw enough action to win that Purple Heart. Ya get hurt bad, buddy?"

Barney and Warren looked at each other saucer-eyed as Harold brushed off any hint of heroism.

"It wasn't much. Just an artillery shell that landed pretty near our tent. For a while there I was a little shaky, but I'm a hundred percent now. I should have taken these darn things off before I got here. The important thing is that we're all together again."

But his protestation only confirmed what Estelle had sensed the moment she had seen him on the railroad platform. He was a sick man.

Luis Castellano was waiting at his front window when the taxi pulled up outside the Livingston house. In an instant, he and his family were on the street, Luis enveloping Harold in his big bearlike embrace. "I've been talking to your picture on the mantelpiece for years," he explained. "I feel like you are my long-lost brother!"

It was a night that burned in Barney's memory forever. Though he was down the corridor from the closed door of his parents' bedroom, he still could hear their voices.

His mother seemed to be crying a great deal, and in tones oscillating between anger and despair kept asking, "Can't you *explain*, Harold? What exactly is a 'thirty percent disability'?"

His father seemed to be trying to reassure her. "It's nothing, hon. I swear there's nothing to worry about."

Then all was quiet. There was no noise at *all* from his parents' bedroom. Barney simply gazed down the hall at their door, wondering.

*   *   *

At breakfast Barney scanned his parents' faces, but could decipher no clue as to what had occurred the previous evening. And watching his mother fuss over someone who was almost a stranger gave him funny feelings that he could not understand. He left early for Laura's house so they could have plenty of time to talk on the way to school.

But as soon as they were alone, he confided to her, "I'm scared. Something's—I don't know—different about my father. I think maybe he's sick."

"Yes, I know."

"You *know*?"

"As soon as we got home last night, Papa took my mother into his office and started explaining to her about something called *'neurosis de guerra.'*"

"What's that in English?" Barney asked anxiously.

"I don't even know what it is in Spanish, Barn," she confessed.

At four that afternoon, Estelle Livingston was seated at the circulation desk in the Grand Army Plaza branch of the Brooklyn Public Library when she looked up and saw Barney and Laura scanning the shelves of medical books. She invited them to her office in the back where they could talk privately.

"Please don't be worried," she said, trying to sound reassuring. "He wasn't hit by anything. It's just a mild case of shell shock. He was very near a big explosion and that sort of thing takes a while to get over. But he'll be back teaching again next term."

She took a deep breath and then asked, "Do you feel a little better now?"

Both children nodded mutely. And then quickly left.

That fall, as Estelle had promised, Harold Livingston returned to his pedagogical duties at Erasmus Hall. And as before, his students found him charming and witty. He could make even Caesar's *Gallic Wars* enjoyable. And he seemed to know all of Classical literature by heart.

And yet now and then he would forget to bring back groceries on his way home from school—even when Estelle stuck a list in the breast pocket of his jacket.

Ever since he had gotten his basketball hoop, Barney had dreamed of the day when he and his dad would play together.

During Harold's long absence, Barney had constantly badgered his mother for details about what his father was like "in the old days." Once he had heard Estelle reminisce about the summer before he was born. By sheer chance there had been a guest tennis tournament at the lakeside resort they had gone to in the White Mountains.

"Harold decided to give it a try—just as a lark. He'd been a wonderful player in his college days—though, of course, CCNY had no tennis team. Anyway, he borrowed a racket, waltzed onto the court, and the next thing I knew he was in the finals! The man who beat him was a PT instructor at the local college—and he said he was lucky that Harold had an off day. He even said that if Harold ever took it seriously he'd be another Bill Tilden. Can you imagine that?"

Barney didn't know who Bill Tilden was, but he could certainly imagine the man whose picture was on the mantelpiece, dressed in tennis whites, smashing a ball to smithereens. He dreamt so often of the day he could show Dad *his* sporting skills. And now at last the time was at hand.

"Have you seen the backboard Dr. Castellano put up on the tree?" he asked his father casually one Saturday, as a kind of overture.

"Yes," Harold answered, "looks very professional."

"Want to shoot some baskets with me and Warren?"

Harold sighed and answered gently, "I don't think I've got the pep to keep up with two dynamos like you. But I'll come and watch."

Barney and Warren raced to put on their sneakers and then dribbled out toward the "court."

Anxious to display his prowess before his father, Barney stopped fifteen feet from the basket, jumped, and shot the ball. To his chagrin, it missed the backboard completely. He quickly whirled and explained, "That was just warming up, Dad."

Leaning on the back door, Harold Livingston nodded, took a long puff of his cigarette, and smiled.

Barney and Warren barely had the chance to sink a few lay-ups ("Good fast break, huh, Dad?") when an irate voice called from across the fence.

"Hey, what the heck's going on, you guys? How come you're playing without me?"

Darn, it was Laura. Why'd she have to butt in?

"Sorry," Barney apologized. "It's a kinda rough game today."

"Who are you kidding?" she retorted. (By now she had bounded over the fence.) "I can elbow hard as you any day."

At this point Harold called out, "Be polite, Barney. If Laura wants to, let her try."

But his admonition was a split second too late, for Laura had already stolen the ball from Barney's grip and was dribbling past Warren to sink a basket off the backboard. Then, after the three players took turns shooting, Laura called out, "Why don't you play with us, Mr. Livingston, then we could have an actual half-court game."

"That's very kind of you, Laura. But I'm a bit tuckered out. I'd better take a little nap."

A look of disappointment crossed Barney's face.

Laura glanced at him and understood what he was feeling.

He turned slowly toward her and their eyes met. And from that moment on they knew they could read each other's thoughts.

But whenever the entire Livingston clan went over for dinner, Barney would marvel at Luis's gift for making Harold animated—even talkative. The doctor was a man of Falstaffian appetites—for food, for wine, and most of all for knowledge.

And his never-ending fount of questions appealed to the teacher in Harold, who delighted Luis with anecdotes from the history of Roman *Hispania*—especially with the revelations that some of the Empire's greatest writers were of Spanish origin—like Seneca, the tragedian, born in Córdoba.

"Inez, you hear that? The great Seneca was one of ours!" And then he turned to his instructor and melodramatically demanded, "Now Harold, if you could only tell me that *Shakespeare* was also Spanish!"

Laura was delighted to hear Mr. Livingston explain why she, quite unlike the stereotyped Latin *chiquitas,* had light blond hair: their family doubtless had Celtic ancestors who migrated to the Iberian Peninsula.

When the two fathers had retired to Luis's study and the mothers to the kitchen, Laura said to Barney, "Gosh, I love your dad. He knows everything."

He nodded, but thought to himself, Yeah, but I wish he'd talk to *me* more often.

Every Saturday afternoon, Barney's mom and dad sat religiously by the radio, waiting for the soft-spoken Milton Cross to announce what the mighty voices of the Metropolitan Opera would be singing that day. Meanwhile, Luis and Inez would take little Isobel for a stroll in Prospect Park.

This left Laura, Barney, and Warren free to attend the children's matinee at the Savoy Theater (admission a quarter, plus a nickel for popcorn).

It was a time when movies were not merely frivolous entertainment, but moral lessons on how good Americans should live. Randolph Scott on his white horse, riding bravely into *Badman's Territory* to save the good; John Wayne *Tall in the Saddle,* riding *his* white horse to tame—it seemed almost single-handedly—the savage lands out West.

In a more tropical setting, Johnny Weissmuller as Tarzan showed every kid the value of swimming lessons, especially if they were caught in crocodile-infested waters.

But their hero of heroes was Gary Cooper. Partly because he was built like a basketball star, and partly because he had helped the Spanish guerrillas in *For Whom the Bell Tolls.* But most of all because he was a courageous physician in *The Story of Dr. Wassell.* As they emerged bleary-eyed from having sat through two complete showings of the movie, Barney and Laura concluded that his was the noblest profession of all.

Of course, they had an equally admirable doctor considerably closer to home. Luis Castellano may not have been as tall as Coop, but in his own way he was a paragon for both his daughter and for Barney (who often daydreamed that his neighbor was somehow his father, too).

Luis was flattered to learn of Barney's ambition, but was quietly indulgent of what he considered a mere flight of fancy on his daughter's part. He was certain she would outgrow this quixotic daydream, get married, and have lots of *niños.*

But he was mistaken.

Especially after Isobel died.

TWO

It was sudden as summer lightning. And like the thunderclap that follows, grief came only later.

Polio was on the rampage that year. The Angel of Death seemed to be stalking every street in the city. Most Brooklyn parents who could afford it were sending their children to the rural safety of places like Spring Valley.

Estelle and Harold had already rented a bungalow on the Jersey shore for the month of August. But Luis insisted upon staying where he was needed, and Inez did not want him to fight the battle on his own. The Livingstons offered to take the girls, and Luis gratefully responded that he and Inez would seriously consider it.

Perhaps he had been too preoccupied with virulent cases of poliomyelitis to recognize that his own younger daughter was showing some of the symptoms. But how could he not have noticed she was feverish—and breathing rapidly? Perhaps because the little girl never once complained of feeling sick. Only when he found her unconscious one morning did Luis realize to his horror what was wrong.

It was respiratory polio, the virus ferociously attacking the upper part of the spinal cord. Isobel could not breathe even with the help of an iron lung. She was dead before nightfall.

Luis was wild with self-recrimination. He was a doctor, dammit, a doctor! He should have been able to save his own daughter!

Laura refused to go to sleep. She was afraid that if she closed her eyes she too would not wake. Barney kept her company in a nightlong vigil of silent mourning as she sat in the suffocating heat of their living room, her insides bruised and aching.

At one point he whispered, "Laura, it's not your fault."

She seemed not to hear him. Her eyes remained unfocused.

"Shut up, Barney," she retorted, "you don't know what you're talking about."

But inwardly she was grateful—and relieved—that he had put into words her feelings of guilt for being alive when her sister was dead.

Estelle was the only one capable of making the funeral arrangements. She assumed that the Castellanos would want a Catholic ceremony, and so contacted Father Hennessey at St. Gregory's. But the moment she announced the plans, Luis bellowed, "No priest, no priest—not unless he can tell me why God took my little girl!" Estelle dutifully called Father Hennessey to say he would not be needed after all.

Then Harold came over and tried to persuade the Castellanos that something had to be said. They could not simply part with their daughter and say nothing. Inez looked at her husband, for she knew it was up to him. He lowered his head and then mumbled, "Okay, Harold, you're the scholar, you talk. Only I forbid you to mention the name of God."

The two families watched in the unpitying August sun as the little casket was lowered into the ground. Barney reached out and took Laura's hand. She squeezed it tightly as if it could close off her tears. And as they stood around the grave, Harold Livingston read a few lines from a poem by Ben Jonson about the death of a brave Spanish infant.

> *A lily of a day*
> *Is fairer far in May,*
> *Although it fall and die that night,*
> *It was the plant and flower of light.*
> *In small proportions we just beauties see,*
> *And in short measures life may perfect be.*

He raised his head from the book and inquired, "Would anyone else like to say something?"

Finally, from the abyss in Luis Castellano's soul came the barely audible words, *"Adios, niña."*

They drove homeward, all the car windows open in the vain hope that a gust of air would relieve the intolerable heaviness. Inez kept repeating in soft, plaintive tones, *"Yo no sé que hacer"*—I don't know what to do.

At a loss for words, Estelle suddenly heard herself say, "My mother came over from Queens. She's preparing supper for all of us."

The ride continued in silence.

As they were crossing the Triborough Bridge, Luis Castellano said to his friend, "Do you like whiskey, Harold?"

"Uh—well, yes. Of course."

"I have two bottles a patient gave me for Christmas. In the war, we sometimes used it as anesthetic. I would be grateful if you joined me, amigo."

Laura was back in her own home, but she still could not go to sleep. Nor would she talk, although Barney sat faithfully nearby. Her mother and Estelle were upstairs in Isobel's old room doing something. Taking off the sheets? Packing her clothes? Maybe even just holding her dead sister's dolls—as if something of her living spirit still clung to them.

Now and then, Laura could perceive from above the almost feral sounds of Inez's grief. But it was mostly the noise of raucous male laughter that filled the house. Harold and Luis were in his study getting very very drunk, Luis bellowing at Harold to join some of the "good old songs—like *Francisco Franco nos quiere gobernar . . .*"

Barney could not help feeling frightened. He had never heard Luis—and certainly not his father—so out of control.

"I guess they're really gonna finish the whole two bottles, huh, Laura?"

"I don't care . . ." She paused a moment and then said, "All I can think of is the times I was mean to her. Last Sunday I yelled and called her a stupid little brat. *Last Sunday!*"

Barney leaned forward and whispered, "You had no way of knowing."

Then she began to sob.

"I should be punished. I should be the one who's dead."

Without a word Barney rose, walked over to where she was sitting, and put his hand gently on her shoulder.

Throughout the rest of that hot, stifling summer, Laura, Barney, and Warren played endless games of basketball, relieved only by their Saturday visits to the air-conditioned Savoy. And Barney did not remember hearing Laura mention her sister's name even once. Until the first day of school when the three of them were walking toward P.S. 148.

"Isobel was supposed to start first grade," she said matter-of-factly.

"Yeah," said Barney. And Warren could but echo, "Yeah."

*   *   *

The death of a child is never a finality. For she lives vividly on in her parents' minds. And the ache of loss increases with each passing year—as birthday after birthday brings new haunting, agonizing thoughts: "She would have been ten next week. She would have loved seeing the circus. . . ."

And thus Isobel never left the Castellano household. The anguish of her absence was a constant presence.

Laura watched with mounting anxiety as her parents moved in different spiritual directions, leaving her abandoned in a loveless vacuum. Each of them sought relief in prayer: Inez for eternity and Luis for oblivion.

Inez began her pilgrimage to reconversion by reading and rereading Saint John of the Cross, the mystical poet who could put the ineffable into words: *"Vivo sin vivir en mí"*—I live without really being alive; *"muero porque no muero"*—I die because I am not dying.

She who, as a young rebel, had denounced the church because it had supported Franco's Fascists, now sought shelter in its all-forgiving sanctuary. For it alone could offer explanation of why her daughter had to die. The local priest was more than generous in reinforcing Inez's own conviction that she had sinned against the Lord and this had been her punishment.

In a certain sense, Luis was also seeking God. But to confront Him with his anger. How *dare* You take my little daughter? he railed in his imagination. And then, when his nightly drinking liberated what few inhibitions he had left, he spoke aloud, shaking his clenched fist at the Almighty in savage fury.

As a doctor he had always felt alone, despite the confident facade he assumed because his patients needed it. Now he felt that he was shipwrecked in a life that had no meaning. And the pain of isolation could be assuaged only by a nightly dose of analgesic—alcohol.

Even when on Saturdays the elder Castellanos went off for walks in the park, he was brooding, she silent, together only in their separateness. Laura gladly joined Barney in the literary sessions, newly established by Estelle.

Each month, Estelle would choose a book that they would read aloud together and discuss after breakfast on Saturdays. The *Iliad* shared pride of place with masterpieces like *The Last of the Mohicans,* and bards like Walt Whitman—he a former Brooklyn resident!

Harold would sit and smoke, listening quietly, sometimes nodding in approval if Barney or Laura made a particularly clever observation. Warren was still young enough to be allowed to stay outside and play basketball. But he soon grew jealous of his sibling's seminars and insisted upon being permitted to sit in.

Life at P.S. 148 went on uneventfully. Barney and Laura did a lot of their studying together, so it was not surprising that they ended up with almost identical grades. Neither, however, excelled in deportment. Indeed, at one point their harried teacher, Miss Einhorn, was driven to write a letter to their parents complaining of their unruliness in the playground and whispering—most often to each other—during class. Laura was once taken to task for throwing a spitball at Herbie Katz.

Barney was the class "wheel." He seemed to be a born leader. Laura was intensely jealous that she could never join the basketball games during recess despite Barney's intercession on her behalf. The mores of the time dictated that girls play only with girls. And worse, she was not favored with the friendship of many girls, since she was skinny, gawky— and much too tall. Indeed, to Barney's chagrin (and her own), she was the tallest person in the entire class. She had broken the five-foot barrier before he did, passed five-one, and there seemed to be no end in sight.

Her moments of solace were rare, but a few were memorable. Like the episode in later years dubbed "High Noon at the Playground."

It was in fact about 4 P.M. on a chill November Saturday. Warren, Barney, and Laura had left the movies early—there had been too much Maureen O'Hara and not enough Errol Flynn. As they passed the schoolyard, a three-on-three half-court basketball game was in progress. After a quick exchange of glances, Barney stepped forward and delivered the customary challenge, "We'll take winners."

But one player objected, "But there's only two of youse."

Barney pointed to his teammates as he counted, "One-two-*three*."

"Come on, buster, we don't play with *girls*."

"She's not just a girl."

"You're right—she's flat as a boy! But no dice—she's still wearing a skirt."

"You want a broken puss, buddy?" Laura asked menacingly.

"Aw, yer mother sucks eggs, girlie."

In an instant, Barney had knocked the offender onto the ground and was twisting his arm painfully behind his back.

"Ow, shit, stop!" he pleaded, "I give, I give—youse guys get winners!"

They did not lose a single game. As the trio strode homeward, Barney slapped Laura fraternally on the back. "Good game, Castellano. We really showed 'em."

"Sure did," Warren chimed in proudly.

But Laura was silent. All she could think of was those wounding words, "She's flat as a *boy*."

It happened almost like magic. During the weeks before Laura's twelfth birthday, her Fairy Godmother must have made frequent nocturnal visits, sprinkling her bedroom with invisible gifts for her endocrine system. Her breasts were growing. They were absolutely, definitely growing. All was suddenly right with the world again.

Luis noticed and smiled to himself. Inez noticed and had to suppress the urge to cry.

Barney Livingston noticed and casually remarked, "Hey, Castellano, you've got tits!"

But Barney was growing, too, and as proof there was the fuzz he liked to call his "beard" that sprouted on his face.

Estelle realized it was time for Harold to inform his elder son about the Facts of Life.

Harold was ambivalent—at once proud and afraid—recalling his own father's introductory lecture three decades earlier. It had *literally* been about the birds and bees, nothing more elevated on the phylogenetic scale. But now *he* would do it properly.

So when Barney arrived home from school a few days later, his father called him into his study.

"Son, I want to talk to you about a serious matter," he began.

He had carefully planned a Ciceronian exordium using Noah's Ark, leading up to a peroration on the male and female of the human species. But, experienced pedagogue though he was, he was unable to sustain the discussion long enough to reach mammalian reproduction.

Finally, in despair, he produced a slim volume, *How You Were Born*, and handed it to Barney, who showed it to Laura at fenceside later that evening.

"God, is this dumb!" she exclaimed, leafing rapidly through the pages. "Couldn't your father have just told you about how babies were made? Anyway, you've known for years."

"But there are a lot of other things I don't know about."

"Like what?"

Barney hesitated. It was one of those rare moments when he was conscious of being separated from Laura by gender.

They were growing up.

THREE

They were graduated from public school in June 1950, the year in which the Yankees once again won the World Series, North Korea invaded the South, and antihistamines became available "to cure the common cold" (at least everybody said so but the doctors).

That was also the summer Laura became beautiful.

Almost overnight, her bony shoulders disappeared—as if some supernatural Rodin had smoothed them while she slept. At the same time her high facial bones became more prominent. And her tomboyish gait acquired a sinuous, graceful sensuality. Yet while filling out perfectly in all the right places, she seemed to remain as slender as ever. Even Harold Livingston, who seldom lifted his face from a book, remarked one evening at dinner, "Laura's become so—I suppose 'statuesque' is the word."

"What about me?" Barney responded with slight indignation.

"I don't follow, son," said Harold.

"Haven't you noticed that I'm *taller* than Laura now?"

His father thought for a moment. "Yes, I suppose you are."

* * *

Midwood High School had the identical red-brick neo-Georgian style with the same proud tower as the halls of Brooklyn College, whose campus it adjoined.

On the wall of its impressive marble lobby was the school motto:

Enter to grow in body, mind and spirit.
Depart to serve better your God, your country
and your fellow man.

"Gosh, it really kind of inspires you, doesn't it, Barn?" Laura said, as they stood there looking in awe at those carved words.

"Yeah, I'm especially hoping to grow in body before the basketball tryouts."

Laura was conspicuous among the freshmen girls for both height and beauty. Very soon, juniors and seniors—some of them hotshot athletes and student leaders—were scampering up the "down" staircase to station themselves in Laura's path and petition for a date.

These were intoxicating days. Men had suddenly discovered her—boys, anyway. And their persistent attention helped her try to forget that she was once a disappointment to her sex. ("Not only am I ugly," she had confided to Barney, "I'm so tall everyone in the world can see it.")

Whereas during their first tentative days at Midwood Barney and Laura ate alone at a table in the cafeteria, she now was so surrounded by upper class suitors that he did not even attempt to join her. ("I'm afraid of getting trampled, Castellano.")

Barney himself did not make much headway. It seemed the last thing a freshman girl wanted to meet was a freshman *boy*. Like a true Brooklyn Dodger, he would "have to wait till next year." And be content with daydreaming about the cheerleader captain, Cookie Klein.

Though the Midwood teams were famously unvictorious, there were always great turnouts for the school's athletic events. Did incurable optimism—or masochism—come with the fluoridation of the Flatbush water?

There was a simpler explanation: The Midwood cheerleaders were extraordinarily beautiful—a spectacle that more than compensated for the debacle.

So fierce was the competition to become one of them that many girls took extreme measures to be selected. Thus Mandy Sherman spent the fortnight of spring vacation undergoing a rhinoplasty, fervently believing that all she lacked was a perfect nose.

Imagine then Cookie Klein's consternation when she approached Laura to recruit *her*—and was turned down flat. In a matter of hours, the news had reverberated around the school.

"I mean, everybody's talking about it," Barney reported.

Laura shrugged. "I just think it's stupid, Barn. Who the hell wants to be gawked at in the first place? Anyway, while all those girls are busy practicing their cartwheels, I can be studying." Then an instant later she added, half to herself, "Besides, I'm really not that pretty."

He looked at her and shook his head.

"I gotta say this, Castellano—I think you've got a screw loose."

Barney was a dedicated student. Several days a week he got up at five to do some extra cramming so he could use the afternoon for playing ball. Since the official season hadn't yet begun, many of the Varsity big guns were out scrimmaging in the schoolyard and he wanted to see firsthand what he was up against.

Long after the other players had started for home, in the gathering darkness dispelled only by a street lamp, Barney would continue practicing his jumper, his hook—and finally his foul shot.

Only then would he step on the Nostrand Avenue trolley and wearily try to study as he rode homeward.

Naturally, he was taking the usual required courses: Math, Civics, English, and General Science. But for his one elective, he had chosen a subject calculated to please his father: Latin.

He loved it—the exhilaration of digging for the Latin roots that made the English language bloom. It made his mental faculties more dexterous (from *mens, facultas,* and *dexter*) and his prose style more concise (from *prosa, stylus,* and *concisus*).

To his delight, all language suddenly became palpable. And, boy, did his vocabulary grow.

He displayed his new verbal pyrotechnicality at every possible moment. When asked by his English teacher if he had studied hard for the midterm, he replied, "Without dubitation, Miss Simpson, I lucubrated indefatigably."

But if his dad was flattered, he was not demonstrative about it even when Barney asked him grammatical questions to which he already knew the answer.

He turned to his mother. "What is it, Mom? Isn't Dad happy that I'm taking Latin?"

"Of course he is. He's very proud."

But if Dad had told *her,* Barney thought, how come he didn't say a word to me?

Then one day he rushed home with his Latin midterm and bolted up the stairs into his father's study.

"Look, Dad," he said, breathlessly handing over the examination paper.

Harold took a long puff on his cigarette and began to scrutinize his son's work. "Ah yes," he murmured to himself, "I'm reading Virgil this year with my kids as well." And then more silence.

As Barney waited anxiously, he could not keep himself from adding, "In case you're wondering, it was the highest in the class."

His father nodded and then turned to him. "You know, in a way this makes me a little sad. . . ."

Barney's mouth suddenly went dry.

". . . I mean, I wish I could have had you in my own Latin class."

Barney never forgot that day, that hour, that moment, those words.

His father liked him after all.

Laura had reached a major—and startling—decision. She mentioned it casually to Barney during the trolley ride from school one day.

"I'm going to run for president."

"Are you nuts, Castellano? No girl's ever going to become President of the United States."

She frowned. "I meant of the class, Barn."

"That's still crazy. I mean, there's only two of us from P.S. 148 in all of Midwood. You won't have a gang of friends to back you up."

"I have you."

"Yeah, but I'm only one vote. And you don't expect me to stuff the ballot box, do you?"

"But you could help me write a speech. All the candidates get two minutes during one of the class Assembly periods."

"Do you know who you're up against?"

"No, but I think I'm the only girl. Now, can you work with me on Sunday afternoon—please?"

"Okay." He sighed. "I'll help you make a fool of yourself."

They rode along for a few minutes, faces buried in their textbooks. Then Barney remarked, "I never dreamed you were this ambitious."

"I am, Barney," she confessed in a lowered voice. "I'm ambitious as hell."

*   *   *

As it turned out, they spent the entire weekend concocting the two minutes that would change the world. At first, they lost a lot of time trying to dream up extravagant campaign promises (free class outings to Coney Island, etc.). Barney finally came to the conclusion that politics at any level is essentially an exercise in making the mendacious sound veracious. In other words, being a convincing liar.

And he was shameless enough to urge Laura to make ample use of that most Machiavellian of words—"integrity."

At Assembly, after three sweating, madly gesticulating candidates had almost set the packed auditorium to laughing with their bombast, Laura's calm and deliberate walk to the podium (Barney had even rehearsed her in that) made an astonishing contrast.

She spoke in soft unhurried tones, now and then pausing—partly for effect and partly because she was so frightened she could barely breathe.

Equally dramatic was the contrast between her speech and those preceding. Simply stated, she said that she was as new to Midwood as she had been to America but a few years ago. She appreciated the warmth of her schoolmates as she appreciated the country that had welcomed her. And the only way she could imagine repaying the debt for all she had received was by public service. If elected, she could promise them no miracles, no pie in the sky, no convertibles for every garage (laughter). All she had to offer was integrity.

The applause was muted. Not because her classmates were unimpressed, but because the sheer artlessness of her words, her manifest *integrity,* and—it cannot be denied—her striking good looks had bedazzled them.

Indeed, by the time the Assembly ended and all were singing the alma mater, her election seemed a foregone conclusion. The homeward ride lacked only the ticker tape.

"You did it, Castellano. It was a total shutout. I'll bet you'll be president of the whole school some day."

"No, Barney," she answered affectionately, "*you* did it—you wrote practically my whole speech."

"Come on, I only made up some bullshit. It was the *way* you performed out there that was the real kayo punch."

"Okay, okay. *We* did it."

That summer, the Castellanos and the Livingstons rented a small house a block from the beach in Neponset, Long Island. There they stayed, breathing healthy sea air, while Luis came out to join them only on the weekends. He was always in a state of semi-exhaustion from the terrible annual battle against polio.

And, of course, for Inez the talk of possible epidemics and the sight of young children playing happily on the beach brought back—though they were never far away—the memories of her little Isobel. If only they had gone to the seashore *then*.

She would stare off into the ocean while Harold and Estelle sat with their faces buried in a book—Estelle reading *Pride and Prejudice* and Harold rereading Syme's *Roman Revolution*.

Meanwhile, an innocently seductive Laura joined her teenage girlfriends running and diving into the waves. And every lifeguard who took his turn on the high wooden seat silently prayed that she would call for *his* help.

Of course, there were dates. Young, bronzed suitors in their parents' Studebakers or DeSotos sought eagerly to take Laura to drive-in movies, or starlit barbecues on the deserted beach.

And necking.

Parking in a tranquil spot "to watch the submarines" or other euphemistic terms for making out—while on the radio Nat King Cole crooned "Love Is a Many Splendored Thing."

Late one sultry August evening, Sheldon Harris put his hand on Laura's breast. She said, "No, don't." But did not really mean it. Yet when he tried to slip his hand inside her blouse, she once again said no. And meant it.

Barney had no time for such frivolity. Early each morning he would wolf down breakfast and start along the still-empty shore, carrying his sneakers (so they wouldn't get sandy) to Riis Park, where games of basketball went on around the clock.

Time was running short. In a mere sixty-one days he would be trying out for the Midwood Varsity. Nothing could be left to chance. He even consulted Dr. Castellano on what foods would be most likely to induce growth. ("Try eating lunch, to start with," Luis advised.) Barney's nutritional campaign was supplemented by periodic sessions on the Riis Park chinning bars. He would hang for as long as he could bear it, hoping his body would stretch in the right direction. On the eve of Labor Day 1951, Barney stood up as straight as possible against the white stucco wall of the porch as independent measurements were taken by Harold and Luis.

The results were spectacular: one tape read six feet and a quarter inch, the other six and three-eighths. He whooped for joy. Laura (who had earlier learned to her great relief that she'd finally stopped growing at five-ten) and Warren (five-four) stood by and clapped.

"I made it, guys, I made it!" Barney squealed, jumping around the room like a rabbit with a hotfoot.

"Not quite." Laura smiled mischievously. "You still have to put the ball through the hoop."

Thus, in the year that saw President Truman relieve General Mac-Arthur of his Far East command and Professor Robert Woodward of Harvard synthesize cholesterol and cortisone, Laura Castellano ascended to the presidency of the sophomore class. And Barney Livingston faced his long-dreaded moment—or, to be precise, three minutes—of truth.

One hundred and eighty seconds was all the time basketball coach Doug Nordlinger needed to distinguish between a live tiger and a dead dog.

The air in the gym was pungent with fear. The candidates were divided into groups of five (Shirts versus Skins) who would go on court to play against one another for three minutes of scrutiny. Each of the ten aspirants had to show his stuff during the same time limit.

Two minutes into his trial, Barney had scarcely gotten his hands on the ball. It looked as if all his dreams of glory would go up in sweat.

Then suddenly a shot was misfired against his own basket. Both he and a taller rival leaped for it. But Barney boxed him out and snatched the ball.

As he started upcourt, several Shirts made desperate lunges for the ball. But Barney pivoted, dribbling with either hand.

Another desperate Shirt approached with murder in his eyes. Barney faked left, ran right, and glided by him. With ten seconds to go he was underneath the enemy basket. He wanted to shoot—but common sense dictated that he should pass to a better-placed teammate. He forced himself to toss the ball to a Skin who was in the clear. As the fellow shot—and missed—the buzzer rang.

It was all over.

The coach lined up all ten in a row. All fidgeted nervously, as if about to face a firing squad—which, in a sense, they were. Nordlinger's eyes went left to right, then right to left.

"Awright, I want these guys to step forward. You—" He indicated a tall, gangly, pimple-faced member of the Shirt contingent.

"The rest of you fellas, thanks a lot . . ."

Barney's heart sank to his sneakers.

". . . except you. Hey, Curly—didn't you hear me?"

Barney, who had been gazing disconsolately at the floor, suddenly looked up. Nordlinger was pointing at him.

"Yes, sir?" His voice was little more than a croak.

"That was smart playmaking there, kid. What's your name?"

"Barney, sir. Barney Livingston."

"Okay, Livingston, you and Sandy go over and sit on the team bench."

As Barney stood in motionless astonishment, the coach turned and bellowed, "Next two teams, hustle out there!"

"C'mon," said his lanky future teammate. And the two started toward the wooden shrine of the elect.

"The coach knew your name already," Barney remarked with curiosity.

"Yeah." The beanpole grinned smugly. "When you're six foot six in Flatbush, a lotta coaches know your name."

At five-thirty that afternoon Barney, Sandy Leavitt (as the beanpole's full name turned out to be), and a third, barrel-chested sophomore, Hugh Jascourt, were measured for uniforms. Official practice would start next Monday, but their satin team jackets—that irresistible lodestone for the co-eds—would not arrive for three weeks. But, hopefully, the *Argus* would publish the good news before that and Barney's social life would move into high gear.

He sprinted off to tell Laura.

FOUR

Late in the second half of the
Midwood–New Utrecht game, the scorekeeper pressed a button. A buzz
reverberated across the gym and into the annals of history. For it was
followed by the announcement: "Midwood substitution, Number Ten,
Livingston."

There was perfunctory applause from the stands. And one delirious
war whoop, "C'mon, Livingston!"

With four minutes left, the New Utrecht boys were getting careless.
Barney was able to intercept a pass and start a fast break downcourt,
finally handing off to captain Jay Axelrod, who sank the lay-up.

Then, with only forty seconds to go, an enemy player charged into
Barney, incurring a penalty. Barney took a deep breath at the foul line.
He had been there so many times in his imagination that summer in Riis
Park. Now it was for real. He took careful aim . . . and sank it: his first
Varsity point!

Laura cupped her hands and cheered, "Way to go, Barney!"

After the game, as they stood side by side under adjoining showers,
Jay Axelrod congratulated Barney on his performance, adding, "That
Laura Castellano must be your one-man fan club. You dating her or
something?"

"No, no," Barney gargled, as he let the warm water spill down his throat. "Why do you ask?"

"I'd sorta like to ask her out."

"So what's stopping you?" Barney inquired.

"I don't know," the captain of the Midwood basketball team replied with sudden diffidence, "I mean, she's so good-looking and . . ."

"Want me to introduce you?" Barney offered.

"Gee, wouldja, Livingston? I'd be really grateful."

"No sweat, Jay. She'll be waiting right outside. You can meet her tonight."

"No, no, Barn."

"Why not?"

"I've gotta get a haircut first."

During the ride home, Barney told Laura of the honor about to be bestowed on her. She laughed.

"What's so funny?"

"Suzie Fishman came over to me after the game and asked if I'd introduce *you*."

"Suzie Fishman?" Barney answered, wide-eyed. "She's one of the best-looking girls in the school. Why does she want to meet me—I mean, I only scored one point."

"She thinks you're cute."

"Yeah? Really? It's amazing what a Midwood uniform can do, isn't it, Castellano?"

"Oh," she said, smiling, "is that all you think you have to offer?"

Inspired by the arrival of his shiny new basketball jacket, Barney began a rake's progress to win the hearts of the Midwood cheerleaders. The team ate lunch together, their conversation filled with erotic braggadocio. If there had been even a modicum of truth to the claims made over tuna fish sandwiches and milk, there was no girl over sixteen in Flatbush—perhaps even the entire borough of Brooklyn—who was still a virgin.

Laura had been dating Jay Axelrod regularly ever since Barney introduced them. They made such a handsome couple that Barney jokingly referred to them as "Mr. and Mrs. Midwood."

That winter Laura took an audacious political step. Instead of just running for junior class president, she entered the campaign for treasurer, the third-highest office in the entire school.

"Castellano, you're really nuts. When the word gets out that a sophomore is running for treasurer, you'll be the laughingstock of Midwood."

Laura smiled. "Fine. They may laugh but at least they'll be talking and that's good publicity."

"God," exclaimed Barney with undisguised admiration, "you really play guts ball, don't you!"

"Look, Barn, my dad always says, '*Si quieres ser dichoso, no estés nunca ocioso.*' "

"Meaning?"

"Meaning, '*Life* is a guts ball game.' "

During an intense practice scrimmage a week before the crucial game against Midwood's archenemy Madison High, Jay Axelrod tripped and fell, badly spraining his ankle. The doctor said it would be ten days before he could even don his sneakers. The next afternoon as Barney was toweling himself at the end of practice, Doug Nordlinger walked by and remarked casually, "You'll be starting tomorrow night, Livingston."

Starting! Unbelievable! Too much!

He could not wait to get home.

"You've gotta come, Dad," he pleaded over dinner. "I mean, it's a Friday night and you don't have to teach the next day. And this is probably the biggest honor I'll ever have in my life."

"I doubt that." Harold smiled indulgently. "But I can understand why you're so excited."

"You'll come, won't you, Dad?" Barney asked again.

"Of course," said Harold, "I haven't seen a basketball game in years."

That Friday, Barney went through his round of classes like a zombie, thinking only of how many minutes were left till seven o'clock.

After school, he went to the empty gym and tossed foul shots for half an hour, then went to George's to fortify himself with a ninety-five-cent steak sandwich and a cherry Coke.

By six, when the other players were arriving in the locker room, he was already suited up, sitting on a bench, his arms on his knees, trying vainly to convince himself that he was cool.

"Hey, Livingston," he heard a nasal voice call. "I've got great news—Axelrod's leg is all better, so you won't be starting tonight after all."

Barney's head jerked up as if jolted by electricity. It was that over-sized moron, Sandy Leavitt, an idiotic grin on his face.

"Ha, Livingston, got you, didn't I?"

"Fuck you, Leavitt," Barney snapped nervously.

Madison was first to take the floor to the clamorous cheering of supporters who had trekked two miles up the road for the traditional Battle of Bedford Avenue. A moment later, Jay Axelrod (in uniform, but on crutches) led the Midwood squad on court as the rafters vibrated, the cheerleaders gyrated, and Barney's heart palpitated.

They quickly began their warm-up routine. As Barney snagged a rebound and dribbled out to try a set shot, he glanced toward the packed stands. His dad had not arrived yet.

The practice continued. It was now almost game time. Barney again sneaked a look at the spectators. Laura was there, with Warren next to her. Thank God. But Dad—where were Mom and Dad?

The buzzer sounded. Both teams returned to their respective benches. Only the starters remained standing as they peeled off their sweats. Barney's fingers fumbled as he unsnapped his jacket.

As the first-string quintets took their positions on court, the loudspeaker droned out their identities.

". . . and Number Ten, Livingston."

He took another glance—just Warren and Laura. His folks were still not there.

"Ladies and gentlemen, please rise for 'The Star-Spangled Banner'. . ."

As Barney placed his right hand in patriotic salute upon the left side of his chest, he could feel his heart racing.

"Play ball!"

The ref's shrill whistle reawakened the athlete in him. Barney instantly latched onto the Madison guard dribbling cockily toward him. In a split second, he rushed forward, stole the ball, and raced downcourt like a rocket.

He was all alone when he reached their basket. Breathe, Livingston, he reminded himself, stay loose and lay it up carefully. He waited another instant and then . . . basket!

He felt almost dizzy with ecstasy.

Midwood was leading by three baskets when Madison called for a time-out. As both teams huddled around their coaches, Barney again looked at the stands. Just Laura and Warren, still!

Had they maybe been in an accident? No, Dad didn't drive. Besides, Warren was there. During the halftime break, they retired to the dressing room and sucked sliced oranges. Barney, his uniform heavy with sweat, slumped on the floor against a locker. Forty minutes later, when the game ended with Midwood a six-point victor—Barney had scored thirteen. Instead of following the rest of the guys to the lockers, he walked slowly over to Laura and Warren.

Laura spoke first. "Papa wouldn't let him come."

"Huh?"

"Right after dinner Dad felt some sort of pain in his chest," Warren explained, "and Dr. Castellano came and examined him."

"What's wrong?"

"Papa thinks it was probably just something he ate," Laura quickly added. "But he made him go to bed to be on the safe side." And then she tried to change the subject. "You were fantastic out there, Barn. I bet you get your picture in the *Argus*."

And Warren added, "I'll remember every single terrific thing you did for the rest of my life."

"Yeah, good," said Barney absently, and started toward the showers.

The next morning Luis drove a reluctant Harold Livingston to King's County for an electrocardiogram. His neighbor had agreed to go only on condition that Estelle not accompany them. ("You're already upset over nothing, honey.")

Later, as he smoked nervously, Harold could overhear Luis discussing the results with the cardiologist, mumbling about P-waves and Q-waves.

Finally, Luis came over and helped Harold to the car.

"Well," Harold asked, trying to mask his anxiety, "wasn't it just indigestion? I seem to be prone to that after all those years on Army food."

Luis did not reply for a moment. Then he remarked, "Harold, the test showed you had some cardiac arrhythmia. That means—"

"I know Greek, Luis. Some sort of irregularity of tempo. Is it anything serious?"

"Well, yes and no. It can be an isolated physiological event that means nothing. Or it can be a warning signal of some underlying pathological process."

"That's just a grandiloquent way of saying you don't know."

"Okay, Harold, I *don't* know. But since you don't know either, I suggest you start taking better care of yourself and having regular checkups. You can begin by cutting down on the cigarettes."

"They relax me."

"You only *think* they do, my friend. Nicotine is a truly poisonous alkaloid and it is actually a stimulant. I can assure you that it would do you no harm to smoke less."

As the car approached Lincoln Place, Harold asked, "What are you going to say to Estelle?"

"Don't you think I should tell her the truth?"

"You've already admitted you don't know for sure."

"May I at least tell her that?"

"Feel free, Luis," Harold answered good-humoredly, "broadcast the inadequacies of your profession all over Brooklyn."

But the moment Luis parked his car, Harold turned to him and said firmly, "But there's no reason to trouble the children about this."

"I agree, Harold. They should not be given additional burdens when they are busy enough just trying to grow up. But I want *you* to worry and remember what I told you."

Barney tried to broach the subject casually.

As they were riding the trolley on Monday morning, he looked up from his Chem book and asked matter-of-factly (in a casual tone he had much rehearsed), "Are you 'going all the way' with Jay Axelrod?"

"None of your business," Laura retorted.

"That means you are."

"No, it just means it's none of your business. How come you're asking, anyway?"

"Well," he replied sheepishly, "some of the guys on the team—"

"The basketball team? The closest those horny nerds have gotten to a naked woman is the statues in the Brooklyn Museum, which I'm sure they'd like to feel up."

"Yeah." Barney laughed. "They do exaggerate, sometimes, don't they?"

"Not just 'they,' Livingston. I hear you've been going around school claiming you've scored with three cheerleaders. Is that true?"

"Absolutely, Castellano, absolutely true."

"You mean you've actually done it?"

"No, but I admit I've boasted about it."

In truth, Barney had been making steady progress in his quest for ultimate sexual fulfillment. On his second date with Mandy Sherman she had permitted a goodnight kiss. On the third, as they were necking in the back row of the Savoy Theater, she had sanctioned a hand under her sweater.

Omigod, thought Barney, both excited and a little apprehensive, this is gonna be it. I've gotta be prepared next time.

But how? He just couldn't walk into Mr. Lowenstein's drugstore on Nostrand Avenue and ask for a "Trojan." The druggist would probably tell his parents, or worse, make fun of him. No, he would have to do it more discreetly—and in foreign territory.

Thus, one Saturday afternoon when he and Warren had traveled to downtown Brooklyn to catch the movie and stage show at the Fabian Fox, he looked around for a suitably large and impersonal pharmacy. Warren was puzzled as his brother stalked up and down Fulton Street for no apparent reason. But he did not dare question anything his hero did.

Just as they reached a large glass door, Barney stopped.

"Oh, shit!"

"What's the matter, Barn?"

"What a dope I am, I'm wearing my basketball jacket."

"I don't get it. So what?"

"So this," Barney replied with nervous agitation, pointing to the left side of his chest where his first name was embroidered in blue script on the white satin. "It's a dead giveaway. They'll know who I am and where I'm from. Maybe you better do it."

"Do what, do what?"

Barney led his brother to a place on the sidewalk where they could not be overheard. "Listen, Warren, I want you to do something for me, something very, very important."

He then gave him explicit directions as to what to look for and, if it was not displayed, how to ask for it. He handed him a five-dollar bill, which was slightly moist from being clutched in his fist.

"But, Barney," Warren protested, "I'm only twelve. They'd never let me buy a thing like that."

"Hey, look, this is downtown. Thousands of people come in and out of that place every day. They'll probably think you're a midget. Now just go and do it."

As his little brother grudgingly entered the pharmacy, Barney paced back and forth nervously, praying that none of his parents' friends, who often shopped on Saturday afternoons at the nearby A&S Department Store, would catch him in flagrante delicto. After a few minutes, Warren emerged, carrying a small white paper bag.

"What the hell took so long?" Barney demanded irritably.

"Heck, Barn, they asked me all kinds of stuff like if I wanted lubricated or unlubricated. I couldn't figure out what to do."

"So, what finally happened?"

"Since I didn't know, I got a pack of each."

"Great thinking," Barney uttered with a sigh of relief, and put his arm around his younger brother. "I'm proud of you, kiddo."

By now Laura was looked upon as such a paragon that many of the older co-eds would seek her advice on matters ranging from makeup to boyfriends to how to handle difficult parents. But Laura did not enjoy this role. She did not really want to soothe, advise, and console other troubled girls.

For how could she be a parent without ever having known the luxury of being a child?

That summer the Livingstons and the Castellanos again rented at the beach. But only Warren went with them.

Luis had arranged for his daughter to be a nurses' aide at the hospital—to expose her to the harsh realities of the medical profession.

During the week, she and Luis commuted together from the house on Lincoln Place, and late on Friday afternoons they joined the stream of sweltering cars inching out of the suffocating city toward the resuscitating breezes of the seashore.

The moment they arrived, Laura would change into a bathing suit and dash into the waves in an attempt to cleanse herself of all the pain and suffering she had had to confront during the previous five days.

Meanwhile, Barney was off in the Adirondack Mountains, working as a counselor at Doug Nordlinger's Camp Hiawatha—the enterprise that provided the real butter for the coach's pedagogical bread.

It was also a unique opportunity for Doug to keep his best players together. Their pay was a meager $75 for the summer—plus any tips they could charm from the campers' parents. ("If one of your kids tells his parents he's having a good time, his father could easily lay a C-note in your hand.")

Barney's cabin consisted of an octet of nine-year-olds, seven of them normal, aggressive boys. The eighth was a painfully introverted kid named Marvin Amsterdam who, because he sometimes wet his bed, was kicked around like a football by his bunkmates.

Marvin was an only child who, when his parents divorced, endured the humiliation of overhearing that neither wanted to have custody of him. He was packed off to boarding school and only got to visit his mother or father during the long Christmas and Easter breaks. Almost the moment school ended, Marvin was again exiled, this time to Camp Hiawatha, where he increasingly dreamed of becoming invisible so the other kids could not see him.

To make matters worse, he was hopeless in every sport. At camp he was always the last chosen and at school he was simply left out.

Barney talked with Jay Axelrod about Marvin's problems as they were having beers one evening in the camp HQ.

"Can't we do something to help the kid?" Barney inquired.

"Hey, look, old pal," Jay responded, "I'm head counselor, not head doctor. I'd really advise you not to get too involved with that kid, Barn. He's doomed to be a weenie for the rest of his life."

Barney walked back toward his bunk through the chirping of crickets and the glittering of fireflies and thought, Jay's probably right, Marvin needs professional help. But I still wish there was *something* I could do for him.

Clearly, he told himself, the boy would never be a basketball player, and anyway that was not something he could learn in just a month and a half. But how about tennis? At least that would make him feel less ignored.

Thereafter, in the late afternoon period designated as "Free Play" for the campers (and unofficial practice sessions for the Midwood hoopsters), Barney took young Marvin Amsterdam and began to school him in the art of racket and ball.

At first astonished, then overwhelmed with gratitude, Marvin tried as hard as he could to live up to the attention suddenly being given him by this new heroic figure in his life. After two weeks he was rallying pretty decently. And by the final days of summer, Marvin Amsterdam was actually beating one or two of the guys in his group.

Barney wrote to Laura, "The coach is pretty ticked off that I'm cutting practice to work with this kid. But I think helping Marvin gain a little confidence has given me more satisfaction than anything I've ever done."

But Mr. Nordlinger was not the only one ticked off at Barney's disproportionate concentration on a single camper. During Parents' Weekend, the other bunkmates told their visiting families that their counselor played favorites. As a result, Barney received a mere forty dollars in tips.

And after he had had a heart-to-heart talk with Marvin's mother and father (making a unique dual appearance), suggesting diplomatically that their son was in genuine need of professional counseling, for the first time in years, the two agreed on something: namely, that Barney had a lot of nerve telling them how to raise their child.

It had not been the most glorious of summers. In fact, Barney could only console himself that he had found enough time to read Freud's *Interpretation of Dreams*. As he wrote to Laura, it had evoked in him a feeling he could only liken to "opening a door hidden behind a Dali painting and finding a new world: The Unconscious."

Otherwise, the only moderately bright spot for Barney had been Laura's weekly letters. And even mail call was a bit disappointing, since there was always a letter on the same stationery for Jay Axelrod.

Barney was not unhappy when the last day came and he stepped out of the Greyhound bus outside Grand Central Station. Most of his charges rushed to the welcoming arms of their parents.

But there was only a temporary nanny to meet Marvin Amsterdam—who was in no hurry to go off with her. The little boy thought desperately of things to discuss with Barney to avoid the wrench of separation. Barney was patient.

"Now don't lose my address, old buddy. I promise I'll answer every letter."

They were shaking hands and Marvin would not let go.

Finally the impatient nanny pried her young charge away. And Barney watched sadly as the boy went off in a chauffeured limousine.

Screw the forty dollars, he thought to himself. It was worth it just to feel that kid's hand.

Relieved that he at last had parted company with Camp Hiawatha, Barney was disheartened to find Jay Axelrod sitting on the porch with Laura when he arrived.

"I guess you two must really be getting serious," Barney remarked the day after Jay left for Freshman Week at Cornell.

"Yeah, maybe. He sort of wanted to get pinned." She somewhat sheepishly showed him her beau's fraternity pin, which she had been clutching in her hand.

"Wow—congratulations—'engaged to be engaged.' You two must be in love, huh?"

Laura merely shrugged and answered quietly, "I guess so."

FIVE

Toward the end of the first month of her junior year, Laura received a letter from Jay Axelrod. It said, in effect, that being far off in the wilds of Upstate New York had been a kind of "Thoreauvian experience." He had had time to take long, meditative walks and concluded that formalizing their relationship had been unfair to Laura. She was still very young and therefore she should be dating other people till she knew her own mind. P.S., would she mind returning his pin.

"This is bullshit," Barney sneered. "It's just a coward's way of telling you to drop dead."

Laura nodded. "If only he'd been honest enough to admit he'd chickened out." She sat for a minute and then slammed her fist on a pile of notebooks. "Dammit! I thought he was such a straight-arrow!"

"I guess most guys are selfish bastards when it comes to girls," he said to console her.

"Are you, Barney?"

"Probably. I just haven't had the chance to show it yet."

Barney was really giving the Midwood fans something to cheer about.

From the opening whistle to the closing buzzer, he fought like a mad demon, blocking, passing, fast-breaking, and playing defense with a tenacity that inspired everyone else on court.

And his accomplishments did not go unnoticed. At the end of the season Barney was selected second-team All-City and voted captain for next year.

"Livingston, you're made in the shade." Laura beamed. "Next year the stands'll be packed with college scouts. You'll probably get as many offers as that shithead Jay Axelrod."

"No, Castellano—I'll get more."

Still sore and grieving from Jay's rejection, Laura tried to commit political suicide.

She failed brilliantly.

She announced herself as candidate for the presidency of the school—a post no girl had ever held. She won, this time with only token assistance from Barney.

Yet to her dismay, even being elected to Midwood's highest office did not heal the wound inflicted on her self-esteem.

That night, the captain and the president met in the garden for a heart-to-heart talk.

As they sat on his back stoop watching the shadow of the oak tree against a backboard of stars, Barney finally summoned the courage to ask, "Why, Castellano?"

"Why what?"

"When we were little, the last thing I imagined you'd want to be was a politician. I mean, you haven't got any crazy ideas of someday being a U.S. Senator or something like that, have you?"

"Don't be silly."

"Then why?"

"Promise you won't hate me?"

"I could never hate you. Come on, spill."

"Well," she began self-consciously, "just between the two of us and that oak tree, I thought it was the surest way of getting into a good college." She paused and then asked timidly, "Do you think I'm disgustingly selfish?"

"Hey, come on, ambition is a normal human feeling," he answered. "I mean, if George Washington hadn't been ambitious, we'd probably still be talking British. Dig?"

"I don't know. Mama says men think ambition in a woman is unattractive."

"No sweat, Laura. Nothing about you could ever be unattractive."

*   *   *

To Barney's amazement, the coach asked him to return to Camp Hiawatha—and as head counselor, at that. Then he learned that it was an honor that came with the basketball captaincy. (He was even able to wangle a job for Warren as a junior counselor at $25 for the summer.)

When he arrived to take occupancy of the camp HQ, Barney scanned the list of campers and found to his ambivalent relief that Marvin Amsterdam was not one of the returnees. Would he ever see the kid again? And if so, would it be at Wimbledon or Bellevue?

In any case, this summer he could not risk the wrath of Nordlinger; the coach's letter would be crucial for his college application.

Like a devoted monk, Barney faithfully spent every day from four-thirty to six in the Rec Hall, working out with Leavitt, Craig Russo, and two new protégés on Nordlinger's new five-man weave offense.

Late one evening in mid-August, his phone rang. It was Laura calling from the hospital.

"Barney, your father's had a stroke."

His blood froze. "How bad is it?"

"They can't be sure till morning, but they're pretty certain he'll pull through. Mama's with your mother—she won't budge from the Waiting Room. Like she's afraid something bad might happen if she went to sleep."

"I'll get Warren and shoot down right away."

"For God's sake, Barn," Laura cautioned, "drive carefully."

He woke his younger brother, then ran to commandeer Sandy Leavitt's car. Two hours and forty-five minutes later, they swerved into the DOCTORS ONLY parking lot. The brothers sprinted upstairs toward the Cardiac Unit, where their mother tearfully greeted them. And then Luis reassured the boys that Harold was out of danger.

"He is sleeping peacefully now, and I think you should take your mother home so she can get some rest."

"What happened?" Barney demanded.

"He had a cerebrovascular accident," Luis explained, "that is a hemorrhage into the brain as a consequence of a clot in a cerebral artery. It is still too early to assess the damage."

"What are the possibilities?" Barney asked anxiously.

Luis tried to be both reassuring and truthful. "It can range from minor loss of movement to complete paralysis, including aphasia. But you must understand there are times when a doctor simply cannot prognosticate. Now, I insist you take everybody home."

"You mean you're staying?" Barney replied.

Luis nodded. "You are his family—but I am his physician."

* * *

Within a week, Harold was well enough to receive visitors and talk in a soft voice, the words perceptibly slurred. But by Labor Day, one thing was painfully clear—he was an invalid. He would never be able to work again.

Estelle went downtown to the Teachers' Retirement Board and began the lengthy bureaucratic process of requesting a medical retirement for her husband. It was then that she learned the cruelty of actuarial tables. Harold had taught for an aggregate of thirteen years and was therefore entitled only to a pension that would be little more than enough to pay the winter heating bill. His Army disability check would help keep up the mortgage payments, but . . .

That evening, she presented the grim realities of their situation to Barney and Warren.

When she finished her brief report, she looked forlornly at her elder son. Barney understood and, without having to be asked, shouldered the responsibility.

"It's okay, Mom, I'll get a job. Seniors finish school at one o'clock, so I can probably find something for afternoons and weekends."

Estelle looked at him with silent gratitude.

Only then did Warren realize. "What about basketball? You have practice every afternoon."

"I know, Warren, I know!" Barney exploded. "I'll just have to quit the goddamn team, won't I?"

Barney sat staring at the contents of his half-open locker. The sneakers, the shorts, the warm-ups, all the paraphernalia of jockhood that had brought him such joy over the years. He could not bring himself to take the damn stuff out and hand it in.

Suddenly he heard the raucous sound of his former teammates entering the locker room. It was an awkward moment for all of them. Finally, Craig Russo broke the ice. "How's your dad, Livingston?"

"Not too bad, Craig. Thanks for asking."

Then it was Sandy Leavitt's turn. "We're really gonna miss you."

"Yeah, me too."

Then, gauche as ever, Sandy added, "Uh—I guess you've heard that—uh—I'm captain now."

Barney was surprised to find Laura outside waiting for him.

"Haven't you got a government to run, or something?" he joked feebly.

"I just thought you might want some company on the way home."

"Oh." He paused, then added, "Thanks, Castellano."

There was no shortage of part-time jobs. That is, if he didn't mind menial labor for low wages.

Barney opted for one that had at least a semblance of variety—soda jerk and delivery boy at Lowenstein's Pharmacy on Nostrand Avenue, just a few blocks from home. Each afternoon, when his last class ended, he rushed to work (he was being paid by the hour) and donned a white jacket and silly-looking white hat to serve up egg creams, black-and-white sodas, and—when the challenge presented itself—banana splits to customers he knew as lifelong neighbors.

Every time his mind drifted off to the pleasurable fantasy of throwing baskets through a hoop in a warmly lit gym, he dragged himself back to the reality of having to trudge through the chill Brooklyn streets, delivering prescriptions.

He tried to console himself with the thought that this part of his job might be regarded as education. After all, old man Lowenstein did let him watch while he mixed the various healing potions.

"One thing, Barney," the druggist would say, smiling, "when you take Pharmacology in medical school, you're a shoo-in for an A."

The pharmacy was officially open until seven-thirty and it was usually after eight by the time Barney got home. His mother always had dinner waiting and, while Warren was upstairs studying, she would keep Barney company. It was her own way of showing him how grateful she was for all he was sacrificing.

For reasons Barney all-too-painfully understood, her conversation seemed like a perpetual series of reminiscences.

"He always had so much pep," she remarked nostalgically.

"Yeah, I've heard that."

"We were always the last couple on the dance floor. I was positively worn out. But then, when he got home, he'd sometimes go to his study and read some Latin author till breakfast time. You can see why he was the most popular teacher in the school."

Barney placed a hand upon his mother's. "Don't upset yourself, Ma. Who cares if he has to use a cane now? At least we can still *talk* to him."

She nodded. "You're right. We should be very grateful." And then she whispered affectionately, "You're a good boy, Barney."

Night after night she would repeat the same cathartic monologue almost verbatim.

Then came the most difficult part of Barney's day—visiting his father.

Harold spent most of his time in bed reading. First the morning paper, then some scholarly work and, when he woke from his afternoon nap, the *World-Telegram*. After dinner he was usually too tired to do anything but sit up in bed and receive visitors.

Feeling guilty about "not doing anything useful," he would take the burden of conversation upon himself, discoursing about current events or whatever book he was involved in at the moment. Yet there was always a barely perceptible tinge of apology in his voice.

Barney sensed this and—reversing the traditional roles—tried to give his father peace of mind by reporting the exciting events in his own intellectual world. One evening he mentioned his fascination with psychoanalysis.

"Hey, Dad," he asked, "ever read any Freud?"

"Why yes, a bit."

The answer surprised Barney. He had expected his father to be uninformed about such "modern" things.

"When I was in the Army hospital," Harold continued, "there was a very sympathetic psychiatrist who would visit us and make us tell him— again and again—how we were wounded. He must have done it a dozen times. And it helped. It really helped."

"How, Dad?" Barney asked with mounting fascination.

"Well, I'm sure you remember how Freud explains the dream process—"

"I know he says that dreams unlock our unconscious mind—"

"Yes. Well, this doctor was helping my psyche to heal by 'dreaming out loud.' Every night I had been reliving that explosion, but talking about it again and again finally put an end to those awful nightmares."

Then a thought occurred to Harold. "By the way, what course are you reading this for?"

Embarrassed, Barney confessed that he was reading psychology in his "spare time." They both knew that he didn't have any, and he fully expected a scolding for neglecting his schoolwork. But again his father surprised him.

"Well, son, it won't do your grades any good. But I've always thought the real purpose of an education was to stimulate the mind to think. Tell me, have you read any Jung?"

Barney shook his head.

"Well, why not look at *his* theory of dreams and the Collective Unconscious—then perhaps we can chat about it."

"Sure, Dad, sure. Maybe Mom can bring back a copy from the library."

"No need for that," Harold responded, "there's a copy in my study—on the same shelf as Artemidorus."

Thereafter, Barney looked forward to these visits with Harold as the *best* part of the day.

It was usually after ten before Barney could sit down and begin studying. By midnight he was often too exhausted to go on and would collapse into bed. Inevitably, he started to fall behind in his classes.

Nor could he catch up on weekends. For Saturdays he had to report to Lowenstein's at 8 A.M. and work the entire day.

That left only Sunday afternoons. But by now Barney had developed a fatalistic attitude: he would not be going to college on a basketball scholarship. And with his grades at their current level, he would probably not be accepted by Columbia at all.

So what the hell, why not use his one free day to go to the playground, throw himself into a few dozen hard-fought basketball games, and let off steam? He would play so long and so hard that, finally, one by one, the other guys pleaded exhaustion and went home.

His first-term grades were, as he had expected, lower than usual. But his aggregate average still hovered above ninety, and that did not automatically rule out the possibility of Columbia. Especially if he did well on the upcoming College Boards.

The crucial part of this nationwide exam assessed a candidate's aptitude in the use of words and numbers. Theoretically, it was like a blood test—something you couldn't study for.

But in practice, during the Christmas vacation, kids attended expensive tutoring courses to improve their "aptitude." Every family with dreams of upward mobility would scrape together the $200 necessary to make their children look smarter than they really were.

Inez Castellano regarded this as a form of "cheating," a compromising of one's *honor.* But Luis was realistic and overruled her. Why should their daughter be put at a disadvantage? He even generously offered to subsidize Barney, who was too proud to accept.

Barney worked Christmas Day (at double pay) since it was Lowenstein's turn to act as the emergency pharmacy in the area. It was lonely for him—especially since Laura never seemed to be around. She was always either at a tutoring class or out somewhere having fun.

She did resurface the week before the SATs, and offered to share some of the tricks she had acquired. These he gratefully accepted, and the two spent several evenings boning up together.

The result was a happy irony. While Laura came up with an admirable 690 in the verbal and 660 in Math, Barney scored 720 and 735.

"Gosh, Barn," she said, "those numbers could get you into any school in the country."

"Listen, Castellano," he answered wryly, "if I could've played ball this year, the only score I would have needed was twenty points a game."

As the harsh winter weather wore him down, Barney began to come home from work a mere zombie. Sometimes he would get as little as four hours sleep. But this was his last term, the home stretch. In a few weeks, they would hear from the colleges and it would be all over but the shouting.

Or the crying.

One Saturday evening, he stayed till nearly midnight, helping Mr. Lowenstein take inventory. He slogged home through the gray slush and staggered up the steps, thinking only of sleep and hoping for no dreams of aspirins, antihistamines, and laxatives.

But as he was removing his coat, his stomach reminded him that it had only been fed a sandwich for dinner and he dragged himself toward the kitchen. To his surprise, the light was still on. And to his added astonishment, Laura was sitting there.

"Hey, what the hell brings you here so late—especially on a Saturday night?" he asked.

"Barney, I've got to talk to you. It's serious."

"Dad?" he asked as an instant reflex. "Has something happened to Dad?"

"No, no." She paused and then added, barely audibly, "It's me, Barn. I'm in trouble. I know you're tired. . . ."

"That's okay, that's okay. Sit down, I'll get a sandwich and we'll talk."

"No, not here. Can we go for a walk?"

"At this hour?"

"Just around the block, you could eat your sandwich on the way."

He focused intently on her for the first time. There was a look of panic in her eyes.

"Okay, Castellano, okay."

He grabbed a handful of chocolate chip cookies, threw on his mud-spattered pea jacket, and they went out into the streets.

They covered the first hundred yards in total silence. Finally, Barney could stand the suspense no longer. "Will you please tell me what's wrong?"

"I . . . I'm overdue," she stammered. "It's been six weeks."

"You mean to tell me you're pregnant?"

She could only nod.

"Oh God, how the hell did this happen?"

"I don't know, Barn. I'm ashamed, I really am. And I'm scared as hell."

He was suddenly consumed by an inexplicable sense of betrayal.

"Why the hell don't you go to the SOB who did it?" he snapped. He could not bring himself to say the word "father."

She shook her head. "Because he's a schmuck. You're the only person I could tell about this."

"Am I supposed to feel flattered?" He took a weary breath and, realizing how desperate she was, tried to master his own feelings. "Okay," he said slowly and deliberately, "can I just for the record know who the guy is?"

"It's . . . Sandy Leavitt."

Barney could not suppress his anger. "Why *him* of all people?"

"Please," she entreated, "if I wanted to get screamed at I could have told my parents." And then the tears came. "Please, Barney," she sobbed, "please help me."

In the quiet winter darkness, he stopped and whispered, "Take it easy, Laura. Let's go back where it's warm and talk this whole thing over. Mom's asleep by now, no one will hear us."

Back in the kitchen they began to pool their mutual ignorance of illegal medical practices and tried to rack their brains for a plan.

It was almost as difficult for Barney to listen as it was for Laura to speak. In his mind, rage was fighting a pitched battle with compassion.

Laura knew two other Midwood girls who had been in her predicament. Each had taken a different measure to solve the problem.

One had paid fifty bucks to a shady character in a dingy two-room apartment on the fifth floor of a tenement near Red Hook. The experience had been horrible and she had been extremely lucky to end up in one piece. As she told Laura, the guy was so filthy she could see the dirt under his fingernails.

The second girl had told her parents who, though horrified, had arranged for an abortion under sterile medical conditions. But this alternative involved going to Puerto Rico—and during the summer vacation, when her absence did not arouse any suspicion.

"Barney, what the hell should we do?" Then, ashamed, Laura quickly corrected herself. "Sorry, I shouldn't have said 'we.' It's my problem really."

"No, Castellano, just stay loose and we'll find a safe solution. Now, first of all, are you absolutely sure you're pregnant?"

"I should have had my period two weeks ago. I'm usually regular as clockwork."

"Okay, then we've got to find a real doctor—closer than Puerto Rico. I sure wish to hell we could ask your father, I mean, pretend it's for someone else—"

"No, Barney, he would see right through it. I'd rather die than have him know."

She turned away. Her whole body began to shake with muffled sobs. Barney stood, walked around the table, and took her by the shoulders.

"Laura, I told you I'd take care of this." And he thought to himself, I only wish to hell I knew *how*.

All of Sunday, Laura's problem drove everything else from his mind. By evening, he had managed to convince himself that he would be able to find someone at school the next day, somebody he obviously just hadn't thought of, someone who knew the ropes.

The two friends hardly exchanged a word as they rode to school Monday morning. Barney was struck by the fact that everything seemed normal. The girl sitting next to him was the same person he had known for so many years. Except now she had someone else's baby growing in her.

When they parted in the front hall, he began to stalk the corridors. After every class he was like a hunter seeking his prey, glancing intently at every passing face. At lunchtime he scoured the cafeteria, still to no avail. By one o'clock, he had made no progress at all.

He arrived at the pharmacy and began sorting through the prescriptions already packed for delivery. As usual, Mr. Lowenstein came over and gave the future doctor a short discourse on the properties of each drug. Barney listened politely, then swept the packages into a small canvas bag and headed out into the piercing cold where he could at least be alone with his thoughts.

It was only on his way back that it suddenly occurred to him. What about Mr. Lowenstein? I mean, he knows almost as much as any doctor and he's in daily contact with dozens of them. Why not ask him?

Because if he gets angry, and I'm pretty sure he will, I'll lose my job.

But then, as he was taking off his galoshes, he glanced at his employer. The pharmacist had a kind face, no question about it. And even though there was no apothecary's equivalent of the Hippocratic oath, he knew the old man never gossiped. When there was a prescription for something potentially compromising, like the time one of his customers had contracted gonorrhea, he would have Barney watch the store while he delivered the penicillin himself, never giving the slightest hint of where he was going.

There were less than fifteen minutes before closing time and Mr. Lowenstein was already locking up the dangerous drugs when Barney approached him and asked if he had a moment to chat. "Sure, Barney, what's on your mind? If it's a raise, you can relax. I was planning on giving you one next month."

"No, no," he replied quickly, "it's about a certain problem."

"What kind of problem?"

"Well—uh—" he hesitated and then blurted quickly, "a girl I know is in trouble."

The old man studied Barney's face and murmured, "And do I take it you're the gentleman concerned in this unfortunate business?"

Barney nodded.

"This is terrible," the pharmacist said, but without anger. "What do you think we sell contraceptives for? Young people, if they want to get mixed up in this sort of thing, they should at least take the proper precautions. To be frank, Barney, I'm very surprised at you."

"Yes, sir."

There was a pause as neither seemed to know whose turn it was to speak.

Finally Barney brought himself to ask, "Is there any way you can help me, Mr. Lowenstein? Believe me, I'm ashamed to be asking you, but she's desperate—I mean, we both are. I don't want her to go to some back-alley butcher. That would be risking her life." He then felt terribly uncomfortable and apologized, "I suppose it was wrong to talk to you about this."

The pharmacist sighed. "Barney, what was wrong was getting this young woman in trouble. But if for some reason the two of you can't get married—and at your age that seems like the case—I suppose you have to take the other alternative. Mind you, I don't know whether it's right. I'm not God. But I'll give you what help I can."

A feeling of enormous relief swept over Barney. He wanted to throw his arms around the old man.

"Lock the store and come into the office," his boss commanded.

Barney hurriedly obeyed and entered the pharmacist's cubicle. He was writing a telephone number on a small index card.

"Don't ask me how I know this," he cautioned, "but from what I hear, this man is extremely careful. He even prescribes post-operative antibiotics just to be on the safe side."

Barney studied the card. "Dr. N. Albritton—in Pennsylvania?"

His employer shrugged. "It's the best I can do, my boy, I'm told he sees patients on weekends, so that would make it a little easier. More I cannot give you. So?"

"I beg your pardon?"

"So, do you intend to make such a call from your own home? Sit down and do it here."

As Mr. Lowenstein tactfully left the room, Barney, in a state of mild shock, dialed the long-distance operator and asked for a number in Chester, Pennsylvania. A few moments later, he heard the doctor's calm voice wishing him a good evening. Now came the hard part.

He tried to pour out his problem as quickly as possible while still being vague enough to protect Laura's identity. But the physician did not seem to want many details.

"I believe I understand the nature of the case. Would it be convenient for you to visit my clinic this Saturday morning? It's just outside Philadelphia."

"Sure, sure, of course. We'll be there any time you like."

"Well, let's say eleven, shall we?"

"Yessir, yessir, absolutely. Thanks a lot."

But the conversation was not over. "Mr. Smith, I assume you are aware of my fee."

"No, no, but we'll bring the money, don't worry. Uh, exactly how much is it?"

"Four hundred dollars. Cash, of course."

Barney was speechless.

Finally, the physician's voice asked politely, "Does that change anything, Mr. Smith?"

"No, no, no, that's fine," Barney hoarsely replied.

As soon as Mr. Lowenstein returned, they tossed on their coats and left through the back door.

Barney was overflowing with gratitude. He turned to his employer and said emotionally, "How can I ever thank you, Mr. Lowenstein?"

The old man stopped and looked up at Barney. "By never mentioning this to anyone. *Ever.*"

"Jesus Christ, Barney, how the hell am I going to get four hundred bucks? I've got less than fifty in my bank account. We're right back where we started from—and there's *nothing* we can do." She began to cry again.

He answered without hesitation. "Listen, Castellano, we're going on Saturday and everything'll be all right."

"What about the four hundred?"

Barney smiled. "No sweat, I've got nearly that much in the bank."

She looked at him in astonishment. "But you worked like a dog for that money. You were saving up for college."

"It doesn't matter. That dough is mine to do whatever I want with. So let's not waste time discussing it anymore and just figure out what the hell we can tell our parents when we disappear Saturday morning."

Laura was overwhelmed with a feeling she could not precisely define. Finally she murmured softly, "I know it sounds stupid, Barn, but I'd have done the same for you."

"I know." He nodded solemnly.

After school the next day, Barney went straight to the Dime Savings Bank and withdrew the $387.56 in his account, while Laura emptied hers of its $46.01 and went to buy the bus tickets—$6.75 each, round trip.

Barney plotted their journey as thoroughly as Hannibal crossing the Alps. Greyhound had a bus leaving at seven that reached Philadelphia just before nine in the morning. That would give them two hours to get out to Albritton's clinic.

Mr. Lowenstein gave Barney the day off, and they told their parents they would be trying to get standing room tickets for the matinee of *Antony and Cleopatra* with Laurence Olivier and Vivien Leigh. Since they'd leave early in the morning, they'd have breakfast at Nedick's in Times Square. And afterwards they might even go to Lindy's or Jack Dempsey's for a sandwich and cheesecake, so they might be home a little late.

It was past midnight and Barney was still tossing in his bed, trying to sleep. Suddenly he heard what seemed like the sound of pebbles thrown against his window. He looked out into the backyard and recognized Laura's silhouette. An instant later he was standing with her.

"Barney, it's come—my period's come."

"No—you mean it was a false alarm?"

She began to laugh and cry. "Yeah, Livingston, yeah, a false alarm. Isn't that great?" She threw her arms around him and they hugged.

"Castellano, you don't know how happy I am for you," he whispered.

"Hey, Barney," she remarked fervently, "I'll never forget this. I think you're the nicest guy who ever lived."

SIX

To no one's surprise, Laura was accepted to Radcliffe—on full scholarship. She was ecstatic at the prospect of attending the college for Harvard's stepsisters, since this would place her in the best position to storm the ultimate citadel—its Med School.

Barney's joy was considerably more subdued. Columbia had accepted him, all right, but on a tuition-only scholarship.

"You'll still be able to play ball, won't you?" Laura asked.

"Only if they practice between midnight and four A.M.," he replied bitterly.

Determined to experience campus life to the full, Barney found a job that would earn enough money both to continue his contributions to the family budget and allow him to live in the dorms.

On July first, he became assistant night doorman at The Versailles, one of the fashionable apartment houses in New York's most elegant arrondissement. It was exhausting but lucrative: by Labor Day he had earned enough to cover his first term's lodgings.

Suddenly, it was time to say goodbye to Laura—a moment he had been unable to acknowledge all summer long. Even when he had gazed out of his window and watched the two sturdy Railway Express men lug

Laura's trunk into their van a week earlier, he had not allowed himself to consider what the event portended.

The night before she was to leave, they sat side by side on the backyard steps, gazing at the outline of the long-neglected basketball hoop.

"Scared, Castellano?"

"Petrified is more like it. I keep thinking I just got accepted by mistake and that I'm gonna flunk every course."

"Yeah," he replied, "I know the feeling."

They fell silent again. Then suddenly Laura whispered, "Shit."

"What's the matter?" he asked.

"Dammit, I wish you were gonna be in Boston, too."

"Hell, I wish I were playing for the Boston Celtics, but we've got to face reality."

"I don't think I like facing reality."

"Then how the hell are you gonna be a doctor?"

"I don't know," she answered candidly. "I really don't know."

Radcliffe College annually published a pamphlet called *The Freshman Register*. It contained the names and pictures of all the incoming girls so they could more easily get to know one another.

But it was a far more valuable document to the Harvard men who could, like racehorse tipsters, study the fillies and circle the probable winners.

In 1954, the photograph of Laura Castellano was ringed in every copy—as evidenced by the tidal wave of phone calls for the newest resident of Briggs Hall.

At first she was flattered. Then amused. But as minute after minute male voices from high tenor to basso profundo parroted, "You don't know me, but—" she finally begged the girl on bells to dismiss any further calls. ("You can say I've got leprosy, for all I care.")

The next morning, she met with her advisor, Judith Baldwin, a lively, fortyish associate professor of Biology who was quite discouraging about Laura's chances of getting into Med School—especially Harvard's. She herself, she confided, had been turned down only twelve years earlier.

"Of course, I couldn't take it personally—it was official policy then. HMS didn't accept its first women until 1945."

"Not even during the war?" Laura asked with astonishment.

Judith shook her head. "Apparently women were still unworthy of Harvard's imprimatur. Nowadays, they only take about half a dozen—

and for them that's a monumental concession. Back in 1881, a group of Boston women offered Harvard something like a million dollars—imagine how much that was then—if they would agree to train a few female doctors each year. Harvard said *no.*"

This did not exactly bolster Laura's confidence.

Meanwhile, Judith added another piquant historical anecdote. "Curiously enough, they did have one woman on the faculty at the time. Does the name Fannie Farmer mean anything to you?"

"You mean the cookbook lady?"

Judith nodded. "Believe it or not, cooking was once a required course in the Med School."

"What on earth for?"

"I'm not quite sure," Judith replied. "But since interns were forbidden to get married, the professors probably thought they'd better learn to feed themselves."

"Sounds monastic," Laura remarked, "but anyway, I still want to give it my best shot, Professor Baldwin. Can you help me?"

"Only if you feel genuinely strong enough to survive rejection, Laura. Take it from me, it's maddening to see the boy who sat next to you in Chem or Bio—whom you practically tutored so he could scrape by with a *B*—get accepted by the Med School, while you and your A still aren't deemed good enough to go there at all. If I sound a little bitter, that's because I am."

"Are you trying to discourage me?" Laura asked.

"Have I succeeded?" Judith inquired.

"No," Laura answered firmly.

"Good." The older woman smiled broadly. "Now let's prepare the order of battle."

Laura returned to Briggs Hall to find a sheaf of telephone messages from suitors she did not know—and a letter from Barney.

Dear Castellano,

This is the very first thing I've typed on the machine your folks gave me for graduation.

I've just moved into John Jay Hall. My room is not exactly spacious. In fact, by comparison, it makes a phone booth look like Grand Central Station. But I've already met a few nice guys and many pre-Meds.

Funny, somehow I don't seem to have run into any pre-Meds who are also nice guys. Most of them seem to want to specialize in

*what you might call "The King Midas syndrome." Recreational
reading seems to be* Medical Economics.

*Columbia is great and even though I've got to fulfil those damn
science requirements, I'm determined to major in English. How
could I pass up the chance of hearing heavyweights like Jacques
Barzun and Lionel Trilling—the latter giving a course on "Freud
and the Crisis of Culture"? Can you imagine, that's a* lit *course?*

*Everything would be great if I didn't have to take organic
chemistry but I want to get the damn thing out of the way so it
won't hang over me like the Sword of Damocles.*

*Just for laughs I went to last week's Freshman Basketball
tryouts. Knowing I wouldn't be able to play, even if by some fluke I
actually made the team, I was cool as a cucumber.*

*The gym was wall to wall with jocks, some of whom looked
like ringers, i.e., tall, musclebound, blond guys from the Midwest
who were probably there on cornhusking scholarships. (Don't say it,
I know I'm jealous.)*

*Anyway, little by little, the wheat was separated from the chaff
(note I continue the agricultural metaphors) and I still hadn't been
shucked. When we were down to the last cut, I went completely
crazy, trying ridiculously long jump shots—even a left-handed
hooker—all of which, by some perverse miracle, went through the
hoop.*

*At the end of the day I found myself being welcomed by the
Columbia Freshman coach, an incredibly couth preppie named Ken
Cassidy.*

*And so, after he had made this incredibly gung-ho oration, I
had to go up to him and say that financial obligations prevented me
from accepting his gracious offer.*

*His reply somewhat shattered his Mr. Perfect image. It was
something like what the hell kind of sonovabitch was I to waste
his blankety-blank valuable time when I knew I wouldn't have the
time, etc. I hadn't heard some of the epithets even in Brooklyn
playgrounds.*

Anyway, I've got to sign off. I'll mail this on my way to work.

Hope you're behaving yourself.

> *Love,*
> *Barney.*

At Christmas they had so much to catch up on that they talked until
4 A.M. From Barney's enthusiasm about the intellectual giants he had

been exposed to, Laura concluded that the average undergraduate at Columbia was getting a better education than the one at Harvard.

But one thing seemed to be exactly the same at both institutions. The pre-meds were, almost to a man (and they were mostly men), ruthless, competitive grinds—who would think nothing of messing up your Chem lab experiment if you so much as left to heed the call of nature.

"That's real dedication," Barney commented wryly, "but you know those are the characters who're going to get into Med School for sure."

"Yeah," Laura agreed, "I wish I knew what the hell made them tick. I mean, it can't just be the money. . . ."

"No," Barney replied, attempting to sound like a professional analyst, "I detect a high degree of social insecurity. These guys seem to view the white coat as some kind of security blanket. Or look at it another way—most of these dorks could only get a date if they went to a fruit store. Imagine the power of being able to say to a woman, 'Take off your clothes and show me your tits!' "

Laura began to laugh.

"I'm not joking, Castellano," he insisted.

"I know—if I didn't laugh I'd cry."

The next day they had another lengthy nocturnal session. This time on a very sensitive topic for them both—their parents.

Harold Livingston had found a way to cope with his guilt at not being a breadwinner. He hit upon the idea of using the skills he had acquired in the Army to translate some of the classics of oriental literature— beginning with the eleventh-century *Tale of Genjii,* the first and most famous Japanese novel.

Barney took pride in his father's courage, reassuring Warren that their dad was not merely performing a therapeutic exercise. He had checked the college bookstore and pragmatically determined that Harold's work could fill an important gap on the lit shelves.

"It could give him a whole new lease on life."

Laura, on the other hand, was anything but reassured. From the moment she entered the house she sensed that the fabric of her family was unraveling. Each in turn, her parents tried to win her confidence, as if Laura's allegiance would validate the opposing paths they had taken.

Inez, who was now so often in church confessing her sins that she could not possibly have time to commit new ones between visits, tried to persuade Laura to come with her.

"I'm sorry, Mama," she replied. "I don't have anything to confess."

"We are all born sinners, my child."

For a moment Laura forgot that Man's first disobedience was the sin of Adam. Instead she thought of another stigma after the expulsion from the Garden of Eden that hit closer to home: the mark of Cain. Am I my sister's keeper? She knew that—at least in her mother's eyes—she was.

Nor did she find solace in her father's company. Indeed it was quite the contrary. As she returned home late one evening, she heard her father's drunken voice calling from the study, *"Venga, Laurita, venga charlar con tu papa"*—come and chat to your father.

She reluctantly obeyed.

Luis was in his shirtsleeves, both elbows leaning on the desk within reach of a half-empty bottle.

"Have a drink with me, Laurita," he offered, his voice blurred and hazy.

"No, thank you, Papa," she answered, trying to keep her composure. "And don't you think *you've* had enough?"

"No, my daughter," he replied. "I can still feel the pain."

"The what? I don't understand."

"I have to drink until I can no longer feel the pain of existence."

"Come on, Papa, don't camouflage it with philosophy—you're just a plain old drunk."

"I'm not that old, Laurita," her father answered, seizing on but one of her adjectives, "that's the pity of it all. Your mother has abjured the world, the devil, and the flesh. She refuses to—"

"Do I have to hear this?" Laura interrupted, feeling increasingly uncomfortable.

"No, of course not. I just thought perhaps you'd understand better why I drink, if you could understand how difficult my life is. . . ."

She did not know how to reply.

In any case, her father rambled on. "At least the bottle does not turn its back on me. It warms me when I'm cold. It soothes me when I'm frightened—"

Laura was finding the conversation intolerable.

She stood up. "I'm going to sleep. I've got some studying to do tomorrow."

As she turned and headed for the door, Luis called after her, "Laurita, I beseech you, I'm your father. . . ."

She did not stop. She did not turn. She merely felt confused and hurt. And lost.

Completely lost.

*   *   *

Estelle could not help noticing that none of the Castellanos touched more than crumbs of the food she had so lovingly prepared for Christmas dinner. Inez sat like a statue. Luis drank wine and Laura kept glancing at her watch, counting not merely the days but the hours and minutes she had yet to endure before she could escape to Boston.

The burden of sustaining conversation had now fallen on the frail shoulders of Harold Livingston.

He turned to Laura, smiling. "Barney tells me that you both got A's in your Organic Chemistry midterms. Keep it up and it's open sesame to Med School."

"For Barney, maybe," Laura remarked, "but my advisor says the medical establishment doesn't look kindly on aspiring lady doctors. Even to get an interview, you have to be something like first in your class, with a letter from God—or at least Saint Luke."

From the corner of her eye, she could see Inez frowning at her irreverence.

"Surely, Laura, you're exaggerating," Harold Livingston commented.

"Okay, then," Laura responded, "I defy anyone to name three famous female doctors in all of history."

"Florence Nightingale," Warren chimed in immediately.

"She was a nurse, schmuck," Barney snapped.

"Well," Harold began slowly, taking up her challenge, "there was Trotula, a professor of medicine at the University of Salerno in the eleventh century. She even wrote a famous textbook on obstetrics."

"Wow, that's a really good one, Mr. Livingston." Laura smiled. "Two to go."

"Well, there's always Madame Curie," Harold offered.

"Sorry, Mr. Livingston, she was only a chemist—and had a hard enough time doing that. Does everybody give up?"

"Yes, Laura," Harold conceded, "but as a History of Science major, you should be able to answer your own question."

"Well, straight from the pages of *The New York Times* I'll give you Dorothy Hodgkin, M.D., who's just discovered vitamin B-12 for treating pernicious anemia. Then I give you Helen Taussig—a Radcliffe girl, coincidentally, though not allowed to get a Harvard M.D.—who did the first successful blue baby operation. I could probably give you a few more but I doubt if there'd be enough for a touch football game against the AMA."

At this point, Luis broke his silence and added, "You will change all that, Laurita. You will be a great doctor."

Under ordinary circumstances, Laura would have been gratified by this unexpected display of parental optimism.

But then Luis was dead drunk.

Later that day when the two of them were alone, Laura told Barney matter-of-factly, "I won't be coming home for Easter."

"Hey—that's lousy news. Why not?"

"Frankly, I think I've already experienced the Last Supper."

Summer came and Barney was still working the night shift on Park Avenue. He sweltered in his doorman's uniform and forced himself to study during every free moment.

Having finished his freshman year with an A-minus average, he did not wish to clip the wings of his ascent to Med School heaven by risking a lousy grade in physics. He therefore decided to take both halves of this required course during the summer session at Long Island University, where the competition among pre-meds was slightly easier.

This ploy was hardly a top secret in the community of aspiring physicians. Laura, too, had opted to take Physics that summer—though at Harvard. As she explained in a letter to her parents, she could not bear the prospect of yet another airless, punishing summer in the melting asphalt of New York. She had no illusions about their sensing the real reason.

But, as she quickly discovered, the only similarity between Harvard University and its Summer School was the coincidence of names. For in July and August the Yard became a sort of country club with the cream of East Coast nubility flocking to Cambridge in the fond hope of snagging a real Harvard husband. Laura was amused by their disarming lack of subtlety. They wore the shortest of shorts and the tightest of T-shirts.

"You'd really go berserk here, Barney," she wrote to him. "There's more cheesecake here than at Lindy's."

I've got labs four afternoons a week and by Friday I'm so full of equations and formulas and incomprehensible concepts like the Doppler Effect (who really gives a damn about the speed of sound anyway?) that all I want to do on weekends is sleep. Maybe you can figure out some way to come up here next summer, Barn. God knows, you'd enjoy it. Meanwhile, please don't work too hard.

Love, "L"

As he walked the LIU campus the next day, Barney looked at some of the passing coeds and suddenly realized that in the matter of sex, he was beginning to be retarded. Indeed Warren had recently claimed to have gone "nearly almost all the way" with a girl from Eastern Parkway. It was unthinkable that his little brother should actually score before he did!

And thus, with horny Machiavellianism, he decided to audit what he regarded as the most promising hunting ground—Modern Drama.

His instinct proved correct—the place was packed with would-be actresses, at a ratio of at least three girls to every boy. Moreover, he quickly discovered that "Columbia" was a magic word to them. Three cheers for the Ivy League.

His first successful seduction could arguably be credited to the rather unromantic initiative of Miss Rochelle Persky who, as they were necking passionately in her parents' living room, whispered tenderly, "Well, are you gonna do it or not?"

He was.

They did.

Naturally, he could not conceal his pride. In his next letter to Laura he gave a few heavy hints, though of course omitting all gross detail. Not really out of chivalry, but for the purpose of aggrandizing his own skills in the enterprise. (He just signed it "Unvirginally yours.")

Barney did not see Laura till she came down to make a brief, reluctant appearance on an August weekend at the house in Neponset —on which the Castellanos and Livingstons had quixotically obtained an option to buy.

Warren, about to enter his senior year at Midwood, was absent, still working as a busboy at Greenwood Manor, the famous Catskill Mountains resort. The tips, he wrote his parents in a message to be conveyed to Barney, were largest for those waiters aspiring to be doctors. His own chosen profession—the law—barely edged out accountancy for second place.

After dinner, Laura and Barney took a walk on the beach in the late-setting sun.

"How are your folks?" he asked.

"I'm not staying long enough to find out," she replied. "I'm taking the train to Boston on Monday morning."

"But it's six weeks till school starts."

"Yeah, but a friend's invited me to his family's house on the Cape."

"Is that serious—or are you just going for the scenery?" he asked.

She shrugged.

He could not tell whether she was being evasive or was genuinely unsure.

"Who's the guy, anyway?"

"His name's Palmer Talbot."

"He sounds like a sports car," Barney remarked. "Is he nice?"

"Come on, Livingston, would I be dating somebody who wasn't nice?"

He looked at her with a sly smile and answered, "Probably. I mean, you've already got a track record."

"Maybe this guy's different."

"Yeah, he's got two last names."

On the way back Laura took a good look at Barney and, for the first time, noticed the fatigue etched in his face.

"This working nights is gonna send you to an early grave, Barn. Can't you get a different job?"

"No, Castellano, I like this one. It gives lots of time to study. And besides, I'm moving up in the ranks. I'll be a first-string doorman next year."

"I still say you're killing yourself," she insisted.

"Listen, you're not a doctor yet."

"Yeah, but at the rate you're going, the cadaver I get in Med School may be you."

1955 would be fondly recalled as the year Americans twice danced for joy in the streets. Once it was for an event unprecedented in the history of Brooklyn—the Dodgers actually *beat* the New York Yankees and won the World Series!

And there was the nationwide explosion triggered by the announcement on April 12 giving the results of a large-scale trial of Jonas Salk's vaccine on the schoolchildren of Pittsburgh. Simply stated, it had *worked*. Science had conquered polio!

The entire country went wild and, as one observer recalled, "rang bells, honked horns, blew factory whistles, fired salutes, kept their traffic lights red in brief periods of tribute, took the rest of the day off, closed their schools or convoked fervid assemblies therein, drank toasts, hugged children, attended Church, smiled at strangers, forgave enemies."

Now there would be no more tragedies like Isobel Castellano anywhere. God bless Dr. Salk.

If only he had found it *sooner*.

SEVEN

It was the Sunday morning of Labor Day weekend. Warren was devouring a jelly doughnut and the Sports section of the *Times*. His father was leafing aimlessly through the Book Review. He seemed paler and more jittery than usual and was already on his third cigarette of the day.

"More coffee, darling?" Estelle asked solicitously.

"No, thanks. I feel a bit stuffy. I think I'll go to the garden and get a bit of fresh air."

"Fine. I'll come with you," she replied.

Harold grasped his cane and struggled to his feet—he was always stubborn about refusing help.

Warren had progressed to the "News of the Week" when he heard his mother's voice crying in panic from the garden, "Help, help—somebody help!"

In an instant he was at the back door and saw his father lying prostrate on the ground. Warren dashed over.

"What happened, Ma?"

"We were standing here talking," Estelle sobbed, "and all of a sudden he just fell. I think he's unconscious—I don't know, I don't know."

Warren knelt and looked at his father, whose eyes were closed and whose face was ashen. He grabbed Harold by the shoulder and shouted—as if to wake him—"Dad, Dad." There was no response. He held his hand under his father's nostrils but was unable to tell whether he was breathing. *He thought so.* He could not be sure. But then he put his ear to Harold's chest.

"It's okay, Ma—it's okay. I can hear his heart. But it's beating pretty fast. I'd better get Dr. Castellano."

She nodded, mute with fear. As Warren sprinted off, Estelle knelt and cradled her husband's head in her lap.

Luis's car was not in front of the house. Warren raced up the steps and rang the bell and pounded on the front door. It was opened by Inez.

"Dad's sick—he's fainted or something. Where's Dr. Castellano?"

"Oh, *María Santísima,* he just left to see some patients. I don't know when he'll be back. Listen, there's a Dr. Freeman very close by on Park Place," she said, pointing to her left.

"Great, great. What number?"

She shook her head. "I don't know—but it is the only apartment house on the block. His name is outside on a brass *letrero* near the front door. You get the doctor. I will go to Estelle and see if I can help."

Less than two minutes later, Warren stood breathless outside 135 Park Place, pressing the button next to OSCAR FREEMAN, M.D. In a few moments, a man's voice came over the intercom. "This is Dr. Freeman. Can I help you?"

"My father's fainted, Doctor. I mean, he's just lying on the ground. Can you please come quickly?"

"Is he unconscious?"

"Yes, yes," Warren replied, now almost shouting with anxiety. "Can you hurry—*please?*"

There was a brief silence.

Then the physician's disembodied voice said unemotionally, "I'm sorry, son, I think you'd better call an ambulance. I can't get involved in this sort of thing—professional reasons."

There was a click. Warren stood motionless for an instant, lost and confused. He had never imagined that the doctor wouldn't come. Oh, God, he thought, what should I do now?

He ran back home, propelled by fear.

The scene in the garden was practically as he had left it, except that Inez had brought a blanket to cover Harold, who was shivering.

"Where's the doctor?" Estelle demanded.

"He wouldn't come," Warren retorted angrily. "Has anybody phoned the hospital?"

"Yes," Inez replied, "they said they would come as soon as possible."

The ambulance arrived twenty-seven minutes later.

It brought Harold Livingston to King's County Hospital, where he was pronounced dead.

Barney was working at The Versailles when Warren called. He raced into the street, flagged a taxi, and leaped in.

"This is a new one on me," the driver jested, "a doorman flagging a cab for himself."

"Spare me the jokes," Barney snapped. "Just get me to King's County Hospital as goddamn fast as you can."

The corridor was badly lit and smelled of disinfectant. At the far end, Barney could see Inez comforting his weeping mother and could hear Luis bellowing, "*Mierda!*—this was stupidity—nonsense! You should never have let him off!"

As Barney came closer, he saw the Spaniard berating his younger brother, who was in a state of shock. "I swear, Dr. Castellano," Warren kept protesting weakly, "I told him it was life and death—"

Seeing her elder son, Estelle rose and cried out, "Barney, Barney." And rushed to embrace him.

The world seemed to stop as he held his grieving mother in his arms, trying to comfort her.

After a few moments, Estelle murmured, "I want to see him again. Will you come with me, Barney?"

Her elder son nodded.

He looked at his brother's face and sensed the qualms he was feeling. "Warren, stay here with the Castellanos till we get back."

Alone with Luis as they both walked to the hospital parking lot, Barney was finally able to ask, "What were you so angry about back there, Dr. Castellano?"

Punctuating his interjections with profanity, Luis recounted the events of that morning.

Barney was confused. "How could a doctor just sit on his ass and let my father die?"

Luis answered through clenched teeth, "The craven bastard was afraid of a lawsuit."

"I don't understand—what kind of lawsuit?"

"My boy, in this great land many physicians will not come to an emergency like this. Because if the patient dies, the family can later sue for malpractice."

"Isn't it a doctor's responsibility to help?"

"Only morally," Luis answered with quiet anger. "Not legally. No law says that a physician absolutely has to come."

"Do you think it would have made a difference?" Barney asked.

Luis shrugged. "We'll never know. Your father's cause of death was myocardial infarction. Time makes a crucial difference when you are dealing with ventricular fibrillations. Freeman could have injected lignocaine—and at least started trying to resuscitate."

Barney exploded with rage. "I'll kill that guy—I'll go and kill him with my bare hands."

Luis grasped Barney's shoulder tightly. "*Calma, cálmate, hijo.* There is no point. You must accept that he is dead. You must be calm for your mother's sake. Remember you are the man in the family now."

It was almost midnight when they got home. Laura had arrived from Boston moments earlier.

"I've—uh—made some coffee and sandwiches," she said diffidently. "I mean, if anybody's hungry. . . ."

The Livingstons' sadness was palpable and yet she could see that Barney was suffering more than grief.

Luis and Inez took Estelle upstairs: he to give her a sedative and she to help her get ready for bed. Warren took a sandwich and an apple and headed for his room—to be alone with his sorrow.

That left only Barney and Laura in the kitchen.

"Hey, Barn, talk to me," she said softly. "I know you're hurting and it'll help to talk."

He lowered his head.

She went over, knelt down, and touched his arm. "Say something, Barn."

Finally, he gave voice to his obsession. "I can't believe it—a *doctor* let him die."

"Barney, that's not important now."

"Well, then, what the hell is?"

She put her hand on his cheek and he grasped it like a drowning man would seize a lifeline.

And allowed himself to cry.

In the days that followed, Estelle Livingston was inconsolable. Barney stayed at home, only venturing to Manhattan for a class or to work a night shift at The Versailles.

Harold's funeral, though planned for only the closest of relations, was augmented by more than a dozen teachers from Erasmus Hall who remembered him with affection, and even by a few former students who had read of his death in the *Brooklyn Eagle*.

One evening two weeks later, Estelle and her sons sat around at the kitchen table to talk about the future. "We're going to be all right," she told them. "Harold was meticulous about these things. We own the house free and clear. His will requests that his two sons share his library. He wasn't more specific. He knew that you'd act fairly with each other."

"I couldn't bear to take any of his books," Barney murmured.

Warren nodded. "Me either. I want to leave everything—you know—just where it is."

Estelle understood. They needed time—all of them.

"He took care of us," she continued. "His insurance from the Teachers' Federation will pay fifteen thousand dollars and his GI policy another ten. That means we won't have any real financial worries."

The two brothers nodded.

"I've given a lot of thought to what to do with this money," she continued. "Barney, I want you to stop working yourself to death. For the rest of the time you're at Columbia, I'll pay all your expenses so you can just study."

Barney raised his hand to protest but she cut him off.

"Please," she insisted, and then said the words she knew would put an end to all discussion. "That's what your father wanted. Don't think we didn't talk about this."

Barney sat motionless, trying to imagine how painful these conversations must have been for his mother.

"I'm putting the same amount in the bank for you," she said to Warren. "So you can afford to go to any law school you want."

"But Mom," said Warren quietly, "what would that leave you with?"

"I'll be just fine. As soon as you graduate from college I can put up the house for sale—"

By unconscious reflex, the brothers answered in unison, "No!"

"Be realistic, boys, do either of you intend to practice in Brooklyn?" she asked. "Besides, Aunt Ceil's been sending us brochures from Florida for years and, frankly, ever since she convinced Grandma to move down, I've been thinking how nice it would be to spend winters without galoshes and umbrellas.

"I know what this place means to you," she continued. "There are memories in every corner. But please believe me—we can sell the house and keep the memories. They'll always belong to us."

"I guess you're right, Mom," Barney said with a sigh of resignation. There was nothing more to say.

At the beginning Barney could not fully grasp the reality that, for the first time in his life, he could do whatever he wanted in vacation time.

The following summer, while Estelle went down to apartment hunt in Miami, the brothers Livingston signed up for a cross-country bus tour— the Grand Canyon, Yellowstone Park, the California Redwoods—culminating with three days in Hollywood.

And for the first time they got to know each other as adults. They talked about their dreams, the "Miss Perfect" they each thought they wanted to marry.

"It's going to be sad," Warren said half-aloud.

"What do you mean, War?"

"I mean, Dad won't be at our weddings. You know, I just can't get used to that idea."

"Me either."

They had always been brothers. But that summer they became friends.

"What the hell are *you* doing here?"

Boyish Ken Cassidy, recently elevated to the post of Columbia Varsity basketball coach, was astounded to see a ghost from the past among the fresh-faced sophomore candidates for the team.

"I'm here just like everybody else, Mr. Cassidy, sir," Barney Livingston said with excruciating politeness.

"Come off it, don't waste my time."

"This is America, sir. Isn't everyone entitled to an impartial judgment?"

"Okay," he sighed. "Take your constitutional rights. Go out there and bounce a ball so I can bounce *you*."

In the initial round, Barney was the only one who sank a shot. And under the boards, he was like an octopus with elbows.

At the end, he had wrought such havoc with the rookies that even the straitlaced coach had to break into a smile.

Oh, what the heck, Cassidy thought, I'll take this clown as fifteenth man. At least he'll give the other guys some aggression during practice.

Now that he felt affluent, Barney would call Laura at least one night a week. She could barely wait for February when Columbia would be coming up to Cambridge to play Harvard.

"Castellano," he warned her, "your milquetoast Harvard guys are gonna see the meanest gutter rat who ever lived."

All during the long bus ride from Morningside Heights, while the rest of the team slept, Barney was wide awake, churned up, ready to unleash himself.

The team ate an early training meal at the Harvard Varsity Club. There were still another four hours to kill before game time. But Barney had made other plans for this hiatus. He strode as quickly as possible through the icy Cambridge streets to the Harvard Square subway station, where he caught the train to Park Street, then changed to a tram that let him off two blocks from Harvard Medical School.

He arrived fifteen minutes early at the wood-paneled office of Dr. Stanton Welles, director of Admissions.

Keenly aware of the legend that Harvard Medical School took not just the finest, but also the most fearless, Barney used the waiting time before his interview to concentrate on the answers he had prepared for the inevitable question: "Why do you want to be a doctor, Mr. Livingston?"

(A) Because I want to comfort and heal the suffering in the world. No, too obvious.

Or perhaps

(B) Because your unrivaled research facilities will enable me to discover new cures, cross new frontiers. Like Jonas Salk, preventing tragedies like little Isobel. No, too pretentious.

Or maybe

(C) Because it's a guaranteed step up the social scale. True, but nobody would admit it.

Or even

(D) Because I want to make a lot of money. (Could be credited for candor—might be rejected for crassness.)

Or better

(E) Because I always looked up to Luis Castellano and want to be a caring man like him.

And

(F) Because a callous doctor caused my father's death and I want to show up all the lousy guys like him.

Answers (E) and (F) at least had the benefit of being genuinely sincere. Still, were they good enough?

Before he could meditate further a voice called out, "Mr. Livingston?"

He looked up. Standing before him was a tall, lean, distinguished-looking man in a three-piece suit that could only have been Brooks Brothers 44-long. Barney leaped to his feet.

"Yes, sir," he replied, very nearly saluting.

"I'm Dr. Welles. Thanks for taking the trouble to come and see us. Shall we step into my office?"

Barney entered a room decorated with an awesome collection of laminated kudos. Besides diplomas, there were memberships in all sorts of societies (national, international, royal, etc.). Not to mention letters signed by what seemed to be every U.S. President since George Washington.

The director ensconced himself behind a grand mahogany desk, and Barney sat straight-backed in a traditional Harvard chair (colonial style— tan wooden arms and a polished black frame bearing the school's insignia in gold).

There was what seemed a long silence. Barney leaned forward, arms on his knees, body poised as if waiting for a jump ball.

At long last Welles opened his mouth and asked, "Do you think you have a chance tonight?"

Barney was taken aback. What kind of trick was this guy trying to pull? How was he supposed to handle this one? Politely say he would do his sportsmanly best? Say that he hoped they would kick the shit out of Harvard? Or ask how can we talk of basketball when there is so much illness and suffering in the world? He rejected all of these alternatives.

"I think so, sir," he replied politely.

But the next question was also from left field.

"Care to put a bet on it?"

Barney could not even come up with a single alternative. So he replied, "Not really—I mean, how would it look if I ended up putting ten bucks in your hand? It might seem like a bribe."

Welles laughed. "Quite right. I never thought of that. Tell me . . ." He paused, then asked, "What drew you to basketball?"

By this time Barney had assumed Welles did not regard him as a serious candidate.

"Because there are no polo fields in Brooklyn, sir."

The doctor gave a little smile. "Hmm. Never thought of that, either." Then he rose, offered his hand, and said cordially, "It's been nice meeting you, Livingston."

"But sir, aren't you even going to ask me why I want to be a doctor?"

"I think you said it all quite eloquently in your application essay. I found it very moving. I'm sure you'll be glad to know that a group of us at HMS are lobbying in the State House for a 'Good Samaritan' bill. So that doctors won't be afraid of attending to a patient who's unconscious— like your father. Sorry I'll miss the game tonight but we've got to dine with some visiting firemen from Tokyo. Anyway, I'm sure we'll see a lot of each other next year."

Heedless of the icy patches on the sidewalk, Barney skipped like a child down the street toward the tram.

The crowd in the Indoor Athletic Building was sparse. Columbia was not exactly a big draw. As the visiting team took the floor, the applause was perfunctory. And only one person felt inspired enough to shout encouragement.

"Let's go, Livingston!"

Barney smiled and, dribbling with one hand, waved with the other.

Good old Castellano, my one-man fan club. But there were actually two ardent supporters—the person sitting next to her was clapping heartily as well. No doubt this broad-shouldered, Harris-tweeded individual was that "parfit gentil knight" of the two last names, Palmer Talbot. My God, he looks even preppier than Ken Cassidy, our all-American coach!

Three minutes or so after the game began, Barney was Columbia's first substitution. More cheers from Laura. Determined to show her all he had learned since she had last seen him in action, he really poured it on. His enthusiasm took its toll: before the first quarter ended, he had already fouled out. Coach Cassidy was furious.

"What are you, Livingston, some kind of animal? What the heck happened to your subtlety?"

"I guess I left it in New York—sorry."

And all through the second half he sat on the bench, head bowed, trying not to look at Laura.

After the game (which Harvard won easily), Laura rushed across the court to embrace Barney. And introduce Palmer. "Nice to meet you at last," said the handsome (and taller!) Harvard man. "Laura's always talked so fondly of you."

"Oh," Barney replied, trying not to act as insecure as he felt. "Too bad you caught me on an off day."

"Come on," Laura consoled. "Some of those calls were pretty dubious. I think the refs were biased."

"Please, Castellano," Barney replied, "don't humor me. I was cottage cheese out there."

"Speaking of cheese, I hope you'll be joining us for dinner," Palmer offered cordially.

Shit, Barney thought to himself, I was looking forward to being alone with Laura to tell her about this afternoon.

"Yeah, yeah, of course."

They went to Henri Quatre, an elegant little bistro on the second floor of a wooden house in a narrow alleyway just off Boylston Street.

"We assumed you'd be tired after the game, so we took the closest place," Palmer explained as they were leaving the gym. "And they do serve a reasonable approximation of haute cuisine."

Feeling insecure, Barney was unable to decide whether the guy was talking down to him or was just physically taller.

They sat, making small talk but unable to find common ground.

Palmer, it turned out, had been graduated the previous year—magna cum laude in Art History, as Laura mentioned when her reticent beau did not. It also turned out he had been on the second eight in crew. He was now in his first year at the Business School (majoring in money?).

He seemed genuinely interested in the topic Barney had chosen for his senior essay: "The Image of the Physician in English Literature."

"I do hope you'll quote Matthew Arnold's wonderful lines about wanting to avoid 'the doctor full of phrase and fame' who comes in 'to give the ill he cannot cure a name'—or words to that effect."

No, Palmer, Barney thought to himself, those are the poet's *exact* words. In fact, he had to concede that this Palmer Talbot was pretty impressive. He might even go as far as to say Palmer was a nice guy.

"By the way, Barn," Laura inquired, "how'd your interview go today?"

"Okay."

"Just okay?"

Barney was bursting to tell her everything—but not before an audience. So he simply shrugged and stated, "Let's just say it was not as bad as my nightmares, so don't worry."

"I can't help it, Barn. I'm absolutely petrified. I mean, they only accept about five or six women a year."

Palmer interposed with an interesting, if questionably relevant fact. "In Russia the majority of doctors are women."

"Are you suggesting I apply to the University of Moscow?" Laura gibed.

"Not at all," Palmer protested. "I don't ever want you to leave Boston."

At eleven-thirty they were standing in front of the gym where the rest of the Columbia squad had already boarded the bus for the long ride back to New York.

"Are you sure you won't stay over?" Palmer asked amiably. "I'd be glad to put you up at the B-School."

"No, no—thanks, but I've got a load of studying to do."

"I must say, all you Brooklynites certainly are ambitious."

"Well, it goes with the territory," Barney responded with as much levity as he could muster. He shook Palmer's hand, kissed Laura goodnight, and turned away, preparing himself to face his teammates' mockery about his laughable performance that evening.

Laura's grades were high. Her recommendations were genuinely enthusiastic, so she knew she would make it at least as far as the interview. But in her case there would not be the usual two appraisals—standard for male applicants—but three. Here again she capitulated to the inequity.

Her first encounter was with James L. Shay, M.D., a noted internist, in his Beacon Hill office dominated by a large window overlooking the sailboats on the Charles.

"You're a very pretty girl, Miss Castellano," he remarked, peering at her over his half-moon glasses.

"Thank you," she replied. (What else could she say—You're not bad yourself, Doctor?)

"A girl like you should be getting married and having a bunch of nice kids, don't you think?"

"With due respect, sir, I don't think medicine and motherhood are mutually exclusive."

"But they are, my dear. Believe me, they are. It's impossible for a woman to pursue a full-time and really fruitful medical career without doing irreparable harm to her children. Now, you wouldn't want to do that, would you?"

Laura was still unsure as to whether he was serious or just testing her.

"I take your point, sir—"

"Good, good—"

"So I'll never get married and just devote my life to medicine."

Dr. Shay peered over his glasses. "Surely you can't be serious, Miss Castellano?"

This was the crunch. But after only a millisecond she responded, "I thought it was you who wasn't being serious, Dr. Shay."

The interviewer had no riposte. He sat for a moment, fumbling with some papers, then rose with a tiny smile and said, "Thank you for coming by, Miss Castellano."

She left his office knowing she had won the round, but fearing she had lost the vote.

In a small cubicle in a lab at "643" (as the insiders referred to Building D at 643 Huntington Avenue), Louise Hoffman, Ph.D., a bio-chemist in her mid-thirties, proved almost more anxious to assert than to inquire.

"I'll be perfectly honest, Laura," she began. "I went through college wanting to be a doctor, too—and I was accepted by HMS, so this isn't sour grapes. But the life of a woman doctor on the hospital floors is a daily humiliation. Some of the men simply refuse to acknowledge your right to be there. Look, you've got a good brain. Why not become a research scientist, where at least you won't be treated as something only slightly better than a mop?"

"But I want to change that—or at least try," Laura protested. "If we all shied away from clinical medicine because it's a rough ride, we'll be mops forever."

Dr. Hoffman smiled. "You've got a lot of spunk, Laura. I think you'll make a wonderful doctor. That's only"—she paused dramatically—"if you survive Medical School."

Two down and one to go. Laura knew the final session—the psycho-logical evaluation—would be decisive.

Dr. Paul Gardner saw his patients in a tasteful, red-brick annex to his home in Chestnut Hill. Laura arrived promptly at six-forty and ten minutes later the doctor beckoned her into his office. When she caught sight of the couch she thought for a split second that she might be asked to lie on it. But Dr. Gardner motioned her toward a chair. In an instant, he was back at his desk, notepad open.

"So?"

"I beg your pardon, Doctor?"

"So you want to be a doctor, Miss Castellano."

"Yes sir."

"Any special reason?"

At least this guy was making some sense. "Well, to begin with, my father's a doctor. . . ."

"Ah, and so you feel a rivalry with your father?"

"No, not at all. I like him. I admire him."

"So then perhaps you are going through this medical business to, so to speak, woo him?"

"I beg your pardon?"

"Your mother is, I assume, not a doctor. So, therefore, by becoming a physician you would displace her as the preeminent woman in the family?"

"Oh, please," Laura protested with exasperation, "this is such a load of—nonsense."

"You can say 'crap,' Laura. You're free to say anything you wish in here."

"Am I really?"

"Yes, yes, of course."

"Well then, Doctor, quite frankly, I think this whole line of questioning is total crap."

Gardner actually seemed pleased at this. "Go on, go on."

Laura no longer felt obliged to observe any decorum.

"Look, Doctor, if you'd taken the trouble to read my essay you would have seen that my little sister died of polio when I was nine. So if you're groping into my subconscious for some deep motives, how about survivor's guilt? How about the idea that the only way I can justify my existence is by trying to make sure that other children don't lose their sisters and brothers?" Then she lowered her voice and without apologizing asked, "Now how does that grab you?"

Gardner looked her straight in the eye (for the first time during the session) and answered, "I think that's most perceptive, Miss Castellano. I do hope you'll consider psychiatry as a specialty."

It had been an amazing year. For in 1957 the Russians had launched Sputnik into space. And to Luis Castellano's delight, Castro and Ché Guevara (a heroic MD) had begun to launch their revolution from their stronghold in Cuba's Sierra Maestra Mountains.

It was also the year the Dodgers abandoned Brooklyn for the greener turf of Los Angeles. (O Perfidy! The very bleachers seemed to weep.)

And on April fifteenth, telegrams of acceptance to Harvard Medical School were delivered to adjacent houses on Lincoln Place, Brooklyn. ·

It was childhood's end.

II

BECOMING DOCTORS

"All generous minds have a horror of
what are commonly called 'facts.'
They are the brute beasts of the
intellectual domain."

OLIVER WENDELL HOLMES (1809–94)
*Professor of Anatomy and Dean of
Harvard Medical School*

EIGHT

Emerson once remarked that Socrates would have liked the atmosphere at Harvard College. A tranquil paradise of Georgian red-brick mansions, graced by wise and ancient trees, the Yard would have been the perfect place to hold a peripatetic seminar.

By the same token, Harvard Medical School would have suited Hippocrates, the totemic father of all doctors (and perhaps even Socrates' own GP). The architecture of HMS is emphatically classical, its verdant quadrangle bounded on the east and west by marble buildings and dominated at the south by a stately temple buttressed with bold Ionic columns. A worthy monument to Apollo the Healer; Asclepius, god of medicine; and his daughter Hygieia, the divinity of Health.

Indeed, a frivolous legend has it that Hippocrates, having grown restless after spending two millennia in the Elysian Fields with the hale and hearty, came back to earth and applied to Harvard Med to observe what progress had been made in the profession since his heyday.

Posing as a straight-A Harvard senior who had scored a perfect eight hundred on the Med Aps and had also run four minutes for the mile, he went serenely confident to his interview. When asked by his interrogator, respected orthopedic surgeon Christopher Dowling, what he considered to be the essential principle of Medicine, Hippocrates confidently quoted himself, "First, do no harm."

He was rejected as unsuitable.

There is considerable debate on what he *should* have said. One school of thought holds that the first principle of latter-day medicine is to find out if your patient has Blue Cross or Blue Shield. But this is cynical as well as incorrect. The true essence of modern medical philosophy, ignored only by a few altruistic renegades, is *the doctor must never admit that he is wrong.*

But how do these erstwhile mortals acquire their infallibility?

There is a hierarchy. First they are novitiates whose faith is sorely tested by autos-da-fé. They have to burn (in midnight oil) four long years. Thereafter, if not consumed, they enter a monastic order infamous for its asceticism—the "Somnambulists" (in other words, interns). After a year of sleepless penance, they can in turn become flagellators for the younger postulants. And in time, they are initiated. Now there is no limit to their advancement in the Holy Order. Bishop, cardinal—even the Vatican.

Except in medicine there are ten thousand Romes: the pediatric papacy, the neurological, the psychiatric (whence the term 'spiritual father'). There even is a Sacred Seat for the proctologist. Saint Peter built a church upon a rock. For many doctors, gallstones have sufficed.

But it all commences in ritual humiliation. And be it Buffalo or Boston, Mississippi or Montana, the rites are similar. Those who aspire to face the agony and suffering of humankind must first themselves become acquainted with it.

Harvard Med School's single dormitory was a colossal architectural chimera—combining the worst of Venice and of Boston Gothic. (A few medical minds had referred to it as a "cacoplastic anomaly.")

The circular lobby was topped by a garish rococo cranium, decorated by what can only be described as a med student's nightmare: writhing snakes, beakers, flasks, and other laboratory vessels—offering a field day for Freudians. Over the door were the famous words of Dr. Louis Pasteur, *"Dans le champs de l'observation le hasard ne favorise que les esprits préparés"*—In the field of scientific observation, chance favors only the mind that is prepared.

A long oak table was manned by several student clerks seated behind rectangular signs bearing letters of the alphabet so that the newcomers could more easily sign in and get their keys. The hum of quiet chatter reverberating in the dome mixed with the nearby strains of a Chopin waltz.

"Ah, the C-sharp minor," Palmer sighed appreciatively, "and it must be Rubinstein."

"No," said a thin, bespectacled young man in a white coat. "It's Applebaum."

Laura spied a familiar group of Harvard refugees from across the river and hurried to join them, Palmer in pursuit.

Barney took his place in line, feeling lost. He was only mildly relieved to discover that they were indeed expecting him—and had even assigned him lodgings.

Actually, "lodgings" was too grandiose a term. His room turned out to be a closet decorated in a style that reminded him of the inside of a cheese box. Surely the inmates of Death Row had more cheerful quarters, he thought to himself—and softer beds. But what can you expect for three hundred bucks a year?

Fearing suffocation, he kept the door open while he unpacked. As he was piling up his Jockey shorts, a smiling face with large exophthalmic brown eyes peeked in.

"You first-year?" he asked, as the rest of him appeared.

Barney nodded and offered his hand. "Barney Livingston, Columbia."

"Maury Eastman, Oberlin. I'm a writer." He took an intellectual puff on the pipe he had been holding in his left hand.

"Then what are you doing in Vanderbilt Hall?" Barney asked bemusedly.

"Oh, I'm going to be a doctor too—but in the sense that Keats, Rabelais, Chekhov, and Sir Arthur Conan Doyle were doctors."

"I thought Keats didn't graduate," Barney remarked.

"He still worked as assistant surgeon at St. Thomas's Hospital." Maury's eyes gleamed. "Do you want to write too?"

"Only prescriptions," Barney replied. "Have you published?"

"Oh, a few short stories in the little magazines—I can slide them under your door. But it's all a kind of rev-up for the first Big One. A few New York houses have already shown interest. If you turn out to be colorful, I'll work you in."

"What exactly is the Big One gonna be?"

"The diary of a Harvard Med student. You know, the pain, the angst—what it's really like to be on the cutting edge. Millions of readers are fascinated by the mystique of medicine—"

"Want to know another interesting fact, Maury? The word 'fascinating' comes from the Latin meaning 'prick.'"

"Come on—"

"Really—my father was a Latin teacher. It comes from *fascinum-i*, neuter noun signifying an icon of the male member. You should try and work that in somehow."

"I must say, Barney, you're an oasis of urbanity in a sewer of scientific snobs."

"Thanks. Uh—see you down at the faculty sherry party, huh?"

"Absolutely. I'm especially anxious to see how the girls interact. I mean the admissions people must have taken Spanish fly this year. Usually they pick dogs or pigs. But this time there's an absolute stunner. I get priapic just thinking about her. . . ."

Oh, shit, Barney said to himself, here we go again. "Yeah—name's Laura Castellano, I think."

"Who?" asked Maury.

What? thought Barney.

"I'm talking about Grete Andersen. She was Miss Oregon a few years ago—and let me tell you, she is built like a brick shithouse."

"Hey, I'm glad you warned me. I'd better shower and shave so I can . . . fascinate old Grete."

"I'll be watching every move you make."

"You do that, Maury. Then you'll believe my theory that the *Kama Sutra* was actually written in Brooklyn."

When the author finally departed, Barney came to a significant decision: From now on he would keep his door closed.

Having made the revolutionary decision a decade earlier to admit women as potential physicians, Harvard had now taken another bold step by consecrating a small section of what had heretofore been a monastery to shelter its handful of female students. Their area of Vanderbilt Hall, officially known as the Deanery, was colloquially referred to by the hairy-chested XY-chromosomal population as "The Erogenous Zone."

It was here that Laura Castellano was required to spend her freshman year.

She was scrubbing off the grime of the journey when a radiant face appeared in the long mirror of the ladies' bathroom.

"Going to the party?" a velvety voice inquired.

Laura nodded. "Just for a few seconds, I've got a date. Besides, for some reason sherry doesn't agree with me."

"It's the congeners," her companion replied, "they really mess up your metabolism—toxic as hell. From a purely scientific standpoint, they really should serve vodka or scotch."

"Fat chance. Around here, chemistry yields to economy."

The girl smiled, revealing a set of incandescent teeth.

"I'm Grete Andersen," she said. "And I'm the scaredest person in the first-year class."

"Wrong—you're *talking* to the scaredest. My name's Laura Castellano."

"How could you be frightened?" Grete asked. "You've already got the cutest boy in our class."

"Thanks. Palmer's terrific, I agree. But he's not a student."

"Then why was he lining up to get a room?"

"Oh, you must be talking about Barney—tallish, black curly hair?"

Grete nodded. "—and extremely cute. I really dig the catlike way he keeps shifting from one sneaker to the other—like a boxer or something. You mean he's not yours?"

"Not romantically. We grew up together in Brooklyn—sort of like brother and sister. If you're a good girl, Grete, I'll introduce you."

"If I were a good girl I'd never have made it here," she replied in a suggestive purr.

Laura smiled and thought, Barney, you're gonna really owe me for this one.

Never again in the next four years would they see so many distinguished physicians gathered in a single Harvard room. The very air was charged with eminence. Since it was clear that the incoming students had little more to offer than hushed reverence, the faculty spoke to one another in a semi-public manner, as their acolytes hung on every syllable.

The topic was perennial: *Who would win it this year?* And they weren't talking about the World Series. Indeed, rumor had it that at least half a dozen professors had bags packed in readiness should they suddenly be commanded to appear in Stockholm.

Indeed, HMS, ever on the lookout for Nobel material, had given ample thought to its future laurels when selecting the class it was now welcoming with Pedro Domecq sherry. Due consideration had of course been given to the "whole man" (and in the case of Grete and Laura, the whole woman). But Havard had also ferreted out a substantial number of brilliant and truly dedicated minds—men with no other interest in life but research, whose libidos much preferred the viral to the virile.

One such specimen was Peter Wyman, a certified genius who already had a Ph.D. in Biochemistry and was adding an M.D. to his name only to be sure of having a passport into every area of the research world.

Peter of the oatmeal face and scraggly hair was the only one genuinely talking *to* a professor, speaking earnestly with a cytobiologist of "going beyond the subcellular."

"God," whispered an awed classmate standing next to Barney, "he makes me want to pack up and go home."

"He makes me want to barf," Barney retorted.

With that, he moved off. For he had spied Laura entering the door—with Grete Andersen.

Instinct told him that he had to intercept the ball before it got any further upcourt.

When Laura began to introduce them he felt like he was going into cardiac arrest. Never in his life had he seen a body like that—not in Midwood, Sunset Boulevard—or even on the burlesque stage in Union City, New Jersey. This is a med student?

He heard the approaching hoofbeats of the rest of the Hippocratic horde. He made the sharpest possible move, asking her to have "pizza or something" right after the reception was over.

The candlepower in the room seemed infinitely brighter as Grete smiled. "That's super—I adore pizza." She would need a few seconds after the party to step into something more casual and would meet him downstairs at seven-thirty. (Great going, Livingston—slam dunk!)

The rest of the party was an exhilarating toboggan ride. Barney chatted briefly and amicably with a few professors, thanked his interviewer— who made an emphatic pitch for orthopedic surgery ("that's real *man's* medicine") and started for the door.

At this point he noticed Laura talking to a tall, handsome student, distinctive not only for his elegant apparel, but also because he was the only black man in the room not carrying a tray.

She caught Barney's eye and waved him over.

It was en route that Barney suddenly realized who the guy was.

"Barney, I'd like you to meet—"

"No need for fancy introductions," he interrupted. "I know a superjock when I see one." Then, looking at her companion, he remarked, "You're Bennett Landsmann, the meanest runner-and-gunner in Harvard basketball history. I saw you play at Columbia four years ago. You scored something like thirty-two points. Right?"

"Something like that," the black man said modestly and offered his hand. "I didn't catch your name."

"I didn't throw it," Barney riposted. "Anyway, I'm Barney Livingston and I'm happy you had graduated by the time I got on the court against your little college. Which reminds me—how come you're only starting Med School? Weren't you two years ahead of us?"

"I guess I'm retarded." Bennett smiled mischievously.

"Don't believe him, Barn," Laura chided. "He was at Oxford on a Rhodes scholarship."

"It figures," Barney said. Then he asked Bennett, "Did you know there's a gym in the basement of this overgrown mausoleum? Want to meet sometime and throw a few?"

"Gladly," Bennett replied. "In fact, a reliable source informs me that there's usually a pickup game at five-thirty. Why don't we check it out?"

"Okay, great," Barney agreed enthusiastically.

"See you there," Bennett said. "Now, if you'll excuse me, I gave my solemn oath to Dr. Dowling that I'd listen to his sales pitch for orthopedics."

Barney watched as Bennett Landsmann moved gracefully through the crowd and thought to himself, I wonder how it feels to be the only black man in the class. I'll bet underneath that air of relaxed charm he must be lonely as hell. Or angry. Or both.

Before he departed, Barney met a few more classmates, among whom was Hank Dwyer, a soft-spoken, porcelain-featured grad of Holy Cross, originally from Pittsburgh. He had been studying for the priesthood when he had suddenly experienced the call to be a doctor—but it was clear he still harbored ambivalent feelings.

"Well," Barney offered, "you have the precedent of Saint Luke."

"Yeah," Dwyer agreed, smiling wryly, "that's what I told my mother. She still doesn't like the idea. In our family, religion is more important than anything."

"What happens if anyone gets sick?"

"You go to church and pray for their recovery."

"Suppose they're dying?"

"Then you call a priest to give them last rites."

Barney somehow felt that the young man's urge to exchange white collar for white coat had been inspired by more than a desire to heal. For he noticed Hank's stolen glances at the incomparable Miss Andersen.

Barney left just before seven and rushed upstairs to don a sportier outfit. He was back downstairs at seven-twenty-four to make certain of being strategically placed when Grete the Great appeared.

Anticipation had sharpened his thoughts. He now realized that taking this Venus de Milo to a mere pizzeria would be like inviting the Queen of England to Dunkin' Donuts.

No, this was not an opportunity that was likely to come his way a second time. *Think,* Livingston, where can you take her that's got a little more atmosphere—and class?

How about the Copley Grille—nice wood paneling, subdued lighting?

But that would blow twenty bucks for sure. Maybe more, if she liked martinis.

He played over in his mind Warren's "paternal" lecture to him on the day before he left for Boston.

His younger brother had assiduously composed a balance sheet and pronounced, "I've got all your expenses worked out, Barn. And I think if interest rates hold up—and you don't go wild buying a car or something— you've got enough dough to carry you all four years. Tuition's a thousand a year, you've got the cheapest dorm room—three hundred and forty dollars for rent—and your meals will run two-fifty per semester—"

"I still say I'd rather cook in my room."

"No way, read the catalogue. All first-year guys have to eat in the dining hall. But if you only go to the movies once a week—"

"Can I afford to take a date?"

"Yeah, yeah," Warren said, smiling indulgently, "you can even spring for two orders of popcorn. Anyway, assuming another hundred and fifty for travel and miscellaneous, you can probably make it for just under three thousand dollars a year."

Dammit, Warren—why didn't you have a contingency plan for sex-bombs?

To hell with it, Barney thought, if I can impress this chick on the first date, I'll gladly starve for a week.

Then he glanced at his watch. It was already eight-fifteen and Grete still hadn't shown. But he waited faithfully, his only company being the legendary physicians in Harvard's history—who appeared to be scrutinizing him from the nearby portraits on the walls.

Oliver Wendell Holmes, a former dean of the Med School, heretofore known better to Barney for his poetry, seemed to be upbraiding him with some of his own immortal lines. "To crawl is not to worship; we have learned a drill of eyelids, bended neck and knee. . . ."

In other words, what kind of schmuck are you to wait this long for any girl?

Calls to Grete's room proved fruitless. Everyone was out enjoying this last night of freedom. By now Barney was tired, hungry and frustrated. But most of all confused. Why the hell had she given him that high-calorie come-on if she hadn't wanted to go out? And she could have canceled, pleading tiredness or something. He was about to put his fist through a portrait of Dr. John Warren (1753–1815) when Palmer and Laura appeared.

"What're you doing down here alone, Barn? I thought you had a date with Grete."

"So did I. I guess she got a better offer."

"Why don't you join us for a bite to eat?" Palmer offered in genuine sympathy. "Come on, food is the next best thing to you-know-what."

Barney smiled appreciatively. As he rose and walked out with them, he inwardly conceded, Castellano was right. Palmer *is* a nice guy.

The next thing he knew he had been crammed into the middle of a Porsche and was zooming toward Jack and Marion's, where Laura insisted he order the gargantuan chocolate cake. "A little carbohydrate-induced hyperglycemia really lifts the mood."

Inwardly she was more troubled than Barney, who by the tenth mouthful had all but shrugged off his feelings of slighted masculinity. I've got to live with this sex-bomb, she told herself—I hope she doesn't drive *me* crazy.

Back in the lobby of Vanderbilt, Laura dispatched Palmer with: "You're at liberty till next Saturday, pal."

"Under protest," Palmer conceded, "but I'll call you." And moving off he waved to both of them, "Ciao, doctors."

Now Laura and Barney were alone.

"Hey, thanks, Castellano. My ego was pretty anemic till you came along. Anyway, I think Talbot's a terrific guy."

"Yeah," Laura remarked as she started toward her room. "He's probably too good for me."

NINE

If the previous night's sherry party had been intended to polish the hard, gemlike egos of the aspiring physicians, the next morning's welcoming lecture by Dean Courtney Holmes shattered them in short order.

They had been astonished to hear that even the most brilliant doctors (like Holmes himself) had such woefully inadequate knowledge of the ills that beset the human body that they possessed an empirical cure for only *twenty-six* of them.

Were they really about to slave for at least another five years to enter a profession that was ninety-eight percent guesswork?

The neophytes were still glassy-eyed as they lined up in the cafeteria for their noontime gruel.

Laura whispered to Barney that she felt gender-bound to join the four other girls, who had already appropriated an exclusive table for the "Honorary Men." He nodded, looked around the cafeteria, saw Bennett Landsmann, and decided to sit with someone he already knew.

Moments later Hank Dwyer joined them, still expressing his bewilderment at Holmes's peroration.

"Are we supposed to *know* all those incurable diseases he rattled off? I mean I haven't even heard of some of them."

He was answered by a classmate sitting on his own at the far end of the table. "How did you ever get accepted to this place? Holmes only cited the most basic medical mysteries—you know, the kind our future research—at least mine—is destined to solve."

The nasal, condescending voice belonged to Peter Wyman.

"Is this character for real?" Barney whispered to Bennett.

"I hope not," his neighbor replied. But Wyman continued to pontificate.

"Shall I start with leukemia and diabetes or can I assume you at least know something about leukocytes and the pancreas?"

"I know he's a goddamn pain in the pancreas," Barney whispered.

"Just what makes you so smart?" Hank demanded of Wyman.

"I'd say heredity, environment, and study," Peter replied.

"What's your name?"

"Peter Wyman, Ph.D., M.I.T., summa cum laude. And yours?"

"Henry X. Dwyer, S.J.—dropped out."

"You made the right choice, Dwyer," Peter commented paternally. "The only true religion is science."

As Dwyer fumed, Barney whispered to Bennett, "I think the priest is gonna punch the pedant."

As Wyman prated on and on, the rest of the table fell silent. They were trying to steel themselves. For in less than thirty minutes they would begin the first of their four hundred and fifty-five required hours of gross anatomy. Those who had taken Comparative Anatomy at college and had dissected frogs and rabbits tried to pretend that the species *homo sapiens* would be a similar exercise. Others had worked part-time in hospitals and had seen corpses. But none had ever put a knife into real flesh and sliced open a human body.

The first thing they noticed was the smell.

Even before they saw the rows of bodies, wrapped in plastic like so many elongated stuffed cabbages.

"Jesus," Laura whispered to Barney, "I can barely breathe."

"We'll get used to it," he murmured back. "That's the stuff that keeps the bodies from decaying."

"Kind of a paradox, isn't it," suggested Maury Eastman, "that we, who have come to preserve the living, must first preserve the dead."

"Bullshit," Barney snapped. He was too edgy to indulge in frivolous banter.

Unflustered, the self-appointed heir to Chekhov's mantle continued to philosophize.

"I wonder which of us it will be. You know, in every class there are guys who can't take this part. Some of them throw up or faint. I've even heard of one or two who walked out of the room and quit Med School completely."

Shut the hell up, Barney kept thinking. We're *all* wondering how we'll cope.

"Good afternoon, gentlemen," called a balding, white-coated figure as he scurried through the double doors in the far corner. It was Professor Charles Lubar, their guide through the human labyrinth.

"I'm especially pleased to be leading our expedition into the mysteries of the human body during this of all semesters, since it is precisely a hundred years ago that Henry Gray published the *Anatomy* which still serves as our basic text. We've assigned four of you to each table. There are name cards. Take your instruments and find your places. As soon as you're set up we can begin."

Barney and Laura had hoped they would be assigned to the same body. But it was not to be. Barney quickly found his station at a nearby table, while Laura went on to search for hers. She cast him a parting glance of helplessness.

"Stay loose, Castellano," he called after her quietly, "it'll be okay." She merely nodded and moved off.

Barney was happy to find that Bennett was one of the other two students sharing his cadaver (in fact the trio itself was lucky, since all of the other tables had a quartet of anatomists). Barney nodded across the acrid-smelling form of what (according to the tag tied around his foot) had been a fifty-six-year-old man who had succumbed to a cerebral hemorrhage.

At the next table another of their classmates studied his tag and remarked, "I think we've got a lousy stiff, guys—cancer. Must have guts like a junk heap." His remark met with disapproving stares from both Bennett and Barney.

"Hey," he protested apologetically, "I'm a little nervous, that's all. Forget what I said, okay?"

"Okay," said Barney. Bennett nodded his agreement.

The third member of their team was a short, bespectacled, frizzy-haired girl whom Barney deduced to be Alison Redmond (Laura had already spoken of the diminutive Bryn Mawr superbrain from St. Louis). She arrived just as Professor Lubar was beginning the traditional homily.

"First, I want all of you to look at the description of the person you are about to dissect. It's highly unlikely, but if you feel there is any chance it may be someone you know, please don't hesitate to ask to be transferred. . . ."

God, Barney thought, that never even occurred to me. Someone I *know*—that would really be grotesque. And then a terrifying, irrational fantasy crossed his mind. What if this were my father!

"All right, gentlemen," Lubar continued, "now I want to be unequivocal on this next point. The bodies before you were once living, breathing, *sentient* human beings. They were generous enough to leave their bodies to science so that, even in death, they could serve mankind. I want you to treat these people with respect. If I see any horseplay or fooling around, I'll kick the perpetrator right out of this course. Is that understood?"

There were murmurs of assent.

Now, in a less cautionary tone, he continued, "Every anatomist has his own idea of where to begin the study of the human body. Some start with the most familiar area—the epidermis or surface epithelium—and work their way through the skin, layer by layer. But I believe in getting right to the heart of the matter."

He then motioned them all to gather around a table in the front row, where the broad, graying chest and abdomen of a male corpse had been undraped.

The face and neck remained wrapped in cloth, giving the impression that "George" (as the professor had chosen to call him) was having an eternal facial massage. Some of those watching half expected—feared—that the dead man would suddenly cry out in pain—for Lubar was holding a scalpel just above the cadaver's neck, poised to attack.

His hand moved swiftly, piercing the body in the jugular notch, about half an inch deep. Like a railway conductor, he rattled off the names of the stations through which his instrument was passing: "epidermis, dermis, subcutaneous fat, superficial fascia, deep fascia, muscle—"

And finally the soft tissue outer wall was breached.

He had run the scalpel downward, a motion that had "unzipped" the skin—which had become as stiff as wax paper. For a moment the instructor paused to draw breath.

Then from a leather case that held what looked like a collection of shiny carpenter's tools, Lubar withdrew a sharp serrated knife and plunged it into the incision he had made at the top of the breastbone. The grating sound made the beholders wince as if their own chests were being sawed open.

The professor once again launched into a rapid burst of anatomical patter, all the while slicing the sternum: "manubrium, xiphoid process, intercostal muscles, thoracic nerves—" Then suddenly, with a snap, the rib cage split open like a cracked walnut, laying bare the innermost engine of human life: the heart. And, embracing it, the lungs.

The students pressed forward for a better look. And as they did, there was the sound of a balloon being deflated—as a body slumped to the floor. All eyes turned to the first casualty of their Medical School education. Sprawled on the floor, looking whiter than the cadaver, was Maury Eastman.

Barney bent over to revive his fallen comrade-in-arms. From above he heard Lubar's unruffled reassurance, "Don't worry, it happens every year. If he's still breathing, carry him outside and let him get some fresh air. If he's not, put him on a table and we'll dissect him."

By the time Barney and a muscular classmate named Tom had lugged Maury halfway to the door, he was already regaining consciousness. "No, no," he protested feebly, "take me back. It's just something I must have eaten at lunch. . . ."

Barney glanced at Tom as if to say, Let's stand him up. As soon as Maury was reasonably steady, they abandoned him to rush back to watch the demonstration.

Lubar gave them a rapid tour of the thoracic cavity—the great vessels of the heart, the thymus gland, the esophagus, sympathetic trunks, and vagus nerve—one of the longest electric wires, extending from the head all the way to the kidneys.

For the students, it was like viewing a faded photograph of the organs they had only seen in vivid color illustrations. All that had once been red and pink and purple was now pallid gradations of gray.

Suddenly Lubar interrupted his own commentary and asked, "What's wrong here?" He gazed from face to face as each student strove to avoid eye contact with him. Finally, he was obliged to appoint a volunteer.

"You." He pointed at the one pupil who seemed too polite to glance away. "What's the matter with George here?"

Hank Dwyer began to stammer, "I—I don't understand, sir. I mean, everything is wrong—his body isn't functioning at all—I mean, he's *dead*."

There were suppressed titters. Not of mockery, but of relief at not having been chosen. They all knew they would have said more or less the same stupid thing.

But Lubar did not denigrate the reply. "Yes," he continued without a trace of irony, "I'd agree that's starting from first principles. But did you notice anything out of the ordinary, Mister—?"

"Dwyer, sir."

"Well, Mr. Dwyer, did you also note that the gentleman was only forty-four when he died? What do you think brought him to such an early end? Do those lungs appear normal to you?"

Dwyer leaned over and took a closer look. The smell of formalin at such proximity was sickening. But he saw what he was intended to see. "His lungs are pretty shriveled up—and they seem awfully black...."

"Which means he was either a coal miner—or a heavy smoker. That blackness is carbon. Do you notice anything else, Mr. Dwyer?"

"There's a lump on his left lung—kind of white and gooey."

"Like marshmallow, you might say," Lubar added with a slight grin. "When you get to Pathology, you'll find those boys always talk in metaphors of food. Anyway, you'll also note the kind of salt-and-pepper effect on the other lung. The marshmallow's the primary carcinoma. And the grains of salt are metastases—newly established colonies from the principal malignancy. So if any of you want to commit suicide slowly, you can puff your way to heaven at an early age—just as this man did."

There was a chorus of murmurs around George's bier. Some, still unpersuaded of their mortality (or the American Cancer Society's report), thought, It won't happen to *me*. I just smoke two or three a day—except maybe at exam time.

"All right," said the professor, "now you can all go back and open up your own hearts."

"What shall we call him?" Barney asked as he and his partners nervously undraped their cadaver.

"How about Leonardo?" Alison Redmond proposed. "I mean da Vinci's anatomical drawings are as good as anything in *Gray's*—and he did them in 1487. In fact, he was a pioneer in the use of undershading to get the three-dimensional effect."

"Fine," Bennett agreed, "I'll go with Leonardo. Those drawings are magnificent. And dissection was probably not even allowed in his day."

"Of course the Italian Renaissance was a rare exception," Alison lectured on. "Leonardo actually dissected a body himself in 1506, probably thanks to his friend, Professor Marcantonio della Torre—"

"Okay, okay, Alison," Barney interrupted, to put a tourniquet on her verbal hemorrhage. "You've made your point. Why don't we get to the nitty-gritty. Who wants to do the first slice?"

Alison and Bennett both volunteered.

"Well, so do I," Barney asserted, "but why don't we just say ladies first."

"You don't have to be patronizing, Livingston," Alison retorted with undisguised hostility. "I'm as good as any man or I wouldn't be here."

"I don't doubt that for a second," Barney replied. "In that case, let's draw straws."

"Sounds fair to me," Bennett commented. "Only who's got straws?"

"We can use some of my fags," said Alison, withdrawing a half-empty pack of Gauloises from her pocket.

"It's better than smoking them," Barney commented sarcastically.

"My body is my own," she countered.

"Sure, sure," Barney said in halfhearted apology.

They were interrupted by the voice of Professor Lubar.

"Please note how I'm holding the scalpel." He was grasping it like a cello bow and making the pronating motion they were intended to imitate. "Try and enter the skin at a ninety-degree angle. Make it swift but light because I want us to study the layers of skin, subcutaneous fat, fasciae, and muscles on the way down. So just cut down to the top of the pectoralis major."

Barney, who had drawn the winning cigarette, imitated Lubar's grasp of the scalpel as best he could. He was just mustering the courage to make an incision when Alison inquired, "Do you want to look at the book before you cut?"

"No, thanks, I'm an ex-jock. We all know where the 'pecs' are."

All three were feeling the tension now.

"Okay, Barney," Bennett whispered in uneasy encouragement. "Go for it."

Barney hesitated for a millisecond. Until he realized that many of his classmates were already at the task. Indeed, at the very next table he saw Hank Dwyer cross himself and then swiftly move his scalpel downward. He wanted to look away, but knew Alison was studying him intently.

He lowered his hand and pierced Leonardo's parchment-dry flesh just below his neck. It felt like cutting into a crunchy autumn apple.

There was no blood. In a way that made it easier. It helped to make Leonardo seem less human—more like a waxen facsimile of life.

"Well done, Barney," murmured Bennett Landsmann at the very same time that Alison, on her own initiative, reached across the chest and with surgical tweezers began to fold back the skin and clamp it.

"God," she muttered under her breath, "this is the slowest table in the room. Get with it, you two. The guys over there are already down to the muscle."

Bennett took a quick glance to the right and then quickly corrected his partner. "Simmer down, Alison, they're only at the axillary fascia."

"What makes you so sure?" She challenged him in a surprised tone that seemed to insinuate that Bennett had done something treasonous—like take the course before.

But his response was merely to hold up their anatomical bible and say sweetly, "It's all right here in Dr. Gray, ma'am."

Sensing that it would be wise to keep the peace, Barney held out the scalpel and said, "Here, Alison, you cut. Ben and I will just take notes."

She took the knife and without another word began dissecting with a deftness and speed that would have been the envy of a senior surgeon.

"God, Barney, you absolutely reek."

It was three hours later and the anatomists, emotionally and physically exhausted, shuffled from the room.

"To be frank, Castellano, you don't exactly smell like a rose yourself."

"I know. I'd like to find a washing machine and stick my whole body in for an hour or two."

"Thank God for the smell," he confessed. "It knocked me for such a loop that I barely noticed I was slicing someone's body."

Just then the doors to the adjoining laboratory opened and another group of classmates emerged from their first session. Among them was Grete Andersen.

"Hey, Castellano," Barney whispered, "did you ever ask Grete why she didn't show?"

"No. She wasn't there when I got back and I went right to sleep."

"Oh," said Barney, reliving his disappointment. "I guess she probably just forgot or something. I'll go and ask her myself."

"Frankly, I think she's bad news," Laura cautioned. "As my mother said when I was five and tried to touch the burners on the stove, 'Cuidado, te quemaras.'"

"Don't worry," he replied complacently, "I'm too cool to get scalded."

Just then the subject of the debate came up and joined them.

"Hi, Barney," Grete said breezily. "How did you and your body get along?"

Shit, can't this girl say *anything* that doesn't have a sexual connotation?

"Fine, fine," Barney answered. And then, as casually as possible, "I—uh—missed you last night."

"Oh yes, Barney, I'm really sorry about our not being able to get together. But I was—well, I guess waylaid is the best way of putting it—by this professor—"

Waylaid or just laid? Barney mused to himself.

"—and by the time I got up to my room, I had this terrible headache. I tried to call you—"

"That's okay," he replied. "We'll just make it another time, that's all."

"The sooner the better," Grete replied enticingly. But she could tarry no longer. For Professor Robinson, her Anatomy teacher, was striding by and Grete suddenly remembered some questions she had forgotten to pose to him. She excused herself and dashed down the corridor, with Barney's eyes riveted on the spectacular movements of her gluteal muscles.

Laura watched him watch Grete and quipped, "I think that formalin has gone to your brain. Let's get these smelly clothes off and take a shower, huh?"

Barney was still distracted. "Christ, would I give anything to see Grete in the shower."

"Okay, Livingston," Laura answered sarcastically, "I'll take Polaroid pictures and give them to you for Christmas."

Barney had grown up with a religious belief in the unfailing efficacy of Lifebuoy soap. But dammit, he had been scrubbing for what seemed like fifteen minutes and instead of his body smelling like Lifebuoy, his soap was smelling like formalin!

"I'm gonna be here forever," he complained half aloud.

"It's like Sophocles' *Philoctetes,*" said a voice in a nearby shower stall.

"Explain the obscure reference," Barney shouted, anxious to take his mind off his odor.

"I'm surprised at you, Barn, I thought you knew your classical mythology cold," Maury Eastman answered. "Philoctetes was this Greek hero in the Trojan War who had a wound that was so smelly his buddies couldn't stand it. So they took him away and dumped him on a desert isle. But then a big-time prophet told them that without Philoctetes— stench and all—they would never take Troy. So they took him back. Pretty good allusion, huh?"

"Not really, Maury—because around here *everybody* stinks."

Back in the room, Barney stuffed his clothing into his trunk, deter-mined to use the same garb for Anatomy as long as possible. But though he put on completely fresh garments and had carefully washed his hair, the formalin remained everywhere, floating above him like a malignant halo.

The odor had the paradoxical effect of bringing the freshmen together—for the simple reason that no one in the cafeteria would sit anywhere near them.

"How much of that stuff are we supposed to remember?" asked Hank Dwyer. "I mean, do you think it'll be enough if we can just recognize the major muscle groups?"

"This isn't kindergarten, Dwyer. You've got to know every one of the three hundred named muscles, their origin, insertion, and action. Not to mention the two hundred and fifty ligaments, the two hundred and eight bones—"

"Goddammit, Wyman," Barney snarled, "we're in no mood to hear you tell us how stupid we are. If you don't shut up, we'll bring you up to the room and dissect you for practice."

Barney forced himself to study till nearly eleven. Then he called over to the girls' wing to see if Grete might be persuaded to have a quick cup of coffee. Laura answered.

"Hi, Castellano, can I speak to Grete?"

"If you can find her. I haven't seen her since before dinner. Should I leave a message that her horny admirer phoned?"

"No, she must have a thousand. I'll just go downstairs, grab a bite, and go to bed. Want to have a cup of coffee or something?"

"Too late, Barn. I've just washed my hair. But I'm touched that you still think of me at all." And then changing the subject, she inquired, "How's the studying coming?"

"So far it's strictly Mickey Mouse—memorize, memorize, memorize. Am I really going to be a better doctor if I can remember the names of every micron of the body? Any *fool* could learn this crap by heart."

"That's why there are a lot of foolish doctors, Barn—they know the names of everything and the meaning of nothing. The way I hear it, we won't see an actual sick person for two years."

"Correction, Castellano. Meet me for breakfast tomorrow and you'll encounter a genuine basket case."

Barney wished her goodnight and walked downstairs to the candy machine, squandering eighty cents on Hershey bars, Milky Ways, Baby Ruths, and Peter Paul's Coconut Mounds.

Ambling back down the corridor toward his cell, he heard the clickety-clack of typing. It could only be one person—the esthetic Maury, whose door was open to allow passersby a glimpse of the artist at work. Barney affected deep inner preoccupation as he passed Maury's room.

But he did not escape.

"Livingston!"

"Oh, hi there, Maur. I was heading for the sack. I'm really crumped out from today—"

"Emotionally drained?"

"Absolutely."

"Traumatized?"

"I guess so."

"And yet deeply moved by your first encounter with a dead body."

"Well, frankly, I prefer encounters with live bodies."

"Hey, that's good. That's really good." As Maury began a frantic burst of typing, Barney tried to edge away.

"Livingston—you can't leave yet!"

"Why not, Maur?"

"You've gotta see what the first day at Med School's really like."

"Are you serious? Where the hell do you think I've been?"

"Come on, you have to see how vividly I've captured all the *Sturm und Drang*." He held out a sheaf of yellow pages, urging his visitor to take them.

Barney was in no mood for anything but sleep. And yet he detected a hint of panic in Maury's voice.

"Okay," he capitulated, flopping down onto Maury's disheveled bed. "Let me see how life is transformed by art." He put down his collection of calorific delicacies.

"Hey, fantastic," Maury remarked with glee as he reached for a Hershey bar and began to unwrap it. And then, turning to Barney, he asked, with his mouth full, "You don't mind, do you, Livingston? I was so involved I didn't go down for dinner."

Barney began to read. Maury had gotten the feelings, all right, the fear and trembling, the thrill of watching a human body being opened to disclose its mysteries. He even had the humorous touch—a student fainting and the compassionate narrator hastening to revive him. But in a not-very-subtle transposition of character, *Maury* was the one observing Lubar with intense excitement, while the fainthearted student was none other than Barney!

Maury leaned over him, a strange grin on his face. "Good stuff, huh?"

Barney felt ill at ease. Why had this guy distorted the truth?

"Your pages, Maury. They're not very explicit about the thoracic cavity. . . ."

"This is a literary book, for God's sake. For the general reader."

"I know. But somehow the general reader doesn't get the impression that you even looked—"

"I looked," he protested almost frantically.

"Then how come you didn't even describe the goddamn heart? Even the *literati* would groove on that."

"Livingston, you're rapidly becoming a pain in the ass."

Barney let this remark sail over his head, like a boxer ducking a punch.

"Listen, Eastman, I want you to give me a straight answer. Did you go back to your table after you . . . were sick?"

"What are you driving at?" Maury answered uneasily.

"I mean, were you there for the rest of the Anatomy lab?"

Maury's eyes had the look of a frightened owl. "You don't understand, Livingston. They were all laughing. You were even laughing with the others."

"What others?"

"You heard them. Everybody in the class was mocking me."

Barney was growing increasingly anxious. He edged closer to Maury and asked gently, "Would you like to talk about what's worrying you?"

"Fuck you, Livingston, you're not my shrink!"

"Do you have a shrink, Maury?"

"None of your business—just get the hell out of here and leave me alone." He buried his head in his hands and began to sob.

Barney understood all too well that this was a plea for him *not* to leave. Yet he also knew that Maury had to get real help pronto.

"I'll leave if that's what you want," he said softly. "But then I think you should call the Health Service."

"I can't," Maury answered with a manic chuckle. "My father doesn't believe in shrinks."

"How come?"

"He is one." And then, almost as a non sequitur, he blurted, "My father hates my guts."

"Why?" Barney asked with outward calm, while feeling desperately out of his therapeutic depth.

"Because I killed my mother," Maury answered matter-of-factly.

"Oh" was all Barney could manage.

"I didn't really," Maury explained. "I mean, I was only two years old when she took all those pills and died. But my father thinks it's all my fault."

Barney knew there was no more time to waste.

"Look, I've got to go to the john for a second. Then I'll be right back."

As Barney turned to leave, Maury's tone suddenly became threatening, "But you better come right the hell back."

There was a phone at the end of the corridor near the stairwell. Barney was out of breath from running when he asked to be connected with Student Health.

A Dr. Rubin was on duty. His voice sounded calm and reassuring, so Barney gasped out the essential details of his friend's plight.

"So what should I do?" he asked urgently.

"I'd suggest you come downstairs so we can continue talking," the doctor replied.

"But can't I leave him with you now? I mean, I've still got a load of studying—"

"Please, Livingston," Rubin replied compassionately, "you don't have to keep up this charade about a 'friend of yours.' There's nothing to be ashamed of. I've already seen several of your classmates tonight with your same . . . difficulties."

"No, no, Doctor. You don't understand!"

"But I do, I do," the physician insisted. "Would you feel better if I came upstairs to see you?"

"All right," he capitulated. "Could you meet me at the third-floor stairwell—as soon as possible?"

Rubin agreed. Barney hung up and, now feeling the strain of the past hour, shuffled slowly back to Maury's room.

He was not there.

And the window was open.

TEN

Barney was struck by the swiftness of what followed. And by the uncanny lack of noise. No panic, no sirens, no shouts. Nothing that would attract attention.

Dashing out of Maury's room, he had practically collided with Dr. Rubin in the corridor. After a split second's explanation, the doctor ordered Barney to call the university police, then grab some blankets and meet him outside. Barney had reacted in motions so frantic that he felt part of a speeded-up movie: he had telephoned, stripped Maury's bed, raced down the stairs trailing sheets and blankets, and sprinted out to the side of the building under Maury's window.

He could hear the groans. Maury was alive. But *how* alive? As he drew nearer, he saw his classmate lying almost inert on the ground.

"Quick, help me," the doctor barked. "Hold his head—keep it in a midline position. We don't want to give him a cervical fracture if he doesn't already have one."

"How is he?" Barney asked, as he knelt down and carefully took hold of Maury's head, hoping that his rapidly beating heart would not unsteady his hands.

"Classic jump case," Rubin commented matter-of-factly. "Heel and lumbar-area fractures for sure." He shone a flashlight into Maury's eyes and then added, "Doesn't look like he's herniating."

"What does that mean?"

"His brain stem seems to be okay. No apparent neurological damage. He's a damn lucky fella."

That's one way of looking at it, Barney thought.

Maury suddenly began to shiver violently. Barney quickly wrapped the blankets around him.

"Livingston, is that you?" he asked in a tone that sounded as if each syllable was painful.

"Yeah, yeah, just take it easy, Maury. You're gonna be all right."

"Oh, shit," his injured classmate gasped. "My father will give me hell for this. Probably say I can't do *anything* right." He made a sound that seemed to come from the no-man's-land between laughter and tears. Then he groaned again.

"He's in a lot of pain," Barney said pleadingly to the doctor. "Can't you give him a shot of something?"

"No, it would dull the sensorium. He's got to be as lucid as possible till we determine the extent of the damage."

Lights flashed. Both the university police and an ambulance had materialized almost simultaneously. Barney had not even heard the sound of the motors. There were soon half a dozen people surrounding Maury, speaking in preternaturally calm whispers.

Barney sensed that they had played this scene so many times before and knew their roles so well, there was no need for dialogue.

The attendants placed a splint on Maury's neck to protect his spine, and were readying him for a stretcher when Dean Holmes arrived. It was an eerie epiphany, his face vanishing and reappearing in the on-and-off flashing beams of the ambulance.

Holmes bent down to look at Maury, and with a borrowed penlight satisfied himself that there was no cranial injury. He gave a slight nod, permission for the patient to be transported to the hospital.

As they were lifting him inside the ambulance, Maury cried out feebly, "Livingston, are you there?"

"Right here, Maury."

"My pages. Please take care of my pages."

"Sure, sure. Don't worry."

The ambulance doors closed noiselessly and moments later it dissolved into the night.

Now there were only three of them out there on the lawn. All the windows of Vanderbilt Hall were dark. Barney glanced at the luminescent hands of his watch. It was 3:45 A.M.

He did not know what to do. He somehow felt he needed their

dispensation to return to his room. So he kept standing, a weary but obedient foot soldier, while his superior officers conferred. Now and then he could distinguish a few words.

"Eastman ... know his father ... brilliant chap ... making arrangements."

At last Rubin nodded, turned on his heels, and headed back for his last few hours of duty at the Health Service. Quite possibly, there were other messages of distress awaiting him.

Holmes walked up to Barney.

"I'm sorry, I didn't get your name."

"Livingston, sir, First Year. I live down the hall from Maury. That is ... where Maury used to live."

The dean nodded. "Livingston, I want you to understand that even as a doctor-to-be, you are bound by the ethics of confidentiality not to mention this to anyone."

"Of course not, sir."

"I mean not even in conversation with your closest friends. It's one of the more difficult aspects of our profession. Besides, this could have unsettling repercussions on your classmates. I'm sure you see my point."

Barney nodded, as much in fatigue as in assent.

"But sir, sooner or later people are bound to notice that Maury isn't around anymore."

"Let me handle that. I'll just circulate a little memo—something to the effect that there's been an illness in his family."

"Yes, sir. May I have your permission to go now? It's very late and I—"

"Of course—Livingston, is it?"

"Yes, sir."

"From what Dr. Rubin tells me, you've been a brick tonight. I appreciate that and I am sure Eastman will appreciate it as well."

"Well, Maury really is a sweet guy. Maybe a bit oversensitive—"

"I mean Dr. Eastman—his father."

"Oh. Yes, sir. Goodnight, sir."

Barney had gone a mere five paces when the dean stopped him. "Oh, Livingston."

Barney stopped and turned. "Yes, sir?"

"What were those pages young Eastman was referring to?"

Barney hesitated, then angrily decided that *something* of Maury Eastman should remain inviolate.

"I don't know, sir. I guess he was delirious or something."

Dean Holmes nodded, which Barney took to be his license to retire. He began his weary way back into the dorm.

As he passed Maury's room, Barney noticed the door was still ajar. He turned on the light and entered. There was a half-filled page in the portable typewriter. Barney leaned over to read it. Thoughts of the narrator after his initial day of medical study:

This was our first encounter with a representative of the Other World. Curiously, we looked inside him and found everything in order. Nothing was missing. What then does Death take away?

Hard-nosed scientists would simply say electric impulses; religious men might say a holy spirit. I am a humanist and what I saw today I took to be the absence of his soul.

Where did it go?

Barney gathered up the dozen or so pages of his classmate's "book," turned off the light, and walked sadly toward his room. He felt a desperate need to shut off his thoughts.

"Christ, Livingston, are you sick? You look like you've been up all night."

"I *was* up all night," Barney answered hoarsely, trying to coordinate a junction between the muffin in his left hand and the jelly on the knife in his right. There were three cups of black coffee on his tray.

"May I sit down, or is this table for grinds only?"

"Sit, Castellano, sit."

Laura sat across from him, drumming her fingers. "Well, are you gonna tell me what happened or what?"

"I was studying epithelial tissue and it was so exciting that I got carried away. The next thing I knew it was dawn."

Laura reached over, appropriated one of his coffees, and retorted, "Bullshit. I know damn well what really happened."

Barney's drooping eyelids opened to near-normal width.

"You do?"

She nodded, smiling. "You had an unexpected romantic encounter. Who was the lucky girl, Livingston—a nurse?"

"Come on, Laura, do I ask you about your sex life?"

"Yes. And I usually don't hold out on you."

"Well, this is different. I've sworn a kind of medical oath. Please don't push."

He was longing to share his feelings of pain and confusion with her.

But he dared not break his word. Not for fear of Holmes, but out of respect for Hippocrates. He took a swill of coffee, commenting, "God, this stuff is awful."

"In my considered judgment," Laura concluded lightheartedly, "you and Grete finally got on the same wavelength."

Barney forced a tired smile. "How did you figure it out?"

"Deductive logic, Barn. Grete didn't come in till after two and you look like an unmade bed. I mean, you haven't even shaved."

"I haven't?" He felt his cheek. "Thanks, Laura, I really didn't notice. Now will you do me a favor before leaving me in peace?"

"Sure."

"Get me another cup of coffee to replace the one you stole."

As she amiably rose to fetch a further dose of caffeine, Barney's headache was compounded by heartache.

Is this what confidentiality is all about? he wondered. I mean, not being able to talk to my best friend in the whole damn world?

"Bad news, Barney—we've lost Alison."

At first he was taken aback. But the twinkle in Bennett Landsmann's eye reassured him that it was not by a misadventure similar to Maury's.

"Apparently some guy at Seth Lazarus's table had to leave school suddenly. And the minute our partner heard, she sweet-talked Lubar into reassigning her—"

"Probably by promising *not* to make a pass at him."

"That was rather ungallant. True, but nonetheless ungallant." Bennett smiled. "Word has it that Seth wields a scalpel second only to Errol Flynn. So Alison wanted to hone her skills with a master."

"Okay with me. Except that leaves us with a cadaver named Leonardo. Do you think we could change it?"

His partner nodded. "How about 'Frank'?"

"Pretty common name," Barney observed. "It could refer to anything from FDR to a hot dog."

"Come on, Livingston, to a true sports fan the only real Frank is Gifford, the New York Giants' immortal halfback—"

Barney's tired face lit up. "Actually, after a real pileup, Frank's looked worse than this."

They could delay no longer the inevitable return to the mutilation of human flesh. They propped *Gray's* open and began slicing carefully down toward the epicardium.

After they had been working twenty minutes or so in silence, Bennett whispered, "You know, I didn't get much sleep last night."

"You too?"

"I kept thinking about this lab. About this guy whose guts we're so blithely pulling apart. Somehow I can understand why it was illegal for so many centuries."

Barney nodded. "I know. It's like a sort of intrusion on his privacy."

"Yeah," Bennett agreed. "And this smell we can't wash off—it's like the mark of Cain."

"Stay loose," Barney replied, "just remember we're not invading the guy's *soul*."

Bennett looked at his lab partner with gratitude. "That's a nice way of looking at it, Livingston. It kind of eases my conscience."

As they returned to the relentless infiltration of Frank's vital organs, Barney thought guiltily, I'm sorry, Maury, I should have quoted you.

"The strain is starting to get to me, Barn."

"Already? For God's sake, Castellano, it's barely been a week—and Biochem has yet to rear its hydra-headed formulae."

They were sitting by themselves, lunching on gelatinous lumps of unknown origin camouflaged by an unidentifiable brownish solution.

"Why does everybody have to lean on my shoulder?" Laura complained.

"Who's leaning?"

"The whole Deanery—it seems like."

"Well, now maybe you know how *I* feel when people choose me as a father-confessor."

"But you like it," she protested.

"Yeah, sure. Actually I get real satisfaction from helping my friends sort out their problems. Besides, it's kind of a dress rehearsal for being a psychiatrist."

"Okay," she conceded, "friends are one thing. But I don't have to advise every girl on the corridor. I mean, I hardly know Alison Redmond."

"Ah, dear old Alison. She jumped ship from my Anatomy table—lured by the legendary silver scalpel of one Seth Lazarus."

"That's not the real reason, Barn. She was—how can I put it?—overstimulated by a certain person's body."

"Mine or the cadaver's?" he quipped.

"Bennett's," she answered with a smile.

"Oh. Well, actually I can't be jealous. He's a really cool guy. But why should that drive Alison away?"

"You figure it out, Dr. Freud. She's scared about getting involved."

"That's a rather unrealistic fantasy. I mean, why should Bennett even look at a rodent like her?"

Laura was not amused.

"He was two years ahead of me at Harvard and I can testify that, regardless of how the package was wrapped, he tended to go for brains."

"How come he didn't get to you?"

"None of your business," Laura replied. But she was blushing slightly.

"Well," Barney continued, "even if he was that undiscriminating—which I still doubt—what's Alison's objection?"

"The truth?" Laura asked. "The honest-to-God truth is she doesn't want anything to distract her from her studies. She's absolutely obsessed about being Number One. It's only the beginning of the term and she's already taking pills to stay awake and study."

"She's a loon. Anyway, spare me any more details."

They were interrupted by the arrival of Hank Dwyer.

"Say, Barn, can you spare a few minutes?"

"Sure," he replied congenially, "sit down and join us."

Hank nodded uneasily to Laura and then answered uncomfortably, "It's sort of private, Barney. Would it be okay if I drop by your room sometime tonight?"

"Tonight? Okay, yeah—fine, great. Is eleven-thirty okay?"

"Couldn't it be a little earlier? I like to hit the sack about then."

"Sorry, Hank, but I've got a shitload of work and I really couldn't spare a second before eleven-thirty."

Dwyer nodded with gratitude—and then respectfully decamped.

As soon as he was out of earshot, Barney quickly turned to a more burning issue.

"Now, Castellano, I want a simple yes-or-no answer: is Grete Andersen a total nymphomaniac or not?"

Laura shook her head. "I'm sorry, that's not a yes-or-no question."

She rose. The consultants' consultation was over.

It is something of a paradox that Biochemistry, which, literally defined, is the study of the life process, is probably the most deadening course a medical student has to take. For living function is reduced to inanimate diagrams and complex formulae scrolled on the innumerable handouts.

"Life is impossible," Professor Michael Pfeifer began dramatically, "without the organic compounds known as amino acids. They are the building blocks of which proteins are constructed, as well as the end product of protein digestion."

Then Pfeifer went on to cast his net a little wider: "There are approximately eighty amino acids in nature. Only about twenty are needed for human metabolism or growth. The ones provided by food are called 'essential.' The others, which can be manufactured by the body, are known either as 'nonessential' or 'glycines.' I've listed both groups on the board. But don't bother to write them down."

At this dispensation from note-taking, the students breathed a collective sigh of relief.

"I'll just read them," said Pfeifer casually. And he did: "Histidine, isoleucine, leucine, lysine, methionine, cysteine, phenylalanine, tyrosine, threonine, tryptophan, valine."

Pfeifer then turned to the second blackboard and reeled off the names of the "nonessential" group, adding, "Naturally, we will be getting back to this in detail later."

Hey, this guy is really easygoing, Barney thought. So much for the myth about Biochem being a horror show. And then it happened.

On either side of the room, assistants began distributing thick sheaves of paper on which—as the students soon discovered—were detailed drawings of structures of everything that Pfeifer had so briefly and amiably touched upon.

If there was such a thing as a collective freshman psyche, it had fallen into a complete collective depression. The room resonated with an echolalia of groans. And then came Pfeifer's cheery coup de grâce.

"Just to keep us on our toes, I think we'll have our first little quiz three weeks from today."

There was a bizarre silence. For a few seconds every single student had stopped breathing. They knew there was a vital question to be asked and all watched to see which of them had the courage to voice it. At this moment Laura raised her hand.

"Yes, Miss . . . your name, please?"

"Laura Castellano, sir. I just wanted to ask if we'll be expected to have this handout memorized?"

Over a hundred heads craned forward, the better to entrap the professor's answer.

"Well, Miss Castellano, that's jumping the gun a bit. We will be covering a lot more material between then and now and it will all be a matter of priorities. After all, can one say that twenty-odd amino acids outweigh the fifty-eight proteins we have in blood?"

"Thank you, Professor." (You sadistic sonovabitch.)

"Any other questions?" Pfeifer asked magnanimously.

Barney, sitting in the back row with Bennett Landsmann, whispered to his lab partner, "Ask him where he parks his car so we can bomb it."

As the class dispersed, Barney called out, "Good going, Castellano, that was guts ball. Now none of us will be able to get a night's sleep."

Barney was angry.

Angry at the way the dean had sworn him to silence about Maury. Angry about Pfeifer's senseless demands upon his flagging memory. About the prospect of having to interrupt his studying to hold unofficial "office hours." He felt almost angry enough to throw a punch at someone. But he settled for the next best thing.

He hastened to his room, whipped off his loafers and jeans, donned shorts and sneakers, and—to warm up—double-timed it downstairs to the gym in the basement.

A full-court basketball game was in progress. He did not know any of the players, except for Bennett Landsmann. Most of them looked like older guys, probably interns or residents. He watched from the sidelines for a few minutes, gaining some vicarious relief from the fact that the contest was being fiercely fought. Obviously, he was not the only guy around this place who needed physical catharsis.

After a little more than five minutes, a rangy red-haired player held up his hands in a gesture of apology.

"Hey sorry, guys, I gotta hold the clamps for Glanville while he does a pelviolithotomy." He motioned to Barney. "You interested in a little roughhouse ball?"

Barney nodded eagerly.

"Okay, guys," said the carrottop, "this poor schmuck wants to break his ribcage. Go easy on him." He then turned to Barney and smiled. "Have fun, buddy boy. Just be careful or those dead-end kids will have you on a stretcher."

Barney nodded again, but could not suppress a sudden memory of the night before.

A half hour later the opposing five had accumulated more bruises than most emergency rooms see on a Saturday night. As they all staggered off court, Barney was out of breath and soaked with sweat. It had been wonderful. Bennett tossed him a slightly used towel and commented admiringly, "God, Livingston, you play dirty. Remind me always to be on *your* team."

"Bennett, coming from you that's a real compliment. You tripped

their center at least four times. Where did your learn your fundamentals—
Sing Sing?"

"Would you believe Torino?"

"You mean Italy? What the hell were you doing?"

"While I was at Oxford, every weekend I flew over and played for
Fiat-Torino. I got three hundred bucks a game and the chance to travel
to a lot of places I would otherwise never have seen. But let me tell you,
what the Europeans lack in basketball finesse, they make up with elbows
and knees. I think the Russkies get a bonus for every pint of blood they
spill."

"You've been up against Russia?"

"Just Spartak, one of their so-called amateur clubs. I was more down
than up."

"Holy shit, Landsmann, I'm snowed, I really am. I'm snowed."

"Don't be, Livingston. Because, frankly, if you ever wanted to
defect, there'd be a job waiting for you in Leningrad."

By the time he showered and had dinner, Barney felt sufficiently
defused to be able to focus on the books. He planned to spend four or
five solid hours of memorization that was somehow misdiagnosed as
intellectual activity.

As he ambled slowly down the corridor, he began to hear music. An
acoustic tidal wave resembling Mantovani's violinists on LSD was emanating from Maury Eastman's room. He shivered inwardly—and tentatively approached the open door.

The inside of the room was blindingly bright. A bar of theatrical
spots ran the length of the ceiling, each brilliant beam focusing on some
sort of artwork—a miniature gallery framed by two enormous stereo
speakers.

"It's not the Flying Dutchman, you can enter," announced a resonant baritone voice from behind him. Barney whirled to discover a
sharp-featured, smartly groomed young man in his early twenties.

"Can I offer you a drink?" he inquired cordially.

Barney cupped his ear. "I can't hear you. Can you turn that racket
down?"

"I'd rather not. Mahler really should be played fortissimo."

"Then get yourself some earphones—there are guys here who can't
study fortissimo."

The music lover smiled affably, walked over to an instrument panel
closely resembling that of a Boeing 707, and turned the knobs that
eventually made the room stop reverberating.

"Thanks." Barney nodded and turned to leave.

"Won't you stay and have that drink?"

"Sorry, but I've a pile of work waiting for me."

"Good God, why is everybody around here so conscientious? Listen, one tiny shot of scotch won't hurt."

Against his better judgment, Barney was mildly fascinated by this character. He requested a Coke.

"With lemon? Lime? A touch of rum to make it Cuba Libre?"

"Neat, thank you. Just a little ice. Uh—are you a med student?"

"Why on earth else would I be inhabiting this dreary dormitory?"

"Yeah, I guess that figures. Up till a few days ago this room was occupied. I mean by someone else."

"Poor bastard." He handed Barney a glass and then poured himself two fingers of Chivas Regal.

"Did you know Maury?"

"Only by name and number—if you get my drift. I understand there was some family crisis or other. Anyway, I was counting on that sort of thing when I kept my housing plans loose for this year. I just didn't think it would happen with such fortuitous celerity. Did you know the *pauvre con*?"

"He was a nice guy," Barney said sternly.

"Wasn't it Hemingway who said 'nice guys finish last'?"

"No, it was Leo Durocher, formerly of the Brooklyn Dodgers."

"Fancy that—*I'm* Lance Mortimer—and I have yet to meet anyone at Harvard Med who could remotely be described as anything but a ruthless, overambitious son of a bitch."

"Including you?"

"*Especially* me. I intend to be a millionaire before I'm thirty-five."

"In that case, wouldn't you be better off at Harvard Business School?"

"Christ, you're sanctimonious. Where are you from?"

"Brooklyn," he answered crisply. "Do you care to pass judgment—or water on that, Lance?"

"Don't be silly, I've heard it's a marvelous place. Lauren Bacall comes from Brooklyn, doesn't she?"

"I believe so."

"Well, if she's good enough for Bogart, she's good enough for me." Mortimer smiled as if tossing off a witty *mot*. "I think I've forgotten your name."

"Likewise—why don't we leave it that way?"

"Oh, come on, old buddy," Lance coaxed, "what do they call you back in Brooklyn?"

"Lots of things. But my friends call me Barney or Livingston. I answer to both."

This was also cause for laughter. "You do realize that all your patients will rib you with 'Dr. Livingston, I presume?' "

"I don't intend to be treating patients who 'presume,' Lance. Now if you can keep your hi-fi down to a dull roar, I'll go study some Histology slides."

"Histology slides?" Lance reacted with histrionic amazement. "Do they actually permit you to take those precious specimens of human tissue out of the lab?"

"A few at a time."

"And what are you using for a microscope?"

"The specialty of the house—an 'A.O.,' ten bucks for the term."

"But that's monocular—and from the Stone Age!"

"My word, Lance, does nothing around here live up to your exacting standards?" Barney asked.

"Please, Dr. Livingston, you misread me. I was merely going to offer you the use of my little jobbie—" And he removed the felt cover from a shining ultramodern *binocular* microscope that was sitting on his desk.

"Wow!" Barney exclaimed—before he was able to stop himself.

"Nikon—state of the art from the friendly elves in Tokyo. I've got two, actually. I've also got two *complete* sets of the slides we've seen in lecture."

"How'd you get them?"

"I won't say until you revise your low opinion of me—"

"What makes you think I have one?"

"Everybody does. Until they come to realize that beneath my obnoxious exterior beats a heart of stone—and a brain of steel. Simply stated, Barney, I'm a born winner."

"If you say so," Barney muttered grudgingly. "Now tell me how you got those slides."

"You can guess *how* I got them. The only detail you lack is how much I paid the poor fish third-year student who runs the projector. And that comes under the heading of medical confidentiality."

Barney had had enough. He turned toward the door, tossing a dismissive, "See you around, Lance," over his shoulder. At which the young man leapt from his Eames chair and chased after Barney like Apollo pursuing Daphne. "Hold on a minute, Livingston—don't you want the microscope?"

"To be brutally frank, I don't relish the prospect of feeling indebted to you."

"But I told you—I've got two of them—and duplicate sets of the slides."

Barney could not stop himself. "Lance, do you have two of *everything*?"

"Well, yes. Most things."

"Two cars?"

His classmate nodded. "Just second-hand Corvettes."

"The same color, though, I'll bet."

Again, Lance nodded affirmatively. "It seemed more practical."

"Oh. Yeah. Sure." And then, swept up by his own morbid curiosity, Barney probed deeper.

"Two girlfriends?"

"There I make an exception."

"Oh?"

"I find women less reliable than cars—so I usually keep three or four on my active list."

"Oh, well that sounds—uh—practical." Barney knew he was navigating in uncharted waters, but convinced himself that he'd enjoy trying to discover what made this character tick.

"Of course, you only have one mommy and daddy."

"What is this, Twenty Questions?"

"Sorry, I just got a little carried away. And I wouldn't want to borrow a microscope from a guy who was—for lack of a better word—'anal acquisitive.' "

"You're a little weird, too. You talk like a would-be shrink," Lance concluded affably. "I like that. You can borrow one of my cars anytime you need it."

"Thanks," Barney remarked casually, and began to gather the various pieces of Lance's super microscope, so he could escape before his benefactor had a change of heart.

"When do you want these back?" he asked, as he lifted the carton of slides.

"No rush. You can keep them all term if you like. I can always get another set."

"You're fantastic, Lance."

"You mean you actually like me?" Mortimer asked with what seemed genuine astonishment.

"Sure." Barney smiled. "You're one of a kind—or maybe I should say two of a kind."

He made ample use of the microscope. It was an exhilarating experience, looking at slices of connective tissue colored by the hematoxylin and resin stain. He was dazzled by the shimmering patches of pink and blue—an ordered chaos that resembled some of Jackson Pollock's paintings. Indeed, only now did his lab instructor's claim take on retrospective validity: *"Histology and art history are complementary esthetic disciplines."*

Just after eleven he felt the need for a carbohydrate fix. En route to the downstairs candy machine, he stopped at the phone to share his excitement with Laura.

An irate female answered.

"If this is for either Grete or Laura, I'm hanging right up."

He recognized the voice. "Hey, Alison, it's me, Barney—you know, we met over Leonardo's dead body."

"Oh, hello," she answered, "how's your dissection coming?"

"Great—how's yours?"

"Not too bad," she replied. "I guess you want to speak to Laura, huh?"

He sensed her loneliness and decided to make the supreme sacrifice.

"Uh, Alison, would you like to meet for coffee a little later?"

"Oh," she said, caught off balance, for she was unaccustomed to even the slightest interest in her as a person.

"Gee, Barney, I've got a lot more studying to do tonight. Could we make it another time?"

"Sure, sure," he replied, inwardly relieved. "Is Laura there?"

He heard the smack of the receiver rebounding from the stone wall as Alison stormed off to fetch Laura.

And, curiously, she answered angrily as well. "Hey, I'm trying to study, who the hell is this?"

"Who were you expecting—Marlon Brando?"

"Oh, sorry, Barney. What's up?"

"Would you believe I've got a complete set of our Histology slides and a Buck Rogers Nikon to look at them?"

"God, how'd you ever get that?"

"Listen, it's too long and thrilling to tell you on the phone. Do you want to come over here and look at beautiful sections of lung tissue stained in silver—not to mention a kaleidoscope of other goodies?"

"Absolutely! How about right now?"

"No, better make it half an hour . . . I've got a counseling session."

"Oh, yeah. Well, see you around midnight, Counselor."

"Sit down, Hank."

"I know how busy you are, Barn. I won't take more than three minutes of your time."

"Well, sit anyway. Why risk getting varicose veins."

Dwyer nodded and perched himself at the edge of the bed.

"Okay, Hank baby. Shoot."

His visitor began to fidget and barely managed to speak. "Barney, I've got this problem. I'd be very grateful if you could give me your advice."

"Sure, sure," he answered, and inwardly thought, What the hell makes him think I know more about *anything* than he does? "What seems to be the difficulty, Hank?"

Dwyer's perplexity seemed to fill the room. Finally, he epitomized his dilemma: "Sex."

"What do you mean?" Barney asked uneasily.

"I've got this problem about sex," Dwyer continued, wiping his palms on his sweater.

Oh no, Barney's instinct for self-preservation was shouting to him. Send this character to a real shrink or you're gonna have guys jumping out of the window on you every night!

"Uh, Hank, don't you think you should talk this over with a—you know—qualified person?"

"No, no, no, Barney, I'm positive a guy with your experience can help me out."

Oh well, Barney joked inwardly, somebody must think I have charisma.

"Okay, Dwyer, spill it out."

"You know I was gonna be a priest?"

"Yeah."

"And I think I told you why I dropped out?"

"Yeah, something along the lines of 'the world, the flesh, and the stethoscope.' "

"It's Cheryl. Cheryl De Sanctis. I lust after her. I'm obsessed about her day and night. I can't study, I can't sleep, I can't learn anatomy because all I want to do is—"

"Sleep with her?" Barney suggested.

"Yes, Barney. You see, I knew you'd understand."

"Frankly, I don't think I do. Because so far I haven't seen any problems, unless Cheryl is married—or a nun."

"For God's sake, what do you think I am? She's just a great girl from my parish—teaches kindergarten. Her family's very religious."

He paused, and then with a groan of longing added, "And she's got the greatest pair of jugs you ever saw."

"Oh," said Barney, trying to grope for a conclusion, "but she doesn't dig you—is that the problem?"

"No, no, she loves me and I'm pretty sure I'd love her even if she didn't have an incredible body. But last night she phoned to say she's coming up next weekend and wants to stay in my room."

"That's no problem, Hank. I mean, as far as I know, the only things we're not allowed to have in our rooms are handguns and reptiles."

"I think she wants to go all the way."

"Great," Barney replied impatiently, thinking, I should only have such problems.

"Th you think it's okay, huh? D'you think we should commit fornication?"

"Hey, look, Dwyer, I'm not a moralist, but it seems to me that if two adults really love each other, that can include sex—"

"Before marriage?"

"Are you seriously considering marrying her, Dwyer?"

He nodded. "I love her, Barney. Now, do I take it I have your blessing?"

"I think you ought to regard it as something a little more secular—like encouragement. I mean, after all, I'm not your priest. Which reminds me, how come you didn't go talk to one?"

"A priest would have told me not to."

Before Barney could consider the manifold implications of this spiritual dialogue, there was a knock at the door.

Dwyer glanced at his watch and rose to go. "Hey, it's past midnight. I'm sorry I took up so much of your time."

Laura's cheery voice called, "It's me, Livingston—are you alone?"

Dwyer looked embarrassed. "Gosh, Barney, I sure wish you had a back door."

"Please, Hank, it's only Laura—"

"Whatta you mean 'only'? You've got the best-looking girl in the class coming up to your room at midnight. How do you do it?'"

He quickly turned and opened the door.

"Hi, Hank." Laura smiled. "I hope I didn't interrupt anything."

"Likewise," he answered shyly.

"No problem. I just dropped by to see if Livingston's microscope lives up to the advance publicity."

"Oh, sure," Dwyer agreed, totally baffled. Then he hurried off to telephone his inamorata.

ELEVEN

"**O**h, oh, oh, to touch and feel a girl's vagina. Ah, heaven."

"Laura, not so loud, we're in *Boston!*"

Palmer Talbot's face had turned the color of the lobster he was eating. His eyes darted self-consciously to the faces of the neighboring after-theater diners in Steuben's restaurant.

Laura was amused. In the course of innocent small talk, Palmer had casually asked her how she and her fellow classmates were able to cope with "the vast quantity of tedious trivia they keep force-feeding you."

She had replied that over the years medical students had concocted several useful mnemonics, unforgettable phrases that could evoke instant recall of vital information from the dusty back shelves of the mind.

"For example?" he had asked.

"Well, there's an absolutely foolproof way of memorizing the twelve cranial nerves—the electric wires that transmit orders from your brain to various parts of the body." She had then cocked her beautiful blond head and declaimed, "Oh, oh, oh, to touch and feel a girl's . . ." et cetera.

At which point the discomfited Palmer had his fit of social apoplexy.

"That sounds like something Barney might invent." He smiled.

"Hell no, I told you it's a classic—part of the folklore. For all I know it may go back to Galen or even Hippocrates. Believe me, it's a stroke of genius. How else would I be able to reel off 'olfactory, optic, oculomotor, trochlear—' "

"I get the idea," Palmer said. "It's certainly not a phrase one would easily forget." And then changing the subject, he whispered softly, "I can't bear being in the same city and only getting to see you on weekends—in fact, not even every Friday night."

"We have classes on Saturday too."

"That's barbaric, Laura, absolutely inhumane."

"That, my friend, is Med School in a nutshell."

An hour later, he was laughing uncontrollably.

"What's so funny, Talbot?" she inquired, playfully slapping his chest with a pillow.

"You've ruined me for life." He guffawed. "I'll never be able to make love again without thinking of the twelve cranial nerves."

"Can you name them?" She grinned.

"No, but I sure as hell can remember that mnemonic!" As he leaned over to embrace her, she pulled away gently.

"No dice," she scolded, "you know I have to go back to the dorm so I can get up early and run my oculomotors over *Gray's Anatomy.*"

"What about *my* anatomy? Can't you stay the night and study with me? I promise to drive you first thing in the morning."

"Sorry. Your idea of first thing on a Sunday morning means after you've read the whole damn *New York Times.*"

"And *Boston Globe,*" he said, grinning affectionately. "And made love again."

She kissed him on the forehead. "Rain check, huh?" And getting up to dress, she added, "Sometimes I get the distinct impression that you'd really like me to drop out."

"I confess the thought has occurred to me at odd moments. But then my conscience reminds me that you're passionately dedicated to your future calling—and that I'm being selfish."

"Good. And does it also castigate you for thinking such thoughts?"

"Not really. Because then I remember that at least a third of your class is already married."

"Not any of the women. We're too busy."

"Doing what—proving you're as good as any man?"

"No, that wouldn't be enough. We have to prove we're better. Can you possibly understand that?"

Palmer was genuinely trying to be fair but he really could not fathom the degree of her commitment.

"Still, ultimately you want to marry and have a family, don't you?"

"I'm about ten years from ultimately," she replied softly. And then added, "I'm not just going to be a doctor, Palmer. I'm going to be a *very good doctor.*"

He looked at her and murmured affectionately, "I love you, Laura, and I'll wait as long as I have to."

He hugged her as if to seal the oath he had just made. As she leaned her face against his cheek, Laura suddenly felt an inexplicable sadness. Jesus, she thought to herself, this terrific guy loves me so much. And I really like him. Why can't I . . . let go? What's wrong with me?

As the Porsche pulled up outside a dusky Vanderbilt Hall, a young couple turned the corner, walking toward them arm in arm. Palmer was escorting Laura to the front door when one of the lovebirds called, "Hey Laura, wait up!"

Hank Dwyer bounded over, a short, plumpish girl in tow.

"Hi," Laura greeted them cheerily, though inwardly surprised that the erstwhile priest was up so late—long past the hour of midnight Mass—and with a girl at that.

"Laura," Hank gasped, "you're the first to hear the great news— Cheryl and I are getting married! Oh, I guess you haven't met each other. Laura Castellano, this is my fiancée, Cheryl De Sanctis—she's from back home."

His raven-haired companion nodded and smiled shyly. But even in darkness the glow in her eyes was perceptible.

Laura introduced Palmer, who politely inquired when the happy couple intended to tie the knot.

"Christmas," Cheryl gushed. "We're gonna get married over the Christmas vacation."

"Yeah," Hank added with a chuckle, "that way I can never forget our anniversary. Isn't that great?"

"I think it's marvelous," Palmer commented, and with a scintilla of irony only Laura could detect, added, "Won't that put a strain on your medical studies?"

"Heck, just the opposite," replied the expansive Dwyer. "When we're together I won't lose all the time I waste now just thinking about Cheryl."

Palmer turned to Laura with a wry grin. "Now that's a refreshing outlook, isn't it?"

"Different strokes for different folks," she said pointedly, giving

Palmer a peck on the cheek. Then she waved to the future bride and groom and hurried inside.

The moment she was alone in the hollow cavern of the lobby, her earlier melancholy returned. Something in the way Hank and Cheryl looked at each other had opened emotional floodgates. The two of them were so obviously in love. Was that the way Palmer felt about her? She was suddenly touched with sympathy for him. And—she could not understand why—sadness for herself.

She found herself wandering in the direction of Barney's room. Just to shoot the breeze if he was still awake. As she approached she could hear his weary voice reciting biochemical formulae.

She stopped, unwilling—or unable—to disturb him with her immature confusion. About relationships. About love—and all that other adolescent stuff.

And so she went to her room, flopped on her bed, opened her Biochem notebook, and tried to immerse herself in the lethean oblivion of amino acids.

Barney had been grinding all evening until the unexpected visit of Bennett Landsmann. He was so elegantly clad in a J. Press blazer with a striped blue tab-collar shirt and what looked like a club tie that Barney was amazed he had merely gone to see the latest Ingmar Bergman at the Exeter Street theater.

"Christ, Landsmann, is that your idea of diversion? I had nightmares for days after seeing *The Seventh Seal*."

Bennett smiled broadly. "But the characters in his films are so morose, they make me feel euphoric by comparison. Anyway, the prospect of studying looks a little less grim. Want to trade questions?"

"Sure. How are you on amino acids?"

"Not bad. I logged five hours' worth this afternoon."

"Okay, then we turn our attention to the trifling matter of protein production in the G-I tract?"

"You're putting me on. Are we supposed to know *that* stuff, too?"

"Well, Mr. Landsmann," Barney replied, trying to imitate their professor's condescending tones, "we only expect you to know the 'important' things. In other words, everything that comes out of my mouth."

To which Bennett replied, "Shit."

And they set to work.

After an hour, they called a time-out so Bennett could sprint to his room and get a couple of Budweisers. They sipped the suds and discussed such trivia as who would win the Ivy crown in football and could anyone *ever* beat Yale in swimming ("I hear they recruit fish," Barney quipped). They even dilated on intercollegiate chess.

As the hour grew late, Barney sensed that his new friend felt more comfortable and he could hazard a few personal questions.

"Tell me, Landsmann," Barney asked genially, "how does it feel to be the Jackie Robinson of Medicine?"

"You flatter me, Barn. I'm a rookie, but I'm certainly not the best player in *this* league."

"Ah hell, you know what I mean, Ben."

"Sure. But it's no sweat for me here, Barney. I've always been the token black. To be frank, I've never known it any other way."

"Where are you from?"

"I grew up in Cleveland. . . ." He offered no more details.

Barney wavered between diffidence and fascination. "What do your folks do?" An innocuous question, that.

"My dad makes shoes," he replied casually.

"Oh," Barney replied, amazed at the magnitude of what a guy from such a modest background had achieved. But he sensed that he had reached the pale of Bennett's private thoughts and could go no further.

So, for another hour and a half, the two men labored. They were in the midst of trying to memorize the oxidative metabolism of pyruvic acid when Laura had approached the door—and turned away.

And it was fortunate she did not linger outside, since before they parted for the night, they had another secular gabfest—this time about the females in the class.

"That Castellano," Bennett murmured, shaking his head in bewilderment, "I knew her when she was at the 'Cliffe. She certainly is an enigma. Beautiful, fiendishly bright—and a real enigma."

Enigma? That was probably the only thing Barney would never have called her. But then he really knew Laura. They were part of the fabric of each other's lives.

You are the enigma, Bennett.

The night before their first Biochem exam, one question united the fearless and the frenzied: What the hell did this gibberish have to do with healing the sick?

"I mean, for God's sake. With all these stupid diagrams it's like training for auto engineering or TV repair," Laura complained.

She was studying in Barney's room, and they were tossing each other questions and intermittently trying to psych out what sort of stuff Pfeifer might be asking on the morrow.

"You gotta stay loose, Castellano. I admit this is like memorizing fifty kinds of macaroni, but they do have a vague connection with the workings of the human body."

"I bet my father didn't have to go through this nonsense."

"I bet he did. Guys were studying metabolism in Greece and China two thousand years ago."

"A *little,* yeah—but they didn't know all the gory details. Besides, dammit, I came here to see sick people."

"Well," he replied with a gallows-humor grin, "look all around you. Pfeifer is a sicko, and all of us are crazy to be doing this in the first place. Want a Hershey bar?"

"No, but I'd love a Coke just to keep me awake. I'll go down and—"

"Don't sweat, Castellano, you stay here and study for the two of us. I need to get the blood moving back to my brain."

He dashed downstairs to the row of vending machines; six of them side by side, each offering products of dubious nutritional value. At this hour of the night they seemed to be grinning at him. And they probably were, because every one of them was empty—even the cigarette machine.

He walked slowly up the stairs, trying to remember who on his floor had a hot plate and coffeepot. Ah, of course, Lance Mortimer undoubtedly had two.

He knocked on the door. There was no answer. Could the guy be asleep? When his second—and louder—knocking still produced no response, Barney tried the door. It was open. And there was Lance, lying in his Eames chair, head back, eyes closed—wearing earphones. *Earphones?* How the hell could the guy be so blasé as to be listening to music on a night like this? He walked over and gently knocked on Lance's forehead.

"Anybody home?" he asked blithely. Lance opened his eyes and uncovered one ear.

"Oh, Dr. Livingston. Where have you been hiding yourself?"

"In my room like everybody else—studying those goddamn chemical structures. Why aren't you doing the same—or don't you intend to take tomorrow's test?"

"Why are you all steamed up? There's no need to panic."

"Maybe, but don't you think there's a need to study?"

"But I am, old buddy, I am. Listen—"

Barney reluctantly placed the instruments on his head. To his astonishment he heard Lance's voice reciting some of the metabolic arcana on which they would be tested the next morning.

"I just play my tapes over and over," Lance explained, "so even if I fall asleep, my brain will be absorbing info subliminally."

"Lance, you certainly are a character."

"I am, aren't I?" His neighbor smiled. "I'm sorry I haven't got any tape to lend you, but I just picked up this apparatus yesterday at Acoustical Research in Cambridge. Can I help you in any other way?"

"Well, yeah. Have you got anything with caffeine in it?"

"Like coffee, tea, or Coke?"

"Coke—make that two Cokes if you can spare them."

"Help yourself," Lance replied, pointing to his fridge. "There's also some camembert you might enjoy." He leaned back in his chair and turned into his prerecorded self-pedagogy.

When Barney got back to his room, Laura was spread out on his bed. Fast asleep.

Barney looked at the dark rings around her eyes and decided she needed the rest more than anything else. He sat down at his desk and studied for another half hour. By then he was too groggy to go on. He glanced again at Laura. She was down for the count; it would be cruel to wake her. He took off his shoes, grabbed a blanket, rolled his lumber jacket into a pillow, curled up on the floor, and fell asleep instantly.

Somewhere in the no-man's-land between night and morning, Laura awoke with a start. It took her a few seconds to realize where she was. Then she saw Barney sleeping on the floor and smiled. He looked so peaceful. She gathered her notebooks and was about to go when she glanced at his desk. He had forgotten to set his alarm. She set it to wake him at seven, then, quietly closing the door, tiptoed into the hall.

There were still lights visible under some of the doors. In fact, one of them was wide open. Lance Mortimer—sans earphones—was drawing diagrams at his desk. He looked up as she passed.

"Hello, Laura," he said, grinning, "how's Barney?"

"Sleeping," she replied matter-of-factly.

"Lucky guy," Lance remarked with a leer.

She looked at him, too tired to be annoyed, and whispered, "Fuck you, Mortimer."

As she reached the stairway, she heard her classmate's response, "Any time, Laura, any time."

They sat bleary-eyed, chewing their pencils or developing ulcers, waiting for Professor Pfeifer's little quiz. Their churning stomachs and throbbing temples were anything but soothed by the weedy, off-key tenor of Peter Wyman humming "Oh What a Beautiful Morning."

The good professor did not disappoint them. Though the first question dealt with the pioneering work on metabolism of recent Nobel Prize winner Sir Hans Krebs, it was nonetheless out of this world:

> *Imagine you were living on the planet Saturn. Reprogram the Krebs cycle using nitrogen instead of oxygen. Draw the diagram in full.*

The second section was (as Pfeifer put it) "a little sweeter." It dealt with glyconeogenesis. In other words, the transformation of sugar to supply the needs of body tissues:

> *Given five molecules of glucose, how much ATP and how much phosphate do you need to make glycogen? How much carbon dioxide do you produce?*
> *Illustrate the steps by which you formulate your answer.*

One hundred and twenty-five right hands reached for the brows above them as they began to grope through a fog of recollection for the appropriate responses.

Somehow the hours passed. As most victims were handing in their exam papers and shuffling out, a few zealous obsessives still continued to scribble madly.

"Now, now," Pfeifer said, as if chastising kindergarteners, "if you can't say it in all that time, you probably can't say it at all. Papers, please."

Outside the lecture hall, expletives outnumbered the ions in the air.

"The guy's a sadistic maniac!" was one typical hypothesis.

Peter Wyman viewed these reactions as sour grapes in the vineyard of medical ignorance.

"Come on, guys," he said affably, "granted there was a lot of writing to do, but the questions were absolutely fair and square."

"Shut up, Wyman," snapped the normally placid Sy Derman, who just happened to hold a black belt in judo, "or I'll permanently stop your basic oxygenation with my bare hands."

"I think Wyman's bluffing," Barney suggested. "I mean, he was the last guy to hand in his paper—"

"Yeah," Laura chimed in, "and you're sweating like a pig, Peter."

"Perspiration is the normal means of removing heat from the body, Miss Castellano," he condescended. "The faster you think, the more calories you burn. I'd say I was putting out five joules per second—at the formula I2Rt."

"Tell me something, Wyman," she replied, "were you born obnoxious —or did you have to take lessons?"

"Listen, lady, as far as I'm concerned, this place started going downhill when they began admitting females."

"*You* listen, kiddo," she interrupted. "If I hear another molecule of sexual chauvinism, I'll give you the old Brooklyn one-two."

"Wow, you'd better be careful," Barney warned. "Laura wields a pretty mean switchblade."

"That I can believe," Wyman sneered. But he nonetheless moved swiftly away.

"Who's in favor of getting smashed?" Lance Mortimer inquired. There was near unanimity among the dozen or so freshmen who had clustered around Wyman. And they paraded off to Alberto's Bar and Grille for a festival luncheon of beer and free peanuts.

For they indeed had something to celebrate: For the first time they had been stretched upon the rack of Torquemada and survived—at least to fight another day. A few brave souls sleepwalked back for the afternoon Anatomy section, but most staggered to their rooms and simply passed out.

In one sense, Harvard Medical School is still like the temple of Asclepius: deep scars can miraculously heal overnight. Thus it was that the next day there was no apparent disfigurement on the faces—and perhaps even the psyches—of the students who again gathered in Room C to hear Pfeifer recount the further adventures of the amino acid's quest for the Perfect Protein.

He at once launched into the thrilling idiosyncracies of the amino acid arginine without so much as a passing reference to the previous session. He knew they were suffering, and they knew that he knew they were suffering. It only magnified the tension.

At last, with some thirty seconds remaining, Pfeifer took a breath and said quietly, "Uh—about the quiz. I'm very pleased to say that some of you did quite well. There were two ninety-eights and even one ninety-nine." He then added with a smile, "On principle, I never give perfect scores."

Pfeifer paused, inhaled again, and continued. "Of course there were those who—how shall I put it—still haven't quite caught on. Indeed, the fact that the lowest score was eleven makes it perfectly clear. But suffice it to say, the majority of you seem to be crowded as it were around the fifty-five mark, and show every possibility of ultimately passing the course."

Agitated murmurs filled the room. Then, as a valedictory, Pfeifer announced, "I will affix the grade sheet in the usual place early tomorrow morning. Good day, gentlemen."

He turned on his heel and exited.

As the students started to follow Pfeifer out, Peter Wyman was heard to mumble audibly, "I wonder what I did to lose that point?"

It was Professor Pfeifer's custom to arrive at the Medical School no later than 6 A.M., so he could get in a few hours of research without the nuisance of having to talk to students. On the days when he had exam results, he would tack them on the bulletin board outside his teaching office—using only the students' initials to preserve their anonymity—and then retreat off to his lab.

Needless to say, there were numerous early risers the next morning. In fact, while the sun was still a faint semicircle on the eastern horizon, half a dozen visitors had gone to what, in recent years, had come to be known as the "Wailing Wall."

Also part of the tradition was the practice of students—even nonsmokers—after they had seen their grades to cauterize their initials with the tip of a lighted cigarette.

Barney arrived at seven o'clock. Bennett was already waiting.

He was not smiling.

Nor, on the other hand, was he frowning.

"What's the score, Landsmann?"

"Livingston," his friend replied somberly, "for us it is neither the best of times nor the worst of times. Voilà."

He pointed to the list and indicated the six names already scorched into oblivion. The recipients of the majestic ninety-nine and the brace of lordly ninety-eights had come and gone. And there were still wisps of smoke emanating from the eleven and the two middle-of-the-roaders who had notched a forty-seven and a fifty-six.

"When did you get here, Ben?"

"I arrived at quarter to and these holes were already here. In fact, you and I seem to be following the essence of Greek philosophy, 'meden agan,' nothing in excess. I got seventy-four. And you got seventy-five."

"How do you know? It occurred to me on the way over that we both had the same initials."

"No sweat. I used my full name for the exam—Bennett A. So I'm the seventy-four."

Barney's face suddenly lost some of its indoor pallor. "Hey,

Landsmann, we're pretty hot stuff. But how are we gonna obliterate our identities?"

"I've got the traditional implement."

"But you don't smoke."

"Of course not, but sometimes I take out unenlightened young ladies who do." He reached inside his jacket and withdrew a silver cigarette case. Removing a long, thin cigarette, he lit it with a matching silver lighter. Both were monogrammed—or at least bore a seal.

"Hey, that's a neat case, Ben. Can I see it?"

He tossed it to Barney. The cover was embossed with a circular crest bearing a silver "A" in a field of bronze.

"What is this?"

"Oh, it belonged to my dad. He was an officer in Patton's Third Army."

"Extremely cool," Barney admired. "My dad served in the Pacific and he didn't get anything like this. What did your father—"

"Hey, come on," Bennett interrupted, "it's breakfast time—eradicate our names and let's split."

He handed him the cigarette.

As Barney went to work on their identities, he quickly scanned the grade sheet for Laura's initials.

They were not there. Which is to say no longer there. Thus she had either done spectacularly well or bombed out.

He would not know what to say if she turned out to be at the bottom. On the other hand if she were at the top (and, Laura being Laura, this was not impossible), he would not know how he'd feel.

TWELVE

"How did your Biochem test go, Laura?"

"Not bad."

"Does that mean you did well?"

"No, it simply means what I said—not bad."

"Come on, we shouldn't have secrets between us. I'm your future husband, after all."

"Just for the record, Palmer, I haven't given an official answer to that one either."

"Okay, Doctor, okay, I capitulate. Now, what are you doing for Thanksgiving?"

"Studying, what else?"

"That goes without saying. But you've got to take some sort of a break. I mean, even prisoners on Death Row eat turkey on Thanksgiving."

"Oh, I'm sure the dining room will come up with a reasonable facsimile—even if it's cellophane with plastic stuffing."

"Then I'll come and eat ersatz turkey with you."

"But what about your parents? Won't they be disappointed not to see you?"

"Not as disappointed as I'll be at not seeing *you*."

Palmer then had a sudden disquieting thought.

"Or did you make other plans?"

"Well, actually, I just assumed that Barney and I—"

"Ah, the good Dr. Livingston—" he interrupted.

Laura frowned. "As I was saying," she continued pointedly. "Barney and I and a few of the first-year chain gang were gonna set up a big table in the cafeteria and pretend we were a family. But there've been a few last-minute defections."

"Namely?"

"Well, Bennett's flying home to Cleveland for the day to be with his folks—"

"That's rather extravagant. He must be well off."

Laura nodded. "I guess so. From the looks of his wardrobe, I'd say he singlehandedly keeps Brooks Brothers solvent. And then Livingston's finked out as well."

"Returning to the family seat in Brooklyn?"

"He didn't say. In fact, he's been acting kind of strangely for the last week or so."

"Why—is he angry with you for some reason?"

She shrugged. "I don't think so, unless he's pissed off because I wouldn't tell him how I did on the Biochem exam."

"How did you do, by the way?" thrusted Palmer, trying to catch her off-guard.

"I told you, Palmer," she riposted, "not bad."

We gather together to ask the Lord's blessing
He chastens and hastens His will to make known.
The wicked oppressing now cease from distressing.
Sing praises to his name; He forgets not His own.

Barney kept the car radio tuned to WCRB as long as their signal held out. They seemed to be the only station in all of New England that had not already begun to sing Christmas carols on Thanksgiving Day. Since he was all alone in one of Lance's Corvettes, he could sing aloud the "Hymn of Thanksgiving," which he remembered with fondness from his high school days.

When he pulled off the Mass. Turnpike at Exit 9, Interstate 86 South was virtually empty. Most travelers had reached their destinations and were already sitting at festive tables. To spend Thanksgiving alone was a fate even worse than a solitary Christmas, he decided. Because outside of Macy's parade on television, there was nothing to do except join your near and dear ones and stuff your face.

Barney's would be one of the few unstuffed faces. He'd had to disappoint his mother, who had naturally expected him to return to Brooklyn. Moreover, all he had offered by way of explanation was that he had to visit a "friend in trouble."

(Curiosity had forced Estelle to ask, "Is it a girl?" Barney had merely replied that it was "nothing to worry about.")

On the northern outskirts of Hartford, he turned off the highway and headed down a series of roads that grew progressively narrower and more primitive. Finally, he squeezed through a narrow dirt path, framed by leafless trees, and suddenly emerged into a vast open space. About a hundred yards away was an opulent house in the French style. A small brass plaque at the large wrought-iron gates read:

THE STRATFORD INSTITUTE

Barney thought for a moment of its colloquial sobriquet: "Château Loco." For here dwelt the aristocracy of the mad. Or at least the plutocracy. Rumor had it that the residents paid nearly a thousand bucks a week.

Christ, he thought to himself, for that money their straitjackets ought to be cashmere. He understood why he was telling himself such feeble jokes. For he had always been told of the paranoia people feel when visiting someone in a mental institution. Even the most confident feel an irrational anxiety that they will be unmasked—and therefore not allowed out.

When he pulled up at the booth to identify himself, he saw that the guard was munching on a turkey leg and looking perfunctorily at a flickering TV screen. He thumbed his clipboard, adding a spot of grease on every page.

"Uh hunh." He nodded. "Dr. Livingston to see Mr. Eastman. Go right in." (Barney had merely said on the phone that he was "calling from Harvard Medical School," but it clearly enhanced his acceptability.)

At the heavy wooden front door he was met by a cherubic matron who politely offered holiday greetings and, somehow assuming Barney was familiar with the institute, indicated that "the Eastman boy" was taking some air on the back lawn, and "Dr. Livingston" was welcome to seek him there.

Barney nodded and started down the long, high corridor.

Unfortunately, he took a wrong turn and found himself standing before a white metal door that was firmly locked. He peered through the rectangular window of wired glass and saw a phantasmagoric collection of patients shuffling, stretching, groaning, each evidently in his own private world, apparently unwilling or unable to acknowledge the presence of anyone else. It reminded him of a Fellini film. Only *this* unreality was real. Jesus, he thought, is Maury in there?

"May I help you?" called a stern female voice. He turned to find a Valkyrie in nurses' garb.

"May I help you?" she repeated an octave lower.

"I'm . . . from Harvard Medical School to see the Eastman boy."

"Well, he's certainly not in there," she protested.

Thank God, Barney thought. "I was told he was on the back lawn. Would you direct me, please?"

She pointed in the proper direction. Barney nodded and hurried off, hoping the fright he felt didn't show on his face.

He found Maury sitting alone on a large, empty stone terrace overlooking a vast, manicured garden. He seemed to be watching the sun descend behind the rim of the Taconic Mountains.

"Hi, Maury," Barney said quietly.

"Hello, Barney," his friend replied tonelessly, without turning his head. "Thanks for coming. Amazing sun, isn't it? Sort of like God putting a shiny copper penny into a slot to buy us a skyful of stars." He still did not turn his head.

"That's a lovely metaphor, you should write it down."

"I don't write anymore," he muttered.

Since Maury would not face him, Barney walked around his chair and leaned against the railing of the porch. Now he could see why his friend was so fascinated by celestial light; his own eyes were like burnt-out electric sockets. The sight made Barney shudder.

"How's Medical School—am I sorely missed?"

"It's kind of a drag, actually. And I miss you, Maur. The guy that's in your room now is a real asshole."

"There's someone in my room? I thought they'd board it up or quarantine it or something so nobody would catch—"

"Stop knocking yourself," Barney interrupted, putting his hand lightly on Maury's shoulder. "I bet you'll be back with us by spring."

"Don't futz me around. I'm gonna be here forever."

Barney gazed into those chillingly empty eyes and thought to himself, This poor bastard was better off when he was manic. At least he was alive.

"Hey, come on, trust me, willya? I'm practically one-eighth a doctor. You're gonna be okay, Maur. You're gonna come out of this and be another John Keats, just like you said."

"Keats died at twenty-six."

"Yeah, right," Barney responded, ill at ease. "That was a lousy example, I guess. But you know what I mean."

Then there was silence. Why? Barney wondered. He knows goddamn well what I'm trying to say. Why won't he let me cheer him up? Why's he so intent on pulling me down into the abyss with him? And why did he ask me to come out here in the first place?

They sat for a few minutes without talking. Then, out of nowhere, Maury whispered, "They're zapping me."

"What?" Barney knew what he meant but didn't want to believe it.

"The doctors call it ECT—Electro-Convulsive Therapy," Maury explained, in the same gray tone of voice. "My fellow inmates call it 'zapping.' You must know about the machines they have to fry your brains. . . ."

"Shock treatment—you mean you're getting shock treatment?"

His friend nodded.

Barney was overwhelmed with disgust. He had always associated electricity with punishment. Shocks for antisocial aggressive types; and for the homicidal, the supreme chastisement—the electric chair. But why this poor harmless guy? . . .

"It's supposed to cure depression." He shrugged and added, "Anyway, my father thinks I'm better."

"Has he been here to see you?"

"No. I mean he's a very busy man and San Francisco isn't what you'd call around the corner." He sighed deeply and continued, "But he calls. He calls Dr. Cunningham, the chief shrink, and makes sure the guy is taking care of me. . . . Hey—I made you come all the way from . . . wherever . . . and I haven't asked about you. Or your wife."

"I'm not married," Barney whispered, growing steadily sicker at heart.

"Oh," Maury answered in a childlike tone. "Didn't you have something to do with that tall blond girl? . . ."

"Laura," Barney said, nodding. "Laura Castellano. She's just my friend."

"She was good-looking, I remember that."

"Good," Barney said, forcing a smile. "If you can talk about pretty girls, then you must be on the way to getting well."

"There's no such thing as 'well' in psychiatry," Maury said with an air of plaintive resignation. "You just progress from one kind of sick to another. You'll be learning that soon, I'm sure."

"What idiot doctor told you a stupid thing like that?" Barney snapped.

"My father," Maury mumbled. "As far back as I can remember, he always said that."

Things look swell, things look great,
Gonna have the whole world on a plate.
Starting here, starting now
Honey, everything's coming up roses . . .

As he drove back up Interstate 86 Barney spun the dials of his car radio, hoping to find something to mollify the dull ache in his gut. But all he could get with any clarity was Hartford's WFDR, a station exclusively devoted to show tunes. And the trumpetlike voice of Ethel Merman blasting out the brand of frantic, mindless optimism so typical of Broadway seemed an ironic mockery of Maury's plight.

He pulled into the first Howard Johnson's on the turnpike, ordered a 3-D burger (which tonight seemed to represent Disillusion, Depression, and Despair), and tried to force himself to eat.

"Gosh, you look down, honey," said the sympathetic, frizzy-haired waitress. "Did you lose your girl or your job?"

"Neither," Barney replied, "but I think I'm about to lose my temper."

He got five bucks worth of change from the cashier, went to the phone booth, pulled a crumpled envelope from his pocket, and dialed San Francisco. After three rings there was a reply.

"Dr. Eastman's office."

It was his answering service.

"Uh—could you tell me how to reach the doctor? It's fairly urgent."

"Are you a patient?"

"No, no. I'm—I'm a doctor, actually. Name's Livingston."

There was a brief silence and a clicking sound, which suggested that wires were being spliced and reconnected.

And then a man's calm baritone voice: "Yes, this is Dr. Eastman."

"Uh—it's Barney Livingston, Doctor. I'm a friend of Maury's. I was the last guy to speak to him before he—you know—jumped."

"Oh, of course. Did you get my little note?"

"Yes, thank you, Doctor," Barney replied, thinking once again of the brevity and lack of emotion in Eastman's letter of thanks. "Actually, that's how I got your number. . . ." Eastman was not exactly helping to keep the conversation alive, so Barney had to keep taking the initiative. "Uh—I've just been to visit Maury, sir—"

"That seems beyond the call of duty," the doctor remarked.

"He's a nice guy, sir. I like him."

"I'm pleased to know that. He generally has difficulties interacting with his peers. Now how can I help you, Mr. Livingston?"

"It's Maury who needs the help, sir."

"I don't follow." There was now a hint of annoyance in the psychiatrist's voice.

"Doctor Eastman," Barney continued, trying to maintain his composure, "do you know they're giving your son shock treatments?"

"Of course."

"Well, if you'll forgive my bluntness, sir, I've just visited your son. And from what I saw, he's a lot worse than he ever was."

"That's not what I hear from Dr. Cunningham," Eastman retorted. "Besides, what makes a first-year medical student qualified to pass judgment on his superiors?"

"Doctor," Barney said earnestly, "all I ask is that you take the time to come and see how these treatments are incinerating your son's brain—"

"That's totally unnecessary, Livingston. I'm extremely familiar with the procedure and in my view it was exactly what was indicated for the boy's depression."

It became increasingly evident to Barney that Dr. Eastman was deliberately avoiding the use of the phrase "my son." As if to absolve himself of any responsibility for Maury's unhappy state.

"Dr. Eastman, I beg of you. Please don't let them zap Maury anymore. He'll be okay. Just let him heal in peace."

There was a brief silence, punctuated only by slight transcontinental static.

"Livingston, I'm grateful for your concern and I'll certainly take up this matter with Dr. Cunningham. I hope you've had a good Thanksgiving. . . ."

Barney was speechless.

"Good afternoon, then," the doctor said in calm and frosty valediction.

Barney hung up and then leaned against the phone like a defeated boxer.

He returned to the medical stockade a little after eight. The library was still open, so he went over to search for the latest literature on ECT. He read feverishly, scribbling notes on index cards. Apparently the strongest indications for shock therapy were (a) immediate high risk of suicide, (b) depressive stupor, or (c) danger to physical health for a variety of reasons.

Granted, Maury was all of the above, but even the strongest advocates of this procedure emphasized that it should be used only when time was of the essence. What the hell was the rush? he asked himself. Maury was just sitting there on the porch, weaving metaphors like an old woman embroidering a sampler.

And there were side effects. In every case there was at least some memory loss, although the studies suggested that this was usually transient. But what if Maury didn't happen to conform to the statistics? Would his powers of recollection be permanently impaired?

Wasn't it Thomas Mann who defined genius as simply the ability to gain free psychic access to past experience? Was not memory the artist's most precious possession?

Maury was an intelligent, sentient, creative guy who deserved at least a fair chance to develop into a full human being. At the very least, to stand or fall on his merits and not be struck down by the thunderbolts of an uncaring Zeus.

These zappers treat mental illness as if it were a gangrene of the brain—to be cut out. There is no human skill involved, Barney decided. When I'm a psychiatrist I'll try to heal those inner wounds, make people whole. And no machine can do that.

Vanderbilt Hall swarmed with gaily chattering students. There was even a crowd around the piano singing Christmas carols. Maybe it would be business as usual tomorrow, but everyone seemed determined to savor this holiday break to the full.

In the cafeteria Barney caught sight of Grete Andersen carrying a tray with food that seemed composed of the same stuff as the linoleum floor. He marveled at the way she made even a camel's hair coat seem like a tight sweater. She undulated over to a corner where Laura was already holding forth to a couple of interns.

He decided to join them.

"Hi, guys," he greeted.

"Ah," Laura called out, "the mysterious traveler. Is it still a state secret, or can you tell us where you've been?"

"I was at Cape Canaveral, helping them put a turkey into orbit."

"Oh, for God's sake, Livingston," Laura complained, "we're not a Senate Investigating Committee."

"Let's just say I was with a friend."

"I bet she was cute," Grete cooed, vouchsafing him one of her radiant smiles.

"Okay," Barney said. "I confess. I spent the day with Jayne Mansfield, sort of going over . . . anatomy problems."

"You know," Grete murmured, "I'm almost prepared to believe

you." And then she added as she moved off, "Maybe that's why you never call me."

The other students gradually peeled away to return to their cells and hit the books once again. Finally Laura and Barney were alone. She looked him in the eye. "You're going to tell me the truth, aren't you?"

"Hey, look," he said uncomfortably, "I really can't. I gave my word."

She gestured histrionically. "Hey, once upon a time we used to be friends."

Barney seized the moment.

"Tell you what, Castellano, I'll trade truth for truth. Okay?"

"Sure."

"I'll tell you where I was, if you tell me how you did in the Biochem exam."

Laura hesitated, caught off-guard. Then, smiling sheepishly, she said in confidential tones, "Would you believe—eleven?"

"No."

She patted him on the shoulder and gave him a lighthearted " 'Night, Barn. Don't forget tomorrow's 'The Big Day' in Anatomy. As Grete might say, you've gotta be 'up' for that."

"The human penis . . ."

It was evident from the relish in Professor Lubar's voice that this was one lecture he never tired of. As a pedagogical tool, he had a large-scale model of the organ before him. It had already stimulated much conversation among the students—all of whom were present—some having even arrived early.

"This is the male organ of copulation and, in mammals, urination. It is cylindrical, pendulous, suspended from the front and side of the pubic arch. If you were to refer to it as a 'phallus,' you would be incorrect, for that is only a valid description of the penis in its state of arousal.

"The human penis can vary in length from five to eight inches, none of which has any physical bearing on the male or female enjoyment of sexual intercourse. Some of you may have heard talk of organs in excess of one foot, but this is mythology—or perhaps someone encountered a horse in the dark."

No one laughed. They restrained their facial muscles out of respect for the professor, their cadavers' genitals, and, most of all, their own.

Lubar held up his penile icon as he discoursed on its three columns of tissue: the urethral orifice, the prepuce, and the life-creating contents of the scrotal sac.

He paused to comment with a wry grin, "I hope you're all following this." And then he asked a question. "Can anybody tell me what occurs when hyperemia of the genitals fills the corpora cavernosa with blood?"

For a moment no one reacted . . . overtly, that is. Could he actually be referring to? . . . Could he possibly mean? . . .

So for no apparent reason the professor called on Laura.

"Yes, Miss Castellano. The result of hyperemia is—?"

"An erection, sir."

The class breathed a sigh of relief.

"Why is it," Lubar asked, "that despite the preponderance of male members in this class only Miss Castellano is familiar with the well-known phenomenon of penile erection?"

No one responded.

Never one to lose the opportunity of cracking a joke at the expense of his female students, Lubar catechized Laura.

"Can *you* think of any possible explanation, Miss Castellano?"

"Perhaps I've just seen more of them, sir," she replied casually.

The professor circumspectly retreated into *Gray's Anatomy,* suggesting that the class begin a careful dissection of the day's featured organ. Those with female cadavers were told to visit a neighbor. And so they set to work.

It was curious. Though after nearly three months they thought they had become inured to the cutting of human flesh, most of the students winced at least inwardly as they began this dismemberment.

"Jesus, Castellano," Barney murmured admiringly as they left the classroom several hours later. "You sure showed up all the guys in the class."

"It was nothing," she replied. "Why the hell didn't *you* speak up?"

"I don't know. I guess I was afraid to stick my neck out."

She fixed him with a mischievous gaze. "*Neck,* Livingston?" Her eyes twinkled.

Just then Grete joined them.

"Wasn't that incredibly disgusting?" she asked with a frown.

"What's the matter?" Laura inquired.

"All those innuendos, Lubar waving that thing around like it was some kind of holy object."

"Actually," Barney remarked casually, "it *was* to the ancient Greeks and Romans. They even worshiped it at festivals—"

"Please, Barney, I've had quite enough for one afternoon. Frankly, I think Professor Lubar is a . . . a . . ."

"A prick?" Laura suggested.

Grete stormed off, flushed with indignation and embarrassment.

If ever proof were needed that the Pilgrim Fathers were truly ascetic Puritans, one would only have to consider the Boston winters. For with the approach of Christmas, the countryside freezes and a merciless wind whips the inhabitants like a penitent's lash. The Pilgrims could, after all, have landed on the temperate shores of Virginia instead of the harsh Rock of Plymouth. They could even, as other Englishmen did, have emigrated to the West Indies, cast off their tightly buckled shoes, and cavorted in the sand.

But the founders of the Massachusetts Bay Colony wanted to suffer. And the New England weather gave them ample opportunity.

Even before the first blizzard, the residents of Vanderbilt Hall were snowed in by an avalanche of work. Time was reckoned not in "shopping days before—" but in hours till the first set of Finals—four of them, right in a row: Anatomy, Histology, Physiology, and the dreaded fourth horseman of the Apoplex, Biochem.

Every dormitory window blazed all through the night. Passersby might perhaps have misconstrued it is a ritual to mark the festivals of light, celebrated by cultures throughout the world at the time of the winter solstice—the darkest days of the year. But inside there was no merrymaking, no caroling, and, most importantly, *no sleep.*

Things had come to such a pass that even Peter Wyman looked scared.

And Palmer Talbot, a medical student by association, also had to make sacrifices.

"Not even *Saturday* night, Laura?"

"Please try and understand. We're like a city under siege here. People are actually freaking out from the tension. Believe me, it's like nothing I've ever experienced."

"Then why are you putting yourself through such torture, Laura? As far as I can see, everything you've done so far in Med School has been fraught with fear. Why would anyone in their right minds put up with it?"

"That's just the way it is. Sort of the price I have to pay."

"And *I* have to pay as well. How can you possibly expect to lead this kind of life and sustain a relationship?"

She sighed. "Palmer, right now the only relationships I can think of are between chemical compounds, cranial nerves, and histological specimens. All of a sudden I'm not a person, I'm a robot studying a human."

"Well, if you hate it so much, why don't you quit?"

"I never said anything about hating it, Palmer."

Though it is a scientific fact that it is impossible for a human being to go without sleep and stay sane, the frenzied med students pathologically ignored this reality. Caffeine helped, of course, and many measured out the nights in plastic coffee cups.

A few were able to avail themselves of recent pharmaceutical advances. If they were lucky enough to know any upperclassmen or—still better—an intern, they could obtain one of the new "pep pills," amphetamine sulphates like Benzedrine to stimulate the nervous system and "conquer" sleep. They were too busy poring over other texts to peruse the small print on the labels. Even the fastidious Alison Redmond neglected to question the safety of the tablets that were, so she felt, keeping her "mind as clear as the sky."

Barney Livingston marched to a different drummer. His own way of vanquishing slumber was with periodic sets of push-ups followed by cold showers. He was regarded as a lunatic by everyone else—except Bennett, whom he had convinced to try the same method.

Laura stuck to cola, and before heading for Barney's room, would fill a large Thermos at the Coke machine. Outside in the corridor students paced up and down, frantically trying to cram the material on countless index cards into their weary, worried brains.

Only Hank Dwyer was oblivious to all the inhuman pressure. While his fellow classmates thought they were in hell, he felt like a purified soul, who in a few brief days would leave this transient purgatory and soar up to be emparadised in Cheryl's arms.

At three in the morning before "Inquisition I" (Anatomy A) Laura and Barney agreed on a five-minute break. They lifted his window to invite the cold air to slap them awake and then opened the door to accelerate the breeze. The waking dead paid them no heed and continued to march, mumble, and memorize. March, mumble, memorize.

"I've seen this sort of thing before," said Barney hoarsely. "This is just the way people move in a psycho ward."

Neither of them laughed. They were too busy trying to remember the origin, insertion, and innervation of the bulbocavernosus muscle.

The tests themselves proved anticlimactic. And a kind of relief, since the freshmen were so exhausted after taking them they would grab a bite, go back to their rooms, and fall into deep and dreamless sleep. On the morrow they would walk into the exam rooms like automata and confront new examinations whose questions would make them so queasy that—almost as a reflex—they would regurgitate information.

At last, with only four shopping days left until Christmas, they were liberated. As she had promised, Laura spent the time at Palmer's place on Beacon Hill. Although she wondered what joy she could bring him by sleeping eighteen hours a day, he seemed delighted to have her to himself—if only as an immobile object.

Meanwhile, Hank Dwyer became the first man in history to fly home on a bus. For he was en route to seventh heaven.

Grete bade farewell to everyone in the Deanery and hurried to the airport to board a student charter to the great Northwest. In the concluding days of the semester she had subtly hinted that there was Somebody Special waiting for her in Portland. This offered a possible explanation for her coyness and coquetry: she had just been practicing. No doubt her beau was tall, muscular, and Nordic and probably named Lars or Olaf. What need for an Eastern Adonis if you have a West Coast Thor?

Bennett came up to say goodbye to Barney the evening after their last exam.

"Have a good holiday, Landsmann," Barney said. "I suppose you've got a different Cleveland beauty for every night of the twelve days of Christmas."

"I'm not going home, actually. I'll be meeting my folks for a fortnight on the slopes."

"Aha, you mean *le ski*?"

Bennett nodded. "And *l'après ski,* which of course is the best part."

"Christ, Bennett, that probably means you'll have *two* girls a day. Whereabouts are you doing your snow jobs?"

"Montana."

"That's pretty far."

"Well, after all, Livingston, I'm a far-out guy."

Peter Wyman's plans were the most ambitious of all. He was remaining in Boston to do lab research with none other than Professor Michael Pfeifer.

At seven on the evening of December twenty-third, Palmer drove Laura to Logan Airport where Barney was waiting to join her for the Eastern Airlines shuttle to New York (only fourteen bucks for a mere hour's aerial roller coaster ride through the turbulent December winds between Beantown and Gotham).

Palmer embraced her warmly, reminded her to choose an early train to join him for the Hunt Club's New Year's Eve fête, and then zoomed off himself toward the ski trails of Vermont where, as he had told Laura, he would sublimate his need for her by schussing himself to exhaustion.

As Laura held their place in the serpentine queue of students waiting to board the flight, Barney excused himself and dashed to the newsstand to buy a *Sports Illustrated.*

He did not sprint back. Instead, he walked slowly in a state of mild shock. Only Laura's voice roused him to action.

"Shake ass, Livingston. We're going to miss the goddamn plane."

He broke into a trot for the last fifty or so yards and joined her just as their turn came to hand their chits to the gate attendant.

"What's the matter with you?" she inquired as they pushed their way into the crowded cabin.

"Nothing, nothing. I guess I'm a little out of shape, that's all."

They found two seats together on the far right aisle, squeezed into them, and began to buckle up. Barney was strangely silent, merely staring at the bald spot of the man in front of them.

"Livingston," Laura persisted, "you look like you've seen a ghost."

"I have—sort of."

Just then the Lockheed Electra's propellers emitted a deafening roar.

Laura fidgeted nervously as the plane sped down the runway and then lifted up over Boston Harbor into the wintry sky. At last the engine noise abated and Laura could again press for information.

"What the hell happened, Barn?"

He shook his head in utter consternation. "I was just getting near the magazine racks when I saw Bennett standing in line for a flight."

"So?"

"He was traveling First Class."

"Hey, we know he's got bucks. It's obvious by the way he dresses. What's such a big deal?"

"He told me he was going skiing in Montana," Barney replied. "But that sure as hell isn't where he's going. I mean, Castellano, the guy was getting on a *Swissair flight to Zurich*! Don't you find that a little strange?"

"No," she replied. "I find that extremely strange."

THIRTEEN

The Swissair stewardess came by, offering champagne and hors d'oeuvres to the First Class passengers. Bennett Landsmann welcomed the caviar, but politely declined the beverage.

"Danke, ich werde vielleicht später mit dem Abendessen 'was trinken."

"You speak German very well," said the bejeweled gray-haired woman sitting next to him. "Where are you from?"

"The exotic city of Cleveland, Ohio, madame."

"But surely you were not born there?" she continued, obviously fascinated.

"No, I lived the first ten years of my life in a little town called Millersburg, Georgia."

"And are you going to Zurich for the holiday?"

"Not really. I'll be meeting my parents to go skiing in Crans-Montana."

"In Valais? Oh, it's a beautiful spot."

"Yes, I'm looking forward to it." He shut his eyes and continued the dialogue with himself. *I may ski in Europe, but I'm sure as hell not German. In fact I'm not even Bennett Landsmann. That is to say, it isn't the name I was born with....*

It was April 1945. The Allied forces had crossed the Rhine and were advancing toward the heart of Germany. With the Red Army on the outskirts of Vienna, it was clear that the Nazis could not avoid defeat.

On April fourth the all-Negro 386th Tank Battalion of Patton's Third Army under the command of Lieutenant Colonel Abraham Lincoln Bennett entered the peaceful village of Ohrdruf.

On the outskirts of the picturesque German hamlet, they came upon a deserted Nazi labor camp. That is, deserted of life. Gruesome piles of contorted, emaciated corpses were strewn everywhere. The bodies were rotting, filthy, crawling with lice, entwined into knots so tight they could hardly be separated.

Colonel Bennett's men had been among the first black soldiers to see frontline duty in Europe. They had landed on the beaches of Normandy the previous June, part of the Allied High Command's desperate rush for replacements to meet the enemy's massive Ardennes offensive. They had seen heavy combat in the fog-rimmed valley of the Meuse River. As a "reward" for their success, they had been transferred to George Patton's Third Army, joining the battle for every inch of icy ground on the push eastward through the Siegfried Line into Germany.

They had seen close friends wounded or killed. They had learned to harden their hearts. But now even the strongest of them were unable to restrain their feelings of revulsion. Some could not keep from vomiting. The stench of death and decay polluted their every breath.

Shocked and disoriented, Colonel Bennett ordered his staff photographer to record the ghastly scene. He was determined to send the photographs to General Eisenhower so that Ike could see this obscenity with his own eyes.

As the tall, heavyset commander stood staring at the carnage, one of his lieutenants approached hesitantly to report. "Sir, we've found sort of a mass grave outside the camp. There must be thousands of bodies. Some are only half buried. Uh—what do you think we oughta do, sir?"

Linc struggled to regain his powers of speech.

"See that they're interred properly, Lieutenant," he answered crisply. "I intend to make a personal inspection." Then he added softly, "And have the chaplain say some prayers."

They remained in Ohrdruf for more than a week, while Linc personally supervised almost all of the "proper" burials. Occasionally when the chaplain's voice began to falter, he would read the prayers himself.

During that whole period, Linc was unable to sleep. The fever and cough that had been plaguing him all through the damp and freezing winter had returned with a vengeance.

Though he had spent many nights sweating and gasping for breath, whenever he thought of seeing a medic, he convinced himself that it was just a lousy little flu.

Finally, on the morning of April fourteenth, three other of Patton's units arrived, the first bearing a welcome directive to press northward. Tired as they were, his men quickly assembled, anxious to leave the atmosphere of this slaughterhouse.

By twilight, as they were moving on the road toward Gotha, small clusters of strange wraithlike figures began to materialize by the sides of the road. One of them, a skeleton who had once been a man, pointed tremulously at the white star on the flag of Colonel Bennett's jeep and called in a hoarse, quavering voice, *"Amerikaner! Die sind Amerikaner! Wir sind gerettet!"*

More living ghosts appeared. The colonel ordered his convoy to halt. Self-conscious at his own well-padded girth, Bennett stepped down from his jeep and walked toward a pale, frightened group of scarecrows. They shrank back as he approached.

"It's okay, folks, there's nothing to be afraid of. We're here to help you." He extended his arms in a gesture of reassurance.

They did not understand his words but were joyfully aware that he was not speaking *German*. One of them, a tall, stoop-shouldered man of indeterminate age, expressed a thousand dizzying, jubilant thoughts in a single phrase, "You are really America?"

Linc nodded. "That's right, we're from the U.S.A."

The next thing he knew the man was embracing his ankles, sobbing, and howling, "God bless America!" Linc could not restrain his tears as he barked at his soldiers to gather these tattered fragments of humanity into their vehicles.

Linc helped the tall man into his own jeep, hoping to learn more precisely who these people were. With halting English ("In Berlin my parents had for me an English tutor") the man explained that most of them had escaped from the Ohrdruf camp a few days earlier as the rest of the inmates were being rounded up for a march to Bergen-Belsen ("Either way it was death, so there was nothing to lose"). He also said the refugees had not eaten for days. Linc had the word passed back to his men to get some food into these people, pronto. Chocolate bars appeared from every khaki breast pocket and were offered to the survivors, who devoured them ravenously.

To the soldiers' horror, in less than an hour three of them were dead—from the shock of overeating.

When he delivered his passengers to a makeshift Red Cross station outside Gotha, the tall man was especially effusive.

"God bless you, General."

Linc could not keep from laughing. "Thanks for the compliment, mister, but I'm not even a full colonel."

"Well, for your kindness, you deserve to be a general."

The two men shook hands and parted. Linc's soldiers then entered the village itself to find several white units of the division had already arrived.

Captain Richard McIntyre of Birmingham, Alabama, was in the process of interrogating one of the local inhabitants—a plump, middle-aged man whose lederhosen made him look like a fugitive from a cuckoo clock.

The captain was at first disconcerted at the sight of a black man in so remote a place. But then, noting the silver oak leaves on Linc's shoulders, he saluted reflexively.

"Who is this gentleman, Captain?" Bennett inquired tersely, inured to the discomfiture of white junior officers when in his presence.

"He's the Bürgermeister—the mayor of this place—uh, sir."

"Have you inquired whether he's holding any prisoners?"

The captain nodded. "He was, sir. There were Jews working in the quarries—but they were marched off two days ago. From what the mayor understands, they were being taken to Buchenwald."

"Why, what's there?"

McIntyre turned and posed the question to the Bürgermeister. He then looked back at Linc and explained, "He thinks it's just another work camp."

"Oh," said the colonel sarcastically. "And that's all he knows, huh?" He then glared at the German. "Just another 'work camp,' huh, Krauthead?"

The mayor, uncomprehending, but trying frantically to ingratiate himself, smiled. *"Na, ja. Ich weiss nichts von diesen Dingen. Wir sind nur Bauern hier."*

McIntyre quickly translated. "He says he doesn't know anything. They're just farmers around here."

"Sure, sure," Linc murmured, and then addressed the officer. "As you were, Captain." McIntyre gave a smart salute which Bennett returned with equal formality, and then started back to the rustic inn his men had commandeered as a temporary HQ.

*   *   *

As senior officer of the battalion, Colonel Bennett was naturally assigned the largest room. His tall narrow windows looked out onto a flowered courtyard.

He sat down at the desk, took a swig from the cognac he had confiscated from the innkeeper, withdrew a sheet of paper that bore the doubly encircled "A" Third Army insignia, uncapped his fountain pen, and began a letter to his nine-year-old son in Georgia.

Somewhere in Germany
April 15, 1945

Dear Linc Junior,

Sorry I haven't written for a while but the tide's been turning in our favor and we've been constantly on the move.

I'd like to say that I'm overjoyed by our successes (our guys have been decorated more times than a Christmas tree), but we've all lost good friends along the way.

I've seen a lot of bad things this past week that I don't think I'll ever be able to describe.

I often think of Pastor Stedman's Sunday sermons about "man's inhumanity to man." But up to now I always took that to mean the way our people have been treated in America.

I wonder what the Reverend Stedman would say about the forced labor camps we've just seen? Men were literally starved to death.

I'll grant the Negro hasn't been treated with kid gloves in America and the Army's not much better. But son, we have never been gassed by the thousands or burned in ovens. . . .

The telephone rang. Linc sighed wearily, took another swig, and picked up the receiver. It was Major General John Shelton, his division commander, calling from somewhere in the field. The connection was faint and full of static.

"Bennett—what kind of shape are your men in?"

"Well, General, to be honest, they're pretty bushed—physically and emotionally. Most of them are just kids, and these past few days they've been shocked by what they've seen."

"But have you seen hell, Linc—absolute hell on earth?"

"Yes sir, I believe I have—two forced labor camps and a huge pit with maybe eight thousand bodies."

"Then you've been in Coney Island, mister. I want your men up here tomorrow by 1900 hours. We're in Nordhausen."

"That's about thirty-five miles north of us, sir?"

"Check. But you'd better prepare your men."

"For what, sir?"

"Nordhausen isn't a labor camp. It's a *death camp.*"

Linc slept especially badly that night. Partly because of the pain in his chest—and partly because of the bruise in his soul. When he did drift off he had terrifying nightmares from which he woke up in a pool of sweat. At 6 A.M. he showered and went downstairs for a cup of coffee.

Standing there like a wizened statue was the tall man whom he had left at the Red Cross station the day before. Linc wondered how long he had been waiting.

"Hi," he said amicably, "will you join me?"

The man nodded eagerly. "Thank you."

The next moment he was seated on the wooden chair across from Linc, gnawing at a chunk of bread.

"Hey, why don't you slow down and put some butter on that, my friend?"

The man nodded, his mouth full. His hands somehow conveyed the message that he had been too hungry to wait. Perhaps he would allow himself the luxury of butter on his next slice.

Linc sipped a mug of coffee and then asked, "Shouldn't you be back at the Red Cross station?"

The man shook his head strenuously. "No, no, no. By Red Cross I meet a woman also from Berlin, a friend of family. She say she saw my wife some few days ago—at Nordhausen. I hear that you go today to Nordhausen. You must take me."

Linc was baffled. He had no idea what the rulebook would say about this. But this nightmare transcended any normal protocol.

"Do you think you're strong enough for the journey, Mr.—?"

"Herschel. Just call me Herschel."

"Don't you have a last name?"

"Sir, until yesterday I had only a number. 'Herschel' is fine."

"Well, Herschel, if you think you're up to traveling in one of my supply trucks, be my guest. I can't promise that your wife will still be there."

They could smell it before they could see it. Even from miles away—and even though the ovens had ceased to operate—there was still the lingering smell of burning flesh in the air.

They passed farmhouses where the peasants were going about their daily tasks as if the sun were not blocked by clouds of death. They were plowing and sowing as if divorced in time and place from this vortex of evil.

Linc studied some of them through his binoculars. They seemed robust and happy, sowing in the farmlands of this fertile oasis in the midst of the Hartz Mountains of Thuringia. The scene could have been the inspiration for Beethoven's *Pastoral* Symphony.

Indeed, Linc could not fathom how the nation that had produced such angelic music could also have committed such satanic atrocities.

No one of the 386th Battalion led by Lieutenant Colonel Bennett would forget that evening. They had been horrified enough at the sight of the gaunt and starving, but now they were beholding the true living dead.

And there were thousands. Though nominally freed by the U.S. Third Army the day before, they were still prisoners of their own wretchedness—too frightened to breathe. The sheer magnitude of their numbers was staggering. And the filth, the excrement, the lice, the rats were worse than in any sewer.

With their sunken cheeks, protruding ribs, and distended bellies, they were barely recognizable as human beings. Their gait was slow and faultering, their movements feeble.

As soon as the convoy came to a halt, Herschel lowered his aching legs to the ground and limped as quickly as he could toward the long rows of bunkhouses from which, even at this distance, the agonized groans were audible.

Linc's soldiers hovered as the medics struggled to keep the "liberated" prisoners alive.

The Nazis might have gone, but the Angel of Death lingered.

Some could manage a faint smile, wave their hands—however weakly—as a welcome to the black Americans. But even happiness required strength and it was there in pitifully short supply.

To endure the ungodly sights and smells, Linc lit one of his fat cigars and tried to keep composed as he walked through the camp to Division HQ to report for duty.

"Welcome to Dante's Inferno," said Major General Shelton, a balding midwesterner in his early forties. The two men shook hands. "Sit down, Linc, you look terrible."

"So do you, General. I only got a quick glance coming over here, but this must be the absolute depths—"

"Shit, man, you think this place is bad? The British entered Belsen up north today and if you can believe it, things are even worse there. Have you seen the ovens yet?"

"No, sir, and I'm not really in a hurry."

"You know, the amazing thing is *this* place didn't even have a gas chamber. They worked the poor bastards so hard that at the end of the day there were enough corpses to keep the crematorium operating around the clock. Of course, they had a little help from dysentery, T.B., and typhus, but most of the credit should go to the boy scouts of the SS."

Linc was speechless for a moment. Finally he asked, "What's being done to help these people?"

"We're commandeering all the medical supplies we can lay our hands on. We've got doctors here and doctors on the way, even some kids from British med schools. But our soldiers have got to help them out. There's so damn many. . . ."

"I know, General," Linc said grimly.

Shelton looked at Bennett's weary face and sensed his fellow officer's dejection. Suddenly, in dramatically exaggerated formal tones he ordered: "Lieutenant Colonel Bennett, will you stand?"

Lincoln rose to his feet, for a split second unsure of Shelton's intent. But then Shelton reached into the drawer and withdrew a small box. It contained a pair of gold oak leaf clusters.

He was about to become a *full* colonel.

"Will you remove your silver clusters?" Shelton requested, again in formal tones.

Linc complied.

As Shelton pinned the gold insignia on Linc's broad shoulders, he remarked, "This promotion's been chasing you all over Europe. Congratulations, Colonel Bennett."

"What can I say, John?" he replied.

"Save your words—'cause sure as God made little green apples, there's a silver star around the corner for you."

To which Linc smiled and retorted, "No, John, I don't think the Army's ready to make the likes of me a general."

That night Colonel Bennett completed the letter to his son. He could not possibly describe what he had seen that day. He could barely allude to it in a way that might be tolerable for an innocent boy. He was a deeply religious man.

All he could think of was Calvary and Matthew's description of Christ's words on the cross, "My God, my God, why hast thou forsaken me?" For clearly both heaven and earth had turned their backs on these wretched victims until it was too late.

His head ached—that damned fever again. And his chest hurt from coughing. Better finish the letter and get some sleep. He merely told his son to keep the faith, give Grandma all his love, and pray that they would be united real soon.

He closed the envelope, folded it into a pocket of his coat, untied his boots, and leaned back on his cot.

At assembly the next morning, Colonel Lincoln Bennett assigned his troops to the various other units already at work. Some were hunting for prison guards who had escaped into the surrounding woods when the Army arrived. Others helped distribute medicine and food. He himself went to join the senior officers whom General Shelton had summoned for a tour of the entire camp.

As they walked past row upon row of bunkhouses whose residents were lying outside, motionless in the spring sunshine, he saw soldiers passing in open trucks piled high with corpses.

An officer from another regiment asked Shelton, "With respect, sir, isn't there a more . . . dignified way of removing the dead?"

The general shook his head. "I sure as hell wish there were, but we've got a problem with the living. There's already an epidemic of typhus in the camp and God knows what kind of pestilence those rotting corpses might bring. Some of these people would drop dead if you just patted them on the shoulder."

Or gave them a chocolate bar, thought Linc.

They saw the "work area"—where inmates had been forced to carry heavy rocks from place to place for no other purpose than to exhaust them. They saw the barbed wire, which until forty-eight hours ago had been charged with electric current.

When they saw the crematoria where human beings were turned to ash and smoke, all Bennett could think was that there was no sense to it at all—no way to rationalize the Nazis' actions within the limited vocabulary of human emotions.

The tour took nearly three hours. They were back at company HQ just after noon. The general announced that Officers' Mess would be at 1300 hours and dismissed the men. As they dispersed, Linc waited to question Shelton.

"Sir, I know you've caught a couple of their guards. What are you going to do with them?"

"Those that make it will go to trial, I'm sure."

"What do you mean by 'make it'?"

"Well," the general replied without apparent emotion, "sometimes the prisoners get to them first. You'd be surprised how even the weakest, sickliest inmates can find the strength to tear those bastards into shreds before we can stop them."

"Do you try to stop them?"

"Of course, Linc," Shelton answered. And then he added in a lower tone, "We just don't make a point of hurrying."

Just then Linc heard a voice calling frantically, "Colonel—wait, sir, please wait!"

He turned to see Herschel hobbling up to him, his eyes ablaze with urgency. "You must help, Colonel Bennett. Please, please, I beg of you. It's Hannah, my wife—"

"You've found her?"

Herschel nodded and then blurted, "She is with the doctors. You must help. Come quickly, please."

Linc tried his best to calm the man. "Hey, listen, if she's getting medical care—"

"No, no. You do not understand. She is *not* getting treatment. They are going to let her die. Come, please."

As Linc and Herschel approached the hospital building, they could see patients lying on litters in the open air, waiting their turn to be brought inside. From the building came the pungent, far-reaching smell of germicide.

Inside was bedlam, cries of pain intermingled with frantic orders shouted by doctors and nurses to one another. Linc lost no time in locating the physician in charge.

Lieutenant Colonel Hunter Endicott, the chief of medical operations, was tall, bespectacled, and white. In fact, being from Jackson, Mississippi, he was extremely white. He was also extremely busy. He had little time to squander on chit-chats with black visitors, even if they were officers.

With Herschel babbling frantically in German a few paces behind him, Linc calmly inquired after the state of health of the former prisoner's wife. Endicott's response was more curt than courteous.

"I'm afraid she's been triaged out," he explained matter-of-factly. "Now, if you'll excuse me, I've got lives to save." As the doctor started to turn away, Linc suppressed the urge to grab his sleeve.

Instead he simply shouted, "What in hell do you mean by 'triaged out'?"

"Hey, look, I told you I'm busy—"

"May I remind you," Linc said quietly but firmly, "I'm your superior officer. And I'm giving you an order. Tell me about this man's wife!"

Endicott sighed.

"Okay, *Colonel*," he said pointedly, " 'triage' is the term we use for classifying the wounded. Now I don't have to tell you how many sick people we have here, or that everybody's got typhus or is damned likely to get it. Our teams have triaged the patients into S, MS, and NS. I know this is going to sound brutal to you, but the first group is 'salvageable,' then there are 'marginally salvageable,' and then there's those who—in our estimation—are 'not salvageable.' I'm afraid this man's wife comes into the last category."

"Why, what's wrong?"

The doctor shook his head. "I really don't think you want to hear this, Colonel—and I'm sure her husband doesn't."

"Correction, Endicott." He glanced at Herschel and persisted. "At this point he can take anything."

"Okay," the doctor replied with a sigh of resignation.

There was an empty cart alongside that once was used for hauling—they did not wish to think of that. Endicott pulled himself up to sit on it as the two men stood nearby.

"Now, gentlemen, listen carefully. For a concentration camp, this place has got extraordinary medical facilities. Not for the prisoners' benefit—but for the Nazi 'scientists.' The doctors performed experiments using the prisoners as human guinea pigs. . . ."

He paused to let the information sink in.

"I've heard sketchy reports about other camps and I know some of their 'research' was pure sadism. But the Dr. Staengel who ran the operation here saw himself as advancing the science of medicine, and so forth. He killed and tortured and maimed—allegedly for the benefit of mankind. Anyway, this bastard had orders from Berlin to come up with something better than sulfa drugs to combat venereal disease. You see, even supermen can get the clap."

He smiled wryly. The other two men merely nodded.

"Well, Staengel was a meticulous sonovabitch and kept a detailed record of everything—so I know exactly what they've done to this woman. On March twenty-eighth they injected her intravaginally with Neisseria gonorrhoeae."

Herschel's face was a chalky, expressionless mask.

"And on April second they started 'treating' her—if that's the word—with an experimental antibiotic they called *RDX 30*. Staengel had the exact formulation down here. But the only important thing is that it contained a small but significant quantity of sodium hydroxide, otherwise known as lye—the stuff your mother put gloves on to clean the drains with because it was so strong.

"Anyway, instead of dealing only with the infection, it acted as an abrasive. The whole lining of her uterus was inflamed and stripped bare. That so-called 'wonder drug' burned through the epithelium and started corroding the blood vessels underneath. She's anemic, she's infected, and her fever's a hundred and four. There's no way . . ."

He paused for a moment and then realized that the patient's husband had just heard him pronounce her death sentence. So he added a few words of consolation. "I'm sorry, sir, but she's too far gone to be saved. Now, if you'll excuse me—"

Herschel suddenly screamed like a wounded animal and fell to his knees.

Before the doctor had taken his third step Linc bellowed, "You wait right here—I'm still in charge here and I haven't dismissed you."

The strain on his vocal cords made him cough again.

Endicott turned slowly with a smirk that seemed to say Fuck you, nigger, but whispered, "I beg your pardon, Colonel. I didn't realize there was any more to say. How can I help you—except by giving you something for that cough?"

"Are you married, Endicott?" Linc demanded.

The doctor nodded and added, "Three kids."

"Just imagine for a minute it was *your* wife that got triaged out. How would you go about saving her?"

The doctor paused for a minute, ransacking his mind.

"Listen . . . *sir*," he finally answered, "nobody here's got the time to perform a hysterectomy—"

"You mean that could save her?" Linc interposed quickly.

The look on Endicott's face told him that he had finally gotten the physician up against the wall.

"Look," Endicott protested as calmly as he could, "she's bleeding so badly she probably wouldn't survive the operation anyhow."

"Don't tell me you haven't got blood," Linc retorted.

"Not enough to waste on hopeless cases, Colonel. *Now* if you'll excuse me—"

"You are *not* dismissed," Linc snapped. "I'm not finished. I want somebody to perform that operation. Christ knows they've suffered enough. They at least deserve a chance."

The gauntlet was down. It was now a question of who would flinch. Linc was taller and his eyes were incendiary.

"All right, Colonel," Endicott said, affecting a cordial air, "suppose I get someone to perform this futile procedure at, say, 2300 hours or so. Where do you propose that he'll get the four or five pints of whole blood he'll need?"

"Just tell me how much and I'll deliver it. . . ."

The physician relaxed, certain that he had now led his adversary into a trap. "Colonel, a man in your position is certainly aware of U.S. Army rules. Under no circumstances are we allowed to use Negro blood on white patients. That is by order of our supreme commander, Franklin Delano Roosevelt. Do you read me?"

"Doctor, I'm afraid you've overlooked one small detail. That woman isn't *in* the U.S. Army. She isn't even an American. In fact she was designated by her own government as a nonperson. So Washington's legislation has no bearing on her case. Do *you* read me?"

In the silence that followed, Linc could almost hear Endicott's teeth gnashing. "If I bring a half a dozen men, will that be enough, Doctor?"

"Yeah—yes. I'll let you know what blood type," Endicott answered wearily and stamped off.

Linc turned and caught sight of Herschel's face. Tears were streaming down his cheeks.

"Come on, man, cheer up. We've got it squared away. I promise you, your Hannah's gonna make it."

"I . . . I don't know what to say. Five years already army soldiers have been torturing us and now you go and do this for me—"

Linc was at once touched and embarrassed. He put his arm around Herschel's frail shoulder as the man continued to weep.

"This Dr. Staengel must have been a real cutie. I sure as hell hope they catch him."

"I don't care," Herschel sobbed, "I don't care about anything except that Hannah lives."

A little after 1 A.M., Hannah Landsmann was carried by stretcher into the astonishingly well-equipped surgery, where seven units of blood had been stacked in an ice bucket. Her gaunt face made her look like a woman of sixty, though Linc knew she was barely half that age. Even the beads of sweat on her brow seemed gray. Herschel held her hand tightly as he whispered reassuring words she was too delirious to understand.

Perhaps out of sheer revenge, Dr. Endicott had assigned his most junior surgeon, Andrew Browning, to perform the complex operation.

Linc's heart sank when he saw the young doctor prop up a dog-eared copy of the *Atlas of Surgical Techniques*. This student needed an instruction book.

At this point Browning turned to them and said, "I'm afraid I'll have to ask you gentlemen to leave."

Herschel still remained immobile. Suddenly a nurse joined them. She looked at Linc and said reassuringly, "Colonel, I've worked with Browning before. He may be new at the game but he knows how to use a scalpel—and he's very, very careful."

Linc nodded in gratitude and then gently led Herschel from the room.

The two men went outdoors and sat on a step to wait. It was a warm spring night and stars dotted the peaceful sky.

Linc had brought cigarettes. Withdrawing a slender silver case embossed with the Third Army emblem, he took out two of them, lit them both, and handed one to his friend.

Linc broke into a rasping cough. His good sense told him that he should not be smoking at all. But, dammit, he needed something to take his mind off all this.

"Are you married, Colonel?" Herschel asked.

"That's kind of difficult to answer, Herschel," he replied uneasily. "We were in the process of getting a divorce when I was called overseas. Only it's hard to find a state that will accept 'mutual disdain' as grounds. I suppose by now she's cut me loose from her life. In any case, she left our son with my mother."

"A son?"

"Yeah—Linc Junior, he'll be ten this summer. To be honest, the thought of seeing him is what's kept me going all this time. What about you?"

"We had a daughter," Herschel answered, seemingly without emotion. "She was nearly four when we arrived at our first detention camp. They told us they were taking her to a nursery. We believed it because we wanted to believe it. But we knew when we kissed her that night it was goodbye."

He inhaled deeply on his cigarette and added, "It's a strange thing, you know. After that, Hannah and I could not even speak her name. We just looked at one another, already feeling so guilty that we were still alive and our little Charlotte was somewhere dead."

There was an aching silence.

Then Herschel continued, "Not much after that they separated us. If you can believe it, I was once a gymnast, strong as an ox. I even belonged to one of the rigorous *Turnvereine* for Christians only. And so they sent me to the quarries as a slave. Until this week I never knew what happened to Hannah."

They had nearly finished all the cigarettes when Browning, still in his bloodstained white overalls, stepped outside, rubbing his eyes.

Both men leapt to their feet.

"How is she?" they asked, almost in unison.

"She pulled through the operation okay," the young man replied. "We just have to hope she's strong enough to heal."

"Can I see her now?" asked Herschel anxiously.

"Really, it would be better to let her sleep it off. In fact that would be the best thing for all of us." Browning took a deep breath and then in the boyish tones of the Oxford student he had been until a few weeks ago, he added, "I mean it, chaps. With all the germs floating around this camp, the best thing we can do for our own health is to turn in."

Linc walked Herschel back to his bunk. There were moans emanating from within. The inmates had been freed in life, but they were still prisoners of their nightmares.

"How can I thank you, Colonel Bennett?"

"For one you can start calling me Linc. And I think we should both say a few prayers and go to bed."

"Prayers?" Herschel asked incredulously. "To whom could I possibly pray?"

"To the Lord, our Rock and our Salvation," Linc replied with conviction. "Psalm One Hundred and Thirty—'Out of the depths have I cried unto thee, O Lord . . . Let Israel hope in the Lord: for with the Lord there *is* mercy.' You know that one, don't you?"

Herschel nodded. Yet something deep inside him could not let Linc's faith go unchallenged.

"God? You talk to me about God? I was once an observant Jew. I led an honorable life. I went every Sabbath to the synagogue—and look at my reward. Do you think I can pray now to a God who allowed my whole family to be killed for no reason? Could I believe in a God that gives punishment where there is no crime? I am sorry, my faith disappeared with the smoke from the chimneys."

Linc could find no appropriate answer. So he merely offered Herschel his hand, which the frail Jew grasped in both his own, and confided, "You know the only thing I can believe in now? I can believe in what *you* gave to me. I can believe in human kindness."

The two men parted. Linc walked slowly back past the sentries, giving them a perfunctory salute, and pondering, How am I going to explain this to my son?

He sat on the edge of the bed, lowered his head into his hands, and began to pray.

He woke up groggy the next morning. His temples throbbed, his back and limbs were aching. That damn flu, he could not seem to shake it. As he showered, trying to clear his head, he vaguely noticed some bluish splotches on his chest and abdomen.

That's all I need, he thought to himself, bugs in the damn bed or something.

He swallowed a couple of aspirins, then put on his warm coat and went out for roll call.

A little before noon he was able to steal a few minutes from his duties to see how Hannah was faring. She had been taken back to her bunkhouse. Herschel was sitting by her side.

"How is she?" Linc inquired.

Herschel smiled. "We have been talking all morning. Her fever is much lower and that young doctor seemed hopeful. Please come over, I want to introduce you."

Herschel presented his American savior in long German sentences that Linc took to be exaggerated praise.

Hannah tried to smile and whispered hoarsely, "Herschel tells how very much you did for me."

"No, ma'am, *he* did it all. I was just the go-between."

"No, no," Herschel insisted. "If we can ever find happiness again, we will have you to thank."

Linc was touched. "Is there anything I can get you folks? I mean, are they feeding you all right?"

"Everything is fine," Herschel replied. "The demons are gone and we can breathe the air. That is what matters."

Suddenly Linc Bennett began to sweat. Perhaps the place was over-heated. No, the Nazis did not bother with heating for these bunks. Maybe he should not have worn his winter coat. He felt dizzy and needed air. He walked as quickly as he could to the door, opened it, and stepped out into the brisk April morning. Then he collapsed and lay sprawled on the ground.

*   *   *

He awoke slowly, and then only to a state of semiconsciousness. He could sense a pillow, so he knew he was in a bed—and he could hear angry voices somewhere in his vicinity.

"Shit, as if we haven't got enough on our hands, this dumb jigaboo colonel has to go and get himself typhus. I mean, considering it's something you can fight off if you're even halfway healthy, the guy must have been actually *trying*."

"With due respect, sir, if you'd just glance at his x-rays, you'll see that he's been walking around with bronchial pneumonia for quite a while."

"Listen, Browning, I don't need a goddamn x-ray, I can hear that cottonpicker's chest from across the room."

"Dr. Endicott, his spirometer is just about fifty percent. He can barely breathe. Isn't there anything more we can do to help him?"

"For God's sake, we're flooding him with sulfamethazine. The only thing I know that's stronger is that Nazi doctor's *RDX 30*. Face it, man, he's a lost cause."

Linc had been sweating, but now chills convulsed his body. In a matter of moments the young medic was at his side, helping a nurse spread another blanket over him.

"Browning, is that you?" Linc gasped.

"Take it easy, Colonel, you'll pull through," he replied, patting him reassuringly on the shoulder.

"Hey, kid," Linc said, his great chest desperately heaving, "I've been in this war business a long time. And I'd say you've already booked this bed for somebody else."

Browning lacked both the experience and composure to be able to respond.

Suddenly Linc groaned softly, "Shit."

"Sir?"

"If I had to die in this goddamn war, why couldn't it at least have been in the field—so my son would have had something to be proud of?"

The young man was almost in tears. "You'll be all right, sir."

"You're a lousy liar, Browning. Wise up, if you expect to make it as a real doctor."

There was a gentle knock as the door opened slowly.

"I'm sorry, no visitors," the young man said quickly but politely.

Herschel pretended not to understand and walked into the room, carrying a small bunch of wildflowers.

"Please," he said, "I have come to see my friend."

Browning shrugged and, as he left the room, simply nodded to

Herschel, saying, "I'll be right nearby, Colonel. Just call if you need anything."

The two men were now alone.

"Flowers for you, Lincoln," Herschel said, holding them out as he attempted to smile. "You know something amazing? Just a few meters past this world of barbed wire, flowers grow and trees blossom. There is still life in the world."

Not for me, Linc thought inwardly. And then he asked, "How's Hannah?"

"Well, well," replied Herschel buoyantly, "almost no fever. Tomorrow maybe I can take her for a walk. We will come to visit."

"Yeah, good, that'll be nice." He then suddenly gasped, "Oh God, my—"

It took a split second for Herschel to realize that Linc was unconscious, then he began to shout for help.

Herschel stood wide-eyed and trembling as the clinical staff tried to revive his benefactor.

"I get no pulse in the carotid," said a voice.

"Nothing in the dorsalis pedis," said another.

"Respiration nil."

"Let's try injecting an intracardiac ampoule of epinephrine."

"I don't think that'll be necessary," said the calm voice of Dr. Hunter Endicott. "With typhus on top of that pneumonia, the guy didn't have a tinker's chance."

The group around the bed stepped aside for the senior physician, who made a thorough and final check of vital signs and said to the head nurse, "Sheila, you'll take care of the paperwork, all right? And make sure everything in this room is disinfected."

She nodded. In a matter of seconds the intravenous drip was removed from Colonel Bennett's arm, the sheet pulled over his face, and the bed wheeled out.

None of them even noticed the witness to all this—a thin, stoop-shouldered, frightened man standing in the corner, a few tiny sprigs of flowers still clutched in his hand, tears running down his cheeks.

Almost involuntarily, his lips parted and a prayer emerged: *"Yisgadal ve yiskadosh shmei raboh . . ."* Extolled and hallowed be the name of the Lord in the world which He created according to His Will . . .

It was the Hebrew Kaddish for the dead.

It was at that moment that Herschel Landsmann swore a solemn oath. That Colonel Abraham Lincoln Bennett must not have died in vain.

* * *

Swissair Flight 127 landed in Zurich on the bright clear morning of December 24, 1958. The tall, black passenger in First Class buttoned his blazer, straightened his tie, slung his cordovan inflight bag over his shoulder and headed toward the exit.

Once down the metal steps, he strode briskly to the baggage area. The carousel brought his matching cordovan suitcases almost immediately. But, like the others who had brought skis, he had to wait for the special cargo to be unloaded.

He glanced through the glass doors at the crowd gathered outside the Customs area and saw the people he was seeking. He smiled and waved affectionately.

And Abraham Lincoln Bennett, Jr., walked out to embrace his adoptive parents, Hannah and Herschel Landsmann.

FOURTEEN

The victims were clamped tightly to metal tables, salivating, their chests heaving. At the center of the room a beady-eyed scientist, brandishing a scalpel in his right hand, was about to demonstrate to his young disciples how to make the incision to lay bare the viscera of one of these creatures. His blond assistant, fresh-faced as a choirboy, held two other instruments—a forceps and a pair of long sharp scissors.

There was an odor of feces and urine, excreted by the patients in a reflex of fear as they were being pinioned.

The demonstrator's arm moved downward at a forty-five-degree angle and slit open the abdomen. There was a sympathetic gasp by some of the beholders.

"Are you sure they're not feeling anything?" a voice asked.

"I've told you many times, Miss Castellano," Professor Lloyd Cruikshank replied. "We're treating these dogs as humanely as possible."

They had returned in January to experience their first encounter with the life systems of a living being. Cruikshank would guide them in the "resection" (a medical euphemism from the Latin *resecare,* to cut off) of one of their dogs' vital organs.

It was also an exercise to develop their tolerance—some would say immunity—toward other people's pain. To hone the mind while hardening the heart.

Laura had so dreaded the prospect that she could think of little else during the Christmas vacation. As a child she would feed and shelter every stray that wandered into their garden—until her mother would discover them and call the ASPCA.

Since they could pick their own team for this exercise, she had begged Barney "as a Christmas present" to assist her through the ordeal. He had agreed but was now discovering it was not all that easy for him, either. Nor for their third teammate, newlywed Hank Dwyer, who today was taking his turn as anesthesiologist—a job Laura envied him, since he could keep his eyes on the heart and respiratory dials and not on the dog's insides. But Hank was upset enough to keep muttering, "Don't worry, don't worry. She's out, she really doesn't feel a thing."

Dissecting the cadavers had been different. After all, these had been, in the most literal sense, inanimate objects. There had also been a comforting anonymity about their faces, which had remained swathed for many weeks and, when finally undraped, were so altered that they were barely recognizable as former humans.

But by now Barney, Laura, and probably every other student in the dog-surgery lab felt as though they were operating on a close friend. For it was their duty to keep their experimental animals alive between resections.

At one point a student nearby was driven to complain aloud, "I can't do it anymore. This mutt is too damn cute."

Professor Cruikshank responded with his traditional "Progress of Mankind" speech.

"We must always remember that we are not doing this out of cruelty to animals, but rather as kindness to our fellow man. We must learn to operate on living beings." And then in a tone slightly less pontifical he added, "Okay, let's get those knives in." And with that, he left the room.

The student reluctantly returned his attention to the beagle anesthetized upon his table. He was both startled and relieved to see that while he had been listening to the professor's sermon, one of his partners had considerately slit the dog's belly open. The student's eyes fixed on the beagle's paw, now pierced—as were all the dogs'—by a needle at the end of a long intravenous tube bringing dextrose and saline to the unconscious animal.

Another difference between dogs and cadavers: Dead people do not bleed. But all afternoon the nervous fumbling motions of the students inadvertently pierced the canines' arteries that spat blood all over them—and quite often their neighbors as well.

"God, I hate this," Laura whispered to Barney.

"Stay loose, Castellano. It's only for a couple of weeks. Just keep reminding yourself we aren't *hurting* them."

At this precise moment a chilling howl filled the room. It was followed by a woman's shriek. The first was from Alison Redmond's collie and the second from Alison herself, whose fury was now focused on the "anesthesiologist" in her team.

"I *told* you he wasn't asleep. I *told* you, I *told* you!" she railed. "You didn't give him enough!"

The choirboy assistant rushed toward her table, syringe in hand. In another instant, the needle was in and the animal silenced. But not Alison's indignation at the pain her dog had suffered.

"You didn't prep him with enough morphine," she complained.

"I assure you I did, Miss Redmond," the assistant replied coolly. "I'm not a tyro at this."

"Then why the hell did it wake up?"

"It didn't wake up," he explained, still unruffled and calm. "What you saw was just a reflex."

"Come on. Screaming and kicking and groaning in pain was a *reflex*?"

"Correction, Miss Redmond. Your *animal* was reflexively groaning and twitching. It was *you* who did the screaming."

As he turned back and started to walk off, Alison exploded, "Fink—I bet you even get a kick out of their suffering! I mean, what the hell kind of a doctor are you?"

"As a matter of fact, I'm not a doctor. All right, everybody, get on with your work. I'll be in Professor Cruikshank's lab if anyone needs me."

The moment the double doors had swung behind him, a puzzled Hank Dwyer asked his classmates, "What the hell did he mean about not being a doctor?"

"Oh," Laura remarked, "aren't you clued in yet? Cruikshank isn't a physician, either. Almost none of our teachers is an M.D.—they're all Ph.D.s. In other words, not lowly practitioners who actually see patients but *pure scientists*."

The final word was left to Alison Redmond: "Fuck pure science!"

Laura was still upset at dinner.

"I feel like Lady Macbeth—I can't seem to wash the blood off my hands."

"Come on, Laura, don't exaggerate," Barney admonished. "Look, I very carefully took out a piece of our pooch's thyroid and he didn't even twitch. Next time you'll remove his spleen and he won't feel anything then, either. Those anesthetics are really powerful."

"Besides," Bennett interposed, "what makes you think it's going to be any different when we've got a human patient on the table?"

"Well, for one thing, *you'll* be doing the job because you're the one who's going to be a surgeon. For another, you'll have a legitimate reason for operating in the first place. And most of all, your patient will be cared for twenty-four hours a day. I mean, there sure as hell aren't any night nurses in the dog labs."

"Don't be childish, Laura," Peter Wyman scolded. "Anyway, what's the difference? Next Friday we saw open their ribcages, take out their hearts, and it'll be all over."

"I'd like to saw your heart open, Wyman," Laura countered, "only I'd probably need a pneumatic drill." She returned to her unhappy musings. "I wonder if our doggie knows what's happening to her. Do you think they gave her something to sleep?"

"I don't believe I'm hearing this," Wyman declared to the universe, adding, "Castellano, I bet you even cried at *Lassie Come Home.*"

"Damn right I did, Wyman."

"Ha—I thought you were the iron lady of our class."

They soon disbanded to return to their book-lined cells. Laura remained, toying with her chocolate chip ice cream. She had barely eaten anything that evening.

"Hey, Castellano," Barney whispered, "I know what you're thinking."

"You couldn't," she said, squashing the ice cream with her spoon.

"For chrissake, I've been able to read your mind since we were in the sand box. You wanna go visit our pooch and see if she's okay?"

She didn't reply.

"Well?" he demanded.

Now she nodded and looked at him with doleful eyes. "And I know you want to come, too."

The corridor was pitch black. Laura pulled out a pen-sized flashlight. Its intense pinpoint ray shone nearly the length of the corridor, lighting the final corner they would have to take.

"Hey, where did you get a neat thing like that, Castellano?"

"It was in my mailbox—present from one of the drug companies. Don't they ever give you any goodies?"

"Yeah, but I never open them. They're just cheap bribes."

As they approached the laboratory they could hear sounds from inside—a soft cacophony of little barks and whimpers. The dogs *were* in pain.

"You were right, Castellano," Barney admitted. "What do you think we should do about it?"

Before Laura could respond, they heard a muffled sound of footsteps padding toward them on the linoleum floor of the corridor.

"Shit, someone's coming," she hissed, immediately snapping off the flashlight. They both pressed themselves behind a column.

The footsteps came nearer. Now there was a silhouette visible against the frosted glass windows of the lab room door. As Laura and Barney watched breathlessly, the figure pushed open the door and glided inside.

A moment later the silence became so pronounced that Barney could hear the rapid pumping of his own heart. And then he realized what was happening.

"Castellano," he whispered, "do you notice anything?"

"Yeah. It's suddenly quiet in there."

"Yeah, very *very* quiet."

A split second later the figure emerged, went swiftly past them—this time at a jog—and disappeared.

"Okay," Laura said, taking a deep breath. "I've had enough thrills for one evening."

"You go back if you want to," Barney replied. "But I've gotta see what the hell went on in there."

"No way, I'm sticking with you even if you go to the boys' room."

They tiptoed the dozen or so steps to the lab doors, which opened noiselessly and swallowed them. Once inside they could hear a tranquil hum, which they easily recognized as the sound of animals sleeping peacefully. There was not a single murmur of pain or distress. Laura relit her flashlight and pointed it at the dogs' cages. They all seemed to be slumbering comfortably. Yet in a few seconds the two realized that several were not moving at all.

"Look at Alison's collie," Barney whispered, pointing to the topmost row of cages. They both drew closer and Laura shined her flashlight into the dog's eyes.

"Jesus, Barney—it's dead."

He nodded and then pointed to a cage below them to the right. "That one looks finished to me, too. Where's our pooch?"

Laura's narrow beam searched high and low.

"There she is—" They both knelt at their terrier's cage. Barney quickly reached inside and touched its bandaged underbelly.

"Alive," he murmured. "Let's get the hell out of here."

"You read my mind, Barney."

When they were safe again among the living, Barney translated their mutual anxieties into words.

"I'm not sure, Castellano. But I'd guess that someone in our class feels pretty strongly about euthanasia. . . . I think there's an argument for calling it humane."

"Yeah, but there's also an argument for calling it weird."

The next afternoon, Professor Cruikshank frowned as he addressed the class. "I'm sorry to have to say that many of you have not shown appropriate care in performing these surgical procedures. We lost nine experimental animals overnight and that means I've had to supply nine new ones just for the final vivisection of heart and lungs."

"But, sir—"

All eyes turned to see who had dared to voice dissent.

"Yes, Mr. Landsmann?" asked the professor.

"Wouldn't it be more economical—and in a way kinder—if the people who lost their dogs joined other tables?"

"I don't think so," the professor responded. "It's too crucial a part of your medical education. No one should miss his own exploration of living vital organs. This is an aspect you can never get in books—or even as a spectator."

Bennett nodded. In any case the whole question was academic, since the animals had already been shackled and anesthetized in submissive anticipation of the explorers' knives.

It had been a strange Christmas for Laura and Barney. They had begun a voyage that was changing their perspective on life. What meager knowledge they now possessed had already begun to set them apart from laymen whose apprehension of the awesome machinery of life was, literally, skin deep.

Still it was wonderful to luxuriate in the amniotic warmth of familial surroundings. Parents were not merely agglomerations of cells, molecules, and tissue, they were embodiments of love and affection. Watching his younger brother gobble sixteen pancakes at breakfast, Barney marveled at the fact that Warren never gave the slightest thought to the effect the glycogenic process he was inducing would have on his metabolism. And it was sheer joy to have conversations that did not require the regurgitation of facts, formulae, or chemical structures.

Warren seemed to have grown in confidence—although that may just have been the impression given by his new mustache. In any case he had admirably filled the role of man in the family during Barney's absence, helping Estelle with the preparations for the inevitable sale of the house and her southward move. Law School was still two years off, but both mother and son had already left Brooklyn—in fantasy.

With his newly honed powers of observation Barney could discern things that he had never noticed before. Like the creaks in the steps to the second floor.

Clearly the house was entering old age. Even the basketball hoop on the oak tree had been shorn of its net during October's hurricane and was corroded by more than a dozen years of winter weather. Rust, dust, creaky boards. Brooklyn itself seemed to be growing tired. So many of their friends had already moved away.

Luis had changed, too. He still described himself as *El Peñon, La Roca de Gibraltar.* But there were deeper furrows in his brow and he was now somewhat disinclined to make house calls at all hours of the night.

Lack of dedication? Lack of energy? If asked directly he would have explained it as a lack of time. His eyes that once would barely glance at calendars were now affected by the movements of the hourglass. He now longed for the weekend. Since he had taken in a Puerto Rican fireball to share his practice, he had let the younger man take Saturdays and Sundays. Meanwhile Luis sat alone in his study, aimlessly skimming through the journals, with the television tuned to whatever football game was being played, as a kind of background music.

And the glass by his side was never empty.

Sunday had ceased to be a special day for Inez Castellano, but only because she now spent every day of the week in penitent prayer.

The already burning zeal had lately intensified, thanks to the advent of Father Francisco Xavier, a charismatic refugee from Castro's Cuba.

"Thank God," she told Luis, "he came in time to save our souls."

"Not mine, *querida,*" he had scoffed, "my soul's well past saving. You can have Francisco Xavier verify it in his next chat with the Almighty."

But he was relieved—if not delighted—that although she talked of hellfire, she at least was *talking.* Better auto-da-fé than autism.

Luis's gentle mockeries had no effect upon Inez's ardor. When not in church confessing or reciting Hail Marys, she would read her Spanish Bible.

"Your mother's studying to be a nun," Luis remarked, his little smile unable to belie the touch of irritation in his voice. Indeed, from what Laura saw, there was more truth to it than jest.

Inez spent her time atoning for sin—her own, her family's, the world's. At first Luis had tried to go to church with her, to sit with her at prayer. But even when her earthly body was mere inches away, her soul was in another world. Their younger daughter was with God already. And his wife was clearly praying for the day that she would join her.

Almost the moment the Castellanos and Livingstons finished Christmas dinner, Inez rose from the table and started to put on her coat and scarf. She could not be late for Vespers and Benediction.

"Let me go with you," Estelle insisted.

"No, no, please don't feel obliged."

"Honestly, I'd enjoy it. The choir is always so beautiful—and I love the sound of Latin—"

She did not add that hearing Latin always brought back memories of Harold, who—especially at this time of year—was very much a living presence in her psyche.

"All right, Estelle, but let us hurry. Father would not be happy if we were late."

"My mother's gone completely bananas," Laura declared to Barney as the two of them began to clear up the dishes from the dining room table.

Warren had decamped for yet another "heavy date." Dr. Castellano had already escaped to the sanctuary of his study.

"Can't Luis do anything about it?"

"What do you want him to do, Barn—give her electric shock treatments?"

"That's not a joke, Laura."

"It wasn't meant to be. I really think she's heading for some sort of breakdown."

She fell silent for a moment, merely stacking plate upon plate. And then she blurted out, "What's wrong with me, Barney? My own mother barely acknowledges my existence. My father's a certifiable alcoholic. It hurts me so much I'm almost beginning to—"

He understood the rest of her unspoken thought.

"I can't help it. I know I should be more understanding. I mean, professionally speaking."

"Yeah, there's the bitch of it, Castellano. You can never be professional about your family. I mean, even if you become dean of the Med School, around here you'll always be treated like an adolescent."

"I know," she acknowledged sadly. "And what's worse, it makes me *feel* like an adolescent. To be honest, since I see you all the time up in Boston, there's no real reason for me to come home any more."

The next morning Laura sat silent as Barney drove her along the Brooklyn-Queens Expressway to LaGuardia in the Castellanos' venerable Studebaker.

Finally he said, "Cheer up for chrissake, Castellano. In less than two hours you'll be in Boston and—as the poet Milton put it so well— 'emparadised' in your beloved's arms. Why the hell aren't you glowing?"

For a moment, she did not reply. And then, just before the Grand Central Parkway exit to the airport, she said, already holding back the tears, "Look at me—two useless parents—one drunk on God, the other on C_2H_5OH."

Barney did not return to Brooklyn, either. Instead he drove back across the Triborough Bridge, then over the George Washington and onto the Jersey Turnpike to begin his long journey toward Pittsburgh, Pennsylvania, where, the following morning, Hank Dwyer and Cheryl De Sanctis would be consecrated man and wife.

The nuptial Mass was celebrated in St. Anthony's Parish Church, in the center of America's industrial heartland. The relatives on both sides of the chapel seemed to be either miners or steelworkers.

The reception in the local Knights of Columbus hall featured such diverse delicacies as mozzarella in carozza, lasagne verde, not to mention turkey, ham, and Irish stew for Hank's relatives. The three-foot-tall wedding cake had the traditional figurines of bride and groom but with a sophisticated difference. For the tiny replica of Hank was also dressed in white, as suited a future doctor, with a miniature marzipan stethoscope around its neck.

But perhaps the most delicious items were the bridesmaids—Cheryl's sister and three friends—all as voluptuous as the bride herself. And Barney's endocrine system suddenly reminded him that he had been celibate since the previous summer.

He therefore decided to try his charm on the prettiest of them, who had the evocative name of Gloria Cellini.

"Any relation to Benvenuto?" he asked, attempting to see if flattery would get him anywhere.

"Yes," she answered, "he's one of my Chicago cousins."

Barney was bewitched and bedazzled by her deep brown eyes, the ivory teeth, and the cleft between the two Italian marble spheres that lay below. For a moment he thought he would make medical history and become the first man to die of unrequited lust.

The five-piece orchestra began playing "Fly Me to the Moon." Barney was already there.

"Are you a doctor, too?" she asked.

"If it will impress you, Gloria, yes. If not, I'll be a lawyer, Indian chief, or whatever you like."

She giggled. "You're funny."

"Would you like to dance?"

"Swell," she replied, and offering him her hand, led him to the bustling dance floor.

Fill my heart with song and let me sing forevermore.
You are all I long for, all I worship and adore.
In other words . . .

Two dances later Barney spied Hank heading for the john. He mumbled something to Gloria about having to check on one of his patients and please not to dance with anybody else until he came back.

Hank was the only other person in the men's room, grooming his hair with greaseless, stainless Vitalis. In the mirror he saw Barney enter and greeted him ecstatically.

"Hey, Livingston. What do you think? I'm actually married!"

"Yeah, Hank, you were great up there. Say, do you know Gloria—?"

"Cellini? Good-looking, isn't she?"

"That's an understatement. But Hank, I'm new to Pittsburgh. I don't know the customs—the ethos, if you know what I mean."

"No, frankly I don't know what the hell you're talking about."

"What I want to know is, can I get that girl to bed?"

"Sure," Hank said, smiling cherubically. "It's easy."

"Easy? Jesus, what do I have to do?"

Hank finished coiffing, popped comb into breast pocket, and on his way out remarked casually, "Just marry her."

Barney had a cold and hungry ride back to Brooklyn.

On New Year's Eve Palmer Talbot was struck by lightning.

At the Hunt Club dance the admiration of the Boston aristocracy for his tall and stunning sweetheart was palpable. He could feel their approving glances as he whirled her about the dance floor to the mellow strings of the Lester Lanin Orchestra. Even he had never seen Laura so beautiful, or, he confessed to himself, so pensive.

This was such an important event on the Boston social calendar that his older sister Lavinia had flown in from England with her husband, Viscount Robert Aldgate, and their infant son, the Hon. Tarquin Aldgate (who had puked his noble three o'clock feed all over an ever-smiling BOAC chief stewardess).

Conviviality was rampant as the witching hour neared. At five to twelve all glasses were filled with Dom Perignon and Lord Aldgate was asked to propose the toast.

"To Mother and Father, good health and happiness. To Lavinia and Tarquin—er—happiness and good health. To Palmer and Laura—um— health, happiness, and—um—marriage."

Palmer beamed as the six Baccarat glasses clinked across the table and, glancing knowingly at Laura, commented, "I'll drink to that."

Laura unexpectedly remarked, "And so will I."

Palmer was so elated that he could not mention it till the next afternoon, and then only when he was dropping Laura off at Med School.

"Laura, did you mean what you said last night?"

She looked up at him and replied, "Maybe."

No sooner had she regained the safety of the Vanderbilt fortress than Laura thought to herself, I said it but I'm not really sure I meant it. So why the hell did I say it?

FIFTEEN

"I've got cancer," Lance Mortimer announced.

"What?"

"I've got more cancer than anybody else in this whole school!"

It took Barney several seconds to realize that Lance was talking about pathology slides of *other people's* carcinomas.

"That's great, Lance," Barney replied. "And I assume, as usual, you've got dupes to share with your friends."

"Absolutely, and that goes for syphilis and gonorrhea, too. This is going to be a terrific semester!"

All during the fall term the students had complained about the "irrelevance" of the curriculum: the dead bodies in anatomy, the lifeless memorization of chemical structures, the total absence of anything remotely related to disease.

The new semester would remedy all this, although it would not go so far as to confront them with an actual live patient.

"Pathology, from the Greek *pathos,* meaning suffering, is the morbid side of histology. Last term you studied microscopic slices of healthy tissues. This course will examine those same tissues when diseased. In other words, pathology is to histology what rotting wood is to mahogany, or, more benignly, what pickles are to cucumbers and yogurt is to milk."

Thus spake Brendan Boyd, professor of Pathology, renowned as the most dynamic lecturer in the school, a man described by one student as "really making death come alive."

"After all," he explained, putting his subject into historical perspective, "the Egyptians were practicing this science nearly four thousand years ago, and we have their records describing various traumata, tumors, and infections. In this respect, Hippocrates was really a Johnny-come-lately and can receive credit only for creating an orderly method for systematizing diseases. The great Galen, personal physician to the Roman emperor Marcus Aurelius, recognized the presence of pus in urine as a sign of internal inflammation in the bladder and kidneys, and discovered the causes of various malignant growths.

"We pathologists have rightly earned a reputation for near-infallibility. For, though our other colleagues in the wards can sometimes miss a diagnosis, a postmortem can invariably find the answer. In other words, we may not be able to cure you, but at least we can tell you why you died."

The students laughed appreciatively.

"I told you," Lance whispered to Barney, "he's really cool."

"I'd call it pretty morbid humor."

"Well, after all, he's a pathologist."

"In the early days of medicine," Boyd continued, "diseases were thought to be caused by evil spirits, and as such were invisible to the eye. By the end of the eighteenth century, however, Van Leeuwenhoek's innovations on the microscope came into use and these spirits were seen to have shape, size, and movement and came variously to be called 'bacteria,' curiously derived from the Greco-Roman word for walking stick; 'viruses,' from the Latin for poison; 'fungi,' from the Greek for sponge or the Latin for mushroom, take your pick; or, generically, simply 'microbes.'

"Among the first modern shining knights to slay these invisible dragons with their equally invisible swords was Louis Pasteur, whose many victories include vaccines to control anthrax in cattle, prevent rabies in humans, not to mention the process for sterilizing milk. The French—whose proclivities for alcohol have raised cirrhosis of the liver to a high art—were astounded by Pasteur's discovery that the fermentation that created wine and beer was actually caused by benign microscopic yeast cells. From this we see that germs can sometimes serve mankind.

"In any case, the battle lines were drawn. Microbes were the enemy—resourceful, insidious, unrelenting, and capable of countless disguises. Medical scientists were the good guys, riding steeds as white as leukocytes, their microscopic eyes scouring that seemingly invisible world for signs of the foe. It would take a Homer—or at least the *Oxford Companion to Medicine*—to do adequate justice to the many heroes in this never-ending battle.

"Shall we sing of Sir Joseph Lister, the Englishman inspired by Pasteur, who came to realize what today is obvious to all, that operating rooms should be germ-free. His great achievement is immortalized far less grandly than Pasteur's in that product familiar to all suffering from breath not fit for kissing—Listerine.

"And no song of antisepsis can forget Miss Florence Nightingale, who almost single-handedly caused armies and civilians to comport themselves in sanitary fashion.

"Then there is Ehrlich of the magic bullet aimed at syphilis. Ask not for whom Nobel tolled—it tolled for him in 1908."

At this, he lowered his voice and modulated his style. "And let us hope it tolls for someone in this room. Just as my own generation saw the conquest of polio by Jonas Salk, perhaps one of you will eliminate a scourge of mankind."

This was the credo at HMS. This is what they had been chosen to do.

It is a common—if crude—metaphor that becoming a doctor involves going through a great deal of shit. But the second-term freshmen soon discovered that their professional initiation would literally require going through human excrement. What is more, it would be their own.

Bacteriology introduces the student to the infinite variety of micro-organisms everywhere in his body, most notably in feces and saliva. Indeed, the professor warned them, even if they brushed their teeth with Colgate ten times a day, they would each have close to a hundred billion bacteria frolicking in their mouths.

The first laboratory assignment was to carry out a bacteriological analysis of feces. They were divided into pairs of lab partners, one of whom's first duty was to supply the specimen.

To be totally democratic the laboratory pairs were chosen in alphabetical order. Barney confidently expected to be doing this unpleasant task with his good friend Bennett, since he assumed that "Landsmann, Bennett" and "Livingston, Barney" would be contiguous on the class roster. He had momentarily forgotten that "Lazarus, Seth" came between them.

In fact, Seth was known to Barney only by sight. Skinny, stoop-shouldered, bespectacled, with unkempt flaxen hair, he always sat in the front row at every lecture and filled page after page with frantic scribbling—but would never raise his hand or ask a question either during or after class.

When they met across the lab table, Barney found Seth to be even shorter and slighter than he had thought. In fact, his physique was distinctly reminiscent of the famous Charles Atlas ads in the comic books of his youth: Seth could have posed for one of the "98-pound weaklings" into whose face the bully on the beach was always kicking sand.

Seth diffidently offered to provide the specimen. And—should Barney feel at all squeamish—make the slides as well.

"No, no, no," Barney replied as swiftly as possible, lest he be tempted. "I'll do half the slides and you do the others, Seth."

His diminutive partner nodded and they set to work. In a matter of minutes all queasiness had disappeared, especially since the stains they were applying transmuted the fecal matter into new substances. Barney applied the swab to the Thayer-Martin medium to see if it would grow the causative organism of one of the nastier venereal diseases, and then went on to prep slides that would reveal intestinal enterococci both friendly and insidious.

For most of the afternoon the two worked in silence.

By five o'clock they had completed their slides and filled the various petri dishes for future reference and effluvience (for the lab assistant had warned them that as the cultures grow, "some of them develop an odor that even makes *me* sick").

As they were attempting to scrub away the residue of their labors, Seth remarked, "You know, there are more germs in our mouths than there are stars in the entire universe. Isn't that fantastic?"

"Only if we don't have to memorize all their names," said Barney, half in jest.

But from the first reading assignment it seemed as if they *did*.

They had to absorb such arcana as which gram-negative rods are common to the gut, and which gram-positive cocci would be likely to be found in sputum. Which bacteria grow in clusters, which in filaments, which show individual patterns on the agar, which swarm over the dish, and which bacteria required anaerobic conditions.

There was no way of getting around it, Barney told himself, for they knew in advance what their final exam would be—a mystery slide that would have to be identified. God, what a colossal waste of time this was going to be. Did anyone—even Bruce the assistant—actually store this stuff in his head after taking the course? It would be like learning the Manhattan phone book by heart while being fully aware that Telephone Information worked twenty-four hours a day.

That midnight, as he was studying, there was a tap on his door. He was in no mood to provide his usual free therapy to the depressed—in fact he needed more than a little himself—so he called out, "Livingston's gone. He left for a padded cell."

His three visitors were not convinced and entered Barney's cubbyhole, which was in a state of neoplastic disarray: sweatsocks lying crumpled next to *Gray's Anatomy,* slides by his microscope piled on a tattered paperback of Emily Dickinson.

The medical Magi—all conspicuous for their height—were unknown to him, except for one with reddish hair whom he vaguely recalled having seen somewhere.

Their leader, who was wearing a white coat and stethoscope, introduced himself as "Skip Elsas—third year," and got straight to the point.

"Livingston, we need your help."

Slightly dazed from lack of sleep, Barney mumbled, "I don't get it. Does this have anything to do with school?"

"Well," Skip explained, "let's say what we need is both tangential and epicentral."

"That doesn't make any scientific sense," Barney answered, more confused than ever.

"May we sit down?" Skip asked politely as they all settled in, without waiting for Barney's response.

"It's like this, Livingston," he began. "Every year there's this friendly basketball game between the Med School and the Law School—"

"—just for laughs—" the redhead interposed.

"—and maybe a few side bets," Skip added. "Over the years it's come to be known as the Malpractice Cup—which will give you some idea how enjoyable it is. Are you interested in playing?"

"Interested—yes. Available—no. I've got so much studying to do I'm thinking of giving up eating and sleeping for the next three months."

"I don't think you understand," Skip continued, now a little more forcefully. "The deans take this encounter very seriously. I don't think they'd look kindly on a conscientious objector."

"Hey, you guys are talking like this was some kind of war."

"It is, Livingston. It is. It's the Armageddon of the professions—and no one who's asked to fight for the cause has ever dared to refuse."

"Actually, it would be suicidal," suggested the second visitor, whose dark, curly hair was not unlike Barney's. "I doubt if a guy like that would stand a snowball's chance in hell if the dean ever learned he finked out. Now whatta you say, Livingston?"

"I say I'm just a mediocre ballplayer. If you're looking for class,

why not ask Ben Landsmann? He's actually played semipro ball for
Fiat-Torino."

"We know," Skip replied in Bogart tones. "We've already had a chat
with him."

"And?" Barney asked.

"He's on the fence," the redhead explained, "says he'd do it if you
did."

"Hey, guys," Skip continued, once again taking the floor. "Ben's
got a much bigger room. Why don't we all go up there and talk this
over?"

Barney took a deep breath and stood up.

"He's not that tall," Curlyhair could not keep himself from remarking.

"Don't sweat it," the redhead responded. "On the court you'd think
he was George Mikan."

The flattering comparison to the legendary Minneapolis Lakers center sent adrenaline coursing through Barney's body. Before leaving with
the trio he grabbed his Columbia Varsity sweater and threw it over his
shoulders. It seemed the appropriate thing to do.

Ten minutes later they were all on their hands and knees on the
carpeted floor of Bennett Landsmann's room, studying various strategic
documents.

"The problem with the damn Law School," Skip explained, "is that
they accept animals. I mean, they actually have two gorillas who've played
pro ball."

And, alluding to Bennett, added, "I don't mean spaghetti leagues, I
mean the NBA. I mean, they've got Mack "The Truck" Wilkinson—"

"The New York Knicks center?" Bennett and Barney said in astonished near-unison, to which Skip added somberly, "All seven-foot-one
of him."

"On the other hand," Barney offered, trying to bolster team spirit,
"the guy's retired. He's old. I mean Mack must be thirty-two or -three at
least."

"He's thirty-five, actually," said Curlyhair. "Moves like molasses."

"Slower than that," said Skip, "the guy can't move at all." He
paused and then revealed the zinger. "I've sent some spies to the Law
School gym to check him out and all he does now is stand in the keyhole
and *lean*."

"Come on," Bennett complained, "that's not legal."

"Tell that to the Law School," Skip retorted. "They've their own
definitions of fair and foul."

To which Curlyhair added, "These lawyers are the dirtiest players you've ever seen. And what they'll be like this year with the Jolly Green Giant makes me absolutely shudder. Don't you agree, Livingston?"

Barney had now become totally involved. "Come on, guys," he urged, "if he can't move, we'll just have to stay the hell out of his way. We can run our plays from the corners."

"You really think you can go sixty minutes without coming into contact with Mack The Truck?" Skip inquired incredulously.

Barney nodded. "If there's one thing you can say about my glorious career, it's that I was the opposite of Othello. I've sinned more than I've been sinned against."

Bennett looked at his classmate with an indulgent smile. "I'm gonna remind you of that when you're in the Brigham with a broken back, Barn." He turned back to Skip. "Are there only five of us?"

"We've got another three or four possibilities," Skip replied, "but our great white hope—excuse me, Bennett, that was a metaphor—is chief surgical resident at Mass General. If he played hookey, we just might be responsible for a few deaths. Anyway, we'll be seven or eight at least, but our real prospects for bringing back that cup are in this room. So let's say we meet for practice in the Vanderbilt gym at midnight, starting tomorrow."

"Midnight?" Bennett cringed.

"It's the only time all of us can break loose. Anybody got anything else to say?"

Fired with team spirit, Barney Livingston pronounced the benediction. "Fellow doctors, may I remind you of the immortal words of William Shakespeare. To be precise, in *Henry VI,* Part II, 'Let's kill all the lawyers.' "

Nocturnal joggers on Avenue Louis Pasteur at that moment were startled to hear several lusty male voices bellowing from a third-floor window in Vanderbilt Hall, "Kill the lawyers!" The simplest conclusion was that a group of their fellow med students had been experimenting with LSD.

Laura had responded to the more grisly aspects of Med School in curiously different ways. In the dog lab she had been hopelessly emotional. By contrast, in Pathology, which brought her into close contact with foul diseases and mephitic substances, she was strangely unruffled. For she had reminded herself that the course would only last a few months, the aggregate discomfort adding up to a mere few dozen hours.

By contrast, her father, when he first came to America, had been forced to work for nearly five years at this stultifying drudgery before he was finally licensed to practice.

The caprices of alphabetization found Laura and Grete Andersen working at adjacent tables in Pathology, each with a male lab partner they were meeting for the first time.

Late one afternoon, Bruce, the diligent assistant, approached them, carrying a rectangular plastic container that looked like the ones that held ice cream in supermarkets.

"I've got a wonderful surprise for you," he announced jauntily. "Your first fresh specimen—straight from an O.R. in the Brigham and barely an hour old."

"What is it, Bruce?" Laura asked warily.

"Never fear, Laura, you don't have to be Professor Boyd to recognize this one." He placed the box on the table. The girls and their partners drew near as he removed the lid.

Grete gave a little gasp and turned her face away in horror. Though even their two male partners were manifestly sickened, Laura resolutely kept her gaze on the contents.

It was a female breast—obviously sliced from a Caucasian woman. The nipple was slightly discolored but still recognizable, crowning a pathetic sack of yellow globules.

"Well?" asked the grinning assistant, "haven't I earned your eternal gratitude? After all, the one sure thing you can count on during your clinical training is cancer of the boob. Uh—you did notice the carcinoma, didn't you?"

"Yeah, we saw it," murmured Laura's partner, a crew-cut athletic type named Sheldon Burns, who was married and unsettled by the notion of this possibly happening to his own wife.

As casually as possible, Laura tapped Grete on the shoulder. "You see it, don't you, Andersen? That little thing there that looks like a piece of gravel. That's the carcinoma. Right, Bruce?"

"On target, Laura. A real nasty little rock it is, too."

Like you, Brucie boy, Laura thought to herself.

"Well," inquired the assistant, affecting impatience, "is one of you gonna take it, or shall I offer this valuable specimen to a rival team?"

The lab partners glanced at one another. It was immediately obvious that Grete was not up to the task. Before Laura could gather the courage to reach for it, Sheldon leaned across her and scooped up the gelatinous tissue with both his hands.

"That poor woman," Grete thought out loud.

"C'mon now, Grete," the assistant chided, "we're supposed to be clinical about this sort of thing."

"Of course we are, Bruce," Laura retorted sarcastically, "that's why next Christmas we're gonna give you a cancerous gonad."

The assistant beat a hasty retreat.

"What do we do now?" Sheldon asked nervously.

"See if we can get some of that carcinoma on a slide," said Laura, trying to maintain a clinical air.

Sheldon nodded and placed the specimen on a lab tray.

"This is very upsetting," he said with candor.

"Yes," Laura agreed. "I wonder how it felt."

"The woman was obviously under anesthesia," Grete asserted.

"No," Laura replied thoughtfully. "I mean, I wonder how the doctor felt when he cut this off."

In the end, Skip Elsas had only been able to recruit a total of eight gladiators willing to face the Godzilla of Mack "The Truck" and company. Med students who had played the lawyers once rarely came back for more.

On the big night, they had their training meal in Howard Johnson's on Memorial Drive: minute steak, baked potatoes, and hot fudge sundaes. Barney was at once heartened and surprised when Skip announced that their meal had been sponsored by the dean's office.

"So they really do care?" Bennett asked.

"Only like something approximating life and death. I've heard an unofficial rumor that Holmes makes an annual bet with his opposite number at the school for ambulance chasers—for one thousand smackers."

"Jesus," one of the athletes gasped. "That means he'll kill us if we lose."

"Let's put it this way," Skip answered with a straight face. "If we don't win, we have every chance of ending up as cadavers for next year's freshmen."

Hemenway Gym was packed. The audience was mostly lawyers and their dates, since the Med School was, after all, far away across the river in Boston.

The visiting doctors took the floor to a tidal wave of boos and booze. But, trained to maintain clinical sangfroid, they went about the business of warming up in orderly fashion. As he stretched and warmed up, Barney noticed that sitting front and center was not merely Dean Holmes but every gray eminence in the entire Med School. What the hell, he said to himself, I've known pressure before. These old farts won't scare me. I'm sure glad I convinced Castellano to stay home and study.

And then it happened.

He was so gigantic that his huge form seemed to block out the overhead lights. Mack "The Truck" Wilkinson, all 348 pounds of him, a colossus that made the sculptures in the temple at Luxor seem like miniatures, lumbered his way to the court—the basketball looking like a grape in his massive paw.

"Christ," Barney whispered to Bennett, "the guy's obese. I mean it, he's clinically obese."

"Would you care to go tell the man himself?" Bennett smiled.

"I just might," Barney replied, "after the game. When I have a running start . . ."

The doctors' game plan was simple: Under the assumption that the lawyers were out of shape—Wilkinson being the prime but not sole example—they would play a running game and exploit the enemy's inevitable fatigue in the second half.

And so they marshaled their energy, so much so that in the initial jump-off, Skip Elsas did not even go through the motions of trying to get the ball, but let Wilkinson slap it to a teammate. To the med students' immense relief, the lawyers were only leading by six points as the halftime buzzer sounded.

In the locker room, Skip addressed his players with professional concern. "Be sure to drink a lot of liquids, guys. It's hot as hell in there. I wouldn't be surprised if those lawyers didn't have the heat turned up on purpose. I sure as hell wish we'd brought some salt pills."

"I've got some tablets," said a distinguished voice, from the other side of a row of lockers. It was Dean Holmes, carrying his black bag. In an instant the players were swallowing a compound that would replace not only their sodium loss but their depleted electrolytes as well.

"How's it going out there, men?" he asked paternally.

"They play an absolutely filthy game, sir," Barney offered, giving what the dean did not realize was an expert opinion.

"I've noticed that, Livingston," the other man replied. "In fact, they seem to be much worse than usual this year."

"Yeah," Barney added, "and then they go and hide behind Wilkinson as if he was a huge redwood tree."

"Indeed," Holmes concurred, "but by the same token he's rooted to the ground." He turned to their leader. "Skip, can't you use his immobility to advantage?"

"Yes, sir. We've been holding back some fast-break patterns for the second half."

"Good," the dean said, nodding. "I'd best leave you to it, then."

It was apparent from the very beginning of the second half that both sides were worn out. Thus the race would not be to the swift but rather to the less out-of-shape. And as the minutes ticked by with excruciating slowness, the game seemed to transform itself from basketball to a kind of homicidal football without pads.

Barney, who had never been afraid to dive headlong for the ball, found himself several times crushed by a *pile* of players who had jumped onto him. His knees were skinned, his ribs bruised. By midway in the final quarter, with the score tied 56–56, the doctors had precisely five players left. But they regained enough adrenaline to resume their running game.

Now, with an electrified crowd on its feet, they slowly began to pull ahead. Two, four, six—then seven points into the lead. And their hands were hot. Skip Elsas grabbed the rebound of a misfired legal shot and tossed it to Barney, who was already at halfcourt. He, in turn, whipped it to Bennett, who was now all alone before the lawyers' basket, save for one guardian—Mack Wilkinson.

Bennett went in for a lay-up. Wilkinson went in for Bennett. There was a crash. A pileup. A whistle. Bennett seemed to have totally disappeared beneath a mountain of arms and legs.

Amazingly, the referees had called a foul against *Bennett*—for charging. But first they had to dislodge the tangled players from the floor. When three of his teammates finally hoisted The Truck, Bennett at last became visible. He was holding his ankle and writhing in agony.

"Ben—are you okay?" Barney asked anxiously.

"Goddammit," he gasped, his face contorted in pain, "I think I've broken something. It hurts like hell."

"Out of the way, out of the way," said an imperious voice. It was Dean Holmes and two other Med School luminaries.

"Give this man air," a second doctor demanded.

Barney and the other players downed cup after paper cupful of water while they pondered their predicament. What if Landsmann were unable to play on—would it be forfeit or four against five? Either way, the situation was grim.

More worried about Bennett than the game, Barney tried to see him. But the Med School eminences had totally surrounded the patient and one of the junior deans waved Barney off. Even the ref was unable to get a glimpse. The mandatory time-out was reaching its limit and he would have to insist the game continue.

Just as he blew his whistle the circle of doctors broke and Bennett once again became visible, being gently helped to his feet by a solicitous Dean Holmes. He stood gingerly on his right foot, then hobbled with a bit more confidence. He nodded to the ref that he was okay and made a reassuring gesture in Barney's direction.

The doctors merely had to freeze the ball to ice the game. They had prepared for this happy eventuality, and though the lawyers threw a full-court press, the medics managed to set up a weaving pattern to kill time and avoid being killed themselves.

When the buzzer sounded, the Malpractice Cup had returned to its proper place—the School of Medicine!

The normally staid Dean Holmes leaped to his feet and cheered. And then, regaining his composure, he walked in dignified fashion to offer his hand to the dean of the Law School (and perhaps even collect the rumored thousand-buck wager).

Skip and Barney quickly helped Bennett to a car and headed for the Emergency Room at Mass General, where their arrival was expected.

As they drove, Bennett began to moan and twist, grimacing in acute pain.

"Ben, are you okay?" Barney asked.

"Hell, no," he answered, grinding his teeth. "The goddamn Novocain is wearing off."

"They gave you Novocain?" Barney asked in amazement.

Bennett nodded. "And some other shot, too. Don't know what the hell that was."

"Well," Barney tried to quip, "just think what they might have injected you with if we had lost."

Bennett did not laugh.

And Barney did not smile. For he was wondering, Did the doctors have to win *that* badly?

SIXTEEN

When they arrived at the hospital, a nurse was already waiting with a wheelchair for Bennett to whisk him—without the usual tedious formalities and paperwork—directly up to Radiology for x-rays. And none other than Christopher Dowling, M.D., F.A.C.S., P.C., head orthopod, was there to check out the pictures. In a few minutes, Dean Holmes arrived. As Dowling gingerly felt his way around Bennett's increasingly swollen lower leg, Dean Holmes said softly, "Good show, Landsmann, those lawyers never knew what hit them."

"Frankly, sir, I'm not quite sure what hit me. What exactly was in those syringes?"

"Xenocaine, which is a state-of-the-art painkiller and—thank God for pharmacology—Ducozolidan, the very latest anti-inflammatory agent."

Skip and Barney had been watching mutely from a corner. At this point the older student whispered, "I've read about 'Duke.' I think they've tried it on horses or something. But I didn't know it was on the market."

"Really?" Barney answered, in a mild tone that belied his mounting indignation. "Maybe if it has some really bad side effects, Dowling can write it up and have another entry for his bibliography."

When the two senior physicians left the room, Skip and Barney approached their injured friend.

"How's it going, old buddy?" Barney greeted him.

"Doesn't hurt anymore," he answered, dry-mouthed. "They gave me some sort of shot. . . ."

At this point Barney didn't even have the courage to ask what further miracle drugs had been administered.

"What's the diagnosis?" Skip inquired, making a vain attempt to sound unperturbed.

"Tear in my Achilles. From the sound of it, a pretty bad one. No bones broken, though."

Barney knew a thing or two about athletic injuries. It was clear to him that Bennett's Achilles could not have been completely torn when they gave him those injections. Their shots had obviously "healed" him enough to make it possible to aggravate the injury to the point where surgery was now required.

Barney could not suppress the angry thought that even had The Truck fractured every bone in Bennett's leg, the standard-bearers of Modern Medicine would have found a way to keep him playing to the bitter end.

"Hey," Bennett said, his voice husky and fatigued, "why don't you guys take off? Especially you, Livingston. I'm gonna need you to take notes for me the next day or so. I may even miss the grand opening of the brain."

"No fear of that," Dean Holmes interjected, arriving on cue. "I'll get our Number One Neurology resident up here first thing in the morning to keep you au fait, Landsmann. Just take it easy."

"Will you be okay, Ben?" Barney asked, already feeling guilty at the prospect of abandoning his pal.

"No sweat—I'll be sure to get all the cute nurses' phone numbers."

The neurologist split Barney's skull down the middle. At least that was the way it felt as he watched Professor Francis James demonstrating how to saw a cadaver's head in two.

What followed seemed an anticlimax. With the skull lying halved like a coconut, the sacred instrument known as the brain—that venerated organ that made man, in Hamlet's words, "noble in reason, the paragon of animals"—looked like nothing more than a small, molding cauliflower.

James quickly outlined its basic structure. "We actually have two brains, or, to put it another way, the right and left hemispheres are mirror images of each other. And we still do not fully understand the reason for this or even the precise function of each side."

He then pointed out the four lobes. "Note that the temporal sits above the hypothalamus, which, though weighing a mere tenth of an ounce, is the control headquarters for appetite, gland secretions, sexuality, and a multitude of emotional states, including the so-called 'rage center.' "

Barney wondered if he was the only one struck by the fact that although science could pinpoint the exact spot in the brain that ignites rage, they had yet to identify the location that produces love.

At lunch, though he tried to conceal himself in the remotest of corners, Laura tracked him down.

"What the hell happened last night?"

"We won," he said dryly.

"You know what I mean. What happened to Bennett?"

"Please, Castellano, I'm not his consulting physician. Also, I'm personally bruised from head to toe—and my soul feels like it's herniating."

Laura sat down across from him. "Livingston, I think Med School is making you antisocial, paranoid, and weird."

"That's exactly what it's supposed to do," he replied. "At this rate I stand a chance of becoming the president of the AMA."

"Please, Barney, *what* happened to Bennett?"

He looked at her with gray-ringed, bloodshot eyes and answered, "He got the best treatment money couldn't buy."

Laura folded her arms in a gesture that said she was determined to wait for an explanation till hell froze over.

"Okay, okay. They shot him up with a lot of newfangled gorp. They had him running around on a torn Achilles."

"I'd say that was pretty stupid."

"Laura, you don't seem to understand. The point is we *won* the game." He sighed and then added, "Now I see why they call it the Malpractice Cup. I wouldn't be surprised if when Mack Wilkinson gets his degree he doesn't help Bennett sue the Med School for a million bucks."

"Why—he's not crippled or anything, is he?"

"Not so far. If he's lucky, in only a few months, Ben'll be able to walk without crutches."

That evening Barney visited Landsmann in his room in the private wing of Mass General. As he opened the door he was startled to find two junior-looking men in white coats pointing to an unusual object on Bennett's bed tray: the same replica of the human brain that James had used in his lecture.

When he noticed Barney, Bennett asked his visitors, "Is it okay if we knock off now, guys? All *my* lobes are starting to hurt."

The two young doctors nodded and the one with the natty bow tie said, "We're both on night duty tonight, Ben. If you get the urge, just have us paged. If not, we'll see you in the morning. Ciao."

Barney looked at Bennett's room. In almost every corner there was a half-opened text, a notebook, or a section of the plastic model. Clearly his friend had not wanted for instruction that day.

"Holy shit, Ben. You can start your own medical school. I guess you won't need these."

He tossed onto the bed carbon copies of the notes he'd taken that afternoon. "I'm beginning to feel jealous."

"Don't, Barn, it sure as hell wasn't worth it."

"Are you in pain?"

"Not really. I'm just worried about sitting in the hospital so long."

"You mean falling behind in your courses?"

"Hell, no." He smiled. "With the kind of help I've been getting, I ought to be ready to practice medicine by the end of the week."

Just then the phone rang. Barney picked it up.

"Good evening," said a voice that seemed to belong to a man in his sixties. "Is this Mr. Bennett Landsmann's extension?"

"Yes. Who's calling, please?"

"This is his father in Cleveland."

Barney handed the phone over. Why the hell does this guy's father have a German accent?

In April 1945 a tornado of flame engulfed the wooden barracks of the Nordhausen concentration camp. The U.S. Army medical authorities had determined that only the complete evacuation and destruction of the infected structures would arrest the ever-widening spread of typhus.

That evening the last of the survivors boarded the Army trucks for transportation to one of the displaced-persons camps set up by the Allies.

Hannah Landsmann was well enough to be able to sit for the journey, although two GIs had to help her into the vehicle. Herschel was at her side.

Inside the truck there was a babel of nervous murmuring. Though the refugees had been told—each in his native language—that they were going to an establishment for rehabilitation and recuperation, they were still mistrustful. How many times during the previous years had they heard their Nazi captors say they were going to a "labor camp," or a "hospital center"?

They had no common means of communication save the wordless language of suffering. Some of the Poles and Germans communicated in Yiddish. But how could Jewish dockworkers from Greece converse with former Viennese schoolmasters? Their equivalent of Yiddish was Ladino, the Spanish spoken by their ancestors who had been expelled from Spain in 1492 and had wandered eastward. A few, like Herschel Landsmann, could speak English.

And so, when the convoy had stopped along the route for a light meal to maintain their malnourished passengers, Herschel approached a young soldier and asked, "Excuse me, sir. Where exactly are we going?"

"Weren't you folks told?" the corporal replied with a New England accent. "We're taking you to a place where you can rest and get better and there'll be people to help you find your relatives, that sort of thing. It's a 'DP camp.' That means—"

"I *know* what it means, sir. Would you kindly tell me *where* it is."

"Our lieutenant said it would be at Bergen-Belsen, sir."

The words shook Herschel Landsmann's frail body. For news of the sheer magnitude of the Nazi atrocities there—the hundreds of thousands lying dead and dying—was already known to all. Was this yet another cruel twist of Fate's knife? Had they once again fallen into the hands of a nation of persecutors?

Herschel shuffled back toward the truck. As he climbed in, a GI offered him some chocolate, which he refused with a shake of his head.

"What's the matter, *liebchen*?" Hannah asked anxiously.

"Nothing, nothing," he replied, making a heroic effort to hide his desperation.

But of course he was wrong. For like Dachau to the south, Belsen was in the process of being transformed from a death camp into a "life camp."

Food and medical care were in abundance and soon there were various relief organizations like the Hebrew International Aid Society, and the Organization for Rehabilitation and Training set up by international bodies to attempt the monumental task of identifying the living and the dead. And to try to reunite families as well as help the refugees go "home"—whatever that word might mean to them. For who of them had the emotional strength to return to a place where their "countrymen" had in so many cases handed them over to the Nazis? In fact, the realistic options were only two: the English-speaking countries or Palestine.

Herschel had a brother who had emigrated to somewhere in Ohio in

the early thirties, and this was enough to make him eligible for im-
migration to the United States. His greatest dream now was to belong to
the generous nation whose ministering angels had liberated him. The
moment the U.S. Camp Commission began its sessions, Herschel and
Hannah made a formal application to live in America.

The interviewing officer asked them a few cursory questions—
including whether Herschel was a Communist. He replied with a good
humor that seemed to impress the official. "Sir, do you think it likely that
someone who once owned the largest leather goods factory in Germany
would be anything but a capitalist?"

Now all he and Hannah had to do was wait while they went
through the process of finding Herschel's brother and arranging for
sponsorship.

And wait they did.

It was midsummer when the letter arrived from one Stephen Land of
Cleveland, Ohio. The correspondent revealed that he was the same
person with whom "Hershie" had grown up in Berlin. Only then his name
was Stefan Landsmann: "I didn't want *anything* about me to be German," he explained. "I even bought a set of records to get rid of every
trace of my accent."

The letter expressed great joy that his brother and sister-in-law had
survived the barbaric genocide, but the rest of the communication was
somber.

"To the best of our knowledge you are the only ones of the family to
escape the ovens. All the Katznelsons, the Spiegels, and the Wiener
cousins were sent to Auschwitz."

But for Herschel and Hannah, his concluding words were the worst
of all.

"I weep with you for little Charlotte. But while I know she can never
be replaced in your heart, you are at least both young enough to have
more children. That is something of a blessing."

Reading these words, Hannah began to sob so intensely that Herschel was unable to calm her. How could he, when he was also weeping?

The bureaucratic process dragged on and on. Autumn came and the
residents of what was now the Bergen-Belsen *village* lived in subdued
anticipation, sometimes punctuated by irritated impatience. They were all
anxious to be dispersed, like seeds to be sown in new earth and, hopefully, to blossom.

By December there were still several thousand inhabitants, among
them Herschel and Hannah Landsmann.

It was Christmastime for the soldiers, and for the Jewish former inmates, the festival of Hanukkah, which commemorated their forefathers' liberation from the tyrannical Syrians in the second century B.C.

Despite the cold and the uncomfortable quarters, it was a time for celebration. The Army chaplains headed a group of volunteers who constructed an enormous candelabrum, each night adding another flame until eight lights, broadcasting the renewed freedom of those celebrants, shone far across the land of their former oppressors. There were songs and dances and rejoicing:

> Rock of ages, let our song
>> Praise Your saving power;
> You amidst the raging throng
>> Were our sheltering tower.
> Furious they assailed us,
>> But Your help availed us;
> And Your word broke their sword
>> When our own strength failed us.

"What's the matter?" Hannah chided her husband. "Why aren't you singing?"

"How can I sing out that 'God saved us' when He turned His back on us? The American Army saved us."

"And who do you think sent *them*?" she demanded.

As the winter of 1946 wore on, Herschel's brother wrote regularly, sometimes enclosing photos of his American wife, Rochelle, and their "two lovely boys." His letters overflowed with optimism: America was the land of boundless opportunity. He himself had established a dry goods shop in downtown Akron and had flourished to the point where he now had a branch in Cleveland, where he made his home.

Since he and Herschel were once again in regular contact, "Steve" felt obliged to offer his brother homilies, like, "In America you can be as big as you dream. Here, if you work, the sky's the limit."

His European brother could not help but remember the signs over the concentration camps: "*Arbeit macht frei*"—work will make you free. Of course, in that case it meant it would free your body from your soul.

When he would complain to Hannah she would try to reason with him. "How can you dislike a man you haven't seen in twenty years? And how can you say his wife is a *yenta* and his children are spoiled when you haven't met any of them?"

"Hannah," Herschel said, tapping a finger on his own forehead, "I can see them very clearly in here. And I don't care what he says, I'm not going into business with my little brother Stefan."

"You mean Steve."

"To me he'll always be Stefan and a know-it-all who knows nothing."

"He was smart enough to get out of Germany before the war," Hannah countered, instantly regretting having brought their badinage to such a painful point. "I'm sorry, Hersh, I went too far."

"No, you're right. If we had gone with Stefan, our Charlotte would be still alive. And *we* would be still alive."

"But we—"

"No," he said solemnly, "we are breathing. But in a world where so many of our brothers have been slaughtered, we can no longer count ourselves among the living."

It was nearly a year after their liberation that they finally touched American soil. The Lands had driven all the way down from Cleveland to meet their ship. And with all the other confused, joyous, guilty-to-be-alive survivors, there was no shortage of tears on the dockside.

Steve and Rochelle had found the Landsmanns a small but comfortable apartment on the fringe of Shaker Heights, the suburb where they had their own "lovely house and lovely garden."

And despite his undisguised misgivings, Herschel went to work for his brother. After all, he had little choice. But he dreamed of becoming independent, of being able to treat his own beloved wife in the luxurious manner Steve treated Rochelle.

Meanwhile, there was a burning priority. Through the U.S. Veterans Administration he succeeded in locating the home address of the late Colonel Abraham Lincoln Bennett. It was in Millersburg, a small village in Georgia about a half hour's drive from Fort Gordon, where the Colonel had been stationed as a career officer.

He tried to reach the family by telephone but learned there was none. He had no alternative but to drive there in person. So, packing a small suitcase, he and Hannah embarked on their first American odyssey during the long July Fourth weekend.

The journey took two days. Late the first afternoon, Herschel searched for a place for them to sleep. The white wooden Dixie Belle Inn just south of Knoxville, Tennessee, seemed comfortable enough and he pulled into the gravel drive, adjusted his tie, and walked in to request a room.

The clerk was unctuously polite—but not accommodating. "I'm sorry, sir, I'm afraid this establishment doesn't accept your kind."

Herschel was taken aback. "Kind? What kind? I'm a human being. I have money—cash. Here—look." He withdrew his wallet.

The clerk merely smiled and shook his head. "No, sir, I'm afraid you don't understand this hotel's policy. It's strictly no Nigras or Jews allowed."

"I don't understand," Herschel said, scarcely believing his ears.

"Understand what, sir?" the clerk inquired. "The connection between Nigras and Jews? In these parts we tend to believe that one's black on the outside and the other's black on the inside. Have a nice evening."

Sick at heart, Herschel returned to the car and related the incident. "How did they even know I was Jewish?" he had wondered aloud.

"Herschel, my beloved, be honest—your accent is not exactly like George Washington's. Now, I suggest we find someplace that will maybe give 'our kind' something to eat and then try to get some sleep in the car."

They arrived in Millersburg the next morning. It was a ramshackle, sleepy hamlet the color of clay baked by the summer sun. Herschel had spent a restless night (parked behind a closed diner), wondering whether on the morrow it would be best to seek directions to the Bennett home from the police or from the post office. With his vestigial horror of uniforms—especially with guns attached—he opted for the post office. It did not stand, as did its Cleveland counterpart, in a great stone edifice. Quite the contrary, it was a sagging appendage to the town pharmacy.

" 'Course I remember the Colonel," the druggist acknowledged with warm southern hospitality. "But—if I may be so bold—whatever would you want with what's left of his family?"

"Uh," Herschel asked hesitantly, "what exactly do you mean by 'what's left'?"

"Why, as y'all must know, the Colonel himself is dead—I assume you saw we put his name up on the Town Hall memorial board right there with all the white men who fell. And it's been years since Lorraine scooted out of this tank town with some fancy Dan from Atlanta. All that's still here's old Miz Bennett and young Linc."

"Can you tell me where they live, please?"

"With due respect, where else would a Nigra live but in Niggertown?"

"Could you direct me, please?"

The druggist chuckled. "My friend, just go to the end of Main Street—and follow your nose."

It was little more than a parallel row of shacks, distinguished only by the fading color of their desiccated wood—formerly brown, formerly green, formerly red. Here and there was a tin mailbox with a name scrawled on it. BENNETT was, relatively speaking, the neatest of the lot.

Under the inquisitive gaze of half a dozen people seated on nearby porches, Herschel and Hannah knocked. A large black woman, white hair pulled back against her temples, answered the door.

"Can I help you?" she asked, curiously scrutinizing her visitors.

"We are looking for the home of Colonel Lincoln Bennett, madam," Herschel said softly.

"Don't you folks know my son is dead?" she asked, anger and sadness both still perceptible in her voice.

"Yes, madam. I knew him in Europe during his . . . last days. My name is Herschel Landsmann and this is my wife, Hannah. Your son rescued me and then fought with the doctors to save my wife. We wanted to meet his family and express our thanks."

Elva Bennett hesitated for a moment, unsure of how to act. Finally she said, "Would you care to come in?"

The Landsmanns nodded. She opened the screen door and led them inside. "Can I offer you some iced tea?"

"That would be very nice," replied Hannah, as she walked into the living room. The mantelpiece was dominated by a large photograph of Linc in full dress uniform. His oak leaves and many medals were also on display.

Mrs. Bennett returned with three mugs and they all sat down, the hostess on a tired armchair and the Landsmanns on an equally well-worn sofa.

"So," said the elder woman, now with a friendly smile, "you knew my Lincoln."

"The finest man I ever met," Herschel said with deep conviction.

Mrs. Bennett concurred. "If he'd been white he'd have made four-star general—and that's the truth."

The Landsmanns nodded. "I have no doubt at all," Herschel stated.

Then came an uneasy silence. How could he explain the purpose of his visit? He tried to broach it tactfully.

"Mrs. Bennett, my wife and I have just lived through a calamity I could not begin to describe—"

"Some of Linc's last few letters gave me some idea," Mrs. Bennett answered sympathetically.

"Your son," Herschel continued, "your son was like a holy angel to us. After all the years of degradation we had suffered, he was so kind. He treated us like human beings. And yet we survived and he did not. I cannot tell you how pained we are."

Herschel was still having trouble getting to the point. Hannah came to his rescue. "We were wondering if there was any way we could help—"

"I don't follow, ma'am," said Mrs. Bennett.

"His son—" Herschel began. "Lincoln was always talking about the hopes and dreams he had for him. We want to be sure these dreams come true."

"Is he all right?" Hannah asked. "I mean, are he and his mother—"

"I'm afraid Linc Junior has no mother," she replied, a sudden flash of anger in her eyes.

"I don't understand," said Hannah.

"Well," Mrs. Bennett started with a sigh, "it's a long and unhappy tale. Those two never did get along even before Linc was called overseas. In fact just about the time he . . . fell in action, the lawyers were finishing up the papers for their divorce. But as soon as she heard, she skedaddled right back."

"Because of the child—" Herschel suggested. "She must have been concerned about him."

Elva Bennett shook her head in vigorous dissent. "Because of ten thousand dollars, Mr. Landsmann. That's GI insurance for the next-of-kin—ten thousand dollars. Every week after that she came all the way out to Millersburg from Atlanta jus' to go by the post office an' see if that check had come. Which, of course, in due time it did."

Her indignation was mounting. "And do you know, Mr. Landsmann," she said, her voice quavering, "do you know that in all those treasure-huntin' trips she didn't once come by to see her son? And the U.S. gov'ment took her for the next of kin! That woman—"

She dissolved into tears.

As Hannah offered the comfort of a gentle touch, Herschel thought out loud, "I'm sorry, Mrs. Bennett, I don't understand. Why isn't he living with her in the first place?"

Elva's mood changed from sorrow to indignation.

"Why should she live with a child she never wanted? She never forgave Linc for not letting her get rid of that baby before it was born. Lorraine fancied herself as a great lady, she didn't want to be 'tied down.' She hated life on the base and was always going off to Atlanta on her own for days at a time. I've raised that boy from the very day he was born."

She dabbed her eyes with Hannah's handkerchief and apologized, "I'm sorry. I shouldn't be speaking this way. The Good Book tells us it's a sin to hate."

Herschel tried delicately to explain their visit.

"Mrs. Bennett, please don't be offended, but may I know if you and your grandson have any financial difficulties?"

She hesitated for a moment, then answered, "We make out all right."

"Please, I ask because we want to do something—anything—to show our gratitude." He hoped his fervor would earn her trust.

Reluctantly the old woman unburdened herself. "Well, naturally, when my son was alive we always got a part of his paycheck. Every month, regular as clockwork. When that stopped I was countin' on the insurance to see us through till young Linc was big enough to work."

"How old is he now?" Hannah inquired.

"He'll be eleven next month. The twenty-seventh."

"So that means he's a long way from seeking employment," Herschel concluded.

" 'Round here, most boys start at fourteen—even earlier if they're tall enough."

"But that is such a pity. I know his father wanted him to have an education, even go to college."

"That dream died with him," she replied softly.

Herschel and Hannah glanced at each other and each knew what the other was thinking.

"Mrs. Bennett," Hannah began, "we owe your son a debt that has no price. We would be honored if you would allow us to be of assistance."

"We are not rich people," Herschel continued, "but I have a job and I can save from it. So when the time comes young Lincoln will be able to attend college."

Elva Bennett was both overwhelmed and confused. "Mr. Landsmann, don't you know there's not a colored school between here and Atlanta that's good enough to prepare him for any college? And there's no chance he could go to a payin' school 'round here."

The Landsmanns felt at a loss. These were barriers they never thought they would encounter. After an embarrassed silence in which none of them knew what to say, Hannah suggested, "But where we live, Mrs. Bennett—in the North—I know there are schools, excellent schools, where I'm sure the boy could go. And that surely would open the doors to a college."

Elva was more confused than ever. Why were these people offering to pay for her grandson's education? Why should any white couple want to do a thing like that? But she continued to explore the issue—and examine the Landsmanns.

"Do you think he could possibly get into one of them northern places? I mean, our Nigra schools barely teach a little reading and writing. There's sixty-one children in Linc's class and frankly I don't think the teacher even knows his name."

Panicked by the thought that she was about to deny their request, Herschel blurted, "But we could have him tutored. Really, Mrs. Bennett, we would get the best tutors. And then he could go to the best *private* school."

Herschel continued, oblivious to the astonishment on his wife's face. "We both mean this with our whole hearts. We want to give your grandson the chance to achieve everything his father wanted for him."

Elva was inwardly torn. If these folks were serious, if they would really send Linc to a private school, what would *she* be left with? Photographs? War medals? Memories? An empty house?

She wondered what the Good Book would counsel. Her thoughts immediately went to a passage in Proverbs: "Blessed is the man who finds wisdom. . . . *Though it cost all you have,* get understanding." She owed it to her grandson. Even more, she owed it to her son. But she delayed the agonizing decision by asking further questions. "What exactly did you have in mind?"

"Well," Herschel replied, "I've heard about these so-called 'prep schools' where he could live with other boys his age. And then again there are the 'day schools' in the Cleveland area." He again exchanged glances with Hannah. She then said hesitantly, "He—Lincoln—could stay with us."

Elva found it difficult to contemplate the thought of young Linc actually living with another family. A white family at that. And not only white, but . . .

"You folks are Israelites, isn't that right?"

"We are Jews, but we are not religious," Herschel replied.

"But you believe in Almighty God?"

Before Herschel could confess his agnosticism, Hannah interposed, "Yes, yes. Of course."

"Could he still go to a Baptist church?"

"I'm sure we could find one," Hannah replied.

The old woman was silent again, deep in thought.

"You people were once slaves of Pharaoh in Egypt?"

Herschel nodded again. "Yes, a long time ago."

"My grandfather was a slave, a short time ago. Mr. Lincoln was our Moses. I suppose that gives us something in common."

"We certainly know what it is to be persecuted, Mrs. Bennett," Hannah added.

Finally Elva asked, "How would you propose to do this?"

Hannah answered tentatively, herself growing intoxicated by her husband's dream. "We could take him up to Cleveland. He could live with us as part of the family. We'd treat him like—" Her voice broke slightly. "—the child we no longer have."

Elva pondered for another moment and then said, "I can't decide this on my own. Linc's gettin' to be a big boy now. He'll have to make up his own mind."

"What time does he get home from school?" Herschel asked, his heart quickening.

"That depends. Sometimes he stays late and plays ball with the other fellas." She smiled. "He's a natural, you know. Just like his dad."

"Perhaps we could go see him—" Herschel hesitantly suggested. "I've got my car outside. If you'd like to come and show us the way . . ."

"Goodness, you don' need to drive there, it's an easy walk. The Nigra school is jus' where it's supposed to be." She smiled ironically. "Across the other side of the railroad tracks."

Herschel could recognize him at once.

Even if he hadn't been tall for his age or by far the best of the players scuffling on the dusty schoolyard court, shooting at a netless metal basket, he would know Lincoln Bennett's son. There was a kind of brightness in his eyes, a zeal, a dynamism that was unmistakable.

"I'll call him over," Elva offered.

"No," said Herschel, "we can wait." And watch, he added to himself. My God, the boy is handsome, he thought. His father would have been so proud.

After a few minutes, the players noticed the strangers in their midst: the white couple staring at them from the sidelines. Who were they— some kind of school inspectors? And why was Elva with them—had Linc done something wrong?

They stopped playing and Linc, still dribbling the ball deftly, first with one hand, then the other, then behind his back, walked up to his grandmother.

When she introduced the couple as "friends of your daddy during the war" he stopped bouncing the ball and grew solemn.

"You actually knew him?" the boy asked.

"We did and he was always talking about you. And how proud he was. That's why we wanted to meet you."

The boy's face wrinkled up as if on the verge of tears.

"Why don't we all go and have some ice cream?" Hannah tactfully suggested.

The others waited outside as Herschel went into a "white" grocery store and emerged with chocolate-covered ice cream pops for all. They then slowly walked back to the Bennetts' home, nervously avoiding any mention of what they were intending to discuss.

Young Linc took an instant liking to Herschel. But the nature of their invitation stunned—and frightened—him.

"You mean leave my granny?" he asked timidly.

"You could come back here for Christmas and vacations," Herschel offered, hastily adding, "and if you're unhappy, you could come back right away."

"Would you like to just give it a try for a little while?" Hannah added gently.

Troubled and in conflict, Linc looked at Elva. She turned to the Landsmanns and said, "I think this is something my grandson and I have got to talk about in private. Could you let us have some time alone?"

Herschel and Hannah agreed almost in unison.

"We could drop by again tomorrow morning if you would like," Hannah continued.

"I think that'll be all right," Elva answered. "I want to pray for guidance. And then we both have got to search our hearts."

"Herschel, are you crazy in the head? Have you maybe forgotten that you're not a rich man anymore? Now you've made that lovely boy start dreaming about private schools—tutors, even. Where did you get such ideas? You know we've got *bubkes* in the bank."

"I know, I know," he said half aloud, "but I want to do it so badly I would give anything. . . ."

"Face it, my darling," Hannah responded. "We don't *have* anything."

They walked two paces before Herschel spoke.

"I do, Hannah."

"What?"

"I have one last possession that I would sacrifice for Lincoln Bennett." He paused and then said, "My self-respect."

Hannah understood at once. "You mean you'd go to Stefan? . . ."

Herschel shrugged, half-embarrassed, half-defeated. "I know we agreed that we should never put ourselves in his debt because accepting his money might mean accepting his values."

He then confessed. "Two months ago Stefan opened a bank account in our names and put in twenty thousand dollars. He said it was for a down payment on a house. I didn't even tell you because I never would have touched it."

Herschel looked at her. "But Hannah, twenty thousand could put Lincoln straight through college. So *nu,* Hannah, do you think that's worth losing my self-respect for?"

She looked at him with love and answered.

"Darling, you wouldn't be losing anything. We would both be gaining something very precious." She threw her arms around his neck and kissed him. "Just please God he says yes."

They were too excited to eat breakfast so they made a walking tour of Millersburg and ended on a bench in the main square in front of the wooden "Honor Roll" of local soldiers who had died in World War II. It was crowned by the crossed flags of the Star-Spangled Banner and the Confederacy.

"He'll never come with us." Hannah sighed pessimistically.

"What makes you say that?"

"Look at this memorial. Look at whose name stands right on top."

Herschel focused on the list before him. Of all the men from Millersburg who had died in the war, the highest ranking was Colonel Lincoln Bennett. Death had given him the respect he had always been denied in life.

When they returned at the appointed hour they both sat nervously facing the boy and his grandmother. Finally Herschel found the strength to ask, "Have you decided, Linc?"

The boy responded with another question. "What about my friends? I wouldn't know anybody. I wouldn't have anyone to play with."

Herschel answered honestly. "All I can say is that we will do our very best to find you some new friends."

"And meanwhile you can call your grandma or your classmates here whenever you feel lonely," offered Hannah.

"Sorry, ma'am, I can't," the little boy replied. "Nobody 'round here's got a phone."

"But you can write," said Elva pointedly. "Your father never phoned us up from Europe and still we always kept in touch."

"Is there anything else that's troubling you, Linc?" Hannah asked.

He nodded shyly.

"Suppose I . . . disappoint you?"

"There's only one way you could disappoint us," Herschel said emphatically. "That is if you don't come."

There was a silence as the young boy looked at his grandma. Now Elva spoke for both of them.

"We both agree his father would have wanted him to go with you."

Though Herschel wanted to leap with joy, he said simply, "That's wonderful. My wife and I will stay here till we organize the practical arrangements." Then to the boy he added warmly, "I promise that you won't regret this."

The Landsmanns left intoxicated with hope while Linc was struck dumb by the awesomeness of his decision.

"Herschel, are you *mishugah*? You mean to tell me there aren't enough *shvartzes* in Cleveland that you have to import another one from the South?"

"Stefan—I mean Steve, I forbid you to talk like that."

Having found a nearby hotel that would accept them for the night, Herschel had phoned his brother in Cleveland to ask if Steve's lawyer could find out what they were legally obliged to do.

His brother had been less than enthusiastic about the whole idea. "Listen, Herschel, be reasonable," Steve continued to argue, "I know you and Hannah want a child. We'll find you one up here. What am I saying—we'll find you *two*. You want three? We'll find you three."

"I want *this* boy," said Herschel Landsmann, in a determined tone of voice.

"All right, all right, Hersh. I'll have my lawyer check out the details and call you in the morning." And then a final admonition: "Only, don't blame me when you get turned down for the Country Club."

The attorney, a young man not long out of Northwestern Law, looked more favorably on the Landsmanns' proposition. There was, of course, the matter of the mother still *de jure* entitled to the child's custody. But judging from all he'd heard about Lorraine, he didn't foresee any problem on that front. It would be easy to prove that the elder Mrs. Bennett had been the actual parent *de facto* and was therefore entitled to transfer guardianship of young Linc to the Landsmanns as foster parents.

There remained but a few minor details for which he would have to consult a law firm in the state of Georgia.

"You folks are doing a wonderful thing," the attorney said sincerely, at the close of their first telephone consultation.

Oh yes, Herschel confessed to himself, at least I know it's wonderful for *us*.

One evening a week later, he found Hannah sobbing.

"What's wrong, my love?" he asked.

"I can't believe it," she murmured, "we're going to have a *child* in our house."

At the beginning the young boy attended the local public school. When they discovered how far behind he was in reading and in math, the Landsmanns hired tutors for him—three hours every afternoon.

Linc did not seem to mind. For he had an unquenchable thirst to learn. And yet, as he confessed to Herschel in one of their heart-to-heart talks, he desperately missed his grandma—and playing basketball. Herschel could do nothing to rectify the first problem, but he could certainly solve the second. Twenty-four hours later a backboard with hoop and net had been set up on the Landsmanns' garage.

Yet the Landsmanns continued to fret, worrying that perhaps they were driving Linc too hard.

"Do you think we're overpressuring him?" Herschel asked late one afternoon. He had come home early from the office and Linc was still closeted upstairs with Miss Alsop, his English tutor. "He may hate us someday for all the time we keep him prisoner with the extra lessons."

"No, honestly," his wife assured him, "I think he enjoys it. There's excitement in his eyes. He wants to learn."

"That's right, I do."

They turned. Linc had just entered. "I love it, really. I wouldn't even mind if I had tutoring on Sundays—'cause then it wouldn't be long before I catch up to the pack."

"And then—?" asked Herschel with delight.

"And then I'll pass them," said the boy with blithe self-confidence.

The next summer, they presented him as a candidate for Shaker Heights Academy. It was not the usual time for admissions. But the headmaster was persuaded by the tenacity of the foster parents, the letters from his teachers and tutors, not to mention a telephone call from their local Congressman (Steve had reluctantly arranged that ploy).

But most of all he was impressed by the young man's intellectual potential. Linc did astonishingly well on the exams they set specially for him. No one would have credited the fact that only months ago he had been scarcely literate.

Moreover, the director of admissions suggested that it might be something of an interesting experiment. That is, to have a colored youngster in the otherwise snow-white student body.

"Sort of like a foreign student, you might say."

"Quite," the headmaster agreed. "And one might also say we're killing two birds with a single stone."

"How so?" his colleague asked.

"Well, not only is the lad colored, but his foster parents are, you know—of Hebrew stock. That would put an end to some of the complaints we've had of late."

They little knew how significant their admission of Lincoln Bennett, Jr., would turn out to be. For—as he had predicted—having caught up with the pack, Linc proceeded to outdistance them. In fact, after a single term they had to promote him to a higher class in English, Math, and Science.

And that was not all.

To no one's surprise, he was the greatest athlete the school had ever seen. But that seemed only natural. For as the coach told the headmaster, his race excelled at any sport involving running fast or jumping high.

At first the other students treated him like a visitor from some strange planet, but one by one he captivated all of them.

Still there were moments of embarrassment. The dances with the "better" girls' schools, for example. After some awkward incidents, the headmaster tactfully agreed that it would be best if he did not participate in such activities.

Linc tried to conceal his hurt from the other kids at school, especially the jocks, who welcomed him on their team, but not in their homes. He would stand in front of a mirror, trying to rehearse a detached attitude with which to confront—and endure—the frequent humiliations.

He confided his true feelings only to Herschel and Hannah. From Hannah he got comfort; from Herschel, strength: "Some day, Linc, you'll be tall and proud and they'll be very ashamed. I know it's hard. But you're being very brave."

Thus, when he had no commitments on the playing fields, he spent the weekends with Hannah and Herschel. Hannah, who in her Berlin Gymnasium had been a whiz in science, was someone he could talk to about matters like Newtonian dynamics, for Linc was now *way* ahead in Physics.

Herschel read his essays and offered detailed comments. Naturally, they sometimes disagreed with one another. But is not an argument the truest index of emotional involvement?

And they did not overlook their promise to his grandmother. They enrolled Linc for religious school and every Sunday they took him to the local Baptist church.

*   *   *

Herschel would have long heart-to-heart talks with Linc. He spoke of Berlin, Hitler's rise to power, the Nuremberg Laws of 1935 depriving Jews of civil rights, and how he wished that, like his brother, he had seen the writing on the wall and left. But he and Hannah had been so comfortable, so seemingly assimilated, that they had never dreamed the Nazis wanted to get rid of *them*.

They both talked compulsively of the camps, of the cruel "Selections" that determined who would live or die. The Nazis only spared the lives of those who looked robust enough to work. After they described how they had lost their little daughter, Linc had nightmares for a week. He could not come to grips with hatred on so vast a scale.

Linc tried to understand their calamity in terms of the faith his grandma had instilled in him.

"Couldn't it maybe have been God's Will?" he asked them.

"His Will?" Herschel replied. "To slaughter all the members of our family?"

"No," the boy said with feeling, "that he spared you two—so we could meet."

Herschel looked at him with deep emotion. "Yes, even I could believe in such a God."

Linc, in turn, would talk to them about his childhood. He had vivid memories of "the Colonel" (as they proudly called him) reading to him from the Scriptures every night. Even before his dad went to war, his mother rarely was around.

"All I remember is her dressing up and driving off to some 'social engagement' in Atlanta. All of us had been living in my grandma's house, and she just called up the General Store and told them to tell us she wasn't coming back."

"Linc, maybe it was for the best," Hannah said understandingly. "Your grandma gave you everything a mother's love could give."

"Oh, I'm not saying I missed her," he replied a little too quickly, bravely suppressing the feeling that had always gnawed at him—that he had somehow been the cause of his mom's departure. "It doesn't matter," he said, giving Hannah a loving smile, "I've got you both now."

Herschel and his brother Steve simply did not get along. Rochelle, Steve's upwardly mobile wife, was embarrassed by their accents and did her best to invite them as seldom as possible. Steve had no respect for Herschel's opinions or suggestions. At best, he was a tolerated employee.

Still, what else could Herschel do? Long ago in Germany he'd built a
thriving business. But Hitler's jackboots crushed it all.

Then, in 1951, all that the Third Reich had brutally snatched away,
the German Federal Republic suddenly returned. Chancellor Konrad
Adenauer announced that his government would pay reparations to its
predecessor's victims.

A specially appointed Court of Restitution ordered that the erstwhile
proprietor of the Königliche Ledergesellschaft could repossess his factories in Berlin, Frankfurt, and Cologne—or else be offered adequate
compensation.

Not surprisingly, Herschel chose not to return to Germany and
accepted monetary "reparation."

As soon as he received the check, Herschel hurried over to his
brother's office and placed a banker's check for twenty thousand dollars
on his desk.

"Thank you, Steve, now you don't have to treat me like a poor
relative anymore."

With his new working capital, Herschel financed a reborn Royal
Leathercraft, first in Cleveland, then Columbus, then Chicago. Within
two years he had become the sole supplier of children's shoes to the
eight-hundred-store "Rob McMahon" chain.

Young Linc was a loving grandson. He called Elva every weekend
(Herschel had arranged to have a phone installed) and visited at Christmas, Easter, and two weeks in the summer.

Yet although his relationship with his grandma stayed reciprocally
strong, his friends—his erstwhile friends—seemed to avoid him. He no
longer dressed like them, or talked like them.

"You ain't a nigger no more," one shouted scornfully. And, after his
second visit, Linc realized that his only remaining tie with Millersburg
was Grandma.

The following spring, that final bond was broken, too—Linc was
called to the headmaster's office and found Herschel waiting sorrowfully
to break the news.

At first he did not cry at all—but later the Landsmanns heard him in
his bedroom sobbing most of the night. His one request was that Herschel journey with him to Millersburg to see his grandma laid to rest. He
stood in the first pew, his head bowed, as he listened to the pastor's
eulogy which hailed Elva Bennett as a saint—but which also had some
covert criticism of her grandson.

"She was a woman of valor. She gave her only son to die for our beloved country and be buried on a foreign shore. She raised *his* only son until the young man left the fold. We bow our heads and join in prayer for Elva, the *last* Bennett to be buried here in Millersburg."

Linc was devastated. On the long ride home Herschel attempted to console him.

"I'm sure he didn't mean it the way you took it, Linc. He's just a country preacher—"

"He knew exactly what he said. He wanted to expel me—and he did."

Herschel sighed. He could feel the boy's sadness. But what could he say to assuage it?

It was Linc who at last broke the silence. He looked at Herschel as he drove and suddenly asked, "Will you adopt me?"

"What?"

"The pastor's right, the Bennetts are all gone. And to tell the truth, I never really knew my father. The Colonel's just a picture on the wall to me. I still sort of worship him, but he's so far away. It's not his fault but, honestly, I've thought about him more times than I ever touched him. You've been a family to me in flesh and blood. I want to have your name." He paused and then began, barely audibly, " 'Cause otherwise there won't be any Landsmanns, either."

Herschel managed to keep his emotions in check till he could bring the car to a halt on the shoulder of the road. Then, weeping unabashedly, he embraced his son.

Barney spent more than two hours in Bennett's hospital room as they discussed the play of the Celtics, the skating of the Bruins, and the prospects of the Red Sox.

As he was holding up his end of the trivial sporting conversation, Barney was asking himself, How come this guy who's probably my closest friend in Med School will never talk about his family? The most he's ever told me is that his father was a shoemaker in Cleveland. What the hell is Bennett hiding?

Finally, at a quarter after eleven—and it did not escape Barney that the nurses had permitted him to stay long after visiting hours—he rose to leave.

"I know you aristocrats have private tutors, Landsmann," he remarked, "but we plebeians actually have to go to class and I've got an eight o'clock lab. Is there anything you want me to bring you tomorrow night?"

"Only if you could manage Marilyn Monroe," Bennett smiled.

"Sorry, Ben, but we're going steady. Do you have a second choice?"

"Well, actually, it would be great if you got me some civilian clothes. I'm hoping to get sprung from this place by the day after tomorrow."

He reached to his night table, picked up a ring of keys, and tossed them to Barney.

"You've got it, Landsmann," Barney replied, and headed for the door.

"Give my love to Castellano and the other guys," Bennett called after him.

As Barney climbed into the white Corvette that Lance had kindly lent him for the evening, he suddenly felt battle-weary. He badly needed sleep. After all, tomorrow he would once again confront the harsh reality of Med School.

Or was it unreality?

SEVENTEEN

Most of them finished their freshman year alive.

But Med School provides perhaps the best substantiation for Charles Darwin's theory of natural selection. For here we see in its cruelest form the survival of the fittest. Not the smartest, as one should expect. But the fittest to cope with the inhuman pressures, the demands made not only on the brain but on the psyche.

This was made abundantly clear by the first suicide among the would-be doctors.

And it was significant, and not unnoticed, that Dean Holmes referred to the tragedy with that qualifying adjective "first," suggesting that he fully expected there would be more.

Professor Francis James had led them upward through the nervous system like Virgil leading Dante on his journey toward Paradise. First, the spinal cord—which sends out the commands for our most basic movements, leading upward to the brain stem, which receives most of our senses. Then the cerebellum—the inner gyroscope that keeps the tightrope walker on his wire, the ballerina on her toe, in fact the orchestra of the entire body playing in exquisite symphony.

Finally, the crowning glory of cerebral hemispheres—containing all the treasure chests of our experiences. The wealth of lessons we have learned from pain and pleasure, food and drink, from fight or flight, from copulating, urinating—and *The New York Times*.

The time for finals was now as close as neurons in the nervous system. In the blinking of an eye, which—sleepless—none of them had time to do, they would be tested on it all. The human body in totality: macroscopic, microscopic, and invisible. (One must recall there are many viruses as yet unseen by any apparatus.)

Barney's gift for friendship made him luckier than most. Lance had lent him a microscope as well as all the slides, so he could contemplate with bloodshot eyes the beauties of a cancer. The slides of carcinoma, viewed bifocally, could radiate like a fuchsia-colored tapestry designed by God.

And for Bacteriology, he had the help of Seth Lazarus—who not only knew the stuff, but had a flair for teaching it to others.

The only problem was he spoke so goddamn softly that unless you sat right next to him, even in these tiny dorm rooms where his acolytes would gather, you could miss a pearl or two. Seth would take notes on the lecture and everybody would take notes on Seth. At times it seemed as if they would canonize him, despite his single eccentricity: He would go to bed at nine o'clock—unyielding as Horatius on the bridge, he wouldn't even compromise for nine-fifteen.

"For chrissake, Lazarus," a desperate fellow student once complained, "you're not a baby anymore. Your mom won't dock you from dessert if you don't make it to your beddie by the dot of nine. Can't you be daring just this once and go at ten?"

Pleas were futile, though he was genuinely apologetic.

"I'm sorry," he said in his characteristic high-pitched whisper, "I think it very important that we all recognize our circadian rhythms. And I know I function best real early in the morning—so I start at five. But a tired brain is like a worn-out battery. So, sorry guys, I've gotta go and recharge. Goodnight."

"I wonder if he still sleeps with a teddy bear?" Luke Ridgeway sneered, when Seth had left the room.

"Hey, can that, Ridgeway," ordered Barney. "The guy's nice enough to give some time to stupid assholes like us. We should be grateful."

"Yeah," Laura chided. "I mean, if I could be as smart as Lazarus I'd go to bed at eight—and so would you!"

"Oh, bullshit, Castellano," Luke retorted.

"Hey, kill it," Barney intervened. "Let's not fly off the handle."

"Fuck you, Livingston. Are you her bodyguard or something?"

"Now listen, guys," said Barney, in what he would later come to regard as his first attempt at handling a group therapy session, "we've got to realize that we're all on the verge of cracking up. I sometimes think that's part of their grand plan to toughen us. But anyway, Seth proved how smart he was by going to get sleep. That's really what we all need."

"Do you know all the cranial nerves, Livingston?" came a challenge from the corner of the room.

"Well, I can name them."

"But can you name their roots and subdivisions?"

"Uh—not by heart," Barney conceded.

"Then *you* sleep while we stay up and learn them all."

Barney stood up. "Well," he said good-humoredly, "there's nothing like a friendly little study session to psyche you up for the ordeal ahead. I'm going to bounce a basketball a few hundred times and get loose. But if you like, Ridgeway, I'll bounce your head instead."

"Jesus," Luke exclaimed, as Barney left the room, "the guy's a dead-end kid. How'd they ever let such riffraff into Harvard Med School?"

"Screw you, Ridgeway." That from Laura Castellano.

"Shit," one of the cooler heads announced, "let's all get out of here before we kill each other."

Even after a hard basketball session, Barney was unable to study. So he went out for a midnight jog. It was a calm spring evening, the scent of summer in the air. He crossed Longwood Avenue to the Med School quadrangle and began running laps around the periphery of its grassy lawn.

The Quad was almost completely dark, with occasional patches of grass visible in the pale light emanating from one or two labs.

About five minutes into his run he knew that he was not alone. At first it was merely the rapid glimpse of someone approaching from behind the great marble pillars of Building A. Could it be some energetic faculty member? No, those guys kept fit by playing murderous games of tennis against each other. At this ungodly hour of the night it had to be another wrought-up student like himself—or, his paranoia suddenly suggested—the mystery dog-killer out to stalk his first human prey.

The figure was moving at a good pace and Barney—having convinced himself he was running for his life—accelerated as well. To no avail, for in another lap the other runner was literally breathing at his shoulder.

"Hi, Barney," came a whisper.

He turned and recognized—Grete Andersen.

"Jeez, Grete," he puffed, "what brings you out here at this hour?"

"Probably the same as you. I knew the pressure would be bad, never like this. I think a lot of guys are going bananas."

"Some people don't realize that nobody ever flunks out of this Med School," Barney retorted.

"I think I'll disprove that," she said, her voice slightly quavering. "I've been struggling to keep my head above water all year and I really don't think I'll make it."

A sudden thought occurred to Barney. Was it Grete who got the ignominious eleven—and the subsequent nine, ten, and thirteen—on the Biochem exams?

"Listen, Grete, the worst that could happen—I know this for a fact—is that they'll make you repeat the first year. I swear, every guy that's accepted gets his M.D. sooner or later."

They jogged a few more steps and Grete tonelessly replied, "Except the ones that kill themselves. I heard that every class loses about a half dozen via the hara-kari route."

Barney's thoughts suddenly returned to Maury Eastman and that early autumn evening. And he wondered if his jogging partner—who for once wasn't going through her sex kitten act—was contemplating self-destruction.

"Let's take a little rest, huh, Grete?"

"Fine with me."

They slowed to a walk. Barney noticed how the perspiration made her face glisten in the moonlight. God, she was a beauty.

"Uh, what made you think of suicide?" he asked as tactfully as possible. "I mean, do you know anyone who is . . . in trouble?"

"I don't know anyone who isn't," she said candidly. "Do you know, the Student Health psychologists are working night and day, and almost everybody in the class has been to see them, at least everyone I know. The tension in the Deanery is thicker than molasses. Never have so many pills been taken by so few. . . ."

"What kind of pills?"

"You know, amphetamines, to keep you up, and phenobarb to cool you down. . . ."

"Where do they get that stuff?"

"Oh, the shrinks give out some on prescription and, well, if anybody knows an intern it's a cinch to get whatever you want."

"Are you taking anything?"

"Yes, sometimes," she said defensively.

"Laura?"

"Probably . . . I don't know. Hell, cut the interrogation, will you?"

Barney, who had embarked on the nocturnal workout to relax, was now more panicked than when he started.

All year long, Laura had never once revealed how she had done on any test. It was so atypical of her that the only logical conclusion was that she was flunking. Christ, he thought, why didn't I insist more? Shouldn't I have realized that she would be too proud to tell me on her own?

By now Barney and Grete had warmed down and were heading back to Vanderbilt. When they had reached the crescent facing Avenue Louis Pasteur, he asked, "Hey, Grete, when you get upstairs, will you ask Castellano to give me a ring?"

"Sure, no problem."

As he began walking back, taking two stairs at a time, Barney glanced at Grete doing stretching exercises and thought, Hurry the hell up, dammit, Andersen. I've gotto know that Laura is okay.

He didn't dare shower lest the phone ring while he was in there. So he just sat on his bed, feeling the warm sweat of his T-shirt turn into a sticky and uncomfortable cold compress. He tried to stay calm.

At last the phone rang and Lance Mortimer—whose room was much closer—was the first to pick it up.

"You must have ESP," he said as he saw Barney sprinting down the hall. "Either that or Miss Roundheels of the class is offering her body as a study aid."

Barney grabbed the phone. "Hello, Castellano?"

"No, Barney, it's me—Grete."

"Is Castellano there?"

"Yeah, but I can't get her to the phone."

"Why not?" Barney asked, his freezing T-shirt now making him shiver.

"She's absolutely zonked, Barney. Dead to the world."

"What do you mean, 'dead'?" he asked anxiously.

"I mean she's so fast asleep I don't think anything but an earthquake could snap her out of it. Can't it wait till the morning?"

What could he say? Should he come straight out and ask Grete to check Laura's pulse and respiration?

"Barney, if that's all, I'd like to go to sleep," Grete said impatiently. "I mean, I've swallowed a tablet and I'm starting to feel a little woozy."

"Dammit," he snapped, "why are all you girls popping pills like M&Ms?"

"Hey, simmer down," Grete replied soothingly. "Every guy—except maybe Seth Lazarus—is swallowing something to get through these exams.

Hey look—" She yawned. "I'll leave a note for Laura that you called. Goodnight."

As Barney slowly replaced the phone, he turned and found Lance standing at his shoulder.

"What's all this about pills?" he asked.

"None of your goddamn business," Barney snapped. "Do you always eavesdrop on other people's conversations?"

"Hey, loosen up," Lance protested amiably. "I'm just trying to help out."

"Exactly what do you have in mind, Lance?" Barney retorted sarcastically.

"Well, I've got red help, green help, and white help. What would you like?"

"What are you? The Old Dope Peddler?"

"Cool it, Livingston. I was only trying to be neighborly."

"Jesus!" Barney fumed and stamped down the hall to his room. He sat on his bed, and took half a dozen deep breaths. And regretted not having accepted Lance's offer of a phenobarb.

He was shocked awake by the hysterical shriek of a siren and the screeching of tires at the front of Vanderbilt Hall.

In panic he sat up, reached to the floor for his trousers, pulled them on, quickly laced sneakers to his bare feet, and began to sprint. As he was speeding down the stairs he caught up with a student he did not know by name.

"What the hell's going on?" Barney asked fearfully.

"I think we've lost a classmate," the student replied, with more bemusement than sympathy. "I guess things got a bit too much for one of our little girls."

"Who, for chrissake?" Barney demanded.

His informant merely shrugged his shoulders. "Who knows? I was just going down to find out."

Barney bounded past him and raced down to the main lobby. Through the open doors of Vanderbilt Hall he could see an ambulance, backed right up onto the sidewalk, its open doors filling the gateway.

There were clusters of students, some half-dressed, others still in pajamas, on either side of the dormitory entrance, all with a look on their faces—so it seemed to Barney—like ancient Romans at a gladiatorial contest, eager to see death.

Suddenly two white-clothed men carrying a stretcher appeared at the bottom of the stairway leading from the Deanery. As they approached the crowd, the orderly in front bellowed, "Out of the way. Give us some room, dammit!"

Barney pushed his way through the crowd to get a glimpse of the stretcher. Whoever they were carrying was obviously dead—and unrecognizable because the entire body was covered by a blanket. He was now face to face with the front stretcher-bearer, blocking his way.

"Who is it?" he demanded.

The man simply growled, "Get the hell out of the way, kid," knocking Barney backward with his shoulder.

Someone touched him on the arm.

"Barney?"

It was Laura, pale as a ghost, but alive.

"Oh, Christ, Castellano," he sighed. "Am I glad to see *you*."

She was in a state of shock. "I had to be the one who found the body. You can't believe how—"

"Who?" he interrupted impatiently. "*Who* is it?"

"Alison Redmond," Laura answered, and then with a glazed expression continued to describe the trauma of her discovery. "She used a scalpel to slit her wrists. The whole goddamn bathroom is spattered with blood." She swayed slightly. "Shit, my head is spinning. I've got to sit down."

Barney put his arm around her waist and helped her to a chair in a corner of the lobby. It was only then that the shock waves began to overtake him. Someone he knew had actually ended her life.

"Laura, do you have any idea why she did it?"

"Hell, I don't have a clue. All I know is . . ." Her voice broke. "All I know is there she was lying in a pool of blood on the goddamn floor." Now she lost all control and she was sobbing too intensely to be able to speak.

"Excuse me, Miss Castellano," said a familiar voice.

Both of them had been too preoccupied to notice the approach of Dean Holmes.

"Laura found the body, sir, I'm sure you understand—" Barney explained.

"Of course," he said, as Laura tried to pull herself together. "Alison was such a brilliant girl. She didn't seem to confide in the other girls, but I'm told she was closer to you, Laura. I was hoping you might be able to help us. Why don't we go down to the cafeteria for something to drink?"

Laura looked up at the older man. His face seemed strangely devoid of emotion. Perhaps that was part of being a doctor—not showing emotion, even if you felt it.

"May I come, too?" Barney asked, knowing Laura needed support.

"Of course, Livingston. Perhaps you can help shed light on this unfortunate event."

They sat in the unlit cafeteria—the semidarkness seemed appropriate for the somber conversation—drinking tea in paper cups from the dispensing machine. An assistant had brought Holmes a folder bulging with Alison Redmond's record.

He took a sip of tea and then began the inquiry.

"Laura, did you notice anything unusual in Alison's behavior?"

Laura shrugged. "I just know she took her classes seriously. She was very dedicated. . . ."

"I'd like to know about pathologies—changes in mood, quirks, that sort of thing."

"Dr. Holmes," Laura began again, "when I said dedicated I kind of *meant* it as a pathology. She was obsessive about her work."

"Ah, obsessive," Holmes remarked, apparently gratified by terminology remotely medical.

"If I might add," Barney interrupted politely, "she was incredibly competitive. I mean, I know we're all that way, but she was sort of like a white-hot locomotive waiting to explode."

Barney paused to see if his contribution had found favor with the dean.

"Can you be more specific, Livingston?"

"Well, for example, she started out at our Anatomy table. But the minute she got wind that Seth Lazarus was a better cutter, she pressured Lubar into switching her to work with Seth. I mean, she had this compulsion about having to be the best. It's my guess that she set incredibly high standards for herself and when she discovered she wasn't Number One, she couldn't deal with it."

The dean was silent for a moment, scrutinizing Barney's face.

At last he spoke. "The girl *was* Number One."

"Oh?" said Barney.

Dean Holmes spread several documents on the table.

"Here's her entire record. She led the class in everything. Even Pfeifer, who's extremely demanding, had her slated for a ninety-nine—which would have been unprecedented."

Holy shit, thought Barney. So *she* was the one on top of the Biochemistry totem pole.

"Did she have any romantic involvements, Laura?"

"No," she replied after a moment's hesitation, and wondered how much more she should say. "To be frank, I think she was afraid of men. I think her aggressiveness was counterphobic—if I'm using that term correctly. I mean, being so much better is certainly one way to keep them away."

Holmes nodded. "That's an interesting hypothesis. I'll see how her psychiatrist responds to that. She was seeing someone in Student Health on a regular basis."

A voice called out in a loud whisper from the front of the cafeteria. "Dean Holmes, could I speak to you for a minute, please?"

The dean nodded his silvery mane and then said to Barney and Laura, "Excuse me, I won't be long."

Barney and Laura waited in the darkness.

"I feel like such an asshole," he said.

"Barney," she countered, "we both said the same things. How the hell could we have known she was Number One until he told us? I mean, she was so damn secretive. . . ."

When the dean returned to their table, he was holding a tan spiral notebook with the Med School seal emblazoned on it.

He did not sit down but merely said, "You've both been very helpful. Thank you."

It was clear they were dismissed. But Barney could not walk away and leave the mystery unsolved.

"Dean Holmes . . . sir, may I ask you what's going on?"

"That's privileged information, Livingston."

Barney persisted. "Sir, just two minutes ago all three of us were having a 'privileged' conversation. If you trusted us then, why won't you trust us now?"

"I suppose you've got a point there, Livingston. And, frankly, but for our little conversation I wouldn't have known what Alison's scrawl could have referred to."

"What scrawl, sir?"

"See for yourself." The dean handed him the notebook. "Look at the last ten pages."

With Laura at his shoulder Barney opened the notebook to the end.

Three words were repeated line after line, page after page:

They're catching up They're catching up
They're catching up . . .

All Barney could think was, Why the hell didn't her shrink pick up on this? What the hell was he doing in these sessions, polishing his nails?

Laura spoke her thoughts aloud. "I should have noticed, I mean, in all those conversations we had. I should have noticed how driven she was."

"Please, Laura," Dean Holmes said gently. "You couldn't possibly have guessed what was on her mind. I mean, it even escaped an experienced practitioner."

As Barney returned the notebook to him, the dean added half to himself, "And now it is my unhappy task to confront the young lady's parents." He sighed. "That's the hardest part. You can be a doctor for a hundred years and still not be able to face the next of kin."

Barney watched the dean walk slowly off and thought, That's the only time I've ever seen him off balance. And if *he* can't absorb all the shocks of medicine, who can?

Which led him to wonder what Alison's shrink might be thinking at the moment. Was he—or she—torn by guilt, crushed by a sense of failure?

And then he asked himself: Why are you thinking about other people's worries? Are you trying to avoid your own emotions?

No, he told this inner voice, I *feel* for Alison. And, curiously perhaps, I don't just wish I had been more of a friend. I actually wish I had been her psychiatrist.

The news of Alison's death electrified the school. Still, for self-preservation, they discussed it as if it had been an event on a distant planet.

Dean Holmes had personally offered to represent the school at the funeral, but her parents had refused.

"I wonder why?" Laura asked a group of fellow students at lunch.

"My honest opinion," said Barney, trying to lower his voice so his hypothesis would carry more authority, "is that they probably viewed her suicide as some kind of failure—flunking out of life, so to speak."

"And what brings you to such a definitive conclusion, Doctor, when you haven't even met the parents?" Hank Dwyer asked.

"Because, Hank, neuroses aren't like viruses, they aren't identifiable things that float around in the air. They come from a definite place and that place is a four-letter word called *home*."

"My, my, we are pontifical today," said Peter Wyman from far down the table. "What about me? What would you deduce about my parents?"

Barney looked, considered, and pronounced, "Well, Peter, I'd say they were extremely unlucky."

Trying to appear unfazed, Peter turned his back on his detractors and walked off.

"Now," said Bennett, "that's a guy I would have tabbed to put a razor to his wrists."

"Don't worry," Barney said with gravity, "you may still be right. After all, statistics say they lose between three and five from every class that way."

"You know what that means," Hank Dwyer offered. "That means statistically one person sitting at this table right now will be six feet under before we graduate."

They exchanged glances.

"Don't look at me." Bennett smiled. "I refuse to die until I'm given written assurance that Heaven isn't segregated."

"Laura, you're going back on your word," Palmer said angrily, as they were sitting in an alcove on the ground floor of Vanderbilt Hall.

"I am not, dammit—I said I would marry you, but not until I graduate."

Suddenly Palmer glared at her and said sternly, "Listen to me, Laura, it's got to be *now*."

She had never heard him so imperious. "Why the sudden urgency?" she asked.

"Dammit, Laura, this is no time for joking." He took a deep breath to compose himself, then said, "I've got my notice from the Draft Board."

"Oh?"

"I've got sixty days, Laura, and I want us to be married before I go. I need that reassurance."

"Palmer, you're putting unfair pressure on me."

Now he pleaded, "For God's sake, Laura, you know I love you."

Yes, she confessed to herself, I know you love me, Palmer. But I still need time to learn if I can love you back—if I can love *any* man enough to marry him.

Painfully conscious she was being unkind, she went on, "And just look at the time you pick to deliver your ultimatum—I've got four finals in the next five days. Couldn't you have waited another week to hit me with this emotional extortion?"

She could see from his expression that her anger had upset him—and she felt immediately contrite.

"Hey, I'm sorry," she said gently. "I guess I went too far. You can't imagine the pressure we're all under—especially after Alison."

He nodded. "I'm the one who should apologize. I picked a bloody awful time to bring this up." Then he added like a humble suitor, cap in hand, "Uh, do you have any plans for Friday evening after your last examination?"

"Well, it's kind of a tradition that everyone breaks out a keg of beer and gets smashed." To which she added quickly, "You know I don't go for that sort of thing. Why don't we have a quiet dinner?"

"Yes, that'd be fine. Will you come spend the weekend at my place?"

"Sure. Maybe. I mean . . . fine."

He kissed her on the forehead, fearing anything more passionate might destroy the frayed and slender thread that bound them still.

It was after midnight when Laura stood outside Barney's room. From the sound of heavy breathing within she concluded that Barney was otherwise engaged. Dammit, she thought, I really needed to talk to him.

Now between each labored breath she could distinguish Barney's voice gasping, "Keep it up—don't stop—c'mon, you're almost there."

Embarrassed, she disappeared down the hall.

In the interim Barney was puffing, ". . . forty-eight . . . forty-nine . . . fifty . . ."

He then stood up, thinking to himself, two days without sleep and you can still bang out fifty pushups. Not bad, Livingston, you're still in some kind of shape.

Very few of his classmates could have made that claim.

"Pregnant?"

"Yeah, I can't believe it, Cheryl is with child!"

Hank had flagged Barney from across the Quadrangle to convey the good news.

"Congratulations, Hank, when is she due?"

"Sometime in August—maybe last week in July. You can't be sure about your first baby."

As soon as Hank had turned to walk away, Barney counted on his fingers and smiled.

He broke the news to Laura during lunchtime.

She was delighted.

"And not only that," Barney continued, "but Hank is going to be a great obstetrician."

"What makes you say that, Barn?"

"He can tell six months in advance that a baby's going to be four weeks premature."

EIGHTEEN

And so they took their examinations. Common knowledge proved correct: only four classmates did badly enough to flunk. Three of them were invited to repeat their freshman year, the fourth to take a breather and begin again in twenty-four months.

Most of the others spent the summer trying to expel the useless memorized minutiae from their brains and preparing their thinking apparatus for more important things. For now there was light—albeit tiny as the ray of an ophthalmoscope—vaguely visible at the end of the tunnel of textbooks, shining on a sick patient waiting to be treated.

Many took jobs as lab assistants, scrutinizing slides of blood, urine, and other substances—for microorganisms, so that their superiors in rank could then exploit their efforts and announce the diagnosis.

Some had more exalted laboratory posts like Peter Wyman, who was actually engaged in original *research* under the aegis of Professor Pfeifer.

Seth Lazarus was going home to a position of responsibility in the Pathology Department at the University of Chicago Med School, where he had already worked for two summers.

As usual, Bennett Landsmann had conspicuously different plans. His original intention, as he had told Barney in confidence ("I don't want the rest of the class to think I'm a playboy"), had been to ski in the mountains of Chile. But unfortunately his Achilles tendon still had not repaired sufficiently to risk so hazardous an enterprise. And so, instead, he had arranged to join his parents for a tour of the Aegean islands. And while they examined the ruins, he would scuba-dive to explore the deep.

Hank Dwyer got a job as an orderly in a private sanitorium. It was near their Boston apartment so he could spend as much time as possible with Cheryl, who was now very pregnant.

Laura had both the good fortune and the bad luck to be asked to do research for Pfeifer. For along with the honor went the fact that the wretched Wyman would be her boss.

At first Barney was puzzled by the eminent biochemist's second choice.

"No offense, Castellano, but why the hell did Pfeifer pick you?"

She merely shrugged. "I have no idea. I'm just glad I don't have to go back home."

But it all came clear the moment the grades were published. Laura Castellano had achieved an astounding A-minus average. It was especially incredible to Barney, who had thought he had done brilliantly in securing a B-plus.

But now the truth was out and he confronted Laura with the evidence.

"Don't deny it, Castellano, you were one of those two ninety-eights in Biochem. Right?"

"Okay, Inspector, I confess, you've got me dead to rights."

"Then why the hell did you keep it such a secret?"

She shrugged. "I don't know. At first I thought it might be just dumb luck, and afterwards I . . ."

But she had no need to finish her last thought, for Barney read her mind. She did not want him to feel uncomfortable.

Barney did not have the luxury of working even in the suburbs of the scientific world. When it was announced that the Med School would be raising its tuition fees, he knew he would have to take a job that paid more money.

So he became a hackie, taking the night shift for Mr. Koplowitz down the block, who owned his own cab.

Barney lived at home for sentimental as much as economic reasons. That autumn there would be a FOR SALE sign in front and someone strange would move into the room that housed so many thousands of his childhood dreams.

Estelle, having officially retired at the end of June, spent the summer in the backyard, sipping tea with Inez Castellano, chatting with her when Inez felt able to communicate, and simply keeping her company when she drifted off into her private world. Then Estelle would gaze around the garden and dream, remembering the days when the three kids had shared their games.

She had breakfast with her sons—Barney just home, Warren about to go off. He was already preparing for his legal career by working as a gofer in a law firm.

Most nights the boys were out—Barney at the wheel and Warren with yet another romantic rendezvous. And with increasing frequency Inez would come over, not merely for company, but for refuge.

By now Luis had progressed from quiet inebriation to loud and rowdy drunkenness. By 9 P.M. he was a raging lion. And lately a lion in triumph. For his idol, Fidel Castro, had just succeeded in toppling Batista to free the Cuban people. Did this call for a Cuba Libre? Or two? Or ten?

Moreover, these sentiments did not endear him to the more patriotic Brooklynites, for Castro had expropriated the U.S. sugar mills. *"¡Viva el pueblo cubano!"* was not exactly on everyone's lips.

The neighbors were beginning to mutter complaints. One or two even approached Estelle to intercede on the community's behalf and get Luis to sober up. Or, at least, shut up.

The once dedicated doctor was getting worse each day. He had already been fined for drunken driving. Another incident would probably deprive him of his license to drive. And perhaps even to practice.

"Can't you do anything to help him?" Estelle asked her friend.

Inez nodded. "I have prayed," she mumbled. "I have asked Our Lady to deliver him from all his suffering."

"Oh," said Estelle, "isn't there anyone—uh—closer who might perhaps speak to him?"

"Father Francisco Xavier has also tried to intercede."

"You mean you actually got Luis to walk into a church?"

"No," Inez replied, "I invited Father to the house last Sunday afternoon."

"And what happened?"

"¡Ay! No me pregunta. Luis was like a madman, yelling at the Father, curses on the Church and all the Spanish bishops who banded around Franco. Father did not even stay for tea."

I'm not surprised, Estelle thought to herself.

Inez suddenly lapsed into prayer. And Estelle was alone to wonder, Why didn't Laura help? How could she ignore her family when they needed her?

She broached it with Barney over breakfast the next morning.

"I think Laura's shirking her responsibility," Estelle declared.

"She's tried, Ma. I assure you she's really tried. But Luis said something unforgivable to her the last time they spoke."

"Like what?" Warren asked.

"Well," said Barney slowly, "among other things, he shouted, 'Don't lecture me as if you were my *son!*' "

There was a sudden silence at the breakfast table, then Estelle said, "Poor little girl."

"That's really a bum rap," Warren agreed. "Both her parents alive, yet she's all alone. I'll bet you anything she's gonna marry Palmer whatsisname out of desperation."

"Don't hold your breath," Barney cautioned. "Palmer's going in the Army, and they've both called a kind of time-out in their relationship."

Estelle was dismayed. "I wonder what will become of her?"

So do I, Barney wondered inwardly.

At 6 A.M. on a steamy August morning, Laura accompanied Palmer to the induction center at the Boston Army Base.

"I'll write to you, Laura. Please drop me a postcard now and then to say I've gotten through—"

"Come on, you know I'll do better than that. But are you sure you want to go through with your plans for OCS? Why spend an even longer stretch in uniform?"

"Laura, if I'm going to lose you, the extra time won't make any difference. And at least I'll be able to drown my sorrows in the Officers' Club."

"You won't lose me, Palmer. I'm not going anywhere."

"Well, I promise I'll be faithful to you."

"Please don't be silly. I don't expect you to become a monk. I mean, it wouldn't be natural."

From this Palmer unhappily inferred that she intended to lead an active social life in his absence.

"Just remember, Laura, you'll never find anyone as devoted to you as I am."

As she drove off toward the Med School (the ever-generous Palmer had left the Porsche in her custody), she thought, He's probably right. Nobody will ever love me as uncritically as old Palmer.

Wyman was already in the lab, pecking on an ancient Underwood portable. He had dark rings beneath his eyes.

"Good morning, Laura. How are you?"

"My, my, what makes you almost mellow this morning, Dr. Frankenstein?"

"Well," said Peter the Great, leaning across the typewriter, "funny you should ask. This happens to be a significant occasion in the history of medicine."

"Don't tell me," said Laura, "you're gonna leave the profession."

He ignored her barb. "Miss Castellano, today marks the acceptance of my official research findings. I sat up all night to complete the paper."

"You're that sure it's going to be published?"

Wyman grinned again. "My dear, Professor Pfeifer is the editor."

But she was to discover in the next few weeks that Peter was not completely accurate in boasting of his authorship. For it was standard practice that every piece of research emanating from a lab bore the name of the senior scientist. Peter's article would appear as the work first of Michael Pfeifer, then of Keith Macdonald, last year's chief assistant, with the genius Wyman bringing up the rear. And at that he was in luck because such articles sometimes have more than half a dozen authors.

Since the U.S. government had been extraordinarily generous in funding Pfeifer's work, he had nine full-time assistants and, as a result, that summer "his" output was amazing. Even Laura's name appeared on one. Although she had dismissed Wyman's ecstasy at bursting into print, when her turn came she felt the same euphoria and longed to share it with someone. She even had an atavistic urge to call her parents, but instantly suppressed it. Who the hell cares what a drunken father thinks? But she knew Barney would rejoice with her.

She was right.

"I know it's the first of a thousand," he cheered on the phone. "And I hope that asshole Wyman gets an ulcer when he hears about it."

Oh God, how well he knows me, she thought to herself as she hung up. Nothing in the world would please me more than beating Peter Wyman—and I *will*.

Seth Lazarus stepped off the broiling bus into the baking sun. Even at seven-thirty in the morning, Chicago was unbearable in the summer.

Fortunately, he had only a few hundred yards to walk to the doors of the hospital where the Pathology lab was kept at an extremely cool temperature to prevent decay in the "patients"—as his supervisor, Professor Thomas Matthews, insisted on calling them.

("When we're finished and send 'em to the undertakers, then you can call 'em corpses.")

This was Seth's third summer in the "death house," as some of the residents called it. It was here he had first learned to be dexterous with a scalpel, to resection tissue for examination, and to have a general reverence for the human body—alive or dead.

By the second summer Dr. Matthews had already entrusted him with the making of incisions, the first general appraisal of the patient's organs, and even suggesting probable cause of death. The doctor, of course, would make the ultimate decision but, more often than not, Seth was right.

The atmosphere in Path was totally different from that of his Anatomy class. Here there was near-silence—a respectful hush for the dead, perhaps. By contrast, the school lab seemed like pandemonium, the students making raunchy jokes to conquer their uneasiness, their newness, and their fear.

Seth was comfortable up here, although at coffee breaks he would stare out the window at the women in the busy streets below and wonder if the fact that he chose to be with these lifeless bodies on the table did not qualify him as "weird."

At college he had an excuse. After all, he was telescoping four full years of studying into three, so impatient was he to become a doctor. It was perhaps understandable that he had no social life.

But then he'd never really made friends of either sex. The only time his fellow students sought him out was during exams, when they'd crowd into his dorm room and plead for his assistance to explain the complex material.

For the past two summers he had merely stared, his nose pressed to the air-conditioned window, observing below him everything he wished to join but did not feel entitled to be part of.

Is that why he had chosen Pathology? As a sure way of not having to tell the next of kin that their loved one was in pain that could not be relieved?

One morning in July his chief asked Seth if he was going to the cafeteria for lunch.

"If you are, I'd like you to pick up an extra copy of the *Tribune* at the newsstand. There's a story about my twelve-year-old on the sports page. He's a hotshot in the Little League—pitched his third no-hitter yesterday."

"Wow, congratulations," Seth replied. And quickly added, "Will one copy be enough, sir?"

The elder man smiled benignly. "Come on, Seth, how many times do I have to tell you to call me Tom—you're not the office boy around here. And, yes, one copy will be fine. My wife has probably bought a dozen."

"Okay. Thank you—Tom."

The midday elevator was crowded with nurses hungry for lunch and doctors hungry for them.

When Seth reached the ground floor he walked over to the newsstand, bought the paper, and was starting to leaf through a copy of *The New Yorker* when he noticed a group of pretty nurses passing by.

One of the trio turned in his direction and cried, "Oh, my God!" Then she was smiling and—more than that—was actually calling his name.

"Seth—Seth Lazarus—I can't believe it. Is it really you?"

"Hey," she addressed her friends, "would you believe, this is the guy I was just talking about? He finished our high school in three years and now look—he's a doctor already!"

Only at this point did Seth remember that he was still wearing his white lab coat with a small rectangular plastic tag on his lapel misleadingly identifying him as "Dr. Lazarus."

"Gosh, I can't believe it's really you, Seth," the girl continued to bubble. "And I bet you don't remember me. But then why should you? I was taking Elementary Chem for the second time so I could go to nursing school and you were helping everybody—me especially—with all those lab experiments. And look—I actually became a nurse."

Seth was unaccustomed to this sort of attention.

He was struck dumb—but not blind. He focused easily upon her name tag. And then summoned the savoir faire to make his debut as a ladies' man. "How could I forget Judy Gordon—of the deliquescent eyes?"

The three nurses giggled. "What does that mean?" one of Judy's friends inquired.

"Oh," Seth answered, somewhat embarrassed by his unwittingly florid rhetoric, "it's actually a term we use in chemistry—it means to melt away."

Judy smiled. "I'm really flattered you remembered me, Seth. And by the way, these are my friends Lillian and Maggie."

"Nice to meet you all," he said. "What department do you work in?"

"The big 'C,' " Judy answered somberly.

"Cancer must be rough." Seth nodded. "I don't suppose you see many of your patients walk out the same door they came in."

"You're right," she replied, "sometimes it can really get to you. There's a pretty big turnover of nurses on our floor. How about you, Seth?"

"I'm in the Path lab. And, by the way, I'm not a doctor yet. I'm just here for the summer."

All during this dialogue, Seth was frantically running his cerebral motors. This was his chance and he was not about to lose it.

"Are you on the way to lunch?" he inquired.

"Oh," said Judy disappointedly, "we've just finished. We're due back in a minute. Maybe we could meet some other time."

"Tomorrow lunch?" asked Seth.

"Terrific." Judy Gordon smiled.

As all three nurses departed toward the elevator, she called out, "Meet you by the newsstand sort of twelve-fifteenish. Okay, Seth?"

He acknowledged her comment with a wave. Then the elevator enveloped them.

For a moment he stood there speechless. He not only remembered Judy, he even recalled trying to ask her out. Only he never got as far as opening his mouth.

As usual, Seth waited to go home till the rush hour had abated. At seven-thirty he boarded a bus that was relatively cool and had room for him to sit and read.

When at last he disembarked the sun was ebbing and the gentle rays of early evening bathed the lawns and flowerbeds of the houses in this unpretentious suburb. Seth knew all the inhabitants by name from the high school days when he had been a paperboy. Even now he remembered which homes had been generous and which housed the Ebenezer Scrooges of the neighborhood.

He reached the village shopping circle, where the Lazarus Meat & Grocery Market had been doing business since the nineteen-thirties. As he passed the front window he saw his father cutting Gouda cheese for Mrs. Schreiber and he waved to both of them. He then went to the back of the store and opened the door that led to their apartment on the floor above. His mother greeted him affectionately.

"Hello, darling. What's new today?"

"Ma," he complained forcefully, for they had run this gamut every day, "nothing's ever new where I work. In Pathology the patients are all dead."

"I know, I know, but maybe you discovered some new cure for death. It's possible."

He smiled. "You'll be the first to know. Have I got time to take a shower before dinner?"

Rosie nodded and went back to the kitchen.

Despite the frequent water shortages of summer, long hot showers were professional necessities for Seth. The smell of death clung to his clothing and his skin and each evening when he came back from the hospital he would scrub himself intensely.

At nine o'clock Nat Lazarus closed the store, and five minutes later the family was at the table.

"So, my boy," he asked, "what's new today?"

"I found a cure for cancer," Seth answered with a poker face.

"That's nice," his father mumbled, his primary attention on the box score of last evening's baseball game. "I tellya," he suddenly announced, "if the Cubs could just get another starting pitcher we'd take the pennant—and that's the truth."

Buoyed up by his experience at noontime, Seth good-humoredly added, "I also found a cure for heart disease, and tomorrow I'll develop something that will wipe out the common cold."

Nat suddenly put the paper down. "Did I hear you say the cold? You're onto something that could cure the common cold?"

"How come that gets a rise out of you and my cure for cancer didn't even make you blink?"

"My boy," his father wisely explained, "you're not a businessman, you don't live in this world. Do you have any notion of how many of those useless snake oils I sell all winter? If you were really onto something that could do the job, we'd patent it and make a mint."

"Sorry, only kidding, Dad. The common cold's the last frontier. It's like the moon for astrophysicists. We'll never reach it in our lifetime."

Nat looked at him and smiled. "Seth, tell your father one thing, huh? Who was fooling who just then?"

"The two of you are crazy with that vaudeville routine of yours," Mrs. Lazarus announced. "Who wants seconds?"

They were digging into Rosie's angel cake and ice cream (homemade, not from the store downstairs), when Seth casually remarked, "Actually, something did happen today. I ran into a girl I went to high school with."

Rosie Lazarus's ears perked up. "Oh yes? Anyone we know?"

"Judy Gordon. She's a nurse in the Cancer Ward."

Nat glanced mischievously at his son. "Sethie, you just be careful not to get her pregnant."

"Please!" said Rosie, "I'll thank you not to talk that way in front of me."

"Excuse me, Madam Queen Elizabeth," her husband replied, "but may I just remind you that if I hadn't gotten you pregnant, Seth wouldn't be here." He turned to his son for verification. "Am I not right, Doctor?"

"Yes, sir," Seth replied professionally. "Mom is what physicians call multiparous."

"And what is that in plain English, may I ask?"

"It means you've had more than one child, Mom."

And suddenly all grew silent. Cold and silent. For Seth had reminded them—and himself, most painfully of all—of Howie.

Howie, who had started life as Seth's big brother but, though still alive, had not become a grown-up human being. For, many years ago while he was sitting in the front seat in his mother's lap, there'd been an accident. Nat was driving and had braked fast in order not to hit a kid who'd run out from between two cars. And Howie had been thrown against the metal dashboard with his mother's weight behind him.

Howie, who'd sustained such massive cranial damage that although he grew, barely learned to swallow food or sit up by himself. Who sometimes recognized his parents and sometimes did not. (But who could tell? For Howie kept on smiling all day long.)

Howie finally had to be sequestered in a hospital. Howie, whom they had to force themselves to visit two or three times every month lest they forget him and believe that their lives could ever be without the shadow of his pain. (Or did he even feel pain?—there was no way to ask him.)

Howie, a never-ending source of guilt, hopelessly crippled but obscenely robust in his lonely nonexistence. For he would not die, although he could not really live.

They finished supper and as Seth helped Rosie clear the table, Nat turned on the television. Fortunately there was baseball on the tube, an anodyne for the ever-gnawing pain of Howie's plight.

As they were in the kitchen, Rosie washing and Seth drying, he inquired, "How is Howie, by the way?"

"How is he?—what a question. How could he be? Maybe when you get to be a real doctor you'll discover something to repair a broken brain."

She was not joking that time. And Seth knew she lived in constant hope that doctors somewhere, sometime, would invent a miracle to bring her lost-but-living son back to his family. Meanwhile, try as she did, she could not lavish her love on Seth. Because he was not Howie.

Seth could walk and talk, could dress and feed himself, while Howie needed help for everything.

When they were through in the kitchen, Seth went out and took a walk to clear his mind so he could complete the paperwork he'd brought home from the hospital. When he returned, his mother had already closed the bedroom door and Nat was jeering loudly at the Cubs' shortstop who had maladroitly muffed a double play.

Aware that Nat was mercifully sedated by his black and white sixteen-inch opiate, Seth did not disturb him. Instead he climbed up to the room which, as a child, had been his own domain, his kingdom—and was now his laboratory. He switched on his desk fluorescent light and plunged himself into the world's pathologies. For this was *his* way of forgetting Howie.

"I'd recommend the tuna fish or chicken salad," Judy Gordon said. "They taste about the same—in fact I have had suspicions that they really *are*."

"Why don't we have one of each and then compare," suggested Seth.

She nodded and he flagged a waitress to take their order.

"So," she said, "I guess we've got a lot of catching up to do."

"I guess."

They reminisced and joked all through their indistinguishable salads. She had a way of making him relax, perhaps because she was so calm, so confident and outgoing.

He ordered chocolate ice cream for dessert, she ordered Jell-O. ("I've got to be careful—it's the bikini season, after all!")

Curiously, Seth could not conjure up an image of her in a skimpy bathing suit, although his knowledge of anatomy enabled him to picture her naked—which was nice enough.

"Do you still live at home?" she asked as they were finishing their coffee.

"Yeah. Guess I'm kind of socially retarded. I still live with Mom and Dad, but I'm only here for the summer."

"Too bad," she murmured, half to herself.

And Seth immediately wondered, What's too bad? The fact I'm living home or that I'm going back to Boston?

As they walked toward the bank of elevators, he mustered the confidence to ask, "Can we maybe go to dinner sometime?"

"Sure. How about tomorrow night?"

"Fine. That would be fine."

"I've got a car—if you could call it that," she said lightheartedly. "But at least it takes me where I want to go. What time do you get off?"

"That's really up to me," he answered. "The patients up in Path don't get upset if we leave early."

"Let's say half-past six? And if there's some emergency I'll phone you in the lab."

"Sure, great. I mean, that's fine," he repeated.

They had an elevator to themselves. Judy pressed five—the Cancer Ward, then eight for his lab.

"Tell me, Seth," she asked, "does working with dead people ever get to you? Do you sometimes feel like you're going crazy?"

"No, I think you've got the harder job. I get them when their suffering is over. You have to watch them die. Isn't that depressing?"

She nodded. "Yeah, and I go home every day and realize how damn lucky I am just to be alive."

They discussed it over dinner at Armando's venerable North Rush eatery, where Seth had never been and still could not afford to be. But this was special.

"You'd be amazed how perfectly normal people are petrified of a dying relative," Judy said. "They shy away because they somehow think that death's contagious. Families force themselves to come, but old friends always seem to have some excuse. So these patients I look after are unbelievably grateful for the slightest kindness we show them. Anyway, if I were on my deathbed I'd sure as heck be grateful to have someone—even if it's a nurse I barely knew—to hold my hand in those last minutes. And frankly, if you'll excuse the insult to your profession— you rarely find a doctor there if he can possibly avoid it."

"Well," he answered, his admiration for her growing by the second, "there are all kinds of doctors, just the way there are all kinds of nurses." Damn, he cursed himself, she'll probably think I'm a callous bastard.

"Is Pathology the kind of medicine you want to always do?" she asked.

"I'm still not sure, to tell the truth. First it was just a summer job I knew would help me get to Med School, then it seemed like it would give me a head start in Anatomy. And I've really learned a lot this past year."

Shyness prevented him from mentioning that Professor Lubar had given him an A-plus—the only time in recent memory that such an honor had been bestowed. "Dr. Matthews thinks our work can ultimately be of use to help prevent some of the things we find as cause of death."

"Oh, I admire that," Judy commented. "But don't you think you're missing something—you know—the emotional aspect that brought us to medicine in the first place?" She sighed and continued, "I think there's nothing more gratifying in the entire world than to hear 'Thank you' from a patient you've been kind to."

Well, he told himself, that's a pretty overt denigration of my work. But do I dare defend myself?

And for the second time in as many days, he found himself saying something that emanated from a part of him he obviously could not control. "Maybe it's because I'm afraid." *Why the hell did I say that?*

"You mean of losing a patient?" she asked. "I know a lot of doctors are that way. It's only human, Seth."

"That isn't what I'm scared of," he confessed again. "It's—it's—the suffering. I think I like Pathology because whatever agony the person's gone through is all over. Even if they're riddled with carcinomas they don't feel it anymore. I just don't think that I could bear to watch a patient in excruciating pain or hooked to a machine that kept him breathing while the rest of him was dead. I guess I don't have the guts to be a real doctor."

As Judy drove him home, Seth became increasingly convinced that he suffered from some rare psychiatric aberration—like a variant of the Gilles de la Tourette's syndrome—which forced him to say things his conscious mind could not suppress. Honest things. But when the hell did honesty impress a girl?

As they neared the bus terminal, he thought it best to liberate her from his craven company.

"It's okay, Judy, I can walk from here."

"No, that's all right. It's nothing for me to take you one or two more blocks."

He nodded and she drove the additional distance again without making conversation. She stopped in front of his parents' grocery, the window illumined only by a neon ad for Schlitz, "the beer that made Milwaukee famous."

"Thanks for the ride," he said. "I'll see you around the hospital."

"No, Seth," she said, "I'm not going to let you go that easily."

Seth was surprised to learn that passion could compensate for inexperience. As she brought her lips close to his, he put his arms around her and held her close as they kissed.

After a moment, as they both came up for air, he asked, "Can we do this again sometime?"

"Which part? The dinner or my shameless pass?"

"Are they mutually exclusive?" he asked. "In any case, I'd better warn you, next time I'll be the one who makes the first move."

"Fine. Who knows where that might lead? 'Night, Seth, and thanks
again."

And, had his parents not been asleep, he would have danced all the
way to the third floor in an ebullient imitation of Fred Astaire.

If ever a list were compiled of where *not* to be in the United States
during the month of August, Boston would certainly make the top ten.
Of course, Pfeifer's lab was air-conditioned—to maintain a constant
scientific environment. But Vanderbilt Hall was not. And it was logical.
Certain specimens if overheated would be irreplaceable, whereas lab
assistants were a dime a dozen.

As she toiled well into the night, Laura began to entertain the
paranoid fantasy that Pfeifer obviously counted on the weather to further
his research by keeping his minions in the refreshing comfort of the lab as
long as possible.

At first she suffered pangs of conscience over Palmer, which she tried
to assuage by reminding herself that at least it wasn't wartime. Still she
knew he would be dissipating some of the best years of his life polishing
his boots, cleaning his rifle—and perhaps even the latrine as well—although
she was not sure whether officers ever had to do that sort of thing.

Then gradually she began to think that she had done what in the
long run would be best for them both.

And she started dating again.

At first it was just beer and pizza with one or another of her
colleagues in the lab. (Wyman excepted, of course. But he did not
fraternize with nontenured people, anyway.)

She went to a Pops concert on the banks of the Charles River with
Gary Arnold, a handsome first-year resident in Neurology. As did several
thousand other couples, they sat on a blanket eating sandwiches, drinking
wine from a Thermos, while they watched the legendary Arthur Fiedler
conduct musical smorgasbords from the latest Broadway shows and a few
snippets from the classics. And when they stood with all the others for
the grand finale, Sousa's rousing "Stars and Stripes Forever," Gary put
his arm around Laura, pulling her close. He was charming, tall, and had a
sense of humor. Perhaps most importantly, he was there. And she was
lonely. So they finished the evening in his apartment on the Fenway.

He visited the lab the evening after to make certain Laura understood that he had no intention of a "serious relationship." She reassured
him she had never had the slightest notion that they would be anything
but friends. For she was well aware that he'd be leaving for Wisconsin at
the beginning of September.

"Look, Gary," she explained with friendly candor, "I was horny, you were horny. When we woke up, neither one of us was horny. That was all there was and that was all there ever will be. Have a nice life."

Inwardly fuming at Laura's beating him to the brush-off, Gary stalked out of the lab muttering something about her being "a real ball breaker."

Her other dates that summer were neither as pompous nor as passionate. Which suited her fine.

Sometimes if she was working late she'd get a call from Barney (at eleven, when the rates went down). He'd usually be phoning from a public booth in Canarsie or some other godforsaken place and always with an entertaining anecdote about his latest passengers. Like the call girl who had offered to pay him in kind.

"It sounds more interesting than medicine. Maybe you ought to consider it as a career."

"Thank you, Laura. Staying up all night is what I always aspired to." Then he would act paternal. "Which reminds me, why the hell are you still working? Even chain gangs have it easier than you. Why not go home and get some sleep?"

"Thank you, Dr. Livingston, I think I'm whacked enough to do just that. Goodnight."

She hung up, went to scrub her hands, and just as she was leaving heard the annoyed voice of Peter Wyman. "Castellano, telephone for you—again. I'm not your private secretary, you know."

Laura hesitated for a moment. If it was Palmer she was not in shape for any kind of conversation. But who else would be calling close to midnight? Maybe something's wrong at home.

"Hello."

"Hi, Laura, it's me—Hank Dwyer."

"Hank," she said, with a happy sigh of relief, "how the hell are you?"

"I tried to call your room at Vanderbilt. They said you might be here—"

"Is something wrong?"

"No, no, it's just the opposite. I need someone to talk to badly." Then Hank announced, "I'm a father and Cheryl's a mother."

"Hey, that's great. Everybody healthy?"

"Yes, *Deo gratias*. But, Laura, I'm in shock—there were *two* of them. I'm the father of twins. I mean, I don't know what to do."

Laura certainly didn't know what he wanted *her* to do.

"I'll tell you what, Hank, when the whole gang's back in town we'll have a monster party for all four of you."

"That would be nice," he replied, in surprisingly solemn tones. "But there's something more important, which is why I'm calling. I mean, you're Catholic, Laura, aren't you?"

"Sort of by birth. But if you'll forgive the irreverence, I've hailed more cabs than I've Hailed Marys."

Hank single-mindedly persisted. "Laura, will you come with me to church?"

"Tonight?"

"Of course. God sent a miracle tonight and who am I to wait till morning to say thank you."

"Sure, Hank," she said softly, "I'd be glad to."

"Oh, that's great. That's really great. Look, Cheryl's mom's here and I can use her car. I'll come around to get you in a second."

They stood in the wide emptiness of the Cathedral of the Holy Cross. That is, Laura stood while Hank knelt and prayed. As he was lost in prayer, she was lost in thought.

I wish I were religious, she lamented inwardly. I don't mean church religious. I just wish I could believe in some Supreme Intelligence to help me steer the boat, to let me know what's right or wrong. As it is, I'm drowning in a sea of doubts. Oh God, I wish I could believe like Dwyer.

When he was saying goodnight to her outside Vanderbilt, Hank was so brimming with joy that he embraced her.

And Laura was sure it was merely by accident that, as he let her go, one of his hands brushed by her breast.

NINETEEN

Their second year began with water and ended with blood.

The first event (not listed in the Course Catalogue) was the christening of Hank and Cheryl Dwyer's twin daughters, Marie and Michelle. Barney and Laura stood in the front pew as the priest sprinkled holy water on the little girls' brows, each time intoning in Latin that he was baptizing them "in the name of the Father, and of the Son, and of the Holy Ghost. Amen."

It was late September and they had been medical students for more than a year without yet having seen a live patient. And there was still eight months of deadening basic science to wade through before they reached the real stuff in the spring—Introduction to the Clinic, and Physical Diagnosis. They took some consolation in the fact that this would be the last winter of their discontent. Spring would bring them into the presence of sick people. But for now they still had no idea what medicine was really about.

Though Laura received a daily letter from the ever-faithful Palmer, finally past basic training ("and with more muscles than Tarzan"), the letters did not relieve her pangs of loneliness. What "social life" she had consisted of fending off the parade of hot-pants interns, residents, now and then even a married attending physician looking for a little action.

She wondered how the sensuous Miss Andersen could deal with the priapic pressure of it all.

Barney certainly was of no assistance. If anything he had joined the enemy camp. For unbelievably, there were a record *six* young females in the first-year class, one of them a radiant Chinese girl named Susan Hsiang.

Barney knew a good thing when he saw it. For Susan had an attitude toward men that harked back to the traditions of the East. What a change from all the ruthlessly ambitious Med School types. To say that he was smitten was an understatement. He was high on the scent of lotus and jasmine.

Laura—though with an ambivalence that she herself did not recognize—agreed that her friend had found the "perfect partner."

As Barney himself was the first to tell her, "She's different, Castellano. She really looks up to me—"

"Of course. She's barely five feet tall."

"Don't joke. I've never known a girl so—I don't know—so feminine. Do you know how to say 'I love you' in Chinese?"

"No, Barney, but I'm sure you do."

"Damn right. *Wo ai ni!* And Susan says it at least thirty times a day. She makes me feel like Adonis, Babe Ruth, and Einstein all rolled into one."

"That's quite a group to carry around, even with your self-image, Barney. But then I suppose whenever your ego gets tired she massages it for you."

But Laura felt a kind of envy not just of Miss Hsiang's unquestionable grip on Barney's psyche, but especially of Susan's ability to find a man she could worship.

By contrast, Laura had grown up with ambition to transcend her gender, to improve her status, to be admired for *herself*.

That did nothing to alleviate her loneliness.

The lovely Miss Hsiang purchased a hot plate, so that after she and Barney had finished their long days in the lab and classroom she could cook dinner for him.

And yet her conversation was seldom concerned with bamboo shoots and the nutritional value of soya beans. Susan could discourse for hours on the medicine of her tradition, which had begun more than two thousand years before Hippocrates with the *Nei Ching,* a classic work on internal medicine.

She also explained to Barney the principle of *I-Ching*. All nature, she said, was composed of two opposing cosmic forces: Yin—female, soft, receptive, dark, empty; and Yang—male, illuminating, firm, creative, constructive. Yin is the earth, Yang is the heavens. Yin is cold, darkness, disease, death; Yang is warmth, light, strength, health, and life. If these forces are in harmony in our bodies, then health prevails. Imbalance brings dysphoria, disease, and death.

And Susan told him about the most mysterious aspect of it all, the phenomenon called *Qi*—which differentiates life from death.

Barney took another sip of rice wine, looked lovingly across at her, and said, "You know so damned much medicine you could already be practicing."

Susan smiled shyly. "In China, perhaps. But now I am here I must learn your ways—and they are very strange. Today I spoke to your Professor Lubar about acupuncture and he told me to 'forget about that sort of nonsense, it had no anatomical basis.' How could he explain the millions of people that are cured every year?"

"I don't know," Barney allowed. "Maybe because they don't teach *Qi* at Harvard."

Her family had arrived in San Francisco from Shanghai via Hong Kong in 1950. But almost immediately her father found a flourishing practice among the Chinese community, which respected his wisdom and did not demand to see his diploma. Since his medicines were herbs and plants, he didn't need a license to prescribe.

Susan, the eldest of three daughters, had inherited her father's desire to heal but wanted to extend her horizons beyond Grant Avenue, the hub of the Chinese settlement in San Francisco. She had gone first to Berkeley whence she'd graduated *summa* in Biochem and then to Harvard and, more specifically, into the kingdom whose self-appointed emperor was Barney Livingston.

He had his sporting reflexes to thank for nailing her before potential rivals could react. He had been in the entrance hall of Vanderbilt listening to Bennett Landsmann rhapsodize about diving for lost treasure when he had glanced across to where the freshmen were signing up and caught a glimpse of the diminutive Miss Hsiang struggling with a large suitcase. Without so much as a word he pivoted and sped across the hall and offered his assistance as a porter.

Two hours later he had introduced Susan to the best in Boston Chinese cooking, namely, Joyce Chen's just across the Charles near M.I.T.

And by the time they had returned to Vanderbilt he was determined to be the Yang to her Yin—or die trying.

* * *

This was to be the year that every member of the class contracted a fatal disease. Lance Mortimer was the first to succumb.

"Barney, can I talk to you?"

"I'm sort of in the midst of dinner, Lance." With a gesture he called his neighbor's attention to his Oriental companion, serving dinner from a steaming wok placed on his desk.

"Oh," said Lance, "I'm sorry to interrupt you, Suzie, but would you mind terribly if I had a word with Barney? It's very important."

She nodded as, with an exasperated sigh, Barney shuffled into the hall where Lance blurted out his terrifying problem.

"I've got it, Barney. What am I going to do?"

"Got what? Make sense, will you?"

"How can I make sense when I'm about to die?"

"You look pretty healthy to me," Barney replied in what he hoped would reassure—and dismiss—him.

"But I'm not, I'm not," Lance protested. "I've got testicular teratoma."

"Have you seen a doctor?"

"I don't have to. I've got every symptom in the goddamn textbook. And what clinches it is that the condition peaks in twenty-four-year-old guys. My birthday was only last week and I felt the first twinge when I was cutting the cake. And I've checked it. Shit, I'll probably have to have an orchidectomy and maybe a scrotectomy—even then it may be too late. Livingston, you've *got* to help me."

"Lance, if you're asking me to slice off your gonads, I can't—till you get a second opinion. Anyway, have you thought of going to the Health Service?"

"Christ, no. It's too embarrassing. Shit, if I had to have cancer couldn't it have been something unsexual? I mean, by tomorrow night everybody in Boston will know I'll be singing castrato. That is, if I even live."

Though legally still unlicensed to practice, Barney nonetheless felt competent to deal with this particular malady.

"Okay, Lance. I want you to go back to your room, take two Bufferin, and keep a cold compress on your scrotum at all times."

"I haven't got Bufferin. Will Excedrin do?"

"No, no," Barney objected. "It's got to be Bufferin. The Charles Street Pharmacy is open late. I suggest you buzz down there and get yourself a large jar. I'll be in to see you about eleven. Okay?"

Lance was overcome with gratitude. "Livingston, if I die I'll leave you all my worldly goods—and if I live I'll give you one of my cars."

As his classmate dashed down the corridor, Barney returned to his room and closed the door.

"Sorry about that, Suzie," he apologized, "but Lance had a little medical problem that I had to deal with."

"And he comes to you?" she said with a touch of awe. "You must be very wise. My father also—"

"I appreciate the compliment," Barney interrupted. "But the truth is I read about Lance's disease over the summer. It's called 'nosophobia.' "

"I have never heard of such a thing," Susan said, her admiration for Barney's sagacity intensifying.

"It's very common among medical students. Nosophobia literally means 'fear of diseases.' It's caused by having to memorize *The Merck Manual,* which has every kind of bizarre illness that ever existed. We'll all of us have a touch of noso during the year. In fact, the way my chest's been feeling lately, I think I'm showing the symptoms of silico-tuberculosis."

He shrugged. "I mean, there's an epidemic in our whole class and the most amazing part is that no two people have the same complaint. For example, Laura believes she's suffering from endometrioma, which shows she's got more sense than Lance because it's benign and can be cured by surgery. In fact this noso craze has made everybody in the goddamn class a hypochondriac.

"Actually, the only guy with a remotely plausible pathology is Bennett. He thinks he's got Albert's disease, which is an inflammation of the connecting tissue between the Achilles tendon and the heel. Considering the fact that he's still limping slightly from last year's friendly game with the lawyers, he just might really have it. Anyway, if *I* don't get rid of this damn cough by next week I'm going to have my lungs x-rayed."

Susan merely smiled.

"Laura, you've got to help me. You're the only friend I have."

She looked up from her desk to see an uncharacteristically disheveled Grete standing at the doorway, terror in her eyes.

"What's the matter, what's happened?"

"Laura," she repeated plaintively. "I've got to have a mastectomy."

"Oh, Grete, that's terrible. When did they find the tumor?"

"I discovered it just now when I was taking a shower. Oh God, Laura, it's like a nightmare come true."

"Don't jump to conclusions, Grete. I mean, we all find little lumps now and then and almost always they're benign."

But Grete sat on the bed and continued her lament. "Oh God, oh

God. What man's going to look at a girl with only one tit? I mean, face it, Laura, what am I if not a body?"

"Look, Grete, why don't you see the doctor first thing tomorrow morning. If you like, I'll come with you."

"I can't," she answered. "I mean, I've got a really important lab."

"More important than a malignant tumor?"

"Well, like you say, it might only be benign. Maybe I ought to wait awhile to see how it goes."

Laura was furious. Didn't that selfish big-boobed brat realize that she was talking to someone who herself had a serious ovarian condition? At least I don't go bothering everybody on the corridor and the only person I've told is Barney, so he'll know what to do if I don't survive surgery.

Nor did the morbid fantasizing stop at the gate of Vanderbilt Hall.

On the contrary, it was perhaps at its most severe in the Dwyer household where Hank's disease, along with normal parental anxiety, combined to create a condition of nocturnal frenzy.

Every time he heard one of the twins cry, cough, or sneeze, he leapt out of bed with his flashlight and pediatrics handbook, fearing the worst. And, on those rare occasions when there was no noise, things were even worse, for he was then certain they had succumbed to crib death and would race to their room carrying a small oxygen tank. He would even call home between classes to make absolutely sure Cheryl had checked the twins' vital signs.

When the mass hysteria had finally abated, the students drew a lesson from this experience. But unfortunately it was one that would actually harm them in later life. For they, whose primary training would be in the observation and detection of signs and symptoms in others, had blunted their own powers to perceive true illness in themselves.

Besides, a real physician almost never seeks another doctor's help. For they all are painfully aware of just how little *anybody* understands about curing the sick.

Their first patient was a Florida orange (California produces less suitable substitutes for human tissue). But this was only for a day.

After their second session in the art of using a syringe they wished there was a specialty exclusively restricted to citrus products. How bold they had become in that first hour, plunging needles into the Sunkist patients without qualms or hesitation; drawing juice or zestfully inoculating the stoic fruits with Boston water.

In session two—the drawing of blood—they had to pick a partner from among their number and take turns being victim and tormentor. Bravado was conspicuously absent that afternoon. Even the masochists and sadists were in short supply, for no one really wanted to inflict and then in turn be inflicted with a needle.

The class, though still a hundred and twenty strong, had come to know if not one another's personalities, at least where their important talents lay. Seth Lazarus could have auctioned himself off. Everybody wanted to team up with him.

The second choice was the women, because in reality the fledgling male doctors did not conceive of them as anything but glorified nurses—and in fact this exercise was normally a staple of nursing school education.

Laura refused all invitations till she offered to exchange stabs with Barney. But he could not bring himself to accept her generosity.

"I just can't, Castellano," he said with regret. "I mean, I can't stand the thought of hurting you."

"I'm not afraid of hurting Laura," Bennett volunteered. And then he gallantly inquired, "May I have your arm, Miss Castellano?"

Laura smiled. "Absolutely. This is my only chance to check the rumor that you have blue blood."

The ever-buoyant Barney found a partner in Hank Dwyer, joking, "Why don't we two stick together?"

This second exercise, venipuncture, was more important for them all, since a substantial part of their medical education would involve scutwork like drawing blood for lab tests.

Barney approached it as a kind of sporting exercise: look eagle-eyed when you see your prey (in this case see the vein) and then move in decisively. It helped that Dwyer was fair-skinned and had a forearm streaked with blue like Roquefort cheese. Or, putting it another way, a veritable hypodermic road map. But poor Hank, still the saintly soul, could not do unto others as his nimble partner had done unto him.

"I'm sorry if I hurt you, Barney," he would preface every move. "I mean, don't take it personally."

And Barney, dying to just get the damn thing over with, had to exhort him. "Go, Hank, go for it! Just stick the damn thing in!"

Words he soon came to regret.

When the ordeal was over, their instructor in Internal Medicine said, "You'll all have your chance to hone these skills, so don't be worried if you haven't fully got the knack."

Indeed, as their experience was soon to prove, aspiring doctors get to draw so much blood during their training that if Count Dracula had known, he would have sold his castle just to gain admission.

> 'Twas the night before Christmas
> And all through the halls
> The students were cramming
> And climbing the walls

Less then half the class went home this last preclinical Yuletide. Had the amount of minutiae they still had to ingest been in the form of sugar, it would have made severe diabetics of them all.

For most the Star of Wonder was not a divine fire in the sky, but the light cast from burning midnight oil.

Once again, Bennett sacrificed his precious study time to go to Cleveland for the holiday.

He could remember the first time Hannah had prepared a Christmas dinner just for him. She had been so flustered about what to serve and what to do.

"It's strange and sad, Linc," Herschel remarked to his eleven-year-old adopted son. "Even before Hitler, Christmas and Easter were often the occasions for pogroms against us. And my father always said how ironical it was—to us Jesus was just a nice Jewish boy who would have hated all these things done in His name."

"Does everybody know that, Dad?" Linc had asked, uncertain as to whether this was secret information.

"Everyone should know," Herschel replied. "But most prefer not to—it confuses things."

"It sure confuses me," the boy confessed. "I don't even really understand the difference between Jews and Christians."

"That's because we have so much in common," Hannah interjected. "After all, the Old Testament commands us to 'love thy neighbor as thyself.' "

"That's a direct quotation," Herschel added. For as a youth he had been an Orthodox believer and known the Bible practically by heart. "It's *Leviticus*, Chapter 19, verse 18."

But with time the near-teenage boy's inquiries were more subtle.

"Dad, if God is just and punishes the wicked—like Miss Hayes, my Sunday School instructor, says—how come He let so many of your people die? How come He let my father . . ."

"This," Herschel confessed, "is something that I wondered myself when I was in the camp, when I saw all my relatives marched off—and *most of all* when I survived. I wondered—was God a parent who showed favorites?"

"And did you find an answer?"

"The answer, my boy, is who am *I* to pose the question? I dare not presume to ask God why my brothers perished. I must only live my life by trying to justify His sparing *me*."

The vestige of his once deep piety was a simple ceremony performed on the eve of Yom Kippur. He lit a candle—just one solitary candle—in memory of those who perished for a reason that was far beyond his comprehension.

And he told Linc, "This flame is burning for your father, too."

This touched the young boy deeply.

As a final act in Herschel's brief ceremony, he would intone the mourner's Kaddish.

The boy was fascinated by the strange, sad language and the fervor that stirred his adopted father as he recited.

"What is that?" he asked timidly.

"It is the traditional Jewish prayer for the dead," Hannah explained.

Linc thought a moment and then turned to Herschel. "Will you teach me how to say it?"

"I don't have to teach," Herschel replied. "It's right here in English on the opposite page. Look, 'Extolled and hallowed be the name of the Lord—' "

"No," Linc insisted, "I want to say it in the holy language."

"That's rather difficult," said Hannah, touched by his sentiment.

"Darling," Herschel corrected her, "that is the one prayer that is always written out phonetically in English letters so whoever cannot read Hebrew can still say it."

He turned to the final page of his siddur and handed it to Linc. "Come, say it for your father. I'll give you a little help if you stumble."

But Linc read it perfectly. *"Yisgadal ve yiskadosh shmei raboh. . . ."* And then he yearned to find out what it meant.

Afterwards, when he had read the translation, he had yet another question for Herschel.

"How come there's no place in the prayer for the dead person's name? All it does is praise God."

"Ah," Herschel replied, "that is because if we remember His name, *He* will remember all the others."

But growing up in such strange circumstances—at once loving and alien—often caused confusion. Especially after Linc insisted upon modifying his name to reflect his dual affiliation. "Ben" was the perfect compromise, since it not only was short for Bennett, but was the word for "son" in Hebrew.

"Dad, what am I, exactly?" he asked Herschel one day.

"I don't understand, Ben."

"Oh, sometimes the guys at school ask me whether I'm Jewish because you and Mom are. And then somebody else will chime in and say that's impossible—I couldn't be anything but 'colored.' It gets me all mixed up. Now and then I feel so confused I just want to go up to my room and lock the door."

Herschel pondered this question—and could not find a clear answer. Finally he simply said, "This is America, you can be anything you want."

"What could he have meant by that?" Herschel asked Hannah when they were in bed that night. "Have there been incidents? . . ."

She shrugged.

"Hannah, when you look at me like that I know you're hiding something."

And then she told him, emphasizing that this was all information she'd inferred from Ben's behavior and from chance remarks. She sensed there had been words—perhaps even fists. That even in such privileged circumstances their son had encountered bigotry. For *two* reasons.

"Besides, it isn't just the *goyim* at his school," she chided. "Your fancy brother and his crowd have been no better. Ben doesn't get invited to his schoolmates' Christmas parties *or* to dances at your brother's temple. When you brought him out last summer to play tennis at Steve's country club, the members almost had conniption fits. He has no real home."

"And what are we, I ask you?" Herschel questioned.

"Two old people—getting older. What will happen to him when we're gone?"

"Are you suggesting we should send him back to Georgia?" Herschel asked facetiously.

"No. I'm simply stating fact. Our son is wonderful. He's the kindest, most loving child I've ever known."

"But we must prepare him, make him strong—"

"For what?" she asked.

"For being not only black, Hannah, but something of a Jew as well. The world will exact an awesome price for that."

It was inevitable. Ben's life in the Landsmann house was a perpetual reliving of the Holocaust. It was in the air; in words both spoken and unspoken.

Once Ben was helping Hannah clear the table after they had eaten in the kitchen.

When she rolled up her sleeves to soak the dishes, he caught sight of the tattoo on her forearm.

"What's that?" he asked ingenuously.

"Just my number," Hannah answered, trying to dismiss the subject.

"What's the number for?" young Ben persisted.

"Let's put it this way," Hannah said, "it was the Nazis' way of keeping track of us."

"That's terrible. Why don't you have some doctor take it off?"

"No, my darling." Hannah tried to smile. "I have survived—and this I'll always keep. It was my lucky number."

Seth Lazarus took a full three days off and went all the way to Chicago.

He felt he was doing well enough in all his courses to be able to sacrifice a few points in his grades to visit Judy. They had arranged to spend a maximum amount of time together while still attending each other's family dinners.

Mr. and Mrs. Lazarus had differing opinions.

"She's certainly a looker," Nat pronounced. "Who would have thought that our little Seth would have come home with Rita Hayworth?"

Rosie was somewhat less effusive. "Do you really think she's right for him, Nat? After all, he's such a shy boy and she's so—well, I don't know—pushy. I mean, did you see the way she held Seth's hand? Right in front of his own mother, she holds his hand. I just think this girl is too fast for him."

"He's over twenty-one, Rosie. He's gonna be a doctor. Let him use his own stethoscope to listen to his heart."

"Are you disagreeing with me, then?"

"When have I ever disagreed with you?"

"Never."

"Then this is a great occasion, because I definitely disagree with you."

Judy's family was considerably less ambivalent. Having assessed his daughter's beau, Simon Gordon had pronounced in the metaphor of his trade, "He's twenty-four karats, absolutely."

"Judy says they all think he's brilliant at the hospital," Mrs. Gordon added proudly. "What a wonderful son-in-law."

"Hey, slow down a minute, he hasn't even asked her."

"Listen, on that score there's no problem. If he doesn't, *she* will."

Outside the Lazarus market, Seth and Judy spent a long passionate time in each other's arms.

"I've booked a room at the Sonesta for tomorrow. Do you still want to go through with it?" Seth whispered.

Judy whispered back, "I only wish it had been for tonight, too. Why don't we go in the morning so we can take full advantage of it?"

"Okay, sure. I'll tell my folks I have to take an earlier flight."

"Very early, Seth. Please."

She was there at nine o'clock the next day, a radiant smile on her face. Seth put his small suitcase in the trunk of her car. They both waved goodbye to his parents ... and drove off in the direction of O'Hare Airport.

It was an odd hour even by the standards of travelers' hotels. The clerk apologized, " 'Dr. and Mrs. A. Schweitzer'—yes, we have your reservation, but we didn't expect you till this afternoon."

"His plane came in early," Judy quickly explained. "Tail winds."

"Oh," said the clerk, trained by years of experience to control his facial muscles. "Well, the girls are cleaning Room 209 right now, if you don't mind waiting."

"Fine," said Seth, affecting a deep baritone. (He somehow felt that a Nobel Prize-winning doctor should have a more resonant voice.) "And, if it's okay, we'll take our luggage up now."

They stood outside the open door to the room, impatiently watching two languid chambermaids changing the sheets on the beds.

"Won't be another minute, folks," said one of them, with a knowing grin. "You newlyweds or something?"

"Uh, does it show?" Seth asked with a blush in his voice.

"I can guess it every time," she replied with undisguised innuendo. "When folks arrive here not looking tuckered out from a flight, they're usually honeymooners. Anyway, we won't be a second. Just be sure and put the DO NOT DISTURB sign on your door."

Seth was a little nervous, but not frightened. He had admitted to Judy that he was a virgin. And she had been equally candid about her "experience." A young intern she dated the previous year had persuaded her of his undying love. The affair had lasted as long as his tenure at the hospital, and when he left for Texas he had sent her the female equivalent of a Dear John letter.

"Don't worry," she whispered, "it'll all come naturally."

"I'm not worried," he replied. "Anyway, I've studied *Love Without Fear*."

"Honestly, Seth, no book can tell you how wonderful it is."

"You mean it was so good with that guy?"

She shook her head. "No, darling. But I know it's going to be beautiful with you."

They had lunch downstairs in the coffee shop. Seth devoured two club sandwiches and a huge slice of lemon meringue pie.

About halfway through the meal, he began to look pensive.

"Something bothering you?" she asked.

He nodded. "Could we take a little drive, Judy?"

"Sure. Where?"

"You'll understand when we get there."

They climbed into her car and Seth, withdrawing a map from his jacket pocket, began to direct her westward. After about half an hour they reached a narrow country junction.

"Seth, we're in the middle of nowhere. Why are you being so mysterious?"

"There's someone I want you to see, Judy," he replied with a curious touch of melancholy. "My brother."

"I never knew you even had a—"

"Yeah," he cut her off, "I try not to think about him."

She drove on as he directed, growing puzzled to the point of apprehension.

Finally, he indicated a turnoff to the right and said simply, "If we're gonna be close, you have to know everything about my family."

They parked in the courtyard of St. Joseph's Home for Children, and a pink-cheeked nun in her early sixties greeted them. "Merry Christmas, Seth," she said warmly. "I know you're anxious to visit Howie, so come right along."

The couple followed her down the corridor, a few steps behind. As they began to climb a wide stone staircase, Judy grew increasingly anxious. "Seth," she whispered, "what's wrong with him?"

"You'll see," he answered quietly.

The sister pointed to a door. "I'm sure he'll be happy to see you." And, as she left, she added, "I'll be down in the playroom if you need me."

Seth waited till they were alone and then said to Judy, "I hope this won't upset you. But you'll never be able to understand me if you don't meet Howie."

Lying on the bed in the cubicle that passed as a room was a man—or a very large boy, it was hard for Judy to tell which—clothed in what looked like a baby's diaper. To say he was thin would be an understatement. He was emaciated, every rib visible through his pale, translucent skin. He gave the impression of living death. He lay back, his head lolling from side to side, his eyes unfocused, spittle dripping down his chin.

Despite all her hospital experience, Judy could not suppress a shudder.

"Hello, Howie," Seth said gently.

The boy did not even turn to look at him.

"Can he hear?" Judy asked as calmly as she could.

"I think he can—sort of—but he doesn't understand words."

There was silence, except for the gurgling sound emanating from Howie.

"Why is he so thin?" Judy asked. "I mean, even if he can't swallow, why don't they give him an I.V. or something?"

"No, it's deliberate," Seth explained, trying to keep a rein on his emotions and speak with clinical objectivity. "They have to keep his weight down so two nurses can lift him when they have to do . . . all sorts of stuff, like change the bedding, shaving him—"

"And the diaper? . . ."

"He's twenty-five years old, but he still needs one." Seth shook his head. "And it's been like this for over twenty years. My folks have really struggled to be able to keep him in a private nursing home. In a state facility he'd probably be dead by now—which would maybe be a blessing."

The room grew silent again, except for Howie's noises. They stood there for several minutes more, Seth looking at his older brother with an expression that she could not decipher. Finally, he said, "It's been good to see you, Howie—take care of yourself."

During the drive back they were both silent. He wondering what she was thinking. She groping to understand why he wanted her to know.

Finally, she asked, "Are you afraid this is something hereditary?"

He shook his head. "It isn't. He was in a car accident when he was four. Thrown against the metal dashboard."

She paused to assimilate this information. "Where were you at the time?"

"Safely cushioned—in my mother's womb."

"Oh," she said. A simple monosyllable conveying that she now understood. "So you feel guilty?"

There was a moment's pause, after which he said very quietly, "Yes. It's crazy, but I can't help it. I have this irrational guilt because I'm out functioning in the real world and he's stuck in that room forever. And my parents seem to reinforce it by the way they treat me. Do you know, there have actually been times when I wished I could have changed places with Howie." He buried his head in his hands in a futile attempt to crush the image from his mind.

Still averting his gaze, he continued, "And do you know the most ironic part? The guy's stronger than me. I mean, I had asthma as a kid, but goddamn Howie's got the constitution of an ox. He'll outlive me."

"I'd hardly say he was living now. Is he in any pain?"

"That's a mystery, really," Seth replied. "The doctors have convinced my parents he can't feel a thing. But I don't see how they can be so sure, since he's got no way of *telling* us. And I just can't bear that place's rigid notion of humanity. I mean, he had pneumonia two years ago when tetracycline had barely come on the market. Why do they *have* to go to all that trouble to get hold of the newest wonder drug merely to prolong the guy's . . . existence?"

"It's wrong," Judy agreed. "And, just between us, that sort of thing goes on in my own ward all the time. There we *know* the cancer patients are in pain. But still the doctors keep on trying this new drug and that new drug. They use the patients for human guinea pigs."

"So I guess you've seen cases like Howie before, huh?"

She hesitated for a moment and then replied with pained candor, "No. I've never seen anything as bad—because it doesn't look like there'll be an end to it."

Seth nodded sadly, wondering if he dared confide in her the secret that was burning in his mind.

That someday he would put an end to Howie's suffering.

TWENTY

The students going off for Christmas vacation in 1959 had no notion that they would be returning to a year of great significance for them. They knew only that they would be paroled from laboratory drudgery.

They could not know that 1960 was to be the year of sit-ins in the South to force desegregation; that Chubby Checker's "Twist" would capture the whole nation; and that Israel would capture Adolf Eichmann.

That it would also turn out to be the year in which Professor Theodore Maiman perfected the first light amplification by simulated emission of radiation, otherwise known as LASER.

That November would see the election of young John Fitzgerald Kennedy.

And perhaps most important for their immediate lives, the first birth control pills would go on sale.

The course was Physical Diagnosis, its purpose to instruct the student—who heretofore had worked only with cadavers, test tubes, and a pinioned dog—in how to deal with patients.

The instructor, Professor Derek Shaw, wore his stethoscope like a High Priest's breastplate and had a manner as starched as his white coat. He began by describing the proper procedure of doing a "work-up" on a new patient—the ROS, or Review of Systems. He pointed out that in disease, more than in any other area, the past is truly prologue—the childhood illness father to the man's disease.

He warned them not to overlook any area of physiological activity—no system, vessel, gland, or organ. And he gave the fledgling examiners a very important piece of advice: "Most patients will be unaware of the medical terms for such functions as urination, defecation, and sexual intercourse. Thus you may have some difficulty making them understand your questions if you pose them in a strictly scientific manner—if you get my point. It may even be necessary to employ more vulgar terms."

Yes, Professor Shaw, the class all thought as one, we know the words you mean.

So after we check respirations and determine if there are any heart and vascular anomalies, prior problems with the stomach, kidneys, glands, nervous system, psychic history, we'll ask them if they're having any problems with pissing, or screwing.

It was finally time for hands on.

"Remember," Shaw intoned, "in medical investigation there is no technology, be it fluoroscope, x-ray—or even microscope—that will ever make the human senses obsolete. The fundamental instruments of diagnosis always will be eyes and ears and nose—some bacteria smell—and hands. And remember that the moment you touch your patient you give the impression that you already have begun to heal him.

"The body is a symphony of sounds which, if harmonious, play a lively melody and, if discordant, indicate that somewhere in the body's orchestra an instrument is playing out of tune.

"Thus our first exercise in diagnosis is the act of auscultation, learning to differentiate between the variety of sounds that are distinguishable only to the well-tuned ear.

"A *bruit* heard above a major artery indicates a vessel narrowing or partial obstruction. And in the thorax, which we might call the pulmonary Carnegie Hall, with the ribs providing the superb acoustics, the oboe-like bleating known as *egophony* will tell us of effusions in the membranes that surround the lungs. *Rales* emitted by the wind section can be designated 'tinkling,' 'whistling,' 'piping,' or 'low-pitched.' In any register they are an overture to bronchial dysfunction. Then the tympanic resonance—a low-pitched drumlike sound when we percuss a patient's chest with our fingertips—reveals the presence of a fluid or infection in the cavity beneath.

"And then, of course, there is the *souffle*—a murmur of the heart that, as it wanders up and down the scale, gives the suggestion that a valve is damaged."

Shaw did not continue his musical metaphors when he went on to the palpation of the four quadrants of the abdomen.

It was the professor's logical notion that the most likely bodies on which to begin examination would be one another's.

But there was instant rebellion. Not from the women, however. They were four and divided neatly into two sets of alternating doctors and patients. And then—for propriety's sake—they were taken to an adjoining room where they could perform the exercise without providing titillation to the masculine majority.

For understandable reasons, at first the men were loath to touch—and be touched—by their fellow classmates. Injecting one another had been one thing. Though painful, it had been merely skin deep. But bodily examination was quite another.

Who the hell would want Peter Wyman groping for his prostate, or manipulating his scrotum?

Professor Shaw was used to mass resistance, but never on such a scale.

It began as a sort of bronchial murmur, quickly escalating into spasmodic gasps of "No way. Nobody's finger's going up my ass." And—yes, quite audibly—"Fuck you, Shaw." But when, out of the corner of his eye, the professor noticed a few students beginning to slip out the rear exit, it became evident that he had a full-fledged mutiny on his hands.

Rather than give the entire class an immediate flunk, he declared new parameters for the initial session.

"Now, obviously, we can't do everything in a single class," he announced, hoping they would not hear capitulation in his voice, "so I think we should limit this first meeting to getting acquainted with heart sounds. The bruit, the murmur, the thrill, and fibrillation."

And to be certain of regaining their goodwill, he offered an enticing inducement for future sessions.

"Since these can sometimes literally mean life or death," he began with deadpan face, "no course of this nature can overlook the correct teaching of a thorough vaginal examination. Naturally, for this procedure we will have to invite some patients of a more . . . experienced nature. But for the moment let us listen to our hearts and learn their music."

The room hushed as fifty-eight stethoscopes lifted to study fifty-eight chests.

*   *   *

The ever-penitent Dwyer offered himself as a diagnostic lamb. He agreed to be Peter Wyman's partner. And his virtue was rewarded. Though he was the pain in the collective class's neck, Wyman nonetheless had great powers of observation.

"You've got tachycardia, Hank," he said, after listening to his partner's chest for what had seemed an inordinately long time.

"Come on, Pete," Hank persisted. "I'm twenty-three years old and fit as a fiddle."

"I'm sorry, Hank, I'll stick by my diagnosis. And if you don't want those kids of yours to be orphans, I think you'd better go to the Health Service. Although, frankly, I don't think they'll tell you any more than I can."

"Okay then, Peter, save me the trip."

"Well," Wyman said, "the first thing I'd advise is that you quit smoking."

"Aw, come on, I only have about half a pack a day. I'm under a lot of tension and it really helps. I mean, when you finish class you go back to a quiet little dorm room. I go home to a bedlam of screaming kids, dirty diapers, formulas, bottles—and a wife who's always bitching that I'm not helping enough."

"Look, Hank, there's published proof that links smoking and vascular disease, but it's your life, not mine. By the way, I also think you're much too overweight."

Hank Dwyer had a very long fuse. But he needed all of it to suppress his anger. "Would you like to know my appraisal of you, Wyman?"

"I'd be interested in hearing your speculation," Peter allowed.

"I'd say that you had a heart of stone and a face to match."

Hank then gathered his notebooks, stormed out of the classroom— and immediately lit a cigarette to calm his nerves.

During Christmas vacation Warren had accompanied his mother to Miami Beach to look at three or four apartments Aunt Ceil had designated as "real possibilities."

They finally found one nearing completion in Carlton Towers. Indeed, Estelle's actual apartment was still only air, as the twelfth floor was yet to be built. But they could imagine what a good ocean view it would have. And most important, in Warren's sage estimation, it was a condominium.

"It's the coming thing, Ma," the lawyer-to-be assured her, "and it's a sound investment."

"But aren't the payments a little high, Warren? I don't dare live over my means."

"No problem. I've worked everything out. With your pension you've got more than enough to live the life of Riley till I'm out earning big coin as a lawyer. And, sooner or later, old Barn'll finish that endless course of his and become a very rich doctor. Besides—Carlton Towers has got that extra little guest room so Barney or I can pop down for a weekend with our wives."

Estelle smiled. "And may I ask whom you intend to marry?"

"Sure. A great girl—fantastically gorgeous—has an A.B. from Barnard, a law degree from Yale, and she cooks like Julia Child."

"Wonderful. Have I met her?"

"No," Warren stated, "and neither have I. But I won't settle for anything less."

"Look," Estelle said with affectionate good humor, "the important thing is that you marry somebody you can talk to—who will be your friend. That was what your father and I had. You don't need these mythical creatures with Einstein's brain and Betty Grable's legs."

"Come on," Warren chided disapprovingly, "isn't Laura gorgeous and smart and nice—?"

Estelle nodded. "Yes, but sometimes I wonder if she—"

"If she what, Ma?"

"Well, unfortunately, I think that deep down she isn't very happy."

"Why?" Warren asked in genuine bewilderment.

"Maybe because she's *too* beautiful and *too* smart and *too* nice."

Even Laura did not have the strength to endure Christmas alone. Three hours earlier she had cheerfully waved goodbye to Barney and Suzie, who were setting out in one of Lance's cars for a cabin in Vermont, where they were looking forward to being snowed in by a blizzard all week.

Sitting in the lonely cafeteria, trying to eat lukewarm turkey that tasted like the artificial plastic decorations that were hung desultorily here and there, she was driven to such a point of unhappiness that she had decided to go home after all—even though her last Christmas there had been so catastrophic.

But when she trudged through the gray slush of Lincoln Place, she realized that her childhood landmarks had become completely foreign to her.

Even the Livingstons' house sat with its empty windows looking down forlornly at the red and green FOR SALE sign in front of it. That was all their neighbors had to offer as a festive decoration.

She walked timorously up her own steps. And was surprised to be greeted by affectionate hugs. Mama smiled and Luis smiled. They were—there was no better word—serene.

And at dinner she discovered why.

The Castellanos had a special Christmas guest—the handsome Cuban priest, Father Francisco Xavier. He said grace in Latin and then blessed all present.

The priest also provided the majority of conversation, too. Or what passed for conversation. It was mostly silence punctuated by, "Please pass the salad," "Some more roast, Father?" "Thank you, it was splendid."

But when they were having coffee, he looked at Laura and remarked, "So, you're going to be a female doctor, I understand."

"I'm going to be a doctor, yes," she replied pointedly.

"It is a noble calling blessed by Saint Cosmas and Saint Damian. Perhaps you do not know of them."

"Actually, I do. They were Christian martyrs who practiced a kind of socialized medicine and are more or less the patron saints of doctors."

"I am happy that you know so much about our religion."

"As it happens, I learned about them in a History of Science course, Father. That's how I also know about Saint Benedict—and the Knights Hospitalers of Saint John of Jerusalem. They were very compassionate people. I especially admire their monastic rule, 'Honor Our Lords the Sick.' "

"That's very good—I like that, Laura," said Luis with quiet pride. "We always should respect our suffering patients."

By Laura's unofficial count it was only the fourth time her father had spoken that evening.

"In fact," Luis continued, fixing his gaze directly on Father Francisco Xavier's face, "I think that's the best notion the Catholic Church has ever come up with. All too often, people worship *doctors*, make saints of us because we stick a little penicillin in them. It should be the other way around."

"That is an interesting point," said the priest politely. "Perhaps I can work it into a sermon."

"Will you be staying long in this diocese?" Laura inquired.

"As long as the Lord wishes me to," he replied softly. "Why do you ask?"

"Oh, I was wondering whether you might want to go back to Cuba now that things are better there."

"Better in what way?" the cleric asked.

"I mean, for the people," she answered. "Batista was a fascist dictator."

"But this Castro fellow is a Communist," the priest remarked with disapproval.

"He believes in all the things I fought for," Luis interposed with far more emotion than he had displayed all evening. "In Fidel's Cuba everyone will get his fair share."

Laura looked at her father with wonder. This is the kind of spirit he used to have. It was astonishing to see it back again.

She merely smiled at Luis. "It sounds like you wish you were there."

At this point Father Francisco Xavier coughed uncomfortably and then it suddenly became clear.

Laura looked at her father and said flatly, "Papa, you're not seriously thinking of *going* to Cuba?"

Luis nodded gravely. "Many doctors from the Batista regime have fled and I am needed."

"But aren't you a little—I don't know—old to be playing Ché Guevara?"

"The revolution is over," Luis answered with fervor. "It is now time to help build a new society."

Father Francisco Xavier bowed his head as if in prayer, and her mother's face was an expressionless mask.

Laura addressed a question to no one in particular. "Is this for real? I mean, is he serious?"

"I am going, *querida*," Luis said with calm resolve.

"And Mama?"

Her spiritual father chose to answer for Inez. "Your mother has made other plans. She will, so to speak, be joining us."

Now totally confounded, Laura turned to her mother.

"You mean you're becoming a *nun*?"

"No, Laurita," Inez replied softly, "I will be what is called a 'choir oblate'—*una lega*."

"A kind of lay sister," the priest interposed.

"I understand Spanish, thank you," Laura snapped at him.

"Calm yourself," Inez chastised. "It was Father who found this convent in upstate New York that needs Spanish-speaking helpers to visit the sick and counsel troubled families in their homes."

Laura was barely able to keep from screaming, What about *our* family, goddammit?

"I will be doing God's work," Inez explained further, "it will help to expiate my sins."

For the moment that was all the information Laura was to be

vouchsafed. She glanced at her father and saw a look of defeat in his eyes. She suddenly felt frightened—and achingly alone.

But to whom could she turn? Luis and Inez seemed to have abdicated their roles as parents.

At this point Father rose and took leave—he had to say Mass early in the morning. Inez stood up to see him out.

"Buenas noches," he said in valediction.

"Be careful walking back," Inez warned.

"God is with me, I have no fear," the priest replied as he went out into the night.

Luis could not keep himself from whispering sardonically to Laura, "Let's hope he's right. Because the Lord certainly wasn't with him when he was mugged three months ago and I had to sew five sutures in his cheek."

Now that the cleric had departed, Laura turned to accost her mother for abandoning her.

But Inez had disappeared. Didn't she even want to *talk* to me?

"Mama goes up early," Luis explained. "She spends some time in prayer, and then she goes to sleep. Come to my study and have a drink, *niña.*" He then added quickly, "I mean a Coca-Cola or something."

Laura nodded and followed her father into his private domain. She could not help noticing how neat it had become. The journals that had once been strewn like so many autumn leaves were now arranged on shelves.

Seeing his daughter's reaction, Luis explained, "Estelle showed me how to catalogue the books and journals. This way they will be much easier to pack. Coke, ginger ale, or club soda?"

"Anything," she replied distractedly.

Luis pried open a bottle of Canada Dry, poured it into a glass, and handed it to his daughter.

"Sit down. You're acting like a stranger here."

"I feel like one," she confirmed bitterly. "I mean, what the hell is going on in this family?"

Luis sat behind his desk, tilted his chair back, and lit up a cigar. "You heard most of it at dinner. I am going to Cuba—"

"For how long?"

"I am going to *live* in Cuba," he explained. "You know my greatest dream is to go back to a free Spain—but who knows if I will live long enough to see Franco dead? I admire Fidel, and Guevara is an intellectual with all the right ideas. . . ."

Laura listened in silence.

"Besides, as a doctor nowadays I spend more time with insurance documents than with patients. In Cuba medicine is free, and I can treat anyone who needs me."

He hesitated and she broke in, "And you're just leaving Mama in that—that nunnery?"

He raised his palms to the sky in a gesture of helplessness and answered, "It was her decision, Laurita."

He shifted forward, leaning his bulky frame on the desk.

"Once upon a time your mother and I were married," he began, "married in every way—the same ideals, the same beliefs, the same concerns about how we should raise our children. You cannot believe the hell we went through when we first were married. She had barely recovered from the bullet wounds when you came along and gave us joy—something to compensate for going into exile from a land we loved. Then Isobel . . ."

He paused and took a weary breath. "After everything else, that was the blow that brought your mother to her knees. Yes, you could say that was no metaphor. She was forever in the church at prayer. We never talked—I mean, of anything substantial. There was no hatred, no dissension, but what there was was worse—a wall of silence. Suddenly a marriage that had everything had nothing. . . .

"So we lived on as strangers. All her conversations were with God. It was as if she had left me all alone. I started drinking heavily. Yes, I know you noticed. But *niña*, there was nothing left I could believe in. . . ."

Laura felt a pang of hurt. Wasn't I any consolation at all—to either of you?

"Then there was Fidel. I saw him as my final chance to live my life out as a *verdadero hombre*. To be useful. Can you understand that?"

She simply nodded.

"When the Cuban Ministry of Health accepted me, I threw every goddamn bottle in the garbage and I haven't even had a drop of *Jerez* since. I have a purpose once again—"

Laura sat, her eyes unfocused, her mind trying to take it all in. "So you two are . . . separating?"

"I'm sorry, *querida*. This is the result of many years. But then, I somehow thought you sensed where things were going."

"And how did you originally plan to announce this to me—in a little postcard from downtown Havana?"

Her voice betrayed not merely fury but hurt as well.

"Everything was not certain until a few days ago," Luis replied by way of apology. "Besides, the only thing we both agreed on was that you were strong enough to take care of yourself. You always have been."

Laura did not know how to react. In all his meditations with himself, in all his grand planning, did her father ever once consider when—or if—or how they'd see each other again?

She did not know whether to shout in anger or break down—but she found herself sobbing.

In a moment Luis was there, his arm around her shoulder. "Please forgive me, Laurita. I know it was my fault. You see, I was afraid to tell you."

"Why are you doing this?" she asked tearfully. "What gave either of you the idea that because I'm grown up I don't still need parents?"

"*Querida*," he whispered soothingly, "soon you'll be married. You will *be* a parent. And you can all come visit with your *papacito* on the Veradero beach."

Laura stood up and shouted, "What makes you so damn sure I'll get married anyway?"

"This Palmer is a wonderful young man—"

"So marry him yourself!" she shouted. "Dr. Castellano, I know damn well you wouldn't do this if I were your *son*."

"That isn't fair," he protested.

"No, you're goddamn right, it isn't fair. Okay, you can read your Marx and Engels, I'm going to bed. I'll leave tomorrow on the first train, so don't look for me at breakfast. And tell my mother not to wait for me to write her."

Laura turned on her heels and walked to the door, but before leaving, whirled around to say, "You might do me the favor of sending my clothes and stuff to Vanderbilt Hall."

She turned again and slammed the door.

Luis Castellano stood thunderstruck. Had he now lost *two* daughters?

When Laura finally staggered into Vanderbilt Hall, it was as cold and empty as a tomb. She was greeted by the only other person pathetic enough to be around on a night like this.

"Hi, Laura. I'm amazed to see you here."

"Frankly, I'm amazed to be here."

"Wanna have Christmas dinner together?"

"Sure—what do you have in mind?"

"How about pizza?"

"Sure. Anything. Just wait till I lug my stuff up to the Deanery."

Fifteen minutes later she was wading through the snow toward Jacopo's Pizzeria with the class charmer—Peter Wyman.

Joy to the world!

Barney protracted his personal winter carnival as long as possible. In fact, he and Suzie didn't leave New Hampshire until after dinner on the last day and hence arrived at Vanderbilt just before midnight.

When they kissed and separated, it was to sleep on their own for the first time in more than a week. On the way to his room, Barney emptied his bulging mailbox. There were the usual bills and a few Christmas cards. Nothing really important. That is, until his eyes lit on an official-looking envelope from someone called "Esterhazy" at—The Morgue, City of New York.

Holy shit, he thought, does somebody want me to identify a body? What the hell can this be?

The moment he entered his room, he tore open the envelope and began to read a carefully typed letter.

Dear Barney,

I learned the ropes. What really happens in the loony bin is not that you get cured (that is a word even a fully analyzed psychiatrist would never pronounce), but, like an actor studying a role, you develop a characterization of a "normal" person. And when you finally get your act together, they're so delighted that they send you off into the world and put another notch in their couches.

Along the way, Dr. Cunningham turned out to be a really good guy—especially when he stopped taking my father's phone calls. He helped me figure out a lot of things for myself.

I still intend to be a doctor—not at Harvard—but somewhere where the rat race is more like a mouse jog. The important thing is going the distance. I've never known a patient to ask a doctor what his Basic Science grades were.

Did Sigmund Freud know Biochem?

Anyway, as you can see from this letterhead, I've conquered my neurotic fears of the viscera of dead bodies by doing the most counterphobic thing imaginable. Deep down, I'm still afraid, but at least I can deal with it—which is the name of the game, as I learned from Dr. Cunningham.

On the other hand, I have ceased to feel guilty about hating my father. He deserves it.

As of this writing he not only doesn't know where I am, he is unaware of who I am, since I have taken the original family name of Esterhazy. Which, I'm sure, he has totally suppressed.

If you are still reading this boring letter I'll close by saying that I will always think of you fondly as a friend and remain grateful for your kindness at a time when I most needed it.

I wish you a Merry Christmas and hope by now you've married that terrific Laura Castellano.

Yours,
Maury Esterhazy (né Eastman)

Wow, Barney thought to himself, "God bless us every one!" Good for Maury. They didn't zap the fire out of him.

This looked like it was going to be a helluva New Year, especially if the letter *he* was about to write got a favorable response.

He had just pulled out pen and paper when he thought he heard the phone ring down the hall. Never mind, it can't be for me. Then there was a knock on his door and the sleepy (and slightly annoyed) voice of Lance Mortimer hoarsely announced, "Phone, Livingston. Don't your admirers ever sleep?"

Barney dropped his pen and sprinted to the phone. Good old Suzie, she misses me already. In a matter of seconds the receiver was in his hand, and he gasped out, "Hi, baby."

The voice at the other end was timidly apologetic. "Barney, I'm really sorry to disturb you so late—"

It was Laura.

"Actually," she continued, "I've been trying to reach you for the past hour and a half. Hope I didn't wake you."

"That's okay, Castellano. What's up?"

"Nothing monumental. Just my whole world falling apart. I suppose it could wait till morning."

"Nothing doing. I'll meet you in the lobby right away."

"Are you sure it's okay?" she asked forlornly.

"Don't be an idiot. I'll be there in a sec."

Barney hung up and went back to his room.

He bent over and began to lace up his sneakers. A second later, as he stood up ready to rush off, he remembered that all-important letter he had been writing.

He went over to his desk and looked at it.

Dearest Susan,
I have two questions to ask you:
    1. Will you be my Valentine?
    2. Will you marry me?

Everything was there but the signature.

Should he sign it and drop it in her mailbox on the way?

No, it no longer seemed the proper time. He picked up the paper, crunched it into a ball and tossed it with an expert hook shot into the wastebasket.

And walked down to see Laura.

TWENTY-ONE

"Castellano, are you sure you haven't taken LSD?"

They were the only two people sitting in the lobby at that hour and their whispers echoed in the dome.

"Believe me, Barn, I wish I had. I'd like nothing better than to block out the reality of what I've just told you. I mean, who ever heard of a mother becoming a nun?"

"Well, she's not exactly taking Holy Orders. Didn't you say she'll only be a kind of lay sister?"

"What the hell's the difference? The point is my whole family's suddenly vanishing. I'm gonna be the only orphan in the world with two living parents." Her despair was palpable. How well Barney understood. For he himself had been grieving at the imminent loss of the beloved house of his youth. But at least he had the comfort of knowing his family would still be within reach. She had no place to go except a lousy little room in the Deanery.

"Laura," he said softly, "listen to me. First of all your mother's convent is just a few hours' drive from the city. And even Cuba's only ninety miles off the coast of Florida. If you get in shape you could practically swim there. . . ."

The absurd image of herself flailing through the ocean waves made her smile—but just for an instant.

"Anyway," Barney continued with quiet fervor, "remember you've still got me. And you'll always have a place to come home to. I mean, Estelle just bought this great big apartment in Miami."

She lowered her head and began to whimper.

"Listen, kiddo. I'm gonna take over the role of parent and give you a strict order. I want you to go up to your room, drink a glass of warm milk, and go right to bed. Now will you do what I say?"

She nodded and stood up. Barney also rose. And for a moment they both stood there motionless, inches from each other.

"Oh God, Barney," she murmured fondly, "what would I ever do without you?"

"Castellano, that's one problem you'll never have to face."

"Cheryl, dammit, can't you keep those kids quiet?"

"They may be twins, but they're separate people, Hank. They wake up at different times, they get hungry at different times, they get wet—"

"You don't have to tell *me*, for God's sake. How the hell am I supposed to study with this infernal racket?"

"And you don't have to shout, Hank."

"Oh, wonderful," he replied sardonically, "you can tell *me* to shut up, but you can't quiet two lousy little babies."

"Is that a way to refer to your children?"

"Oh, get off my back, willya?" He stood up, clapped his book shut, picked up his notes, and grabbed his coat.

"Where are you going?" Cheryl pleaded.

"Someplace quiet—the library. I've gotta learn every tiny detail of Physical Examination by tomorrow."

"Try examining your head while you're at it," she called after him. But her words were drowned out by the slamming of the door.

Let it not be said that Harvard Medical School was all work and no play. For, to be precise, it was all work and *one* play: the traditional second-year show. It was the uncensored product of exhausted, regressed, vengeful minds and a masterpiece of transcendental vulgarity.

It afforded a dramatic experience unique since Aristophanes. For the students knew that the targets of their wit (if you could call it that) were actually sitting in the theater as they were insulted.

This year's offering, entitled "Pubic Relations," marked a new high for low blows.

As in the rhapsody to their Anatomy teacher:

> *Lubar is a necro–phi–li–ac*
> *He loves to hump cadavers in the sack*
> *We ask him why he lives this kind of life*
> *He says that it reminds him of his wife.*

The triumph was due in large measure to the creative talents of Lance Mortimer. As soon as the curtain fell, Dean Holmes rushed over to compliment the author.

"Mortimer, you've got a truly amazing gift for filth. I think you should have become a pornographer, not a doctor."

"I may have to, sir, if I don't pass Biochem." As he proceeded to the reception, Lance congratulated himself on his instinct. Tonight's scatological extravaganza had won the hearts and dirty minds of the guys that count.

To help them put their studies in a proper context, the students were offered a brief series of lectures under the generic title Social Medicine. Those expecting spiritual uplift were disappointed when the first speaker, a representative of the American Medical Association, inveighed against socialized medicine. "Let us not forget that Lenin declared that 'socialized medicine is the keystone to the arch of the socialist state.' "

And he went on to denounce disability insurance as "another step toward wholesale nationalization of medical care."

"What do you think?" Barney asked Lance as they shuffled out of the room after the passionate harangue.

"Oh, I don't know, he had some interesting things to say."

Laura arrived just in time to hear Lance's comment.

"Lance, it's a fact that poor people get sicker and have shorter lifespans than rich people. Do you think that's fair? That guy was preaching a sort of elitist medicine: 'pay now, live later.' I only wish I'd had eggs to throw at that bastard."

Barney smiled at her outburst, while Lance meekly countered, "Well, Laura, different strokes for different folks."

"No, Lance, the *same* strokes for the *same* folks. And I hope you notice we've not heard anything from the opposition. I mean, they should have had somebody here from the Committee for the Nation's Health. They're good guys—only they're practically as poor as the people they're fighting for. The AMA spends millions of dollars every year just to undercut any kind of national health insurance."

"Well," Lance allowed liberally, "it's a free country, Laura."

"No, it isn't, Lance, in the world of health care it's a very expensive country."

"Oh, come on, get off your soapbox, willya?"

Laura did not deign to answer. She merely turned and walked off.

"Is she some kind of Communist?" Lance asked Barney.

"No, old buddy, she's just a sensitive human being with a real social conscience."

"Well, if that's the case," Mortimer quipped, "she's certainly come to the wrong place."

None of the men could sleep the night before the next class exercise. What, they asked themselves—and sometimes each other—were they so afraid of?

"After all," Barney reasoned, "we're acting as if we're going into uncharted territory. But the vagina is really one part of the body we've actually been on *both* sides of. In one way we could look at it as a sort of homecoming."

"That is first class bullshit," Bennett countered as he distributed bottles of Heineken to the coterie that had gathered in his room to share—and hopefully exorcise—their anxieties about having to perform their first pelvic exam on the morrow.

"Yeah," Lance agreed, "why don't you admit it, Livingston, you're scared. We all are."

"I didn't say I wasn't scared, I was just trying to help us 'calm out.' Anyway, why don't we listen to the voice of experience?"

He pointed to Skip Elsas, his one-time basketball teammate, a fourth-year student and therefore someone who had actually been through this ordeal.

"Come on, Elsas, give out," Bennett urged.

"To be absolutely frank, guys," Skip began, "that first pelvic exam is one of the scariest things you'll ever have to do. I don't care how much experience you studs have had, you've never shone a lamp a few inches from the honeypot and examined it clinically. Besides, if you don't know what you're doing, you can cause the woman a lot of pain. The first thing to remember is to warm the damn speculum. I mean, how would *you* feel if somebody put a pair of cold metal tongs into one of your orifices?"

A hand rose for a question. "Can't we use lubricant?" asked Hank Dwyer.

"No, no. Your first job is to take clean cell samples—Pap smear, that kind of thing. Oh, yeah, and a culture for gonorrhea, too."

"You mean we're going to be sticking our noses right into potential VD land?" Lance complained with outrage.

"Nobody said anything about using your nose," Skip responded with a tiny smile.

There was scattered nervous laughter.

"Okay," he continued, "when you get the speculum in, you open it, and—if you've positioned it right—you'll be able to get a view of the cervix, which is down and posterior. You'll know when you've found it 'cause it looks like a big pink eye. Then you do your smears and gently get the hell out."

Now a collective sigh of relief.

"Wait," Skip protested, his arms raised like a policeman stopping traffic, "that's only half the job. Now you can put some K-Y jelly on the second and third fingers of your examining hand (he demonstrated) and do your bimanual exam. That's two fingers into the vagina—which may be a more familiar procedure to some of you."

He waited for appreciative chuckles, but they were not forthcoming.

"Anyway, you put your other hand on the abdomen and try to assess the size and condition of the uterus—which normally feels sort of like a lemon. The secret is trying to look like you know what you're doing. The whole damn thing should take less than five minutes. Oh—and one last thing, you're going to have to keep a tight rein on your feelings because, believe it or not, the first few times it can be kinda . . . sexually stimulating."

He paused and then said, "Any questions?"

Hank Dwyer's hand shot up frantically.

"Yeah?" Skip inquired.

"You did say that the cervix is *pink,* didn't you?"

He nodded.

"Well," Hank continued self-consciously, "I've been, uh, doing a little practice. You know—with my wife—"

"Yeah?" Skip urged him on. "And what seems to be the problem?"

"Well, I kinda flipped my lid at what you said. I mean, my wife's cervix looks—well—*blue.* Could something be wrong?"

"Well," their expert replied, "I can see you haven't studied your textbook, old buddy. That's called 'Chadwick's sign.' "

Hank's usual pallor turned white. "Is that serious?"

"Well," Elsas said, "that depends on you and your wife. A blue cervix means she's pregnant."

To which the erstwhile priest replied, "Holy shit!"

The murderer struck again. A year after his first visit he (or she) entered the dog labs in the dead of night and randomly killed six specimens.

The faculty was tempted to call in the police but Dean Holmes cautioned against it. The Humane Society had always been agitating against the use of animals for lab experiments and this unfortunate incident would only be a call to arms for them.

"I think the best course is, as it were, to let sleeping dogs lie," he suggested in a secret strategy session with Professor Lloyd Cruikshank and the lab assistants. "We've got to solve this mystery in-house."

The dean pressed on. "Do we have any clues? We know he used overdoses of the usual painkiller, but is there any kind of pattern to this character's behavior? I mean, did he always kill the same breed—bigger ones, smaller ones . . ."

Mike, one of the assistants, raised his hand. "Well, the dogs were pretty well mutilated, sir."

"I don't follow."

"Well, as you know, some of those students are better with their scalpels than others. The lousy ones can really butcher the dogs' insides."

"And cause them pain," the dean suggested.

"Well, they're anesthetized but, yes, some of the dogs probably suffer during the last few procedures."

"I take your point, Courtney," said Professor Cruikshank, speaking directly to the dean. "Do you think we're dealing with a self-styled mercy killer?"

Holmes nodded. "I think all the evidence points in that direction."

Professor Cruikshank continued, "This started last year so wouldn't it be safe to say it would be someone now in the sophomore class?"

"Do any of you know any crackpots or nutty overaltruistic types from last year? Usually they make themselves known by delivering a sermon on cruelty to animals."

Cruikshank and his assistants were again deep in thought. Finally, Mike remembered. "The day after last year's incident, that black guy kind of objected to Professor Cruikshank bringing in new dogs just for the final experiment."

"That would be Bennett Landsmann," the dean offered.

"Yes, sir, I believe that's his name."

"If he's the perpetrator, I'm afraid we'll have to hush this up," the dean commented.

"Come now, Courtney," Cruikshank retorted. "Just because the chap's a Negro—"

"I didn't hear that," Holmes replied sternly. "Now, Dr. Cruikshank, may I speak to you privately?"

The professor motioned to his junior men, who quickly made themselves scarce.

Then he demanded, "What the hell is the big secret?"

"I take it the name Landsmann doesn't mean anything to you, Lloyd. Don't you read *The Wall Street Journal*?"

"Of course."

"Then you may have read that Federated Clothing has just bought out Royal Leathercraft—wholly owned by Mr. Herschel Landsmann—for twenty-eight million dollars. . . ."

"And?"

"To mark the occasion, and to express his gratitude to the university for educating his son, Mr. Landsmann has given us a donation—which he insisted be anonymous—of one million dollars."

Cruikshank whistled. "My God. Do you know the young man?"

"Yes, a bit—and he's a solid citizen and he doesn't seem the type. It's very possible he isn't the culprit."

"I guess that means we're still stuck with a lunatic stalking the halls."

"Let's not get carried away, Lloyd, he's only killed a few dogs."

"So far, Courtney," Cruikshank cautioned.

A group of them stood outside the gynecology examination room, uneasy in their ill-fitting white coats. They felt slightly fraudulent, pretending to be experts when they were little more than tourists in a land to which they had no visa.

Grete Andersen emerged, a look of smug satisfaction on her face.

"How did it go?" asked a nervous classmate.

"No problem. The patient was really happy to see a woman examiner who *knows* what it feels like." And she undulated off, while one or two of them fantasized about what examining *her* might be like.

Barney's name was called. He entered the room tentatively and was taken aback by what he saw. For his patient was already lying in the "lithotomy position," her heels in stirrups with a paper sheet draped across her from the waist down—so *she* would be unable to examine him examining her. A small blue-white spotlight was illuminating the precise area he would scrutinize.

Following correct medical procedure, a female attendant was present, as chaperone and assistant. She helped him don his surgical gloves, then moved away so he could perform the examination.

Barney looked at the patient. She was a peroxide blond in her middle forties, perhaps a little heavily made up.

"Hi," he said in what he hoped would be a reassuring tone, "I'm Dr. Livingston and I'll be doing a cervical checkup just to see if everything's okay. Please be relaxed and be sure to tell me if it hurts. I mean—it shouldn't hurt. I've done this thousands of times." (This was an addition that Skip had suggested privately.)

To which his patient replied with a single word: "Bullshit."

Refusing to believe what he had heard, Barney proceeded to examine the external genitalia to see if they were inflamed, atrophied, or otherwise. Gingerly he separated the labia and dictated to the nurse, "No vaginal discharge, no abnormalities of the clitoris."

A further perusal assured him that the thighs, mons veneris, and perianal region were all normal.

Now it was time to use the speculum. He picked it up from the tray—it was the Pedersen model that looked roughly like a duck's beak. It felt cold and he asked the nurse to run the hot water tap so he could warm it.

Once again he told his patient to relax. Then, taking a deep breath, he separated the labia with the gloved fingers of his left hand and inserted the speculum into the vagina in a downward direction (to avoid the urethra).

He reached the cervix with, he thought, minimal discomfort to his patient. At least all he heard was one murmured "Oh shit." Okay, he was there. Now it was time to fix the blades in an open position by tightening the screw lock at his end. He then took a cervical spatula and gently scraped the interior of the vagina for mucus, which he put onto a specially prepared slide. Then he handed the Pap smear to the nurse who would—at least theoretically—send it to the lab to be analyzed.

He had to spray the slide with some kind of cytologic fixative to keep it pristine. Trying to lower his voice half an octave—to sound older and wiser—he ordered, "Spray please, nurse."

Without another word she handed him a bottle of—no, it couldn't be—Revlon hair lacquer. He stared at her in disbelief. She smiled and replied ingenuously, "That's what *all* the doctors use, sir."

"Oh," Barney replied. "Yes, of course. Many thanks."

He was halfway through. Now the manual. As he held his hand out and the nurse squeezed lubricant on his fingers, he thought it might be good bedside manner once again to reassure his patient. But, paradoxically, having probed her private parts he was now embarrassed to look her in the face.

"Okay," he said confidently, but with his eyes averted, "if we just stay relaxed this next part won't hurt a bit."

To which his patient replied, "*I'm* relaxed." Which did wonders for Barney's confidence.

Putting his left palm on her abdomen he began to insert his lubricated fingers into the vagina, at which point he heard the disconcerting sound of the patient breathing in low rapid breaths.

"Are you all right, ma'am?" he asked anxiously.

"You forgot to tell me to do this, Doc. Short breaths keep the abdominal wall from tensing."

"Oh. Yes. Of course. Many thanks."

With his patient gently guiding his left hand, he was able to locate the uterus and determine its position, size, consistency, contour, and mobility. Then he swiftly checked the ovaries, and, in the words of the great not-quite-doctor Elsas, "got the hell out."

He concluded the visit with a gallant "Thank you, ma'am, you've been a good sport."

"Thanks, kid, you weren't too bad yourself."

At the best of times meals in the cafeteria were strictly stag affairs, though Laura was frequently an exception to this. But tonight even she conjoined with others of her gender.

It was a natural reaction. For the female students alone had truly empathized with the creatures whose heels were fixed in the stirrups as they opened their private parts to the maladroit manipulation of the opposite (tonight it was more like opposing) sex.

But the men were not insensitive to the fact that several of them had caused their patients anxiety, discomfort, and pain.

Bennett was one of the most penitent. "I know I hurt this woman," he kept repeating. "She sort of stifled her moans. But I just couldn't find the cervix. Anyway, it felt like hours till I did."

"I'm glad I didn't get yours, Landsmann," Barney remarked frankly. "I mean, my patient had more fun than I did. When she wasn't putting me down she was just sort of laughing under her breath. Who the hell would want to be a gynecologist?"

"Oh, come on, Livingston," Lance protested. "These weren't garden-variety Mary Poppins types. These were pros."

"What do you mean, pros?"

"You're a jock, Livingston, let me put it in sporting terms. What Bill Russell is to basketball, these gals are to sex."

Barney's jaw dropped. "No way—you're just putting us on."

"Really," Lance replied. "Scout's honor. The next time you want to do a pelvic on one of them it'll cost you twenty-five bucks at the Hotel Berkeley."

* * *

"Cheryl, why the hell didn't you tell me you were pregnant?"

"Hank, I wasn't sure. I mean, how did you know?"

"Well, as it happens, I could see by the color of your cervix."

"I don't understand. Are you angry because I'm pregnant, or just because I didn't tell you?"

He took a moment before answering. "A little of both, I guess. I mean, haven't we got our hands full with the twins? How are we going to pay for all this?"

"Your Harvard insurance will cover the maternity part. What other sacrifice is involved?"

"Well, you may not think so, but I regard sexual deprivation as a sacrifice."

"Not *all* the time, Hank. I mean, modern obstetricians say—"

"Don't tell me what doctors say, dammit—it's *my* place to tell *you*. And don't say you were enthusiastic after the twins were born. I practically had to rape you."

"Are you trying to say we should have used some sort of birth control?"

"Well, there are pills—Enovid, Ovrol—on the market now."

"We're Catholic, remember?"

"Oh, come on, honey, join the twentieth century. I bet you even John F. Kennedy's wife is on the Pill."

"She happens to be pregnant right this minute, Hank."

"Jesus, you've got an answer for everything, haven't you?"

Suddenly tears were coursing down Cheryl's cheeks. "I don't know you anymore, Hank. You're blaspheming all the time. You keep shouting at me. I thought I was marrying a saint, and you're turning into a monster."

He could not bear the sight of her crying. He took her in his arms and whispered, "I'm sorry. I must be overworked or something. Actually I think it's great. Maybe this time we'll have a boy."

Barney was immersed in study when there was yet another series of knocks on his door.

"Hey, come on," he grouched, "can't you see that DO NOT DISTURB sign?"

"Hey, loosen up, Barn," came a voice from the other side. "This is your distinguished colleague, Dr. Landsmann."

Well, Barney thought to himself, at least Ben isn't here to ask my spiritual advice. (Come to think of it, why not? He's the only one who never has.)

He opened his door. "Quick, Landsmann, I'm studying to be a doctor. What's happening?"

"I bring earthshaking news from Olympus!"

"Which is?"

"The Malpractice Cup—"

"No way," said Barney, waving his arm as if to hold off a missile. "There's no force on earth that's going to get me back on that court."

"Calm out, Livingston," Bennett said jovially. "Listen to the tidings I bring." He reached in his jacket pocket, withdrew a piece of paper, and handed it to his agitated friend. "I suppose there's one of these waiting in your mailbox as well—this year's competition is canceled."

"What?" Now Barney's face betrayed disappointment. "Why?"

"Well, the official word from Dean Holmes is something to the effect that medical studies involve too much dedication to allow for such frivolities. . . ."

"Like hell. What's the real story?"

"Well, my humble guess is that since the Shysters have now got—in addition to Mack the Truck, who's still only in his second year—two new freshmen who've played in the NBA, Dean Holmes is going the Falstaff route."

Barney nodded. " 'Discretion is the better part of valor.' And, no doubt, the series will resume as soon as the Truck and his Trucklets graduate."

Bennett smiled. "I think we ought to have a drink to celebrate. I've hidden two bottles of suds outside your door."

Good man, Bennett. I wish I had more guests like you.

Barney kept the celebration brief, since he was expecting Suzie. Scarcely a half hour after Bennett's departure, there was another knock on Barney's door. And it was not followed by Suzie's dulcet voice.

"Livingston's not here," he called out.

"Please, Barney. I've got to see you."

It was Laura. Her expression reflected her tone. She looked on the verge of tears.

"I'm sorry, Barn, I know I'm being a real pain in the ass. But it's something that can't wait." She entered, carrying her green book bag behind her.

"Sit down," Barney offered hospitably, pointing to his twelve-dollar, fourteenth-hand easy chair.

She shook her head. "I'd rather stand, if it's okay. I was doing some extra work in the lab so I didn't get my mail till just now. That noble

Father Francisco Xavier was helping my mother clear out the house when he found what he calls a treasure trove of my father's writings. There's one in particular that shook me to my boots."

"Can I see it?"

"It's in Spanish." She fumbled in her book bag for the tan envelope. "Read the first one. I'll translate if you have any trouble."

She handed Barney a sheaf of yellowing lined paper. He scanned the first page, and read, *"Llanto para un hijo nunca nacido."* He looked up at her.

"Elegy for an unborn son," she translated.

"I understood that," Barney said softly. "I was just a little surprised that he carried his fantasies so far."

"It wasn't a fantasy. It's about a boy he had to abort from a woman. . . ."

"Your mother?"

She nodded. "It seems that she was pregnant when she was wounded—though neither of them ever bothered to tell me. And Luis had to sacrifice the child—his *son*—to save her life." In a futile attempt to shrug off this burden, she commented, "It's pretty lousy poetry."

Barney stood, took her hands, and led her to the chair. "Will you sit down, for chrissake?"

She obeyed him mutely. He tried to offer some mitigating insights.

"This explains a lot of things, Castellano. I mean, not just his obsession with having a son, but the fact that I've always felt your mother was angry at him for something. Now we know why."

She looked at him, dark rings around her wide blue eyes. "And what the hell good does knowing do? Luis resented the fact that I was alive and his 'son' wasn't, and *she* resents the fact that I'm alive and my sister isn't. I feel like obliging both of them and jumping out the window."

"No way, Castellano. I can tell you from personal experience that a leap from this height will merely break your bones and send you to the loony bin. My professional advice is that you remain alive."

"And do what?"

"Sit here and talk to me," he answered quietly.

He went to the door, replaced his DO NOT DISTURB sign, and returned to listen to Laura for the next three hours.

TWENTY-TWO

"Suzie, what the hell happened to you last night?"

It was breakfast time. Suzie was sitting in a corner, now and then nibbling her blueberry muffin or taking a sip of coffee. But never looking Barney in the face.

"Please, Suzie?"

Still averting her gaze, she said softly, "You made a fool of me."

"*What?*"

"I know when I got to your room you had someone there already. That wasn't very gallant of you, Barney. You should at least take a break—like a fighter between rounds."

He sat down across from her and pleaded, "But you don't understand, it was only Laura."

"What do you mean 'only'? You had a beautiful girl in your room when you were supposed to be waiting for me."

"Please, Suzie, how many times do I have to tell you she's just a friend?"

"Then how come you didn't answer when I knocked?"

"I didn't hear you. Maybe you just weren't loud enough."

"Look, I didn't want to make a French farce out of the whole thing, so I rapped quietly. It was enough humiliation for me to do that."

Barney slapped his palm to his forehead in frustration. "Jesus, Suzie, you know I wouldn't lie to you." He looked across the table, his eyes pleading. "Suzie, I love you. Haven't I told you that a million times?"

"Yes," she answered shyly, "and I wanted to believe it."

"I mean, I want to marry you," he blurted out.

There was a ripple of surprise in her otherwise impassive demeanor. "Do you?" she asked softly.

"Yes, Suzie, really. Really, really."

"I wish I could believe you," she said wistfully.

"What the hell's stopping you?"

"You said 'really' too many times. Like you were trying to convince yourself—not me."

At which she rose, and gracefully left the cafeteria.

Barney sat there, his head in his hands. And, like a child being pacified, distractedly finished Suzie's muffin and coffee.

He did love her, he assured himself. But then he was forced to concede that he didn't really, really, *really* love her.

Clinical rotations began and the doctors-to-be were overjoyed at the prospect of working with patients in Harvard's many teaching hospitals. They did not, however, realize that their duties would entail what was colloquially known as "scutwork." Unqualified as doctors—or as nurses— they were the lowest caste of all and therefore saddled with countless menial tasks. Like trudging back and forth from the patients' bedsides to the lab with blood, urine, and other samples. When they were not occupied with such duties, they had to write up the case notes and—worst of all—deal with filling out the endless insurance forms. It didn't take long for them to realize that they were paying thousands of dollars tuition for the privilege of saving the Med School money by doing unskilled labor for no salary at all.

They began to regard the task of drawing blood as a rare privilege. And sometimes in the middle of the night they were awakened to be accorded the dubious honor of reinserting an I.V. needle. But that was because the upperclassmen were too smart to get out of their beds for something so trivial.

The clinical rotations were to acquaint them with the major specialties of the healing art so they could choose which path (or pathology) they would ultimately follow.

Surgery and Internal Medicine were obligatory. After that there was a broad spectrum of specialties and subspecialties like Obstetrics, Pediatrics, Psychiatry, Neurology, Ophthalmology, Urology—even, for those so inclined, Proctology.

The once more-or-less cohesive class was now fragmented into tiny groups. Whereas before they had been able to take some solace in the fact that all one hundred and twenty of them were suffering at the hands of tyrants like Pfeifer, they now had to face the equally formidable physicians in groups of two to ten.

Barney and Bennett counted themselves lucky that they were assigned to the Brigham. For although more often than not they would go on different ward rounds with their respective clinical instructors, they were at least in the same building and could enliven each other's drudgery. Barney devised an entertainment which he dubbed "the Schleppers' Olympics." It involved several unusual disciplines, all of which forbade the use of the hospital elevator.

First there was the four-floor dash with hands free. Then followed sprints carrying various implements, samples, etc. And Bennett devised a "mini javelin contest." The challenge was how many patients' veins you could get into on the first shot with your needle and draw blood. The loser had to pay for dinner, during which they would discuss that week's "accomplishments."

Though they were on the same Internal Medicine rotation, it was impossible to believe they were doing the same tasks. For they had diametrically opposed views of them.

"There's no action, Barn," Bennett complained. "No wonder the internists are called 'fleas.' They just crawl around on the outside, peeking into little corners. I mean, I can't see spending a lifetime hypothesizing about what may or may not be happening inside a person's body."

"I think it's fascinating," Barney rebutted, "the detective work involved in putting little clues together to solve a mystery. Why not go in for Radiology, Landsmann? Then you could spend all day alone in the dark with x-ray eyes."

"No thank you, Dr. Livingston. I'm for surgery, the real *vita activa.*"

"Well," Barney remarked, "you know the old chestnut about the different kinds of doctors: The fleas know everything and do nothing, the surgeons know nothing and do everything."

"Yah—and psychiatrists know nothing and do nothing."

Barney laughed. Bennett followed up his thought. "Why are you bent on spending the rest of your life in an easy chair acquiring adipose tissue on your ass and telling people they shouldn't love their mothers?"

"Come on, Ben, there are literally millions of walking wounded out there who need help. Sometimes I think we should all be institutionalized."

"And indeed we have been, Doctor," Bennett chuckled. "We're all in the hospital already."

They had both come off duty at 5:30 P.M. and were not expected in the hospital until seven the next morning. And as they were ambling slowly back to Vanderbilt Hall in the gathering twilight, Barney risked a question.

"Ben, you've never really told me what made you go into medicine. I mean, you once said your dad was a shoemaker. Was it a kind of dream of your folks that you go into a profession?"

"No," Bennett answered, "they didn't push me in any direction. I just decided to go into something that might make the world a little better."

"Come on, Landsmann. I'm not interviewing you for admission. I'm your buddy. Can't you come up with a more plausible reason? God knows I've bored you with the details of my Brooklyn youth. And I'll bet your childhood is a helluva lot more interesting."

"Okay, Livingston." Bennett smiled. "As a special favor to you, I'll search my soul right here in the middle of the street. I guess the reason I went into medicine is because a young doctor—actually, he was only a med student—saved my mother's life."

"Now we're cooking," Barney replied passionately. "What happened? Was she in an accident?"

"No," Bennett said quietly. "Not unless you call Hitler an accident. One of the Fuehrer's medical apostles used her for a human guinea pig."

"Holy shit," Barney whispered under his breath.

"When the Allies liberated the camp, my mother was in the terminal stage of an acute endometrial infection. This British med student did emergency surgery in the most primitive conditions and saved her life."

"Jesus!" Barney exclaimed. "But hey, I never knew there were blacks in the concentration camps."

"My mother is Jewish," Bennett replied.

"Ah," said Barney, smiling, "now it all comes clear. Let me conjure up the rest of the romantic tale. Your father—obviously with Patton's Third Army, since you've got that cigarette case with his insignia—liberated the camp and they fell in love. Right?"

"Half right."

"Which half?"

"This is going to confuse you, Barney. My *father* liberated my *parents*."

"Hey, wait a minute, Ben, I'm lost. Can we start with first principles— like birth? Who the hell is your father?"

"My father *was* Colonel Lincoln Bennett, Senior, U.S. Army, deceased 1945. My 'parents' are Herschel and Hannah Landsmann of

Berlin, Nordhausen Concentration Camp, and, currently, Cleveland, Ohio. You see, Hannah was in really bad shape and it was my natural father who browbeat the doctors into trying to save her life. But then, ironically, *he* died of typhus. When they got to America the Landsmanns tracked me down and, to make a long story short, when they adopted me I took Bennett as a first name."

"Okay, I think the pieces are starting to fit. Now do I take it that it's Mr. Landsmann who's the shoemaker?"

Bennett nodded.

"By the way you dress and jet-set around, I guess he must have a pretty successful store."

"Well actually, the shoes are made by his factories. His 'shop' is called Royal Leathercraft."

"What a story," Barney murmured. Then the thought struck him. "But what about your natural mother? Where is she in all this?"

Bennett's face tightened. "I don't know, Barn. I don't have a single memory of the woman."

"Well, you're luckier than most. You've actually got three parents that you're proud of. Most people don't even have any."

Bennett laughed and put his arm around his classmate. Barney was touched by this unprecedented demonstration of affection.

Laura was doing her Internal Medicine rotation at the Mass General. Running in the pony express between patients and lab, learning how to take pulse, blood pressure, and palpate the major organs for anomalies— and taking endless medical histories from new patients.

She was already encountering the difficulties of being a woman in a man's profession. When she tried to record medical details from a construction worker with kidney stones, she found him less than cooperative about discussing anything below his navel.

"But sir," she protested, "I've got to write this up or you'll never have your operation. Do you want those kidney pains forever?"

"Look, lady, I got nothing to hide, but if I gotta talk about personal things like passing water and private parts, I'll tell it to a doctor, not some blond nurse."

"I beg your pardon, sir," she retorted. "I take umbrage at that."

"The hell you will," he responded. "The only thing I'll let you take is my pulse."

Grete was not having it any easier. Yet her worst experience came from a doctor, not a patient.

She had chosen Surgery as her first rotation and was doing the usual scutwork: holding retractors to keep wounds open while the Big Knife himself entered the body in order to, as they always put it, "cut to cure."

On rare occasions some of the more advanced students were allowed to put in the final sutures. And Grete got her chance when Dr. Malcolm McBride invited her to join him in sewing up. In good pedagogical fashion, he took each of her hands in his, helped her grasp the needle in her right and move along with him down, through, and up in order to close the incision.

Grete immediately began to sense that something was wrong, for not only could she feel the surgeon's body behind her but, with every movement of his arms, he was brushing by her breasts.

Did anybody notice what he was doing to her? Did they notice that their teacher's breathing had become more rapid? Or were they mesmerized by the suturing hands?

"I can't go back into that room. I just can't."

As soon as she returned to Vanderbilt Hall, she had rushed to tell Laura.

"What should I do?" she asked tearfully. "Besides rubbing my breasts with his arms, he was pushing his . . . inguinal area against my backside. I felt like stabbing him with the needle."

"You should have," Laura replied.

"That's easy to say," Grete protested. "But would *you* risk flunking Surgery for something no one else could see?"

The question gave Laura pause. No, she probably wouldn't have done anything if the guy had stopped short of rape.

"Think of it this way, Grete," she said reassuringly. "It's just a lousy little 'feel.' I mean, if the guy's so twisted that he's satisfied with that kind of cheap thrill, have pity on him. I mean, we'll be damn lucky if we get through the next two years with nothing more than this."

"Bless me, Father, for I have sinned. Since my last confession, I have committed fornication."

"Yes, my son."

"And often lately."

A pause.

"First there were those girls in the Med School class. Grete—and then Laura. I feel worst about her, Father, because she's a Catholic, too. Actually, we've even prayed together in this church. What shall I do, Father?"

"My son, we must all be careful to avoid the occasions of sin and particularly the sins of the flesh. But above all you must endeavor to uphold the teachings of the Catholic faith. Pray for strength, my son, and I will pray for you."

"Yes, Father."

"For your penance, say The Stations of the Cross three times. Now make a good Act of Contrition . . . *Absolvo te in nomine patris et filii et spiritus sancti.*"

"But Father—I'm still scared."

"Of what, my son?"

"These were only fornications in my *mind*. I'm scared I might actually do it."

There was no reply from the other side of the confessional box.

Hank Dwyer left the cathedral, his soul cleansed and his spirit renewed.

Laura hated Surgery.

Not just for the more obvious blood-and-guts aspect but because it was so physically exhausting to stand guard on a retractor for two or three hours—as vessels or viscera were detached, resected, ligated, or removed. She had seen enough of the "heavy work," too: broken leg bones being repaired like pieces of wood by a carpenter, then everything stitched over with materials as varied as nylon, kangaroo gut, and silk. It somehow seemed like an assembly line in Detroit.

She felt more at home talking to pre-op patients, trying to calm their dread and watching them surrender to the anesthetic with the help of her tranquilizing words.

The post-op room was harrowing. Now and then she had the joy of seeing a patient to whom she had spoken revive smiling, happy, and on the way to health. But usually, even if the procedure had been successful, they were in considerable pain and nothing in her vocabulary could relieve their distress.

And then, of course, there were those who did not wake up at all. . . .

She would return from the hospital each evening well after dinner, and barely have the strength to go down to the sandwich machines.

Almost every day there was a letter waiting from Palmer. Or "Second Lieutenant Talbot" as he now sometimes referred to himself.

God, she thought, why did I push that guy away? Here he is going to exotic places in the Pacific, probably meeting dozens of pliant, nubile maidens. Though his letters vowed fidelity and implied celibacy, she was sure he was really having a hot time.

For her part, she maintained her sexual independence and had a couple of desultory affairs with interns that did not amount to much. And, after incessant pressure, she even gave in to the importunate Gary Arnold, the narcissistic neurosurgeon back in Boston for an interview.

But their second encounter was equally short-lived. Gary had an irritating tendency to pontificate.

Late one Sunday evening, as they were lying in bed, he stared up at the ceiling and murmured, "You don't like sex, do you, Laura?"

"What?" She had been half-asleep.

"I simply observed that you don't seem to enjoy making love."

"Are you implying that I've got a problem, Gary?"

"Well, to be perfectly honest, I think you should perhaps talk to someone about it some day."

"You know," Laura replied, gradually growing more and more awake, "you may have a point there. The more I think of it, the more I realize that sex isn't all that much fun—"

"Ah," said the doctor, in the same tone that Archimedes had long ago said *Eureka*.

"No, Gary, what I mean is *I* don't enjoy sex with *you*."

As the suddenly autistic neurologist groped for an appropriate response, Laura dressed, put on her coat, and headed for the door, leaving a farewell present for the good doctor.

"You know *your* problem, Gary? You confuse your mind with your penis—which is perfectly understandable, since they're both pretty pathetic."

At which she smiled demurely and tiptoed out of his life.

A dutiful son, Seth Lazarus called home every weekend. His mother would always ask, "What's new?" And he would run their tired—almost vaudevillian—gambit of, "Nothing much. I just cured cancer, heart attacks, toothaches, and mosquito bites." To which she would then offer her usual comment, "And what *else* is new?"

After this his father would get on to monologize away about the various Chicago teams and their prospects.

The dull, disheartening formula never varied. Seth wondered why he bothered to spend the money.

But one weekend he got no answer. Neither at home nor downstairs in the store. They could not have gone off on a vacation because they never did. Indeed, they must have made a kind of tacit vow not to after Howie went into the hospital. They probably thought themselves unworthy of any further joy in life. But where *were* they?

He phoned Judy, an activity he usually saved for weekday nights from one minute past eleven ad infinitum. She knew immediately why he'd called.

"I'm sorry, Seth, but your parents made me promise not to say anything. It's Howie. . . ."

She paused and Seth succumbed to the secret wish that this would be the long-awaited news that his brother was . . . out of pain.

"What's happened?" he asked quickly.

"He's had some sort of brain hemorrhage. He practically died."

Seth completely lost control. "You mean he's *still* alive?"

"He's still breathing. They've got him on a respirator. Your parents have been sitting by his bedside all week."

Seth exploded. "Why in God's name do they do it? He hasn't really been alive for twenty years. What the hell kind of hospital is that?"

Judy sighed. "I don't know, Seth," she said softly. "But I do know your mother is in that room all the time to be sure that Howie's being 'supported.' "

"I'll get someone to cover for me and take the first plane tomorrow," Seth announced decisively. "I think it's American at seven-thirty."

"I'll meet you," Judy replied affectionately. "It's a hell of a thing for you to come back for, but I'll be very glad to see you."

"Me, too," Seth answered.

The instant he hung up, Seth threw on his blue windbreaker, hurried downstairs, out of Vanderbilt, across Longwood Avenue to the Med School Quad, and then darted into Building D.

Half an hour later, he was back in his room, filling an overnight case with what he would need for tomorrow's journey: shirt, tie, Jockey shorts, socks, toothbrush, toilet bag.

And, finally, a hypodermic needle.

TWENTY-THREE

"Gosh, you look exhausted, Seth."

"I couldn't sleep all night. This is a pretty terrible thing I've gotta do."

"*We,* darling," Judy corrected him as they walked arm in arm down one of the long corridors at Chicago's O'Hare Airport early the next morning. "We're in this together."

Crowds of harried businessmen sprinted past them, rushing for their flights. They reached level three of the garage where Judy's car was parked, and their voices echoed in the stark concrete maze. Seth was silent as Judy backed out and started down the ramp.

"You're having second thoughts, aren't you?"

"I'm not sure I'd call it that. To tell the truth, I'm scared out of my wits."

They were on the highway when she tried to reassure him.

"Seth, it *is* the right thing."

"Some people would say it's playing God."

"I don't believe God wants a human being to suffer needlessly—especially when the sick person isn't even aware that he is technically 'alive.' I mean, you've said practically the same thing to me dozens of times."

"I know," he acknowledged. "But what if I'm caught?"

She had no answer for that. Indeed the prospect had haunted her ever since they discovered that they both believed it was right to end an unviable, pain-wracked life.

And he had gone even further by confiding that if he ever had such cases he would—if they wanted—"help them die."

"Another thing," Seth warned out loud, "I can't just walk in there with my valise. It'd be too obvious."

"I thought of that," she replied. "There should be enough room in my handbag."

He nodded, and said, "I wish I could just pull the plug out of the damn respirator. I mean, if they had any humanity the doctors *there* would do it. When horses are in pain, they 'put them down' to stop their suffering. Why don't they do that for a human being?"

"I guess most people believe that God loves humans more than horses."

"No," Seth corrected her. "He obviously loves horses more—because He lets us end their pain."

They drove into the St. Joseph's parking lot and pulled up in a distant corner. Seth opened his small suitcase and withdrew the syringe. It suddenly looked huge. And then from his pocket he produced two vials of liquid.

"What is it?" Judy asked.

"Potassium chloride," he answered. "It's a very common mineral we all have in our bodies. It's needed by the electrolytes in the brain. If you infuse too much of it intravenously, it causes cardiac arrest. It can never cause suspicion because no one would question its presence."

He pierced the cap of the tube and began to draw in the liquid. "At least this is the last time I'll see Howie suffer."

Howie. He had pronounced the name for the first time that day. All through the sleepless night and on the plane he had been trying to depersonalize "the patient." This is not your older brother, he had told himself, this is just a suffering mass of useless organs with no real identity.

He emptied the contents of the second ampoule into the syringe and handed it to Judy. She gingerly wrapped it in her handkerchief and tried to cushion it in her purse.

"We're bound to lose some of this just in the jostling."

"Don't worry," Seth answered blankly. "It's . . . more than enough."

She closed her handbag carefully. They left the car and walked side by side, their footsteps crunching on the gravel courtyard.

Just as they were entering the main door, an exhausted and un-shaven Nat Lazarus emerged from the elevator.

"Seth," he exclaimed in a husky voice, "what a surprise—your mother will be glad to see you." Then he turned to Judy and, without rancor, added, "I thought you promised not to—"

"It's my responsibility, Dad," Seth interrupted. "When I couldn't get you on the phone, I called Judy and made her tell me what was going on. Uh, how is he?"

His father shrugged. "How is he? With a boy like Howie that's not a question you can really answer. Under other circumstances I might say he was a little worse—but he was already as bad as you could possibly get."

"How's Mom?"

Nat sighed. "Another question you could answer yourself. How do you think she is? She stays there all day and all night talking and talking to him about current events, about the latest diet fads in Hollywood—whatever's in the magazines. I don't see how she has any voice left."

"Does she get any sleep?" Seth inquired.

"She made them fix up a bed for her right next to him. 'In case he needs me,' she said. Me, I can't breathe in that room, so I'm going to our motel and lie down."

"You're right, Dad. It'll do you good. See you around lunchtime."

"Yeah, sure." And then Nat wearily added, "Nice to see you, Judy."

Seth held Judy's hand as they approached the room.

The nearer they came, the more distinguishable was the whining pneumatic sound.

The door was slightly ajar, and the gray head of Rosie Lazarus was visible above the green cloth-padded armchair. She was facing the pillow end of the bed, where presumably she could see her elder son's face. For all that was visible from Seth and Judy's vantage point was an enormous metal respirator.

"Hello, Ma," Seth said softly. There was no response.

"It's me, Ma," he said louder, thinking, That goddamn contraption is so noisy she can't even hear the voice of her living son.

He walked into the room, Judy a step behind. His mother jumped with a start when he touched her on the shoulder.

"Oh, Seth," she wailed, as he embraced her, "Howie's so sick. The doctors here can't make him better. Maybe you know a specialist from your hospital we could call."

He shook his head. "I don't know anyone, Ma."

"Then we'll just have to sit and wait," his mother answered. And then she noticed the second visitor. "Hello, Judy, dear. How nice of you to come."

Now for the first time Seth looked at his brother's face. It was dwarfed by the apparatus. His eyes were closed, his brow perspiring. He must be in pain, Seth told himself. And I know that if Howie wants anything it's for it all to *end*.

He turned again to his mother. "How about you, Ma? Are you taking care of yourself? Are you eating?"

"It doesn't matter about me. I'll be all right."

"Have you had breakfast, Mrs. Lazarus?" Judy asked solicitously.

"Is it time for breakfast? I thought it was still yesterday."

"I noticed a Howard Johnson's just down the road," Judy offered. "I'd be glad to drive you—"

"No, no, no," Rosie quickly protested. "I can't leave Howie that long. Be a darling and bring me a little something, will you?"

"What can I get you, then?" Judy asked.

"Nothing. Anything. I'm really not hungry. Frankly, all I need is a strong cup of coffee."

"Well, in that case, I think there's a machine in the lobby," Judy replied. "Why don't you come with me just to stretch your legs?"

Rosie sighed. "Actually, I could probably use a tiny walk." She pushed against the arms of the chair to help herself stand up.

"Come, dear," she said to Judy. Then she enjoined her other son, "Seth, you stay with Howie, and if anything happens you ring right away for the nurse."

"Fine, Ma," he replied, his words still halfway in his throat. Then he reached in his pocket and withdrew a handful of loose change. He placed the coins in Judy's hand, adding, "If you happen to find another vending machine, get me a sandwich or something."

"That's right," Rosie said approvingly, "you should eat something, too, Seth. You're as thin as a stick."

The moment the two women were out of the room Seth hurriedly closed the door and rushed over to where Judy had left her purse.

And then he began what he had rehearsed so many times before in dreams and fantasies. Especially all the previous night.

He went to the far end of the bed, where his hands would be hidden by the respirator should one of the nurses or doctors chance to come by.

He snapped open Judy's handbag, reached inside, and hesitated for a moment, not even daring to breathe, as he listened for footsteps in the hall outside.

There was nothing but the sound of the respirator.

In the I.V. drip leading into Howie's arm there was a burette, a hollow glass tube to indicate the amount of medication being administered.

Seth quickly unscrewed the narrow tubing and placed the needle of his syringe into the burette, and emptied the massive dose it held. Then with trembling hands, he hurriedly restored the I.V. to its normal function, returned the syringe to Judy's handbag, and sat down again at his brother's side.

He knew his brother's heart would soon stop beating. But the mechanical ventilator would continue to pump air into his lungs. And since Howie had already been unconscious, the nurses might not find him D.I.B. for at least five minutes. Or perhaps as long as an hour.

Seth did not know if he wanted his mother to be present to say a last irrational goodbye—or to miss the moment when Howie's agony would finally be ended.

He himself could not take his eyes from the face of the brother with whom he had never been able to speak.

Goodbye, Howie, he said in his thoughts. If there is some supernatural way you can possibly know me, then you'll understand that I've done this because . . . I love you.

The funeral, like Howie's life, was restricted to the four of them. Even Judy did not attend. For it was Rosie's wish that "the family should be alone together one last time."

Seth stood impassive at the graveside as he listened to the cemetery's Unitarian minister eulogize his brother's goodness. The only thing that brought him comfort was the fleeting references to Howie's being "laid to rest" and "now at peace."

In the limousine ride from the cemetery, Rosie consoled herself by endlessly repeating what the doctors—who tried in vain to wake her Howie—had said.

"At least, thank God, he didn't suffer. It was painless. His heart just stopped. There was nothing anyone could have done."

Judy was waiting in front of the Lazarus market. She offered her condolences to Rosie and Nat, both of whom nodded in mute appreciation and, arm in arm, walked toward the back door.

Seth and Judy were alone.

"How do you feel?" she asked.

He was going to tell her fine. But suddenly a deluge of guilt overwhelmed him and he murmured, "Oh, Judy, what have I done? What have I done?"

*   *   *

They were working in different hospitals for their next rotation, so Barney and Bennett rarely saw each other except for the occasional midnight foul-shooting contest, in which the score now stood at 2,568 to 2,560 in Barney's favor.

But early one morning, as Barney was completing a three-mile jog, he caught sight of Bennett going crazy—like Gene Kelly in *Singin' in the Rain*—madly leap-frogging over parking meters along Avenue Louis Pasteur. Barney sprinted to catch up.

"Hey, Landsmann, have you blown your mind?" he puffed.

Ignoring the question, Bennett blurted ecstatically, "I've done it, Livingston. I've just delivered a real live baby."

"Hey, no shit." Barney smiled and held out his hand. "Congratulations. Only eleven to go and you can graduate."

"I'll do a million more with pleasure. Can you imagine what it's like, Barn, to reach into that bloody goo and pull out a tiny human being!"

"You mean you got to do the actual delivery?"

"I really lucked out. It was five A.M. The resident was doing an emergency operation, the intern had been up all night transfusing a bleeder and told me to go ahead and do it on my own."

"Great!"

"Of course," Bennett continued, "the guy might have been slightly influenced by the fact that the mother was a welfare patient from Roxbury. But anyway, I did it—although I have to admit that the nurses gave me a little help. And the woman herself had been through it all before. But you'll never believe what happened next."

"Landsmann, from you I'd believe anything." Barney grinned.

"Well, then, dig this—the woman looked up at me and said that though this was her ninth kid, it was the first ever delivered by what she flatteringly referred to as a 'gen–u–ine spade doctor.' So she insisted on giving her my name."

"*Her*—it's a girl?"

Bennett shrugged joyfully. "Can I help it if there's now an eight-pound little lady in the Beth Israel maternity ward called 'Bennetta Landsmann Jackson'?"

"She even got the Landsmann part, too? Lucky you didn't mention Abraham Lincoln."

"To tell the truth, I did. But she's already got a kid with that name."

"How's the labor coming, Laura?"

Attending obstetrician Walter Hewlett had peeked into the labor room to see how Laura was coming with her patient, Marion Fels, a thirty-six-year-old prima gravida.

"Contractions four to five minutes apart, cervix about six centimeters dilatated, eighty percent effaced—minus three station."

"Scared?"

"No, I'm all right."

She was lying, of course.

Laura was sure of the information she was conveying, which explained exactly the position of the baby in Marion's birth canal. But she was far from being all right.

They had already determined that it would be a cephalic presentation—i.e., that, like ninety-five percent of all babies, Marion's would be arriving head first. But the information she had just given Hewlett suggested that they were not likely to see the baby crown for at least two hours.

And she was terrified that Hewlett might go off to find a quiet bed and try for a little shut-eye.

"Listen, Laura," he said, "it's obvious we've got plenty of time. I'm going to step out . . ."

That's okay, Laura thought to herself, you always go to the same place in the parking lot to light up a cigarette.

But then she heard the end of his sentence.

". . . and get something to eat. I've just *got* to go to Blue Hill Avenue and get a corned beef sandwich with a big half-sour."

Blue Hill Avenue? she thought. That's *miles* from here! For God's sake, Walter, you can't leave me alone like this. I know there are nurses around but I'm the only doctor—and I'm not even a doctor.

"Think you can hold the fort?" Hewlett smiled.

She was determined not to chicken out. "Sure, Doctor, no problem," she said, wondering where she got the strength—much less the breath—to utter such a falsehood.

"Great," said Hewlett. "Can I get you anything?"

She shook her head. "Thanks." All the while thinking, you could get me a qualified obstetrician.

"How are you feeling?" asked the head nurse.

"Fine, thank you," Laura replied.

"I was asking Miss Fels, Dr. Castellano," she retorted.

"Oh," said Laura, trying to hide her embarrassment.

"I'm okay," the patient answered.

The head nurse smiled. "If you need anything, just holler."

"Can't you do something about these damned contractions?"

"Stay loose, Marion," Laura interposed, "we'll be able to give you some medication very soon."

"Yes," the head nurse confirmed, "we've got you scheduled for a saddle block."

Florence Nightingale withdrew her smirking face from the doorway. Laura thought to herself, Isn't it wonderful to be getting such support from the teammates of my gender, who resent my wearing a white coat instead of a white hat. Please, Walter, eat that damn sandwich before this woman is fully dilatated!

She tried to regain the patient's confidence by taking her blood pressure and then checking her cervix, which—to her alarm—had dilatated to nearly eight centimeters. The labor was progressing more rapidly than anyone had expected.

As soon as the patient's contraction ended, Laura asked her gently, "Did I hear her call you 'Miss'?"

Marion smiled wanly and replied with some difficulty. "Yeah. I didn't want to marry him—mainly because he was married to someone else. Still, I'm not getting any younger and I wanted to have a kid before it was too late."

"What do you do?" Laura asked.

"Work for *The Globe.* I was so busy being successful that I didn't take a look at the biological clock. Are you married, Doctor?"

"Please call me Laura. And the answer's 'Not yet.' "

Suddenly Marion blurted, "Quick, Laura, your hand!"

As Marion moaned and squeezed her hand tightly, Laura murmured, "Relax. Try to breathe normally. It'll be over soon."

When she caught her breath, Marion inquired, "How much more of this till I get my baby?"

"Not much," Laura replied reassuringly, inwardly praying that Walter was already speeding back along the Fenway. "I'll just check you again."

To her consternation she discovered that the cervix was fully dilatated and the baby was at the *plus two* station.

Christ, it was first down with goal to go! She rang for the nurse.

"This is it," Laura whispered to Marion.

"Thank God, these contractions are starting to kill me."

A squad of nurses bustled in and began to wheel the mother-to-be to the delivery room. In a split second Marion was gone.

Suddenly a voice behind Laura whispered unctuously, "Hadn't you better scrub up?"

Shit, it was the friendly head nurse.

"Yes, of course," she responded in a state of mounting panic. "Uh—when Dr. Hewlett comes back, be sure and tell him where I am."

"Of course, Doctor."

Laura sprinted down the hall, stopped at the sink outside the delivery room, and began to scrub.

All the while she struggled to control the rapid beating of her heart.

She pushed open the door and entered the O.R., where a second nurse was waiting to help her into a sterile gown and gloves.

From a distance she could hear Marion groan with pain.

"Where's the anesthesiologist?" she asked. "He's supposed to be giving her a saddle block."

"Nico's just been called on a Code Blue. He may be quite a while."

Oh God, Laura thought to herself, I ought to call him back on a Code Blue—'cause I don't think I can keep breathing on my own. And I *know* I can't do the anesthesia on my own.

She stood motionless, trying to remember what a real obstetrician would do in a situation like this. He would administer a pudendal. She had observed a few of those procedures, but had never actually done one.

Now she had no choice—Laura took a deep breath and walked into the brighter lights that flooded the operating room.

Then suddenly the miracle occurred. To her astonishment she was no longer shaking. She found herself moving calmly toward the table, where Marion's legs had been strapped into the stirrups for delivery, her abdomen draped with sterile towels and sheets. The head nurse stood nearby at a small table on which she had tidily arranged the surgical instruments.

Laura rapidly rehearsed all the instructions she had memorized. First and foremost, do not hasten delivery or you might cause serious damage to the mother and child.

Depress the perineum to stretch it and let the newborn's head clear the opening of the vagina.

From beyond her field of vision, Laura heard one of the nurses cry, "Look, the baby's crowning."

With an icy calm Laura instructed the Head Nurse to fill a syringe with ten cc's of Xylocaine.

As she was waiting, she inserted her left hand past the baby's head and felt for Marion's ischial spine. Then, with her finger on the pudendal nerve, she asked for a "trumpet," a metal tube that she inserted to guide her eight-inch needle. Taking the syringe with her other hand, she put it through the trumpet till she felt the tissue at the side wall of the vagina. She then withdrew the needle slightly to be sure there was no blood. And finally injected the painkiller.

At that moment Marion had another excruciating contraction.

"Shit," she gasped. "The goddamn drug's not working!"

Laura answered in what she hoped would be reassuring tones. "Xylocaine needs about two or three minutes to take effect, Marion."

Indeed, less than five minutes later, all was well—for Marion, at least. Laura was able to perform an episiotomy. With a pair of straight Mayo's scissors she made a three-inch cut from the base of the vagina toward the rectum to facilitate the baby's grand entrance.

And Marion did not experience the slightest twinge.

Yet now things seemed less clear. A torrent of blood and mucus was pouring everywhere. But somehow Laura's hands found the infant and she gently helped it clear. Its face and chin—and then the neck.

Functioning like an airplane on automatic pilot, Laura carefully rotated the infant and disengaged its shoulders from the mother's pelvic inlet.

Slowly (*every movement must be slow,* she kept reminding herself) she turned the baby so that its face pointed downward. Now the second shoulder was free. The rest would be a cinch. But *don't hurry, Laura, goddammit.* Your heart can go as fast as it wants, but keep removing the baby gradually and gently.

An instant later she was holding an entire infant in her hands. At least it would look like one when all the vernix, blood, mucus, and other matter were washed off. Christ, it was slippery. What if I drop it? No, I'm holding it the right way—by the back of its heels. Then someone cried—or was it a wail? In any case it was the first utterance of the newest arrival to the world.

Laura looked at the gravy-coated being she was appropriately holding like a chicken and called out, "It's a girl. Marion, you've got a girl!"

She placed the baby on her mother's stomach, as the nurses wrapped it in warm towels. As soon as the cord ceased to pulsate Laura clamped it, cut it, and tied it.

Just then a tall, stoop-shouldered doctor in an ill-fitting white coat entered the room. It was Nico, the anesthesia resident. "I'm sorry, Laura. But a code's a code. Shall we get this show on the road?"

"Sorry, Nico," Laura said with a breeziness born of relief, "I'm afraid the show's over."

"What did you use for anesthesia?"

"I did a pudendal."

"Yourself?"

"No, my fairy godmother helped."

Nico looked at the mother communing peacefully with her new baby, then glanced at Laura.

"Hey, Castellano, not bad."

He took a final glance at her patient and then about-faced to return to his code.

Laura started to sleepwalk toward the exit.

"Wait, Doctor," she heard the head nurse cry out. "Don't forget the placenta." Laura returned to the table and, like an automaton, awaited the arrival of the afterbirth, and closed the episiotomy cut with chromic catgut.

Finally, she checked Marion's general condition. The bleeding was slight. There were no lacerations or cervical damage.

"You're okay, Marion," she murmured.

To which the ecstatic mother replied, "You're okay yourself, Laura. Thanks."

Even after they had wheeled her patient out, Laura stood alone in the empty operating room, her feelings of relief now changing to pride. And then to jealousy. Marion really had things in the right perspective.

It suddenly seemed to Laura that for a woman the greatest joy was to hold a baby in her arms.

And now she realized that however much she wanted to succeed, she wanted *that*, too.

Barney was proud to be operating with the First Team, though he knew the best he could hope for was to be called upon to hold a clamp.

At least he would be watching Thomas Aubrey ("the surgeon's surgeon") and anesthesiologist Conrad Nagy ("the best gas-passer in Christendom") do their stuff.

Today's procedure was a cholecystectomy. What would usually be the routine removal of a gallbladder was this time made a "little more interesting," as Aubrey put it, "because our patient, Mr. Abrahamian—as you will have read in his notes—has had a complex childhood history that included rheumatic fever, and practically every allergy you can think of. We have to be alert for surprises.

"Dr. Nagy has administered atropine as a pre-op, induced anesthesia with sixty milligrams of methohexitone, and used salcuranium for good neuromuscular harmony. To keep the patient asleep he is using nitrous oxide and oxygen in a 70:30 ratio.

"So much for prologue, now we open the curtain."

Holding the scalpel like a cellist's bow, Aubrey made a Kocher incision, then beckoned to a nurse on his right and another on his left to come forward and hold the abdominal drains. Aubrey put his right hand into the wound to move the liver and thereby expose the gallbladder. He grasped the organ with a ring clamp and lifted it toward the surface.

His first assistant, Dr. Lipson, kept the opening wide with a broad-bladed Deever retractor. He then signaled to Barney to take a narrow-bladed retractor and place it under the costal margin—the bottom edge of the rib cage.

"Now, gentlemen," Aubrey announced, "we have maximum exposure. A careful surgeon must take his time in inspecting the entire area he has exposed."

He took them on a guided tour of the duct system and arterial supply before removing the gallbladder. Thereafter he led his intrepid explorers in a search for any possible bleeding points that he had not already tied. At this point he turned the show over to Dr. Lipson to close the wound while Aubrey continued to narrate.

"Please note that Dr. Lipson is carefully avoiding the capsule of the liver, since sutures passing through that organ would cause bleeding. When all is ready, we will insert the drain—"

Suddenly, the anesthesiologist broke the spell of placid pedagogy.

"Problems, Tom," he said, an unmistakable edge of worry in his voice.

"What's up?" the surgeon asked calmly.

"This guy's sizzling. Blood pressure's sky-high. Pulse is one-eighty."

Dr. Aubrey quietly ordered, "Somebody get a rectal temperature."

Barney stood mesmerized, as one of the nurses inserted a thermometer. He began to sweat, yet did not dare wipe his brow for fear of losing his concentration on the retractor he was holding. He glanced at Nagy. The anesthesiologist's forehead was furrowed and his eyes broadcast anxiety. Aubrey's attention remained riveted on the open wound as if dissociated from the panic all around him.

After what seemed an eternity, the nurse removed the thermometer.

"My God!" she gasped.

"Just read it, Helen," Aubrey ordered in quiet clipped tones.

"It's almost a hundred and eight, Doctor."

"Shit," Nagy cried out, "malignant hyperthermia. Let's get some ice, stat."

Barney heard footsteps racing toward the door. He felt that he, too, should be reacting to this emergency, but how? Frightened and confused, he turned to the chief surgeon.

"Should I help them get ice, Doctor?"

"Did I give you any orders, young man?" Aubrey snapped in his first display of emotion. "Just keep holding that retractor and stay out of the way."

At this moment the anesthesiologist blurted, "Tom, the EKG is going crazy."

Aubrey ripped off a glove and reached for the patient's groin to feel for the femoral pulse. Barney could tell from the expression above his mask that he had found none.

"No heartbeat," another voice called out.

"EKG flat," Nagy announced. "He's dead."

There was a sudden flood of silence. No one *dared* speak until Dr. Aubrey decided on a course of action.

At last he ordered, "Dr. Nagy, continue aerating the lungs."

The anesthesiologist nodded and obeyed.

Why the hell is he doing that? Barney wondered. This poor bastard's dead.

The surgeon then tapped his assistant's shoulder. Lipson understood and moved aside, ceding the task of suturing Mr. Abrahamian to the swift and dextrous hands of the chief surgeon.

Barney watched in growing disbelief. Why the hell is he sewing so carefully—sewing at all, actually? They're only going to reopen the guy for a postmortem.

By now Barney had removed the retractor and was merely a helpless and confused bystander as oxygen continued to inflate the dead man's lungs.

Aubrey tied a locking half-stitch, which squared the last knot. "All right," he said quietly, "take him to the recovery room. I'll be there in a few moments."

As the late Mr. Abrahamian was wheeled off, Aubrey turned and strode coolly back to what must have been the star's dressing room.

Lipson re-entered from post-op and saw Barney rooted to the ground. "What's up?" he asked.

"I don't understand what I just saw," he answered.

"Which part?"

"The guy was dead and they still—"

"Oh that," Lipson answered. "How much surgery have you been in on?"

"This is the first week of my rotation," Barney replied, and then demanded, "Now will you please explain to me why the hell you pumped air into a guy who's so dead he had no pulse or heartbeat?"

"Calm out, amigo," said the young doctor, "you've just learned why no patient ever dies on Dr. Aubrey's operating table. Thanks to the balloon work of Aubrey's gas-passer, Mr. Abrahamian will be pronounced dead *after* the operation by somebody in the recovery room."

"You mean just for Aubrey's ego?" Barney replied with astonishment.

"No," Lipson protested, "Tom's a bigger man than that. But you can't imagine how much paperwork he's saved—even though I usually do it for him. All the damn certificates, hospital papers, insurance forms— that bureaucratic crap takes hours. Now it'll be a job for the boys in post-op. So you've learned something today, eh, amigo?"

"Yeah," said Barney, "I've learned that I don't want to be a surgeon."

Just before their fourth and final year, Second Lieutenant Palmer Talbot flew into Boston from California—military rate—on United Airlines. A week later he could have winged home without a plane, so inebriated was he by the heady wine of Laura's newly affectionate behavior.

For her part, Laura was delighted at having a Stage Door Johnny outside the operating theater—a man whose qualities she respected, who treated her like something other than a sexual brass ring on the medical carousel.

Palmer had determined to make his Army years an educational experience. He had been accepted by the Army Language School in Monterey and had begun the study of Chinese. It would mean a commitment to the military for an additional year. But it had seemed worth it, especially when Laura had been so cold and indifferent to him.

Now he had a Laura who preferred sitting by a fire in the living room of his Beacon Street house and talking about everything—as long as it was nothing to do with medicine.

She told herself she had forgotten how well read he was, what a good listener—and how loving. There was no one in the world, she convinced herself, who cared for her as much as Palmer Talbot. What a fool she had been to risk losing him in the smug confidence that she was yet to meet "Mr. Right." For she had now decided that it could never be "*Dr.* Right."

She tried not to burden him with the deep hurt she still felt at the disintegration of her family. The separation had become all the more definitive when earlier in 1961—in January to be exact—the United States government completely severed diplomatic ties with the Castro government. And then the Bay of Pigs invasion, launched by exiled Cubans from Miami intent on "liberating" their homeland, reduced relations between the two countries from absolutely nothing to overt hostility.

"Now I couldn't see Luis even if I wanted to," Laura commented wryly.

"Well, actually you *could*," Palmer offered. "It's still possible to go to Mexico and fly over from there."

Laura looked at him and tried to sound resolute when she pronounced, "I've no desire to visit Cuba, Fidel, or my father."

"Haven't you had any contact at all since he left?"

"A few crummy letters. I didn't even bother to answer them. I mean, the guy's more than *un poco loco* to be a revolutionary at his age. He claims his greatest aim in life is for me to join him in Cuba and be a doctor there."

Palmer shook his head. "I read somewhere about men doing outlandish things at his age—sort of menopausal madness. Even if you wanted to, I wouldn't let you follow him."

"Don't worry, there's no risk of that. Or of my joining my mother in her religious retreat."

"How is she, by the way?"

"Oh, we've spoken on the phone a few times. She claims she's happier than she's ever been since she 'found her calling'—as she so piously put it. I think she expects me to visit her, but I'm in no mood to see a mother who would rather be a 'sister.' "

He touched her on the shoulder. "I know what you must be going through."

"I don't think you possibly can. You know, with both my parents going loony, I'm kind of scared I'll flip out, too."

Palmer smiled. "How about flipping out over me?"

"I think I already have," she replied, and put her arms around him.

There was now a good chance that the Army would send him back to Boston. Sponsored by the NDEA (National Defense Education Act), he could do his final year of service taking advanced courses in Far Eastern languages at a "recognized college or university." Since the army "recognized" Harvard, he had come to discuss their program with its director, Simon Rybarchyk.

And to find out how things stood with Laura.

The night before he had to leave, as they were lying in each other's arms by the fire, he said, "Look, Laura, I'd really like to come back East and study. But I can't settle for what Shakespeare called 'living in the suburbs of your affection.' I know you're not ready to get married. So I'm willing to play it any way you want, as long as we can be together— and I mean *live* together."

Laura looked at him for a moment and then said, "Palmer, the girl who didn't believe in marriage isn't here anymore. Actually, I think 'Laura Talbot' sounds very pretty."

"I don't believe I'm hearing this. Are you actually telling me you're willing to become Doctor Laura Talbot?"

"No," she said, smiling playfully, "I'll be Mrs. Talbot but *Doctor Castellano*."

"You're actually going to marry that schmuck?"

"I thought you liked Palmer," she protested.

"Listen, I like Elvis but that doesn't mean you should marry *him*. You're only doing this because you suddenly imagine you're all alone, and Palmer is the path of least resistance."

"Barney, he loves me."

"I know, Laura, I don't question that for a minute. What I do question is whether, deep down, you honestly love him."

TWENTY-FOUR

There is a time of supreme crisis in the life of every fourth-year medical student.

As he is completing the last few "elective" rotations, doing a little more Surgery or Internal Medicine if he intends to be a cutter or a flea, he suddenly looks at the calendar and notices that in June *of that same year* he will be officially granted the title of M.D.

At that moment of acutely painful awareness, he realizes that he is not remotely prepared to become a doctor. Shit, he says to himself (or "Gosh," if he is Seth Lazarus), people are going to think I know what I'm doing. They're going to expect me to recognize what's wrong with them—and cure it. How am I going to deal with that?

Now, retrospectively, the days of tedious scutwork seem like Paradise Lost. How infinitely better to be schlepping up and down the stairs and holding clamps while others operate. The worst he might come home with nightly is a pair of aching feet. But his conscience never aches.

Doing scutwork, he takes everything—but the responsibility. He is not yet obliged to be infallible.

Some who pass this crisis have the honest self-awareness that they always will be students; they will never have learned enough. But such candor cannot protect them from their patients' pain. And ultimately, be it ten or twenty years, the strain becomes too much for some of them whose hearts break metaphorically—and even physically.

And they become members of that species known as the "impaired physician," a euphemism for a doctor with a damaged soul.

The other—far more common—way by which the fledgling healer copes with this apocalyptic moment is *denial*. He deludes himself that taking the Hippocratic Oath is tantamount to baptism. That with the diploma come superhuman powers that—like microbes—are invisible except to the initiate observer.

The syllogism runs along the lines of Descartes' "I think, therefore I am." But in medicine the formula is, "I have a Degree, therefore I am a Doctor."

Those who can successfully perform this satisfying self-hypnosis will win friends, awards, promotions, and—with perseverance—even a Mercedes SLC.

It was time for Barney to decide upon a specialty.

As had been his practice since his earliest memories, he held an inner dialogue with himself. Question: What makes you happy, Livingston? Answer: Making other people happy.

Well, that doesn't help much—to do that you could play Santa Claus in a department store. Can you clarify these thoughts?

Yes, upon reflection I can translate my ambition—to treat unhappy people and make them see the joy in life.

The more he searched himself, the more he found the evidence that he was cut out for psychiatry. First and foremost, troubled people had been turning to him for as long as he could remember.

Hadn't Laura always chosen his shoulder to cry on? Didn't he derive enormous satisfaction from what he accomplished with little Marvin Amsterdam at summer camp? (Where are you, Marvin? Are you well and happy?) And he'd lost count of the classmates who had sought assistance from him at both college and Med School in their times of desperation. Yeah, I'm like some magnet for the melancholy.

And yet the first thing a psychiatrist must be is honest with himself. So, come on, Livingston, try to analyze your own decision. You already know what you would do for others, but what would psychiatry do for *you*?

Come on, then, this is the hardest part.

The "equilibrium" that people see in me is really an illusion. I am as flawed as anyone. It's only that I seem to have the knack of hiding it. Psychiatry would help me, first of all, to heal myself. Because let's face it,

Livingston, you're nearly twenty-five years old and haven't ever had relationships with women that transcend the superficial. And surely something's wrong with that.

Besides, the mere fact that you want to be the man dispensing wisdom is a way of self-protection. Be honest, you're afraid to look inside yourself and see what's going on.

Yeah, the choice of specialty is often a reflection of the doctor's inner need. I want to understand myself. I want to know the reason why I allow myself to act as everybody's father figure. Could that be a way of hiding something deeper—like the fact that what I want to be is just a father?

Having decided on psychiatry, Barney thought it sensible to take an extra neurological rotation to get a better idea of how the brain functions organically.

He found himself once more performing literally what he would spend his life trying to accomplish with mere words: probing the human brain.

Bennett Landsmann, whose eye was fixed upon the gleaming scalpel, took an extra round of surgery and filled out applications for a surgical internship in the Boston area.

"Hey, look, Ben," Barney tried to tell him diplomatically, "be honest with yourself. Even if your name were Bennett X and you had all the Black Power in the world, it wouldn't help. There's never been a black surgical intern at any of the Boston biggies."

"There's never been a woman either," Bennett countered, "but Grete Andersen's applying."

"Hey, listen, my friend, you may be as handsome as Sidney Poitier, as great a jock as Jackie Robinson—and even more Jewish than Sammy Davis—but to those guys, you're still a horse of a different color. And as far as Grete is concerned, for once she's gonna learn that she can't wiggle her way into a male closed shop. Anyway, that's her problem. Why don't you wise up and apply for an internship with me in New York?"

"I have a sentimental attachment to Boston, Barney. The Symphony runs rings around the New York Philharmonic. Even the art museum—"

"Don't give me any of that cultural bullshit when I'm trying to tell you facts, Ben. These surgery departments are not about to break tradition—they'll only break your heart."

"But what about you, Barn?" Bennett said, turning the tables. "What attraction could New York possibly have for you now that your mother's sold the ancestral mansion and moved to the land of sun, fun, and skin cancer?"

"Well, my brother Warren's at Columbia Law. . . ."

"But he's living with some girl, right? He didn't invite you to play *Jules and Jim*, did he?"

"Come on, Ben, New York is the capital of the world. It's certainly as good for psychiatry as Boston, and besides—"

"Besides—it's two hundred and fifty miles away from Laura Castellano."

"What does that have to do with anything?"

"Come off it, Barn. You've been in a lousy mood ever since she got officially engaged."

"He just isn't *worthy* of her, dammit!"

"All guys feel that way about their sisters—and I suppose, some day, their daughters. No one's ever good enough for them. From everything I hear, Mr. Talbot is very cool."

"He is," Barney confessed, "there's nothing I can say against him except he's wrong for Laura."

"And you feel so strongly about it that you don't want to hang around and watch her suffer when the bubble bursts."

Barney poised to retort and then paused. A wan smile crossed his face. "Christ, Landsmann, it hurts me to say it, but you've sort of hit the nail on the head."

"Well," Bennett allowed, "I guess I was being selfish. I thought if we were both in Boston we could share an apartment and maybe change our foul-shot competition into something more elevated—like numbers of damsels seduced. Hell, I don't wanna lose you to New York."

Barney looked up and grinned. "Then marry me, Bennett."

"I can't, Barney. You're not Jewish."

Barney felt certain he was having a heart attack.

Then the psychiatrist in him made him realize that death was merely a wish-fulfillment fancy.

The truth is he was petrified. For this morning he was about to deliver his first neurological "presentation," the write-up of his examination, analysis of symptoms, and "differential diagnosis" of a real patient. And it would be before, of all people, Professor Clifford Marks, world-renowned neurologist and a ruthlessly demanding teacher.

Barney was certain from the various symptoms he had been analyzing so intensely that the patient he was about to present would survive. Barney's only question was, would *he*?

He reached the fourth floor just as Marks, the portly, gray-templed professor, was marching from the elevator, surrounded by a cluster of students and interns.

They exchanged perfunctory salutations as the senior consultant led them down into the Neurology ward. It was not a pleasant place. Those lying in their beds seemed to be divided into opposite extremes: They were either twitching and convulsing or else paralyzed.

At last they reached the bedside of Mr. Aldo Moretti, a balding, middle-aged man, who at first appeared out of place in this ward. For though his hands and feet were bandaged, he was apparently able to move his limbs without paralysis or palsy.

Moretti was delighted to see so many doctors coming to pay homage to his fascinating symptoms and warmly welcomed these new pilgrims.

When all were gathered around, Professor Marks nodded to Barney. "All right, Livingston, let's hear the problem."

Barney turned to the group and opened the manila envelope containing official forms, as well as the copious notes he had made for himself.

As he was about to begin, his subject interposed with a cheery greeting, "Hi there, Barney. Howdja feel this morning?"

"Fine, fine. Thank you, Mr. Moretti," he muttered. And then he went back to his prepared text.

Again Moretti interrupted, this time addressing all the other white coats. "This kid was so tired last night when he admitted me he could barely keep his eyes open. If I hadn't felt so lousy, I'd have gone back home and let him sleep."

"Hmm, yes," the professor remarked. And then he added, "Proceed, Livingston."

Barney cleared his throat and then recited, "The patient is a forty-two-year-old male business executive—"

"I'm in trucking, actually," Moretti footnoted. "I own a fleet of trucks." At which he turned to Barney, urging, "Go on, kid. Go on."

Barney continued. "Last Sunday he was entertaining his in-laws for dinner and was cooking a large pot of spaghetti—"

"How many times do I have to tell you, Barney, it was *vermicelli.*"

Barney worked up the courage to talk sternly to a man nearly twice his age. "I'd be grateful if you'd just let me finish this, Mr. Moretti. Then if you've got anything to add, you can do it afterwards."

Determined not to give Moretti another chance to hold the floor, Barney barreled on, "As he was carrying the boiling pot to the sink, he suddenly dropped it, causing extensive second-degree burns to his hands and lower extremities."

"I can't understand it," Moretti apologized. "I mean, nothing like this ever happened to me before. And what the hell I'm doing with all these spastics, I don't know."

Barney took a deep breath and continued. "When admitted to the E.R., the patient was in a confused state and couldn't recall even dropping the boiling water on himself."

"Yeah, I was in a real fog," Moretti commented.

"He was admitted because of the extent of his burns and put on I.V. hydration. At this point he presented no focal neurological signs.

"This morning he developed a high fever—probably secondary to his burns—had temporary loss of consciousness, smacked his lips, and kept turning his head to the right. He had a tonicoclonic seizure lasting less than a minute. When Neurology was called in, he had been groggy for over half an hour."

"The kid hasn't missed a thing," said the voice from the pillow, which Barney pretended not to hear.

"What was your initial impression?" the professor asked.

"Well," Barney suggested—trying to sound as if it had just come to him rather than being the result of frantic research—"it's just possible that the high fever he spiked may have caused a seizure. There's also the possibility that he could be septic from an overwhelming bacterial infection introduced by the burns."

Following protocol, Barney then offered his "differential diagnosis," one based on a comparison of Mr. Moretti's signs and symptoms with those of other diseases with which they could be confused. In addition to the obvious possibility of tumor, there was AVM, a circulatory malformation that causes similar problems. There was even the possibility of multiple sclerosis. Encephalitis could not be ruled out unless they did a spinal tap—

There was a sudden bellow, "*No way!* Nobody's sticking a needle in my spine. A friend of mine had it and it hurts like hell."

Barney was now beyond rage, on a transcendental level of calm, as he replied to the latest outburst, "We'll keep that in mind, Mr. Moretti."

Then he turned back to the white coats. "Anyway, Professor, as you keep reminding us, seizures are only signs, not diseases in themselves. As far as I could tell, the patient has no family history of seizure disorder except for one incident he mentioned in conversation—that his grandfather fell off a horse and sustained what was obviously a post-traumatic seizure.

"The neuro exam was normal, including assessment of the twelve cranial nerves. The examination of sensory and motor nerves fails to reveal any abnormalities. Tendon reflexes are normal and there was no Babinski sign. Mental status is within normal limits."

At which point the bedridden commentator shouted, "Bet your sweet ass I'm not loony."

"In conclusion, sir," said Barney, sensing relief was just a few syllables away, "the patient's seizure seems to be . . . idiopathic."

Idiopathic—the most useful word in the medical vocabulary. Any doctor who is unable to diagnose a patient's ailment can always employ that valuable adjective "idiopathic," which is simply Greek (related to "idiot"), meaning of unknown origin. In other words, the physician is telling the truth but keeping the patient from understanding his confession of ignorance.

The professor nodded. "Excellent presentation, Livingston, your family history thorough, your differentials were all relevant, and your neurological work-up complete. I congratulate you."

"Hey, what about me?" roared the indignant patient. "Give me some credit, huh? I mean I'm the guy that told that stuff to Barney. He just wrote it down."

Unruffled, Marks continued to address his student. "Can you tell me why you ruled out TLE?"

"Well, sir," Barney began, frantically excavating his brain, "temporal lobe epilepsy would have been a possibility except he didn't suffer from déjà vu or micropsia—the classic symptoms you associate with TLE."

To which the eminent neurologist replied, "Hmm."

Marks then bent over to make a long and careful study of Moretti's face. At last he turned to address his acolytes. "Gentlemen, if you look carefully at the patient's face you will note a very slight asymmetry. You will also note that his left eye is slightly higher than the right. We call this a 'soft' neurological sign."

The students were duly impressed but could not see where Marks was leading.

"Now, if I may ask Mr. Moretti a few questions."

"Me?" the patient said, his ego doing cartwheels. "Ask me anything."

"Can you remember your birth?" the professor inquired.

"Of course," Moretti answered, "the twelfth of February."

"No," Marks interrupted. "I mean the circumstances of your birth. Do you recall your mother saying there were any difficulties?"

Moretti thought for a moment and then offered, "Actually, she did. I think they had to pull me out with those tongs."

"I suspected so," said Marks, with a little smile of satisfaction. And then to the students, "Forceps birth, facial asymmetry . . ." He pointed to the left side of the patient's head. "Since he turned to the right when he seized, the lesion in the brain would be here. I think that, with due respect to Livingston's conclusion, we are still dealing with a temporal lobe epilepsy, which can be confirmed by EEG."

He then turned to his resident and said, "George, take the ball from here. If it checks out, we'll get Moretti started on Dilantin."

As Marks and his group of worshipers moved on to the next neurological enigma, he commented to Barney, "That was a tough one to call. You did a splendid job. Too bad you're opting for psychiatry. You should become a doctor."

Pharmacology, though given relatively short shrift among the last of the preclinical courses, is in fact a discipline that can help determine the success or failure of a medical career.

It is not just that students learn about the composition of innumerable drugs, their actions, uses, and contra–indications. For all this can be found in the various expensively bound reference books behind a doctor's desk. Rather, it is the physician's ability to write a really good prescription and thereby win hearts and influence minds.

No patient will feel comforted unless he receives some sort of prescription—that little document with cryptographic scrawl—that proves his physician really *cares*.

In Barney's view, which he somewhat unwisely put to Morris Cohen, the professor, "It's like a door prize, isn't it? I mean, the patient sort of feels unloved if you don't *give* him something tangible. A souvenir or sop."

"I beg your pardon, Livingston, you might display a little more respect for scientific research. Does polio vaccine or penicillin qualify as 'soppish' to you?"

"Please, sir," Barney said, quickly backtracking, "no disrespect intended. But isn't it true that sometimes just an ordinary aspirin dressed up in fancy terminology can act as a placebo? I mean, a prescription can make a patient feel he's starting to recover from the second he gets it in his hands. I think there's literature that backs this up."

"Well," Cohen retorted in defense of his important discipline, "a good doctor should be able to determine if his patient's ailment is psychosomatic in the first place."

A voice inside Barney was shouting, Shut your mouth, you idiot— you need this course to get your damn degree. And so he shut his mouth.

Professor Cohen had already sensed that Barney had more to say. "Please, please," he coaxed sarcastically, "feel free to carry on the dialogue. Say whatever's on your mind."

"Uh, well," said Barney, with exaggerated diffidence, "it's just that psychophysiological symptoms still are symptoms that need treating."

Then he swiftly put in a word for his sponsor. "As you've often put it, sir, there's a 'dosis for every diagnosis.' "

The guy looked like a cat who had just been stroked. "Well put, Livingston. Now we're back on track," he purred. "All right, gentlemen, let's take a look at those abbreviations."

Cohen proceeded to explain why doctors still composed prescriptions in Latin abbreviations. "For centuries this was the universal language of medicine. Indeed, Latin had been the language of instruction, too."

But Barney thought—and this time made sure *not* to say—You're full of shit! We're taught to write in Latin just to add to our mystique. The patient cannot translate q.i.d *(quater in die)* as "four times a day" and p.c. *(post cibum)* as "after meals," and so he feels he's in the hands of a great healer.

A doctor must be very careful never to employ a foreign phrase his patient might possibly understand. For instance, he will never write *per rectum,* but instead abbreviate it to "p.r.," when he prescribes a medicine to be shoved up the ass.

After that particular session, Bennett raced over to berate his friend.

"What the hell is wrong with you? You pull that psychiatric bullshit with a pharmacologist and he'll flunk you sure as 'Lucky Strike Means Fine Tobacco.' "

"Don't sweat it, Landsmann. Didn't I retreat with finesse?"

"Not noticeably, Barn."

"Hey, listen, I held back. I didn't mention that no fancy doctor on Park Avenue would write a *readable* prescription—or he'd lose his mystique."

"Livingston, I do believe you're turning cynical."

"Hell, Landsmann, isn't that what Med School is supposed to do to you?"

Laura could not get the children out of her mind.

Of all her clinical rotations, she felt the greatest involvement during Pediatrics. Perhaps it was a latent maternal instinct, but she regarded every patient she saw—whether gashed dangerously near the eye, racked with pneumonia, or horribly disfigured from an automobile crash (a chronic danger)—as her child, too.

Every ward in Children's Hospital held scenes that often moved her to tears. There were the terminally ill with diseases like cystic fibrosis, hemophilia, thalassemia, muscular dystrophy, and *worse*. Some of their lives would be measured in days, perhaps months—at best a few years. But all were incurable.

At first she felt drawn to a life in the laboratory, which she would dedicate to the quest for cures for these child-killers. But then she realized what she wanted was to be *with* the children, if only to make their deaths a little easier.

But the battle was not always one-sided. There was the joy of having a pediatrician detect near-invisible diseases like galactosemia—potentially fatal but simple to cure if discovered *in time*.

But Laura's most profound feelings were reserved for the premature babies, born twelve to fourteen weeks early and unable to breathe for themselves. They were so light and fragile (some less than two pounds) that they would actually turn blue if merely touched by a physician's stethoscope.

These tiny incubator patients fought pathetically for every breath, and the battle to save them might take days, even weeks. And, at that, they were lucky to rescue one out of four.

Barney might say it was her lingering guilt over Isobel's death, but she didn't give a damn about the reason. She only knew that what she wanted to do with her life was save babies.

So she applied for an internship at Children's Hospital. And was accepted.

"Laura, open up!"

"Go away, I just got off duty and I've gotta sleep."

The knocking grew louder and more persistent.

"Please, I have to talk to you," a frantic female voice called.

"Oh, shit," Laura grumbled to herself. She sat up in bed, threw off the covers, and went to the door. "Sometimes I wish I had an unlisted room number."

She opened it to find Grete, in tears.

"What's wrong, Andersen?" she muttered.

"Laura, I've been rejected by every single Harvard hospital. I feel like killing myself."

Laura made Grete come in, sit down—and calm down. First she let her get the crying out of her system. Then she tried to bolster her spirits by appealing to her ego.

"Look at it this way, it's Harvard's loss, not yours. I mean you've been accepted at dozens of places—and they don't have a monopoly on good surgeons here. Pick a place where they *want* you."

"Well, I've got offers from Johns Hopkins and Georgetown. So I guess I'll be spending the next few years somewhere in the vicinity of our nation's capital." And then she added, with a smile, "Maybe I'll even get to date President Kennedy."

"Sure," Laura replied, "JFK would work a bombshell like you into his heavy schedule. . . ."

She giggled. Grete was herself again. The Queen of Innuendo.

Bennett Landsmann was also refused a surgical internship by the three Boston hospitals to which he applied.

It surely wasn't something he lacked. After all, he was a Harvard summa, a Rhodes scholar, and had outstanding grades in his clinical rotations. As Barney once again explained, "I tell you, Landsmann, it's just too much melanin—black's *not* beautiful in surgery."

"You want the truth, Barn? I deluded myself into believing I was different. Somebody had to be the Jackie Robinson of surgery, and I thought I would be the guy. Anyway, it hurts like hell."

Barney grabbed his friend. "Fuck 'em, Bennett. Fuck 'em all. You've been accepted in a million places. Go to Philadelphia, Chicago, Baltimore— you're gonna be such a great cutter they'll be on their hands and knees asking you back as full professor."

Bennett looked at him. "You're a real mensch, Livingston."

"I'm flattered, Landsmann. And, if it means anything, I think you're one."

"Ah yes, Dr. Livingston," Bennett replied with a less broad smile than usual, "but I'm a *black* mensch."

The cases of Grete and Bennett were exceptional. For the most part the M.D.'s of 1962 would be going to internships at the hospitals of their first choice.

Even Lance Mortimer, the lowest on the totem pole, was accepted by Mount Hebron in Los Angeles.

Although—as he confided to Barney—his father, screenwriter Terence Mortimer, had to get none other than John Wayne to phone the chairman of the board and threaten to lead a battalion of cavalry against the hospital if they didn't accept "my buddy Terry's boy."

TWENTY-FIVE

Their anointing as full-fledged doctors took place in June of 1962 at a ceremony in the Medical School Quadrangle. The podium erected in front of Building A was surrounded by a semicircle of spectators on wooden chairs.

On this hot and humid afternoon in the presence of the medical pantheon that had been their teachers, and of the parents whose dreams many of them would be fulfilling, they were to receive their diplomas. And, most importantly, they would be initiated into the sacred priesthood of the healing arts by pronouncing the Hippocratic Oath.

Estelle and Warren were both there, Warren's camera recording the historic occasion for posterity.

But who was present to observe Laura's consecration? The elder Talbots and her fiancé, of course, but none of them could really qualify as "family" quite yet. There was no one from Lincoln Place. Laura had specifically told her mother by telephone not to attend.

"But why, *querida*?"

"May I refer you to the story of *The Little Red Hen*? You didn't help me bake the bread. So I don't want you to come and eat it."

She had acted from hurt but ended by feeling guilty.

Just before the ritual began, as Laura was adjusting her cap and gown, two Catholic priests approached her. One was young and cherub-cheeked, perhaps a novice, the other elderly and, as his darkened glasses seemed to indicate, blind.

"Señorita Castellano?" asked the younger man.

"Yes?"

"Miss Castellano, this is Father Juan Diaz-Pelayo."

Before she could respond, the old man started to address her in the pure Castilian of her mother tongue.

"I have come to bless you," he announced, his voice quavering with age. "I was with your honored father in the Civil War—there were not many of us from the Church. And I had the misfortune to fall into—shall we say 'unfriendly' company. Your father saved my life. I am sure he and your mother will have pride from you this day."

His palsied hands then made the sign of the Cross, as he said: *Benedicat te omnipotens Deus, Pater et Filius et Spiritus Sanctus.*

"Amen," added the cherub.

They vanished as quickly as they had appeared. Who had sent them? Her cloistered mother? Her father, somehow passing on the message through some secret network all the way from Cuba?

Barney had seen the encounter from afar and was at her side the moment the apparitions evanesced.

"Are you okay, Castellano?" he asked. "You look a little pale."

"To tell the truth, I feel like there was LSD in this morning's coffee. These two characters came to bless me." She shook her head in disbelief. "I wouldn't be surprised if the next thing that arrives is a chariot of fire. Don't let them take me off, huh?"

"I'll keep my eye out. Stay loose, Castellano."

The Dwyer family was represented by Hank's and Cheryl's parents. Each grandma held a twin; the little boy sat on his mother's lap. They were ecstatic at the prospect of this "coronation" of a simple kid from Pittsburgh.

Out of curiosity, some of the graduates-to-be surveyed the alabaster crowd to see if they could catch a glimpse of Bennett's parents. But there was not a single black among them.

Barney had had dinner with Bennett and the Landsmanns at Maître Jaques the previous night. Their affection for one another seemed to him stronger than any he had seen among "real parents" and their children.

But in fact there was a modest crowd of blacks waiting to raise a hearty cheer when Bennett strode onto the podium to get a handshake and a diploma from the dean. Of course, they were not seated in the sacred semicircle, but rather at the windows of the other buildings. The school's custodial staff—janitors and cleaning ladies—were acutely aware that there were only two soul brothers (and *no* sisters) in the entire school.

The ritual began with the usual congratulatory and self-congratulatory speeches, followed by the presentation of various awards.

Professor Georges de la Forêt, a Nobel Prize winner for his work in molecular biology, emerged from his laboratory only once a year—for this ceremony. He came before the congregation to announce the winner of the John Winthrop Prize for the most original work in medical research by a member of the graduating class.

After mumbling a few unintelligible remarks in what was variously construed as French, English, or Esperanto, he squinted at a small scrap of paper and announced, "Ze winner zis year—"

Then he departed from his prepared text to offer a personal opinion, "and in my view perhaps ze most original mind to come here since myself." He then called upon Peter Wyman.

The triumphant winner rose from his seat to acknowledge the thunderous ovation of the crowd.

But there was none.

There was polite applause from the parents' section and from his classmates a few scattered boos. And by the time Peter had mounted the podium and shaken Professor de la Forêt's hand, the idea of expressing their collective opinion had so inspired the class that their chorus of deprecation seemed to resonate to the heavens.

By contrast, Seth Lazarus—honored as the highest-ranking student— was greeted with cheers more appropriate to a football stadium.

Nat and Rosie were sitting with Judy Gordon in the third row. Though proud, Rosie chastised herself, How can I be happy when my little boy is dead? At the same time, her husband inwardly rejoiced, Thank God I have one brilliant son alive.

Suddenly, as if activated by some celestial switch, decorum returned and the audience hushed.

Dean Holmes, looking more than ever like a high priest in his crimson robes, bade the students rise and repeat after him the sacred physician's Credo—the Hippocratic Oath.

"*I swear by Apollo the physician* . . ."

"I swear by Apollo the physician . . ."

"*To hold my teacher in this art equal to my own parents* . . ."

"To hold my teacher in this art equal to my own parents . . ."

"*To consider his family as my own brothers and to teach them this art . . . without payment* . . ."

Even as he repeated these last words, Barney reflected on the irony
that most of his fellow students were not exactly going to do missionary
work.

"I will use my best judgment to help the sick and do no harm . . ."

Bennett Landsmann could not keep from thinking: The Nazi doctors also took this oath. How then could they have done what they did to
Hannah?

*"I will not give fatal drugs to anyone—even if I am asked. Nor will I
suggest any such thing . . ."*

Seth Lazarus moved his lips, but did not say the words. For this was
something he could not swear to.

"I will not give a woman any medication to cause abortion . . ."

Laura Castellano was startled to find herself thinking of that time—so
long ago—when she and Barney actively sought out a doctor who would
not honor this tenet of the Oath.

"I will be chaste and religious in my life and in my practice . . ."

Hank Dwyer, already sweltering, began to sweat still more profusely.
Will this be like the priestly vows I couldn't take? Am I, even here, being
tested by the temptations of the flesh?

I will not use the knife, not even to remove the stones within . . ."

Most of the future surgeons among them wondered at this injunc-
tion. Yet they were aware that for many centuries cutting human flesh
was considered a menial procedure, often done by barbers. There was
apparently little distinction between cutting hair and amputating legs.

But then again perhaps there was a reason for this interdiction. A
religious one: the body was a sacred temple. Do not enter. Do not trespass.

"I will not abuse my authority to indulge in sexual contact . . ."

Sitting on the podium with his distinguished colleagues, the surgeon
who had made the pass at Grete Andersen tried not to hear this stern
commandment of the vows *he'd* taken long ago.

At last the Oath concluded:

*"I will never divulge the secrets of my patients, regarding them as
holy . . ."*

"I will never divulge the secrets of my patients, regarding them as
holy . . ."

And then Dean Holmes announced, "You are now physicians. Go
out and do honor to your profession."

There is no experience in the world to match it. One might argue
that it rivaled the taking of a marriage vow—or Holy Orders—yet for the
one there was the institution of divorce and for the other the possibility
of renouncing the commitment.

But the Hippocratic Oath could *never* be abjured.

That afternoon they'd made an irreversible commitment to serve humanity and give healing comfort to the suffering.

Furthermore, unlike the vows made in matrimony and religion, theirs was made not to God, but to *Man.* If renouncing God would bring perdition, they would know it only in another world. But should they fail to serve Mankind, they'd know in *this one.*

And so they sallied forth to do battle with disease and death. And one another.

III

BEING DOCTORS

"He that sinneth before his Maker,
Let him fall into the hand of the Physician."

ECCLESIASTICUS 38:15

TWENTY-SIX

In 1962 advances in medicine and automotive mechanics seemed to be moving in parallel lines. A new electric shock device could revive an apparently lifeless patient—the way an emergency jump-start revitalizes a dead car battery.

And in cases where the patient's own heart failed, physicians were now able to replace the faulty valves with artificial ones—made from such substances as plastic, Dacron, and the like.

The only difference was that spare parts for a car come with a warranty and medical repairs do not.

Were such physicians imitating and perhaps arrogating the work of God? If so would they, like Prometheus, be punished?

Another event was interpreted by some as the visitation of divine wrath against the medical profession when a "harmless" tranquilizer called Thalidomide that doctors had confidently given to pregnant women was found to cause grotesque birth defects.

And that was followed by the moral issue. If women, reassured by their physicians, had been innocently ingesting this hidden poison, were they not entitled to have their pregnancies terminated? Or did medical ethics force them to run the risk of giving birth to malformed children who would lead an impaired and painful life?

The new direction of medicine was affirmed by the bestowal of the

Nobel Prize on James Watson and Francis Crick for ther discovery of DNA, the stuff of life itself. Despite its daunting nomenclature, deoxyribonucleic acid had a surprisingly simple structure. Shaped like a double helix with, among other things, thiamine and sugar, DNA might ultimately enable scientists to bake "live" gingerbread men. In other words, to create human beings in the laboratory.

Was this not the ultimate outrage to the Chief of Services in Heaven?

And while this brave new world beckoned on the horizon, humanity would more immediately be served by what would quickly become the most frequently prescribed drug of all time. The saver of souls and soother of psyches, the indispensable palliative for the Age of Anxiety, the miracle of medications: Valium.

The orchestra struck up "Here Comes the Bride." Laura took Barney's arm, and all the guests remarked upon her beauty and on the handsomeness of her escort.

It was three days after graduation and the sun was shining through a clear blue sky. But there were some shadows upon what should have been a wholly bright occasion. For the loving relatives and friends were all too painfully aware of who was absent, since, by default, the duty had fallen to Barney to give the bride away.

As they slowly walked down the makeshift aisle created by the rented chairs arranged in the garden of the Talbots' home, Barney wondered what Laura was feeling. She seemed tranquil, dignified, and calm, the loveliest of brides.

But was she happy?

In scarcely half a dozen measures of "The Wedding March" they reached their destination: Reverend Lloyd, the Talbots' local vicar, and, on his left, a triumphant Palmer and his Best Man, Tim—"the blond-bland Polo nut"—as Barney thought of him. (How ill-at-ease he looked without his horse.)

When all were at their posts, the minister began.

"Dearly Beloved, we are gathered here in the sight of God and in the face of this congregation to join together this Man and this Woman in Holy Matrimony."

After emphasizing the sanctity of the occasion, he asked if anyone present could show just cause why Laura and Palmer should not be joined together. Barney—who believed he could—nonetheless resolved forever to keep his peace. When the reverend asked who giveth this woman, Barney indicated that he gaveth.

At this point, he relinquished Laura to the custody of Palmer, who duly promised to take her as his wedded wife. And she promised to "love, honor, and obey" till death did them part.

The equestrian Best Man then handed over the ring, which Palmer placed on Laura's finger, and after a few well-chosen platitudes from Reverend Lloyd, the couple kissed for the first time as man and wife.

Instantly, the strains of Mendelssohn's immortal wedding theme announced that the time had come for all present to feed their faces and get completely smashed.

Uncertain what his role now was, Barney stood and watched the newlyweds disappear into a flurry of well-wishers.

"Lovely couple, aren't they?" asked Reverend Lloyd.

"Yeah," Barney replied, feeling a curious melancholy, "my brother Warren's in there taking pictures."

"Are you married?" asked the vicar.

"Uh, no, sir."

"Well then, Doctor," Reverend Lloyd said heartily, "with any luck, you may be next!"

It was about this time that Bennett Landsmann began to suffer an identity crisis.

Though he was no stranger to racial prejudice from the total segregation back in Millersburg to the less overt (and therefore more insidious) social ostracism in Cleveland, he had always been able to roll with the blows. And now he had naively thought that his status as a Harvard M.D. would make people look up rather than down at him.

But he was mistaken. For he was quick to realize that his fellow citizens still saw only the black skin beneath the white jacket.

Living in New Haven for his surgical internship—and hopefully residency—in the prestigious Yale–New Haven Hospital, his eyes were opened and his mind perplexed.

The hospital was not just near the city's ghetto, it was at its very epicenter. And although he himself lived—and parked the new Jaguar with M.D. plates, which Herschel had given him—in a modern air-conditioned apartment building across the parkway near the Old Campus, he spent almost every hour of his day encountering the anger of New Haven blacks.

The university and its nearly all-snow-white students were the rich and privileged; the blacks were the demeaned, neglected, consigned to poverty. The road built off Route 95 between the college and the ghetto was considered a Machiavellian ploy on the part of Yale—a sort of highway-moat to keep the riffraff out and leave the patricians in their tranquil citadel.

Not that the hospital was segregated. Both blacks and whites garbed in medical regalia were visible in equal number. The only difference was that the surgeons who performed the operations were white and the team that mopped the blood up later were descendants of the slaves that Lincoln freed.

Bennett tried to keep his equilibrium and his sense of humor. But he was lost—caught in no-man's-land between two separate and distinct societies. And he did not feel at home in either. Worse, *neither* was claiming him as their own.

A day did not go by without some sort of disquieting reminder of his "otherness."

Once, while working in the E.R., he admitted a black family who had just sustained minor injuries in a car accident. The wife, who had been hurt the least, was merely in a state of shock. A shot of epinephrine seemed appropriate. To save time Ben decided to take his own prescription to the drug dispensary.

The pharmacist looked at the paper and then stared at him.

"Dr. Landsmann, eh?" he asked. "He must be new."

"I beg your pardon?" Bennett said politely.

"Boy, you should know the rules. We're not allowed to give this kind of stuff to orderlies—only to a doctor or his nurse. You tell that lazy Landsmann he'd better come himself."

"*I'm* Doctor Landsmann," Bennett answered, hoping that his voice sounded calm and dignified. For he was too embarrassed to be angry and too wounded to be hostile.

Their glances met.

"Oh, gee, I'm sorry, Doctor," the pharmacist said deferentially. "I didn't know—I mean, most of the staff—"

"I understand," said Bennett softly. "Just make up the prescription. I've got a patient in distress."

"Of course. Of course." The druggist turned and brought the epinephrine with uncanny speed.

The following Saturday evening a territorial war between Italian and black gangs produced nearly a dozen casualties, including one young black shot in the chest by a zip gun.

Bennett was assigned the gunshot victim. He and a nurse swiftly wheeled the young man into the first Trauma room on the corridor. As she scurried off to prepare a hypodermic, Bennett took a closer look at the bullet wound. But when he reached to cut open the patient's shirt, he gasped with difficulty, "Hey, shit! Don't touch me, man, I want a doctor."

"I am a doctor," Bennett said as soothingly as possible.

"Don't jive me—there's no nigger doctors in this place. Get me The Man himself."

Bennett was on the verge of protesting that he did in fact qualify for the distinction when Herb Glass, a fellow intern, entered to ask advice about the multiple knife wounds he was treating.

As Bennett turned to have a sotto voce dialogue with Herb, his own patient screamed, "There, there—I want *that* guy. My fuckin' chest is gonna kill me. Tell that doctor I need help."

Bennett quietly explained the situation.

"Fuck him," Herb whispered indignantly. "He should feel lucky he's got a doctor with hands like yours."

But Bennett's self-respect had been so bruised that he persuaded Herb to switch patients.

Without another word, he walked across the hall to begin suturing the stab wounds of a patient he hoped would either be more tolerant or—better still—unconscious.

"For Heaven's sake, can't you try and see sense!"

Henry Dwyer, M.D. (as Hank now felt he should be called in view of his new status), was trying to reason with Cheryl, as she was nursing their fourth child, Rose Marie. It was barely dawn and he had just come back from a grueling thirty-six-hour shift on the wards of Boston Memorial.

"Hank, will you please stop bellowing—you'll wake the kids."

"What do I care? They never let *me* sleep after I slave my guts out just to put bread in their mouths."

"Hank, they're only little children. How do you expect me to explain to them what an intern is?"

"That's *your* problem, Cheryl. You're the mother. In my house Dad was always treated like a king."

"Oh, pardon me, Your Majesty. Do I take it you were born toilet-trained?"

"That's beside the point. You're dodging the important issue."

"Honey, it is *not* an issue. The Catholic church explicitly forbids birth control. Or have you completely lost your faith?"

"Look, don't try hitting me with that lapsed priest business. I don't feel guilty anymore. Besides, if you want to throw the Good Book at me, how about Saint Paul, *I Corinthians*: 'It is better to marry than to burn'?"

"What on earth is your point, Hank?" So emphatic was her gesture of exasperation that her breast pulled out of Rose Marie's young mouth.

Hank was nearing the end of his rope. How could a sexy—or at least a once-sexy—woman like Cheryl not understand that men in their prime needed regular intercourse, even if certain prudish, straitlaced Catholic girls thought it was slightly dirty?

He squatted down beside her, his quadriceps femoris aching from his climbs up and down the hospital stairs. "Honey, I burn. I give that damn hospital my heart and soul, but there's one special part of me I save especially for you. Now am I being clear enough?"

Little Rose Marie let out a wail. Hank frowned as if she meant it as a reprimand to him. Cheryl put the baby's tiny head back to her breast.

"Hank, I understand that you have needs, but you're a doctor. Don't you realize that a woman who's just given birth—"

"I deliver babies day and night, so don't tell me about so-called 'postpartum' depression. That's just your excuse for keeping me away."

"Come on, that isn't fair. I didn't say I was depressed. I'm just tired. I'll get my old enthusiasm back again."

"Oh sure, and then get pregnant right away."

"Not while I'm nursing."

"Look, I *know* a nursing woman can't get pregnant. I was simply implying that four kids is plenty for any struggling doctor's family."

"But, Hank, the struggling's almost over. Once you're set up we won't have any problems. And besides, you know my parents want to help us now."

"I have my pride," he countered sanctimoniously. "I don't take handouts from my in-laws. All I want is respect. Every husband needs respect."

"I do, honey. You know I worship you."

"Then why don't you respect my needs?"

Cheryl was crying, the tears spilling down her cheek onto her breast and moistening her baby's brow.

"Hank, I'll do the best I can. Tonight—when everyone's asleep—"

"Fat chance," he sneered sarcastically. "Someone's always crying for attention."

She was desperate to placate him. "And we'll practice . . . some control." She could not bring herself to say the actual word "contraception."

Hank smiled triumphantly. "Good, that's my girl. I've read the literature and they've refined the Pill to—"

"I didn't say the Pill," she interrupted hesitantly. "Catholic families can only use the rhythm method."

"The rhythm method?" he exploded. "You can dare to say that, when what's sucking at your breast this very minute was conceived that way? Besides, that's just a lame excuse to keep things down to once or twice a month."

And then he stopped. He realized that he'd gone too far. Cheryl was now weeping uncontrollably, bending over Rose Marie as if to shield her from her father's anger.

He knelt down again and murmured, "Hey, I'm sorry, hon. But you try going without sleep for two straight days and maybe you'll know how incredibly strung out I feel. I'm really sorry."

"Oh, Hank, I love you. Please don't let us fight like this again."

Father, mother, child remained entwined for several minutes, rocking back and forth.

And Cheryl was assuaged. "Do you want breakfast, hon? I'll make you some French toast as soon as Rose Marie's asleep."

"That's okay, I had some garbage at the hospital. Interns are like goats—we'll eat anything."

He rose and started for the bedroom as a second thought occurred to him.

Interns share another trait with goats: we're always horny.

On Saturday nights Bellevue Hospital's emergency room is like a MASH unit. To Barney, who'd been assigned thirty-six hours there, it seemed as if a world war was being waged on the streets of Manhattan.

Paradoxically, the knife and gunshot wounds were the easiest to deal with. By the end of the first few weeks he had sewn up so many miles (or so it seemed) of lacerated tissue that he found himself thinking of Luis Castellano's description of the Spanish Civil War: "I was more a seamstress than a doctor."

Gradually Barney was learning to suture skin in a semicomatose state so he could at least rest his mind while dealing with the battered victims of urban violence.

There was never a chance of getting any actual shut-eye since, at least from Barney's standpoint, New York lived up to its reputation as "the city that never sleeps."

He tried to console himself by recalling that he had been forewarned about the rigors of internship.

But why, he asked himself, as thousands had before him, why do we have these inhumanly long shifts?

Surely no airline would ever let a pilot fly for half as long as Barney worked. How come interns were subject to such punishment?

Ironically, doctors—the very people who knew physiology best—

seemed to ignore the fact that human beings cannot function normally when tired. That the interns were being driven to the edge of collapse.

He had had the temerity to ask a senior member of the staff the logic of allowing young physicians to punish their bodies in a way that would be deemed pathological in their patients.

The distinguished elder statesman merely replied, "That's the way *we* did it—and *we* survived."

"No, no, no, sir," Barney argued back somnolently, "even if you ignore our state of health, what about the unlucky patient who is seen by a doctor who can barely stay awake? Is it in *his* best interests that he be treated by a zombie? Tired people make mistakes."

The doctor looked at Barney scornfully. "Livingston, this is part of your education and you know what they say: If you don't like the heat, get out of the kitchen."

And so Barney soldiered on, although he felt his blood was turning slowly into coffee and his brain to soggy white bread—with a slice of cheese on top. There was one consolation: He was too tired to be worried that he knew so little, too exhausted to realize that if he ever lost his trusty *Merck Manual,* he would have no idea what he was confronting or what to do about it.

One relatively quiet weekday night a man announced to the nurse at the admissions desk that he was "dying from cancer." But when asked to be more specific he replied, "I can only tell it to a doctor."

The nurse assigned the case to Barney.

He took the man into one of the examination rooms, sat him down, brought a cup of coffee for each of them, sat across the table, and asked for the usual information—name, occupation, and most importantly for the hospital, what health insurance.

The patient turned out to be one Milton Adler, an accountant aged thirty-five—who had Blue Cross and Blue Shield.

"Fine," said Barney, putting down his pencil and trying not to choke on the fumes of the strong cigarette the man kept puffing. "Would you like some sugar in your coffee?"

The man grew agitated. "Jesus, what the hell kind of a doctor are you? I'm sitting here dying and you ask me whether I want sugar in my coffee. Did they saddle me with some student? I mean, haven't you got a superior I can speak to?"

"Mr. Adler," Barney answered firmly, "I am a qualified doctor. I know all about carcinomas, neoplasms, and any oncological pathology you might have. And frankly, based on my experience, I think you've still got enough time to talk to me for fifteen minutes."

"Is that all?" the patient asked anxiously. "You mean I have less than an hour to live?"

"I didn't say that, Mr. Adler," Barney responded, as gently as he could. "But we may *both* die of old age if I don't get some more details."

Something in Barney's manner (perhaps it was the ease with which he had pronounced "carcinoma") convinced Adler of his young physician's competence. "Okay, ask me."

"Now where exactly is your cancer, Mr. Adler?"

The man thought for a moment and finally replied, "I don't know, I'm not sure. Hell, you're the doctor, you should be able to find it."

Barney was beginning to get the picture.

"Mr. Adler, everything except skin cancer is invisible to the naked eye."

"Then take me to x-ray, for God's sake. What are you waiting for?"

Barney picked up a piece of blank paper and tried to sound concerned. "I think that's a good idea, Mr. Adler. But first I'll have to tell them what part of you to photograph. Do you hurt anywhere in particular?"

"My heart, Doctor. I think I've got cancer of the heart. Is it curable?"

"I can't say till I've got more information," Barney answered. "If you could tell me what symptoms you have—and when they started."

"I'd say it began last Sunday." And then he noticed Barney's pencil was still. "Aren't you writing all this down?"

"Don't worry, Milton, just keep talking."

"Well, that's it. I just told you, the pains started on Sunday."

"Did anything else happen over the weekend? I mean, was it otherwise uneventful?"

"I don't know what you mean. Isn't terminal cancer enough?" And once again he grew suspicious. "Are you sure you're not a medical student?"

Barney ignored this question and asked one of his own. "You're married, Milton? Is that right?"

But by now Adler was frantic. "You asked me that already for the goddamn forms. Now get me your superior or I'll call my lawyer!"

For a split second neither man moved. And that second stretched into several minutes as patient and doctor sat silent in the little examination cubicle.

Then Barney asked very delicately, "What made you think of your lawyer, Milton?"

"What do you mean?" the patient retorted angrily.

"You said you wanted to see another doctor. Why would you possibly need a lawyer for that?"

Adler was at a loss to answer but rose to his feet in protest.

"Sit down, Milton," Barney ordered softly but firmly. The man complied like an obedient child.

Barney leaned his elbows on the table. "Now Milton, are you in some kind of trouble?"

"No, absolutely not."

"Are you okay financially?"

"Yes, yes." He waved dismissively. "Stop asking these stupid questions."

Then Barney asked, "How about your marriage?"

"What marriage?" he suddenly exploded. "If I still had a marriage, why would I be calling my lawyer? She's hired the biggest barracuda in New York. And my guy's such a weakling he'll probably even lose me visiting rights to the kids. Christ, I could die."

He buried his head in his hands and began to weep.

After a moment Barney softly suggested, "You mean you want to die, isn't that really what you're saying, Milton?"

"Yes, yes." He nodded, his hands still covering his face. "I love her and I love my kids. What do I have if they're gone—just an empty goddamn apartment. You can't imagine how terrible I feel."

"I think I can," Barney said sympathetically. "I'd say you feel as bad as a man who has cancer of the heart."

It was Barney's first successful psychiatric diagnosis—and his first failure.

Although he immediately prescribed medication to lift the patient's mood, he felt that Adler was too close to seriously cracking up to let him go home.

He called the Psychiatric Ward and explained the situation. The chief resident there, a very tired guy called Barton, was annoyed. "Listen, kid, if we had to bug every depressed person that walked into E.R., we'd need Central Park to house them all. Besides, we're packed up here. It's strictly standing room only. Give him some Librium and send him home."

"But, Dr. Barton," Barney remonstrated politely, "I think this man might try to kill himself."

"Well, that's different," came the voice over the phone. "If he *does* try that, call back."

Barney returned to the examination room, handed Adler two black and green capsules, and a paper cup of water.

"Take one of these now, Milt, and the other tomorrow after breakfast. This ought to calm you down and let you sleep. But I want to see you back here first thing in the morning, okay?"

The patient nodded obediently and swallowed a capsule.

Barney walked his patient to the entrance and flagged him a cab.

Adler did appear the next morning. On the front page of the *Daily Mirror*. He had jumped fourteen stories from what the reporter called "his lavish East Side penthouse." When interviewed, his grieving wife, who had been in the country for the weekend with their children, sobbed, "I should have known. Poor Milton was feeling so depressed. I should have known."

Trying to steal a few precious winks of sleep, Dr. Ivan Barton was dozing at a desk in the nurses' station, his bearded chin cradled in his hands, when he was awakened by what sounded like a sledgehammer a few inches from his ears. He looked up with a start and saw an unfamiliar figure in a soiled white coat.

"Are you Barton?" growled an unkempt young doctor.

Having been up for the last thirty-six hours, the Psychiatric resident was slightly disoriented. He replied fuzzily, "Can I help you?"

Barney pushed a copy of the *Mirror* at him. "Take a look at this," he fumed. "This is the guy you refused to 'bug' last night because you didn't take me seriously."

"Hey, hey, slow down, old buddy," the slightly older doctor responded, gaining control of his faculties and (so he thought) his clinical technique. "You must be really new here."

"What the hell's the difference? Maybe if you'd taken the trouble to interview Adler last night, you'd have seen what I saw. The guy was desperate."

"C'mon, kid, you weren't that sure yourself or you'd have leaned on me a little harder. Am I right?"

"No," Barney bellowed, and immediately thought to himself, It probably *is* my fault. I'm responsible for that poor bastard's death.

"Do you want to talk about it?" Barton asked solicitously.

Barney shook his head and sat down. "I'm sorry if I flew off the handle. This is the first time I—"

"Lost a patient?" Barton finished his thought.

Barney nodded. "It's terrible. If only I'd been on the ball, I'd have saved the poor guy's life." He then looked up and asked, "Have you ever lost a patient?"

"Yes," Barton confessed, "and if it's any consolation, it actually gets worse each time you do."

"You mean you've lost a lot of patients?" Barney asked in shocked surprise.

"Listen, kid, it's a statistical fact that med students 'kill' an average of three patients before they qualify. And *nobody* keeps track after that."

Barney shook his head in anguish. "I don't think I can ever go through this again."

"Then don't be a psychiatrist," Barton advised sincerely. "Take up something safe like dermatology." He paused. "Just like an orthopedic surgeon needs physical strength, a shrink needs a lot of inner resilience. The sad fact is the world is crawling with unhappy people—and that even includes psychiatrists. In fact, do you know our own suicide rate?"

"I've heard it's pretty high," Barney murmured.

"Nine—*nine* times higher than the general population. You've chosen a very dangerous specialty, my friend."

Barney knew doctors could not save every patient. That was a fact with which he was prepared to come to terms. Hadn't a mugging victim he was treating just died on the table while an I.V. dripped blood into him?

But now at once he realized what the difference was. A knife is swift; life's blood pours swiftly from the body. A psychiatrist may be dealing with a similar phenomenon, but in *slow motion*. His job should not be sewing up the wound as much as trying to deflect the knife.

"Hey, when do you get off?" the psychiatric resident inquired.

"Half an hour ago," Barney replied.

"I leave as soon as Sarah Field comes in, which should be any second now. Want to grab a little breakfast?"

"No, thanks," said Barney, still in shock. "I just want to sleep. I want to crawl into bed and block out all of this." He turned and started off.

"Don't count on it," Barton called after him. "Most interns can't distinguish between sleeping pain and waking pain. It's *all* one fucking nightmare."

"Thanks," Barney responded, "you've been a real help."

TWENTY-SEVEN

Seth Lazarus had been the bonus baby of the graduating physicians.

Even Peter Wyman conceded this, although he might have claimed that unofficial honor for himself, had not Harvard made him a preemptive offer. Professor Pfeifer wanted him around, since Peter had become indispensable for his *own* research. As Peter saw it, Mike (they were on first name terms now, of course) wanted to "ride on the comet's tail." Thus Peter had applied only to hospitals within walking distance of the Biochem lab. He was, naturally, accepted by all.

His mentor had seen to it that Peter's meager intern's salary was supplemented by funds from the National Institutes of Health.

Thus for Peter nothing changed, except that the stationery he had printed now read: Peter Wyman, M.D., Ph.D.

Seth had established a record unprecedented in Harvard's history: he had received A-pluses in every one of his clinical courses. Hospitals had wooed him the way the colleges courted prize high school quarterbacks. Moreover, because of his multifaceted talent, he had been offered special rotations in whatever discipline he felt he wanted for his specialty.

Think of the prestige of Surgery, said half-a-dozen chiefs of service. You've got virtuoso hands. You cut like Jascha Heifetz plays the fiddle—with finesse, dexterity, and absolute precision. You could be another Harvey Cushing.

Needless to say, Seth was deeply flattered by the comparison to Harvard's legendary neurosurgeon and physiologist.

But he declined with thanks.

As he confessed to Judy, he did not want to consecrate his life to treating human beings who were passive and unconscious. He even reasoned that this was a possible explanation of the clause in the Hippocratic Oath which prohibited "cutting for the stone."

For almost the same reasons, he turned down an invitation from his old boss, Tom Matthews, to join the Path team full-time. Matthews all but guaranteed Seth would succeed him as department chief. But Seth had viewed Pathology merely as a means to an end—the way to recognize what made a human body die. In that department patients reached the doctors far too late.

No, if surgery was too much like the work of plumbers, or carpenters, Path was archaeology. It is no consolation to a widow to find her husband's cause of death. But think what happiness you'd bring a wife if you could decipher all her husband's symptoms. Then if you had time and expertise enough you could possibly save his life.

So Seth chose a middle course: Internal Medicine, where astute diagnosis might even spare the patient the necessity of surgery. So what if internists were sneered at by surgeons as mere "fleas"?

Despite the blandishments of San Francisco, Houston, and Miami— not to mention Boston and New York—he wanted to go home to Chicago. He felt a special tie to his old hospital. His heart was there. His future wife was there.

Unfortunately, he had not reckoned with the fact that Mom and Dad were also there.

For in the time since Howie died, his mother had undergone a metamorphosis. Although she visited the cemetery as regularly as she had the nursing home, she now began to obsess about her other son.

Seth in his naïveté made a strategic human error. He and Judy had decided that the following June, when his internship concluded, would be the ideal time to marry. They both agreed not to tell their parents. So when he returned to Chicago right after graduation he had chosen the path of least resistance and lived at home.

Rosie, who had barely noticed when he'd stayed past dinnertime to study in the high school library, now fretted if he was not at the dinner table every night. Although he'd always telephone her from the hospital to let her know, more and more she viewed his absence as filial disloyalty.

Moreover, as this new obsession grew, she would not fall asleep until her son returned. Sometimes it was even *after* Johnny Carson. And while some movie from the Stone Age flickered on the TV screen, she'd still ignore Nat's pleas to shut it off and let him sleep in peace.

"Not on your life," she'd answer sternly and would stay awake to hear Seth's footsteps climbing toward his room.

One night when *The Late, Late Show* featured a classic from the silent days, she provided sound track by engaging Nat in dialogue.

"What do you think he does at this hour?" she asked.

At first her husband did not answer, for he had found a way of sleeping with a pillow over both his ears. Rosie had to shout again: "What do you think he's doing, Nat?"

That was the very minute Seth entered and began tiptoeing upstairs. And so, unwittingly, he overheard a kind of verbal primal scene between two senior citizens. His father said, "For God's sake, Rosie, the boy's almost twenty-five."

"And what if she traps him? Girls are known to do that. Everything is hunky-dory, or should I say hanky-panky, and Poof!—suddenly she's pregnant."

"Good," said Nat. "Then you'll be a grandma that much sooner."

Seth remained on the stairs, spellbound by the conversation.

"Judy isn't good enough," said Rosie wistfully, "he could do better."

Nat raised himself onto his elbows and retorted, "She's a sweetie and they love each other. What do you expect, for heaven's sake, Princess Grace?"

"I expect better."

"Hey, listen, Rosie. Seth's a lovely boy. He's got a good head on his shoulders. But Prince Rainier he's not. This girl makes him happy. What more can you ask?"

During the pregnant pause that ensued, Seth told himself to get upstairs and out of earshot. But his thoughts could not activate the appropriate motor areas in his brain.

And then he heard his mother say in a lugubrious voice, "I don't want to lose him, Nat. It's bad enough I lost Howie. I don't want to lose my other child."

"Who's talking about losing? The boy's in perfect health. He's simply going to take a wife."

"Take her where, Nat? That's the point. I won't allow my Seth to marry her. And that's my final word."

To which her husband answered, "I sincerely hope so, Rosie. Goodnight."

*   *   *

The following Saturday, Seth Lazarus and Judy Gordon drove to Evanston and in the sight of God and in the face of a congregation— consisting of Daniel Carroll, Justice of the Peace, his wife, and a second witness (who cost five dollars) but not, alas, of their parents—were united in Holy Matrimony.

Those whom God hath joined let no mother-in-law put asunder.

It was Laura's first experience with a disfigured baby.

Twelve hours earlier Mrs. Kathleen Paley had given birth to a seven-pound baby boy. The attending pediatrician, Dr. Paul Fedorko, had brought along his favorite intern so that Dr. Castellano could observe how to handle a newborn in the initial moments of its life.

The young mother had been in a state of panic when she arrived at the hospital. Her obstetrician, Dr. Jack Lesley, concluding that it would be easier on his patient and on himself if she were heavily sedated, administered a hundred milligrams of Nembutal to put her out and then "scoped" her—in other words, gave her a hundred milliliters of scopolamine—to *keep* her out.

Laura was astonished—it seemed enough medication to keep an elephant asleep for a couple of days. Mrs. Paley had been all but decorticated; it was as if the outer layer of her brain had been shut off. To Laura it seemed miraculous that the woman was still breathing.

It had been a breech delivery, which Lesley had handled expertly, but which served to delay discovery of the impairment till the very last minute.

The mother slept unaware of the shock awaiting her.

For her otherwise perfect little boy had been born with a partial cleft palate—the tissues in the area of the mouth and nose had not fused. In addition, the infant had a harelip that made him look as if a dog had bitten him and torn his mouth.

Fedorko had warned Laura to prepare herself for this possibility, since Kathleen's family had a history of these malformations.

Laura had seen pictures of babies with cleft palates in textbooks but, although she tried to remain clinically detached, she shivered at the sight.

Dr. Lesley signaled the pediatricians to take the infant away. Laura and Fedorko wrapped the baby in blankets and the nurses rushed him out on a small isolette to Intensive Care. Meanwhile the mother was wheeled to her room where, because of the sedation, she would remain unconscious for at least half a day. This would give Lesley and his team enough time to steel themselves before confronting the parents.

Laura learned an important lesson that day. When a doctor has good news to tell a patient, he presents it on his own. He is like an opera star; he stands center stage and sings an unaccompanied solo. By contrast, when all has *not* gone perfectly, a different tune is sung—more like an oratorio for as many voices as possible.

To put it more bluntly, in times of crisis doctors believe there is safety in numbers.

Laura was drafted for the team—comprising Lesley, his chief resident, and Fedorko, who was now the child's official doctor. They reassembled twelve hours later outside Room 653.

"All set, Paul?" Lesley inquired.

Fedorko nodded. "I've got the book," he said and turned to Laura. "Are *you* okay?"

"No, to be completely honest," she replied. "I mean, I don't know what I'm doing here in the first place."

"Well, if you're going into pediatrics, this is something you'll have to learn. Also, frankly, these things are always easier if there's a woman present," Paul answered.

Shit, Laura thought, it's my job to keep the mother from "acting like a woman"—in other words, getting hysterical. What am I supposed to say—I've been through it, too? Or is there some special cliché that's appropriate for "just us girls"?

She turned to her preceptor. "What's in the book, Paul?"

"You'll see," he said, and then smiled. "Don't worry, Laura, this is one of those occasions when we can almost guarantee a happy ending."

Lesley knocked.

A man's voice bade them come in. They entered, their number making the little room seem crowded. Mort Paley was sitting by his wife's pillow, holding her hand tightly. She was clearly still more or less comatose, but her husband leaped to his feet the instant the doctors entered.

"Hello, Mort," the obstetrician said, deliberately using the first name to reinforce the effective parent-child relationship that always gives a doctor the upper hand. "Congratulations."

"But there's something wrong, I know," Kathleen called out. "I mean, I've been asking every nurse on the ward and they just keep saying 'Wait till Dr. Lesley comes.' Something's the matter—it's on your faces. All your faces."

The obstetrician began again, "Let me introduce my colleagues."

Mort listened impatiently as Lesley presented each member of the team by name and function. It was more obvious than ever that they were not there to bring glad tidings.

Laura empathized with him. Why are they taking so damn long? she wondered. Can't they just tell the truth and calm these poor people? Christ, they must think the baby's dead.

"There's a little problem," said Lesley finally, without emotion.

"What? What's wrong?" Mort demanded. "I mean is he sick or something?"

At this point Lesley ceded the floor to the pediatrician.

"Dr. Fedorko will explain. It's really his department."

Paul coughed and put on a show of confidence as he began.

"Now, Mort, I am sure you know that there's a history of cleft palate on Kathleen's maternal side—"

"Oh, no," the father gasped. "You mean the kid is gonna look like Kathleen's uncle? The guy is practically a freak. He can't even talk normally."

"What is it, Mort?" his wife asked. "Is our baby like Uncle Joe?"

He took her hand to comfort her as she began to moan. "No, no, please tell me it's not true."

"Mort and Kathleen," the obstetrician interrupted, "this is 1962. We've got the know-how to correct this sort of deformity. Just let Dr. Fedorko show you what wonderful work pediatric surgeons do these days."

Once again he called upon—or rather, it seemed to Laura, passed the buck to—his colleague.

"Look at these pictures," Paul said soothingly, opening the photograph album.

"Oh, Christ." Mort Paley cringed.

"But those are the 'before' pictures," Fedorko insisted. "Look at those same children after they've been operated on. Aren't they marvelous?"

Mort was not assuaged. He was still stick at the thought of what their baby looked like *now*.

He stared at the doctors and entreated, "Please don't show these to her now. Can't you at least wait a day?"

"No, Mort," Lesley answered categorically. "This is something the two of you have got to face so you can start to deal with it right away."

What for? Laura asked herself. What on earth could possibly be gained by giving bad news to this woman now? The poor girl's been in labor half the night. They won't be operating on the kid for weeks, so why don't they let her rest a little longer?

But then, as the senior pediatrician continued to show photographs of malformed children before and after corrective surgery, Laura suddenly understood Paul's haste: he had no tolerance for pain. He empathized too much and needed to unload the burden as soon as possible.

For the first time Laura understood why it was said that to be a doctor—or at least to survive as one—you have to build a fortress around your feelings to withstand all the assaults of emotional involvement.

You can try to help the suffering and mitigate their pain, but you must not *feel it*.

She wondered if she could ever be that strong.

An hour later Fedorko suggested, "Laura, why don't you help Nurse Walker take baby Paley to his mother. She's got to breastfeed him."

"Can she do it, Paul?"

"Physically, yes. The kid's able to suck. Psychologically—I don't know. That's where your bedside manner will come in. I'd really prefer not to use a Breck feeder. Why use a syringe when, from the baby's standpoint, the best source is 'Château Maman'?"

"But, Paul, I'm so new at this I don't know what the hell to say."

"Tell her the harelip will be perfect in six months. Anyway, if you can just get her to take the baby in her arms, Nature'll do the rest."

She stood outside Room 653, took a deep breath, and then said to the nurse, "You wait here. I'll see what I can do to prepare her psychologically."

"But Dr. Castellano, that's not our usual practice. I mean, we normally bring the baby right in."

"Well, if you don't mind, I'd like to try it my way."

"All right, Doctor," she capitulated.

Kathleen's first reaction had been precisely what Laura had expected: "No! God! I don't want to see it—take it away."

Her husband was still there and gave a wordless gesture to Laura, seeming to convey, Can't you stop torturing her?

A little frightened by the task forced upon her, Laura persisted. "Please, Kathleen, he's a lovely little boy with a few . . . malformations that we can easily set right."

"But he's like my Uncle Joe," she protested. "It's my fault. When Mort sees him he won't love me anymore."

"Please, honey," her husband whispered, "it isn't your fault. And I'm certainly not going to stop loving you."

To relieve the tension, Laura changed the subject slightly. "Have you chosen a name yet?"

"We were going to call him Mort Junior," Kathleen began. "But now—"

"We're still going to call him Mort," her husband interrupted reassuringly.

Laura looked at him, as if to say, You're a good guy. She's damn lucky to have you.

"I'm going to bring little Mort in now," Laura said gently. "He's ready to be nursed, and I'd like you at least to give it a try."

Kathleen could not answer. Instead, Mort, putting a hand on his wife's shoulder, looked at Laura and said, "Go on, bring our baby in."

There is an ironclad rule: As long as a doctor holds a baby it still belongs to him. The moment a mother actually touches it, the child is hers forever. And no matter what he looks like he is beautiful.

So it was with Kathleen Paley.

Laura put the newborn infant into Kathleen's arms, and the mother lifted her son to her breast—and sighed.

"Look, Mort," Kathleen murmured lovingly, "he's feeding." With her free hand she stroked the baby's fuzzy head. "He's cute, isn't he, Mort?"

"The cutest baby in the whole world, darling," he replied, and *meant* it.

Laura thought to herself, Good thing you didn't look inside his mouth—you could see directly to his nose.

"Thank you, Doctor," Mort said with emotion. "Thank you very much. We'll be seeing you again, I hope."

"I hope so, too," Laura answered sincerely, and made a mental note to follow up on baby Paley's progress. And be sure that she was present when they made him really beautiful.

Johns Hopkins Medical School
Baltimore, Md.

Dear Laura,

I was really glad to get your letter and very touched by your story of the cleft palate baby. If the pediatric teams are anything as good as they are here, that little boy will be fine.

My own surgical experience—if you can call it that—has consisted almost exclusively of holding retractors while other people cut. A second-year resident promised to teach me the trick of holding a clamp and sleeping on my feet at the same time. He claims it's the only way you can get through the ordeal.

On the more personal front, there's been a kind of change in my life. One night last month, I was on call with this really neat resident who's married with two kids.

You know how it is when it's very late and the rest of the world's asleep—you find yourself saying things you otherwise never would. We got to talking about careers and marriage, and this guy said straight out, that if he had to choose between being Surgeon General with no home life—or being a GP in Greenland with his wife and kids—he'd go the family route without a second thought. By the time he had finished asking me why I wasn't a wife and mother, he had me asking myself the same questions. And I couldn't come up with any good answers. So I figured it was maybe time to stop being an adolescent and talk to somebody who could help me do it.

The upshot is that I've started seeing this really good psychiatrist—you may even have heard of him. Andrew Himmerman. He's a really bright man who's written half-a-dozen books and about a zillion articles. The only trouble is he practices in D.C. and driving from Baltimore to Washington three times a week at 5 A.M. may send me to an early grave. But, at least I'll go with my act together. Anyway, I'm scouring the Washington area for a Surgical Residency so I won't have to commute for shrinkery.

Your letter wasn't very specific about married life. But then I guess since you knew Palmer so long it hasn't made that much of a change. On the other hand, having seen what the long days (and nights) at the hospital have done to some interns' marriages, I suppose there's strain involved. But then I sometimes forget you're Wonder Woman.

Got to run and scrub.

Please write soon,

Love,
Grete

Laura folded the letter just as Palmer appeared in their kitchen, yawning and unshaven. She rushed to kiss him.

"Gosh, you look like you've been up all night," she murmured.

"So do you."

"I was," she answered with a weary smile. "I saved two lives. And you can't imagine how great that feels. So what's your excuse?"

"I was waiting for you to come home."

"Did you forget that I was on? I mean, I wrote it all down." She pointed to their "Harvard Through the Seasons" calendar on which she had written out the timetable of her hospital comings and goings in green ink.

"I can read, Laura," said Palmer, drowsily going through the motions of making himself instant coffee. "But being an old Army man, I construed 2300 hours to mean eleven P.M. and figured you'd be home by midnight."

"Oh shit," Laura responded, tapping her forehead. "We got this emergency call from Manchester to pick up a pair of preemie twins and take them to Intensive Care. I rushed up with one of the interns. And you won't believe this, we had a flat tire on the way back."

"No, actually," he replied coolly, "I don't believe it."

"Lucky the respirators were on a generator or we would have lost the kids—" She stopped abruptly when Palmer's words finally sank in. "Are you calling me a liar?"

He tried to be nonchalant. "Laura, Manchester is in the sovereign state of New Hampshire and I'm sure they've got their own pediatricians—"

"Of course they do. But you know why so many people move to New Hampshire—because there's no state tax or anything. But that means their hospitals can barely afford a box of Band-Aids. There was no way of saving those twins except by putting them on the respirators at Children's."

She gave Palmer a pleading look.

"Anyway, I know I should have called, but it was all such a rush. I'm sorry, darling."

She went to kiss her husband, but he moved slightly to avoid her embrace.

"Are you playing hard to get?" She smiled affectionately.

"I'd say you were the one who was doing that," he retorted.

"Palmer, what the hell are you insinuating?"

"*Primo,* though I'm willing to believe they've got spartan facilities in Manchester, I'm not prepared to accept that they don't have an ambulance that could have transported those unfortunate infants.

"*Secundo,* I have never heard of an ambulance being driven by two doctors—and certainly not one that had a flat tire.

"*Tertio,* the way you've been waxing rhapsodic about your medical colleagues, I figured it was only a matter of time until you were, as the Bard puts it in *Othello,* 'making the beast with two backs.' "

The rage center in Laura's brain was sending the signal to explode. But the rest of her was too exhausted.

"*Primo,* my loving husband," she began her rebuttal, "you should remember that Othello was *wrong* about his wife. *Secundo,* Manchester doesn't have portable incubators and we were in a station wagon, not an ambulance. And, *tertio,* I think you are a paranoid shithead for not believing me. I mean, how the hell do I know you weren't with some floozy last night? Now, get out of my way, I've only got four hours to sleep before I'm due back."

As she was disappearing through the kitchen door, Palmer called after her, "That was a good idea you just gave me, Dr. Castellano, I might just start my own private Intensive Care Unit. To take care of *me.*"

At the heart of it all was the problem that Laura and Palmer each had different expectations from a marriage. Yet she had never found the courage to discuss it openly with Palmer.

He was still traditional enough to think his wife should be a companion, helpmate, mother of his children, and of course a sparkling hostess. After all, his own mother had been such a model wife to his father. And certainly Laura filled every one of his criteria.

She, on the other hand, had no paradigm for marriage. She knew only that she did not want a relationship like her parents'. The fact that Luis and Inez had lived together for more than twenty years before they separated certainly did not prove that they were ever welded as a couple.

Indeed, there had been a long time during her early Med School years when she doubted that she was fit for any kind of marriage. For the only thing her parents had succeeded in imparting to her was the quality of self-reliance. And wasn't marriage a relationship of mutual dependence? Not out of weakness, but of two strengths fusing to become a greater force—two beams leaning on each other to sustain a greater weight.

But all through their courtship, what Laura had found most attractive in Palmer was the way he protected her. He seemed—though she could never see it that explicitly—so fatherly. And he had led her to believe that marrying would simply change her name, not her life-style.

They had honeymooned at the exotic Hotel Byblos in Saint-Tropez. Every morning they would walk along the water's edge from the beach of Pamplon (Plage de la Bouillabaisse) to the beach of Tahiti—trying not to look self-conscious (or even look, for that matter) as they passed the nudist colony that lay in between.

Palmer did not disguise the fact that he enjoyed this kind of sightseeing and he tried to tease her into taking off her bra. But to his amusement he discovered she was not as uninhibited as either of them thought.

After lunch they would go to bed, and then siesta. Later, as the sun grew orange, they would sit in Le Senequier near the marina, and observe the bronzed and beautiful as they paraded by.

They sipped Pernod, while a few hundred meters off, the fishermen were busily unloading what would be their dinner at Leï Mouscardins.

Their nuptial voyage had been a dream, but their return to Logan Airport was an uncomfortable awakening. For Laura, whose sensuality (even in a bra) had put the other women on the beach to shame, now donned a baggy white coat and drove off to Children's Hospital at dawn.

Palmer was left with half a summer to burn, not knowing how to occupy himself till the fall term began. At first he tried to work on his Chinese. But he was driving himself crazy with the sound of his own voice trying to imitate the tones of pronunciation that differentiate the various meanings of the same word.

He would sometimes take a book and walk along the Charles to find a shady spot and read. And when he tired, he would watch the sailboats— like albino butterflies—dash to and fro across the placid water.

The dark would arrive with half the evening gone. He would then return to Beacon Street, defrost a dinner, open a bottle of Chablis, play Vivaldi on the stereo, and fantasize that he was on a date with Laura.

He was a patient man and Laura—still radiant and energetic from their honeymoon—made the nights she was off duty compensate for her absences.

But the internship weighed heavily on her shoulders and fatigue set in. Then she would come home, kiss him, take a shower, have a bite to eat, and then plunge like a deep-sea diver into many-fathomed slumber.

Gradually she started to give up the eating. After a few more weeks she would leave the shower for the morning, kiss him, throw off her shoes, and then go to bed in what she had been wearing.

But let the record show—she always kissed him first.

Once—miracle of miracles—she got the medical equivalent of a two-day Army furlough.

Palmer was delighted and proposed a little drive up to Vermont to see nature's brushwork on the autumn trees, have dinner at a cozy inn, and then, as Edgar Allan Poe put it, love with a love that was more than love.

"I'm up for the last part," Laura said, smiling wearily, "but couldn't we do it a little closer to home, like in our own bed?"

"Come on, Laura, where's your sense of adventure?"

"I think I lost it after my first all-night surgery."

"Laura, darling, is it really worth all this?"

She saw the sadness in his eyes, knew the loneliness he felt, yet answered, "Yes, Palmer, it is to me."

The phone rang.

Bennett Landsmann opened one eye while trying to keep the rest of his body asleep. It was 2 A.M. and he had just gone to bed after thirty straight hours in the E.R. But the ringing persisted relentlessly and finally with a sigh of defeat he picked up the receiver.

"This is Dr. Landsmann," he said gruffly.

"This is Dr. Livingston, but you can call me Barney."

Bennett opened his other eye and sat up.

"Hey, do you know it's the middle of the night?"

"No," Barney quipped. "But can you hum it?"

"Are you high on something?"

"Not unless you count Nescafé and chocolate bars. No, Landsmann, this is the first time I've sat down in what seems like a month. I must have interviewed several million patients and written up histories for every damn one of them. I've lost count of the cuts and lacerations I've sewn. I got so dazed that the chief resident actually told me to lie down.

"Anyway, being a man of leisure for the next fifteen minutes, I thought I'd see how they were treating you up there at Yale. Were you actually *sleeping,* Landsmann?"

"No, of course not. I was doing some extra research in my spare time. Trying to invent a cure for bullshit. Anyway, how's your ass?"

"Aching just like the rest of me. Well, how about you, old buddy? Are you at least doing any horizontal dancing in the sack?"

"One or two nurses have looked favorably upon me. But there's even a pecking order in that department, and senior residents get the best talent. Anyway, I'll survive. What do you hear from Castellano?"

"Nothing. I mean, what do you expect? She's working as hard as we are. And whenever I do call, old Palmer claims she's out. Half the time I'm convinced he's giving me the straight-arm."

The friends were exchanging Casualty Ward anecdotes—some of which were so grisly that only gallows humor made them tolerable—when Barney innocently touched a raw nerve.

"So, in other words, outside of total fatigue and sexual deprivation, you're happy in New Haven?"

There was a silence.

"Hey, Landsmann, are you still there?"

Bennett hesitated. "Well . . . it's kind of a long story."

And he then recited a litany of ugly incidents.

When he finished, Barney said, "I can imagine how you feel."

"Can you really?"

"I'd say your mood was pretty black."

"Right on, Livingston. And getting blacker all the time."

TWENTY-EIGHT

Informed observers of the American scene predicted that 1963 would be remembered as the year of Black Awareness. That is until the events of November twenty-second. Now the hallmark of the year would be John F. Kennedy's assassination.

Not only was the body politic in turmoil, but the human body also featured prominently in the news. It was the beginning of a new era.

All over the country there was news of successful replacement of diseased and dying organs. Dozens of people received the gift of life when the kidneys of another were transferred to them.

At the University of Mississippi, the first lung transplant was performed. In Houston, Dr. Michael De Bakey used an artificial heart to maintain the circulation of the patient's blood during heart surgery.

And when they lacked a human donor, the laboratories came to the rescue. Thanks to man-made corneas, some who were blind could see again.

But not all the medical news was good. For the American Hospital Association reported that the average daily cost per patient had more than doubled in five short years. From $18.35 to $36.83.

And before Jack, another Kennedy died that year. On August seventh, JFK's second son, Patrick, was born five and a half weeks premature, weighing four pounds ten and a half ounces and suffering from RDS (respiratory distress syndrome). His lungs had not developed sufficiently. He could inflate them but could not retain any air.

Wrapped in a blue blanket and placed in a little plastic box, the infant was rushed from Hyannis Port to Boston Children's Hospital, where the entire staff was mobilized in the fight to save him. The hospital had an apparatus unique in the world—a huge oxygen chamber thirty-one feet long and eight feet wide. Two specialists worked inside the machine in a desperate attempt to force oxygen into the baby's system.

But without success. After a mere thirty-nine hours of life, the baby died.

(Ironically, only a year later, a new technique of treating RDS was perfected by doctors at Children's Hospital in Louisville, Kentucky.)

By the end of 1963 the Harvard Medical School class that had received diplomas a year earlier had ostensibly completed all requirements to practice medicine in America. They were, most of them, between the ages of twenty-four and twenty-nine.

They were also, most of them, far from ready to practice, because the end of internship most often signals yet another beginning.

True specialization demands intensive concentration on a specific aspect of medicine. Like anesthesia or pharmacology. Or on one tissue, like skin or blood. Or one area, the chest or abdomen. Or one organ, the eye or heart. Or one physical technique, the art of surgery. Or even one mystery (though some insisted it was not a science), the workings of the mind: psychiatry.

Thus, Barney Livingston, M.D., having duly fulfilled the requirements of internship and wanting to become a psychoanalyst, needed to spend three years in psychiatric residency (and thereafter another optional twelve months).

And if he wished to be a full-fledged member of a psychiatric institute he had to have the insides of his own head probed by a senior analyst. This was intended to get himself in better touch with his unconscious, and thereby help his patients to get in better touch with theirs.

Thus, assuming that he did not stumble along the way, Barney might be free and clear of all the pedagogical requirements in another six or seven years. This would put him on his own at last in 1970, at the age of thirty-three. In other words, he'd just be *starting* when professionals in other fields (like little brother Warren, who would receive his Law degree that year) would have been off and running—not to mention earning a real living—for pretty close to a decade.

And this, always assuming he had fulfilled his military obligations somewhere along the way.

And Barney's road was not the longest. Graduates aspiring to surgical careers, like Bennett (who had been invited to stay at Yale) and Grete (who had switched to Georgetown Hospital in Washington), had at least five years of postgraduate training to complete—one as an intern, two as assistant resident, one as first assistant, and, provided they had not collapsed or reached senility by then, a final year as chief resident. Of course, if they were going into a *sub*specialty, like pediatric surgery, there would be still further years of training.

Doctors are often accused of callousness, venality, and self-infatuation. But they remind us that they have sacrificed the springtime of their lives, completely lost the precious years between their twenties and their thirties acquiring skills to benefit their fellow men.

Furthermore, they have suffered deprivations. Most of them have not had more than a dozen real nights of sleep in all this time. Many have sacrificed their marriages and have lost the unique opportunity to see their children grow.

So when they argue that the world owes them some compensation— in the form of wealth, respect, and social status—their demands are not entirely without cause.

Also, as the grim statistics show, they often suffer worse than any patient. For no one can repair a broken marriage or restore the children damaged by their father's ostensible neglect.

Laura had been at the hospital when the Kennedy baby was rushed in. Although she had no direct contact with the case, she remained there in a kind of mass vigil with most of the staff.

She had been awake for more than forty-eight hours when White House Press Secretary Pierre Salinger, himself on the brink of tears, announced that "Patrick Bouvier Kennedy died at 4:04 A.M. this morning. The struggle of the baby boy to keep breathing has been too much for his heart."

And she shared in the collective grief and sense of failure that pervaded every corridor.

When she heard one of the new interns say, "At least the Kennedys have two other kids, it's not all that terrible," she turned on him.

"What the hell kind of attitude is that? The point's not what she has, but what she's *lost*!"

The chastened intern retreated.

*   *   *

As a first-year resident in pediatrics, Laura had at least a few serious responsibilities.

For instance, when the time came for Kathleen and Mort Paley to bring their six-month-old in to have his lip repaired (the palate surgery would be done later), Laura stood right at the surgeon's shoulder. She watched intently as Fedorko meticulously closed the ugly tear, concluding with near-microscopic nylon stitches to connect the outer skin. The disfigurement had all but disappeared.

The Paleys were ecstatic. Three days later, as Kathleen was putting on the baby's coat and hat, Mort commented to Laura, "It's worked out just the way you promised, Dr. Castellano. We're extremely grateful—all three of us."

As they shook hands, Laura thought, Words like that are what make most of us go into medicine.

But Laura was sleepwalking by the time she returned home after her twenty-four-hour rotation. One of the few neurons still working in her brain reminded her body that it needed some food in order to perform the basic functions of life.

She opened the Frigidaire, pulled out two yogurts, and sat silently at the kitchen table force-feeding herself, too tired to read even the newspaper lying nearby. She reached for a small pile of letters—bills, mostly—and aimlessly leafed through them. There was nothing worth staying awake for except one embossed "Georgetown Medical Center, Washington, D.C." She picked up a knife and opened the envelope with surgical precision.

Dear Laura,

Great news. Yesterday I actually got to make an incision on my own. Okay, so it was only a routine appendectomy. But the patient was an 18-year-old cheerleader-type whose greatest anxiety was whether she'd be able to wear a bikini again. Anyway I'd been practicing my technique (mostly on peaches and oranges) so when the Chief suddenly turned and handed me the knife and told me to go for it I was truly ready.

I took the scalpel, pronated my hand, went for it and made a really neat (I thought) transverse incision. And then he let me keep going until I had incised the peritoneum. I felt so high—I had finally been initiated.

I seem to be making progress in my therapy, too. Andy says that at one time or another almost every medical student has to seek psychiatric help. And he told me about a study made by the Markle

Foundation a few years ago, and I went to the library and looked it up. Would you believe that out of 219,000 doctors in this country, only a lousy 11,000 are women?

And what really shocked me was that the divorce rate for female doctors is five *times higher than for men—and God knows* they're *not doing so well. Even a super guy like Andy is stuck with a pretty unsympathetic creature for a wife.*

I'm due on in about three minutes and I've been writing this naked as a jaybird—so I'd better hurry and get dressed.

Please write and let me know how you *are.*

Love,
Grete

Laura smiled. Same old Andersen, always goes back to her body. I wonder when her shrink will get around to working on that?

And then it struck her. "Andy"? Does she call her psychiatrist by his first name? And how the hell does she know about his marriage? Is that something they would discuss in a therapy session? But she was too tired to give it any more thought.

She removed her shoes in the living room and walked on tiptoe up the stairs. The bedroom lights were still on. The bed was empty.

And unslept-in.

Laura sensed that she should have been upset. But she was so exhausted that even the disappearance of her husband could not overcome the beckoning of Morpheus.

It was only at eight o'clock the next morning that she was able to grasp the fact that Palmer had vanished. No note. No explanation. No nothing.

Her imagination ran the gamut of possibilities. Maybe he was in an accident. Maybe mugged and taken unconscious to a nearby hospital.

She thought of calling his parents but did not want to alarm them.

After making herself a cup of coffee, she studied the bulletin board in the kitchen where they had each put their individual time schedules.

Her eye fell upon the previous day's agenda. Palmer had taken a seminar on "Anglo-Chinese Diplomatic History" that night—7 till 9 P.M. She had made up her mind to call the professor to find out if Palmer had been there the previous night, when the object of her inquiry suddenly appeared.

"Good morning, Laura," he said cheerfully.

"Palmer, you had me worried to death."

"Really? I'm glad to know you care."

She knew the remark was intended to provoke a fight, so she let it pass.

"Where the hell have you been all night?"

"With friends," he answered, the better to annoy her.

"That's it? That's your entire explanation?"

"Have I ever asked *you* for a detailed account of your activities outside the house? You just tell me you've been at the hospital and that's the end of it."

"You had a seminar last night."

"Indeed I did."

"And?"

"And that's the end of it."

"You don't expect me to believe that the discussion was so stimulating it lasted all night."

Palmer grinned. "Laura, darling, that's the sort of report I'm always getting from you. Your lovely green handwriting says you're due off duty at eleven and then you appear at dawn, and just toss off some line about having an emergency. What if I told you that we had a little crisis—the appendix of Professor Fairbank's book fell out and we used heroic efforts to suture it together."

"If that's supposed to be a joke, I'm not laughing."

"Laura, I've not been laughing since the second week of your residency. I am by nature a gregarious person. Of course, you're the person I'd most like to be around but you seem to be in scarce supply. Therefore, when some of the lads in the seminar suggested we go out for a few beers, I joined them."

"Didn't you even try to call?"

"Yes, darling, I did. I tried you every half hour from eleven-thirty onward. There was no answer at the house and the hospital switchboard couldn't locate you. Finally I just gave up and accepted a fellow student's invitation to sleep on the couch."

"You're very vague about this student's gender, Palmer."

"Do I ask you about your fellow doctors' gender?"

"Cut this sophistry, goddammit," she exploded. "You know my job requires me to be on duty all night long. It's not the same thing."

"Excuse me, but from my standpoint it is. Did you enjoy your solitary sleep last night?"

"Of course not, I was—"

"You were feeling what I feel almost every night," he interrupted.

"Come off it, Palmer, don't tell me you didn't know how residents and interns live—if you can call it living. Do you think I actually enjoy being so dizzy from lack of sleep that I can barely see straight? I'm not some kind of masochist."

"That's two of us," he countered. "You don't enjoy your night shifts in the hospital and I don't either." He paused, then added, "My class-mates are all married, having kids—and having fun. Meanwhile, for all intents and purposes I'm living like a hermit. In a nutshell, Laura, I will not go on this way."

They stood there like two people on opposite banks of an ever-widening river.

At last she spoke. Her voice was weary. "Obviously I won't give up the hospital."

"Obviously."

"So what do you propose as an alternative?"

"Well, I think if we want to stay together, we'll have to decide on some sort of compromise, some modus vivendi."

"On the contrary, Palmer. I think you've already made the decision for both of us." She took a breath and then asked, "So where exactly were you last night?"

He answered, with no apparent emotion, "Getting laid."

"Incurable" is almost a taboo word in the medical vocabulary. Though most doctors can pronounce the word "terminal," they seem allergic to the special connotation of "incurable." It somehow seems to reflect pejoratively upon them. It's also dangerous. Relatives of the unfor-tunate patient might have the temerity to ask, "*Why* can't you cure him, Doctor?"

In ancient days the poor unfortunates who contracted leprosy were exiled, isolated from the rest of all humanity—and not only for their awful aspect or the terror of contamination, but also because society prefers to hide mistakes that simply will not disappear.

Leprosy can nowadays be cured quite easily with Dapsone. But it has its modern analogue in mental illness.

Though psychiatry is more compassionate in this regard. Its wards are carefully divided into "curables" and "chronics": those for whom the only therapy is a lethean medication like Thorazine, and others who might possibly be rescued from the dusky cavern of delusion.

Barney Livingston began his psychiatric residency that July of 1963 by being exposed to the psychotic (read "incurable") section of Bellevue Hospital. Like every neophyte he had hopes of helping all the sick of soul. Thus when he pushed open the door of the Blenheim Ward, he did not see an overcrowded museum of waxwork figures. He did not see five dozen people, each of whom was living all alone inside a private world. Instead he looked on it in the manner Dante gazed upon the souls in purgatory, determined that he would help them leave.

One thing struck him almost immediately. At this moment the streets of Manhattan were hot enough to melt the asphalt, and yet the vast majority of inmates here were dressed like King Lear for the tornadoes of the heath.

He reminded himself that chronic schizophrenics often wear winter clothing all year round in terror that it might be stolen or—still more unlikely—lost in this warehouse of a room.

Psychiatry is often dubbed "the talking cure." But Barney realized why *this* patchwork quilt of persons had been thrown together.

They were silent.

Now and then there was the sound of shuffling feet. A cough. A sneeze. But even these were rare. The inhabitants seemed mute. Or else humming to themselves some otherworldly mantra.

It was bizarre, none of them seemed to acknowledge the existence of another. His arrival did not catch even a single pair of eyes. Good God, he thought, how could people get this way?

A huge, muscular black man, wearing a white shirt open at the neck, came up to him.

"You look a bit lost, Doctor," he said amiably.

"Hi, I'm Dr. Livingston," he greeted his interlocutor, obviously the ward attendant.

"Yes, Doctor, we've been looking forward to your arrival. Let me guide you to the nurses' office."

"Thanks," Barney said, but his eyes kept darting left and right.

Passing through a set of double doors they saw to their right a gray-haired man, his head leaning toward his left shoulder, the fingers of his left hand dancing, his right hand moving back and forth across his left forearm.

"That's Ignatz," the black man explained, "he's practicing."

"Oh," said Barney. And then he worked up the courage to ask, "Practicing what?"

"Why, Doctor, don't you see his Stradivarius?"

"Oh, sure, sure. It's just I had a little trouble hearing it."

"Ah, but Doctor, 'Heard melodies are sweet, but those unheard/Are sweeter . . .' "

Barney smiled in appreciation. "Very apt," he said admiringly. "John Keats—himself a doctor. By the way," he added, holding out his hand, "I still don't know your name."

"Oh," the black man said, "I would have thought they'd told you in the palace."

"I beg your pardon?"

"Don't you know that Pontius Pilate plans to crucify me?"

"Jesus Christ!" said Barney, momentarily off balance.

"Yes, my son. And when I see my Father on Friday night I'll put in a good word for you."

Suddenly an irate voice shouted out, "Mr. Johnson—what have you been telling that young doctor?"

The big man turned to what seemed to be—at least Barney hoped—the ward head nurse, who was marching toward them shaking an admonitory finger at his guide.

He whispered to Barney, "Beware, my son! That woman is a succubus—she's Satan in a female form."

At this point, the nurse reached them. "Good morning," she said. "I'm Jane Herridge. You must be Dr. Livingston."

"Dr. Livingston?" the black man said with fascination. "Then I must be Henry Stanley."

"Now, Mr. Johnson, you go off and spin your tales and let me talk to Doctor here. He'll come and visit you again, I'm sure."

The nurse led Barney away, all the while assuring him that Mr. Johnson's multifaceted delusions were quite harmless.

"Actually he doesn't live here, he's from the acute ward. But he sort of acts as an unofficial orderly. We're very shorthanded. And he's so outgoing and has such a way with people."

Probably because he *is* so many people, Barney thought to himself. He looked over his shoulder at the looming figure of Mr. Johnson, who now lifted his arm in valediction.

" 'O now, forever, farewell the tranquil mind!' "

"That's Shakespeare," Barney confided to the nurse. "But I'll be damned if I can remember what play."

From afar off, the great man cried, "*Othello,* act three, scene three, line three hundred and fifty-one!"

A moment later they were safely sheltered behind the almost soundproof glass of the nurses' station, sipping coffee from paper cups with plastic holders.

"That guy's some kind of genius," Barney remarked.

The nurse replied, "Doctor, I think the saddest thing about this ward is all the wasted talent that's imprisoned here. And I don't mean by bolts and bars. It's locked deep inside them. And there's nothing to be done."

"Are you sure—?"

Mrs. Herridge interrupted him. "Please, Dr. Livingston. I mean no disrespect, but every summer a new resident comes on this ward and thinks he'll turn it into some institute of higher studies. But the truth is that it's just a loony bin and they're so far gone that they can't fend for themselves in the outside world."

She took him on a tour of the "facilities." The prisonlike windows were not new to him, nor were the rooms with padded walls. (He could not bring himself to speak of them as "cells.") But what astonished him was where they slept. Their dormitory was like a bunkhouse in a summer camp, but instead of half-a-dozen beds there were—"How many, nurse?"

"Sixty," she replied. "This was only built for forty, but you know our problems."

Barney wondered if he did. Was there an epidemic of madness in the world?

"How do you treat them?" he asked.

"Well, we don't exactly 'treat' them, Doctor. We just try to get them through the day. Believe me, it's quite a task to wake up sixty patients, from sixty different planets, march them into breakfast—"

"March?"

"Well, not exactly. But we do try to get them standing two by two. They're easier to manage."

"Like Noah's Ark," he said absently. And then he asked, "What comes after that?"

"For those that can make *some* communication, we've got arts and crafts. We've even tried a dance class now and then. But most of them just stand around and do . . . whatever you just saw them doing till it's time to eat. Then they get their medication and that's it."

"That's it?"

A look of impatience crossed the head nurse's face. "Dr. Livingston, there are sixty of them and eight of us—and that's including Mr. Johnson. We have to keep them sedated or it would be sheer chaos."

Barney nodded. "If it isn't too much trouble, could I go through some of the case histories?"

"Certainly," she answered, and led him back to her office.

Holy shit! Even after a cursory glance at the records, Barney was stupefied by the quantity of drugs these patients were receiving.

"God," he said to the head nurse, "even Superman would fall asleep on the doses that you're giving these poor people."

Mrs. Herridge did not answer—just glanced at him from the corner of her eyes. He began to think she was looking him over, perhaps examining *him* for traces of psychosis.

"Is something wrong, Mrs. Herridge?"

"No, Doctor. I'm just surprised that you'd want to spend so much time reading those histories."

"Well, that's my job, isn't it?" Barney replied.

"Well, if you actually read the complete files of everybody in this ward your rotation would be over. Most of them have been with us for as long as I can remember. Mrs. Ridley would be celebrating her twenty-fifth anniversary here—if there were some way we could let her know."

And Barney thought to himself, But what if whatever they had that brought them here wasn't as bad as what they turned into just by *being* here?

"Mrs. Herridge, can you tell me if anyone has ever been released from this ward?"

"Not in the usual hospital sense, Doctor. I mean, they're mostly elderly and—"

"—just dying to get out, eh?"

He thought he detected a movement of her facial muscles, the fleeting manifestation of a proto-smile.

But she glanced impatiently at her watch. "If you'll excuse me, Doctor, I've got to see that everything's in order."

Barney nodded. To make sure all the inmates are drugged up to their eyeballs?

He rose politely. "I guess I ought to go, too. I'll be in early tomorrow morning and make a fresh start."

But he was concealing the real truth: he was genuinely frightened of being left alone among the ghosts of living human beings.

He followed several paces behind the head nurse, trying to keep his gaze on her footsteps.

Just as they were arriving at the far end of the gigantic hall, he heard a sound—like a whine—that, though lacking words, still struck him as a kind of plea.

He stopped and slowly turned toward the left. There was a youngish man—at least he seemed not as antiquated as the other patients.

Motionless, he stood emitting intermittent moans. And staring into space.

Then something happened.

Their eyes met. At least Barney thought they had made contact.

And, for a fleeting instant, he sensed a glimmer of recognition.

Did this man know him? Had they ever met beyond these walls—out in the world?

As he stood puzzled, Mrs. Herridge said quite audibly, as if she assumed the patients, if not deaf, were at least uncomprehending, "Pay no attention, Doctor. He's a tragic case—tried to kill his wife and children. Dreadful story. Shall we go?"

Barney began to walk toward the guard at the door. But before he left, he stole a furtive glance at the groaning man and repeated to himself, I swear to God I know that guy.

Theoretically, Bennett Landsmann had the last two weeks of August free, to catch his breath, some sleep—or even a fish or two.

A few years earlier, Herschel and Hannah had bought a summer house at Truro on Cape Cod. Hoping that it would make their son feel more at ease when he came to visit with a lady friend, they deliberately chose one with a separate guest cottage.

It was here that Bennett had spent the final weeks of August 1958, when he returned from Oxford to begin Med School.

The Landsmanns were overjoyed that he had brought along Robin Winslow, about whom he had written so often. From everything they had gathered, they assumed she was the girl Ben had chosen to marry.

Now and then Ben and Robin went off together to explore New England. Hannah was certain that on one of these trips she was consulting with officials at Harvard about the possibility of transferring.

Robin was a raven-haired fellow Oxonian who had won a much-sought-after exhibition to Lady Margaret Hall where she was reading physiology.

What had made her achievement all the more remarkable was that she was South African. And—at least in Bennett's eyes—shared with him a singular quality: she was neither black nor white. For she was born in her native country's no-man's-land for racially mixed "Cape Coloreds."

The Landsmanns liked her immensely. She was full of good humor and, despite all she had gone through, not embittered. And it was clear to them that Ben was totally smitten.

Just before Labor Day, when they all drove Robin to Logan Airport, they affectionately promised one another to spend Christmas together. They assumed that holiday would coincide with an engagement party.

And yet, to his parents' astonishment and sadness, after less than a week of Med School, Bennett announced without emotion that he and Robin had broken up. There were no details given—and none demanded.

"He's a grown man," Herschel argued, "and he doesn't owe us any explanation."

*   *   *

Though he still went to the Cape every August, after that summer he was always alone. Again, they never asked him why. But in the summer of 1963 Bennett did not come at all.

"I'm going down to join Dr. King's March on Washington," he told them on the phone.

There was silence. Neither of his parents knew how to react. The papers had reported numerous threats of violence by white supremacists. Although they knew Bennett wouldn't throw the first stone, they were equally sure that he would be the first to spring into action if one came from the other side.

At last Herschel responded, "I admire Dr. King and I'm proud you're going. But Bennett, promise you'll be careful."

"I will. Don't worry," Bennett answered. "I promise not to engage in conversation with anybody wearing a sheet."

Herschel replied with a nervous laugh, "Goodbye. But call and let us know you're okay."

"I will. Love to you both."

When they had hung up and rejoined each other in the kitchen, Herschel suggested to Hannah, "Why don't we go for a walk?"

"At this hour? In the dark?"

"Come on," he urged, "we've got the moon and when it's shining on the seashore, it'll be at least as bright as Cleveland in winter."

So they put on sweaters and went out to stroll hand in hand along the peaceful desolate beach.

"All right, Herschel," Hannah said at last. "What's on your mind?"

He seemed to be watching the waterline recede as he finally answered, "Well, it had to happen some day."

"What?"

"We've lost the boy," he whispered.

"Lost? Because a twenty-eight-year-old won't come to see his parents at the beach?"

"Adopted parents, Hannah. Ben's going home."

"His home's with us," she said.

"No, my darling, we have to count our blessings. We just had him on loan. His home is with his people."

TWENTY-NINE

"Oh, deep in my heart
I do believe
We shall overcome some day."

On August twenty-eighth, 1963, the crowd seated in the hot sunshine before the Lincoln Memorial in Washington numbered nearly a quarter of a million. Every one of the District's six thousand policemen had been mobilized. Four thousand Marines were poised on standby. But the march had taken place without the slightest incident. For this multitude was not a rebellious mob but a congregation heeding the call of Martin Luther King, who had "subpoenaed the conscience of the nation."

There were speeches by representatives of Civil Rights groups, ranging from the venerable NAACP to the newer, more activist Congress of Racial Equality (CORE) and the more volatile Student Nonviolent Coordinating Committee (SNCC). But whatever their conviction, all of them were galvanized by Dr. King's passion.

I have a dream that one day this nation will rise up and live out the true meaning of its creed: "We hold these truths to be self-evident, that all men are created equal" . . . *I have a dream* that my four little children will one day live in a nation where they will not be judged by the color of their skin but by the content of their character.

His words brought the gigantic, cheering congregation to its feet. Many, overcome with emotion, began to cry. Some fifty feet from where Bennett Landsmann was standing, a young black woman collapsed, victim of the scorching sun and fever of excitement.

Ben pushed his way through the crowd that quickly clustered around her, shouting, "I'm a doctor, I'm a doctor." In an instant he was kneeling at the girl's side.

"Is she okay?" asked several members of the crowd hovering nearby.

He nodded. "We've just gotta get her to one of the first-aid stations fast."

"There's one right around the side of the monument," a youth replied, pointing beyond President Lincoln's marble chair. "I'll lead the way."

Careful to keep her head elevated, Bennett picked up the patient and ordered the milling crowd to clear a path. Moments later they reached the shade of a white tent flying a Red Cross flag.

"Hey, somebody—we've got a bad case of hyperthermia. I need an I.V. of saline and some cold towels stat. And let's get a blood pressure."

"Stay loose, brother," a volunteer called out. "Just lay her on the cot and I'll go get the doctor."

"Take it easy, girl," he replied. "I *am* a doctor, so give me a hand, huh?"

As the volunteer helped Bennett stretch out the unconscious woman on a cot, he could not keep from thinking, Jesus, right here in the shadow of Abe Lincoln with Martin Luther King's words still reverberating in the air, this soul sister didn't take me for a real medic.

Just then an official doctor responded to the call and, rushing to the scene, began to laugh.

"Landsmann, where the hell've you been all afternoon? I could really have used some help."

It was Laura. He smiled broadly.

"Castellano, what's a nice girl like you doing in a place like this?"

"What does it look like—baking cookies?"

One of her student assistants arrived on the run carrying an I.V. apparatus and a bottle of saline solution.

As Laura set up the drip, Bennett inserted the needle into the forearm of his still-unconscious patient.

"Just like the old days, huh?" he asked.

"Yeah." She smiled. "But it seems like a million years ago that we were injecting oranges."

Laura wrapped a nylon cuff around the comatose girl's right arm, and pressed her stethoscope to the inside of her elbow.

"God," she exclaimed, "blood pressure's sky-high. We've got to wrap her in wet sheets."

"Do you have any?"

"I've got a pile of towels and a few cans of cold water. That'll have to do. I'll get them while you take her clothes off."

Laura dashed off and Bennett turned to look at the young woman. With the tube going into one arm, it would be impossible simply to remove her T-shirt. He grasped it by the neck and tore it down the middle.

She had not been wearing a bra. Her breasts were now completely exposed. Bennett suddenly felt a twinge of embarrassment.

Laura returned with the wet towels, and the two of them swathed the young woman from back to chest.

"What about her pants?" she asked impatiently. "We've got to wrap her legs, too. Hurry up and take her jeans off."

"Yeah, sure," he answered, trying to regain his clinical detachment.

"Come on, Landsmann," Laura urged, "I'm getting soaked from these towels."

Bennett tore open the bronze snap at the front of the Levis, unzipped the fly, and began to pull down her trousers. The jeans were so tight that he was dragging off her underpants as well. An instant more and she was entirely naked. Her abdomen was firm and flat, her coffee-toned thighs beautifully shaped.

Before he could chastise himself for unprofessional thoughts, Laura dropped several towels in his hands and ordered, "Okay, Ben, finish looking, then make sure she's covered. I've got half a dozen hyperthermics I haven't even started on."

Before Bennett could reply, Laura was out of earshot. He knelt down by the Sleeping Beauty and reviewed the procedures for treating heatstroke he had memorized in Med School.

The important measures had been taken but he knew there was still a chance—depending on the gravity of her condition—that she might start convulsing. He checked her I.V., for she needed both salt and liquid badly. Then he knelt again and started to massage the only uncovered parts of her body, her feet and hands.

After several minutes the first aid began to work. The young woman started to shake her head as if trying to pull herself from unconsciousness, and then she awoke.

"Where am I?" she muttered groggily. "What's all this stuff wrapped around me? I'm cold."

"Good," said Bennett, "that's a good sign."

"Who are you?"

"Don't be frightened, you're in a Red Cross tent. What's the last thing you remember?"

"Dr. King . . . 'I have a dream' . . . What happened after that?" she asked.

"Well," Bennett said, smiling, "I guess you had a dream, too."

"In other words I fainted, huh?"

He nodded. "You had one helluva case of hyperthermia. You still do, so lie back down. Think you can take liquids orally?"

"How the hell else do people take them?" she retorted with a little smile.

"Ah," Bennett replied, "take a look at your arm, it's been drinking for the past half-hour. But you're starting to act sassy so I guess you must be getting better. By the way, what's your name?"

"Anita—and I would like that glass of water. What's *your* name?"

"Right now it's Gunga Din. Stay loose while I go fetch the H₂O."

He dashed off and in a second returned with a cup. "Here, drink this," he said, propping her up with his right hand, "it's got electrolytes."

"It's got what?"

"All kinds of ions to replace the minerals you've lost."

"You talk just like a doctor," she remarked.

"Well, maybe I am one," he joked.

"How much longer do I have to stay here like a mummy?"

"Just till we're sure you're okay. In the meantime I'd better try to get you some clothes."

"Clothes? Shoot—what happened to what I was wearing?"

"I'm sorry, I had to tear it off—in the performance of my clinical duties."

"Come on," she teased, "I bet you had a nice long look."

"Whatever you say," he added with a grin. "I did manage to salvage your jeans though. Are you here with anybody else?"

She nodded. "A group of us came up from Spelman College in Atlanta."

"Good, then I think they're right nearby. I saw a bunch of girls waving a school pennant. I'll go see if one of them's got a shirt you can wear."

Outside the tent, the afternoon heat had at last begun to abate. Bennett found a covey of Anita's friends, one of whom had retrieved her knapsack when she fainted and now handed it to him.

"Aha," he said as he approached her cot again, "you really came prepared. Did you maybe think you'd get invited to the White House?"

"Don't jive me, brother. By the time The Movement gets itself together, there'll be someone with a lot of soul right up there in the Oval Office. And I don't mean vacuuming the floor."

"You actually think we'll live to see that?" he asked sincerely.

"Brother, I won't die till I do—even if I have to hang around a hundred years before I croak. What's *your* dream?"

"Well, at this stage in my medical career I'd say it was to get a night's sleep."

"That's all, Doc?"

"My name is Bennett. And yeah, if I really want to go all the way in surgery I'll be lucky to sleep twenty hours a week for the next five years. Matter of fact, I'm supposed to be on duty at this very minute. But I conned one of the more liberal residents into taking my shift—which means when I get back tonight I'll have to work for maybe fifty hours straight."

He stood up.

"Which reminds me—I've got to hustle to make my seven-thirty plane. Can I drop you anywhere, Anita?"

"You mean from the plane?"

"Are you smoking, or are you always this kooky?"

"Except when I conk out from heatstroke, I'm a barrel of fun."

Bennett looked at his watch. And then he looked again at Anita, quickly weighing the possible alternatives. If he caught the flight he would lose the girl, but if he stayed, the hospital might "lose" *him.*

He watched as two of her college friends helped Anita into a fresh T-shirt. She was some woman.

Oh, what the hell, he thought, I may not ever get another chance like this.

"Uh, Anita, might I have the pleasure of inviting you—and your friends, of course—for a little farewell meal before we go our separate ways? I think I should keep an eye on you and be sure you're forcing liquids."

Anita said yes. Her fellow co-eds were even more enthusiastic.

"Great," he responded, "just let me sign off with one of my colleagues."

Bennett dashed inside and found Laura starting yet another saline I.V.

"Thank God the sun's going down," she said as she saw him approach. "Can you wait awhile so we can have a drink, Ben?"

"Sorry," he replied with frustration. "I've just made a previous commitment."

"Okay." Laura smiled knowingly. "I realize how serious your commitments are. Some other time, huh?"

"Sure, sure. By the way, how's Palmer?"

She sensed he was anxious to leave so she simply uttered, "Fine. I'll give him your regards."

As he hurried off, Laura thought to herself, Palmer *is* fine, and *I'm* fine for that matter. It's just our marriage that's sick.

During dinner at a nearby Sloppy Joe's, Bennett could not help wondering why Anita had insisted that her friends sit next to him while she sat across the table.

Except for this enigma, all of them had fun. The afternoon's demonstration had been powerful. They had something to be proud of. Bennett checked his watch again. The final shuttle was now airborne. He would have to stay the night in Washington.

Alone?

The other Spelman girls dropped graceful hints that they would gladly mitigate his loneliness. But Anita remained aloof.

He decided to make a final try as he accompanied the girls to their bus. He managed to maneuver himself to Anita's side and hold her several steps behind.

"Hey," he chided, "remember me? I saved your life this afternoon. Don't I even get your phone number in gratitude?"

For the first time she was ill at ease. "Hey, Bennett, you're a cool guy and I'm grateful. But I've got a fiancé."

"Oh," Bennett said, trying to conceal his disappointment. "What does the lucky man do?"

"He's in the Marine Corps—just about to start Officers' Candidate School. We're getting married when he graduates."

"Oh, well, maybe you'll invite me to your wedding."

"Sure," Anita said, smiling. But both of them knew it was just idle chatter.

As soon as the girls' bus pulled away from the curb, Bennett headed for Union Station and bought a ticket for the milk train to New Haven. During the long, slow journey he tried to catch up on some much-needed shut-eye, yet found himself unable to sleep.

Barney had been up all night. He was still haunted by the sight of that last inmate in the Blenheim Ward. Tomorrow at eleven there would be a meeting of the ward staff under the general director. Perhaps he would learn then who the guy was.

He stayed in bed as long as possible, but by 5:30 A.M. he had to find out. He got up, pulled on his clothes and walked, yawning and bedraggled, to the "Land of the Incurables."

The security man scrutinized him with curiosity. Barney then realized that he had not bothered to comb his hair or tuck in his shirt. How would he convince this guy that he was legit?

"Good morning, Doctor," said the guard in friendly greeting.

Barney could not keep himself from asking, "How can you tell I'm a doctor? I mean, I look like such a slob." As he spoke he was hastily putting his shirt in his pants.

"You forgot your fly, Doctor," the guard replied amiably, "but the fact is *all* you doctors look the same after the night shift. It's the patients who get medication to keep them snug as a bug in a rug."

Barney entered the ward and walked as softly as possible across the vast hollow "Activities Room" toward the nurses' station where a young, pretty Puerto Rican woman whose nameplate read N. VALDEZ was seated. Even though Barney knocked politely, she was startled. *No one* ever came in at that hour in the gray zone between night and morning except for an emergency heralded by the ringing of alarms.

"Can I help you, Doctor?" she asked.

"Yes, I'd like to see the file on one of the patients."

"Now?" she asked, looking at her watch. "I mean, doesn't the committee—"

"I'm the new resident," he replied. "I'm anxious to get an early start."

"Certainly, sir," she replied, still unsure of Barney's precise motives. "Which one of the patients are you referring to?"

"Uh, I don't exactly know. But if we can go to the dormitory I can point him out."

Nurse Valdez complied. After seven years on the psycho wards, no behavior by patients *or* staff surprised her.

The patients were all still asleep when Barney and the nurse entered the huge dormitory, their snores, mumblings, and groans forming a kind of nightmarish symphony. She began to shine a flashlight on the faces on each pillow. Barney suddenly touched her arm.

"Him! That guy—what's his name?"

She directed her beam to the foot of the bed where the patient's chart was hanging. Barney bent over and read "CASSIDY, Kenneth. Date of birth: 17 July 1932."

Barney was staggered. That wraith? Could it actually be *Ken* Cassidy, the boy-scoutish basketball coach at Columbia?

He knew that it had to be.

"Thank you," he whispered, trying to keep his composure. "I'd like to see his records now, please."

Barney sat in the nurses' office drinking cups of brackish coffee laced with too much sugar, reading the report on Ken Cassidy.

The patient had been admitted two years earlier, after going violently berserk. Though he had exhibited no prior symptoms of psychological degeneration, he had suddenly begun to destroy his house with an axe, while his wife and daughters cowered in the kitchen. Had not the police—alerted by the neighbors—arrived in time, he would most certainly have massacred them. He was originally seen by a resident whose initials, VM, Barney did not recognize and was assigned to Blenheim by Professor Stanley Avery, the general director.

"Good morning, Doctor Livingston, *you* are up early!"

It was Nurse Herridge reporting for duty so that she and Valdez in tandem could rouse the patients two by two.

A few seconds later, their multifaceted orderly appeared.

"Good morning, Mr. Johnson," said Barney.

A gloomy look crossed the big man's face. "Mr. President," he said, "I feel terrible at having let you down."

"How so?"

"As Supreme Commander U.S. Army of the Pacific I should have held on to Okinawa. But believe me, sir, I shall return."

"I am sure you will, General MacArthur," Barney replied. "What say we all go rouse the troops?"

Johnson stood to attention and saluted his commander in chief. "Yessir, right away, sir!"

Barney observed the ritual awakening, helping out where he could (he really did not know quite what to do). As soon as Cassidy had been coaxed to wash his face and brush his teeth (no shave today; that was done for them by Mr. Johnson on a rotating basis), Barney took him by the arm and led him to a quiet corner.

"Mr. Cassidy, yesterday it seemed like you recognized me. You do remember me, don't you? I was the dirty player—the guy who was the pain in your ass on the Columbia basketball team. You still like basketball, don't you, Ken?"

Cassidy stood like a granite statue, eyes unfocused, his expression giving no indication as to whether he understood any of what his interrogator was saying. Barney grabbed the man by the shoulders as if trying to wake him.

"Basketball, Ken," he repeated, "throwing the ball through the hoop, *slam dunk!*"

He was getting nowhere. He raised his voice as if the sheer intensity of decibels would penetrate this sick man's skull. "Roar, Lion, Roar! Go Columbia!"

Barney's intemperate shaking took effect. Cassidy suddenly lashed out, landing both hands against Barney's chest and knocking him half-way across the corridor.

Ever on the alert, Mr. Johnson came bounding up to protect a staff member. He grabbed the flailing Cassidy in an overwhelming bear hug, cautioning him.

"You watch what you're doin', Mr. Cassidy. I may be retired from the ring, but ole Joe Louis still has plenty of fight in him. Don't forget the number of bouts I went without a defeat!"

Cassidy continued to kick and punch even as "Joe Louis" increased his grip. Johnson looked solicitously at Barney, who was picking himself up off the floor.

"You okay, Doc?" he asked.

"Yeah," Barney replied, "thanks. Thanks for saving me, Mr. . . . Louis."

"That's all right," Johnson replied, "he's no Max Schmeling. Should I get the nurse to give him a shot?"

"Yeah, I guess so," Barney answered, feeling responsible for the poor man's paroxysm.

Twenty minutes later Ken Cassidy lay heavily sedated on his bed as Barney, Johnson, and Mrs. Herridge looked on.

"He missed breakfast," Barney observed guiltily.

"Don't worry, Doctor," the nurse assured him, "I'll see that he's fed as soon as he wakes up."

"When do you think he'll be coming around?"

"I'd say he will be conscious but tranquil in less than an hour."

"Good," Barney commented. "I'll go down to the cafeteria and come back."

"You do remember there's a staff meeting at eleven o'clock, Doctor," Nurse Herridge reminded him.

"That's why I want to be back before ten," Barney answered.

He returned in an hour, shaven, kempt, and presentable for the conference with his colleagues. But meanwhile, he had some professional research to perform. With the head nurse at his side, he went to Cassidy's bed.

As she had predicted, the patient was now marginally awake. Barney withdrew an ophthalmoscope from his jacket and began to look into Cassidy's eyes. He checked his left eye routinely. But when he gazed into the right, he remained motionless for several minutes.

"May I ask what you think you are doing, Dr. Livingston?" Mrs. Herridge asked, a trifle impatiently. "This man has been given a thorough physical examination."

"How long ago?" Barney asked.

She handed him a folder. "See for yourself."

Barney scoured the pages, looking for the relevant information, and then found it. "Eighteen months ago. Christ, no wonder!"

"I beg your pardon, Doctor?"

He stood up. "Thank you, Mrs. Herridge, you've been great. I'll see you at the staff meeting."

There were seven of them: Barney; Joseph Leder, the second-year resident; Vera Mihalic, a straight-backed, intense young woman with thick granny glasses, who was chief resident; Professor Avery; and three nurses. Mr. Johnson was not deemed qualified to attend these sessions, even though for nearly a month the previous year he had been Sigmund Freud.

Avery introduced Barney to his colleagues and they proceeded to discuss the new admissions—a brace of paranoid schizophrenics—both of whom were desperately in need of hospitalization and for whom they just had to find two extra beds.

Nurse Herridge objected. "With due respect, Professor, we're overcrowded already. If we keep squeezing in extra beds, we'll end up like the Black Hole of Calcutta."

"Point taken, Jane," Avery replied. "Is there anybody we could possibly move?"

Barney's hand shot up.

"Yes, Barney?"

"I think we could give Mr. Cassidy's bed to someone else, sir."

There was mild consternation in the room, since everyone had already been informed of that morning's fracas.

"Are you serious?" Avery protested. "Wasn't his behavior today ample testimony to the severity of his condition?"

"Yes, sir," Barney replied. "But he's not psychotic."

"I beg your pardon?" Avery asked in the voice of a man whose professional toe had been stepped on. "And just what ward do you suggest is appropriate for that coiled spring of physical violence?"

"Neurology, sir," Barney replied. "I think his antisocial behavior is the result of intracranial pressure."

"Surely that would have been picked up at his physical, Dr. Livingston—or do you happen to possess x-ray eyes?"

"No, sir," Barney answered, "but I checked him with an ophthalmoscope a little while ago."

"Well," said Avery, "so did Dr. Mihalic and I when he was admitted, and I believe she checked him again a little more than a year ago. What new data are you offering us?"

"Sir," Barney continued confidently, "the meningioma in his right eye might not have been as apparent then."

Vera Mihalic protested. "I've also done a neurological residency, and let me assure you, Dr. Livingston, had there been the slightest trace of intracranial growth compressing his cerebral functions I would have picked it up. The man is a paranoid schizophrenic with homicidal tendencies."

And you're a tight-assed bitch who's afraid to be called wrong, Barney thought to himself.

Avery interposed to avoid the growing disharmony among his staff.

"Wouldn't an empirical recheck be the best way to deal with this?"

"Obviously," Barney and Vera answered almost in unison.

At eleven-thirty, while Mr. Johnson held a sweating and disheveled Ken Cassidy's hands tightly behind his back, first Professor Avery, then Dr. Mihalic, then Dr. Leder, and finally Barney peered at the patient's brains through the white of his right eye. None of them could deny the presence of a tumor.

By noon Ken Cassidy had been transferred to Neurology and scheduled for surgery the following morning. Twenty-four hours later the growth was removed from his frontal lobe and within a few days the neuropathologists declared it benign.

Barney soon learned another vital lesson on the privileges of the medical hierarchy. It was Avery—in the company of the neurosurgeon—who "volunteered" to convey the good news to Ken Cassidy, as he lay in his new room holding his wife's hand.

Barney had to sneak into Ken's room at the end of visiting hours that evening. Before he even tried to introduce himself, Cassidy smiled weakly and muttered, "Livingston, you ornery bastard. What the hell are you doing here?"

"It's the latest thing in medicine, Ken. All the hospitals are recruiting basketball players for the Bedpan League. Interested in coaching us?"

"Sure," he whispered, and grinned like a man who had just had a weight taken off his mind. Or in this case a cranial tumor.

Barney went off to begin his night duty, so full of adrenaline he was able to stay awake without a drop of coffee until noon the next day.

Before condemning him to eternal silence, Vera Mihalic called him every name in the book—and quite a few that were in no book or back alley he had ever encountered.

"Why are you so pissed off?" he asked. "I mean, you don't have to give me a Nobel Prize, but I think I at least deserve a little pat on the head for saving a guy's life. Just what the hell did I do wrong?"

She looked daggers at him. "You should have come to me first."

"Oh, for God's sake. I discovered it at ten and the meeting was at eleven. And besides, the diagnosis was right. Isn't that the only thing that really matters?"

"How did they ever allow a naive schmuck like you into the program?" she sneered. "Little boy, you'd better learn that there's a pecking order if you want to make it in this game."

She turned on her heel and marched off before Barney could respond.

Little boy? Pecking order? *Game?*

Thereafter at Thursday meetings, with a skill bordering on genius, she was able to avoid addressing anything to him. The best he could hope for was a third-person mention, such as, "Perhaps Dr. Livingston doesn't realize . . ."

It was 1964—a year for medical controversy in the outside world as well.

The doctors who served their country during World War II had come home to discover that they had to wage another battle. This time the enemy was not Hitler or Tojo but Harry S. Truman, President of the United States. He had been determined to establish a program that would offer *free* medical care to every member of society. The American Medical Association was up in arms. This was creeping socialism and they would fight it to the end.

The battle lasted nearly twenty years. In 1964, President Lyndon Johnson pressured Congress to pass his Medicare bill, which offered free medical care to people over sixty-five and the disabled of all ages.

His victory was all the more heroic because the AMA had spent many millions of dollars and had at least twenty-three full-time lobbyists in Washington to prevent what they viewed as an infringement upon their lives and livelihood.

Also in 1964, the Surgeon General issued his long-awaited report on the effects of smoking on health, presenting evidence linking it to lung cancer, heart disease, and various respiratory conditions—as might be expected from a product that filled the human lungs with the same kind of poison emitted by automobile exhaust pipes.

But the tobacco industry had its own scientific teams, who counter-attacked with equally "conclusive" proof that smoking could actually be beneficial as a "relaxant" for people under pressure.

On another front, the U.S. Public Health Service charged that insecticides were killing thousands of fish in the Mississippi River and would wreak further environmental havoc if stringent controls were not immediately initiated to stop the pollution.

On a smaller but no less important front, a long-standing dispute was settled by an uneasy truce between Henry Dwyer, M.D., and his wife, Cheryl. By sheer weight of scientific evidence, sophistry—and unremitting verbal harassment—he had persuaded his wife to go on the Pill.

Cheryl wanted only to follow the dictates of her religion. But ultimately she was convinced that the latest drug Hank was proposing—containing, as it did, merely estrogen and progestogen, both related to *natural* hormones already found in the female endocrine system—would, in fact, come closer to obeying God's dictates than any other precaution yet devised.

Hank was a first-year resident in Gynecology at St. Damian's back in Pittsburgh, where they were again among close friends and had two loving grandmas more than anxious to babysit.

Needless to say, he was spending more than half his nights on call at the hospital. He enjoyed the thrill of bringing new lives into the world. Holding up a baby in the bright, festive light of the operating table and announcing grandiosely—somewhat like the Lord's M.C.—"Mrs. Jones, you have a lovely boy/girl/set of twins. . . ."

Many of the residents were married and detested night duty for keeping them away from their wives and children. But they always found in Hank a willing stand-in. Since they were so grateful, he did not feel obliged to tell them that the pleasure was entirely his.

For being on call gave him access to a quiet room with a bunk bed on which he could get more sleep than he did at home. (Children, unlike alarm clocks, cannot be set to sound at a specific hour.)

Moreover, he had discovered that the legend that babies are born in the early hours of the morning was, in fact, true. (No one knew exactly why, but perhaps it was connected with cortisol levels peaking at the time.) Thus he could have a midnight rendezvous with the stork—even a few of them—and then be able to creep into bed in his solitary cell for a few undisturbed hours.

He had also found that, if spoken in the right tone of voice, at the right hour of night, to the right nurse, the phrase "Miss——, you have a lovely ass/bosom/legs . . ." could alleviate his monastic asceticism.

Most residents were constrained by the demands of their schedule to regard the hospital as their home away from home. By contrast, Hank Dwyer began to regard his home as a mere entr'acte in the true drama of his life.

As the former priest rationalized, It is better to dally than to burn.

THIRTY

Although Martin Luther King had received the Nobel Peace Prize a year earlier, by 1965 his whole philosophy was under fire from new militants in the Civil Rights movement.

In founding the Black Nationalist party, Malcolm X argued, "The day of nonviolent resistance is over." Ironically, within a few months, Malcolm himself was shot to death by a black revolutionary who regarded Malcolm himself as not violent *enough*.

James Baldwin had been "right on" when he predicted "the fire next time."

The relationship between Laura and Palmer also reached a stage of bellicosity. That it was war she had no doubt. And, for the first time since the Army had sent him to grad school, Palmer was actually wearing his uniform.

That was the way she found him when she returned from one of those increasingly draining thirty-six-hour stints.

"Oh, Palmer, are you going to a costume party—or are you dating a WAC?"

"You may recall, Laura, from the days when we were still on vaguely civil terms, the Army Reserve commits me to meetings one night a week and one weekend a month. When I first signed up, I thought it would be a sacrifice. But, frankly, it'll be a great relief."

"Screw you, Palmer."

"Well," he quipped sarcastically, "if you won't, there are others who will."

Laura sighed deeply. She was sick of this intramarital sniping.

"Palmer, I know you're too busy perfecting your Chinese to read the papers, but there's a new thing called 'no-fault divorce' and since we have what I diagnose as a case of marital rigor mortis, I think we should avail ourselves of it."

"Don't be silly," he replied. "We're just two willful people who happen to love each other despite the temporary bifurcation of our roads. I'm willing to wait because I think we belong together."

"Is that why you screw around?"

"And you *don't*? What about all those lusty young interns and residents?"

She began to cry, more out of frustration than sadness.

"Oh God, Palmer, can't you understand we're working our guts out to save sick babies? That if we ever do get five minutes to lie on a bed, we use it for sleep? Can't your lascivious brain comprehend 'commitment'?"

"Well, Laura," he said with a world-weary air, "I'm certainly not qualified to give you a lecture on hormonal impulses. But I'd have less respect for you if you *weren't* at least getting a little on the side."

He was wounding her and they both knew it.

She asked herself, Why do I put up with this?

Vera Mihalic made Barney an astonishing proposition.

The chief psychiatric resident, who for the past two months had been studiously avoiding him, inexplicably walked up at the end of morning rounds and invited him for a cup of coffee.

Anxious to mend fences, Barney readily agreed. He even offered to buy her a Danish, but instead she bought him one and insisted on paying for everything. ("After all," she joked, "I'm in a higher income bracket than you.")

Barney thanked her politely. Then, as they were sitting at a quiet table in the hospital cafeteria, he felt brave enough to add, "I thought you hated my guts, Vera."

"Don't be silly, I'm in analysis. I learn to work these things out."

"Oh, I'm glad," he responded. "I'm looking forward to my own Training Analysis."

At which she quickly added, "That still doesn't mean I like you. It's just that I know *why* I dislike you. It's because you're so much smarter than I am," she explained with a quiet candor. "And not only that, you relate to patients so much better. You should be proud of the progress you've made with some of them—especially since we always throw the hopeless cases to the junior people. I mean, we all broke our hearts for the first year, so why shouldn't you?"

Barney smiled. "I know at some point I'm supposed to say thank you, but I can't seem to fit it in anywhere. Is there some particular reason for all this flattery? Like maybe to inform me that I'm being dropped from the program?"

"Of course not."

"Oh," Barney said, now completely at a loss as to why he had been invited to this coffee klatch. And he wasn't helped by Vera's next question.

"Where do you sleep when you're not on duty?"

Was he being led into some trap by this neurotic nexus of ambivalence?

"I've got a room in the student dorm. It's practically just for changing shirts, I'm there so little."

"Have you thought of an apartment?"

"Sure. I've thought of the Waldorf-Astoria, too. But as one of the guys worked out, residents get paid something like thirty-four cents an hour."

"I mean sharing an apartment."

"With you?"

"Well, actually, there were four of us—two guys and two girls. A neurosurgical resident, a pediatric resident, and a girlfriend of mine who's working on Wall Street. But we've just had a vacancy. The neurosurgeon dropped out."

"In the middle of the semester? Why?"

"He jumped out the window."

"God!" Barney exclaimed. "You mean he killed himself?"

"We're on the fourteenth floor, Livingston—so take a guess. Anyway, your share of the rent would be twenty-seven-fifty a month, and cleaning the kitchen once a week. What do you say?"

"Gosh, Vera, I'm flattered."

"Does that mean yes or no?"

"Am I gonna have to sleep in the neurologist's bed?"

"Unless you want to sleep on the floor."

"Well, okay," Barney conceded, "as long as you change the sheets. But I still don't understand why you asked me."

"I don't either. But my shrink and I are working on it."

*   *   *

One of Seth's rotations in his Internal Medicine residency was a stint in the Oncology Ward.

Although published statistics indicated that nearly one-third of all cancer victims were being saved—salvation being defined as continuing to live five years or more—the place still seemed like a torture chamber. Those not facing an unspeakably painful death were suffering from the awful discomfort of "the cures." Radiation or chemotherapy often made them so sick that they felt they were enduring a punishment worse than death.

What made life tolerable for Seth was the fact that Judy was now second in command of the nursing staff and they could often steal time for lunch, coffee, or at least a kiss.

Mrs. Alpert, a patient with incurable bone cancer, caught sight of the doctor and nurse embracing. Seth and Judy were embarrassed and apologetic. But the patient surprised them.

"Go on, children," she said, smiling. "It gives me pleasure to know that life goes on."

But for some, life was going on too long.

Mel Gatkowicz, a steel worker, was living—or rather dying—proof of the validity of the Surgeon General's report. For his two packs a day had finally succeeded in giving him lung cancer, angina pectoris, and Raynaud's disease, a circulatory malfunction that progressively diminished the blood flow to his extremities. This meant that his fingers and toes were becoming gangrenous and needed to be amputated.

By now he was too sick to smoke, too sick to eat, and growing ever more incoherent. The only thing he could convey with any accuracy was the agony that none of the drugs could sufficiently alleviate.

In a controlled experiment sanctioned by the U.S. Health Department, he was treated with heroin, but even *that* did not end his anguish.

Seth was assisting Dr. Bart Nelson when Mel's wife, Doris, cornered him in the corridor.

"I can't bear to see him like this, Doctor," she sobbed. "He's in such pain. Why can't you *do* something?"

Her three sons stood behind her, their own wives beside them, as a kind of Greek chorus intoning a litany of sorrow.

"I'm afraid we've done all we can," Dr. Nelson replied as compassionately as he could. "We'll simply have to wait for Nature to take its course."

"How long will that be, Doctor?" the eldest son asked anxiously.

Nelson shrugged. "I honestly don't know. He could go any time. On the other hand he's so tough he could linger for days—maybe even a week."

Doris now turned to plead with Seth. "Don't you think it's inhuman to see such a strong man end like this? It isn't my Mel lying in that bed anymore. That's not the man I was married to for thirty-five years. He wouldn't want to go this way, I know it. Not even a dog should suffer the way he's suffering."

Seth nodded in agreement.

Doris turned again to Dr. Nelson. "You know, when I leave the hospital every night I go to church. I get on my knees and I pray, 'God, take this man. He wants to go to Your arms. He never did no wrong to nobody. Why don't You kiss him and take away the breath of life?' "

Both doctors were moved, but Nelson had seen many Doris Gatkowiczes and had built up a kind of emotional immunity.

"I think we're all praying for that," he said quietly. He patted the grieving woman on the shoulder, nodded to the sons, and set off, his eyes to the ground.

But Seth could not extricate himself from this group half-mad with pain.

Doris's eldest son tried to comfort her. "It's okay, Ma, it won't be long."

"No, no, even another minute is too much. Why doesn't God answer me? Why doesn't He rescue him and let him die? I feel like going in there and tearing out all those tubes in his arms."

"Easy, Ma, easy," her son murmured.

"I don't care, I don't care," she shouted. "I want him to stop suffering."

The Gatkowicz family gathered around their mother as if to insulate her from the pain they all felt emanating from their father's bed.

They hardly noticed the young physician who had stood there, a silent witness to their agony.

Seth had coordinated his schedule so that his nights "on" would coincide with Judy's. He was sitting in the on-call area, berating a fellow resident, Joel Fischer, for smoking.

"How the heck can you do this, Joel, when every room on this floor has got proof of what you're doing to your own body?"

"I can't help it, Seth, I really can't," he protested. "Stupid as it sounds, the only thing that gives me relief from their pain is a few puffs."

"Okay," Seth said, getting up for some fresh air. "But I'm not going to sit here and let you take me with you to an early grave."

As he walked into the darkened corridor Judy came up and whispered, "Francine's gone down to supper. We're alone."

"What about Joel?" he said, motioning to where the young doctor was enjoying his nicotine pacifier.

"I'll chat with him," she said reassuringly. "What does he like to talk about?"

"Sex." Seth grinned. "He's going through a divorce. Tell him about all the promiscuous girls you could fix him up with."

"But I don't know any."

"So dream some up. Just give me five minutes."

Judy nodded. But before she could turn away, Seth grabbed her by the arm and whispered, "Is this the right thing—am I doing the right thing? I'm scared."

"I know," she answered. "But that poor man shouldn't have to suffer like that."

"But I swear if he isn't conscious enough to give me his consent, I won't do it. He's got to give me his consent."

Then they each walked off in a different direction.

At the nurses' station, Seth picked up the medication prepared for Mr. Gatkowicz for midnight *and* 3 A.M. He had an extra vial in the pocket of his white jacket.

He entered the sick man's room. It was hard to tell whether Gatkowicz was awake or asleep, since he lived in a kind of drugged gray zone that offered the comforts of neither state.

Seth approached the bed. There were I.V.s attached to both of the patient's arms, but his right hand was outside the covers. Seth took hold of it and whispered, "Mr. Gatkowicz, if you can hear me, please squeeze my hand."

Seth felt the man's callused fingers close firmly on his.

"Now, Mel, I'm going to ask you some simple questions. If the answer is yes, squeeze me once, and if the answer is no, twice. Do you understand, Mel?"

The man's fingers tightened . . . once.

"Mel," Seth continued his catechism, "have the doctors told you that you are going to die?"

One squeeze.

"Are you afraid?"

Two squeezes. He was prepared for death.

"Are you in great pain?"

The patient squeezed his hand with more force than ever . . . once.

"Would you like me to help you? Would you like me to put you to sleep forever so you won't feel any more pain?"

The sick man gripped Seth's hand and would not let go. To Seth he seemed to be saying, "Take me from this earthly torture. In the name of God, let me go."

"I understand, Mel," Seth whispered. "Don't worry, I'm going to help you."

There was no problem about a hypodermic needle. Seth had merely to detach one of the I.V.s temporarily and insert the midnight morphine.

In a moment the patient was unconscious. Then Seth administered the three o'clock dose of morphine and finally the vial he had secreted. He pocketed the three empty ampoules, looked at the patient's peaceful face, whispered, "God bless you, Mr. Gatkowicz," and tiptoed out.

Later that night Mel Gatkowicz was discovered dead. The certificate, indicating cause of death as multiple carcinomas with attendant respiratory failure, was signed by Joel Fischer, M.D., and Seth Lazarus, M.D.

When informed by telephone, the widow broke into tears and cried, "Thank God, thank God."

Once the inmates of the chronic ward were given their sleeping pills, Barney Livingston had relatively few problems on night duty. There were, of course, occasional calamities in the E.R., but these were mostly the result of Saturday night intoxication. Unable to sleep in such proximity to what he imagined were horrifically painful nightmares, he filled the empty hours by reading. And very soon by different activities.

First he began to telephone various classmates he knew were also on the graveyard shift. (Laura tried to synchronize her nights "on" with his.) Barney could also call the West Coast where, because of the time difference, some people were actually going off day duty to get the now-mythical good night's sleep.

During one of the latter types of conversation, Lance Mortimer casually remarked, "By the way, I've given your name to Lindsay Hudson."

"Who the hell is he or she?"

"Well, in Lindsay's case I don't think he's made up his mind yet. But anyway, the guy went to college with me and now he's an editor of the *Village Voice*. He asked me if I knew any literate doctors, since they're apparently rarer than benign tumors. So I suggested you."

"Hey, thanks, Lance," Barney replied, genuinely flattered. And then he joked, "How come you didn't give him *two* names?"

"Dr. Livingston, I honestly couldn't come up with a second."

*   *   *

True to Lance's word, Hudson of the *Village Voice* called Barney two days later and asked if he would do a short piece on the psychodynamics of Albee's *Who's Afraid of Virginia Woolf?*

Barney enjoyed the task immensely and dropped heavy hints that he would be receptive to similar invitations.

He was obviously a natural to appraise John Huston's cinematic biography of *Freud,* a film that Barney concluded was "probably the Master's two least successful fifty-minute hours."

This piece caught the eye of an editor from the recently launched *New York Review of Books,* who invited Barney to lunch at Four Seasons, an honor so staggering that Vera agreed to cover for him.

The next day, a copy of Pasternak's *Doctor Zhivago* was messengered to him, with the request for a "think piece" about physicians in literature, using *Zhivago* as a springboard.

"I must have been crazy to take on the assignment, Castellano," he reported that evening. "It's tantamount to intellectual hubris."

"Come on, Barn, from what little I've read that's what the whole *Review* is based on. Besides, I know you can do a terrific job."

Just as he was about to end the conversation, she suddenly added, "Hey, this is a first, Livingston."

"What do you mean?"

"It's the first time *I've* had to bolster *your* confidence."

Vera Mihalic was becoming less and less able to maintain platonic— or for that matter professional—distance from the literary colleague with whom she shared a sink and shower and, occasionally, even toothpaste.

Sex had long figured prominently in her analysis—which, of course, is as superfluous as saying that a whale plays a role in *Moby-Dick.* Vera's particular problem had been a fear of men. As she epitomized it to impress her doctor: "They're either too phallic or too encephalic"—i.e., beneath contempt or above reproach. It was, she theorized, the feminine version of the so-called *"dual imago"* complex, which separates men's views of women into antithetical categories.

The doctor had evinced considerable interest in this concept—both when Vera had articulated the notion, and again when she inquired if it seemed worthy of writing up for one of the journals. She even felt she could be daring enough to posit a paradigm of normalcy based on the qualities she perceived in Barney Livingston.

So, for the sake of research, curiosity, as well as the hope of not turning thirty still a virgin, she decided to give herself to Barney body and soul (reserving her psyche for the couch).

Naturally, she could not violate the entente cordiale in the apartment, and so she decided to offer herself when Barney was on night duty.

Her roommate Peggy was curious when she saw Vera preparing to go out just as the eleven o'clock news was beginning.

"I thought you were off tonight, Vera," she said.

"There's a lunatic in the Chronic Ward," she replied, dabbing *Joy* behind her ears.

"Aren't they all lunatics? Isn't that why they're there?"

"This is a special case," Vera replied.

"What's the problem?" Peggy asked with interest.

"Dual imago," Vera replied.

"I've never heard of it."

"It's very new," she explained. "In fact, I'm thinking of writing an article about it."

"Oh Christ, Mihalic, can't you ever think of anything but work? Why don't you seduce one of those cute young doctors? They're supposed to be starving for sex."

"How do you know?"

"Barney mentioned it."

"He did?" Vera asked suspiciously. "When was this?"

"This morning. At breakfast. Over corn flakes," Peggy replied.

"Oh," said Vera. "Corn flakes, that's fine. See you later."

"Will you be gone long?"

"I don't know. It's my first experience with a case like this."

Barney was bushed. One of the chronics had a paradoxical reaction to the sedation and had gone so wild that he needed his hands and feet tied while they administered a massive dose of Thorazine.

Since he was the first on the scene, Barney had to wrestle with the guy till security arrived. By the time he got back to the on call room he was too tired to type any further. So he lay down on the bed, picked up the phone and asked the operator to get him Children's Hospital in Boston.

Strictly speaking, of course, it was quite unethical for him to be making a personal call. But weren't these doctor-to-doctor conversations?

"This is Dr. Castellano," came a weary voice.

"Hey," Barney replied, "you sound as tired as I feel."

"Oh, Barney, you can't believe what this evening's been like. Why do kids always seem to spike their fevers at midnight?"

"Who knows," he remarked, "maybe they get lower rates like the telephone."

"No," she replied, "they get *me*. And I'm afraid I'm the best resident on my shift. I mean, I'm not joking. It's just that the other guys are real dorks."

Laura was in the midst of telling him how much he had risen in Palmer's esteem since he had begun to publish in *The New York Review of Books* when Vera Mihalic stepped off the elevator at Barney's floor.

"Typical of that schmuck," twitted Barney, "always impressed by the externals. Why don't you come back to New York where you're really appreciated? In fact, why don't you come down on your next free weekend? I can put you up."

Vera stopped out of sight, but not out of earshot.

"I thought you lived with someone," Laura said.

"Oh, but that's a strictly business arrangement," he replied. "I mean, Vera Mihalic is to sex what ants are to a picnic."

Vera's eyes were moist as she hastened toward the elevators. Hence she did not hear Barney's mitigating compliments.

"But she's a real good person, Laura. I mean, looks aren't the only thing."

"Now that's a revolutionary statement, coming from you, Barney."

"Listen, Castellano, I'm starting my Training Analysis soon and I want to clean up my act so the guy will get me through it quickly. I'm working on temporarily moderating my libido."

Laura laughed.

"What's so funny, Castellano?"

"Your libido will wane when pigs fly, Dr. Livingston."

"Is that a compliment or a criticism?"

"It's a fact, Barney. Hey, listen, my light just went on. They need me in the E.R. Call me after midnight on Thursday."

"Okay. Give my love to Palmer."

"Why not," she said wistfully. "He doesn't seem to want any of mine."

Barney hung up and shook his head in consternation. Why the hell does she stay with that cold preppie nerd?

When he was finally relieved at 7 A.M., Barney walked the half mile to the apartment just to get some air in his lungs and blood in his legs.

The place was empty when he arrived, and he went to the bathroom to brush his teeth before going to bed.

There was broken glass everywhere. All of his toiletries—especially the aphrodisiacs like Old Spice aftershave, deodorant, etc.—were either broken or shattered all over the floor. Written in shaving cream on the mirror was "Drop dead."

He took it to be an unprovoked expression of hostility from Vera.

Just as he had swept up every shard of glass (he hoped) and put some order to the chaos in the bathroom, the phone rang.

Christ, he thought to himself, I hope it's the Violent Ward to tell me they've got Mihalic in a straitjacket.

"Hello," he barked, "this is Dr. Livingston."

"Barney, can you tell me why all psychiatrists are crazy?"

It was Laura. And there was irritation in her voice.

"Castellano, can you tell me who the hell broke all my bottles?"

"What are you talking about? Now I know you're as crazy as the rest of them."

"Hey, Laura, I've been up for nearly two days straight. The atom bomb's just hit my bathroom and I'm so freaked out I'm gonna grab my stuff and move to the nearest 'Y.' "

"Livingston, before you go I'd like you to hear the letter I just received from Grete Andersen."

"Can I pass on that? I'm really not in the mood."

"No," she replied sternly. "Shut up and listen to this."

Dear Laura,

Hope you're well. I'm certainly as high as a flag on the Fourth of July, having conquered my phobias and joined the human race as a full-fledged woman—

"Laura, for God's sake," Barney protested, "do I have to hear her gush about how the earth moved?"

"Just listen to the rest of this." She read on:

What's more, I've really lucked out. It's true love. Andy says he's never known anyone as wonderful as me—

"Who the hell is Andy?" Barney asked.

"Andrew Himmerman," Laura replied flatly.

"*The* Andrew Himmerman? You mean the guy who wrote that great book on ego development in teenagers?"

"The very same. Apparently he's been working on Grete's ego— from the knees up."

"What?" Barney said in righteous indignation. "That's absolutely unprofessional and just what I'd expect from a hysteric like Grete Andersen. Laura, you had a psychiatry round in Med School. Haven't you ever heard of transference?"

"Excuse me, Barney, this is a little more than transference. It's more like transportation. Apparently they've just spent a weekend in South Carolina."

"Do you believe that idiotic fantasy?"

"She wrote me on Hilton Head stationery."

"So she went there on her own to fantasize."

"And I suppose the Polaroid picture of the two of them by the pool is also a figment of her imagination."

"So it might have been a conference."

"Then why are they twisted around each other like a pretzel?"

"Jesus, that's terrible. I've heard this sort of thing sometimes happens. I mean, he's not the first to violate the Hippocratic Oath."

"No. But he's the first to violate Grete and that's a whole lot worse."

"Castellano, if this is true, Himmerman deserves to be bounced. But I also think that you're yelling at me because you wanted a good reason to scold somebody else for wronging another woman."

Laura thought for a minute.

"I guess you're right, Barn," she answered quietly.

"Is Palmer screwing around?"

"Well, let's just say at the moment he's dabbling in promiscuity."

"You don't deserve that, Laura," he said softly.

"Forget it, Barney. I called to talk about Grete."

"I'm sorry, Andersen can take care of herself. She's a big girl."

"I'm a big girl too, Barn."

"No, you're not," he said affectionately. "You need someone to take care of you."

There was a sudden silence at her end.

"It's okay, Laura. It's okay to cry. That's what pals are for."

"Oh God, Barney," she said. "What did I ever do to get a friend like you?"

"Moved to Brooklyn," he answered cheerfully. "Now go to sleep and we'll speak again tonight."

THIRTY-ONE

Psychoanalysis differs from all other medical disciplines in one major respect. While fledgling cardiologists, for example, do not have to lie on the table and have their chests cut open in order to qualify for their specialty, a psychoanalyst *must* learn what it feels like to be on both sides of the couch. Again, as opposed to the surgeon, he will be dealing not with a passive patient etherized upon a table, but with an active individual, agonizing with him.

At its best, psychoanalysis can be the most exciting and humane specialty of medicine. At its worst, it is unquestionably the most destructive.

Barney was accepted as a candidate for the Psychiatric Institute and began a Training Analysis with its president, Fritz Baumann, internationally renowned for his incisive writings and respected by his patients as a wise and caring therapist.

But Barney quickly discovered that analysis itself is far from enjoyable.

Freudian analysis, Dr. Baumann explained, is like a repertory company of two actors, with the patient playing himself at various ages and the analyst playing all the other characters in his psychological development (or lack of it). By analyzing the scenes he recreates, the patient is then able to understand how long-ago incidents might have influenced the behavior patterns of the rest of his life.

In the abstract this sounded like fun to Barney. But all too soon it became clear that repressed thoughts are painful. And there is no way that the analysis, even of an ostensibly "well-balanced" candidate, as he considered himself, can be anything other than brain surgery without knives.

Barney arrived for the first session jaunty and high-spirited, certain he would impress Dr. Baumann as the best adjusted patient he had ever had. He was determined to transform what is traditionally a marathon into a hundred-yard dash.

He had, in a sense, been studying for this exam from the first moment he had taken Freud's *Interpretation of Dreams* from the Brooklyn Library to read during the summer nights at Camp Hiawatha. From then on he had consciously tried to analyze the motivations for significant actions in his life. And he was determined to show Dr. Baumann that *he* really knew what made him tick.

He entered the brown-carpeted, wood-paneled office with the narrow leather couch against the far wall, eager to dispense with the preliminaries and get down to the business of inner exploration.

Dr. Baumann asked the usual questions—family history, siblings, childhood diseases, etc. He went on to explain that the bill (at a special discount for candidates) would be rendered monthly. Finally, he inquired if Barney understood the procedure.

"Yes, sir," he answered. "I've got to say anything and everything that comes to my mind, to repress nothing and get down to the primary material."

He then got on the couch perfectly prepared to disclose any number of repressed (or so he thought) secrets, the "shameful" sexual things he had done as an adolescent. Even the erotic fantasies about his kindergarten teacher. Surely that was the sort of stuff an analyst would have difficulty in dredging from a recalcitrant patient with a psyche sealed in cement.

And so he filled his first fifty-minute hour with what he proudly regarded as the most generous exposition of carnal activities since Krafft-Ebing's *Psychopathic Sexuality*.

It took him eleven sessions—and one or two subtle hints from Dr. Baumann—to recognize that he was offering spicy revelations simply to show that he was a "good analysand" and thereby currying the analyst's favor.

"Why the hell should I be so uptight just because I want you to like me? I mean, it's perfectly normal, isn't it?" he finally asked.

Barney suddenly became aware that despite the air-conditioning in the room a cold perspiration bespangled his brow.

"Can you explain that, Dr. Baumann?" he reiterated.

When there was still no reply on the part of the master psychiatrist, his apprentice realized that they had struck analytic pay dirt. And that he himself would have to wield the pick and shovel to mine it.

Gradually, and with surprising difficulty—and Baumann's total silence—Barney came to understand that he had recreated the most troubled relationship of his life.

It was a discovery made through anger.

"Why the hell don't you ever say anything?" he repeated with growing frustration. "I mean, I'm paying out good money and you won't talk to me. And don't think I haven't noticed you don't even say good morning. Christ, all you've given me to take away is 'Our time is up.' Now what the hell am I supposed to do with that?"

Dr. Baumann did not reply.

"Okay, now I'm catching on, Fritz," said Barney with undisguised hostility (as evidenced by his irreverent use of the distinguished doctor's first name). "You actually want me to get pissed off. Well, you've succeeded—I *am* pissed off."

Dr. Baumann did not reply.

"Okay, okay, I'm clued in now. I mean, I've read all the literature. And I know what's coming next. I'm supposed to say that it's really not you I'm angry at but the person I've turned you into. You know I'm right, Fritz. You should at least give me some credit for self-awareness."

Dr. Baumann did not reply.

"Of course," Barney snapped, continuing his tirade, "you want me to say that—" He stopped, unable to finish his sentence. For he was not yet capable of articulating who in his life had behaved to him as he imagined Dr. Baumann was acting now.

Oh shit, he thought to himself, maybe I should go into dermatology. You don't even have to get a rash for that one. Why am I putting myself through this stupid exercise? What do I care if Baumann likes me nor not? He's just a fat, balding old man.

"What are you thinking?" Baumann asked.

At first Barney was startled by the unexpected sound of the doctor's voice. He then replied with a feeling of cathartic aggression, "I was just thinking you were a fat, balding old man."

There was a pause. Then Baumann asked quietly, "What is your association?"

"None, none. I have no association." Barney simply could not reveal the embarrassing connection he had made.

Finally, he remarked, "I don't think this is getting us anywhere, Fritz."

There was another silence, before at last the doctor said, "Our time is up."

It took Barney over a month of daily sessions—and innumerable repetitions of the same scene under various guises—to summon up the courage to admit to Baumann that the phraseology he used to denigrate his analyst had a significant association.

"Yeah, yeah," he said, "I know what you think I'm thinking—that 'old man' is just a slang way of saying 'father.' But you're wrong. That's a stupid idea."

Once again, he could not come to full grips with it.

"Jesus," he complained, "I sure haven't gotten much for nearly three hundred dollars."

And suddenly he thought to himself, Why am I behaving exactly like a typical textbook patient? Why am I bitching about the fee? That's so goddamn classic. Why can't I be different?

Then a new idea struck him. Maybe Fritz will like me better if I fit into the usual pattern.

In 1965 the impending storm in Southeast Asia finally broke. Indeed, the first series of President Lyndon Johnson's bombings was ominously codenamed "Rolling Thunder."

In June the White House announced that General Westmoreland could commit U.S. Army troops to battle as he saw fit.

To say that a small flame would grow into a conflagration would be more than metaphorical. For this was the year in which the first antiwar demonstrator reached into his wallet, pulled out a small piece of paper, and put a match to it. It was the first burning of a draft card—and far from the last.

While their contemporaries were now too old to be conscripted as foot soldiers, those who had become doctors still owed a debt to the military. And they were asked in increasing numbers to honor it by service in Vietnam.

At first there was no opposition of any magnitude. Perhaps it was because the Administration was attempting to obscure its growing involvement in this little Southeast Asian country.

Curiously, the classmate least likely to be drafted was the most eager to serve. Hank Dwyer volunteered. His domestic situation had become intolerable. Since there was no peace at home, he decided he might as well go to where there was a real war. Cheryl at first saw no objection. In fact, she—and the folks back home—admired Hank's display of patriotism. And besides, she was sure that a gynecologist would be posted to some stateside Army camp to care for the officers' wives. None of them anticipated the extent of Hank's zeal, which led him to sign up for a special Army program that instructed physicians in the treatment of battlefield trauma.

As preparation for this, Army sharpshooters would fire at partially anesthetized sheep and then the doctors would race to try to "save" them. This was difficult at first—especially for young men brought up on such tender melodies as "Little Bo-peep" and "Mary had a little lamb."

As it turned out, Hank was motivated by more than fervent patriotism. In the Officers' Club at Fort Devins, Massachusetts, he had heard fascinating accounts of the exotic delights of Saigon.

One experienced Regular Army captain, who had already been on a brief inspection tour, put it in a nutshell.

"You guys remember what Havana was like before that prick with the beard stopped all the fun? I mean, fantastic—right? Like one long party. It was like their primary resource was rum and cooze. And I mean the most beautiful girls you ever saw in your life. I always wondered what became of all that when Fidel Shithead took over—and now I know. They just transferred their operations lock, stock, and barrel to Saigon."

"Is it really that good?" asked a wide-eyed colleague.

"No," the captain insisted, "it's ten times better. I get horny just talking about it. Let's have another beer."

"It's my turn," volunteered First Lieutenant Hank Dwyer, M.D., U.S. Army Medical Corps. As he stood watching the barman siphon out three more glasses, a tall captain strode up. And motioned to the bartender. "Two gin and tonics, Horatio, and take it easy on the tonic."

"Be right with you, Captain," he responded politely.

Hank turned and saw a familiar face he could not put a name to.

"Excuse me, don't I know you from someplace?"

The captain looked at Hank and immediately noticed, "You're in the Medical Corps?"

"That's right."

"Then you may have known my wife at Harvard."

It all came together for Hank. "Now I remember. You're Laura Castellano's husband, aren't you?"

"That's one way of putting it," Palmer answered.

The two men reintroduced themselves and shook hands.

"What brings you here, Palmer? Thirty-day reserve stint?"

"No, I've gone back on active duty."

"Gosh," Hank remarked, "Laura must be pretty unhappy about that, huh?"

"Well, matter of fact," Palmer replied, "she's so busy healing the sick I don't think she'll notice I'm gone for at least a month."

"Yeah. My wife complained that I was spending so much time at the hospital, my children were forgetting what I looked like."

"I know the feeling," Palmer commented.

"Got any kids?" Hank asked.

"Uh, no."

"Well, you're playing it smart," Hank offered. "We have a menagerie at home. I can't get anything done. Frankly, I envy you. It would've been great to spend a few years alone with Cheryl—just the two of us. You know, every night like Saturday night—if you get my meaning."

"I get your meaning," Palmer replied curtly.

"Laura's a great-looking girl," Hank continued, undeterred. "She's cute as any cover girl—and I really mean it."

"Thanks. I'll be sure and tell her." At which point Palmer was rescued by Horatio's arrival with the beverages.

It had been nearly two months since Barney had moved into a huge if somewhat seedy SoHo loft, and he still did not have the slightest clue as to what had provoked Vera Mihalic's paroxysm of bottle-breaking.

When he had angrily inquired the morning after the event, Vera had snarled that she had only wrought devastation on his toiletries "because I couldn't get ahold of your head." This was the behavior of a trained psychotherapist? He began to wonder if she probed her patients' brains with a hammer and chisel.

Thank heaven she would be leaving in a few months, and he would no longer have to endure her murderous stares at the hospital.

Meanwhile, he was taking childish delight in his own continuing ascent in the world of literary freebies. The pinnacle was an invitation to dine at Lutèce (where the cost of the wine exceeded his monthly salary as a resident). His host was Bill Chaplin, senior editor at Berkeley House, an imprint so distinguished that its very name was an imprimatur of quality.

And Barney found Chaplin enormously well-read, equally at home discussing Plato or the *nouveau roman*. But he admired even more the quality and flair of the assistant Chaplin had brought along—a willowy nymph with long genuinely blond tresses.

They were already at the table when Barney arrived.

"Sally is just going to sit in while we chat, if you don't mind," Bill said deferentially.

Somehow Barney *knew* with certitude that Sally Sheffield (Bryn

Mawr '63) had fantastic legs even though they were underneath her skirt, which itself was underneath the table.

Though relatively inexperienced, Barney was not naive. He knew that Chaplin had not invited him to discuss Flaubert or Proust or Faulkner—though all of them did come up in the course of conversation. But he had to wait until after the soufflé, the brandy, and the (contraband) Havana cigars before they got down to business.

Barney knew that it was nitty-gritty time when the lissome Miss Sheffield excused herself for leaving early, charmingly explaining "My boss is a slave-driver, and he's given me a pile of homework. Nice meeting you, Dr. Livingston."

Barney's eyes were fixed on the golden tresses disappearing across the room. God, he thought to himself, she's even blonder than Laura.

"Barney," Chaplin began, rediverting his attention, "I hope I've conveyed to you how impressed I am by your work. It's fresh. It makes exciting reading because you don't use psychiatric mumbo-jumbo."

"I'm flattered, Bill," he answered sincerely.

The editor smiled. "I'd very much like to publish you, Barney."

"I'd very much like to be published *by* you," Barney replied.

"Have you been kicking around any ideas?"

"As a matter of fact I have. Ever since I was a kid I've been fascinated by sports. I think practically everyone in the world at one time or another has fantasized about being a champion."

Bill nodded. "I was going to be an All-American halfback. Unfortunately, I stopped growing at five-six."

"I always dreamed of playing pro ball for the Knicks," Barney continued. "But the fact is, some people actually get to *live* this fantasy. A runner like Emil Zatopek—the Czech "Ironman"—there's got to be something special in his head that drives him beyond human limits. But there are literally dozens of examples."

"The Brown Bomber would be another logical choice," Bill offered.

"Absolutely. Joe Louis is a fascinating case. There's a guy who couldn't even *talk* till he was seven, ending up the Heavyweight Champion of the World—

"—and then there's a whole category of athletes who started out with crippling handicaps. Hal Connolly, for example. Imagine—he's born with a bum left arm and, of all things, chooses the hammer throw, an event which *emphasizes* his disability. He ends up winning the Olympic Gold in '56 and breaking the world record seven times."

"That would be terrific," Bill agreed, warming to the idea.

The maître d' arrived with the check, which Barney's host quickly signed and returned.

"Thank you, Mr. Chaplin," said the maître d' with a little bow and genuflection in his voice. In an instant the two men were alone again.

"Well," said Bill in summation, "I think you've got a wonderful idea. And I'm certain we'll be able to arrange something that will satisfy your people."

People? Barney said to himself. What the hell does he mean?

Chaplin's next utterance clarified the matter.

"Have them call me in the morning. Listen, I'm sorry to leave you like this, but I've still got a long manuscript to get through tonight. But do stay and have another brandy or whatever. By the way, who does represent you?"

Barney dredged his Bordeaux-logged memory and, after what seemed to him an eternity, replied, "Uh—Chapman, Rutledge, and Strauss—"

"Ah, attorneys," said Bill approvingly. "Thank heaven we don't have to deal with those wretched ten-percenters. Ciao."

The maître d' groveled up again. "May I get you something, Dr. Livingston?"

"Uh, yes, matter of fact, I'd be grateful for a glass of mineral water. And do you have a phone?"

"Right away, sir." The genie vanished.

This guy is going to carry a phone to me? Me, Barney Livingston, late of Brooklyn, New York, who's been stuffing nickels and dimes into slots all his life, now gets a phone served on a silver platter? God, I can't wait to tell Fritz about this.

But there was more pressing business at hand. He dialed the number.

"Who's this?" said a sleepy voice.

"Warren, it's me—I'm sorry to wake you."

"Barn? Are you in some kind of trouble?"

"Sort of. But it's nice trouble. I need 'people.' "

"Are you sure you haven't flipped from lack of sleep?"

"No, no, but I think I forgot the name of the firm you work for."

"Chapman, Rutledge, and—"

"Good, good," Barney interrupted. "My brain is still slightly intact. Listen, Warren, find out who the best contracts guy in your office is and ask him to call me at the hospital. I've just sold a book!"

"Hey, wow! Congratulations, Barn! Wait till Mom hears about this. You must be in seventh heaven."

"Actually I'm in Lutèce. But that's as close as I've ever been. 'Night, kiddo. Thanks."

*   *   *

It had been a relatively quiet night in the pit, as doctors often referred to the E.R.—the usual broken bones, febrile babies, car crash victims, etc.—until the police suddenly alerted the Admissions nurse that two victims of a particularly brutal mugging, both of whom had received multiple stab wounds and were bleeding badly, were on their way to the hospital.

In a matter of minutes Seth heard ambulances and police cars and a split second later there was bedlam in the E.R. There may have been only two patients, but the attendants and policemen rushing them in on stretchers were themselves smeared with blood.

"Who's in charge here?" barked a police sergeant.

"I am," Seth said. "Tell me quickly, I don't think we have much time to lose."

"Sorry, Doc, sorry. From what I could see the woman got the worst of it. She seems to have more wounds—and I think she's been raped, too."

"Thanks, Sergeant," Seth said quickly. "I'll take care of her myself."

He motioned to a pair of nurses and Tim Bluestone, an intern, to take the man into the second trauma room. Meanwhile he, another intern, and a third nurse would work on the woman in Room 1.

Before the wheels of the trolley had even stopped revolving, Seth's assistant was starting an I.V. in one arm while he himself started a second and began transfusing blood.

The nurse had stripped off what was left of the woman's torn garments. Though she was spouting blood everywhere, the patient lay so comatose with shock that she seemed beyond pain.

As he tried to gauge the quantity and severity of her wounds, Seth heard angry and indignant voices around the table saying, "Animals, absolute animals. How could *anybody* do a thing like that?"

"She obviously put up a hell of a fight," Seth remarked quietly. "She's mostly cut up on her arms and shoulders. There are only two lacerations on her abdomen and they're well below the heart and too superficial to have damaged an organ."

He looked at the younger doctor. "Check her for internal bleeding and start sewing. I'll give you a hand as soon as I see how Tim is doing."

He walked quickly across the corridor and opened the door to find the other E.R. team strangely motionless.

"What's happening?" Seth asked.

Tim Bluestone answered hoarsely, "He was knifed right in the heart. He's dead."

Seth looked at the cardiac monitor: the printout looked like a straight line. The victim lay immobile on the table, a small red stream leaking slowly from a cut on the left side of his chest.

"Take his blood pressure again," Seth ordered as he withdrew a tiny flashlight from his pocket to peer into the man's eyes.

"I've already checked them," Bluestone commented. "His pupils were dilated and didn't react at all."

Almost as if he had not heard, Seth asked, "What's the blood pressure?"

"Zero," Bluestone answered. "I told you, he's dead."

Again Seth seemed to ignore his colleague's verdict. "Give me a needle and a syringe stat."

"With what, Doctor?" the head nurse inquired.

"Just a hypodermic," he snapped.

The syringe was placed in his hand. To the astonishment of all present—especially young Dr. Bluestone—Seth swiftly plunged the needle into the man's chest, almost as close to the heart as the wound itself. Slowly he let the syringe fill with blood, relieving pressure from around the man's heart.

"I'm starting to get a heartbeat," said the incredulous nurse at the monitor.

Seth nodded slightly to acknowledge her report and turned to the other nurse. "Give Dr. Bluestone ten mils of epinephrine." He then glanced at the younger doctor and said, "Put it straight into his heart, Tim."

Without another word, Seth reached into the instrument tray, withdrew a scalpel, slit open the man's chest, and with a wide retractor snapped two of his ribs. Now there for all eyes to see was the heart—beating.

Seth covered the knife wound with one hand and squeezed the heart with the other. The head nurse dashed out to see if the surgeons on call had arrived to complete the work Seth had already begun.

Bluestone was speechless. All he could manage was, "Jesus, that was quick thinking." And then it occured to him. "But it's against hospital rules for anyone but a surgeon to open a patient's chest."

"I know," Seth replied in quiet annoyance. "But try telling that to his widow."

Seth's hands continued to pulsate the heart, his eyes fixed on the man's face.

After a few minutes the patient began to groan, "Ellen, where's my Ellen?"

"She's all right," Seth whispered. "I'm Dr. Lazarus and your wife's in the other room. You're both going to be all right."

An hour later, when the two doctors had managed to wash the blood off their hands (though their jackets were still streaked with red), they had a chance to reflect on what had happened.

"I don't know what to say, Seth. I feel so goddamn guilty. If you hadn't come in—"

"Forget it, Tim. We all screw up sometimes."

"Not you. I've been watching you for a whole year now and I've not seen you miss a single thing."

Seth smiled. "That's a procedure they never teach you in Med School, Tim. It's called C.Y.A."

"What?"

"Covering Your Ass."

THIRTY-TWO

It was a year of rebellion. In 1966,
America was scorched by no fewer than forty-three race riots.

And the black community in New Haven was making plans to assert
its own identity and demand its inalienable rights. Yet, sadly, Martin
Luther King would have been an unwelcome guest at their planning
sessions. For the struggle here, as in most northern cities, was going to be
blazing and bloody.

And Bennett Landsmann would inevitably be caught up in the
whirlwind.

As a junior surgery resident, he now had increased responsibilities
and even an office (if one could flatter his cubbyhole by calling it that).

He was busy writing up a patient he had just admitted for an
inguinal hernia when there was a knock at his door. His visitor was a
muscular black orderly he knew only as Jack.

"Am I interrupting, Doc?"

"No, not at all. Come in and sit down."

Jack entered but did not sit. Bennett returned to his desk, looked up
at the younger man's worried expression and asked, "Is there something
wrong?"

"You might put it that way, Doc."

"Please call me Ben. Now, what's the problem?"

"It's about all of us," the orderly answered with diffidence. "I've been sort of deputized to sound out the brothers and sisters on the hospital staff. By that I mean the nonjanitorial and nonmenial."

"That's quite a job."

"Not really, Ben. Do you wanna know how many black doctors and interns there are?"

Bennett smiled. "I've a feeling I wouldn't run out of fingers and toes."

"You wouldn't run out of fingers, period. Listen, Ben, a lot of us are sick of sitting on our asses writing letters to Congressmen—or marching like Boy Scouts around New Haven Green. There's a group getting together for some heavier action. We want what's coming to us—and we want it now. Do you fathom?"

"I fathom," Bennett replied.

"We've having a kinda rap session Thursday night. Can you make seven-thirty?"

"I think so. What's the address?"

Jack stood up, withdrew a slip of paper from his pocket, and handed it to Bennett. "I reckon you'll find it an eye-opening experience." He turned to leave.

"By the way," Bennett called after him, "does this group have a name?"

"Yeah," Jack replied, "we call ourselves the Black Panthers."

He raised his arm in a clenched-fist salute and left the room.

"I've got it all figured out, Fritz," Barney explained to the analyst he hoped was awake and listening. "My father was away in the war, so naturally I fantasized about him and probably wondered now and then if it wasn't maybe because of me he went away."

The doctor did not affirm or deny.

"You know, Fritz, I keep telling you it would be a great help if you'd just let me know if I'm right or wrong." He paused. "I'm sorry, Doctor, I shouldn't take out my frustrations on you. I do understand that what I say is right because it's what I'm really thinking. Isn't that right?"

The doctor still did not reply.

"Naturally I went through my early childhood looking for a father figure. And Luis Castellano was right there, fifty feet away. Great big, bearlike, paternal. I guess there's a part of me that became a doctor just to be like him—although he didn't have much faith in psychiatry. He used to joke that it was just 'confession without absolution.' "

"That was G. K. Chesterton," Baumann offered, in a rare intervention.

"Well, maybe," Barney replied, "but it's also Castellano. I'm sure he didn't read Chesterton—the guy was a conservative Catholic propagandist, everything Luis wasn't."

Barney went on expostulating about his surrogate father for the better part of a month. It was only then that Dr. Baumann felt it necessary to intervene.

"But of course you did have a real father," the analyst observed.

"Yeah, yeah. Did you think I was trying to avoid talking about him? Oh, come on, Fritz, I'm not that hung-up." He reflected and then said softly, "I guess I am, huh?"

He interpreted the doctor's silence as assent.

"I used to dream about him when he was away—except that after a while I kind of forgot what he looked like. I mean, I was seeing all these heroic soldiers in the war films and I kind of fantasized that my dad was some Audie Murphy type."

Barney paused for a moment, his mind going back to the day when they met Harold at the station—and once again relived his disappointment.

"I had imagined he was big and tall but this guy that came limping toward us seemed so small and frail."

He stopped abruptly, for he felt on the brink of tears. He took several deep breaths before he continued.

"But still he was my father and I was desperate to please him. I mean, could you believe I took Latin just to show him I was interested in what he taught? I guess it wasn't such a big deal—"

Again Barney paused, and then reflected bitterly, "At least it wasn't a big deal to *him*." He was growing angrier.

"I know I've told you this about a million times. I was a pretty good basketball player in high school and I could really get those Midwood fans excited by setting up a real fast break or something. I wanted my father to see me in action, you know, getting the crowd's approval. . . . But he never came." He paused, still trying to keep control of his emotions. And then he said, "Sometimes I hate him." And continued bitterly, "I hate him for dying before he could see me . . . see me grown up."

And Barney could speak no further. He was crying.

Barney was seeing charity patients at the hospital on a regular basis—some weekly, some twice-weekly—and from them confirming Thoreau's view that the majority of the men lead lives of quiet desperation.

His textbooks had stated that as much as twenty percent of humanity suffered from depressive symptoms. But the despondency that Barney saw hour after hour made this estimate seem pathetically low. There was an epidemic of despair—in New York, at any rate.

A precious few had bipolar syndromes. They at least oscillated between a high of inexplicable euphoria and a low of equally unmotivated desperation.

On the other hand, his textbook had been right in saying that this malady occurred more frequently in women. They had more "vulnerability factors." For many, the home—even without children—was solitary confinement, unmitigated by the support of a "confiding relationship."

Sometimes after a long day's journey into nightmares, Barney would come to the conclusion that there was no such thing as a happy marriage. But then, he rationalized, the happy ones wouldn't be coming for therapy, would they?

He found that much of Freud's *Melancholia and Mourning* still offered the most insightful explanation of depression. For those who suffered from it were, in a sense, mourning the loss of their self-esteem, their commitment to life.

And he explained to Dr. Baumann that he was preoccupied by this problem because he was worried about Laura.

"That girl's got everything, she's beautiful, bright, generous, she's got a sense of humor. And yet she still lets her sonovabitch husband walk all over her because she thinks she's worthless. Christ, I wish she'd see a doctor."

But in fact, Laura *was* seeing a doctor. Which is to say she was dating Robbie Wald, a psychologist she had met when he had come to Children's on a special consult. He seemed to her to have some of Barney's charm and optimism—with a few special gifts of his own. He was also a talented pianist who taught at the New England Conservatory.

And whenever they went to a jazz club he would inevitably end up taking the pianist's place and jamming with the rest of the combo.

Robbie was warm and attentive, often showing up at ungodly hours during Laura's night shifts with bagels from Ken's, or a multiflavored gallon of Baskin-Robbins ice cream.

There was always plenty of Rocky Road—Laura's favorite—though she never told him that her predilection for this flavor was due to its name, which she considered a wry comment on her marriage.

Yet the affair troubled her. She had suffered no qualms whatever about seeing other men during her long courtship with Palmer. Yet now that she was married, she felt guilty. She believed—or wanted to believe—in the sanctity of the vow she had taken.

Still, Robbie's engaging manner had finally won her over. Besides, she was lonely. Except for her telephone conversations with Barney, she really had no one to talk to. Even her mail consisted of little more than bills, occasional postcards from Palmer and infrequent epistles from Grete.

As she felt increasingly at ease with Robbie, she began to mention Grete's problem.

"Correction," Robbie had answered, "her biggest problem is her own doctor. Andy Himmerman may be the world's greatest expert on adolescents, *and* have a profile like Cary Grant, but he's a pretty screwed-up guy himself."

"What do you mean?" Laura asked.

"My guess is he feels insecure about his masculinity. But why he had to abuse his position and seduce a patient sure beats me."

Laura was taken aback. "How come you know so much about him?"

"I can't violate professional ethics. Let's just say I treated a patient he messed around with and messed up."

"But Grete swears he wants to marry her."

Robbie chuckled. "To paraphrase Dorothy Parker, 'If all the women Andy's promised to marry were laid end to end—I wouldn't be a bit surprised.' "

"Robbie, this isn't a laughing matter. Grete doesn't know the first thing about men. That's why she was seeing Himmerman."

"Oh, God," Robbie muttered to himself, and then fell silent.

Laura had to ask. "Did you straighten out that patient of his? I mean, is she okay now?"

Robbie squirmed. "She was a very sick girl."

Laura picked up on the past tense. "Was?"

Robbie nodded solemnly. "I almost told the coroner to list cause of death as: Andrew Himmerman, M.D."

"Jesus!" Laura exclaimed. "Why didn't you report him?"

"I tried," Robbie answered tonelessly. "But the only witness couldn't testify."

Bennett was having trouble getting to sleep—even with the two milligrams of Valium he had taken. Yet he knew it was crucial that he be sufficiently rested or he might not be alert enough to cut. There are no Monday morning quarterbacks in Surgery.

Finally, he overcame the reluctance—to pick up the phone.

"Dr. Livingston's not here," said a voice that sounded exactly like Barney Livingston.

"Hey, man, it's me, Bennett. Did I wake you?"

"Ah, Dr. Landsmann," Barney said, now in a theatrically professional tone of voice, "could I get back to you? I'm in the midst of seeing a patient."

"At your house in the middle of the night? I tried the hospital and they said you were off duty."

"Dr. Landsmann, I'm afraid you'll have to call me during my regular office hours tomorrow morning."

Bennett finally caught on.

"You with a chick, Doctor?" he asked quietly.

"Yes, Doctor," Barney replied pointedly. "The patient is in very serious need of my immediate attention."

"Sorry. Don't let me interrupt the progress of medicine."

Barney put down the phone and returned to his room, muttering histrionically, "It's endless. Doctors keep calling for consults night and day. I mean, just because it's morning in Europe doesn't mean that they have a right to disturb me now."

Then he asked his patient, "Now where was I?"

"Right here," replied Sally Sheffield.

Bennett could not believe his eyes.

Crammed into the small, flamboyantly postered living room on the upper floor of a two-family house near Dixwell Avenue were more than two dozen blacks, half of them women with Afro hairdos. Most of the men dressed like leather fetishists or storm troopers (or both). For the official Panther uniform was black leather jacket, beret, shirt, and pants. And, of course, black boots.

The room was decorated in wall-to-wall rage: pictures of Malcolm X, Ché Guevara, Stokely Carmichael, and Ron Karenga—the most militant black nationalist of all. The posters seemed to be shouting a chorus of revolution: "burn the peckers," "kill whitey."

Bennett entered uneasily and was grateful to see Jack. The orderly hailed him, then walked over and escorted him to the center of the room, where he was introduced to the gathering as "Brother Bennett."

In his Varsity sweater, open shirt, and jeans, Bennett felt like an alien.

He tried desperately to tune into these people who, for all their violent intentions, were acting to redress a genuine injustice. Curiously, he was reminded of an essay Barney had once given him to pass on to Herschel. It was by Bruno Bettelheim on human behavior "in extreme situations." In this case it had been the concentration camps, but the principles were the same. Extreme pressure brought out astonishing reactions among the suppressed.

Jack got up to speak, but he was no longer referred to by his "slave name" but rather as Brother Jamal.

"We've got brothers who've been in the military and can teach our men guerrilla warfare. We've got instruction in karate for every kid not big enough to hold a rifle. We're also organizing a course in house-to-house fighting. If the white man's preparing for war, then war he'll get!"

There was applause, and enthusiastic murmurs of "Right on."

Brother Jamal asked for questions.

Bennett hesitated, then raised his hand.

"May I ask what evidence you have that, uh—'whitey' is preparing for war?"

Jamal-Jack responded, "I've got written proof that the U.S. Army is training seven task forces—do you read me?—*seven* task forces to cope with the 'uppity' behavior they're expecting from us. Only we intend to crush *them*."

This drew another salvo of "Right on's" from the audience.

"Matter of fact," the speaker continued, looking at Bennett, "we want you to teach a first aid class and, since you're a surgeon, train a medical corps to treat bullet wounds. Now, are you with us, brother?"

Bennett was taken aback.

Jamal-Jack prodded him. "Come on, man, you know what Eldridge says—'If you ain't part of the solution you're part of the problem.' Now, just where *do* you stand, Brother Bennett?"

There were murmurings among the crowd.

Bennett stood up and responded as calmly as he could manage.

"I'm probably the oldest guy here and so maybe I can put the struggle for equality—our struggle—into some kind of perspective. The little town in Georgia where I grew up had a beautiful high school for the whites and a hovel for the 'Nigras.' Since then, the Southern schools and even the universities have been integrated. Now there's a black Senator from Massachusetts—"

"You hold it right there, Uncle Tom," an angry voice barked.

It was Jomo Simba (Swahili for "lion"). "We know just where your head is, mister—right near the white man's ass."

There were mocking chuckles from the Panthers, and Simba continued.

"We're here 'cause we're sick and tired of all that honky 'look how far you've come' shit. You'd better straighten up and fly right, man. Or when the smoke clears you're gonna be little pieces of black dust."

There were louder "Right on's."

"Okay, wise guy," Bennett retorted, "let's see if you can come up with answers to some heavy questions. One—what good was it to burn Watts or any other inner city when we were setting fire to our own houses and our own businesses? And, closer to home, have any of you ever been treated in the Yale–New Haven Hospital? Where the hell would you go if you burned *it* down?"

"They've got about two and a half black doctors on the medical staff," yelled a shrill female voice.

"Granted, granted," Bennett retorted. "But they still *treat* all of black New Haven in the Emergency Room."

"What the hell kind of progress is that?" the woman lashed back.

Bennett lowered his voice and replied with studied deliberation, "Just give me a second to tell you a little story. The guy who pioneered the techniques for blood transfusion was a black doctor named Charlie Drew—one of the most multi-talented men who ever lived. In 1950 he was hurt in a car crash in Alabama. But because he was black, he couldn't get admitted to a goddamn hospital for the *only thing* that would have saved his life—a *blood transfusion*. Do you dig? Have any of you ever had that problem?"

They did not answer.

"What I'm trying to say is that I can understand wanting to burn bridges behind you. But why the hell would anyone want to burn the bridges in front of him?"

They were stunned into silence, which was broken by a Panther from across the room.

"We don't need your goddamn opinion. We need your ass in the front lines."

Bennett tried to leave the stage as calmly as possible.

"Hey, look, guys," he said quietly, "you've laid a very heavy trip on me, and I need time to think. I'd be happy to teach first aid in the ghetto—it could do a lot of good. I'm just not ready to put a bomb under Lyndon Johnson's chair."

Then, pleading hospital commitments, he excused himself and headed for the door. Jamal-Jack caught up with him in the corridor.

"Listen, Bennett," he said in an uneasy whisper, "my job brings me sixty-eight-fifty after taxes and I've got a wife and kids to support. You won't mention this—?"

"Of course not, Jack. Don't sweat."

Bennett turned and rushed down the stairs to the street, for he was ashamed of being seen in his nine-thousand-dollar Jag.

THIRTY-THREE

It was an awesome moment to be thrust into the world. Yet in the years 1967–68 most of the doctors who were graduated from Med School a half-decade earlier would at last be freed from supervision and out on their own, honored with the crown of omniscience, but cursed with the awareness of their limitations and fallibility.

It was a time of such confusion that military leaders were pronouncing on the value of life and physicians were redefining the moment of death. Moral schizophrenia was epidemic.

General Westmoreland told the press that Orientals, like those his troops were trying to kill in Vietnam, held human life to be less important than did those in the more enlightened West.

Blacks ran riot in the cities, incurring the white man's wrath. Yet, paradoxically, when some of these same men put on khaki uniforms and machine-gunned the Vietcong, white generals pinned medals on their chests.

This contradiction, this schizophrenic attitude toward violence, was epitomized by Cassius Clay (as white men called him) or Muhammad Ali (as his brothers and a handful of the liberal left referred to him). The great warrior stood on the steps of the induction center and declared that he would not employ the talents God had given him for mayhem to square off against the Vietnamese. He who had willingly leapt into the ring to make opponents "dive in five" or "hit the floor in number four" refused to join in the destruction of a people who could not even afford the price of boxing gloves.

Ali was diagnosed as mentally incompetent for Army duty. ("I said I was the greatest—not the smartest.") The times they were a-changing.

Meanwhile doctors now were asking, "What is death?" In other words, when could they remove the organs of a man deceased to use them as replacements for defective parts of men diseased?

In a country so close to the South Pole that it was sometimes lit by the aurora australis, Dr. Christiaan Barnard was waiting for a death to be declared so he could graft the corpse's heart into another's body.

At Groote Schuur Hospital near Capetown, surgeons added one more dimension to the debate on whose life was of more importance. Dr. Barnard's third patient, a white Capetown dentist, was rescued from death by the gift of a "colored" man's heart. How would the sages of apartheid now classify this patient? Which part of the bus, which toilet, and indeed which township would be home for Philip Blaiberg, Barnard's most successful—and most controversial—patient?

Still there was a good prognosis for the world. Transference of the heart from one chest to another stole the headlines in 1967, yet in that self-same year in a quiet laboratory in Cleveland, Ohio, a doctor took the entire brain out of a monkey's skull and transferred it into another's.

The prospects defied credulity.

There is no graduation day in psychoanalysis, for in a sense it never ends. Indeed the most significant part of the therapy begins only when the patient rises phoenixlike from the ashes of his inhibitions, stands vertical, and walks out into the labyrinth of daily life, his psyche now a compass that will—hopefully—lead him to the right decisions.

It was with ambivalence—pride and relief alternating with sadness and apprehension—that Barney faced his final session with Dr. Baumann.

Though his analysis officially was at an end, he was still aware that he would always carry with him unresolved emotions.

Indeed, throughout his inward odyssey from memory to memory, Barney had discovered that Harold's illness and his early death had robbed him of the father he had so desperately needed. And there was no changing that.

Dr. Baumann's help had also taught him how to understand what he was doing—or at least *why* he was doing it. He could look forward to the greatest gift analysis can give—the rare ability to act as an adult.

That was the good part. But there was still a precinct that remained off-limits—a character in the drama of his life who seemed to appear in almost every scene, but whose function never was explored. And Dr. Baumann knew full well that Laura Castellano was hardly a "walk-on."

His patient had so vividly described this girl, not merely her virtues, but also her troubled psyche, that Baumann often found himself wondering what she was really like. Yet he knew that he had failed to help the young psychiatrist disclose exactly what this mythic figure meant to him.

With merely minutes left and Barney free-associating about entering his thirtieth year, he remarked, "Well, Castellano's turning thirty, too. I feel so guilty being optimistic when I know that she's so damn miserable."

Fritz intervened.

"About Laura—"

Barney interrupted.

"I suppose you're thinking I've been holding out on you and that I maybe harbor—I don't know—romantic feelings about Laura. But I don't."

The analyst did not reply.

"I mean, I've been completely honest with you, Doctor. I don't deny that once or twice through all the years we've known each other I've had—call it sexual—thoughts about her."

There was a silence.

"Are you sure you aren't camouflaging something?" Baumann asked directly.

"Sure I'm sure. But with due respect, sir, it's a new world. Nowadays it's possible for men and women to be just good friends."

"It has always been possible," Baumann replied. "I just wonder if you are certain it's that way with you and Laura."

"It's how she feels about me, I'm sure about that."

"And you?"

"I don't know. I really, honest-to-God don't know."

"Well perhaps this is something you might work on in the future."

Though he had not yet completed the two supervised analyses necessary to be admitted to the Institute, Barney was nonetheless Board-certified to practice general psychiatry, and could now see private patients outside the hospital in an office of his own.

Through the widening contacts he had made among older colleagues, he learned that one of the Senior Fellows, Brice Wiseman, had just lost to the Army the young psychiatrist with whom he'd shared an office.

Barney found himself in turmoil. He sat down in his newly purchased Eames chair, closed his eyes, and tried to look within himself to find
out what was bothering him.

Was it perhaps the fact that Brice Wiseman's office was on the East
Side of New York, close enough to Park Avenue with all the connota-
tions of privilege emanating from that legendary street? Yes, that was part
of it.

And then there were the furnishings. His predecessor had collected
exotic art and artifacts and had made his office a sort of poor man's
museum.

Ah, but isn't that the point? No poor man would be likely ever to be
treated in such regal splendor, he told himself. If I'd needed help when I
was just a kid in Brooklyn, would I have had the chance to see the
well-intentioned Dr. Livingston in his offices between the avenues of
Madison and Park? Then he thought immediately, in his own defense,
that he was also seeing troubled people at the hospital for nothing. He
pondered longer, trying to plumb the deeper reasons for his discontent.

And, finally, he knew.

It was not the address, the fancy decor, or the pictures. It was the
price. For at the bedrock of his qualms he found what was disturbing
him: he had to put a value on *himself*.

On the surface it seemed ridiculous that he had never thought of this
before. But then up to now all he had ever wanted as reward was a good
night's sleep. The hospital paid him a salary—if you could call it that.
And his writing brought a little extra. That at least was work he could
somehow quantify.

But how could he assess himself—his brain? And if the people a
psychiatrist sees are already in such distress, how could he impose yet one
more burden on them? True, Freud believed financial sacrifice was part
of the incentive for successful treatment. But not *everything* the Master
said was right. For after all, when he psychoanalyzed himself, he clearly
didn't send himself a bill.

Barney found himself recalling childhood incidents. Like overhearing Luis Castellano talking to the mother of a child whose broken arm
he'd just set.

("How much do I owe you, Doctor?" she had said.

"Is five dollars too much for you?" he had asked.

"No, no," she had said hesitantly. "But is it okay if I pay you some
now and some later?"

And Luis had reassured her, "Fifty cents a week will do. But I'm not
in any hurry. We can talk about it when I take the *niño's* cast off.")

But then Luis did not have to pay a hefty office rental or half the salary of a receptionist.

Yet does a doctor really need these trappings?

"I know how you feel," Brice said the next day. "But even if you were Rockefeller and had all the goodwill in the world, you'd have to charge. It makes the patients take you seriously. It's documented in the literature—not just by Freud, but Ferenczi and plenty of others. Of course, you'll make exceptions where there's indigence involved. But, otherwise, if I were you I'd peg my fee at somewhere between twenty and thirty bucks a session."

But Barney's conscience was still not assuaged. "In ancient Babylonia a doctor only got paid when he had cured his patient."

Wiseman laughed. "Hammurabi made that rule back in 1800 B.C. Nowadays I think the AMA would tend to look upon that as a bit outmoded."

And then he once again addressed the point: "You're providing a service, Barney. See yourself, if you will, as a taxi driver transporting a patient from sickness to health. The meter has to run, doesn't it?"

Unwittingly Wiseman had hit on a metaphor that corresponded to a genuine experience in Barney's life. He had been a hackie.

He broke into an impish smile. "The only difference is we don't take any tips. Right, Brice?"

Wiseman grinned and said, "Only if it's on a stock or on a horse."

By the spring of 1967 there were nearly half a million U.S. troops in Vietnam, few of them understanding what exactly it was they were fighting for. Meanwhile, all across the United States there were at least as many protesters marching against their country's involvement in Southeast Asia. General Lewis B. Hershey, the director of conscription, let it be known that men who had been given a student deferment from service to complete their education would forfeit that privilege if discovered participating in an antiwar demonstration.

A great many doctors had their military obligations to fill and would have to make a moral decision if asked to serve in Vietnam. By now large colonies of young Americans who had been conscripted were turning into self-made refugees and fleeing the country. Canada and Sweden suddenly became the centers of the draft evaders.

But there were other ways of keeping out of uniform. A doctor's note declaring a young man unfit for service, for example. Since certification of mental instability was probably the most effective draft deterrent, Barney found himself under extreme pressure.

For what kind of doctor would he be if he declared a well man sick? He and Laura discussed it endlessly in their after-midnight "consultations."

"Thank God the only boys I deal with are just a few days old," she commented, "so I don't have to worry about this sort of thing."

"Don't be so sure, Castellano. The way things are going, this war may be still on when they grow up."

"Anyway, you're in the hot seat *now*. How're you going to deal with it?"

"I'm gonna declare that General Westmoreland's insane and the whole war is lunacy."

"I agree with you," she said, "I've already marched my feet off. And I sympathize with the bind you're in. I mean, nowhere in the Hippocratic Oath is it written that a doctor can lie to keep his patients out of battle. There's no moral precedent."

"There *is*," Barney countered. "The Nuremberg Trials proved that morality transcended nationality. And don't forget, if these guys just sit here and set fire to their draft cards, they'll be thrown into jail. Now isn't *that* immoral? Besides, doctors are supposed to save lives. And whoever I declare unfit won't go out there and kill people."

"Gosh, Barn, you're really taking a big risk. I admire you. What are you gonna say is wrong with them?"

"I'll say anything I think is appropriate—foot-fetishism . . . schizophrenia, homicidal tendencies."

"Oh, they'd just *love* a guy with homicidal tendencies."

"Speaking of murderers," Barney interrupted, "how's that sonovabitch husband of yours?"

"He's doing something in Washington."

"That wasn't my question. How are you two getting on?"

"Oh, I don't know," she answered. "Let's just say it's on hold. Anyway, he's flying in tonight."

"Don't you think he's bounced you like a yo-yo long enough? That's pretty self-destructive, Castellano. Why don't you give him some sort of ultimatum?"

"Look, Barn, I've already extended a cordial invitation to divorce. He didn't accept. He says he likes things the way they are. Frankly, as far as I'm concerned, I'm too tired to care."

Laura was so involved in this conversation that she did not notice the door opening. Or Palmer entering the room.

"To be frank, I'm probably to blame for his screwing around. I mean, maybe his affairs have just been to get back at me for my 'liberated' policy before we got married."

"Christ, Castellano, you've got a unique talent for always making yourself the guilty party."

At which point, Laura screamed.

"Hey—what the hell's going on?" Barney asked.

She turned and was relieved to see it was Palmer who had playfully nipped her on the neck. As he kept his arm around her waist, she reassured Barney.

"It's my wayward husband trying to be Dracula. I think I'd better go now."

"Okay, Castellano, only work up the courage to have him put up or shut up."

She hung up.

Suddenly Palmer was undoing the buttons of her blouse, murmuring in a tone she had not heard for years, "I've really missed you, Laura."

Thirty minutes later as they were sitting before the fire, Laura kissed him and remarked, "That has to rank as the greatest conversion since Saint Paul went catatonic on the road to Damascus."

"You know I've always loved you, Laura. It must have been delayed adolescence. I mean, I won't pretend I was celibate in Washington. It's a bit of a sexual carnival down there. I mean, I hope you didn't see that ugly little rumor in the columns about myself and Jessica Forbes. I just happened to be sitting next to her at dinner. But I guess everything a Senator's daughter does is grist for the gossip mills."

Laura wondered if this "confession" was not also a poorly disguised attempt to boast. But she wanted so badly to believe his renewed expression of love.

"Look, Palmer," she answered, "you don't have to cite name, rank, and bra size. Let's just say we both had a kind of vacation from monogamy."

He then asked tentatively, "Has there been someone . . . special in your life?"

"Why don't we change the subject?" she said gently, knowing that if she had been candid about Robbie it would have injured Palmer's ego. She responded with a question.

"How long are you staying?"

"I've got a two-week pass," he answered. And then he added softly, "If you can possibly wangle any time off, I'd like to spend as much as I can with you."

"I could maybe manage a day or two—"

Just then the phone rang. Neither of them moved.

"It's probably for you," he whispered.

"Forget it. I don't want to break the spell."

The ringing persisted.

"Go on, Laura," Palmer urged. "You're a doctor and it may be important."

As she walked slowly to the phone, Laura could feel his eyes following her.

"Hello, this is Dr. Castellano."

"Hi, Laura, it's your ever-lovin' Robbie. Can I tempt you for a late drink and a few bars of music?"

"I'm sorry, I'm kind of snowed under. I'll see you tomorrow after morning rounds."

"Is anything wrong? Or am I maybe interrupting something?"

"Thanks for understanding."

"Sure, sure," he said disconsolately. "See you in the morning."

She could hear the disappointment in his voice.

"Who was it?" Palmer inquired casually as she returned to the fire.

"Nothing," she replied. "Nothing that means anything."

"May I ask you something?"

"Sure."

"Are you taking the Pill?"

She grinned. "Don't tell me you're worried about knocking me up. Anyway, set your mind at rest, I take it as faithfully as ever."

A fleeting expression crossed his face that seemed to say, For whose benefit have you been practicing birth control for all these months?

"If you stopped, how long would it take you to get pregnant?"

Laura was speechless. She answered reflexively by the book.

"The body's endocrine system is pretty unpredictable. Sometimes when women come off the medication it takes six or seven cycles—or even a year. But then there are also cases where stopping actually stimulates immediate fertility."

"Let's hope you're in the second category," he said.

She was still in a state of mild shock.

"Why this sudden urge to parenthood?"

"Well, we're neither of us getting any younger. Women should be having their first babies by the time they're in their early thirties. And since your residency ends this year and you won't be on such a punishing schedule you could sort of work it in."

"What's your real reason, Palmer?" she persisted.

"Well, I'd like an heir to carry on the family name."

"No," Laura demanded, "I want your absolutely honest reason—the whole truth."

He looked her straight in the eye and confessed with a touch of apprehension, "I'm being transferred—I'm not sure exactly when—but I'll be going to Vietnam."

"Laura, you've got to be joking!"

"I'm sorry, but I have to."

"But he's treated you like dirt—are you just gonna let him back into your life and screw up your head again?"

Robbie was beside himself. Laura had just told him over coffee that they could not see each other anymore—except as friends. Robbie could cope with that part of her announcement. He was a mature adult. At various stages of his life he had won and lost—and had an ex-wife and two messed-up kids to prove it.

But the idea that a woman like Laura would even consider going back to Palmer after the shabby way he had treated her totally confounded him. All the more so because he knew firsthand that it was often feelings of unworthiness that kept a man and woman together, even when they were both well aware that it was mutually self-destructive.

Robbie believed that he was better for her than her husband. For Robbie could see the little girl inside the woman, and she brought out all his protective instincts.

Now this Palmer bastard waltzes in, snaps his fingers, and she goes straight back for more punishment. On reflection, maybe Laura really wants to be miserable. Okay, Robbie, he told himself, let her go—the grief you save may be your own.

All of this ran through his mind as they were standing at the nurses' station stoking up on caffeine. He was glad he had resisted his first impulse to berate her. He felt calmer, more rational.

"Are you sure you're making the right decision?" he asked.

"I haven't made any decision at all, Rob."

"You mean choosing between me and Palmer was no contest?"

"No, it was no *choice*, Rob. Palmer's my husband. I thought long and hard before I married him."

"You *do* have a choice—you know damn well I would marry you."

Laura took his hand tenderly. "Robbie, listen—what we shared was lovely—and I'm very fond of you. But honestly, you're better off without me. I'm not bad for an affair, but I'm not really what you'd call good wife material."

Robbie was hurting—as much for her as for himself.

"Laura, listen carefully, this is my closing speech." He paused, drew breath, and then said softly, "God's played a dirty trick on you. He gave you everything. Only He was probably so snowed by the result, He just forgot to add that final touch of confidence. Okay, so I wasn't the guy. It won't be easy but I'll deal with it. I only hope that someday someone pounds a little sense into that gorgeous head of yours and makes you *like* yourself."

He turned around, ashamed to show his tears.

And walked away.

THIRTY-FOUR

In the early autumn of 1968, the Black Power movement literally reached an Olympian peak.

At the Games held in the mile-high city of Mexico, American athletes Tommie Smith and John Carlos won the gold and silver medals in the 200-meter dash. Standing on the podium as the band struck up the "Star Spangled Banner," the two athletes raised black-gloved fists in a gesture of protest at the way white America was treating their brethren.

This new rage had begun to boil the previous year, when Rap Brown became Chairman of the Student Nonviolent Coordinating Committee. His inaugural speech gave a hint of how little his group's name now meant when he offered to assassinate Lady Bird Johnson, the President's wife.

And he also introduced a new theme to the militants' dogma—anti-Semitism. Suddenly American Jews were viewed as the primary cause of the black man's suppression.

This was a strange tactic for organizations like SNCC and CORE, which had in large measure been supported by former residents of the original ghettos.

For Herschel Landsmann it was a dagger in the heart. He had up to now been a passionate and generous supporter of the black man's cause; he and Hannah felt betrayed. But their greatest anxiety—so disturbing that they dared not broach it even to each other—was how would this affect their relationship with Bennett?

By now Barney had completed over two hundred pages of *Mind of a Champion* and could no longer withstand Bill Chaplin's persistent pleas for a look at the manuscript. With much trepidation he delivered the material to the Berkeley House building.

From nine that evening, he phoned Bill Chaplin at least twice an hour, pleading for some sort of response.

"Is it good, Bill? Is it good? I mean, is it okay? Or is it terrible? Is it pretentious? Is it superficial?"

The bemused editor replied, "Look, I can't read if you keep distracting me. Why don't you take a pill and go to sleep."

"I don't want a pill, dammit, I want know what you think."

The pages he had given Bill contained analytic observations on such varied champions as sprinter Jesse Owens, boxer Joe Louis, and Roger Bannister, the first four-minute miler.

They also included an interview completed merely days before his death with Donald Campbell, the man who set speed records both on land (403.1 mph) and water (276.33 mph). This was an especially intriguing case since Campbell's father had also been in the "speed game," having been the first man to break the 300 mph barrier on land. Was it something in the genes? Was it something in the psyche? How did he feel about "defeating" his own father?

But Barney felt that the best chapter so far was on his boyhood hero Jackie Robinson—grandson of a slave and the first to break the color barrier in baseball.

At half past eleven Bill called him.

"This material's terrific," Bill exclaimed.

"You mean you like it?" Barney asked incredulously.

"No, I *love* it. How soon can you finish the rest?"

"Hey, listen," Barney retorted, "you sometimes forget I'm a practicing doctor."

"I know, I know," Chaplin conceded, "but we've just gotta get this onto our spring list. If it's money you're worried about, I can get you another advance so you can take a sabbatical from your other commitments and just concentrate on the book."

There was a sudden pause.

It seemed to Bill that they had been cut off.

"Barney, are you still there?"

Barney answered in tones that barely disguised his resentment.

"Bill, let me tell you for the millionth time that a psychiatrist is like the father of an extended family. Our patients aren't like people who go in for an operation and then leave a week later. When they make a commitment to me, I make a commitment to them—to be there when they need me—even if it's for *years*. Would you like your pilot to start his sabbatical while you're midway across the Atlantic Ocean?"

Bill was duly chastened. "I'm sorry, Barn, I'm sorry. I got carried away. I realize your priorities. May I withdraw my offer—with no hard feelings?"

"Sure, no sweat."

"Okay then, Barn, I'll sign off," his editor said, anxious to retreat, but not before adding, "still, if you could finish by August—"

"Goodnight, Bill."

"I've just killed someone—what the hell am I gonna do?"

It was 2 A.M. Tim Bluestone, junior resident in Internal Medicine, was distraught. His superior, Seth Lazarus, tried to calm him down.

"Hey, take it easy, Tim. Try to get hold of yourself. Sit down and tell me what happened."

The young doctor obeyed like an automaton. And then he buried his head in his hands. "Oh, Christ, I'm a murderer," he groaned.

Tim raised his face and wiped his eyes on his sleeve.

"It's Mrs. McNaughton. She was—"

"I know," Seth interrupted. "She was scheduled for an exploratory tomorrow. Keep talking."

"The nurse was doing a routine check of vital signs and the old lady's blood pressure was suddenly dropping like hell, so she got me from the on-call room. I ran up and could tell, even before putting the cuff on her, that there was severe hypotension. She was blue in the face. . . ."

He paused and then said, "I feel like such an asshole. I know I should have called you, Seth. You wouldn't have let me screw up."

He looked forlornly at the chief resident. Seth simply said, "Go on."

"Well, I thought I knew what to do. I mean, I actually did know what to do, except I—"

He stopped himself in mid-sentence. For he was about to admit the fatal error.

"Her damn diastolic was down to thirty, so I told the nurse to bring me Aramine, stat. I knew it would increase the blood pressure right away."

"That's right," Seth commented, "a vasopressor agent was indicated. So far I don't see any irregularity."

"Well, the nurse brought me half a dozen ampoules. She just dumped them there and ran off down the hall—somebody was hemorrhaging. I mean, I suppose part of this is her fault because she should have brought me Aramine that was more diluted. No, shit, *I* should have looked more carefully. But I was so goddamn tired I really didn't know what I was doing.

"Anyway, I pushed ten mils into Mrs. McNaughton's I.V. and waited for a response. It didn't come. Then her pressure suddenly shot up— and I panicked. I was scared she might have ventricular failure, infarction, or a cerebral hemorrhage."

"So you lost your cool and gave her another ampoule," Seth anticipated.

Tim nodded. "Then suddenly she just conked out." He paused and then murmured, "She was dead. Finally, I did what I should have done in the first place. I picked up her chart. It was then that I saw she was a severe diabetic—"

"Bad move," Seth commented matter-of-factly. "Aramine is contra-indicated for diabetics because it constricts blood vessels that are already diseased and can cut off the blood supply."

Tim began to pound the desk with his fists.

Seth stood up and said quietly, "Have you spoken to anyone else?"

The younger man shook his head.

Without another word, Seth began to walk toward Mrs. McNaughton's bed, Tim following. On either side of her, patients were snoring. Mrs. McNaughton was still.

Seth carefully checked her vital signs and shone a light in her eyes. He looked up at Tim and said, "You're right, I'd say she had a massive cerebral infarct."

Tim stood motionless, paralyzed with guilt, as Seth continued.

"Go back to the office and wait for me. I'm going to tell the on-duty nurse to take care of things. Then you and I will write the death certificate."

For a split second neither spoke. Then Tim repeated in a tiny frightened voice, "I killed her, Seth, didn't I?"

To which Seth responded simply, "I'll see you in the office." And then walked off.

When Seth reached the on-call room about fifteen minutes later, the air was thick as London fog. Bluestone must have been smoking two at a time, he thought to himself.

Seth handed Tim a pen and a document. Tim glanced at it mutely.

"Just sign it, Bluestone, will you?" Seth urged.

"You list cause of death as Massive Cerebral Infarct."

"So? That's perfectly correct."

Tim looked at Seth, his facial muscles frozen, and said, "You know damn well *I* was the cause of death."

"Listen, Bluestone, there isn't a doctor in the world who hasn't lost a patient by human error—especially if he's been without sleep as long as you have. That certificate tells the truth." Seth paused and then conceded, "It just doesn't tell the whole truth."

Tim stared at the senior resident with gratitude. "Thanks, Seth, I'll never forget this."

For a few moments neither of them spoke. Then Tim asked haltingly, "Tell me, Seth, have you ever killed a patient—I mean, by mistake?"

Seth weighed his answer carefully, and replied, "I told you. We all do."

Barney's career—as well as his mood—was definitely on the rise. He used what seemed to him a princely advance from Bill Chaplin as a down payment on an apartment in Gainsborough House, where from his living room window he could survey his massive front lawn—otherwise known as Central Park.

Moreover, he spent almost every elevator ride in the company of a noted writer, artist, or musician. He still could not believe his career had reached such heights, and the little boy in him was often tempted to ask his ninth floor neighbor to hum a few bars of whatever it was she was currently singing at the Met.

"Great news!"

"It damn well better be for a call at midnight."

Barney, who had been working late into the night writing up patients' notes, had just dozed off when Bill Chaplin's phone call awakened him.

"Listen," Bill said excitedly. "I've just had dinner tonight with the top enchilada at *Sports Illustrated*. Last week I sent them your Jackie Robinson chapter—and they want to print it in their big April baseball issue—to show how things have changed. Barney, you've no idea what this could mean."

"But Bill, my chapter's much too long—"

"Of course, they'll cut it, old boy. And don't worry. I've made sure you've got the right to approve the final abridgment."

"Great, Bill, great," replied Barney. "But do you mind if I go to bed now? I've got my first patient at six-forty-five in the morning."

"That's really New York for you, isn't it, Barney?" Bill enthused. "People go bananas every hour of the day. Well, here's a thought for you to sleep on: When this book is published, you are going to *happen*."

Barney was too tired even to care about "happening." "Good night, Bill, and pleasant dreams."

"I never dream," Bill answered parenthetically. "I've got these great red pills that make my mind a total blank."

"Terrific," Barney said in valediction. And as he hung up thought, Good luck, Chaplin. When your brain turns into Silly Putty you'll be really glad you hooked yourself on Seconal.

Lance Mortimer was probably the only man in Los Angeles who could keep an entire room convulsed with laughter without having to tell a single joke.

He had found that one of the many advantages of choosing Anesthesiology as a speciality is that it can get you invited to a lot of "A-list" Beverly Hills parties that might otherwise be above your station. Even his father, a highly successful screenwriter, had never been so honored by the upper echelons of Hollywood society. Lance's special appeal as a guest was that he would show up, not only with two beautiful girls, but with a tank.

That is, a tank of nitrous oxide—colloquially known as laughing gas.

Lance had chosen to become an anesthesiologist only after careful investigation and intense deliberation.

First he eliminated the really "chain-gang" alternatives. Like Obstetrics, for instance. Who wants to get up in the middle of the night? But for that matter, who wants to go to other people's houses for anything but a party? So that meant Internal Medicine was out, too.

And Surgery was too damn much hard work. And the responsibility too heavy a trip.

At one point Dermatology held his favor. First of all, that specialist does not get called up at ungodly hours. Or lose a patient. Or need to memorize a large pharmacopoeia. As Lance saw it, you either give the patient cortisone or penicillin. Or if you are less imaginative (and less acquisitive), simply tell the patient that the skin disorder is most likely to clear up on its own.

And there was dough in Dermatology: one guy he knew of had converted his Beverly Hills office into five separate miniconsulting rooms, each no bigger than a broom closet. He would dart from booth to booth, casting his eyes—and sometimes a magnifying glass—upon the rash, or wart, or other symptom. He'd then make an instant diagnosis and say something short and charming to the patient. Thereafter a nurse would give out all the forms and the prescriptions—and make another follow-up appointment for the next week.

The only problem, Lance decided, was that Dermatology was boring. Seeing minor variations of the same rash a hundred times a week would be like having to look at a single painting all the time. If you were forced to stare at it hours on end, day after day, even Mona Lisa's smile would get on your nerves.

Next case: Urology. Recent studies in *Medical Economics* showed that genito-urologists now led the league in the crucial area of bucks per annum. Here again you never had to make a house call. That was good. The ratio of customers per hour was also good. And, like Dermatology, you never lost a patient. (For if you did detect something like cancer, you immediately referred the carcinoma to a surgeon or oncologist.)

But then, Lance told himself, the work was hard. And the responsibility considerable. You'd have to keep up with the literature, master new techniques, and generally take your practice seriously. Moreover, some of your patients really would be sick—might even die (albeit on someone else's operating table). And the notion of spending the day looking up people's asses with a proctoscope was not exactly thrilling.

The task of an anesthesiologist seemed to him far more attractive: to reduce his patient to a cozy state of muscle relaxation, induce a peaceful slumber, and to keep his breathing stable. Meanwhile, at the other end of the table the surgeon—under constant stress—painstakingly cuts and slices, grafts and sews, always risking danger. And if the operation fails, the surgeon nearly always gets the blame.

All the while the friendly "gas-passer" just checks his dials to balance breathing and blood pressure. Then when the operation is successful and the patient wakes, he overflows with gratitude for his new gift of life.

What's more, Anesthesiology pays very well. Its hours are flexible. The patients are in no condition to complain or contradict or even question you. And if you choose, you can arrange a schedule that gives you maximum free time to live a normal, wealthy life.

And get invited to the A-list parties for your charm—and nitrous oxide.

Barney's days were now so busy he had half-forgotten that *SI* was going to publish his Jackie Robinson chapter. One Saturday morning in late February, on his return from spending two hours with a patient who had called in mortal panic the night before, he was just changing into his sweats to jog out some of the pain he had absorbed by osmosis, when the phone rang.

"Hello, Dr. Livingston, sorry to bother you on a Saturday, my name's Emily Greenwood. I'm with *Sports Illustrated*. I guess you know why I'm calling."

"Oh, sure, your magazine's amputating—or should I say 'editing' the chapter from my book."

"Let's put it this way: We have to cut, but we don't necessarily have to mutilate. Would it be convenient if I brought our proposed text to your apartment today? We're sort of racing a deadline."

"How much time do I have?"

"Well," she hesitated and replied apologetically, "since this is 'soft' news it has a long lead time. In other words, we go to press on Monday."

"What? That's ridiculous!" ("Soft," yet!)

"Please, Dr. Livingston, we're a news magazine and your piece has to go in when it's slotted. Besides, I think you'll be pleased with the way it's been cut."

"Well, in that case, could you have it messengered over to me?"

"No problem, it'll be there in half an hour," she replied.

Barney went to his desk, pulled out his copy of the chapter, and began to reread what he had written months ago.

Twenty-five minutes later the bell rang. He opened the door to a petite young woman with large brown eyes and short reddish-brown hair.

"Hi, I'm Emily Greenwood. Are you the good doctor?"

"That's me," Barney replied, trying to hide his disappointment at being regarded as a second-class writer who had to make do with an editorial assistant.

"I've got the manuscript," she said cheerily, holding up a manila envelope.

"Great—uh—would you like to come in for a cup of coffee?"

"Well," she replied, smiling, "I guess I'll have to—that is, unless you want to go over my edits in your hallway."

"*You're* my editor?" he exclaimed.

"You bet. I wouldn't have let any of my assistants go near this. I think it's a great piece."

Flattery—if it was that—smoothed Barney's ruffled feathers.

"Come in . . . come in," he said, motioning with an exaggerated bow. "Why don't you get set at what I grandiosely call my dining table while I boil some water?"

"Fine," Emily replied, entering Barney's living room. Piles of clothing were scattered everywhere, each suggesting the end of a specific activity—running pants and jogging shoes, assorted socks and a squash racket, etc.

"I hope you don't mind instant," he called out from the kitchen alcove.

"You're the doctor," she replied agreeably.

In no time he was back with two mugs of coffee, and as he set them down on the table, remarked, "I guess I owe you an apology."

"Don't worry, it happens all the time. Everybody takes me for my own secretary—it must be my childish enthusiasm for sports. But why shouldn't a woman be the next Grantland Rice? I believe in what Virginia Woolf said about the 'androgynous mind.' "

Apt allusion, Barney thought—and responded by indicating that he knew the source.

" 'A Room of One's Own' was really a landmark essay for women writers. And there's plenty of clinical data that each of us needs some of the qualities of the opposite sex to be able to function creatively."

"Well," said Emily, "I'm not exactly Virginia Woolf."

"That's okay," he replied, "I'm not exactly Sigmund Freud."

"Fine." She smiled. "Now that we've exchanged mutual expressions of humility, let's put on the gloves and start fighting over the cuts."

And fight they did. To Barney every excision felt like an incision.

"Emily, no, no, that's 'the most unkindest cut of all.' "

"C'mon, Barney," she countered, "we've got to make the focal point Robinson's gut feelings on that very first day in the major leagues. Don't you agree?" She gazed at him with those wide brown eyes.

"Frankly, Emily," Barney confessed, "you keep looking at me like that and I'll end up letting you cut the whole damn thing in exchange for your phone number."

"C'mon," she chided like a miniature football coach, "let's get this over with."

"Listen, Em—you don't mind if I call you Em?"

"Not at all—it's the first letter in mother, so I'm sure it must have some psychological significance for you. But don't tell me until we finish the job. Now I suggest we start when Robinson first walks into Branch Rickey's office. I think that's the most astonishing part."

"How so?"

"I mean, I don't know about you, but everybody's recollection of Jackie in that first incredible year—when they were throwing insults at him from the bleachers and baseballs at his head from the mound—was that he was above it all. He seemed so noble that he never felt rage or the urge to retaliate."

"That's what I thought, too. And it really knocked me out when he told me that Rickey actually made him swear an oath to lock up his emotions for three whole seasons. Only a saint could have kept his cool for all that time."

It took them less than an hour to extract what Barney had to admit was better than his own original chapter. Jesus, she was bright.

And not bad-looking, either.

No, no, stop lying to yourself, she's pretty, Barney admitted to himself. In fact, she's very pretty. Goddamn, a girl like that must have a boyfriend for sure. Better not risk asking her to dinner or we could ruin our editorial relationship.

"Now," said Emily, as she closed her notebooks with a dramatic slap, "I hope you'll give me the pleasure of your company for a late lunch at the restaurant of your choice."

"*You're* inviting *me*?" he asked.

"Well, let's say I'm inviting—and the magazine is paying. So give your appetite free rein."

"Okay then, how about The 21 Club?"

"Then '21' it is. I know the Kriendler boys, so if it's okay, I'll just use your phone to tell them we're on our way."

It was indeed late, even for a Saturday afternoon, and the upstairs room was filled mostly with waiters clearing tables.

Seated in a corner table, oblivious to all else, was a pair of sports freaks trying to top one another with recondite reminiscences of the Brooklyn Dodgers. Emily accepted Barney's challenge, and he began testing her knowledge by demanding she identify the players by their uniform numbers.

"One—"

"Pee Wee Reese, shortstop—good glove, so-so bat, lifetime average .261."

"Four."

"Irwin 'Duke' Snider—center fielder, long ball hitter, best season 136 RBIs."

"Six."

"Carl 'The Reading Rifle' Furillo—right field, greatest throwing arm in baseball—lifetime batting average .299, led the league in '53 with a .344."

Their game ended in a tie, each having scored all hits and no errors. Then, just as they were moving from numerals to topics requiring verbs, a thought occurred to Barney.

"Do you realize, Emily, that all the early Dodger heroes had a single-digit uniform? Then Jackie Robinson shows up and they give him forty-two? Do you think that's just coincidence?"

"No, you've got a point," she answered, "because they gave Campy—the second Dodger black man—number thirty-nine. As a doctor, what do you make of that?"

"Well," Barney began, "in my professional opinion, I'd say—absolutely nothing. I personally always used to ask for number ten—not in the major leagues, I hasten to say."

"I know," said Emily Greenwood cheerfully.

"Know what?"

"I know you used to be a basketball jock—before you got so intellectual. Actually, I've got a confession to make—I hope you won't psychoanalyze it too much." And then she confided, "I used to have a thing about your legs."

Barney did not know quite how to react. Was this some trendy new locution among the East Side swingers? ("Would you like to come up and see my kneecaps?") He responded with a similar tone of levity.

"That's very flattering, Em. I mean, I don't think anyone's ever said anything that nice—or off-the-wall—to me."

"Don't worry, I'm not some kind of fetishist. I was two years behind you at Midwood."

"You were at Midwood—how come I never noticed you?"

"Well, I guess you were too busy romancing the cheerleaders. Anyway I used to photograph the games for the *Argus*. Actually, I've always wondered why you didn't play senior year—you would have made All-City First Team for sure. I mean, you weren't just good on offense, you were a tiger on defense. Whatever happened?"

Elated by her admiration for his erstwhile sporting exploits, Barney replied in laconic, Gary Cooper fashion, "It's a long, sad story, Emily. I don't think you'd want to hear it."

"I've got plenty of time," she said, smiling.

Her innocent remark made him glance at his watch. It was four-fifteen.

"Hey, Em, the captain's looking razor blades at us. I think he'll kill us if we don't get out of here."

"Don't be so paranoid, Barney, Dimitri lets me stay forever. I'm his connection for tickets to the Super Bowl."

"Don't you have a date—or work to do?"

"No, to the first; yes, to the second. And you?"

"The same. But let's forget the pages yet unwritten. And as the Latin poet says, 'Seize the Day.' "

"You're right," she answered. *"Carpe diem."*

And as they walked out Barney thought to himself, I'd really like to "seize" you, too, Emily.

After another few blocks of high-spirited conversation, Barney realized, *Now* I really know what euphoric means.

THIRTY-FIVE

It was a November Saturday morning, crisp as an autumn apple, and the normally brown and stone-gray Yale campus was enlivened by blue-and-white football scarves, blond-haired Vassar girls, and undergraduates' cheeks red from excitement, football fever, and the cold.

Bennett had gotten off duty at 10 A.M. After assisting Rick Zeltman on an eight-hour "plumbing job" (which is how the senior surgeon had referred to the complex genito-urinary procedure), he was bushed from the mental strain as well as the physical effort. But much too excited to go straight to bed.

He strolled over toward the college campus with the thought of dropping by the Co-op and picking up a book to take his mind off blood and guts.

Street vendors were out in force, hawking balloons, pins, and other paraphernalia. The undergraduates looked like children to him. Christ, he thought, have I grown old so quickly? What's been going on since I was locked inside that concrete and linoleum dungeon where there's no day, no night, no change of season? Ten years ago I walked in like a young lion, and now I suddenly feel like an old goat.

As Bennett crossed Chapel Street toward Broadway, a young black selling newspapers approached him.

"Hey brother," he called out, "have you got the news? Are you tuned in? If not, better buy this document. Just two bits, brother, and you'll find out where it's at."

Bennett reached into his pocket, gave the boy a quarter, put the paper underneath his arm, and walked away.

Half an hour later he was home with fifteen dollars worth of books that, if he was lucky, he'd read between that afternoon and next July. He turned on his stereo, kicked off his loafers, and sat down to read.

But he was so zonked from cutting, tying off blood vessels, suturing—and most of all worrying if he was doing everything correctly—that even the stylistic pratfalls of Tom Wolfe's *Electric Kool-Aid Acid Test* could not hold his attention. As a kind of last resort, he started to glance over the latest Panther news.

The paper's rhetoric was strident and virulently antiwhite. Hell, Bennett thought, I'll skip the heavy stuff. Maybe they've got a sports section.

He flipped through the final pages and was happy to come upon some cartoons. Ah, he thought to himself, just the level of literature I need right now.

And then he began to read one. But after the initial obscene caricatures of "Filthy Jewpigs ripping off Blacks," he hurled the paper to the floor and stormed out of his apartment into the chill New Haven wind.

He found Jack in the orderly room.

"Hi there, Ben baby," Jack greeted him—forsaking the usual hospital formalities, since the other orderlies regarded Bennett more or less as "one of them."

"I'd like a word with you," Bennett said sternly.

"Certainly, Doctor."

The two men stepped into the empty corridor. Bennett was about to explode with the tirade he had prepared en route to the hospital. ("Is this all you can write in that filthy rag of yours?")

But he realized that to vent his anger on poor Jack would serve no purpose. He was not the editor, he was not a leader, he was just a simple foot soldier fighting for a cause in a foreign land known as America.

So he reined in his fury and said simply, "I'd like to come to the next meeting, Jack."

"Change of heart, Doc?"

"You might say that."

"Okay, I'll let you know."

*   *   *

The chief resident had been in the Emergency Room of Boston Children's Hospital admitting a nine-year-old girl with a dangerously high FUO (fever of unknown origin), which she suspected signaled endocarditis.

By the time Laura had finished writing up everything, it was after midnight. She was heading for the on-call sleeping room when she noticed that the normally sedate voices at the nurses' station were unusually loud and excited.

One of the women called from afar, "Laura, did you see the eleven o'clock news tonight?"

"No," she said, too exhausted to be aroused by anything other than World War IV (she was sure she was tired enough to sleep through World War III). "What did I miss?"

"It's wild, Laura. Absolutely wild," said the youngest—and normally the most reticent among them. "It's a really raunchy Washington scandal about two doctors—the woman surgeon was from Harvard and about your age."

Laura instantly knew who this had to be. Her heart began to race and she blurted out, "Did one of them commit suicide?"

"Tried to. Nearly three hundred mg's of Valium. But they reached the stomach pump in time. The woman doctor was positively gorgeous."

Laura, half in shock, muttered, "Grete Andersen?"

"Yes," a nurse replied. "That was her name. Did you know her?"

Laura asked anxiously, "Was there any brain damage? Just what did that damn psychiatrist do?"

The nurses looked surprised.

"Why, *he* was the one that took the pills," one of them replied.

Laura held her head, for she was growing dizzy.

A nurse named Nida came up and asked solicitously, "Laura, are you all right? Is Dr. Himmerman a friend of yours as well?"

"No, no," she said still in confusion, allowing herself to be led to a plastic armchair in one of the waiting alcoves. "I'd be grateful if someone would tell me just what the newscast said."

"Well," Nida began, "this doctor is supposed to be a really world-class honcho in psychiatry."

"Forget the credentials. What did he do?"

"Well, to put it mildly, what he shouldn't have been doing with a patient. Your friend was very cool—"

"—and brave," said another nurse.

"She called a press conference at the Georgetown Hospital."

"She what?" Laura asked, certain she was imagining all this. "Why the hell would the press come to listen to some surgical resident?"

"First of all, she's stunning," Nida answered, "and, most of all, they love this sort of juicy scandal. Anyway, she said that she'd gone to Himmerman for treatment and he'd ended up in bed with her."

"But how the hell could she prove it?"

"Oh, that was the interesting part. At first this Dr. Himmerman—who's incredibly handsome, by the way—spoke to the cameras and denied it all. He said it was some kind of paranoid delusion and that 'the poor girl' should be in a mental institution. He was very convincing."

"I'll bet he was," Laura muttered.

Nida's next words were a bolt from the blue: "Then he just turned and walked up the steps of his townhouse—a beautiful place in George-town, by the way—went upstairs, and swallowed all those pills."

"Oh," said Laura, now elated. "So the sonovabitch turned out to be his own worst enemy. Hurray for Andersen."

"Grete, are you okay? I've been trying to reach you for nearly two weeks."

"Sorry Laura, it's just that I've had to move in with a girlfriend because my phone was ringing off the hook. I should have called you sooner—I'm sorry."

"Hey, how did you get the guts to blow the whistle on that unethical bastard? What made you do it?"

"Somebody had to. Do you know that Andy swore he'd leave his wife and marry me? Then I found out he used that line about a million times."

"How'd you find that out?"

"From none other than Mrs. H herself. We met as I was coming out from my session. She looked me up and down and suddenly flew off the handle and said, 'You must be Andy's latest Barbie doll.' Then she stormed right into his office and started screaming. What happened after that will probably appear in the next *National Enquirer*."

"Oh, Grete, I feel so sorry for you. I hope this lousy experience doesn't turn you off men in general."

"Well, to tell the truth, they're not my favorite gender at the mo-ment. And as for male *doctors*, they're just about the lowest form of life. I'll give you three guesses who has to get out of town as a result of this scandal."

"What are you talking about?"

"Well," Grete replied, "it seems the Surgical Department here thinks I'm not cutting it—to coin a phrase. So they've offered someone else the senior residency and informed me that, though I was 'welcome to stay,' I wouldn't have a stipend and I'd have to slog my guts out as a volunteer."

"In other words, they fired you."

"Well," Grete replied sarcastically, "you might say so. In fact, 'fired' was the only word they *didn't* use. These doctors are like a fraternity or some secret society. My sin apparently wasn't that I allowed myself to be seduced, but that I told the press."

"Grete, I'm absolutely speechless. You mean that creep is gonna get away scot-free?"

"Probably. I mean, naturally they're going through the motions. He'll have to testify before some County Board—in private, naturally. But he still maintains that I'm a hysteric who fantasized the whole thing. Anyway, I'm resigned to leaving, so I'm writing to practically every hospital from here to Honolulu. And if all else fails, I'll join the Army."

"What?" Laura said with incredulity.

"I'm serious. They need surgeons badly. They would probably even ship me to Vietnam." And with the pain audible in her voice, she commented, "Frankly, Laura, if I got my head shot off it couldn't hurt much more than it hurts now."

For the first time in their marriage, Laura and Palmer had almost identically punishing schedules. No longer did he complain when she came home at 4 A.M. For he himself was wide awake, having spent the midnight hours in the intensive study of Vietnamese.

As she entered the room he removed his reading glasses, looked at her, and smiled. "You know, my darling, I'm beginning to have respect for what you're going through. I mean, this lack of sleep is absolutely killing me."

"Actually, Palmer, it's a tried and true technique for breaking prisoners of war. I'm told it's very popular in Southeast Asia."

"Oh? Who told you that?"

"The New York Times."

"And you believe that Commie rag?"

"My God, Palmer," she remarked, only half in jest, "sometimes you make Barry Goldwater sound like a Berkeley radical."

Laura poured herself a glass of orange juice, sat down wearily, and mused, "I'd like to know just what the hell it is about you men that makes you go on having wars and killing one another. Maybe it's all that testosterone—I mean, the androgen's a potent stimulant."

"I just thought that it stimulated sex," Palmer said, smiling.

"Well, there's always been a vague connection between love and war, hasn't there? Take Helen of Troy—"

"At this point, I'd rather take you," said Palmer, rising from behind his desk.

"Do you think tonight was the night?" he asked.

They were lying side by side in bed, relaxing drowsily.

"Palmer," she replied sleepily, "if Medical Science had invented a machine that could pinpoint ovulation I would have sneaked it home from the hospital under my raincoat."

"Well, anyway, it's not necessary," Palmer reasoned. "I mean, if we do it every night we're bound to catch the right time, aren't we?"

"Speaking professionally, Palmer, it takes the average 'Olympic' couple, as they call them, four to six months to conceive a baby. And sometimes longer if you've been on the Pill."

"I think a lot of it is psychological," he commented. "If you really put your mind to it, I'm sure you could succeed straight away. Take my own parents—I doubt that they've made love more than half a dozen times in their entire marriage, but they've got me and my sister to show for it. Anyway, what do you think we should call him?"

"Him? Who's him?"

"Our child—my son. The one that we're busily conceiving."

"How about Miraculous?" she asked. "It would be very appropriate." Then she quickly added, "And Miracula if it's a girl."

"It won't be a girl," Palmer assured her.

"It may not be anything at all," Laura said.

"Well, I'll face that problem when I have to," Palmer answered. "Meanwhile, you don't mind these little exercises in procreation, do you?"

"No," she said, "but I'd prefer to think of what we're doing as making love."

"Of course we are. That's the beauty of the whole exercise."

Laura paused for a minute. She was happy for the first time in a long while and did not want to break the mood. And yet she could not keep from asking, "Palmer—why this sudden urge to procreate? I mean, it's too late to keep you from going to Vietnam. . . ."

"That's just the point, darling," he replied. "To be brutally frank, I'm frightened about not coming back."

A fortnight later, Laura was driving him to the airport.

"You know, you still haven't explained to me exactly what you'll be doing over there."

"Because I honestly don't know, Laura. That's why I'm going for a week of briefing in Washington. Outside of Washington, actually—at the fabled estate of Senator Sam Forbes. There—I shouldn't even have told you that much."

"Forbes is a Hawk's hawk," she commented.

"I knew you'd say that. In any case, please keep it confidential. We won't even be allowed to call out."

"Oh—and will his lovely debutante daughter Jessica be there as well?"

"Darling, she's an empty-headed social butterfly—a two-watt bulb."

"Yeah. But how are her other assets?"

"I won't even dignify that with a reply, Laura."

They rode on in silence for a while, reaching the end of Storrow Drive and plunging into the Callaghan Tunnel. In the midst of what seemed an endless, dimly-lit tiled bathroom, he returned to the most pressing issue of the day.

"Can we name him Palmer?"

Laura nodded. "Only if it's a boy," she said blankly.

Flight 261 to Washington was already boarding. There was only enough time for a hasty goodbye, a final fleeting exchange of thoughts.

"Laura, tell me again—did you really stop taking the Pill?"

"Yes, I swear."

He smiled, turned, and strode onto the plane.

The small apartment was more crowded than ever. Not only had the Panthers gained some new recruits, but others had flocked there on learning that the principal speaker would be the Yale "Soul Surgeon."

Bennett's heart was pounding. He was not even sure how he would begin until he was actually standing in front of them. But an almost supernatural voice brought forth the words.

"I believe that every black man in America should get a square deal and a fair deal. As the Constitution says, '*all* men are created equal.' " He now approached the minefield. "But *equal* does not mean superior. We are no worse than any other people—but we are no better, either."

"What the hell you talkin' 'bout?" a voice called.

"That rag you call our paper blames the black man's troubles on so-called 'Jewpig Fascist Zionists.' "

Cheers of approbation. "Right on, brother!" "Kill the Jews!"

Bennett tried to remain calm. "Just why exactly have you singled out this ethnic group for annihilation?"

"Oh, man, don't you dig?" called out another angry voice from across the room. "The Jewpig is the slumlord, the pawnshop owner, the man who takes your car away if you're a little late in making payments—"

Bennett all but lost control.

"Now hold it right there, brother!" he shouted angrily.

His outburst brought a sudden silence to the room. But a silence that crackled with electricity.

"Let's get one thing straight," Bennett began. "Some Jews may be slumlords but, goddammit, so are some blacks. And there are plenty of Jews *helping* our cause. How about Mitchell and Schwerner, those two kids who got killed by the Klan in Mississippi?"

There was universal agitation.

"Dr. Landsmann," Chairman Simba said with deliberate formality, "I don't think the brothers know where you're coming from."

Bennett was drenched with sweat as he tried to continue.

"My father fought and died in World War Two because he had respect for what this country stood for. And he had to take more shit than any of you guys could ever dream of. Not just segregated units, or 'colored only' bathrooms—but if one of his soldiers got shot, the Red Cross had to give segregated *blood*.

"Yet he could write me the day before he died that he had seen atrocities more terrible than anything our people have ever known. He saw the Nazi death camps—"

He was cut off by buckshots of abuse. "That's a load of shit," and even "Hitler didn't kill enough!"

Bennett was quickly losing all control. But he had to finish.

"After my father died I was adopted by a Jewish couple who were both survivors of those camps. With their own eyes they saw their little daughter taken to be gassed and the rest of their family burned in ovens. Has anybody *here* gone through that?"

Mouth parched and cheeks wet, he nonetheless managed to conclude.

"I came here to tell you that we blacks don't have a franchise on suffering. And that *every* Jew is not our enemy. Because if we believe that, we become our *own* worst enemy."

He paused and then said quietly, "Just think about that, brothers."

Bennett let his eyes come into focus, looking at the spectators for a reaction. They were immobile. In fact, the only movement in the room came from his own hands, now trembling with emotion.

The chairman, in an expressionless voice, asked, "Are there any comments?"

A man in the back raised his hand.

"I would like to say to our distinguished visitor: Fuck the Jews, and fuck *you*."

Though the crowd remained motionless, Bennett was suddenly frightened. He had an eerie sense of otherness that made him feel he was seeing all this through distorted mirrors.

As he began walking toward the door, a path of people split before him like the Red Sea.

Barney first learned the news when he arrived at the hospital. John Warner, one of his junior residents, came rushing toward him shouting, "Livingston, have you seen today's *Times*?"

"No," replied Barney dryly. "Have we set some new record for napalming children?"

John, a hawkish Republican, ignored Barney's jibe.

"Didn't you go to school with Peter Wyman?"

"Yeah," Barney replied, "but it's not something I like to boast about."

"You will now," the resident asserted. "Look."

He handed Barney the paper. In the lower left-hand corner was a picture of Peter in a white coat. He had the usual smug smile on his face, although fewer hairs on his head.

The story announced, "New Clue to Cancer Structure Found" and the subheading "Young Harvard researcher invents pioneering technique in genetic engineering."

Barney studied the paper and thought, He kept telling us how bright he was. Maybe we should have believed him. After all, it says here he's already published sixteen papers and a zillion abstracts.

But he sure likes publicity. I mean, his findings won't be published for another six months. So is this press conference just to give the Nobel people more time to get familiar with his name?

Anyway, he rationalized, Peter's not got everything. I mean, there's no mention of a wife or kids.

But then Barney's superego challenged *him*. Who are you to throw stones, Dr. Livingston? Where are the wife and kiddies waiting in *your* glass house? To which his ego responded, give me time, I've got to finish this residency, start up a practice. Besides, I'm almost married.

Barney was intending to bring the subject up with Emily that evening.

Theirs had been a whirlwind courtship that had traveled the whole spectrum of American sporting life: football, basketball, boxing, baseball, hockey, tennis, and track and field in Europe. (That August during a meet at Malmö in Sweden, he was even able to spend two days interviewing the retired "Ironman," Emil Zatopek, for the final chapter in his book.)

They were synchronized, they were symbiotic, they even jogged at the same pace.

If this was not the kind of match made in heaven, it would at least be as durable as Astroturf.

Barney was weary of merely helping other people achieve happiness and decided it was time to try it himself. After all, he had endured much ribbing the year before, at his brother Warren's wedding to Bernice ("Bunny") Lipton—who was halfway to being a lawyer herself.

During the reception an uncle from Houston even castigated him, demanding, "When can we expect to get some pleasure from *you*, Barney?"

At the time he had been tempted to say, speaking as a psychiatrist, that if all marriages were as idyllic as his uncle painted them, his couch would be empty save for the occasional schizophrenic.

Indeed, as he himself had written in the *Journal of Modern Psychiatry,* during these troubled times the marriage relationship had almost come to mirror the malaise of the external world. But, as the unprofessional side of him well knew, marriage was best described by Dr. Johnson as "the triumph of hope over experience."

In any case, he and Emily would be different. They had a wonderful relationship, open and aboveboard. And though happy in each other's company, they each had a life beyond the household. It would bring that perfect equilibrium that marriage seeks but rarely finds.

He broached the subject to her over a late dinner at her apartment after they had seen the Lakers make mincemeat of the Knicks. The menu consisted of Zabar's finest take-away delicacies. Which meant that all Barney had to do was chill the wine and open it. After filling her glass and then his own, he raised a toast.

"To happily ever after—or more appropriately—Emily ever after."

"After what?" she smiled.

"After marriage," he replied.

Her glass stopped halfway to her mouth. And though she tried to hide it, Barney caught a hint of melancholy in her expression.

"What's the matter, Em? Did I say something wrong?"

She nodded. " 'Marriage'—"

"—is the wrong word?" he finished her thought.

"It is for me. I think you'd make a lovely husband."

"Well, then, why can't I be *your* lovely husband?"

Her eyes were downcast and she was shaking her head.

"No, Barney, no," she repeated, "it just wouldn't work."

"Is there someone else?" he asked, the frightening thought just occurring to him.

"No, no," she protested.

"And don't you at least care for me?"

"Of course. Do you even have to ask?"

"Then why, Emily? *Why?*"

She took a sip of wine and answered. "I can't be a wife. I'm ruthless, selfish, and ambitious."

But now the girl who had just referred to herself as insensitive and hard was weeping copiously. "You deserve better, Barney."

"That's crap."

"No, it's true."

Barney felt like a man who had gone out to plant a rosebush, put his shovel in the luxuriant soil, and suddenly struck a piece of unyielding stone.

There was no mistake about it. Emily's "no" meant absolutely not.

"Hey, look, forget my whole proposal. I withdraw it. This offer is void where prohibited, which happens to be everywhere. But might I ask you for something on a less contractual level?"

"What?"

"Move in with me. I'll make an office for you in the extra bedroom. We can be singular by day and plural by night. And if you don't want to come home for any reason you won't have to bring a parent's letter. Now is that fair enough, my little bird who won't be caged?"

Emily did not answer. She merely leapt up and threw her arms around him tightly, sobbing all the while.

As he hugged her with a matching affection, his mind could not close his office door. For an analytically perceptive voice was saying, Something's odd. Now, Doctor, can you figure out just what it is?

"I'll come over tomorrow and help you pack your stuff," he said.

"Thanks for understanding," she whispered in a tone of profound gratitude.

As they stood there in each other's arms, Barney could not help wondering, What am I supposed to understand?

Peter Wyman was a controversial figure. He was perhaps the only man ever to receive a degree from Harvard Medical School who outspokenly loathed sick people.

During his first year of postgraduate fellowship he was disdainful of his laboratory colleagues and demonstrated only a semblance of civility to Professor Pfeifer, his boss and patron. Pfeifer had not hired Peter as his assistant on the basis of his charm. Rather, he knew Wyman was a precious resource and was loath to let the enemy get hold of him (the enemy being everyone else in the field).

But Pfeifer had assumed that a clever boy like Peter knew the rules of the game: You help me to the podium and when your time comes I'll reach down and help pull you up. Meanwhile I'll see to it that as an Assistant Professor you live comfortably on federal grants and get to work in what is arguably the best biochemical laboratory in the world.

Peter was by nature mistrusting. Aware of his own lack of scruples, he assumed that everyone else would be equally without conscience. In other words, he was his own best friend. And his own worst enemy.

He had discovered the "Victoral factor" while doing research to corroborate one of Pfeifer's own hypotheses. He therefore felt it was his and his alone. And no sooner did his first control studies yield promising results than he went to the Medical School's trumpet section—the Press Office.

Director Nicholas Kazan was delighted by what Peter told him. Rather than calling a press conference, he recommended that they invite the medical editor of *The New York Times* up for lunch at the Ritz and give an exclusive to the paper of record.

"If I assure him he's the one and only, I can almost guarantee you'll make the front page. After that it'll be child's play."

Peter had only one important question.

"Do you think I should wear my contact lenses?"

Kazan proved to be an astute stage manager. After the first piece broke in the *Times*, he engineered an exclusive television exposure on the *Today* show. NBC sent Barbara Walters up to Boston to do the interview.

Peter had accomplished something brilliant. He'd taken a significant step toward the ultimate control of cancer. But it was not a *cure*.

His work could best be likened to a road map leading to buried treasure. Although the way was now discovered, it remained for other scientists to travel it.

Still, for a week thereafter, frantic callers besieged the Med School switchboard, pleading for the chance to benefit from Wyman's new discovery, before it was too late for someone in their family.

During the TV broadcast, Miss Walters naturally brought in Professor Pfeifer for his comments. And he told the camera, "Peter is a remarkable young man, a very remarkable young man."

As soon as the little red light on the camera blinked off, the older man asked his acolyte to breakfast with him—at his club.

Pfeifer waited till they had reached their second cup of coffee to initiate dialogue.

"Tell me, Peter," he asked casually, "do you have any notion why I've asked you here this morning?"

"To celebrate, perhaps?"

"And what precisely would our joyous reason be?"

"Well, the breakthrough—the whole project. The good publicity Harvard's got. . . ." His voice trailed off.

"I rather think you got more publicity than Harvard."

"Are you implying that I've stepped out of line, sir?" Peter asked ingenuously. "I've followed protocol and included your name in the actual article in the *NEJ*. I respect the hierarchies, sir."

"I'm extremely flattered," Pfeifer answered. "And glad to share a little of the credit, if only as director of the laboratory."

"Oh, sir," Peter unctuously persisted, "you did more than that. You've taught me everything I know."

At this point Pfeifer changed his tone.

"Cut the groveling, Wyman, you're not very good at it. I know I'm credited as coauthor of this. But then I'm the editor of the journal and I would have put my name in even if you'd 'forgotten.' What puzzles me, Peter, is two of the other scientists whose work you cite."

Peter's oatmeal face began to blanch.

"I'd like to think I knew the big boys in our field, and on occasion I've collaborated with a few of them. But I've never met this fellow Charpentier of the Institut Français de Recherches Médicales in Lyons or van Steen of Amsterdam—which certainly is curious, since both of them ostensibly collaborated with us on this breakthrough."

"Uh . . . well, actually they're both rising stars. They're very young and haven't published much."

"Then you were lucky to make contact with them so they could perform their own experiments and corroborate your data independently."

"Yes sir. That's true."

And suddenly there was silence. All that could be heard were the murmurings of distinguished Bostonian gentlemen politely discussing—or perhaps even deciding—the fate of the nation, the world economy, and Harvard's chances against Yale.

Meanwhile, Pfeifer sat and stared at Peter.

The older man was patient; he could wait. But then Wyman had remarkable endurance, too. So, in the end, Pfeifer capitulated. And broke the silence.

"Unless it was established in the last two weeks, Peter, there *is* no

Institut Français de Recherches Médicales in Lyons and that would make it quite difficult for 'Charpentier' to work in such a place. Of course, the University of Amsterdam exists. That's why I could ring up my good friend Harry Joost and ask about the mythical van Steen. . . ."

He stared at Peter, astonished at the younger man's ability to face his exposure unflinchingly.

"Dr. Wyman, without the benefit of data from the large-scale studies allegedly done in Amsterdam and Lyons, your conclusions are—to put it mildly—premature and fragile."

"My theory is correct, Professor Pfeifer," Peter said softly. "You could run another dozen tests and the results would be the same as mine."

"But Peter, if you were so certain, why not have some genuine investigations made to prove your point? Why were you in such a hurry?"

"The pressure—I didn't want anyone else to beat us out with this. So I took a calculated risk."

His mentor did not react. Peter continued his plea.

"You don't know what it's like out in the world of research now. Sir, why should another doctor help me out just for a thank-you in the footnote?"

Pfeifer thought for a moment before answering.

"Peter, I know that medical research can be like a street fight in an alley—there's so much at stake. But there are only two ways one can deal with it. Either show integrity above reproach and damn the cheats—or be crooked and get away with it. I'm afraid that you did neither."

Peter sat frozen, waiting for Pfeifer to pronounce sentence.

He did so in a hushed tone lest he disturb the distinguished breakfasters.

"Peter, listen carefully. I want you to go back to the lab, take everything that's yours—and make sure everything you take *belongs* to you. And be out of my sight before the end of the day. You have an hour to write your resignation, which the dean will most regretfully accept this afternoon. I can't run you out of town. But my advice would be to stay clear of the Boston medical community for, shall we say, the rest of your life."

Peter felt like wood—hard, dry wood. Dead.

He had to force himself to breathe.

"Is—uh—any announcement going to be made?" he asked finally.

Pfeifer smiled. And with undisguised disdain he replied, "If we were to let this reach the press, it would reflect badly on Harvard. Besides, we prefer not to wash our dirty test tubes in public."

"And—what about the article?"

"It will be published in due course. After all, despite certain short-comings, it's an important piece of work. And don't worry, you'll get your credit. I can easily find two colleagues to take the credit for the mythical Charpentier and van Steen."

He rose, with Peter still glued to his chair.

"Goodbye, Wyman. And good luck in the profession of your choice."

THIRTY-SIX

The mere fact that in 1969 both Grete Andersen and Peter Wyman lost their jobs for diametrically opposite reasons reinforced the paradoxical nature of the practice of medicine. While the woman surgeon had tried to invoke professional ethics, Peter had defied them. Yet both suffered a similar fate.

Of course, Grete had the not-inconsiderable advantage of being the injured party, and so appealed to those physicians in America who believed that a medical degree was not a license to transcend morality.

Washington's medical establishment may have declared her "persona non Grete" (as she had quipped to Laura on the phone), but even they could not rewrite the past. They could not change her superb classroom and clinical grades in Med School, or "deep six" their once-enthusiastic evaluations of her hospital work.

She was welcomed into the surgical program at Houston's University Hospital where, in fact, the most interesting work in surgery was currently being done—the repair and replacement of human hearts.

Peter, in his own opinion, had not been dishonest but rather merely expedient, for he self-righteously believed that history would prove him correct. The wretched bureaucratic machinery for determining scientific proof was a waste of valuable time.

Although he had a dossier listing some twenty publications, letters from his Ph.D. mentors at M.I.T., and even a note from Professor Pfeifer indicating that he had "a solid research brain," Peter nonetheless found it difficult to get another academic job.

But this did not come as a surprise. For he knew that what is done in a letter can swiftly be undone by a phone call. And Pfeifer, in whitewashing Harvard, was clearly blackballing him.

So Peter scoured the private sector to find a laboratory that would accept him. Dale Woodburn and Art Nagra, two recent Stanford graduates, had started up a private biochemical concern in Palo Alto for research and development.

Both partners at Neobiotics liked Peter's ideas. They liked his credentials. They liked his diplomas on the wall. And even though they didn't like *him,* they knew a winner when they saw one.

Woodburn and Nagra had tuned in early to the new, disquieting events in the world of medicine. Study after study, journal after journal, was documenting the alarming fact that, as one put it, "if penicillin is not dead already, it will be in the next decade."

The incidence of venereal disease had quadrupled in just ten years. And other bacteria were beginning to show strong resistance to the miracle antibiotics of a generation before. In fact, in the previous year alone, seventy-five thousand patients had died from infections *contracted while in the hospital.*

Such is the power of our enemy—Disease.

"Laura? Can you hear me?"

"The connection's perfect, Palmer. Sounds like you're around the corner. Where are you?"

"Nowhere that you'd like to be," he said evasively. "I was just calling to find out how things are."

"Everything's fine. I've written you a letter."

"Good. I'm sorry that I've been so uncommunicative but I've been rather involved, you might say. Are you sure you haven't got any other news to tell me?"

Though she knew to what he was alluding, she ignored the question.

"Palmer, I get up at five. I drive to the hospital. I see patients getting sick. I see patients getting well. I come home and I flake. The only thing of import I can say is that they're offering a special residency in neonatology—that means treating infants the second they're born—and I've been accepted in the program."

"Oh—that's wonderful. You must be looking forward to working with the babies."

"Yes, it's very exciting—although it can also break your heart."

"I understand. Uh—while we're on the subject, I was wondering—"

"No, Palmer," she said softly, "I'm not."

"Oh."

"I told you it doesn't automatically work the first time. The odds were heavily against it."

Palmer's voice suddenly became more businesslike. "I—uh—shouldn't really be hogging the phone for so long. There aren't many lines and there are so many others waiting—"

"Palmer, promise me you'll write even if it's only to tell me that you're safe. Otherwise I feel I'm married to a one-way mailbox."

"You're always in my thoughts, Laura. I hope you believe that."

"And you in mine."

Laura was more confused than ever. She even castigated herself for not having gotten pregnant for him. Perhaps Palmer's genuine desire was to consolidate their relationship. She wanted him to love her as he had years ago.

"Well, I guess it's goodbye for now."

"Yeah, sure. Goodbye."

From NONFICTION FORECASTS, *Publishers Weekly,* March 6, 1970:

MIND OF A CHAMPION: A Psychiatrist Looks at Sporting Greats, *Barney Livingston, M.D.* Berkeley House, $7.95.

A practicing psychiatrist examines the psyches of champions in various fields of athletic endeavor from Olympics to boxing to baseball. Enormous research and interviews in depth went into this attempt to find what separates the extraordinary from what Livingston calls the "layman athlete."

Each of his twelve chapters focuses on a single great champion, e.g. Jesse Owens ("What Makes Jesse Run?"), Sandy Koufax ("The Left-Handed Bullet"), Doctor Roger Bannister ("Four Minutes of Physiology").

Livingston offers some provocative observations, e.g., that for some runners their races are fantasy re-enactments of sibling rivalry.

A lucid jargon-free study that should appeal to legions of sports fans, as well as all those interested in what makes people tick.

First serial to Sports Illustrated. (April 20)

Bill Chaplin was so excited by the preview in the bible of the book trade that he convinced his colleagues to increase the first printing of Barney's book from ten thousand copies to fifteen.

They also decided to subsidize a selective author tour and arrange a launch party for what might prove to be the "sleeper" of the year.

He was disappointed that Barney did not jump for joy.

"How many times do I have to tell you, Bill, I work for Sigmund Freud, not P. T. Barnum. I don't want to be marketed like a new detergent. I've written a serious book, and I want it to be taken seriously."

"Barney, you want your book to be *read*. To do that we have to spread the word. We're only proposing that you make one or two television appearances, go to Washington and Boston—"

Barney interrupted, "Bill—I'm a psychiatrist, for God's sake. My patients have enough difficulty trying to deal with my persona without having to face it over their scrambled eggs at home."

Chaplin sighed in frustration. "Will you at least let us kick the whole thing off with a dignified reception at the St. Regis and a few interviews with important—do you hear me?—important journalists?"

"Why would any of them want to meet an unknown like me?"

"Aha," said Bill, "that was my brainstorm of the day. We'll make the party not just for your book but for the people in it. Wouldn't it be wonderful to have all those living legends in a single room?"

Barney was excited by the notion but still fearful about letting himself be caught up in a three-ring circus.

He covered the mouthpiece of the phone and turned to Emily. "Bill wants me to—"

"I know. He was talking so loud I could hear every word."

"What do you think, Em?"

"I think he's right that you have to get some media exposure. Just make sure you can veto the publications."

Barney returned to the phone. "Okay, Bill, my spiritual advisor persuades me that you know best. Only make sure I approve everything. And keep it respectable. I mean, I draw the line at exclusive interviews for *Screw* magazine."

"You leave it to me," Bill said gratefully.

Barney hung up and looked at Emily. "Pretty good news, huh?" he asked.

"I'd say it was fantastic news—how come you don't seem excited?"

I am, Barney thought to himself. But I know what's keeping me from celebration.

Though he had promised not to broach the subject when she had moved in with him, he could not restrain himself from dropping unsubtle hints.

As they would jog through the park, he would point to little children playing with balloons, or mothers wheeling tiny babies, and say, "We'll have one of those some day—and then you'll have to marry me."

But Emily would always come up with the same response. "We're happy as we are, Barn. Let's make the most of it for as long as possible."

Since she would repeat the phrase like a litany, Barney had begun to worry what the hell she meant by "as long as possible." That we'll keep on having fun before we take on the responsibility of children? Or—she couldn't mean—as long as we're together? Could she?

Tu-doh Street in Saigon was known to most GIs as "Joy Street." Its corridor of gaudy pink and blue neon-lit attractions fulfilled *all* the wildest dreams of sensuality that a cloistered monk could be expected to repress.

Thus, Captain Hank Dwyer, M.D., felt he was in a sensual Disneyland, whose wonders never paled. And he would return to this fleshly paradise every chance he could.

The girls were so beautiful—delicately, slender ivory statues, whose exquisite hands could rouse a man to passion with a single touch.

True, they accepted money for their company, but in return they offered more than physical delights. They were aware that men sought out their company to cure loneliness as much as sexual desire. They gave them comfort, company, and—there is no other word—a kind of worship.

For men have huge psychic appetites and a hunger for assurance that they are the kings, the ruling gender. And whether they are in battle in the Wall Street jungle or the paddies of Vietnam, they come home hungry every night and need to stand on their pedestals and be replenished.

But the Americans in Southeast Asia were secretly upset by the news that reached them of the changes taking place back in the U.S.A.

Rumor had it that their pedestals were actually being chipped away.

For at the very moment they were firing their weapons here in Nam, at home there was another kind of war. Only, instead of burning villages, the combatants were setting their bras on fire.

To the soldiers in the field, the news of Women's Liberation was disquieting. How could they fight to free a foreign country if they faced the specter of returning home to be a prisoner?

Hence, here on Joy Street, they found refuge in the arms of the most captivating women they had ever seen. The jet-black hair and eyes, beguiling smiles—and, most of all, the childlike sensuality, for many looked like budding-breasted teenagers in early bloom.

And the nectar and ambrosia! How could a country that—beyond its capital—was wracked with strife, bloody and staggering, obtain the finest French cuisine and vintage wine? Though peasants were starving in the villages, here in Saigon itself there was no shortage of *pâté de foie gras* or champagne. In fact, there was nothing you could get in Paris that you could not get in Saigon—except peace.

A mere dozen miles from Joy Street, eighteen-year-old soldiers—farm boys from the fields of the Dakotas, blacks from urban ghettos like Chicago and Detroit—were being killed and maimed, never really understanding what they had been fighting for.

And yet many of their countrymen back home were cursing them for following the flag and dying for their country.

There are only two ways for a doctor to confront the gruesome wounds of war: by hardening his senses—or by feeding them.

Hank Dwyer chose the latter course. And as the fighting grew fiercer—in a single day he might see ten soldiers whose legs had been blown off by hidden mines—he was so steeped in blood that he grew numb. The only time he felt alive was in the arms of Mai-ling.

They had met on Joy Street under what were then commercial circumstances. But he soon assured himself these porcelain goddesses were from educated families that had dispersed, disintegrated, or just disappeared—that they, too, came to Joy Street hungering for real companionship. And after a week of nightly visits, Hank persuaded Mai-ling to come and live with him in the air-conditioned villa he shared with two other officers who had also acquired Oriental "brides."

Indeed they had the makings of a small commune. For one of the other women had a child already, one was pregnant, and Mai-ling, the new arrival, soon learned from them that her ties with America would be greatly strengthened if she were the mother of a child whose father was a U.S. Army officer.

Hank took the news impassively. If it had been Cheryl who'd announced this, he would have lost his temper and insisted that the pregnancy be terminated.

But here in Southeast Asia things were completely different: the taking care of children was accepted as exclusively the province of women. And besides, Mai-ling understood that every man by nature was polygamous, and she would wait patiently all night till he came home to her . . . from Joy Street.

*   *   *

Barney Livingston, M.D., was born on June 16, 1937, in King's County Hospital, Brooklyn. He was "launched" on April 20, 1970, in the Versailles Room of the St. Regis Hotel, New York.

In the interim, between the preview *PW* rave and publication date, Berkeley had engineered a sale to a paperback house for fifteen thousand dollars, a price Bill Chaplin considered modest but one that so staggered Barney he spent half the day writing the figure on his notepad.

In a festive mood, he went out to be fitted for a made-to-measure suit.

My God, he thought to himself, as the tailor measured him from every conceivable angle, he's more thorough than a doctor.

Nothing was left to chance. The master tailor even asked him, "Which way do you dress, Dr. Livingston?"

The question totally confused him. I mean, how did anybody dress? He said nothing.

"I beg your pardon, sir," the tailor said respectfully, "I didn't hear your answer."

"I didn't really understand the question."

The tailor tried to rephrase it. "The way your member falls— "

"My what?"

"Your member, sir," he answered, indicating Barney's crotch as unobtrusively as possible. "In the majority of men, it usually rests on the left."

Unreal! This guy is asking me on which side I hang my cock!

"Well, let's go for the left," said Barney, choosing the statistically preponderant alignment. And also hoping that the measurements would not get any more detailed.

"My God, do you look great," said Emily enthusiastically. "I'd better watch out at the party or some woman will seduce you on the spot."

He took her in his arms and said, "Listen, kid, when you're in a room with me, I wouldn't even notice Raquel Welch."

"Is Bill's new 'Playmate of the Year' going to be there?"

"Yes," Barney answered with a grin, "his editorial assistant has made all the arrangements."

"Bet she's a knockout."

Barney sighed. "Oh, Em, you know I want to be monogamous. I want to grab you by the left hand and squeeze a ring onto your finger."

Emily was not reassured. She was conscious that when limelight suddenly shines on some men they get priapic thoughts.

"Then there's the golden goddess of physicians—"

"You mean Laura?"

"Am I finally going to meet this creature—or is she someone you dreamed up just to make me jealous?"

"I'm sure she's much too busy," Barney casually replied. "I had Bill send her an invitation just so she'd know I would have wanted her to be there."

Twenty minutes later, they were in the lobby of the St. Regis. Estelle, Warren, and his wife Bunny (looking very pregnant) were waiting nervously.

"Why didn't you go up?" asked Barney cheerfully. "The early people get the best hors d'oeuvres."

He hugged his mother, who had arrived from Florida that morning.

"Thanks for flying up," he said.

"Oh, Barney, do you think I'd miss a grand event like this? I was a librarian, remember? To me, the greatest thing a man can do is write a book."

Warren did his best to conquer all his pangs of jealousy. "C'mon, let's go and see what kind of goodies Berkeley House is serving in the author's honor. If they're inadequate, I'll file suit tomorrow."

They were not the first to arrive. Indeed, most of the champions were already there. Breathless with excitement, Barney introduced his mother, brother, sister-in-law, and Emily to the immortals of the sporting pantheon.

"That Rafer Johnson is the handsomest man I've ever seen," Estelle whispered to Barney.

And as the other brand of heavyweights appeared—the heroes of the media—the Fourth Estate was snowed.

The festivities were at their height when an unexpected visitor arrived.

And Emily knew instantly that it was Laura Castellano. Though simply dressed in a dark navy suit, unadorned by anything but her golden hair, the doctor looked breathtaking.

Barney rushed to welcome her, exchanged a kiss, and immediately brought her over.

"Em, meet Laura—my best friend since kindergarten."

Both women answered in unison, "I've heard so much about you—"

"I'm glad you could come," said Emily, "I know how busy you must be."

"I wouldn't have missed this for the world. Barney's my dearest friend. And I think Mind of a Champion is brilliant."

"I do, too," said Emily, "and if you liked the piece SI excerpted, you'll go wild when you read the book."

"But I've read it all—Barney sent me galleys."

Emily's worst fear was confirmed. She'd sensed from the beginning that Barney's deepest feelings were pledged to the quasi-legendary Laura—however many times he protested that their friendship was platonic.

She found herself unable to sustain the conversation. Spying a co-editor from *SI*, she excused herself and hurried off.

"Isn't this terrific?" came a sudden voice from behind Laura.

She turned and there, looking handsome and sartorially elegant as usual, was Bennett Landsmann.

"Ben," she cried, and they embraced warmly. "How are you?"

"You know the answer to that," he said, grinning. "How is any resident? He's either half-alive or half-dead. On this exceptional occasion, however, I'm happily half-drunk."

"So what do you think of our mutual friend's success?"

"You and I both know it couldn't happen to a nicer guy," Bennett replied. "And how about that Emily? She's a real winner, isn't she?"

"She's lovely," Laura answered. "We haven't had much of a chance to talk yet, but she seems like a real live wire. Are they happy?"

"Barney loves her, I know that," said Bennett. "He wants to marry her. Yet for reasons we might diagnose as cryptogenic, she keeps saying no. But Barney figures they'll keep going as roommates till he wears her down."

"Hey, listen, Landsmann," Laura chided, "no offense, but I didn't fly all the way from Boston just for a class reunion. I wanna meet the stars. Where's Jackie Robinson?"

Bennett pointed. "Do you see that mob across the room? Behind it is the man himself. I haven't met him either, so I think I'll ask the party boy to introduce us."

"Great. You run interference through this crowd and I'll be right behind you." And off they set.

Bill Chaplin was ebullient. The party had exceeded his expectations.

To see Jesse Owens talking track with Roger Bannister (flown over just for the occasion), and watch Joe Louis and Muhammad Ali strike pugilistic poses for the cameras. God, what a fight that would have been—the Brown Bomber in his prime against the self-styled Greatest.

Bill had asked Bannister, now a practicing neurologist in London, to propose the toast.

He was brief and to the point.

"Having had both experiences, I can safely say that four hours talking to Dr. Livingston is far more stimulating than four minutes on the track.

"I think Barney should be congratulated for his imagination and for his insights, which demonstrate that an athlete has a soul as well as a body."

There was appreciative applause, and as the two doctors shook hands for the cameras, Muhammad Ali shouted, "Hey there, Doc, you forgot to mention *me*—I got the most soul in this room!"

Barney glanced over at Estelle and Warren. His brother looked as if he'd burst with pride. His mother was dabbing her eyes. And he thought, Oh God, if only Dad were here.

"I got everybody's autographs."

"Oh, Bunny, you didn't. That's so corny," Warren chided.

"They didn't seem to think so. Ali even scribbled a poem on a napkin for me."

Barney had arranged for a small group (what he called the "home team") to come back to the apartment for deli sandwiches and champagne.

"Hey, Bun, that's wonderful," said Laura as Warren refilled her glass. "Can we hear it?"

Bunny withdrew the cloth napkin from her pocket. "It's a little short but it's genuine Ali: 'Livingston may be the latest star/but me Ali is still the best by far.' "

There was suitably appreciative laughter.

"Save that, Bunny, it may be valuable some day," Barney advised.

"I'll do more than that," she replied happily, "I'm going to frame it."

Emily brought out a huge platter of the best cold cuts the Carnegie Delicatessen could offer, and everybody munched as they continued to consume champagne as if it were Doctor Brown's celery tonic.

"Hey, Barney," Laura asked, a little tipsy, "just among the gang here, who did you think was the most impressive guy you interviewed?"

"I honestly don't know," he answered, even woozier than she, "but I can tell you one thing. If I had to choose a single person in the world to have dinner with—" He paused for dramatic effect and then concluded, "—it would be Emily."

The little group of inebriates applauded.

"So when's the wedding, Barn?" called Bunny.

Barney's wits were too sozzled to come up with an immediate answer. But Emily took over.

"Bunny, you'll be the first to know," she replied, feigning gaiety.

"No, no," Barney protested. "*Me* first."

* * *

Just after ten, Laura stood up.

"I hate to be a party-pooper, but I've got to catch the last plane back to Boston."

Then Bennett rose as well. "I think it's sack time for this young surgeon, too. But Laura, can I drop you? La Guardia's right on the way to Yale."

"Fine, Ben. You can fill me in on how you've been 'cutting up' lately."

The two of them made the goodbye rounds. When Laura reached Barney, she whispered in his ear, "Emily's terrific. Don't let this one go."

"I won't," he whispered back. He accompanied Laura and Bennett to the door. When he returned to the livingroom, Warren was putting on his jacket.

"I don't know about you guys," he jested, "but I work for a living, Bunny's got to take the kids to school, and Momma's looking kind of tired. So we'll leave you two to bask in glory."

He then turned to Emily and said, "Make my big brother come to Sunday dinner some time, willya? He's so irresponsible."

At last the population had decreased to two.

"Well," said Barney, beaming at Emily with affection, "how did you like this evening?"

"She's absolutely gorgeous."

"What?"

"How come you never told me Laura was so beautiful?"

"Because she's not," he said straightforwardly. "I mean, compared to you—"

"C'mon, compared to her, I'm nothing. I'll be frank with you, Barney. Just talking to her makes me feel incredibly insecure."

"But why? She's Mrs. Palmer Talbot. And we're just—"

"Don't give me that 'platonic' line again. Why don't you admit there's some special bond between the two of you? I mean, you did send her galleys of your book."

"She's a doctor—*and* a sports fan. What do I have to say to reassure you, Em?"

"You can't."

"What if I said marry me and I'll never speak to Laura Castellano again? I won't even ask her to the wedding."

"Oh, Barn," she moaned wearily, "let's not go through this thing again."

"All right, then," he said firmly, "let's just have it out once and for all. Why can't you marry me? What the hell is stopping you?"

Emily began to cry. "I knew it. I just knew it would come down to this."

"To *what*, goddammit?" This time he was determined not to let her off.

"I know you, Barney. Probably better than you know yourself. You don't just want a wife, you want a family."

"So what? It's only natural when a man and woman love each other."

Out of the blue, like a machine gun, she said, "Barney, I can't have children."

For a moment there was breathless silence.

"How do you know?" he asked softly.

"I had some problems when I was in college so they did a laparoscopy. They looked inside and saw my tubes were blocked, completely blocked. And before you ask—it can't be cured by surgery."

Barney did not know what to feel. But he knew what to say.

He knelt by her chair and whispered, "Emily, it's you I love. Not some child I've never met."

"Look, Barn, I've lived with you and I know the thing you want most in life is to be a father."

Her sobs increased and her last words were barely audible. "And I can't make you one."

"Em, believe me," Barney pleaded, "it won't matter. We can always adopt—"

"You'd hate me for it some day," she said with a tinge of anger, "even though you'd do the 'noble' thing. You'd stick with me and live in your *own* pain because you didn't have your own kids."

Then they both were silent.

In one sense Emily had proved she was right. Barney was in agony already.

"You won't leave me, will you, Em?" he pleaded softly.

"No, Barn, I'll be here until you kick me out."

At least I'll have another chance to talk to her, he thought—and to myself.

As usual, the annual meeting of the American Psychiatric Association was a chaotic potpourri of squabbles, tantrums, and an extraordinary amount of antisocial behavior. (After all, it was their area of expertise.)

Barney read a paper in the Literary Analysis session on "*Moby-Dick* and the American Psyche" and was gratified not only by its warm reception but the subsequent invitation to join the editorial board of the Association's journal.

His joy, however, was not unalloyed. For, to his consternation, at the final plenary session the prize for the most distinguished work in Adolescent Psychiatry was awarded to the notorious Andrew Himmerman. So what if the guy wrote a brilliant monograph? How could a Society whose basic principle was to straighten minds honor someone who had so betrayed their code of ethics?

Maybe everything boils down to politics, Barney thought, but if I ever come face to face with that lecher, I'm going to tell him what I think of him.

Fate has a consistent caprice: She has ordained that in any men's room—be it one with twenty, fifty, or even more urinals, if there are only two gentlemen present they will end up standing next to each other.

And this is how, at 4:38 P.M., Barney Livingston encountered Andrew Himmerman.

"Very much enjoyed your paper, Dr. Livingston," the elder psychiatrist remarked.

Barney ignored him.

"Thought it was right on target," Himmerman continued affably. "I assume you'll be publishing it in the *Journal*."

Barney was doing his best to make haste and retreat from this uncomfortable situation.

Himmerman was confused. "Have I done something to offend you, Doctor?" he inquired politely.

"No," Barney finally retorted. "But you certainly did a job on a friend of mine."

"Oh," the psychiatrist said calmly, "and who may that be?"

"Sorry," Barney replied sardonically, "I forgot there've been so many in your life that you can't keep track. I was referring specifically to Grete Andersen, M.D."

"Oh, Jesus," Himmerman groaned.

They were washing their hands now, this time separated by three sinks' length.

"I'd like to set the record straight, Dr. Livingston."

Barney chose not to reply.

"You may not believe this," Himmerman persisted, "but I never touched that girl. I don't deny having acted improperly several years ago, but—"

Barney cut him off with a line of Marlowe's, " 'But that was in another country: and besides, the wench is dead.' "

Himmerman blanched. When he finally could answer, it was obvious he was having trouble finding the proper words.

"I can't tell you how that girl's death hangs over me. My marriage is a shambles, my wife is paranoid now every time I talk to an attractive woman. I don't sleep easy, I promise you."

"You seem to have slept easily enough with Grete."

"No, no! I had nothing to do with that girl. She was a complete hysteric. It was a total fantasy."

"Dr. Himmerman," Barney said, striving to control his temper to demonstrate his own psychic stability, "I've seen a photograph of the two of you. You were wearing tennis shorts. She had on a very skimpy bikini and you had your arms around each other. Eastman Kodak doesn't sell fantasy film."

"Oh, no," Himmerman muttered under his breath. And then he asked angrily, "Did you study that photograph carefully?"

"Not under a microscope, but I gave it a good, hard look."

"Then you should have noticed that she had her arms around me but not vice versa."

"Are you denying that you took Grete to Hilton Head for a weekend tryst?"

"Dr. Livingston, if I told you there was no tryst, that the girl took *herself*—and, as far as I know, is still a virgin—would you believe me?"

"It would be difficult," Barney responded.

"Well, let me offer you some irrefutable facts," he persisted, anger rising in his voice. "The Psychiatric Association of the Southern States held its annual convention at Hilton Head over the weekend of April seventeenth and eighteenth, 1966. I was president at the time. Do you think I'd be crazy enough to take a patient to something like *that*?"

Barney still withheld judgment.

Himmerman continued. "I went down to the pool during our lunch-time break and all of a sudden this hysterical creature pops out of the bushes and gives me a hug. She had sweet-talked one of the life-guards into taking that picture. I told her right on the spot that our professional relationship was over and not to show up for her hour the next Monday."

He paused, sighing at the uncomfortable recollection of the unhappy incident, and asked, "Does this sound plausible to you, Dr. Livingston?"

"Yes," Barney conceded, "but why did you take the pills?"

Himmerman lowered his head. "I'm trying to be brutally honest. And it's not easy, Doctor."

"I know," Barney said sympathetically.

"This girl's problem—and now I'm speaking confidentially, doctor to doctor—is a morbid fear of men. She's a classic hysteric, who gets frightened when she titillates a man and then runs away—"

He paused, and continued, "It's my guess—and I hope it doesn't sound too self-serving—that the transference was working and she was petrified of her feelings toward me. Her only escape was to discredit me as a love object. How the hell she did it I still haven't found out, but somehow she got a look at my dossier in the Association's files. Up till then it had all been kept out of the papers. I had sworn to the Ethics Committee I'd go back into therapy myself. That was the only condition under which my wife agreed to stay with me. Now this sick, sick woman was threatening to call a press conference and announce herself as the latest in a long string of sexual victims."

He looked Barney in the eye and asked quietly, "If that happened to you—your career, your marriage, everything—all about to go up in smoke—for a lie—don't you think you might momentarily lose control. . . ." His voice trailed off.

"Yes," Barney said gently, for he now believed the man. "I guess I would. I'm sorry, Dr. Himmerman."

THIRTY-SEVEN

Death reaped an awesome harvest in 1972.

Princes, presidents, and poets. Ice-cream men and athletes all left the earth a poorer place.

Ezra Pound—genius, traitor, madman—perished from the earth, leaving, in his own words, "a deathless adornment/a name not to be worn out with the years."

Charles Atlas, he who had begun life as a ninety-eight-pound weakling and become a paragon of muscles, the inspiration for all adolescent boys, could not chase off the bully Death when it kicked sand in his face. The hero who had once held up the world now had to leave it.

That pugnacious president, Harry Truman (who once threatened to beat up a critic who had panned his daughter's singing), lost his final bout with life.

Maurice Chevalier, quintessential Gallic charmer, though perhaps less chivalrous than his own name implied (he'd entertained the Nazi troops), was taken only God knows in which direction.

The Duke of Windsor, who'd forsaken the role of king to become the slave of love, had now to abdicate his life.

A Being of still greater power than J. Edgar Hoover tapped the FBI chief's line to say his time was up.

There really was a man called Howard Johnson, the inventor of the sundae. His life ended in this year, surely accompanied to heaven by an angel's choir of no less than twenty-eight voices.

All too soon, The Reaper took off Jackie Robinson, aged only fifty-three.

Younger still were all the U.S. soldiers in Vietnam, whose death toll neared the fifty-thousand mark.

Indeed, perhaps it was no accident that in this devastating year the magazine called *Life* expired.

And Barney's wounds from having been shot down—albeit metaphorically—had still not healed.

Publishers Weekly's prediction had lulled him into expecting that *Mind of a Champion* would receive at least a modest critical welcome.

But it had never come. There had been no further praise. There had not even been any further pans. His book had suffered the worst possible of fates: it was totally ignored.

"Bill, tell it to me straight," he had demanded three months after publication, "is my book dead in the water?"

"Let's put it this way," Bill replied, "sales have been a little slower than we had hoped, but then the paperback is bound to reach a wider audience."

Chaplin hesitated, hoping some felicitous, mollifying rhetoric would pop into his head. But then he realized painfully that there was no evasion.

"Yes," he said, "I'd say that rigor mortis has set in."

Had the experts of the *Guide Michelin* dined at La Renaissance, in the heart of Saigon near the French Hospital, they would have surely given it three stars.

This at least was the opinion of Major Palmer Talbot, who dined there often—especially when he was anxious to impress a visiting government official or an important journalist.

("Ironic isn't it, Major, to find the best French restaurant in the world halfway 'round the globe from Paris. You would think that the war would cramp the chef's style. You know, keep him from getting the ingredients."

"I think the left-wing press likes to exaggerate the situation here just for the sake of selling papers. I mean, it's clear we've got things fairly in control—which is, of course, what you've come to see. And I hope you've been convinced that it's a matter of a few more months till we bring peace to this lovely, benighted land."

"Well, frankly, I'm impressed. And I'll share my impression with the boys on the Hill.")

It has often been said that war is hell. Yet it is rarely admitted that for the privileged few war can be a hell of a good time.

Certainly Palmer Talbot's tour of duty in Vietnam had thus far been enormously enjoyable. He had acquired the knowledge of Vietnamese not for the purpose of going out into remote villages to ask if Ho Chi Minh's bullyboys were in the vicinity. Rather it was to help coordinate the actions of U.S. troops and their South Vietnamese colleagues by acting as liaison officer with their high commands.

He also had the enviable job of winning the hearts and minds of a steady stream of distinguished visitors, who were flying in and out on so-called "fact-finding missions." Palmer always saw to it that whatever else they might have seen, they at least knew that a place like La Renaissance was still flourishing, so the war couldn't be *that* bad.

He was therefore not surprised when upon arrival in HQ one morning, there was a message for him to call the chairman of the Senate Armed Services Committee.

"Will you get Senator Forbes on the phone for me?" Palmer asked Marie-Claire, his Eurasian secretary. "I'll take it in my office."

"No, Major. He specifically requested that you use one of the 'safe' phones. It must be something of a high security nature."

As he walked toward the soundproof room where the "scrambler" phone was kept, Palmer took a cursory glance at the message she had handed him—it was the Senator's home, not his office, that Palmer was to contact urgently.

The call went through in a matter of seconds.

"Hello, Senator, this is Palmer Talbot in Saigon."

"Oh, Palmer, good man. Thanks for calling. I guess it's already tomorrow where you are."

"Yes, sir. May I be of help to you, Senator?"

"Matter of fact, you can, Major. You can do me an enormous favor."

"What's that, sir?"

The Senator paused momentarily and then replied laconically, "Marry Jessica."

"Jessica?" Palmer asked, slightly off balance.

"That's right, Major Talbot. My daughter, Jessica, whom you

got pregnant while you were being briefed at my estate. If it's all right with you, I'd like to announce it to the press immediately."

"But that's impossible, sir," he stammered. "I'm already married and I can't abandon my wife."

"It's nice to hear you so protective, Major. But that's the way I also feel about my little girl. I would advise you in the strongest possible terms to see things my way."

The unspoken message was loud and clear. Forbes had enough power to have Palmer sent to the front lines where the mortality rate of officers could be measured in minutes.

"Now don't you worry, Major Talbot," the Senator continued. "I realize there'll be a stumbling block or two on the way to the matrimonial aisle. But if the current Mrs. Talbot is the generous person I'm sure she is, she'll agree to a quickie Mexican divorce and we'll be high and dry."

Palmer was shaken. He didn't want to hurt Laura. And he especially did not want to confront her fiery Spanish temper.

"Uh, Senator, with due respect," he mumbled, "you're asking me to do an outrageous thing."

"And do you not regard what you did to my Jessica as outrageous?"

Palmer was at a loss. "Sir, I'd like a little time to organize my thoughts before—"

"I quite agree," the legislator replied. "That's why you'll be receiving ten days furlough as of 0900 hours today. If you hurry—and I dearly hope you will—you can be in San Francisco by tomorrow. And in Boston the day after. Meanwhile, to expedite matters I'll have one of my former law partners begin to draw up the necessary papers. Is that all right with you, Major?"

"Uh, sir, yes, fine."

But when the conversation ended, Palmer sat there in a state of shock, his head buried in his hands, murmuring over and over to himself, "Laura, oh Laura. What should I do?"

Contrary to popular belief, it is possible for a human being to live normally in New York at night.

For as the sky grows darker the metabolism of the city slows down, its hypertensive pulse rate decreases, and the general mood descends from daytime manic to a relatively tranquil hypomania.

Barney walked out to the terrace and gazed down at the city, which seemed like a hive of glowworms.

Emily was in Switzerland, covering the European ski championships. To fill the lonely hours he had planned to finish a paper on schizophrenic thought disorder. But then Laura had called, and now he was agitated and unable to concentrate.

She had been too distraught to be specific. All he could gather was that something terrible had happened between her and Palmer and she could not bear to be alone in Boston.

Barney naturally insisted that she fly to New York as quickly as possible. She had protested that Emily would not like it. But on learning that Emily was away on assignment, Laura said she would try to make the last shuttle from Boston.

Just after eleven o'clock the doorman buzzed him that Miss Castellano was on her way.

Her eyes.

They were the first thing that struck him when he opened the door. Her eyes were huge red circles, as if they had been bruised in a fight. She had obviously been crying for several hours. Her voice was hoarse, as if she had exhausted all its strength.

"Hi," she said softly.

He took the suitcase and said, "Come in. Sit down. I think you could use a stiff drink."

She nodded.

"For chrissake, Laura, what's the matter?"

"Palmer showed up. . . ." she began and then burst into tears again. "I can't, Barn. It's too unbelievable."

"I thought he was in Vietnam. How come he's suddenly home—was he wounded or something?"

"No, Barney," Laura answered, "it's *me* who's wounded. He wants a divorce."

"Hell, I've seen that coming for a while. I'm sure you must have, too."

She shook her head. "No, no, we had sort of a reconciliation. Everything was fine and then he just shows up and shoves a piece of paper in my face."

"What kind of paper?"

"Consent to a *rápido* Mexican divorce."

"Hey, this is crazy, Castellano. What's the goddamn hurry?"

Laura told him haltingly.

Barney was unable to retain his professional objectivity.

"You know what, Castellano? I say good riddance to the bastard. Any guy that isn't faithful to you isn't really good enough to be your husband."

She shrugged her shoulders. "Maybe I just wasn't good enough to be his wife."

Barney could not bear this self-deprecation.

"Laura, for chrissake," he shouted, "just because he treated you like shit doesn't mean that *you* have to go along with his opinion. Screw him, Castellano! Let him go to hell and some day you'll find someone worthy of you."

She shook her head. "No way, Barney. I'm convinced that as far as men are concerned I'm a born loser."

He sent her to bed in the guest room. Then he gave her a glass of water and two pills, and sat down next to her. "I know you won't believe me, but I promise you that the sun will come up tomorrow morning. And that'll mean you'll have one day of recuperation to your credit."

She took the pills and, emotionally exhausted, lay back on the pillow.

"Thank you, Barn," she whispered softly.

He sat with her till he was sure she was asleep, then tiptoed out.

And went back to his typewriter, ripped out the unfinished schizo piece, put in a new sheet, and began to type.

MEMO
To: L. Castellano, M.D.
From: B. Livingston, M.D.
Subject: 101 Reasons why life is still worth living.

And he brought it to her with a cup of coffee the next morning.

Barney was on the telephone when Laura entered the living room. He hung up and smiled. "You look better already, Castellano."

"I bet," she answered wryly. "I just took a look at myself in the mirror. I look like I've gone ten rounds with Muhammad Ali."

"No, you don't," he corrected her. "Ali is a *clean* fighter." And then he imperiously pointed to the sofa and said, "Sit down."

When she had obeyed he told her, "I've been on the phone to your Chief of service and explained—without really explaining—that you're ill and have to have a week or so to recuperate. He was very understanding."

"What am I supposed to do in the meanwhile?"

"Take long walks, think nice thoughts. In fact, why not buy yourself a whole new wardrobe?"

"This hardly seems like professional advice, Barn."

"Listen, Castellano, just for this morning I've had a temporary switch of roles. Look upon me not as a doctor, not even as a friend, but as a parent. You're going to listen to me and do what's best for you."

"Yes, sir," she said with a wan smile. "But have you retired from the medical profession? I mean, don't you have any patients to see?"

"I had the secretary cancel everything before lunch, but if you're okay, I'll see my afternoon people."

"I'm okay, Barn. I'm okay. You don't have to screw up your life just because I've screwed up mine."

"No back talk," Barney retorted. "Remember, today I'm the parent."

He left her after lunch, certain that she was sufficiently better to be able to undertake a trip to, say, the Museum of Modern Art—anything rather than letting her sit around.

When he returned at seven-thirty, he was surprised to see that Laura had prepared dinner.

"Well, I didn't actually do anything more than heat the stuff up. It's amazing what precooked goodies you can buy on Fifty-seventh Street. So sit down and tell me how your day was."

Barney gave a verbal sketch of the four cases he had been treating that afternoon, as well as the boisterous meeting he had attended at the hospital.

"I mean, Castellano, if a master psychiatrist ever walked into our hospital while we were having one of our staff get-togethers, he wouldn't be able to distinguish between the doctors and the nuts."

"Some of our conferences up in Boston are like that," she replied. "By the way, I think the paper you're writing is terrific."

"You mean the schizo thing?"

"It shows a lot of new insights. When are you going to finish it?"

"Well, it's overdue already. But it's so late, I might as well leave it another few days."

"No, Barn," Laura said firmly, "let *me* play parent now. When we finish this magnificent banquet, I want you to march over to your typewriter and finish the article. And that's an order."

Barney smiled. "Yes, Mother."

Three hours later Laura was perusing his final pages and expressing her approval.

"Good job, Livingston. I think you've got a future in medicine."

"So do I, kiddo. Now while I stay up and proofread, I want you to go and get another good night's sleep."

She rose like an obedient child, kissed him on the forehead, and went to bed.

*   *   *

They had a swift and early breakfast the next morning before Barney left for his full day's agenda.

It was then that Laura told him, "I'm not going back to Boston."

"What?"

"I just can't. I know I couldn't walk into that house and I wonder if I could even walk into Children's Hospital without feeling—I don't know—humiliated. Can you understand that?"

"Certainly the house part. But what are you going to do?"

"As soon as you leave, I'm going to sit at your desk and start making phone calls to see if maybe somewhere there's an opening in a neonatal unit."

"Not in the middle of the year, Castellano—the places will all be taken."

"Ah, Barney," she grinned, "you obviously know nothing about the world of hospital medicine. Even as we speak, some doctor somewhere is slitting his or her wrist or freaking out or something. I mean—look at me."

Barney called Laura from his office at noon. She sounded almost happy.

"You may not believe this, but I think I've got a job."

"That was pretty quick. How'd you manage that?"

"Well, actually, my old pediatrics supervisor called a friend at Queen's Hospital, Toronto. And even though they're not starting their program till next year, they've already got the funds—so I can start any time."

"That's fantastic."

"I can hardly believe it myself," she replied. "But to make sure it doesn't disappear, I'm going to fly to Toronto tonight."

"Come on, Castellano, not so fast," he cautioned. "You've just been hit with the atom bomb, you need at least another twenty-four hours to get back your equilibrium. Besides, I've booked a great Indian restaurant."

"I don't think—"

"That's precisely right, Laura, don't think. I'll be doing that for you till you're released from my care. So just be ready by seven-thirty."

She decided he was right. She needed at least another day to get her logistics straight—and to buy some clothes for the harsh Toronto weather.

Fifteen minutes later, as she was completing her shopping list, the front door opened.

And in walked Emily, struggling with a large suitcase.

She caught sight of Laura sitting comfortably at Barney's desk and was struck dumb.

Neither of them could find the appropriate words.

At last, Laura said simply, "Can I help you with that bag, Emily?"

"No, thank you," she replied, her facial muscles still frozen.

As Emily carried the valise toward the bedroom, Laura remarked, "Barney wasn't expecting you till tomorrow."

"I can see that," she said quietly. "I got a hitch with the ABC plane. I didn't realize that by coming home a day early I would be an unwelcome intruder."

"Emily, you don't understand."

"I'm afraid I do."

"I mean—Palmer and I are divorcing. Actually we're divorced already, thanks to the government of Mexico."

"That also stands to reason," Emily replied frostily.

"I was going to leave tomorrow," Laura continued, still trying to get Emily to unlock the gates of her prejudgment.

"Well, don't hurry on my account," Emily retorted. "I'm leaving now."

Trying to avert catastrophe for Barney, Laura gathered all her strength and shouted, "Wait, goddammit, Emily—I want to say something to you!"

With the door half open, she turned to Laura, "Okay, talk."

"I was in trouble," Laura began softly, "very bad trouble. And there wasn't anybody in the world I could call but Barney. He let me stay out of pity, that's all. I slept in the guest room. I mean, Emily, please—he was the only person I could turn to."

Laura suddenly ran out of words. She realized that in this situation the truth seemed like the wildest fiction. How much better it would have been had she concocted some extravagant lie.

"Hey, Laura," Emily said quietly, "Let me be totally frank with you. There were two reasons why I wouldn't marry Barney. And you were one of them."

At which she closed the door.

"Castellano, it's not your fault. I told Emily a million times about our relationship and if she still doesn't believe me, too bad."

"Now look who's being a martyr, Barney."

"I'm not, I'm not, we had no future. She was never going to marry me."

"Come on, you made a perfect couple. I mean, you loved her, didn't you?"

"Yes."

"And you still love her?"

"Yes. But it doesn't change anything. It's just that I'll have to start getting over it now instead of later."

"She said I was one reason why she couldn't marry you. What was the other?"

"I think that's a private matter, Laura."

"Barn, under any other circumstances I wouldn't ask you. But if you're going to help me get this off my conscience, you've got to tell me that there really was another reason."

Barney paused for a moment and said, "She can't have children. I said it didn't matter. I said that all I wanted was our marriage."

"And—?"

"She didn't believe me," he said softly. He was lost in thought for a moment. And then he added, "Do you know something, Castellano, I'm ashamed to say it—but in a way she was right."

Seth was puzzled by the nurse's identification of his final patient of the day. It was in fact a trio—a man in his mid-sixties and what looked like his son and daughter.

They entered his office without a word and stood respectfully until Seth signaled them to chairs.

"Are you Dr. Lazarus?" asked the older man.

"Yes, I am. But who are you? Why didn't you give your names to the receptionist?"

Seth waited for a moment, as the trio looked at one another.

Then the father said uneasily, "We didn't want anybody else to know about this. I mean, this will all be confidential, won't it?"

"All physicians have taken the Hippocratic Oath and are sworn to secrecy about what's told them."

"That's not always true," the daughter interposed.

"I'll grant there are indiscreet doctors, Miss, but I can assure you I'm not one of them. Now may I know your names?"

"Carson," said the older man, "like Johnny—only no relation." He gave the kind of chuckle that must have become second nature to him by now.

"I'm Irwin," the man continued. "This is Chuck, my son, and Pam, my daughter."

Seth looked at them and wondered out loud, "Who exactly has the problem?"

To Seth's surprise, the father answered, "We all do."

At this the elder Carson sat forward on his chair and spoke in hushed tones.

"It's actually about my wife—their mother—she's very ill."

"Where is she?" Seth inquired.

"Back home. She's much too sick to travel."

"Where's home?"

"In Hammond."

"You came here from Indiana? Just what exactly's wrong with Mrs. Carson?"

The older man bit his lip, looked first at his daughter, and then at his son, both of whom nodded to indicate that he should continue his plea.

"A year ago they found a malignant tumor in her stomach. They operated. They took it out."

"And?" Seth inquired.

"Well, it was tough at the start, but we helped her to sort of readjust. For a while there, things seemed fine. I even took her on an anniversary trip to the Caribbean."

He paused, breathed deeply, and continued. "Then it sort of started all over again. So we went back to see the doctor. He did some x-rays. Would you like to see them?"

"Yes, of course,"

Seth took the large envelope, withdrew the films, and put them up against an illuminated cabinet.

He saw the situation at once. "To be frank, they don't look very promising."

"We know," said the young man.

At which the father took up the narrative again. "I asked the doctor if he'd operate again. And then he said—"

He broke into tears.

"Sorry, Dr. Lazarus. I'm really sorry," the old man sobbed. "It's just the awful way he answered me. It was so brutal. He said straight out, 'No, it's not worth the trouble.'"

"That was hardly the kindest way of putting it," Seth remarked. "But these pictures do show a large growth at the juncture of the digestive tube where she was operated."

At which point, the man tearfully repeated, "When I pleaded with him, he just waved me off."

"Didn't he suggest any other possibilities of dealing with the neoplasm?"

"Well, there's x-ray treatment. But even our G.P. told us that in stomach cancer it's almost useless."

"I'm afraid your G.P. was correct, sir," Seth commented.

Mr. Carson's narrative accelerated. "So then he comes up with the idea of chemotherapy, another useless procedure. I mean, the only thing it's guaranteed to do is make your hair fall out—and turn you into a tired skeleton."

Seth merely nodded.

"So what was left? Nothing. Zero. They just sent her home to die."

As he continued, Carson's voice became more and more of a supplication. "Doctor, she can barely swallow anymore. We have to feed her baby food. Things like Gerber's applesauce."

"And even that is getting difficult to keep down," the daughter added.

"Now," said the son, "she needs antispasmodic drugs and tranquilizers just to be able to swallow sugar water."

"So we went to the doctor again," the elder Carson said, picking up the tale. "Now, all of a sudden he's back to the idea of an operation: 'gastro—' I can't even pronounce the name."

"A gastrostomy," Seth explained. "It's what you might call a re-plumbing of the whole digestive tract that would bring the food directly to the intestines through a tube into the skin."

Seth paused to await further details.

"Well, Doctor, I don't have to tell you," Carson said, raising his voice and betraying some of his bitterness, "that it's a hell of an operation and the guy actually admitted it wouldn't stop the cancer growing. He wasn't even sure it would stop the pain. He just said it would give her more time."

Seth wanted to get to the heart of the matter. "I'm sorry to say, from what you've told me, I don't think there's any possible way of saving her. I mean, certainly nothing within my knowledge or power."

"We know that," said the father, as the son and daughter echoed, "Yes, we know. We know."

"That's why we're begging you to *help* her, Doctor," the elder Carson said.

"I don't understand," Seth answered, with a troubling intuition that he did.

"Doctor, don't let her just sit there and become a subhuman thing with plastic tubes everywhere. Don't let her suffer like this. Let her go now, while her life still has a shred of dignity. She wants to die."

There was a pause and then Carson spoke his concluding words. "Please help us, Doctor. I mean, help *her*."

The rest was silence. They had said their piece.

Seth was dumbfounded. And petrified at the thought that his long-ago "act of compassion" for Mel Gatkowicz had somehow escaped the confines of the hospital—and even crossed state lines.

"How did you get my name?" he inquired as calmly as possible.

"A new internist in our hospital. Dr. Bluestone."

The older man broke the silence.

"Will you help us, Doctor?" the elder man implored again. "For the love of God—"

No, said Seth to himself, for the love of man.

"Have Dr. Bluestone call me this evening at my home." He stood up.

The family rose at once, as if a prelate of the church were passing by, and walked out into the darkness.

Seth put out the office lights. And as he locked the door and headed for his car, he thought of the consequences of what he had all but pledged to do.

Now death would make a house call.

THIRTY-EIGHT

The moment he arrived home, Seth recounted the whole incident to Judy, who shared his apprehension.

"If that's what Tim wanted, why didn't he do it himself?" she said angrily. "He's put *all* our lives in jeopardy."

Seth merely acknowledged her words with a glance. He was all too aware that what they regarded as mercy would be seen by many others as murder.

"Tim's supposed to be calling tonight," Seth reminded her. "I don't really know what to say."

"You've got to tell him to go to hell."

Seth was deep in thought. At last he said quietly, "What about the Carsons?"

"Oh, God," Judy responded with agonized frustration, "you're not thinking of doing what Tim's asked—"

"I don't give a damn about Bluestone," he replied, eyes focused in the middle distance. "But I care about those people. The whole family is in torment—and there doesn't seem to be an end to it."

"No, Seth," Judy objected. "Don't take the risk...." Her voice trailed off. For she could sense that he was so sympathetic to Mrs. Carson's plight that he had already made up his mind.

A little after 9 P.M. the phone rang. It was Tim Bluestone calling from Indiana.

"Seth," he began, "I think I'd better explain—"

"You certainly had," Seth interrupted. "I want to know exactly what you told the Carsons and why."

"I told them I knew a very compassionate doctor who might be able to help. I haven't got the guts to do it alone, Seth. Besides, I saw you leave Mel Gatkowicz's room the night he died. And afterward I wondered."

Seth could not answer him. And dared not ask whom else he had told.

"These are special circumstances, Seth," Tim pleaded. "The Carsons are good, decent people. And Marge—that's the wife—is just a fragment of a human being. She's in excruciating pain. I've put the significant data in a letter to you. You'll probably get it in tomorrow's mail. Look, the family is so desperate they asked me if I wouldn't—you know—do something. At first I resisted the idea. But these past few days, watching Marge deteriorate, I think they're right." He paused and then blurted out, "If we could just do it together, Seth. That would kind of share the burden."

Tim, you fool, Seth thought to himself, don't you realize this is something you can't share? Even if you collaborate, you still get the full weight on your shoulders.

"Okay, let me read her case notes and I'll get back to you."

"At my home, not my office, please."

"Obviously," Seth replied, not disguising his annoyance.

The dossier was in the next morning's mail. Seth called Tim a little before ten.

"You're right," he said, "nobody deserves to suffer like this. We should go ahead on your ... proposal. But it'll have to be on the weekend."

"Yes. Of course."

"Now tell me exactly how to get to their place."

After giving him specific directions, Tim added, "Thank you, Seth— God, this whole thing is frightening."

Seth did not even address Tim's statement. For that would have meant haranguing him about the ghosts he saw in countless dreams. Bluestone had nothing to teach him about fear.

"Listen, Tim, where do the son and daughter live?"

"The boy's an Engineering grad student up at Northwestern. The daughter's married to a guy who owns a restaurant. Sometimes she helps him out as a cashier."

"Well, make sure neither of them is around this Sunday. Can you do that?"

"Sure, sure."

"Now I've got to know one last thing—is the woman conscious?"

"Most of the time. It's just that to give her some relief from pain, we have to drug her very heavily."

"I'll have to talk with her, so make sure she's lucid Sunday evening. I'll be there at nine."

It was a typical lower middle-class suburb with nearly identical two-family houses, each with the same shrubbery and a similar tree in front. It was 9:05 P.M. The road was pitch dark. And Tim Bluestone was pacing nervously in front of the Carson house when Seth suddenly materialized.

"Bluestone?" he said softly.

"Hi, Seth. What happened to your car?"

"Never mind. I'm parked in a suitable spot. Let's go inside."

Seth did not add that he had taken Judy's station wagon—which lacked "M.D." plates.

From outside the front door they could hear the sounds of baseball on the TV. Seth suspected that the husband kept it loud to drown out—from his ears if not his mind—the sounds of his wife's suffering.

"Hello, Doctor," Irwin Carson said, in a voice drained of emotion. "Thank you for coming."

"Where's Mrs. Carson?"

"She's upstairs. Her bedroom's upstairs. Uh—she's expecting you."

Seth merely nodded. "Would you like to go up and speak to her?"

Her husband thought for a moment and then replied, "We've done nothing all afternoon but talk. We've said goodbye, I don't think I can . . ." His voice trailed off.

The two doctors nodded and walked slowly up the stairs.

"Good evening, Marge," Tim said, "this is Dr. Lazarus."

The woman was barely a wraith, her face like a skull. An I.V. ran into her right arm, sustaining her life drop by little drop.

She reached out a bony hand toward Seth and, with effort, whispered, "Thank you for coming, Doctor."

Seth nodded and sat down to exchange a few words with the pain-racked woman.

"Mrs. Carson, it must be hard for you to talk, but there are things I have to know. Are you aware of why we are here tonight?"

"Yes, Doctor."

"Were you absolutely sure of what you asked Dr. Bluestone? I mean, have you had any second thoughts since then?"

"No. I want to die." To which she added, almost in a moan, "*Please, Doctor.*"

At this moment Seth's eyes hit upon a small replica of the crucified Christ on her night table. She was a Catholic, and yet by inviting him this evening, was she not committing a kind of suicide—a mortal sin? Marge answered the question before he could ask it.

"Don't worry, Doctor," she murmured, "do what you have to do. The rest will be for me to face. I've prayed to Him so often, I know He'll understand."

At this point Seth looked at Tim to see if he, as her family physician, wanted to say anything. But he seemed unable to speak. Seth turned again to Mrs. Carson.

"I'm just going to put some medicine into your I.V., Mrs. Carson. In a few minutes you'll go to sleep—"

"—and no more pain?"

"No, Mrs. Carson," Seth answered softly, "no more pain."

The woman began to cry, her tears zigzagging down the crevices that once were cheeks. "Oh, God," she murmured, "thank You for sending Your angel."

Seth continued to talk calmly, conscious that his words were comforting her. As he inserted the small vial into the needle in her right arm, he noticed Tim Bluestone turn his back. *He couldn't even watch.* Seth took hold of Mrs. Carson's hand and held it tightly as the life and pain ebbed out of her.

The two physicians left the room and rejoined Irwin Carson, who was staring unfocusedly at the tiny figures on the screen. He stood up.

"She's at peace," Seth replied to his unasked question.

Carson crossed himself and began to cry. Perhaps from sorrow, perhaps from relief. Perhaps both.

"I . . . I don't know what to say," he sobbed.

The younger doctor did not know how to respond.

As he was putting on his jacket Seth offered, "Mr. Carson, I want you to know that the last thing Marge said was that she wanted this because she loved her family."

Still weeping, Carson nodded, indicating that he understood.

"Dr. Bluestone will come by in the morning to see how things are. Goodnight."

Irwin Carson remained rooted where he stood, as the front door quietly closed.

The two doctors were once again outside in the darkness.

"How can I thank you, Seth?" Tim whispered with emotion.

Seth took him by the shoulder and replied, "Don't call me again. Ever."

And he disappeared into the night.

"I don't think I've ever been so depressed in my entire life."

"Statements like that could make people lose confidence in psychiatrists," Bill Chaplin said. He was trying to lift his author's mood with a friendly dinner at Elaine's.

Barney tried unsuccessfully to smile.

"Bill, I'm only human. Besides, you don't need to be happy to help other people—otherwise there wouldn't be a single therapist in New York. I've got a lot of tangible things to be miserable about. For one, Emily's left—she won't even take my calls at *SI*. In fact, one of my so-called 'well-wishing' friends has informed me that she's getting involved with some guy from ABC Sports. My pal Laura's somewhere in the wilds of Toronto two steps away from a nervous breakdown, and nobody wants to read my book, even in paperback."

"Come on, Barney," Bill urged, "quit mourning, it's been long enough. Let's talk about your next book."

"I haven't got one," Barney replied disconsolately. "My cupboard's bare. I mean, I thought I had a great idea in the sports book. I honestly believed that people wanted to know what goes on in the heads of heroic figures."

Bill stared intensely at Barney. "You're right, they do. And I don't think you should change your approach one iota. Why not just focus on another type of heroic figure?"

"No way, Bill. Achilles is dead, Sir Lancelot is dead—and the Beatles have broken up. You can't have idols in an age of cynicism. I mean—"

Suddenly Chaplin interrupted:

"Barney—I've got it!"

Bill, in fact, had gotten it so loud that half the restaurant turned to glare at him.

But Bill was too electrified by his own idea to care.

"Barney," he continued, "there are all kinds of religions in America, but everybody agrees on one thing—God is a doctor or vice versa."

"What? Chaplin, you keep talking like this and I'll have you certified. From my experience, doctors are as far from being heroes as any group I have ever known."

"*You* know that," Bill stated, "but the average person doesn't. The man in the street thinks the doctor is a priest with a hotline to God. We worship them. We're scared of them. If you can somehow convey what really goes on in doctors' heads—"

Barney began to smile. "Bill, there's no such thing as a collective medical psyche. Doctors come in more varieties than Heinz. But most of the ones I know are dedicated people struggling to do a Sisyphean task, just hoping that the rock won't roll over them. It's not as glamorous as Ben Casey and Dr. Kildare."

"*You* know that, Barney, but *you're* on the inside. Doctors I've encountered are venal, insecure schmucks in white coats who use the letters *M* and *D* as crutches to hold them up in society. Am I right?"

"No," Barney answered quietly. And then added, "But you're not completely wrong, either. I've come across some of those characters—the kind who read *Medical Economics* instead of the *American Journal*—and they demean the reputation of our whole profession."

Bill all but leaped across the table to grab Barney by the lapels. "Come on," he demanded, sounding like a drill sergeant. "Show me— show me what's behind those masks, the minds inside those inflated heads. Show people what doctors *really* are."

Barney pondered for a moment, and then calmly inquired, "Are you asking me for a hatchet job?"

"I'm just asking you for the truth, Barn. If the public image of doctors is distorted, set it straight."

Bill's voice lowered. "You listen to me, Livingston. We've tapped a nerve and you're not leaving this upmarket McDonald's without a signature, even if it's on a napkin."

And then, half to himself, Bill murmured, "Oh, Dr. Jorgensen, for years I've been wishing you dead. But now I hope you live long enough to read this book!"

"Who's Dr. Jorgensen?"

Bill suddenly grew somber.

"The guy that killed my eye," he murmured. "I went in for a routine cataract job. This guy messed up and I walked out with a dead eye. I even sued and the bastard won."

"Come on, Bill. The chances of that happening are about a million to one."

"No, Barn, you don't get the point. Some kind of incident like this has happened to almost everybody in the world. This topic hits *everybody*. I'll bet even in *your* life you've had a bad experience with a doctor."

Barney was suddenly jolted by the image of a scene he had never beheld and yet had conjured up in countless nightmares: his father lying face down in the garden, while his mother screamed and Warren ran . . .

And Dr. Freeman didn't come.

He did not realize how deep in reverie he was until he heard Bill say, "Okay, are you gonna write that book?"

Barney shook his head. "I don't think you'd want to read what I'd produce, Bill. The majority of doctors are so dedicated and involved, their rate of suicide is something like ten times the norm."

"Is that really true?" Chaplin exclaimed.

Barney nodded. "Their drug and alcohol addiction is a *hundred* times the norm." And Barney added, "Because caring takes a toll."

"So you want to write an apology, a defense?" Bill inquired.

"No," replied Barney, "just the truth: that doctors are like every other human being."

"Okay," Chaplin conceded, "write it any way you want. Only promise me you'll write it."

Barney looked at his watch and stood up. "Listen, if I don't leave now I'll be late for my three o'clock patient and I'll have to include an exposé of myself in this damn thing. Thanks for lunch, Bill. I only wish to hell we'd talked about baseball."

"How come?"

"Because now I have to write that goddamn book."

As usual, Lance Mortimer had a mistress called Lady Luck. His mentor at Mount Hebron was a man regarded with awe by many of his colleagues. For Patrick Knowles was the first in the profession to reduce his entire hospital obligation to forty-eight hours a month.

What is more, these were forty-eight *consecutive* hours. There were some in the medical community who wondered how Knowles could remain alert throughout his arduous two-day stint. But then the specialty of this transplanted Englishman was waking people up as well as putting them to sleep.

He was a great teacher. He painstakingly instructed Lance in perhaps the most delicate maneuver required at the outset of an operation, namely getting an endotracheal tube down the patient's throat and into the lungs, so the anesthesiologist could do the unconscious patient's breathing for him.

("Here's the whole trick, old boy," Knowles explained. "Remember that the trachea is in *front* of the esophagus. Be absolutely sure you *see* the tube passing through the vocal cords, then you should be able to hear breathing sounds over the anterior chest—which means you're home and dry.")

Lance also quickly learned how to avoid a common error of apprentice anesthesiologists—namely, knocking the patient's teeth out while trying to insert the tube.

Fortunately, the one time he did this Knowles was at his side and quickly took over to aspirate the teeth before they could get stuck in a bronchus or a lung, where they might cause a nasty pneumonia or a still nastier death.

Lance was also blessed (Lady Luck showing unusual fidelity) in the fact that his victim—so to speak—was a charity patient and was overjoyed at the prospect of getting dentures that actually improved her smile.

There was another factor that contributed to his mentor's extraordinary success in Tinseltown.

Not only was Knowles a rich and handsome man of many parts but he looked a full twenty years younger than he really was—and this without apparent surgical enhancement.

One night (i.e., one of his monthly two) he was on call with Lance and he imparted this secret as well. It was not merely the fact that he massaged his face with Dr. Niehan's magical formula, made from the embryos of sheep at the famous clinic in Switzerland, but that he knew enough to "avoid *hassle* with determination."

"If the surgeons—most of whom, as you've probably noticed, are prattish twits—think they know better, don't argue. Ninety-nine times out of a hundred they take the rap if the patient doesn't make it. And most of the time you don't even have to show up for the ritual of telling the next of kin.

"And—thanks to those lovely, efficient nurse-anesthetists—you can work three O.R.s at once, nipping back and forth to see how the patients are doing. And since we 'gas passers' don't need to scrub up, you might even steal a sec to call your broker and see how *you're* doing."

Lance revered the man. Up to then, his dream had been only to work *two* operating rooms at once.

"Hey, Bennett, I've got a patient in about ninety seconds. We've got to make this quick. What's up?"

"*I'm* up, Livingston. I just got the telegram saying I've been accepted for the heart transplant program in Houston."

"That's great, Landsmann. You'll be the first guy in medical history who can transfer a heart with a little soul!"

"Hey, that was actually fairly witty."

"For that compliment, Ben, I'll buy you the dinner I was going to buy you anyway, but you can have two desserts."

"When and where?"

"Why don't we meet halfway? There's a steakhouse right off Exit Thirteen on the Connecticut turnpike. How about Friday night at around eight-thirty?"

"Great. Go back to your shrinking, Barn."

Two evenings later Barney pulled his new Ford Pinto into the parking lot of The Red Coach Grille and circled slowly, spied Bennett's Jag, and parked a few spaces away.

Inside the restaurant it was loud and crowded. Still, there was no problem in finding Bennett, who was taller and of course darker than most of the clientele.

After greetings were exchanged and congratulations bestowed, they sat down and told each other how exhausted they looked. And speculated as to how many years this kind of schedule would take off their lives.

They ordered two T-bones and a bottle of Mondavi Cabernet Sauvignon, then headed for the salad bar to overload their plates.

When they got back to their table, Bennett was eager to share the excitement of his new position with his best friend. But it was getting progressively more difficult for them to hear each other. There was a large table of noisy and jolly people nearby—getting noisier and jollier all the time. Finally Barney and Bennett were forced into silence.

Apparently it was some kind of family celebration and their leader, a balding, rotund little man, was telling anecdotes in a loud nasal voice.

The guy was actually amazing to watch. His effort to hold the limelight, not only of his table but of the entire restaurant, made it obvious to both doctors that he was trying to compensate for an inferiority complex.

This became ever more evident when the waiter, in a white cook's hat, came by with a large wagon under whose massive egg-shaped stainless steel cover sat a long, succulent cut of London broil, waiting to be carved to the clients' satisfaction.

"Let's hear it for the cows," squealed the roly-poly man. His clan applauded, whistled, and cheered.

Then the fat man made an astounding proposal.

"Who bets I can swallow that whole roast in one gulp?"

"No way, Carlo," said one of the male relatives dismissively. "Even a horse couldn't do that."

Carlo affected indignation.

"Wanna put money on it, Chet?" He reached in his pocket, withdrew a roll of bills, and peeled off a hundred dollars.

"I got a C-note says I can swallow that roast beef whole. Put up or shut up."

"Okay," Chet replied with a laugh, "this will be the easiest 'century' I've ever made. Let's go."

With all eyes in the restaurant upon him, Carlo had the carver stand aside and began to circle his prey like a matador.

Finally he stepped forward, grasped the roast in both hands, and held it above his head for all to see. There was applause and various encouraging sounds from what seemed like every table except that of the two doctors.

Barney heard one of Carlo's relatives remark to a tablemate, "I seen him swallow big ones before, but this'll make the *Guinness Book of Records*."

Suddenly the crowd hushed and tension rose.

Carlo began to stuff the enormous roast into his mouth, as the crowd went wild.

A moment later he was on the brink of death.

His throat was completely blocked and he was unable even to draw breath. Clutching his gullet, he staggered, desperately trying to pull out the roast. All the while his face was turning a cyanotic blue.

His wife shrieked. Yet everyone in the restaurant seemed paralyzed.

Barney and Bennett reacted instinctively.

"Heimlich Maneuver," said Bennett.

Barney shoved his way through the rapidly gathering crowd. He rushed toward the choking man.

Carlo's wife was frantically trying to help her husband remove the roast when Barney arrived and brusquely pushed her aside.

"What the hell—?" she screamed.

"Give me room, give me room—I'm a doctor! Get out of my way," he shouted harshly. This was hardly a moment for bedside manner.

Barney began to apply the standard technique for removing a foreign body from the trachea, where it is preventing the flow of air to the lungs. He positioned himself behind Carlo, locked his arms around the victim's chubby waist, making a fist with his right hand. Then he began to squeeze the abdomen between the navel and the ribcage with quick, forceful upper thrusts.

He did not succeed. The air passage was too tightly blocked. Now Bennett was at his side.

"The Heimlich won't do it, Ben," Barney called out. "What now? He'll be dead in half a minute!"

Bennett knew the next move. "Tracheotomy—lay him down quick."

The man had lost consciousness and was limp in Barney's arms as he set him on the floor. The spectators were too stunned to speak. Bennett grasped a steak knife from a nearby table, kneeled down and jabbed the point of the knife into the base of the victim's throat. Blood poured from the wound.

Carlo's relatives were suddenly jolted into outrage. There were hysterical cries of "He stabbed him." "The nigger's trying to kill him." "Help!" "Police!" "Murder!"

As Barney valiantly tried to hold Carlo steady, one of the burly bartenders attempted to drag Bennett away.

"Stop, you asshole," Barney shouted. "My friend's a surgeon. He's saving the guy's life."

The bartender either did not hear Barney or did not want to hear him. He continued to pull Bennett to his feet. There was no time for polite explanations. Bennett smashed his left fist into the bartender's solar plexus and sent him reeling.

The crowd recoiled in fear.

"I'm a doctor, dammit," Bennett shouted, barely able to control himself.

Meanwhile, Barney called from the floor. "Come on, Ben. Get something we can use as a trocar to give this guy an air supply."

Bennett's eyes darted around quickly and saw nothing. Then he noticed a nearby waiter with a ballpoint pen in his breast pocket. In a single motion, he grabbed the plastic pen, snapped it in two, pulled out the ink cartridge, and handed the hard, outer cylinder to Barney, who immediately plunged it into the incision to keep the air passage open.

Pausing for a moment, he shouted to Ben, "What about the bleeding? Can we use something for clamps?"

"No, Barn. Just stay down there and make sure the opening is—"

The rest of his sentence was drowned out by the sound of sirens. For the bartender had pressed his silent alarm, which had roused the State Police eight hundred yards down the road.

Suddenly the troopers were everywhere.

They quickly sized up the scene: a black man with a knife was standing over a white man with blood pouring from his neck. They took swift, decisive action.

Three of them set upon Bennett, two holding his hands, a third ferociously pounding his face and body till he slumped to the ground, where they continued to kick him.

Barney knew he *had* to keep the air passage open and could not come to his friend's rescue. Instead, he bellowed like a wounded bull, "He's a doctor, you bastards. He's just saved this man's life—leave him alone!"

That was the last thing he remembered.

The cold wind awakened him.

At first Barney fought to regain his senses, but all he could see was a psychedelic flashing of lights. The back of his head felt like it had been hit with a sledgehammer.

An ambulance attendant was breaking an ammonia capsule under his nose to bring him back to consciousness.

"Are you all right?" the man asked.

No, Barney thought to himself, I feel like I've dived head first into an empty pool. But something hurt even worse than his head.

"Ben—where's Ben?"

"You mean the other doctor?"

"He's a surgeon," Barney protested groggily.

"He'll be all right," said the medic.

"All right?" Barney gasped. "Where is he?"

"On his way to the Ridgetown hospital."

"You mean he's still taking care of the patient?"

"Not exactly," the attendant replied. "He's in a separate ambulance."

Barney could finally focus his eyes. And he stared with anger at the man who had just spoken these words.

"He was pretty badly beaten up," the man explained uneasily. "I guess the troopers didn't know who he was. They thought—"

"He did an emergency tracheotomy, you schmuck. He saved that fat idiot's life."

The attendant did not know how to respond. For lack of anything better, he spoke the truth. "Yes, that was fantastic. Both of you were really great."

"Take me to him," Barney ordered, still slurring his speech. "I wanna see my friend."

"I'm sorry, but we've got orders to x-ray you for possible concussion. And then take you to the station."

"Don't need a railroad station," Barney mumbled. "Got my own car."

"No," the medic said apologetically, "I mean the police station. The family is filing a complaint."

Once again, Barney had to wake his brother in the middle of the night.

"Hey, Barn," Warren groaned, his mind still caught in the cobwebs of sleep, "don't tell me you've sold another book."

"I'm afraid this time I've *been* booked."

"What?"

"Please wake up and listen. The cops allow you only one phone call."

"Cops! What's the matter?"

"Well, I'm not sure. But I think the charge may be something like attempted murder."

"Holy shit!" Warren gasped, now jolted fully awake.

As the surly policeman overseeing the call impatiently tapped his boots, Barney explained to his brother as quickly and coherently as possible what had happened.

Warren tried to remember the relevant material. Luckily, he had read about a similar case in one of the recent law journals.

"Now Barney, I know you're tired. But I'm gonna ask you some very important questions and I want you to think carefully."

The policeman's boot-tapping became louder and louder. Barney gave him an imploring look and said with all the politeness he could muster, "It's my lawyer, Sergeant. I think I'm allowed to speak to my lawyer for as long as I need to."

The officer merely coughed as if to say that he would be the judge of how much time was genuinely necessary.

"Now," Warren began his pretrial examination, "did you state clearly that you were a doctor?"

"I shouted it at the top of my lungs."

"Did the patient either ask for or refuse treatment?"

"Warren," Barney said, his exhaustion exceeded only by his exasperation, "the guy was nearly dead. If we hadn't—"

"Please, Barn, just answer my questions. Was there anybody there from his family?"

"Yeah, yeah, I suppose so. What the hell are you driving at?"

"It's something called the 'Good Samaritan Law,'" his brother replied. "Since the fifties most of the states have passed some kind of legislation that allows doctors to intervene in emergencies without running the risk of being sued for malpractice."

"Hey, look, it was a matter of life and death. There wasn't time for me to show my diploma."

"So, in fact, you're saying you identified yourself, and neither the victim—who was medically and legally non compos—nor his family refused medical care?"

"That's pretty close," Barney said quietly.

"Okay, listen, Barn. I've got to make a few calls to find out what lawyers our firm uses in Connecticut. And then I'll get up there as soon as possible to arrange for bond."

"And what do I do in the meanwhile?" Barney asked with exasperation.

"I don't know," his brother answered, trying to calm him. "Read the paper, play cards with Bennett."

"Ben's not here," Barney said with concern, "he's in the Ridgetown hospital."

"Well, phone him and tell him not to worry. I'll take care of this as quickly as I can."

"Can *you* speak to Ben?" Barney pleaded. "I get only one call and you were it."

"You mean in Canada, too?" Barney was holding the telephone in his less-bandaged hand.

"Yeah, Barn," Laura answered, "one of the wire services must have picked up the story. The papers here made a big deal out of it. There was even an editorial."

"For or against?"

"C'mon, don't be so paranoid. Of course it was favorable. They used you guys as an example of the need for a nationwide 'Good Samaritan' law. You did the right thing. It was wonderful."

"The guy's family didn't seem to think so."

"But they dropped the charges, didn't they?"

"Yeah. They sure cooled down fast—although I'm still waiting for my box of candy or a thank-you note."

Laura fell silent.

"Hey, Castellano, are you okay?"

"I was just thinking," she replied, a strange sadness in her voice. "This was probably the most important thing you've done since you became a doctor."

"What do you mean?"

"I'm gonna find out if that bastard Dr. Freeman is still practicing in

Brooklyn and I'm gonna send him all the clippings. Maybe it'll remind him that he's got your father's blood on his hands."

Barney thought for a moment. She's right. Perhaps the adrenaline that came to me so swiftly in the restaurant had been dammed up since my childhood, waiting for the moment I could show the doctor who refused to treat my father what he *should have* done.

Even as Laura and Barney were exchanging thoughts, an infuriated Herschel was standing by his son's bed in Yale–New Haven Hospital (to which he had insisted Bennett be transferred by ambulance, despite the local orthopedist's vehement objection).

Seated patiently on the other side of the room were two middle-aged men, one in a three-piece suit, the other in a lumber jacket. Neither looked like a doctor.

Bennett was lying on his back, head and chest heavily bandaged, with plaster casts on so much of his body that he seemed like a latter-day mummy.

An hour later Barney arrived, himself swathed in gauze and walking with difficulty.

"How is he?" he asked Herschel.

"Let's put it this way," Bennett's father answered, "those troopers did a thorough job. If there was any bone they could possibly break, they broke it."

Just then Bennett stirred and returned to the world of the conscious.

"How do you feel, Ben?" Herschel asked anxiously.

"Hi, Dad," he answered, still half comatose. "I don't feel anything yet. What happened?"

"To change the old chestnut, Landsmann," Barney said, "the operation was successful—but the doctor died!"

"We saved his life?" Bennett asked, his mouth dry from lack of fluids.

Barney moved to pour some water. "Of course. From now on you can do your operations with a steak knife—maybe graduate into forks and spoons."

Bennett smiled. "Ow, don't make me laugh. It hurts."

"Sorry, Ben," said Barney, bringing the cup to his friend's lips, "I was just ribbing you."

Bennett groaned again. "Dad, please get this crazy man out of here." He rested for a moment, took a few breaths, and asked, "Who cut me up?"

"The best, my boy," said Herschel, "the head of your department."

"I'm at Yale?"

"Yeah," Barney replied. "Our original idea was to get you to operate on yourself at your own hospital, but your boss said you were too junior."

Bennett's ribs again twinged with laughter. "Who sent you, Livingston, the Ku Klux Klan? Get serious. Read me the O.R. notes."

"Be patient, Ben. I think they'll be in several volumes, but the radiologist's promised to bring all your pictures over when you were awake."

"I *am* awake," Bennett said slowly. "Get me those pictures so I can assess the damage."

"I've already checked it out," Barney answered in a calming voice. "They broke the radius and ulna in both arms. You've cracked a femur and they scored at least four goals with your head. Let's just say they made a jigsaw puzzle out of your bones."

Bennett could sense that his friend had omitted something. "Come on," he ordered, "if that's all it was, you wouldn't have that hangdog look, Barney. What else did they get?"

Barney hesitated and then said as casually as possible, "There was a fracture dislocation of the cervical spine. Your boss is gonna do a 'reduction' as soon as you're well enough to take some more gas, and then you'll be as good as new."

"Don't jive me, Livingston. That puts me out of action for at least twelve weeks."

"Don't worry, Bennett," Herschel interposed. "It won't affect your appointment in Texas. And meanwhile, if you're up to it, I'd like you to discuss some things with these two gentlemen."

At this point the sartorially ill-matched pair came forward and introduced themselves. They were attorneys of such eminence that Bennett immediately recognized their names. One was the renowned champion of civil rights, Mark Sylbert, "defender of the underdog." The other was regarded as the most persuasive courtroom speaker in the land.

"We can't sit here and watch this country abandon its basic principles," Sylbert argued. "This is a clear-cut example of what our society's come to, and I'd like you to let me fight it, Dr. Landsmann."

"Dad, I think it's wrong," Bennett said, wincing as he spoke.

"No, son, the most wonderful thing about America is that a man can get real justice—"

"—that's if he can afford expensive lawyers, Dad."

"Excuse me, Ben," said Herschel, his indignation rising, "you've got at least a dozen broken bones, and damage to your spine as a reward for doing something noble."

"That's right," Sylbert interrupted. "They just saw the color of your skin and took for *granted* you were in the wrong. That, to my mind, is the most virulent form of racism. This is a chance to call them to account."

"The story's in the press already," said the other advocate.

"Well, then," Bennett commented, "I'd say the point is made." He looked at Herschel and inquired, "How much would it cost to take a suit like this to court?"

"Ben, money is no object here. I'll pay as much as necessary."

"Okay," Bennett replied, the strain of talking making him more uncomfortable than ever. "Don't waste the dough on scoring legal Brownie points. Send whatever it would cost to the Southern Christian Leadership—in memory of Dr. King."

THIRTY-NINE

To prepare himself for his unprecedented exploration into the physician's mind, Barney composed a questionnaire, which he sent out to all his friends and Med School classmates. Clearly, they would have witnessed behind-the-scenes dramas inaccessible to him. Naturally, he promised total anonymity. The respondents were even given the option of omitting their own names.

Lance Mortimer was one of the first to reply and did so at some length, prefacing his contribution with a personal letter.

Dear Barn,

I think you're on to a brilliant idea (I kick myself for not having thought of it first). As a matter of fact, I've seen so many unbelievable things that I started keeping a diary about two years ago, and I will go through it carefully and send you the juiciest bits. (I can't just xerox the entire thing—I don't tell even my shrink about my sexual exploits.)

I enclose my record of an incident that occurred in the early morning of June 6th 1970. Obviously, I have disguised the names— not to protect the innocent, but to save my own neck.

Now, obviously, you know these incidents took place in Los Angeles, but I have invented a private hospital called St. David's at

Newport Beach. And I'd be grateful if you kept my little fiction. You could blow the whole profession sky-high—if they don't destroy you first.

Regards,
Lance

P.S. *Your* Champions *book was reviewed in the* Los Angeles Times *by Vera Mihalic a couple of years ago. I didn't think it was something you would want to see, so I didn't send it along.*

As Barney first began to peruse Lance's initial contribution, he smiled at the Hollywoodisms. But by the time he had finished, he felt deeply unsettled. Obviously, he had opened up Pandora's box.

After reading the report for the third time, he felt the need to share his anxiety with someone. And since Dr. Baumann would hardly be amenable to a midnight call from a former analysand, there was no alternative.

"Hi, Castellano. Did I wake you?"

"Not really, I've given up sleep for Lent. What's up?"

And then he read the document aloud.

No one will ever forget the masterful Oscar-winning performance of Luke Jamison (not his real name) in Stanley Walters' (not his real name) production of (let's call it) Starless Night. *Nor will the performance of June Sommerville (not her real name)—in real life Mrs. Jamison—as the deaf-mute girl ever fade from memory.*

It was thus that to an obbligato of excitement the hospital received the news that June was on her way in a private ambulance with a suspected ruptured appendix.

Surgeon Steve Ross (not his real name) woke me from an exhausted sleep in the on-call room and told me to be ready for the procedure stat. I barely had time to run a razor over my face and comb my hair, before dashing to the O.R.

For those who have never seen June Sommerville in real life, let me tell you that her beauty was not the result of makeup or trick photography. She was gorgeous.

As we were rushing her in, I couldn't help but notice that our hospital director himself had appeared, to invite her husband Luke to wait with him in the comfort of his own office.

After injecting Miss Sommerville with sodium pentothal to relax her, then quickly inserting a tube into her trachea and pump-

*ing the ambu bag to inflate her lungs, I began to induce her into
"comfortable sleep" with the usual mixture of Halothane and oxygen.
I asked her to name her ten favorite film roles. She had barely gotten
to Ben Hur when she was in the second stage of anesthesia, a
Nirvana-like dreamland. I signalled to Dr. Ross that the patient was
"under."*

*He then asked for his trusty scalpel and made a flawless incision
in her ivory-white abdomen. In a matter of minutes—Ross is a superb
craftsman—the offending appendix was removed and paracentesis (the
draining of the infected fluid) of the abdominal cavity had begun.*

*But then disaster struck. So dazzled had we been—or most
specifically Dr. Ross—that a star of Miss Sommerville's magnitude
was making a guest appearance in our operating theater that an
appropriate medical history had not been taken prior to the procedure.*

*Thus it was not realized that she was allergic to penicillin until
she suddenly went into anaphylactic shock. As I was struggling to
get her oxygenated, there was yet another catastrophe—cardiac
arrest.*

*Here again Ross wasted no time and opened her magnificent
thoracic area to massage her heart. The moments ticked by, she
was still out—her perfectly chiseled features becoming bluer and
bluer.*

*After several minutes I suggested to Ross that we stop our
efforts, as it was a lost cause.*

*"No, you a--hole," he shrieked at me. "We can't let Luke
Jamison's wife die on our table—it would kill the hospital's
rep. And I'll be socially blackballed all over town. Keep f----g
pumping!"*

*I protested that even if we did revive her now there would be
irreversible brain damage. He again told me to intensify my ventilation and shut the f--- up.*

*After eighteen minutes and thirty-three seconds, June Sommer-
ville's heart began to beat again.*

*"Thank God," I heard Ross exclaim to himself. Bad career
move, I myself said to the Almighty.*

*As soon as her breathing had stabilized, Ross tore off his mask
and headed at a sprint for the director's office to convey the news to
Mr. Jamison that the operation had succeeded.*

*But if anybody wonders why June Sommerville has not made
any films recently, it is not—as the press agents have put out—that
she prefers the privacy of her Bel Air rose garden. It is because she*

*is in a very exclusive nursing home where she is too brain-damaged
even to recognize her award-winning husband.*

*I was kind of upset—especially when Steve Ross demanded that I
give my write-up to him personally. Not being a total innocent I
realized that Ross realized that even a first-year med student knows
that after five minutes of cardiac arrest brain damage is inevitable.
And there was no point in adding to Mr. Jamison's grief.*

*Subsequently I learned that he comes regularly to worship
the living effigy of his wife, bringing her each time a bouquet of
red roses.*

*But for some reason, however, Steve Ross never asked me to be
his gas passer again.*

As Bennett was wont to remark in moments of levity, which—
except when Barney was visiting—were becoming rarer, his progress
toward health was similar to the peeling of an onion. For every time they
took a bandage off, there was another one beneath, and plasters covered
plasters, so that it almost seemed there was nothing left of Bennett at the
core.

After the fifth week of recuperation, the pain began to be less
physical than mental. It was torture for him to be inactive and to worry
about what was happening to his muscles under those casts.

"I'm atrophying into nothing," he told Barney during one visit.

"Listen, Landsmann," Barney joshed, "you're the envy of the surgical residents' world—you've already spent more time in bed than most of
them do in ten years."

"I'd trade, you know I'd trade," Bennett murmured, irritated, annoyed, and frustrated. "That's why I've used my irresistible charm on the
orthopods to get me started on physiotherapy right away."

"Now? In all that plaster? What sport are you gonna go in for—para-
chute jumping?"

"No, Dr. Livingston," Bennett replied, "I'm just starting with two
balls."

"Well," quipped Barney, "so do all the rest of us."

"If you don't mind, I'll start with squash balls."

One day Jeffrey Kirk, Professor of Orthopedic Surgery, came to visit
bearing instead of chocolates something else that Bennett had long been
yearning for: his x-rays. They went over them together.

"Well, Jeff," Bennett pronounced jauntily, "I can give you my
professional opinion that this patient's bones are healing beautifully."

But then he came to the last set, pictures of the seven vertebrae that form the spine between the head and shoulders.

"Hello there," he remarked, "I'll bet this was a sticky wicket, Jeff. But the 'reduction' you performed looks perfect. Now how soon till you let me out of here and back into the O.R.?"

The answer took him by surprise.

"Is tomorrow morning soon enough?"

Except that both his legs were bandaged, Bennett would have skipped for joy.

"I'll be there with bells on, Jeff."

It was then that Kirk announced the one proviso.

"I don't want all my beautiful reduction work to go for naught, Ben. You're going to have to wear a halo apparatus."

"No. You're kidding. I'd look like a man from Mars."

"That won't matter," Kirk replied, "your colleagues think you are already."

He did indeed look like a creature from another planet. They had put a metal band around his head and screwed it into his cranium. Another rigid metal strip went down to his shoulders. All this would immobilize his neck to keep him from reinjuring what Jeffrey Kirk had so expertly restored.

"I tell you," Bennett remarked to Barney when they spoke that evening on the phone, "I'm like a copper replica of Tonto."

"I hope you're taking pictures to send out as Christmas cards," Barney suggested.

"No, my man, the Christmas card you'll get will show me standing tall in Texas in a cowboy hat."

Curiously, Bennett did not notice people staring at him in his halo apparatus. For by now he was inured to people looking oddly at a black man in a white man's territory.

Until the brace was removed, he would have to be content with high-class scutwork: suturing—at best, perhaps a simple appendectomy incision. His squash-ball exercises had paid off for, if anything, his forearms looked more muscular than they had before the incident.

Finally, he demanded his reward. "Take this stupid thing off my head, or I'll unscrew it by myself," he told Professor Kirk. "I want full flexibility so I can get back to some serious procedures."

Kirk frowned. "From what I hear, you've passed the red light anyway, Ben. Walls have ears—even through the noise of the emergency room."

"Yeah," Bennett confessed with a sheepish grin. "There was a bus crash and they really needed me. Well, can I do it with a green light now?"

"Yes," Kirk smiled, "as far as I'm concerned, you're perfect."

"Come on, Doc," Bennett retorted, "nobody's perfect." And then added, "but I'm sure as hell trying."

Bennett was so elated by his clean bill of health that he found himself whistling a happy tune as he donned his surgical blues.

His first "real" assignment was an extremely complex portacaval shunt, a procedure in which the portal vein in the liver is joined to the vena cava inferior—the principal vein draining the lower portion of the body.

As Bennett approached the operating table, he noted that there seemed to be an unusually large number of surgical personnel present. In addition to his first assistant, Terri Rodriguez, he saw two senior surgeons, one the Chief of service.

He knew full well why they were there. They wanted to see if he still had it. Whether the severe trauma he had suffered had caused any loss of skill—or of nerve. Bennett told himself that it was just like a crucial athletic challenge—where the game would be won or lost by the guys who could keep their cool.

He was determined to give no outward sign of anxiety. And make no mistakes.

He smiled at his spectators and said breezily, "Good morning, all. This is going to be a long procedure, so I suggest we begin right away. . . ."

After the first half hour, the Senior professors nodded to each other and unobtrusively left the room. They had seen enough.

Feeling triumphant, Bennett told Barney all about it on the phone that night.

"Christ, Landsmann, you must have nerves of steel. I would have been shaking in my boots. How the hell can you say you actually enjoyed it?"

"Dr. Livingston," Bennett replied affably, "be sure you put in that book of yours that most of us crazy surgeons actually *groove* on pressure."

This book is one of the most important contributions to psychoanalytic thought in at least a generation. Surely it will occupy an important place in the literature of the entire discipline.

Barney perused the words excerpted from the most recent edition of the *American Journal of Psychiatry*—a publication not normally given to superlatives. The encomium had been reprinted on a poster in the entrance hall of the Psychiatric Institute announcing the forthcoming lecture of its distinguished author, Maurice Esterhazy.

"Have you read it yet?" asked Brice Wiseman, peering over his office mate's shoulder.

"It's almost impossible to get hold of a copy," Barney replied, "and I'm dying to see it—that guy was my neighbor in Vanderbilt Hall."

"Oh, come off it, Livingston. Harvard can't claim *every* genius in the field. The flyleaf explicitly says that Esterhazy did all his training at the Maudsley Hospital in London."

"Okay, I'll quit waving the flag. But I do know the guy. Anyway, have you read his book?"

Wiseman nodded. "I was up till three last night—I just couldn't put it down."

"That means you could lend it to me so I can be insomniac this evening," Barney suggested.

"Sure, I'll bring it to the office tonight."

"Thanks, Brice," Barney replied. "It's amazing just to think that a medical book might be that exciting. But then, even the title is provocative."

"*Freud's Legitimate Daughter*—it almost sounds like a novel."

The two men parted, each to make rounds at his particular hospital.

It was a clear winter day and Barney decided to walk to Bellevue. In truth he wanted to be alone with his thoughts. To ponder the astonishing metamorphosis of Maury Eastman, whom he had last seen fifteen years ago as a tortured would-be suicide, his soul all but incinerated by electroshock, into Maurice Esterhazy, distinguished graduate of what was arguably the best psychiatric hospital in the world.

He tried to disentangle his web of feelings. Joy for Maury, of course. But even stronger, gratification bordering on *Schadenfreude* that a downtrodden son could achieve such remarkably appropriate revenge on the father who had persecuted him. For, despite his rank in the American Psychiatric Association, the elder Eastman had published many articles but never an entire book. And certainly nothing with the spectacular success Maury's was enjoying.

He was so anxious to read Maury's masterpiece that he canceled his dinner date with the nubile first-year resident in Cardiology who had recently arrived from Holland.

He made himself a nutritionally dubious baloney and cheese sandwich, sat back in his favorite chair, and began to read.

The cover said it all. *Freud's Legitimate Daughter* was subtitled "The Psychology of Melanie Klein."

The controversial British psychoanalyst who had died a few years earlier had begun her career as a strict Freudian before going on to make pioneering insights into the psychology of children far younger than Freud believed could possibly be analyzed.

Much to Klein's chagrin, the patriarch of analysis rejected her theories, somehow unable to recognize they were merely carrying his own work an important step further.

Maury's dramatic title encapsulated his subject's dilemma. For there had been a constant hostility between Klein and Freud's own daughter, Anna, who understandably considered herself to be the true perpetuator of her father's theories. Maury not only demonstrated that Klein was the better "Freudian," he also presented powerful justification of Kleinian theory buttressed with insights of his own.

It was one-forty-five when Barney read the last page. He had been so spellbound by Maury's book he had failed to notice that the needle on his hi-fi had been grating on the label of the last of his stack of records.

The next afternoon brought another surprise: a phone call from Fritz Baumann, whose tone was collegial.

"Barney, I suppose you know that Esterhazy is lecturing at the Institute next Thursday. Elsa and I are giving a little dinner for him afterwards, and he specifically requested that we invite you. Can you make it?"

"Absolutely," Barney replied, "I look forward to it."

He hung up and thought, Christ, my own analyst has asked me to dinner!

Barney had never seen the auditorium at the Institute so packed. Many had come up from as far as Baltimore and down from as far as Yale. It was Standing Room Only, with perhaps twenty candidates standing in the back, notebooks open. Fritz Baumann introduced Maury as "probably the most innovative analytical thinker of his generation."

Barney was taken aback by Maury's change in appearance—and accent. The former Maury Eastman looked like an English don—long hair, wire glasses, and a corduroy suit that looked very much lived-in. And he radiated confidence. One could feel that he was completely at ease with his audience. And with himself.

Maury began with a few lighthearted quips about the difference in orientation between British and American psychiatrists—and said that his own position could be described as "somewhere over Greenland." The audience was charmed.

Then he began to discuss "The Paranoid-Schizoid Position in Early Infancy." Speaking mainly without notes, he occasionally referred to the single index card he had brought with him. And to his watch to make certain he did not exceed the time limit.

It was a performance all the more spectacular for its total lack of flamboyance. In calm, leisurely tones, he presented his own theories of child analysis, which impressed even the most reactionary of Freudians.

The question period was long and spirited and demonstrated the breadth of Maury's medical knowledge.

The dinner at Fritz Baumann's home was restricted to the gray eminences of the Institute, with three exceptions. Maury and Barney were under forty, and Maury's wife, Antonia, was under thirty. She was also strikingly handsome. And herself a neurobiologist.

At the cocktail session before dinner, Maury was encircled by analysts deferentially asking him questions. He remained the sedate Englishman until he saw Barney. At which point he broke through his ring of admirers and rushed to embrace him, calling out, "Livingston, it's great to see you."

As they still had their arms about one another, Barney whispered, "Maury, could you tell me your secret? Is it something simple like eating Wheaties every morning?"

"No, try seven years of analysis. And a good woman," he replied affectionately. He then turned to his host. "Dr. Baumann, I hope you're proud to have this wonderful chap in your Institute."

Barney looked at Baumann, who was pleased.

And Maury continued to address his old friend as if no one else in the room mattered.

"You *must* have dinner with us tomorrow night, or I'll take irreparable umbrage."

"Of course, Maur," Barney replied, "and I'll even give you a copy of my own book. In fact I'll give you ten—since nobody seems to have bought it."

"I read it, and thought it was an insightful piece of work. So did Antonia. But we'd be grateful for a signed copy. Oh, and please bring a guest. Are you married?"

"Only to my work," Barney answered, feeling slightly self-conscious.

"Actually I was sure you would end up marrying Laura the Magnificent. Whatever became of her?"

"That's a long story, Maur—"

Just then the *other* Dr. Esterhazy, Antonia, came up behind

Maury and whispered, "Darling, your presence is being clamored for. Why don't you go and scintillate while I talk to Barney?"

Maury kissed her on the cheek and went off to rejoin the senior psychiatrists.

"Maurice has spoken so affectionately of you," Antonia said as soon as they were alone. "Apparently you were the only one who gave a damn about him when he was in trouble."

"I was only being human," Barney answered shyly. Then suddenly Antonia changed the subject.

"Could we possibly have a quick word in private?" she asked.

"Sure," Barney replied. They stepped into the still-unoccupied dining room.

"Have you ever met his father?" she whispered.

"Not exactly, but you could say we've encountered one another. Why do you ask?"

"Maurice is speaking in San Francisco next week. Frankly, I'm worried what might happen if the wretched man actually appears at the lecture."

"I don't blame you," Barney agreed. "Why the hell did Maury agree to it?"

"I suppose he needs to prove something to himself," she replied. "But I think it's playing with fire. Don't you?"

"No," Barney replied. "I'd say it was more like playing Russian roulette—with five bullets in the gun."

I'm not a human being.

This was the conclusion Barney reached as he lay on his bed later that evening after having watched Maurice Esterhazy, brilliant psychiatrist, loving husband, and father—in other words, a total mensch.

It was scarcely believable that the individual he saw tonight had once been so manic-depressive that he had needed electroshock treatment.

It made Barney realize yet again that what *he* had achieved—or not achieved—was so unsubstantial, superficial by comparison.

Yeah, he told himself, in Robert Frost's words, I've got "miles to go before I sleep."

Bennett had been working like a demon, as if to make up whatever ground he had lost while "benched," as he put it, because of injuries. To the residents with on-call duties on the weekends, he was a veritable Santa Claus—offering them a sleighful of free time. The extra assignments actually made him feel less tired, since he was repairing the damage to his confidence that had kept him awake all those nights he was recuperating.

On several of the more violent New Haven Saturdays, he even managed to perform emergency cardiac procedures—psyching himself up for next year's big challenge.

"Can't you slow down, Ben?" Terri complained.

"Want me to get another assistant?" he had replied amicably.

"No way—I'm learning too much. I just wish you'd ease up for your own sake."

By April, four months after the operation, Bennett was back leading the "normal" life of a chief surgical resident—merely his share of the 36-hour shifts.

He was just tearing off his blues after a grueling stint when Terri popped her head through the door of the men's dressing room (there wasn't an equivalent for the women surgeons—they had to dress with the nurses).

"Ben, Professor Baye just called down from Hematology. He needs a splenectomy on a leukemia patient. He specifically asked if you'd do it. But we're booked solid from eight-thirty on. What should I tell him?"

"Tell him we'll do it at *six*-thirty—if he can get up that early."

"Dr. Landsmann," she cautioned good-humoredly, "keep this up and you'll die young."

"Too late for that, Ter. Anyway, tell Baye to send down the guy's charts and I'll study them tonight. And make a copy for yourself—just in case I get senile halfway through the procedure."

A spleen removal in patients suffering from lymphocytic leukemia is carried out either because the organ has become so enlarged that it is painful, or because it is causing a symptomatic reduction of platelets—small blood cells that help control bleeding.

Bennett arrived at the hospital a little before 6 A.M. and fortified himself with chocolate chip cookies and several cups of coffee. Although he had all but memorized it the night before, he took yet another look at the medical history of his patient, Harry Scanlon, thirty-nine-year-old male Caucasian.

At 6:30 A.M. sharp he was stationed at the head of the operating table.

He acknowledged the two professors with a polite greeting and then, like an orchestra conductor, glanced at his concertmaster, in this case the anesthesiologist. The latter nodded and in a matter of seconds murmured, "The patient is under, Doctor."

Bennett received the information with a wordless nod and immediately set to work, deftly making a long midline incision. With an intern and nurse holding retractors to give him more visibility, he began the standard exploration of the viscera his incision had disclosed.

He then checked the liver for cirrhosis and infiltration by neoplastic cells, palpated the gallbladder for possible stones, and explored everything up to the upper border of the pancreas. No anomalies. He could proceed.

He slid his right hand gently across the light pink convex surface of the spleen, placed the organ into his left hand, and pulled it up toward the abdominal incision.

He craned his neck to get a better look at what he was about to excise—and at this moment he felt an inexplicable tingling in the little fingers of both his hands. He ignored it, thinking that perhaps Terri was right—he had been pushing himself too hard. But this was no time for such thoughts.

He quickly dissected the spleen artery and vein from the surrounding tissue, motioning to Terri to affix clamps. He held out his hand and requested, "Scissors." When they were slapped into his hand, he cleanly cut free the spleen.

The next stage would be messy but routine. He had now to tie off the two little tubes that were artery and vein. Bennett took the silk to ligate them and tied what felt like firm knots.

"All right," he spoke to himself out loud. "We can take the clamps off." He reached over to remove the metal instrument from the vein.

And suddenly there was blood. Blood everywhere.

There was a barely audible gasp from the onlookers. Bennett was shaken. He had never seen anybody make this kind of gaffe. But there was no time to berate himself. He had to repair the damage as quickly as possible.

He called for suction to retrieve the vein, and this time resutured it successfully. He then casually ordered Terri to close up shop, and walked back to the dressing room, trying to affect a confidence he did not feel.

He sat down and tried to comprehend what had occurred. It could simply be tension, he tried to convince himself. Or human frailty . . . but what the hell was that tingling he had felt in his fingers?

As he was sitting pensively in the surgeons' dressing room, there was a gentle knocking at the door, after which Terri Rodriguez called out, "You alone in there, Bennett?"

"Yeah," he replied, "come on into the sanctum."

"Are you all right?" she asked.

"Why shouldn't I be all right?"

"I don't know, I just thought you might be upset by that little accident. It was really nothing."

"Come on, Ter, you're too good a doctor not to know better. That was a horror show. Stop lying to me and I'll stop lying to you."

For a moment she was silent and then said, "You've got a radical mastectomy in half an hour. Do you feel up to it?"

"Why the hell shouldn't I feel up to it?" he barked angrily.

It was the first time in the year she had worked with him that Terri had seen him lose his temper.

"Okay, Ben, okay. I'm going to grab a roll and coffee. Can I get you anything?"

"No. Thanks, Ter. I'm sorry I flew off the handle."

"No problem," she replied and retreated from the domain on which she had been trespassing.

For once in his life, he sought psychiatric help. Or at least the help of a psychiatrist. He asked Barney if he knew of any cases where surgeons get "stage fright" or something similar which might account for his sudden maladroitness.

"There're plenty of surgeons who panic," Barney replied. "My partner sees them all the time. But then it's usually a total freak-out—they can't even go near their patients. No, Ben, I don't think it's in your head. If I were you I'd see a neurologist as soon as possible."

"Can you fix me up with someone in New York, Barn? I'd hate like hell for the word to get around Yale, especially this close to the end of the year."

"Hey, Landsmann, be reasonable. If it's nothing then who cares who knows about it? And if it *is* something, you sure as hell don't want to go on operating till it's fixed. Am I right?"

"I'm afraid so," Bennett replied, trying to suppress his own fears. But dammit, he prided himself on always being honest with his patients. Now he knew he owed it to them to be honest with himself.

Unable to take refuge in the psychosomatic, Bennett screwed up his courage to go back to Professor Kirk. He now had too many symptoms: backaches, intermittent numbness in his arms and fingers. As he himself diagnosed it, "Jeff, this poor muscle function in my 'intrinsics' has got to stem from the eighth cervical root."

Both doctors knew a CT scan of Bennett's cervical spine was called for, and both men knew instinctively what it would show. Bennett's fracture had slipped marginally, resulting in nerve root impingement.

Moreover, his neurological deficit would progress unless he had an immediate operation to fuse the vertebrae.

"I don't want surgery!" Bennett roared.

"And I don't want to go deaf, so quit shouting into the phone," Barney replied. "For chrissake, Landsmann, do you want to risk becoming a basket case? You know that Kirk's the best cutter in the business. What the hell are you worried about?"

Bennett put it in a nutshell. "I'm a surgeon, too—remember? I know this operation's only successful . . . *most* of the time."

FORTY

As she sat in the audience, Antonia Esterhazy could feel the tension. This time the size of the crowd at the San Francisco Institute of Psychiatry was not merely because of Maury's eminence. Many of them had come hoping to see some kind of confrontation between their esteemed colleague, Frederick Eastman, and the man they had learned was his estranged son.

Maury was already seated on the platform when one of the Senior Fellows began to introduce him.

His eyes darted here and there through the audience to find his father. He knew that as former president, Fred Eastman *had* to make a showing.

In fact, Dr. Eastman had taken the least obtrusive seat in the back of the room, where only a few spectators could savor the drama of watching his facial reactions when the lecturer took the podium.

Meanwhile, the introduction continued.

"We are especially gratified, since Dr. Esterhazy was born and raised in this very city and has, in fact, some familial ties with our Institute."

There was a smattering of nervous laughter. Now all eyes were focused on Maury to see how he would react. He gave nothing away.

But a sense of foreboding drew the blood from Antonia's face and made her squirm uneasily in her seat.

Maury rose, acknowledged the polite applause with a friendly smile, and took the podium.

"I'm sure you are all familiar with the song 'I Left My Heart in San Francisco.' At the very least, I can say with certainty that I left my childhood tricycle. My psychiatric colleagues can think what they like, but I've come to retrieve it for my kids."

His reassuring smile encouraged the audience to be at ease. He was not about to denigrate his father. Or praise him. Or even mention him.

Dr. Frederick Eastman sat ramrod straight and expressionless.

Maury's lecture elicited the same warm response that it had in New York, Philadelphia, and Boston. If anything, the dialogue during the question period was more deferential to him than it had been on the East Coast.

At last the audience began to disperse, with murmurs of praise coming from every corner.

But now came the dilemma. The Senior Fellows had arranged a dinner in honor of their guest speaker. Dr. Eastman had naturally been invited to attend and was reassured—to his own surprise—that Maury had no objection. His son's reply, conveyed to him verbatim, had been a monosyllabic "Fine."

The party was in a huge house so high on Nob Hill that, as the host was wont to remark, "On a clear day you can see Alcatraz."

Frederick Eastman entered the room and glanced uneasily at the crowd of admirers surrounding his son.

"Dr. Eastman?" inquired an English-accented voice. He turned to his left and saw an attractive young woman.

"I'm Antonia Esterhazy," she said, offering her hand. "I'm sure you're anxious to see Maurice, so why don't I extricate him?"

"I—uh—that would be very kind."

Earlier she had asked the host's permission to use a quiet corner of the house—and the doctor had suggested they use his own office.

It was thus that, beneath a photograph of Sigmund Freud, Maury and his father came face to face after more than a decade.

Maury could sense his father's uneasiness. But he felt incapable of compassion. Years of analysis had purged him of rage, but still could not replace it with forgiveness. That was for saints.

He was determined to make his father speak first. For the important thing was no longer what he had to say to his father—but rather what his father had to say to *him*.

And Fred Eastman quickly realized that was the way the scenario had been preordained. The only decision left to him was the choice of opening dialogue. At last he said, "I knew Melanie Klein. She was a very clever woman."

"A magnificent analyst," Maury added. "It's a pity she isn't appreciated more."

And then a pause. Eastman himself was determined *not* to say too much. For when he had tried to probe his own psyche to find some buried or repressed affection for his brilliant son, he had been unable to discover anything but feelings of rivalry and resentment.

He had rationalized that this was the result of his inevitable anger that Maury's very existence was a living reminder of the pain he had felt when the boy's mother had died.

And of course Maury had always known it. He had been made to feel he owed his father an eternal apology simply for being alive.

"Your wife is charming," Fred Eastman allowed.

"Thank you."

Another silence.

"In your lecture . . . you mentioned children. The joke about the tricycle . . ."

"Yes. We have two boys."

"Oh."

Yet another silence, until Maury finally said, "Look, I don't think we have much to say to one other." He was careful not to use the word "father."

"Is that the way you want to leave it, Maury? Is that all you came here to say to me?"

"I came here because I was invited to give a lecture. You were just a member of the audience."

At that instant, Antonia poked her head in. "Don't forget, Maurice, we've got to catch the eleven-thirty to Los Angeles."

He turned back to his father, who then asked, "Well, Maury, have you gotten your revenge?"

"Yes."

"Do you feel better now?"

Maury paused. And then quietly answered, "No."

Laura liked Toronto best when it was swathed in snow. It was then that the normal pace of the city slowed to a peaceful immobility. Moreover, unlike the flakes in Brooklyn which turned gray almost the instant they hit the ground, here the heavens' sprinkling of white feathers stayed pure, creating a sense of pristine tranquillity.

Not that she ever did much more than tramp in the snow behind the hospital. Since she had no desire for a social life and was working night and day in Queen's Hospital, it had seemed logical to live there as well.

When she had first arrived she had caused the usual flutter of masculine hearts. But the romantic tachycardia was quickly cured by her indifference. As she told Barney on the phone, the last thing in the world she wanted was "a date."

"I have this kind of Pavlovian response to the guys who ask me out—the more attractive they are, the more I think I'll end up hurting. So I'm now the fulfillment of both my parents' dreams—a doctor *and* a nun."

All she could think of was the babies. It was as if she regarded every new hospital admission as a member of her family. No matter what the problem—trauma, febrility, orthopedic, or respiratory, she seemed always to be there trying to help.

And all this in addition to her official training in a neonatal program that involved a lot of hands-on treatment of those unfortunate infants whose fate it was to enter life already sick or dying.

As never before in the history of medicine, the progress of technology was influencing doctors. And nowhere was this more evident than in the treatment of the newborn. The definition of prematurity and viability seemed to be changing at a dizzying pace. Until recently a baby born even a few weeks before the expected forty-week gestation was regarded as a "preemie" whose life was in peril. Now doctors realized that not only these, but younger babies were savable. Their increasing ability to detect anomalies in children yet unborn gave the experts in neonatology a chance to rectify problems as soon as the baby saw the light of day.

The new presence of the neonatologists in the delivery room inevitably created a kind of custody battle for the unborn infant. Traditionally both mother and child had been the obstetrician's responsibility. But now the pediatricians were proving that in critical circumstances the baby needed its own individual specialist.

In every case it had become standard procedure to assess the baby by giving it an Apgar score, a technique named after its originator, Dr. Virginia Apgar. It involved an evaluation of the five crucial elements of the baby's condition—one minute after birth and five minutes thereafter. The baby would receive either zero, one, or two points for heart rate, color, respiration, tone, and responses to suction.

An infant who scored over seven on the first exam could already begin training for the Olympic event of its choice—whereas one whose

Apgar was less than four would be fighting for life and need all the help that medical science could offer.

Laura was learning more each day she spent at Queens, but she had not made many friends. She had a few acquaintances with whom she might have conversations over coffee at the nurses' station, but she was generally viewed as severe and distant.

She constantly complained of hospital bureaucracy, the amount of paperwork involved in, for example, getting a sick baby from the front door to the Pediatric Ward. She was openly critical of mistakes on the part of her colleagues, senior and junior.

"We're human beings," an ICU nurse once dared to remind her. "To err is human—"

"No," Laura had retorted. "To err is fatal."

She had somehow lost the ability to catch brief snatches of slumber during night duty, but made the best use of her insomnia by reading professional literature and outlining articles of her own. She had become interested in the problem of hemorrhaging in the newborn, which was almost always detected too late. If only some kind of early-warning technique could be developed, so many more could be saved.

At three one morning when she was in the on-call room studying, the phone rang. It was Christian Lemaistre, the department's leading obstetrician.

"May I speak to the on-call pediatrician, please."

"This is Dr. Castellano," she replied.

"Oh." He had obviously been expecting a baritone and not a soprano.

"Can I help you, Dr. Lemaistre?"

"I've got a woman having problems with her labor and I may have to do a caesar. Can you be scrubbed and ready in fifteen minutes?"

"No problem, Doctor." She hung up the phone, put on her shoes, gulped down the now-cold coffee that had been on her desk, and raced for the elevator. The obstetrician had already dressed and scrubbed. As she quickly did likewise and hurried into the O.R., she could not help noticing that—even with his mask on—what she could see of Lemaistre's face substantiated his reputation as disconcertingly handsome.

Twenty-five minutes later, the obstetrician had pulled out a tiny baby boy. Laura pressed the O.R. stopclock, rushed the baby under a radiant heater, and as a nurse dried him with a warm towel, began her assessment. His breathing was poor—in fact, in the next instant she announced, "Respiration nil."

The infant was in grave danger, as was evident by the score she gave him, "One minute Apgar . . . zero."

"I would say one or two, Dr. Castellano," Lemaistre overruled from behind her.

"Either way he's more cyanotic than a blue blanket. We've got to intubate and get him some oxygen stat." And then she called to a nurse, "Get me a three-O tube."

"I would think two-five would suffice, Doctor," Lemaistre disagreed.

"Three-O," Laura repeated and, turning back to the baby remarked to Lemaistre, "This kid is big for his gestational age. He's got a pretty good chance." She called out to the nurse, "make it eight-five centimeters."

As the nasotracheal tube was being fixed into a valve, Laura turned the baby on his back and positioned his head to minimize nasal trauma. She then lubricated the tip of his nose to ease passage of the tube.

"I'd better take it from here, Dr. Castellano," Lemaistre offered in a tone that sounded more like a command. "It's a very delicate maneuver. If it's not placed perfectly in the trachea you might go too deep and pass into the main bronchus and—"

"I know that, Dr. Lemaistre," she snapped. And thought to herself, dammit, I've probably done it more times than you. But if you insist upon pulling rank. . . .

She stepped away as the nurse handed him the apparatus, which he began to insert in the baby's nostril. The nurse immediately returned with an oxygen tank and Lemaistre quickly began administering it to the baby. The arrow moved relentlessly around the dial of the small stopclock, reaching the five-minute mark. The baby was pinkish and both Laura and Lemaistre agreed that the Apgar was now up to seven-plus.

The obstetrician smiled. "All's well that ends well," he remarked, and then turned to his neonatologist and said, "You can take over from here, Laura. If you need any help, I'll be in my office writing it up."

He handed her the oxygen, nodded to the nurses, both of whom replied practically in unison, "Goodnight, Dr. Lemaistre," and left the room.

The nurses were closing up shop when they heard Laura suddenly call out, "Shit! The tank's empty. Get me the backup, stat!"

One of the nurses hurried to the wall, took the emergency oxygen tank from its fixture, and handed it to Laura. She took it and a second later shouted "Goddammit, this thing's empty, too. What the hell kind of hospital is this?"

She turned to the nearest nurse and commanded, "Try to ventilate him with an Ambu. I'll be back as quickly as I can."

Even as she was rushing frantically out of the O.R. she realized that she should have stayed and used the ventilation bag while someone else sought the oxygen. Yet at the same instant she reminded herself that only she was aware of how grave the situation was and would therefore move fastest.

The nurse at the station far down the corridor was startled to hear a frantic voice calling, "Oxygen—somebody get some goddamn oxygen!"

She looked up and saw Laura in her O.R. greens, sterile covers still on her shoes, racing toward her like a lunatic. She was reaching for her keys to the supply just as Laura arrived, out of breath and furious.

"I'll get it for you right away, Doctor," she said nervously, turning around and starting to open the supply room door. In her panic, she was fumbling for the correct key.

"Hurry, dammit," Laura urged.

The harsh admonition only made the nurse more flustered. Laura finally snatched the keys from her hand, opened the door, grabbed a small oxygen tank, and lugged it with all her strength down the corridor as fast as she could.

At first the baby was obscured by the two nurses ministering to him.

"Let me at him," Laura barked.

The nurses stepped to either side and Laura saw the baby. He was a very deep blue. And motionless.

No amount of oxygen could revive him now.

Laura stood in the middle of the room like a statue of ice, clutching the now-useless tank of oxygen. People seemed to be swirling around her. Her ears perceived fragments of words: "Call Dr. Lemaistre. . . . Tell the mother. . . . Take the child. . . . morgue . . ."

Then suddenly things came into focus again. For Lemaistre had called out to her in a manner that sounded like a captain upbraiding a sloppy private.

"Is this the first time you've gotten hysterical during a procedure, Dr. Castellano?"

She did not reply.

Then he added with ironic indulgence, "Perhaps you should arrange not to be on call when you're having your period."

Laura refused to let herself be provoked.

"That baby could have lived," she stated calmly . . . and categorically.

"The result might have been more favorable," Lemaistre conceded.

"Come on, Doctor," Laura replied with annoyance. "You know damn well the baby *should* have lived. It was a screw-up. The hospital screwed up. Are you denying that, Dr. Lemaistre?"

"Perhaps you are perfect, Dr. Castellano. But in my somewhat greater experience, I've found that even with the best of intentions, normal people can make mistakes."

"Not this kind of stupid, totally avoidable mistake, dammit. This was negligence—inexcusable negligence."

He was still unruffled. "I have also found, Dr. Castellano, that normal people do not enjoy being reprimanded by children. If you feel so strongly about what happened, why don't you speak to the head of your department? Or, for that matter, my department? Now if you'll excuse me, I've got another patient in prodromal labor."

He turned and started to walk calmly away. At first Laura thought to herself, prodromal labor means she won't be ready for at least five hours. Why didn't you at least flatter my intelligence by giving me a more plausible excuse for chickening out? And then she called out, "Dr. Lemaistre."

He stopped. "Yes, Dr. Castellano?"

"Have you told the parents?"

"Yes. I'm not the kind of doctor who is afraid to convey bad news. And I've already placed the mother under sedation."

"May I ask how you put it to them?"

"I said that the baby was born in very poor condition and our very best efforts could not sustain him. Would you have put it any differently, Dr. Castellano?"

Before she could reply, he had turned again and was nearly out of the room.

Laura stood there, too worn by her efforts, the baby's death, and the postmortem dialogue to be able to think clearly. One of the O.R. nurses came up to her.

"Laura, please don't take offense if I tell you Dr. Lemaistre is a skilled man—and a good man. I'm sure deep down he was as upset as you are. But none of us can do this kind of job and mourn for every one we lose. We would go mad."

Laura mutely nodded her thanks. And as the nurse departed, she thought to herself, you don't understand either, Sister, I'm not mad— I'm angry.

Up till now, Laura had taken a kind of perverse pride in the fact that she did not know how to type. It was yet another part of her self-assertion that she would not fit into the cookie-cutter stereotype of the "typical woman." She therefore had to impose upon the good graces of one of the day nurses, just now coming on duty, to sit with her in the ward nurse's office and type up a letter—in quadruplicate. It was addressed not to her own chief of Pediatrics and the chairman of Ob/Gyn— they of course would receive carbons—but to Ivan Caldwell, M.D., director of the hospital.

After relating the night's events as concisely as possible, she asked Dr. Caldwell if he would take some action to avoid a repetition of "this sort of stupid, tragic ineptitude."

The young nurse typed furiously to keep up with the swift flow of Laura's outrage. As the nurse was reading back the letter, she remarked pointedly, "I think you left something out, Dr. Castellano."

"Oh?"

"You didn't name your next of kin."

"I don't follow. I'm not about to die, nurse."

She shook her head in disagreement. "That's not how I see it. I'd call this a suicide note."

Laura was late for rounds, and so, as soon as she had addressed envelopes for three of the letters, she picked them up, rushed downstairs to hand them to the hospital receptionist, and hurried to the Pediatric wards. She sleepwalked through the rest of the day.

She finally got off duty at five-thirty and went to grab a quick sandwich in the cafeteria.

Then, en route to her room, she stopped by her mailbox to see if there was yet any reply from Washington about her application to the National Institutes of Health. But there was only some junk mail (mostly circulars from drug companies), a phone bill—and an envelope with "Dr. Laura Castellano" written by hand.

She suppressed a yawn as she opened it but was wide awake by the time she finished reading.

Dear Dr. Castellano:

I would be grateful if you would stop by my office at seven P.M. *this evening. If you have another engagement, please cancel it, as the matter I wish to discuss is of some considerable urgency.*

Yours truly,
Ivan Caldwell, M.D.
Director

She glanced at her watch. It was six-fifteen; barely enough time to go up and take a shower—and perhaps two aspirin.

The director's secretary knew Laura's name without having to ask when she arrived just before seven.

"Good evening, Dr. Castellano. Go right in. I'll buzz Dr. Caldwell."

Even before she had fully opened the door to the director's office, she realized that this was not going to be an intimate tête-à-tête. On the contrary, it looked like a committee of white coats—or perhaps more accurately, a posse—had been organized to confront her.

"Come in, Dr. Castellano," said the director, the only one in civilian garb, as he stood up politely. "Is there anyone here you don't know?"

Laura glanced around the room. She recognized her chief of service, Lemaistre, and his boss, but was unfamiliar with the bony, bespectacled, gray-haired woman who quickly rose and introduced herself.

"I'm Muriel Conway, head of Nursing." She smiled, offering her hand.

"Please sit down, Dr. Castellano," the director said, pointing to a chair at what had to be the epicenter of the large room.

She sat obediently, too numbed by fatigue to be nervous.

"Well," Caldwell began. "I suppose you know why I've asked you to come by."

"I think so," Laura allowed, "but I'm kind of surprised that it's turned into such a . . . group affair."

"I thought the reason would be evident, Doctor," the director replied, "for your unfortunate letter tacitly implicates everyone present."

"With due respect, sir, I would apply 'unfortunate' to the *situation* my letter describes."

The director let her comment fly past him. He then gave what he deemed the correct version of the situation.

"Since receiving your note, I've made a thorough investigation into the events of this morning and it's clear to me that you've behaved extremely unprofessionally."

What the hell is he talking about? she thought to herself. She struggled to retain her poise, for her intuition warned her that Caldwell was trying to provoke her into an angry outburst so he could fire her on the spot.

But she surprised him by conceding, "I've thought about it, too, Dr. Caldwell, and I know I was intemperate. I should not have been so emotional in the O.R. It didn't help matters any, and it certainly couldn't bring the baby back to life."

She paused and then added pointedly, "Only oxygen could have done that."

This remark elicited a few uneasy coughs.

"Anyway, I'm very sorry I flew off the handle."

"That's very mature of you, Dr. Castellano, and I thank you. But I'm afraid you're missing the larger point."

"Sir?"

"We are conscientious physicians. And we've also, as the young people say, 'lost our cool' at one time or another. One of the great and inevitable burdens of this profession is that we often get emotionally involved with our patients."

Dr. Caldwell leaned across his desk and said, "But it is a cardinal rule that one doctor never impugns another."

"With due respect, sir, I've never read that anywhere. I mean, it's certainly not in the Hippocratic Oath."

"Dr. Castellano, I will not dignify that remark with an answer. Let me just repeat that it is universally accepted that doctors must take for granted that their colleagues have the best possible intentions."

"And what if you see a mistake that's so egregious that you can't accept this 'article of faith'? I mean, if someone, say, saw a drunken surgeon kill a healthy patient?"

"Don't be absurd, Laura. Then of course you would report that to his superior."

He paused till he could discern a look of relief on her face, then added, "But never in writing."

Again there was a sound of people shifting in their seats. The director rose.

"I think I've made my point, Dr. Castellano. Thank you for dropping by."

As Laura was walking down toward the elevators, she felt a hand on her shoulder. She stopped. It was Dr. Lemaistre.

"Laura," he said, smiling, "you are a very beautiful woman."

"And what is that supposed to mean, Doctor?"

"It means you will have no trouble whatsoever finding another job for next year."

FORTY-ONE

Barney had finally convinced Bennett to let him be present when the surgery was performed.

"What the hell good are you gonna do me when I'm out cold?" Bennett asked.

"But you forget my specialty is the unconscious, Landsmann. I might do a little groping in your brain while they're working on your spine. Anyway, you know that doctors are always on their toes when they're being watched—and I actually remember some of my neurology."

"I'm sorry, Livingston, you still haven't given me a convincing reason."

"Hey, Landsmann, this may come as a shock to you because you've never heard the word, but I'm your *friend*."

Barney won the day.

Barney was there to joke with Bennett as they administered the pre-op injection, and his was the first face his friend saw when he regained consciousness.

"How did it go?" Bennett asked sleepily.

"It went, Landsmann," Barney reassured him. "Kirk tells me the pictures are pretty. No one will ever accuse you of not having a strong backbone."

Bennett was quiet for a moment and then asked, "Can I withhold laughing at that?"

"For how long?" Barney asked.

"Till the neurologist confirms I can cut more than a Christmas turkey."

"Landsmann," said Barney affectionately, "you *are* a turkey."

Bennett smiled.

But in the days that followed, Bennett did not smile again. Anxiety had made a prisoner of his facial muscles. Because he knew his whole future depended on a few basic and painful tests he would undergo at the hands of Laszlo Farkas, Yale's senior neurologist.

Barney once again insisted upon being present.

"I've heard of Farkas," he said reassuringly. "He's got a great rep as a diagnostician."

To which Bennett commented, "Unlike his rep as a human being."

"How's that?" Barney asked.

"He isn't one," Bennett replied. "You've heard of doctors who have nerves of steel. They say this guy has a heart of cast iron."

"Screw his personality, Bennett. At least he won't sugarcoat the truth."

"I'm not sure I want to know the truth," Bennett said with a sense of foreboding.

At first, it seemed that the icy-mannered Professor Farkas could speak only one word—and even that was in an unknown language. He prepared Bennett for an EMG (electromyelogram) simply by using a series of gestures interspersed with exclamations of "Aha" in various tones of voice. This definitive test would measure the impairment, if any, in the normal transmission of impulses from Bennett's brain to his precious hands.

Bennett asked Farkas to allow him to look at the oscilloscope during the procedure. The professor replied by oscillating his fingers in a negative gesture. He seemed to be saying, "However skilled you may be in your area of medicine, you do not merit collegial status with me."

But, in fact, there was no need to see the screen, or even to exchange any words. For both men (all three, since Barney was lurking in a corner) would be able to hear the hisses and creaks of the EMG's loudspeaker, giving an auditory impression of the electrical impulses being transmitted through Bennett's peripheral nervous system.

For Bennett it could just as well have been the electric chair.

Although he did not wince at the painful shocks the doctor kept applying to his arms, the sounds that he was hearing confirmed the agonizing truth. Farkas had already indicated that he suspected—without even having to test—that Bennett had nerve entrapment in his cervical spine. He even went as far as to say that his diagnostic instinct told him it would be irreparable.

But that had been merely a doctor's cold, clinical hypothesis.

Now the sounds made clear to all three doctors that the news was bad.

Thus, when Farkas—with a smile of satisfaction that his diagnosis had been proved correct—exclaimed "Aha," he was in fact signing the death warrant to Bennett Landsmann's career as a surgeon.

Barney insisted upon driving him home. For once there was no protest, and Bennett slumped into the front passenger seat and let his head loll back.

"Feeling dizzy?" Barney asked.

"Yeah," Bennett answered. "But that's the least of it. Tell me, Dr. Livingston. What does the surgeon do when he can't be a surgeon anymore?"

That was the question. How could anyone who had trained for nearly twenty years and was just about to *start* a surgical career be told that all those years of sleepless nights, sweat, and toil had been annihilated by a policeman's boot? And all because Bennett had acted in the noblest manner of a physician.

Herschel was waiting back at the apartment. He had known this was the day and wanted to be present when his son received the verdict.

Bennett told him the news in words deep from the abyss.

"Look, it's not the end of the world," Herschel argued. "My son, you're still a doctor. There are other specialties—"

"Like mine, for instance," Barney offered. "You could be paralyzed from the neck down and still do lots of good as a psychiatrist."

"No, thanks," Bennett joked bitterly, "I'd only do your job if I was paralyzed *above* the neck."

Barney went out to the Greek pizzeria on Howe Street and brought back dinner for the three of them. By the time he returned, it was clear that Herschel had proposed to Bennett every imaginable medical specialty in which his injured arm would not be a drawback. Yet his son was adamant.

"Dad, I told you I don't want to be a shrink or a flea. And I couldn't bear the thought of doing anesthesia while somebody else was cutting. Dammit, those are different ballgames. And I don't feel that temperamentally I could hack it in a single one of them."

He looked at Barney. "Livingston, do you think you would be happy doing kidney transplants?"

"No way," Barney answered with painful candor. He turned to Mr. Landsmann. "Sir, I'm afraid that Bennett's really right. In the old days surgeons were actually a group completely separate from doctors. Bennett was a natural surgeon. He had the reflexes, the right mentality, the courage to move quickly—and the dedication—"

"Cut the eulogy," said Bennett wryly. "Save it for when I'm relaxing in my coffin."

He put his hands on his temples and complained, "God, what a headache. It must be from that damn anesthetic—or the mickey I got slipped by you two characters. I gotta get some air."

He walked to the door of his terrace and pulled at the handle. It was stuck. He pulled again.

And then he realized Barney had locked it. He turned to his friend and said, "Very cute, Livingston. But don't you think if I wanted to kill myself I could find better ways? I mean, I still can wield a scalpel. I could slice myself like a salami."

Then he muttered, barely audibly, "Besides, I'm already dead."

Barney rose and grabbed his best friend by the shoulders.

"No, you're not, goddammit, Bennett—You're alive! Just stop feeling sorry for yourself and sit down and talk. Let's all see if we can think of what move to make next."

"For one I'll sue the whole state of Connecticut," Bennett said with anger.

"And after that?"

Bennett sat down and shook his head from side to side.

"I don't know, Barn," he replied, giving in to the assaults of helplessness. "I really don't know what to do. Help me."

He looked up at his friend. "Please."

Barney sat down across from Bennett. "Listen, kiddo, doctors shouldn't treat their own families." And then he added, "And I consider you a brother. So let's call this unofficial."

"Okay, Barney," Bennett answered dryly, "let's hear your fraternal words."

"Well, first of all you really know your medicine. You're *capable* of being great at almost any specialty. That's intellectually—but not emo-

tionally. You're too angry, Ben. And our profession has just one outlet
for a rage like yours."

"Yeah, what?"

"Forensic medicine."

Bennett's face showed that Barney had struck a chord. Herschel
looked confused.

"Excuse me, Barney," Herschel interposed politely. "I am not familiar with this specialty you're suggesting."

"*Forensic,* Mr. Landsmann, comes from the Latin *forum,* meaning
'place of debate,' and *ensis,* meaning 'sword.' In other words, the practice
of medicine in a court of law. It's probably the most challenging discipline in either profession."

He looked at his friend and continued. "But I know my pal Bennett
likes a challenge. And he's got all the equipment—knowledge, speed—
and most of all, the courage to deal with the unexpected." He turned
once again to Bennett. "Will you think about it? A sword is even sharper
than a scalpel."

In the brief time Barney took to explain his suggestion to Herschel,
Bennett had been debating with himself.

"Hey, guys, we're talking three more years of school—"

"Maybe four," his classmate admitted. "But in the end you are both
a doctor's doctor and a lawyer's lawyer. And you'll have the thing your
psyche needs the most—a place to *fight.*"

Bennett lowered his head as Barney and Herschel waited patiently
for his reaction.

"Dad, what do you think?" he asked.

"I can't presume, Ben. I can only offer my opinion and let you
decide. But what I feel is . . . Barney has a good idea. It all depends on
whether you could take going back to a classroom and starting over."

"It's not quite starting over, Dad. I might be able to look at it as
another kind of residency."

"Then you'll consider it?" asked Herschel anxiously.

"Yeah, I guess so. I mean, if I can somehow convince myself I have
the guts."

"Sleep on it, Ben," Barney suggested. "Nothing's gonna change
overnight—except hopefully your mind. Fair enough?"

"Fair enough."

Herschel put on his coat and said goodnight to them both.

"I've booked into the Park Plaza. I think I'll go try and get some
sleep. I'll bring fresh rolls for breakfast. I noticed a bakery along the
way."

He turned to Barney and said, "You're a good boy," and then to Bennett, "and you're not so bad, either."

He smiled and took a pinch of his son's cheek.

They waited at the elevator with him. He waved a mute goodbye with the semblance of a smile.

Bennett turned to Barney and remarked, "Okay, you're dismissed, soldier."

"The hell I am," Barney retorted, and then joked, "I bought you dinner. The least you could do is let me stay overnight."

"You crazy shrink. Do you still believe that I'd try and 'off' myself?"

"No," Barney protested, "I just don't want to . . ."

He stopped himself. He owed his friend the truth. "Yes, Landsmann. Because you haven't gotten through the worst part yet."

"Namely?"

"You're gonna sleep peacefully. That's the good part."

"And? . . ." Bennett asked.

"Sometime tomorrow morning you'll wake up and have to face the world—and that's the hardest part of all."

"Okay, old buddy, you may be right."

Bennett put a hand on his friend's shoulder and they walked back into the apartment.

Barney slept fitfully and finally surrendered to insomnia just after six, when he got out of bed and padded from the guest room to the kitchen for some coffee that would clear his mind.

His glance wandered to the terrace door—and suddenly he noticed. Ben was standing there motionless, simply staring at the city.

"Hey, Landsmann, want coffee?" Barney asked.

But Bennett did not answer. He was in some kind of trance.

"It's funny . . . from this high up I can see the whole hospital. I've been looking at it since it started to get light. From here it suddenly looks like a giant tombstone. And it is—that's where I buried the ten best years of my life."

"A cat has nine lives, Ben," Barney retorted. "You're a very cool cat, so that leaves you with eight more."

Bennett remained motionless, looking out at the slums behind the hospital.

"You were right," he said softly.

"About what?" Barney asked, handing him a cup of coffee.

"I think I would've jumped yesterday, Barn. You must be a real psychiatrist . . . you really read my mind."

"That's not professional technique, Ben. That comes from being someone's friend," replied Barney softly.

"You know something else?" Bennett continued, his eyes fixed on the still-sleeping city. "There were only three things keeping me from the high dive—Mom and Dad. And you."

Then they sat down to have coffee and discuss the latest crises in the field of sport.

Herschel returned a little after seven-thirty, bearing a cornucopia of still-warm rolls and pastries.

"Hey, Dad," joked Bennett, "we're not feeding the whole university. It's just the three of us."

"Don't second-guess me," he replied. "Probably the one thing you're not is a parent. So come on, boys, dig in."

And Herschel was correct. A half-hour later there was scarcely a crumb remaining.

And the matter of Bennett's decision had been studiously avoided.

At last the former chief resident in Surgery at Yale announced, "It's gonna be a bitch and I don't know if someone kicking forty still has the patience to slog through those lousy courses."

Herschel and Barney exchanged expressions of relief.

"Okay, guys," said Bennett. "Let's say I try it."

"Good man," Barney exclaimed. "What school are you going to honor with your presence?"

"Ah," Bennett replied, "therein lies the rub."

"I don't understand," said Herschel.

For the first time since he'd received the bad news, Bennett smiled. "Do you think the world is ready for a Jewish spade with *three* degrees from Harvard?"

Barney reinforced his friend's good mood. "Christ, Landsmann, do I envy you. Not only will you go back to the womb, you'll also be in walking distance from the 'Cliffe."

"No, Livingston. You're way off base," Bennett remarked mischievously. "I'll make history as the only guy who played for *both* sides in the Malpractice Cup!"

"I'll drink to that," said Barney, raising his cup to clink with Bennett's.

"I'll drink to that as well," said Herschel.

To which his adopted son added, "*L'Chayim.*"

While Bennett was planning his return to Cambridge with the deans of Harvard Law School, half a world away his former classmate was busy mapping an itinerary of his own. Hank Dwyer and the two officers who had been his neighbors in their Saigon pleasure dome had to make hard decisions.

Nixon was pulling the GIs out of Vietnam as fast as they had once poured in. And the three men would imminently be getting tickets stateside.

And so the trio sat down to discuss what steps to take about their Vietnamese "families." One of them did not have a wife back home, so his course was simpler. He took the attractive Oriental girl-woman who'd borne his son and daughter to the U.S. Embassy, where a great part of the staff were working night and day to process new Americans, register their births and marriages, and plan their journeys home.

The second officer had decided to go back alone to start divorce proceedings to get rid of his pushy and aggressive American wife, and then import his docile, worshipful companion and their child from this beleaguered country. For though the U.S. had lost the war, he at least had found what true domestic bliss could be.

For Hank, things were not so clear-cut. Though he appreciated Mai-ling and enjoyed the company of Gregory, his two-year-old (especially since he could see him only when he *wanted* to), there was the matter of his already considerable contribution to the U.S. population back in Boston.

Dealing with Cheryl had been easy from his current vantage point, which was, however, also a point of no return.

For Hank himself had changed. He had seen life beyond the city limits, so to speak. His world was larger than before and his horizons wider. Cheryl simply wasn't his idea of the kind of woman he needed now. Yet getting a divorce from a religious Catholic would be difficult enough. With Mai-ling and young Gregory around, it might even be impossible.

"I've got no choice, guys," he concluded to his fellow officers. "If it's all right with you two, I'd like to leave Mai-ling in the house and—you know—make arrangements on the other side."

"Well, you'll register them at the Embassy, won't you?" one of the officers asked.

"Uh, sure," said Hank. "That won't obligate me to—import them, will it?"

"No, but your kid will be a U.S. citizen. And a U.S. passport could come in very handy if we should lose—I mean, if they should lose Saigon."

For Hank it was simply a case of peer pressure.

*   *   *

He found himself in the midst of pandemonium. The lines of soldiers and their families stretched far beyond the compound's high white
stuccoed walls. There were children of all ages and widely varied pig-
mentation. Some of these "Amerasians" were as white as snow and yet
had inherited their mothers' high cheekbones and almond eyes. Those
who had been fathered by black soldiers had the golden color of
Polynesians.

The sheer number of them was staggering, even more so since the
Embassy officials estimated that barely a quarter of the GI-fathered
children had been put on record.

Hank and his colleagues had to wait for several hours in the baking
sun to place their unofficial families underneath the protective canopy of
the Stars and Stripes.

Naturally, Hank lied. By now it had become a well-honed skill. He
did nothing to dispel Mai-ling's impression that her fate would be like
that of her sisters in the villa. She would have to be patient, of course—
that was one of the attractive features of these Asian women. But the time
would come and Hank would send for her, and they would be together
once again.

Not long afterwards, Hank received official word that he was being
transferred home. Since he had served not one but two entire tours of
duty, he could of course be honorably discharged.

But he was much too patriotic—and perplexed—to make so bold a
move. And so, to the surprise of his superiors, he asked to be transferred
somewhere—anywhere—as long as it was on the West Coast. This would
disengage him from the Vietnamese connection and still enable him to
deal long distance with the "situation" back in Boston.

The night before he left Saigon, Hank made a sentimental journey
back to Joy Street. He brought a camera with fast film so he could
remind himself in later years it had not been a dream.

Some of the neon lights were flashing still. But even those that were
aglow seemed to be fading rapidly. The place and its activities were
running down.

For old times' sake he went to Mikko's, where he had met Mai-ling.

"Hello, Captain," said the proprietor, grinning. The only thing
apparently intact in his establishment was his good humor. "Good to see
you. Everybody seems to go now."

"Yeah," Hank agreed and looked around at the empty chairs and
tables, some piled up for storage. The spotlights that once made the

crowded dance floor brighter than day were shut off. Even the jukebox seemed to glow more dimly.

"You want your usual?" asked the proprietor (who was now his own doorman, bartender, waiter, and chef).

"Yeah," Hank replied distractedly, regretting that he had made this visit, which would cloud his memories of the euphoria he had known when Joy Street was in flower.

He leaned on the bar and looked around.

There still were women. They were not in short supply in a country that had seen a generation of their brothers decimated.

"We have a brand new girl," said Mikko, handing Hank his drink. "Fresh from the country. Like a flower. And she virgin. You would like I introduce you?"

Before he could answer, the enthusiastic Mikko was presenting one of his harem to him.

"Captain Dwyer, this is ... Dio-xi, but we call her 'Dixie' for short."

"Hello," said Hank, seeing how exquisite the very young girl was—like some painted cherub or angel on a chapel wall.

"Can I buy you a drink, Dixie?" he asked.

She glanced at Mikko for instructions.

"It's okay, Dixie, Captain Dwyer's a friend," he said kindly. "I'll make you a ginger ale."

With Hank's rudimentary Vietnamese, and Dixie's broken English, they sat at a table trying to have a conversation. And of course he asked the inevitable question. The old what's-a-nice-girl-like-you-doing-in-a-place-like-this gambit. Apparently her village had been overrun—not once but three times. First the Vietcong, then the GIs, and then as soon as the U.S. soldiers left, the Communists took over again. And wrought bloody revenge on those who had collaborated with the Americans.

Her father had been shot. Her mother had been raped and shot. She had hidden in a tree and escaped everything except the worst experience of all: having to watch and feel powerless. And her flight inevitably ended here on Joy Street.

Hank listened, and from somewhere in his well-insulated conscience took pity on the girl.

"How old are you?" he asked.

"Sixteen," she replied.

"How old are you really?" he persisted.

She lowered her head and confessed. "Twelve."

There was an awkward moment, after which Hank murmured with embarrassment, "I'd like to give you money, Dixie."

"You must first speak to Mikko about that," she answered bashfully.

"No, no, no," he quickly interrupted. "I want to give you money to get out of here. Like maybe find a real job. I know there are even some convent schools where you wouldn't have to . . ." He couldn't even bring himself to say the words.

"You really kind," she answered softly. "But I cannot."

"No, no, I insist," said Hank, and pressed two fifty-dollar bills into her tiny hand. He stood up.

"I've gotta go now, Dixie. Take care of yourself, okay?"

She nodded, lacking the emotional vocabulary for the acknowledgment of kindness.

Hank waved to Mikko and walked out into the street.

He had taken barely twenty steps when he discovered that he'd left his camera on the nightclub table. He quickly hurried back. Now there was no one in the bar but—minor miracle—his camera was still there.

Then he heard voices from the corner and glanced over. It was Dixie, handing over everything he'd given her to Mikko.

The jewel in the crown of the U.S. Medical Establishment, the National Institutes of Health, is a twenty-minute drive from the White House in Bethesda, Maryland. There are sixty-three different buildings, most of which are of red brick. Their tranquil setting resembles a college campus.

Yet the NIH hospital itself is the largest red-brick building in the world, with no fewer than nine miles of corridors.

And genius is the norm.

At least eighty-eight Nobel Prize winners have worked in the area behind the huge hospital, which is dotted with laboratories of all kinds. Here pioneering research goes on three hundred and sixty-five days a year to fight cancer, heart disease, neurological disorders, and other more arcane but equally savage afflictions.

The tenured Senior Fellows supervise those lucky enough to have run the difficult gauntlet of application and been appointed for a two- or three-year Junior Fellowship. Selection depends largely on the importance of the proposed research project and the committee's estimation of whether the applicant is gifted enough to pursue it.

Very few of the Fellows do any work in the hospital. They mostly remain buried in their red-brick labs, peering with electronic microscopes, waiting for a minuscule miracle to swim into their field. Within the profession, they are sometimes jokingly referred to as "Rat Doctors."

But it is an unassailable fact that a country doctor who trudges five miles in the snow to treat a patient in a log cabin is far better equipped if he is carrying the latest drug discovered in an NIH lab.

Laura Castellano had known that her chance for acceptance as a Research Fellow was particularly small. For working at the NIH could fulfill a doctor's military obligation. And the average physician preferred Bunsen burners to burning villages.

But Laura's project also impressed the selecting committee for several important reasons.

First, those still in the process of building a family realized that an early-warning system to detect imminent hemorrhaging in preterm babies might be of genuine value to them personally. Her proposal was sound and pragmatic:

> *Thanks to the latest developments in ultrasound scanning, we can now document the* timing *and* extent *of the hemorrhages and correlate the temporal relationship between the* onset *of a bleed and other important events occurring in the baby.*
>
> *For instance, we would regularly measure blood gas tensions (oxygen level, carbon dioxide level, degree of blood acidosis). Fluctuations in blood pressure would also be carefully recorded, as well as monitoring of the neonate's clotting ability to detect any tendency toward a bleeding diathesis. . . .*

Furthermore, Laura's project seemed like one that could produce results in a relatively short time and would be useful to cite when Congress deliberated the size of its appropriations to the Institutes.

And yet Laura never knew how close she came to having her application rejected—that it was only the new "Equal Opportunity" laws that saved her.

For as long as anyone could remember, applications for schools, colleges, and civil service jobs had to be accompanied by a photo of the applicant—whereby the ethnic background of a candidate could be revealed.

In this braver, more democratic world created by Congress, candidates were to be judged on their merits alone: it was strictly forbidden for the referees to make any allusion whatsoever in their letters to the candidate's race or creed.

Of course, it was clear to the blue ribbon committee that Laura Castellano was female—a point in her favor. But the lack of a photograph kept her from being rejected on other grounds: the damning fact that she was beautiful.

For it has been common knowledge since time immemorial that beauty and brains cannot possibly go together. Thus, had the arbiters known what Laura looked like, they would have instantly rejected her as a dumb blonde.

During her final weeks at Queen's, Laura made the rounds of Toronto's used car dealers to find herself the wheels that are indispensable for anyone working in the Washington area. Her depression had done wonders for her bank account. All that winter, her obsessive commitment to the neonatal ICU rarely allowed her into the light of day, much less a shop that sold anything more than milk and graham crackers. She had not even picked up a newspaper. Her idea of leisure reading was the *New England Journal.*

She was thus able to afford the two thousand dollars "Honest Ernie" was asking for a "slightly pre-used" Chevrolet Nova. Laura was even canny enough to get him to throw in a new set of tires.

On the last day of June she said goodbye to the few friends she had made—two ICU nurses and the cashier at the cafeteria. She loaded the trunk with her bag and some cartons of books and headed south.

In two hours she had crossed the bridge over Lake Erie into Buffalo, New York, and headed toward Pittsburgh. Only *then,* having long passed the latitude of Boston and New York, did she turn east, stopping only to feed herself and her car.

She reached Washington at sunrise, which made the still-sleeping city look like a travel agent's poster. A few lines of Wordsworth popped into her head from the distant memories of Midwood English class—"This city now doth like a garment wear/the beauty of the morning."

After more than a year of unrelieved gloom, she felt hopeful. Maybe Washington would not belie its outward beauty. Maybe she would find happiness here.

Laura had rented an apartment in Bethesda but was too excited to go "home," even to freshen up. She drove straight to the NIH, where—to her delight—she saw that at 7 A.M. she was far from the earliest arrival. By noon she was ensconced in her lab and had already started looking over her protocol notes.

As she was taking off her fresh white coat with its tiny blue and white nameplate, she heard a woman inquire after her from across the lab.

"Has Dr. Castellano arrived yet? I have a long-distance call in my office for Dr. Castellano."

Puzzled, Laura made herself known and followed the secretary to the director's office where she picked up the phone.

"Hey, Castellano. Welcome back to the land of the free and the home of the brave."

"Barney! Hey, did you lose my extension number or something?"

"No, Laura," he whispered at the other end, "this was just a ploy to get you into the director's office so you could casually meet him—or at least his secretary. Be *real* nice to her—they're usually the power behind the throne."

"Dr. Livingston," she said, now trying to sound as formal as possible, "I don't believe I should be tying up this phone, so I'll get back to you sometime this afternoon. Is that all right?"

"Of course—but mark my words, this call will reap dividends. So long."

As Laura hung up, the secretary inquired, "Friend or colleague?"

She knew the right answer to that one.

"Colleague. Dr. Livingston's on the faculty at NYU." As of three months ago, she thought but did not say.

"What sort of research is he engaged in?" the secretary asked politely. It was inconceivable to her that a doctor could actually be treating patients.

"I'm afraid I'm pledged to secrecy," Laura replied apologetically.

"Oh," she answered, with undisguised admiration. "I can appreciate that. And it's quite proper of you not to tell me. My name is Florence, and if you have any problems, just come to me."

Laura thanked her and headed out, thinking to herself, Florence, you'd flip if you knew that the lab animals in Barney's research project were not rats or mice or even monkeys. Just doctors.

Laura's high expectations of Washington were not dispelled. She daily rubbed white-coated shoulders with some of the greatest medical minds in the world. And as far as resources were concerned, there was no book, no journal, no piece of apparatus—however exotic or outlandish—that could not be produced inside of sixty minutes.

And the Institutes did not seem to have that cutthroat atmosphere so characteristic of college campuses. The Juniors knew that they were there for a limited time and were aspiring to get enough done—and results published—so they could obtain tenure at their own universities. This was not like Chem 20, where your neighbor would sabotage your experiment if you so much as looked out of the window for a moment at an autumn leaf.

The two other young pediatricians with whom she shared the lab and its computer were both congenial—and happily married. The proof of this was the swiftness with which they invited Laura to dinner at their homes. They wanted their wives to have an entire evening to satisfy themselves that the "Boston Bombshell" (as she was referred to behind her back) was not about to explode in their household. And Laura fully understood that if she hoped to have company while working late, she had better reassure the wives that any nocturnal activities she would undertake with their husbands would be strictly intellectual.

Laura's commitment to Pediatrics was genuine. But it was a measure of how estranged she had become from her own motivations that she failed to recognize that it also demonstrated a powerful maternal instinct. And she was thirty-six years old. Time on her biological clock was running short.

She began to have terrible nightmares. Though she had no idea where Palmer and Jessica were now living, she was aware that in the same year she and Palmer were divorced, unto them a child was born. A little "preemie"—miraculously weighing in at a hefty eight pounds. Her nightmares re-enacted fantasies of meeting the new Mr. and Mrs. Talbot, seeing their child, and crying out "No, no, no, he's mine! That baby is mine!"

Yet despite Barney's badgering, she was reluctant to seek psychiatric help. For she was terribly afraid of many things: of letting it be known around the Institutes that she was anything but Wonder Woman, or *El Peñon*—that rock of rocks, Gibraltar. And, more importantly, she was afraid to confront the desperate conflicts in her own mind. She even had bizarre dreams in which she had played two roles; she was her own mother cursing and castigating herself as "Little Laura" for being too unworthy to survive an angel like her sister.

In her waking life there was only one Laura Castellano she had any respect for at all. The one who, along with her supervisor, Dain Oliver, had a paper accepted by the *American Journal of Pediatrics* before her first Christmas at NIH. (Even by sprinting superbrains this was considered a fast start.) Moreover, she would get to read it at an international congress in Mexico City during the third week of January. As she told Barney on the phone, "I'm flying!"

At least she admired her own academic achievements.

FORTY-TWO

The first International Conference of Neonatologists was scheduled for Mexico City from January seventeenth through twenty-fifth, 1974. From all indications it would be an important event. When it comes to saving babies, there are no political divisions East or West. There is no Third World, just one single global family. No country had an infant mortality rate of zero; which meant there were battles yet to be won.

The group from NIH came close to being the official "American Delegation," and all of them were staying at the Maria Isabel Sheraton, where the general meetings were to be held. All during the flight Laura sat next to Dr. Oliver and coaxed her kindhearted director into listening to her fifteen-minute paper again and again.

"You'll be fine, Laura, you'll be fine," he reassured her. "You don't have to memorize it—after all, you'll have the text right in front of you."

"I know, Dain, but I keep having this terrible premonition that I'll get up there and suddenly forget how to read."

Oliver laughed. "I hardly think that's likely, Laura. Just remind yourself of how far you've come since the first grade. But I can understand your panic. I still remember being unable to keep my breakfast down the day I read my first paper."

"Oh, I'm not worried about *that*," Laura replied. "I don't intend to eat any."

Just then the plane descended from the halo of smog that constantly crowned La Cuidad de Mexico and began its final approach.

There was a polyglot hum in the crowded hotel lobby. Stretched above the elegant marble registration counter was a banner reading ¡BIENVENIDO A LOS SALVADORES DE NIÑOS! Under which was the same welcome to the English, French, and Russian guardian angels of children.

Like her other colleagues from NIH, Laura was preregistered—one of the few real benefits of working for the government, she told herself. There were two messages for "La Doctora Castellano." One was a telegram whose contents she intuited before opening: good wishes from Barney in some macaronic approximation of broken Spanish, which concluded, "*Buena suerte y Breaka un leggo.*"

The second message came in a handwritten envelope on hotel stationery. She had been looking forward to seeing some old friends from Boston and assumed this was a harbinger of those reunions. Instead it was an astonishing communication.

> *¡Querida doctorcillita!*
> *¿Porqué no presentas tu disertación en tu lengua materna?*
> *No te olvida que todavía eres una verdadera castellana.*
> > *Besos y abrazos,*
> > *Tu afectuoso papacito.*

[*Greetings my beloved little doctor. Why aren't you reading your paper in your mother tongue? Don't forget that "Castellano" means a true Castilian. Hugs and kisses, your loving father.*]

"What's the matter, Laura?" asked Dain, who was standing in line behind her. "You're pale. Is it bad news?"

She shook her head, unable to respond.

"It must be the altitude," Oliver concluded. "It takes a while to get used to it. Why don't you go sit down and I'll take care of the bureaucracy for you."

She nodded gratefully and looked for the nearest chair in the lobby. As soon as she was seated she tried to assemble her thoughts. What the hell is my father doing here?

How would she get through the hours between now and eleven-fifteen tomorrow morning when she was scheduled to speak? As soon as she got to her room she tried to call Barney—without success. Why tonight of all nights did her workaholic friend not answer his home phone? She called his office—maybe for some reason he was still there.

But all she got was his answering service. "Is this an emergency?" they inquired solicitously.

No, she thought to herself, I can't have them page him. Forget it—take a couple of those tablets you prescribe for yourself and go to sleep.

She was slightly dizzy the next morning—but that could have been the pills, the altitude, or even the *carne asado* she had tried to eat for dinner. She revived herself with coffee and gave herself a special dispensation to add sugar—which as a doctor she knew was unhealthy and therefore normally eschewed.

Where would her father be sitting, she wondered. This wasn't the U.N. after all. The physicians from any one country might be sitting together, but not necessarily in alphabetical order. Luis might be far away. Or be waiting right inside the door closest to the podium, waiting to pounce on her with a huge embarrassing paternal hug.

In any case, it was too late for speculation. She could hear the public address system quite clearly from outside; the speaker preceding her had finished answering his final question from the floor.

The chairman of the morning session was a ruddy-cheeked Rumanian who insisted upon making his introductions in French (one of the official languages of the congress). It was the first time she had ever heard herself referred to as "*Docteur* Laura Castellano."

She gathered her courage and headed for the podium, eyes downcast, looking neither left nor right. Though the whole purpose of her many hours of rehearsal with Oliver had been to be able to make visual contact with the audience, she read her paper in a hasty monotone, never once looking up from the text.

Chairman Ardeleanu thanked her in florid French and then turned to the audience to ask if there were any brief questions. He recognized a youngish Latin physician who, according to protocol, first identified himself and his provenance: "Jorge Navarro, *Faculdad de pediatría, Universidad Popular de Havana.*"

Laura had been forewarned. The State Department had told them they could expect some provocation from "the usual leftist political plant." But she had never in a million years imagined that the stooge would be directing his fire at *her.*

Why was it, asked the good Dr. Navarro in rapid Spanish, that in the

United States, infant mortality for blacks and Hispanics was higher than for whites?

There was a muttering in the audience, some cries of encouragement but mostly groans of distress and disapproval. Even among those of Navarro's political persuasion there was some dissent at his ungallant choice of an obviously naive young woman as his propaganda target.

"Do I have to answer that?" Laura asked the chairman. "I consider it to have nothing to do with my topic."

The Rumanian either did not know English or pretended not to. He bowed slightly and said, "*Madame peut répondre.*"

Okay, thought Laura, her anger at being singled out momentarily overcoming her stage fright, I'll answer this dogmatic little schmuck with some sophistry of my own.

She responded to the Cuban in the language of his question— indeed, the pure Castilian version. Where did he happen to run across such statistics? Did he know that the black birth rate was twice as large as the white—and that Hispanics had the largest families of any ethnic group in the United States? (She was careful to avoid using the term "America" to refer to her country—which *Latin* Americans always deemed arrogant.)

She lambasted him with excruciating politeness, humbly asking if "our distinguished colleague from the Republic of Cuba could possibly explain the reason—if not the relevance—for his inquiry." No mere straw man, Navarro rose to the task.

"In a so-called 'developed' country, the rate of infant mortality is an unerring reflection of its attitude towards the future generation—and especially to ethnic minorities."

The audience was warming to the debate and the chairman saw no reason to deprive them of this unexpected entertainment by enforcing the five-minute limit on discussion.

"I find that an interesting philosophy, Dr. Navarro," Laura said, taking time to formulate her reply. "And I sympathize with the *Cuban* mothers who suffer an infant mortality exactly *double* that of ours in the U.S. But then of course you are an evolving nation (she was careful not to say "underdeveloped"), and we hope that scientific exchanges at congresses like these will help rectify the situation as soon as possible."

She paused to take a breath, during which time the irrepressible Navarro interrupted, "You are avoiding my question, Doctor."

"Not at all," Laura responded calmly. "You were stating the belief that infant mortality rate reflects the majority's attitude toward minorities. Am I not correct?"

Navarro smiled and folded his arms with satisfaction. "That is indeed the question, Doctor."

"Well then, how would *you* explain, Dr. Navarro, that your patrons in the Soviet Union—I hope you do agree that Russia is a developed country with innumerable ethnic groups—have a mortality rate more than *three* times as high as the United States'. In fact, it is even fifty percent higher than Cuba's."

The air was filled with the silent shouts of "Olé" as Navarro, a wounded bull indeed, sank back in his chair.

Though at this point few still remembered the content of Laura's actual paper, she left the platform to a warm round of applause.

Dain Oliver rushed up to offer her a hearty handshake and a proud pat on the back.

As she glanced over the shoulders of the congratulating colleagues who had surrounded her, she saw him.

Or at least she saw a gaunt, bony man who vaguely resembled her memories of Luis. But once he caught her eye, there was no longer room for doubt. Still he did not move forward and merely waited till she could break free and come to him.

Moments later Laura moved through an ocean of people, wondering how she should act toward her—long-lost? one-time?—father.

If he opened his arms with paternal affection, should she respond? If he merely offered his hand, should she take it as if meeting a stranger? Even in these fleeting seconds she realized that the issue was wholly up to him.

Thus, almost as an act of self-preservation, she stopped short several feet from where he was standing.

He smiled warmly. And the look in his eyes left her in no doubt as to the pride he felt.

When he realized she would come no closer, Luis spoke quietly in Spanish.

"Dr. Castellano?" he asked.

"Yes, Dr. Castellano," she replied.

"How are things?"

"Not bad," she answered. "You've lost weight, Luis."

"Yes," he acknowledged. "That is my only criticism of Cuban democracy—all you can get to drink is rum and I somehow got bored with it. Besides, all civil servants have compulsory exercise. And it hardly befits a member of the Ministry of Health to be drunk or obese—"

"The Ministry of Health?"

"Don't be impressed, Laura. I'm just a functionary. I mostly translate medical articles. I'll print yours if you like."

They were interrupted by Chairman Ardeleanu's voice through the loudspeaker delivering a grandiloquent introduction for the next participant, a professor from Milan.

"Shall we have a cup of coffee, Laurita?" Luis asked.

He's using the old affectionate diminutives, she thought.

"Why not?" she replied blankly.

They turned and left the auditorium together, she still not believing that this was really happening.

"The coffee shop is downstairs," she said, motioning the way.

"Are you crazy?" Luis remarked. "They charge three dollars a cup here! Let's go somewhere and mix with the people."

They walked along the Paseo de la Reforma and after a few minutes turned down what was probably the only street in the *zona rosa* shabby enough for her proletarian father. She was right, and they sat on rickety chairs at one of the outdoor tables.

Luis made some cryptic motions to the owner perched by the till behind his laminated counter. The man waved back in what Laura took to be a gesture meaning, "Got it, Luis."

"That's my old pal Jaime. He's deaf. He likes me because I take the time to 'talk' to him. Also he's very sympathetic to the Revolution."

Luis was looking her over—as if about to begin a complete examination.

"You, too, have lost weight. Are you dieting?"

"No." She smiled. "I've discovered a foolproof method for weight-loss—it's called insomnia."

Suddenly, Luis leaned across the table—closer to her than he had been in all these years. He whispered, "Laura, I must know—please tell me—" He paused and then added anxiously, "Am I a grandfather?"

"I'm no longer a wife, Papacito."

"Oh. I'm sorry."

"He was a shit," Laura replied without rancor.

"Oh well, in that case," Luis responded, "you did well to divorce him."

"He divorced me."

This stopped Luis. "I am sorry for you, *niña*. Truly sorry." But he quickly added, "These days one doesn't have to be united in the church to have a child, you know."

She did not know how to react. And then she realized it was not a question but a preamble to a declaration *he* wanted to make.

"You have another sister and a brother, Laura. Very nice children, both of them."

He said it so matter-of-factly, as if people did this sort of thing every day.

Laura felt hurt and betrayed.

"Aren't you still married to Mama?"

Luis shrugged. "I suppose a priest might say so. But in Cuba the Church is just a tolerated ornament."

Laura asked—as she knew he wanted her to—"Do you have any pictures of your children?"

"Do you really want to see them?" Luis asked gently.

Before she could answer yes, he had his wallet out and was extracting little photographs, which he laid upon the table like a dealer would a hand of cards. One was a picture of herself and Isobel. Another was of Laura alone. Though touched by these, her eyes immediately darted to the boy.

"His name's Ernesto," said Luis.

Somehow she knew it was before he said so.

"And of course you call him 'Ché.' "

Luis nodded, smiling. "Of course. The little girl is . . . Isobel."

Up till now Laura's reactions to her father's revelations had been of astonishment. But now she was actually shocked.

"You named her after—"

Luis nodded. "An act of love, Laurita. I hope you'll meet her one day."

Where, I wonder? Laura asked herself—in Gorky Park?

"Tell me about yourself, Laurita. Tell me how you've been."

She looked back at him. His gaze was unmistakably affectionate, compassionate. And for the first time in her life she believed he loved her and he really wanted to know.

And she started telling him everything.

But first she had to weep.

Darkness was falling as they walked back to the Sheraton. The afternoon session was just breaking up. Dain Oliver spied her and looked manifestly relieved. She waved to him as if to say, I'm fine, I hope you weren't worried. And then she turned to face Luis.

"That's my boss, I think I'd better go back or they'll think that I've defected."

"Of course, of course." Her father nodded. "Just remember *I* am on your team as well." And then he added parenthetically, "The Cubans are not staying at this place."

"I guessed as much," she said. "You're probably at something like the 'El Fleabag,' am I right?"

"Well, fleas are human beings, too," Luis said, parodying himself. "Maybe some day they, too, will rise and break their chains." He then said quickly, "Laura, I must go. I've been playing hookey. But write to me at the address I gave you. Do you promise?"

Laura nodded.

"And I promise I will answer—I can send it via Mexico. I want to know your news. And don't just send me articles. I want a photograph of grandchildren. You hear me, *niña*?"

She nodded once again. Luis opened his arms, wrapped his eldest daughter tightly in them, and whispered something.

Something Laura dared not even think about in her most private thoughts.

She returned to Washington still unaware that for all its power and influence, the nation's capital was just a simple village where the huts were marble. Its only industry was government, its only conversation politics, its paper *The Washington Post*.

Thus what had seemed to Laura no big deal—for her exchanges with Navarro were insignificant in her mind compared to the reunion with her father—was, for Washingtonian consumption, quite a tasty tidbit. And by the time her plane had landed and she returned to her apartment to drop off her bags, the phone was ringing off the hook.

"Hello, Laura, this is Florence at the Pediatrics Institute. Have you seen today's *Post* yet?"

"No, I haven't had a chance—"

"Well, look at page fourteen—Maxine Cheshire gives you a lovely pat on the back. Have you got a copy?"

"Yes. Thanks, Florence. I'll see you in a while."

Laura started to boil the kettle to make instant coffee and then picked up the newspaper from where it was lying inside the door. Maxine, the doyenne of Washington society, had reported:

At a recent international medical conference in Mexico City, a Cuban representative tried to browbeat a young woman NIH doctor with anti-American propaganda. Blond and extremely attractive **Laura Castellano, M.D.** *not only held her own but castigated the Castroite in his native tongue. Bravo Dr. Castellano!*

She read the item over several times and tried to figure out how she felt about it. *Why do they always have to mention my looks? It makes it seem as if I couldn't have done it if I was Quasimodo.*

She was interrupted by an unnerving whistle. She turned and was relieved to see that it was only her kettle.

It was a little before one when she got to the Institute. Dain Oliver was already in the cafeteria.

"It's the usual Wednesday get-together of the division heads," Florence explained, "but I'm sure he wouldn't mind if you went over."

"I don't know," Laura thought aloud, "I guess I should wait, but I really want to see him as soon as possible and assure him that I'm not a publicity hound."

"Whatever do you mean, dear?" Florence inquired.

"I mean, I don't want him to think I gave out the story. I have no idea how the paper got it."

Florence was surprised at her ingenuousness. "Why, Dr. Oliver called Maxine himself, Laura."

"He did? Whatever for?"

"To enhance our visibility, of course."

"Why should we need visibility?" Laura asked her.

"Because every time the Senate votes on us for funding, it really helps if members of the Committee can recall that they've read something positive about us recently. And let me tell you, Laura, *everybody* on the Hill reads Maxine Cheshire."

"Oh, I see," Laura said. And then she remarked, "That makes me think of my old high school. When I ran for office we'd use every trick to publicize my name."

As she walked out of the director's office, Laura thought some more.

It really is *like Midwood in a lot of ways. Was it that we were so mature then, or is this really just an adolescent game?*

In the ensuing weeks she would find out firsthand.

At first Laura consoled herself with the thought that her sudden notoriety was just a flash in the pan. Her little verbal tiff with the dogmatic Cuban wasn't really such hot stuff. Surely journalists had better things to write about—like Congressmen found cavorting with naked playmates in a public fountain near the Jefferson Memorial.

And yet the invitations kept cascading in.

Celebrity is self-perpetuating. Once your name is known in Washington—especially if it is for something that requires brains—you are invited once or twice to find out if you are also a charming dinner partner.

And of course, in Laura Castellano's case, her personality came wrapped in such a gorgeous package that she soon became a much sought-after guest. It was refreshing to be able to invite a hotshot doctor, especially if hostesses were short of a female to match up with a bachelor Senator (or a married Senator who kept his wedding ring back home and brought it out just for elections).

At first Laura enjoyed it. At least she tried to tell herself that she enjoyed it. She could smile and sparkle, show her sense of humor, charm the others present—male and female. In short, she became The Perfect Guest.

Still, Laura saved all *passion* for her work. Manufacturers of medical equipment were now seeking her out so they could be part of the important breakthrough she was nearing. Though her whirlwind social life had not abated, she sometimes had her dates drop her at the Institute so she could spend the quiet early hours of the morning working on her data. And while all the party talk was Watergate and whose head would be next to roll, she burrowed on. For infant hemorrhages have no political affiliations.

Her second paper was accepted. And her third. There was no question that she would have her Fellowship renewed. And, despite what was essentially a research appointment, she had the unique gratification of being able to save some newborns in the NIH hospital. In almost every sense she was fulfilled. She was successful and admired. The satisfaction she derived from her work surpassed her fondest hopes.

Everything was perfect. Except she was still unhappy.

FORTY-THREE

To the canon of the greatest loves in history—Antony for Cleopatra, Romeo for Juliet, Tristan for Isolde—could now be added the passion felt by Barney Livingston for Shari Lehmann.

The only problem was that Shari was his patient.

For once, an analytic hour was more painful to the doctor than the patient.

Shari was a twenty-five-year-old dancer with the American Ballet Theatre—a sensitive, intelligent young woman with striking Mediterranean looks. Her marriage had disintegrated six months earlier and her depression was so severe that the company physician had suggested she seek professional help. A senior member of the Institutes recommended Barney as a potential analyst.

Barney could not help but think that Shari's case confirmed one of his long-held theories: that it is almost always the less attractive mate who has the extramarital affair. Because unconsciously he or she does not feel worthy of the other partner.

Shari's husband was a well-respected cellist twenty years her senior, and pathologically jealous.

"I just couldn't reassure him," Shari complained, "even when I offered to stop dancing and go with him on his concert tours. In fact, that's what made everything explode."

She always wept when they discussed her break with Leland, which could more accurately be described as his rejection of her.

"Why, Dr. Livingston? If I only knew why. I could come to grips with it and maybe pull myself together. Now I'm just a big neurotic mess. . . ."

No, you aren't, Barney thought. The guy who has the problem is your husband.

Meanwhile, Barney's agony intensified. Why couldn't he have met Shari socially so he could tell her—without compromising ethics or the Hippocratic Oath—that he was desperately in love with her?

He wished that he could treat the hurt she felt by putting his consoling arms around her, whispering, You're okay, Shari. What you need is someone who appreciates you.

Me, for instance. I'd do everything to make your wounded, beautiful young soul rejoice again.

But he had to suffer all of this in silence.

What made matters worse, her analysis was going well. Which is to say transference had occurred. The stage in which the patient recreates her neurotic syndromes with the analyst as star of the scenario. She had already confessed with difficulty—but with courage—"Dr. Livingston, I know this sounds silly. But I have this sort of . . . crush on you. I've read your book—and all the articles I could get my hands on. I guess that's classic in analysis. And anyway, I've always been attracted to older men. . . ."

Her last remark slapped Barney on the ego. *Older men?*

"I mean, I'm sure all of your female patients feel the same way. I took a course in Psych in college and I suppose this is what's called 'transference,' but I feel so terrible just saying this, Doctor."

As Barney sat dumbly he wondered, Did you also learn about the formidable problem of *counter*transference?

For inevitably, if analysis is to work, the doctor and his patient must establish a relationship. But of course, as Freud observed, the therapist must learn to use these feelings wakened in him for the patient's good. To draw the line of involvement at "suspended attention" and merely do what Theodore Reik described as "listen with the third ear."

To put it bluntly, the worst thing a psychoanalyst can do is take advantage of the privilege that his patient has bestowed upon him—the private key to her unconscious thoughts—and use it to gratify himself.

And for a while it got dangerously close. Barney found himself having "unprofessional" fantasies. *Why* should our relationship—so intimate and caring—not be consummated?

Because it's wrong.

The pitched battle between his id and superego seemed never-ending. He knew of one or two cases of psychiatrists who had married their patients. Granted, they had been training analysts, but still . . .

And then he thought of Andrew Himmerman. Oh God, don't let me be like Andrew Himmerman.

Barney tried to tell himself that this was different. All he wanted was to be with Shari till death did them part.

Week after week he would sit there during Shari's hour, never taking notes, for he remembered everything down to the slightest detail.

"The first one is the worst one, Barn."

This was all he could get from Brice Wiseman, with whom he shared office and coffeemaker.

"You mean you've felt the same way?" Barney asked.

"For God's sake, Barney, we're not robots. Analysis can only work if it's an alive and shifting interaction. *You're* responding to her feelings as well as she to yours."

"Do you think she knows how I feel, Brice?" he asked.

"I'm sure she does—to some extent. But then she probably tells herself she's projecting it on you and that it's all her imagination. That's the only saving grace."

Barney shook his head.

"Brice, I'm in trouble. I want to give up everything for her. I'm the only person on this goddamn earth who knows how wonderful and caring this girl is."

"She's also beautiful," Brice commented. "I've seen her in the waiting room."

"Look," countered Barney forcefully, "I've seen 'beautiful' in my day. I'm telling you that girl's real beauty is *inside*."

He heard his intercom buzz. It was time for his next patient.

Wiseman said, "Let's talk about it later, Barn."

He walked back to his office, opened his door, and called in a new patient sent to him for consultation and evaluation. It was a man not much older than himself, although his inner torment made him pallid, and dark circles accentuated his eyes.

"Mr. Anthony?" Barney asked.

"Yes," the man replied as Barney closed the door, "I'm Dr. Anthony."

For the second time that day Barney was furious with himself. He'd read the patient's whole history a dozen times the night before. But now he'd been so worked up about his own intemperate behavior that he had forgotten his new patient was presenting something he had never dealt with—a pathology that rapidly was turning into a clandestine epidemic.

Anthony was classified as an "impaired physician." Or what some psychiatrists had come to call a "wounded healer."

They sat facing each other across Barney's desk. And Barney resorted to the usual preamble. "What brought you to me, Doctor?"

"I'm in internal medicine," Anthony began. "I've got a wife and kids who love me, even though I see them less than I probably should. All in all, I think I'm a pretty decent father—and a loving husband. What I mean is, Doctor, there is no external reason for me to be anything but satisfied with my whole life. I'm on the Board of the *American Journal,* and I get more referrals than I can handle. . . ."

Barney did not offer a comment. Or pose a question. Because at this point he had no idea what could possibly be lacking in this doctor's world.

"I like my patients," Anthony continued. "I'm devoted to them, really. When they're in the hospital I visit every morning—and if possible before they go to sleep."

"That must be stressful," Barney offered. "I mean, especially with the terminally ill."

The physician nodded. "I'm afraid I carry all their problems around with me. And to be honest, I've—well—needed a sort of crutch to get me through the day."

He paused and then said with embarrassment, "I take a lot of tranquilizers."

Barney nodded understandingly. "Which you've prescribed for yourself?"

"I need them, Doctor," Anthony replied. "Look at the broader picture. Each of my patients has a family—who share the stress of their illness with them. Multiply that by a dozen—no, by twenty—and you'll get some notion why I need . . . comfort now and then."

He then continued apologetically, "I'm not a drinker, I've got self-control. But I do need a little Valium to get me through the day. I mean, it's for my *patients'* sake."

"How much do you take?" asked Barney quietly.

"Well," he answered hesitatingly, "ten milligrams—"

"How often?"

"A few times a day," the doctor replied evasively and looked at Barney, whose expression communicated that the answer was unsatisfactory.

"Well, I would say my average intake in a day is about fifty to sixty mils."

"The normal maximum dosage is forty," Barney commented quietly.

"Yes, I know."

"And since it acts as a central nervous system depressant, by now it's probably having a paradoxical effect on you."

"No, no," Anthony protested, "I've been fine. I mean, I know the dosage's high, but I've been functioning okay."

Suddenly, he slammed the desk and shouted, "I'm a good doctor, dammit!"

Barney waited a moment and then asked gently, "You still haven't answered my question, Dr. Anthony. What brings you here?"

"I'm here," he said with difficulty, "for reasons that I still can't understand. Last Sunday—no, two weeks ago—when my wife was at her mother's with the kids—" He paused and then finally encapsulated his trauma in five words. "I tried to kill myself."

"Barney, I'll be honest with you, I'm in love with all my patients."

"Very funny, Castellano. Be serious. I'm really in a bind."

"Barney, you knew this could happen. It's an occupational risk in your specialty. Don't you think other caring docotrs go through hell?"

Her words recalled to Barney that there were physicians who had far more anguished souls than his. And he mentioned Dr. Anthony to Laura—though not by name.

"What's bothering the guy?" Laura asked sympathetically.

"You won't believe this, Laura, but his problem is he *cares* too much. I'm just beginning to discover that it's like a special form of cancer that's restricted to the good physicians. Some of them put armor plating on their feelings and treat their patients like a butcher treats his meat. And when I see a poor sensitive bastard like this suicidal doctor, I can't say I blame the others. It's self-preservation."

"I suppose you're right," she conceded. "If I let go and grieved for every little preemie that I lost, I think I'd crack. In fact, I probably will sooner or later."

"Laura," Barney said with genuine concern, "I've told you and told you and told you, you should be talking to someone."

"C'mon, Barn, you know I'm okay. I really am."

"Oh yeah? Tell me the truth. How much Valium do *you* need to get through the day?"

She hesitated and then evasively conceded, "Not that much. I've got things under control."

Oh Jesus, Barney thought, I wish I hadn't brought it up.

* * *

In retrospect, the Watergate scandal seemed to have whetted the media's appetite for circus antics in the center ring of government. The public seemed to crave the live excitement of another Congressional investigation. But Gerald Ford was too damn decent to give anybody food for gossip.

Though in a sense politics has always been theater, now it had become a spectator sport as well. And at last there was a promising middleweight bout on the horizon.

By 1972 the Department of Health had succeeded in banning cigarette advertising on television—and made the manufacturers put warnings on each package that what purchasers were about to smoke *might* possibly be harmful to their health.

Now, two years later, government health officials needed to go further. They were most concerned at this point with the damage done to unborn babies whose *mothers* smoked. Government health officials wanted the public to be aware that an uninformed mother might be puffing her own child's life away.

The tobacco industry was, of course, prepared. Indeed, their forces were always on alert, ready to attack as soon as the first match was lit. By contrast, the busy Senators and Representatives who sat on the Joint Health Committee had to rely on their assistants' briefings to confront their single-minded, better-rehearsed adversaries. Besides, some of them were from states whose principal income was derived from tobacco.

Capitol Hill veterans of the earlier clash sat in skull sessions with their advisors, thinking of a more exciting way to present the facts—which themselves were frightening, but would be buried by the suave rhetoric of the opposition.

One junior Senator put forth the idea that they call as witnesses mothers who had lost children as a direct result of their heavy smoking.

"That idea won't fly, Richard," said their chairman, Tom Otis (D-Minn), "the industry's lawyers will smart-talk those poor gals into inarticulate wrecks. That's the physician's province. We need some big-league doctors who can talk in words of less than six syllables."

"Did you have anyone in mind, Senator?" added the junior man.

"Absolutely," Otis answered. "I'm surprised that you, as a young father, didn't come up with it first: the most famous baby doctor in the world—Benjamin Spock."

There was an antiphonal buzzing in the meeting room: "No, no, no," clashing with "Good, good, good."

"With due respect, sir," said the junior Senator, voicing the opinion of all the hawks among them, "Spock's still too political. He's too identified with all those Vietnam protests."

A Republican Senator agreed. "He's right, Tom. Spock's too damn controversial."

"Goddamn," conceded Otis. "I'm afraid you're right. What say we adjourn till nine tomorrow and meanwhile call our contacts in the AMA to see what suggestions they come up with."

That very evening Senator and Mrs. Otis attended a small dinner party at the home of socialite Anne Harding. Also present was the bureau chief of *Time,* his wife, and a young Kissinger assistant, who was partnered with Dr. Laura Castellano of the NIH. Otis, as he told his colleagues next morning, considered it "sheer dumb luck."

For this doctor was a pediatrician specializing in illnesses of newborn children.

"And she was so in touch with the whole subject."

"Again, with due respect, Senator," Congressman Richard Moody tactfully dissented, "Dr. Castellano isn't what you might call well-known beyond the city limits."

Tom Otis fixed the younger lawmaker in his gaze and said, "My boy, I would think even a freshman like yourself would know the power of the media. Just by putting this gal *on,* she *ipso facto* becomes known."

Although a debate on cigarette package warnings is hardly as big a draw as the peccadilloes of a President, there were nearly four million spectators watching PBS that morning. Some had a vested interest. Wall Street traders had their little Sonys tuned to see if any unexpected bombshell might affect the value of tobacco stocks.

There were also a few aficionados of the English language who reveled in the brilliant use of words that was the trademark of the spokesman for the industry, M. Arnold West (often mocked by his detractors as "M. Arnold *South*").

As always, his argument was neat and simple. The issue was not whether smoking was harmful—for this, he said, was a matter that only qualified scientists can determine—but of civil rights. . . . It was a familiar but effective ploy, to tie the tainted object to a sacred cow and thus protect it by association.

"It is also a matter of free enterprise," West continued, using more patriotic buzzwords. "For after all, we know that drunken drivers kill or maim innumerable innocents in tragic accidents all over this great land.

But has anyone yet suggested that the breweries put warnings on their labels that their beverage might indirectly cause injury to others?

"Now to the point before us: that the tobacco industry should warn that 'smoking by pregnant mothers may cause birth defects or stillbirths.' "

He paused to scan the faces around him to assess if he was reaching them, and then continued.

"I'd like our distinguished Senators and Representatives, as well as all our visitors in the gallery, to look first to their left and then to their right." And he then urged them, "Go on, go on." The audience—at least in the gallery—were somewhat puzzled but did what they were told.

"And now," said West, "I ask you. Does your neighbor look crippled? Does the person next to you look sick? Or—I know this is ridiculous—'brain damaged'?"

The advocate picked up the ball. "My point, distinguished members of Congress, ladies and gentlemen, is that it is statistically impossible that all those in this room, who, thank the Lord, are hale and hearty, were born of mothers who were nonsmokers. That is a statistical impossibility, and I defy—nay, I invite—a refutation of this point."

The murmurs from the gallery suggested his sophistry had won this round. He ended in impassioned peroration:

"All we ask for is our civil rights. Let us be free. Let us be free to earn a living—and here I speak not only for smokers but for thousands upon thousands of our citizens who till the soil. Let us not allow a small hysterical minority to impinge upon the liberties our Founding Fathers fought for when they forged this nation."

He turned to the chairman and said, "Senator Otis, sir, that is all I have to say for now. I would be happy to answer any questions your committee might have."

"Thank you, Mr. West," the lawmaker replied. "But since this isn't a trial, let's postpone the questions till we've heard from the supporters of this proposition. And, quite candidly, I count myself among them. We believe this is a medical issue and so we should like to call on expert witnesses." He looked down to his left and said, "Would you take the microphone please, Dr. Castellano."

All eyes and the electronic cyclopean stare of the television camera focused on Laura.

The director of the broadcast knew a good shot when he saw one and communicated to the cameraman's earphone, "Stay tight on the broad's face and just let Otis's questions play voice-over."

Laura stated her name, her educational background, and her current position. Her A.B. and M.D. from Harvard may have especially pleased the Eastern viewers, but her current position as Research Fellow at NIH, trying to improve the fate of newborn babies, touched the nation.

Moreover, Laura had come prepared, and not just with data and key phrases on blue index cards. She had brought to that hearing what all the eloquence and fire of Mr. Arnold West could never have produced—photographs.

("Castellano, you've gotta remember that it's a visual medium," Barney had warned as they discussed her forthcoming appearance long into the night. "You've got pictures of the damaged lungs of babies, those little break-your-heart preemies struggling to breathe inside their isolettes—and be sure to get enlargements big enough for TV cameras to pick up. There's nothing more eloquent than the sight of a sick little child.")

And so for once the dominant impression left by Laura Castellano was not merely that of a willowy blond beauty, but of a doctor explaining what the terrible pictures on the TV screen had meant.

Mr. West interrogated Laura relentlessly.

"Ladies and gentlemen, as a father, I assure you that I am as touched as anyone in this room by the tragic pictures we have seen. But, with due respect, Miss Castellano—excuse me—or is it Mrs. Castellano—or Ms. ?. . ."

He had thereby conveyed to the spectators that the expert witness *was not herself a mother.* Of dubious bearing on the matter, but an emotionally solid hit.

"You may call me *Doctor* Castellano, if you don't mind," Laura said quietly.

"Excuse me, *Doctor* Castellano, but you have not given us documentation that these poor unfortunate babies were brought to their sad condition because their mothers smoked. Is it not true that literally thousands of such babies are born every day, even to nonsmokers?"

"Yes, sir."

"You did say it could happen even to nonsmokers?"

"Yes, sir, I did."

"I think I've made my point," Mr. West said, and sat back from his microphone.

"Now I'd like to finish mine," said Laura. "This isn't show business, Mr. West. This is medical science. We don't have stunt men or doubles or stand-ins. We don't retouch our pictures to make patients look more sickly." And then she raised her voice. "Let me give you some hard facts: Babies born to women who smoke tend to be two hundred grams *lighter* than babies born to nonsmokers.

"When a pregnant woman smokes, she inhales various poisons—not just nicotine, but carbon monoxide. Most of this crosses the placenta and reaches the baby."

She paused and then directed her next question to the tobacco advocate himself. "I ask you, Mr. West, would you put any child of yours near the exhaust pipe of a car even for a second—much less *nine* months?"

There were murmurs in the hearing room. Across the land, viewers leaned forward in their seats.

"I realize the Committee's time is precious, but let me cite one more bit of information: With every cigarette she smokes, a pregnant woman directly increases her chances of having a stillborn baby.

"I have photocopies of these data for every member of the Committee."

Game, Set, and Match to the Health Mafia.

This time *The Washington Post* carried her picture. It was—as Laura had somewhat perversely hoped—a rather unflattering one, for she had scowled as she encountered the jostling swarm of paparazzi, urging her to "Look this way, Laura," and "Give us a smile, please, Dr. Castellano."

She and Barney had a postmortem session late that night.

"You did good, kid," he enthused. "Just don't let this go to your head. I don't want you posing for *Playboy*."

She laughed. "Let me tell you, Barney, I was really scared. That West is brilliant. I had no idea where he would be coming from in the question period. I hate to say this, but if I ever got sued for malpractice, I'd want that barracuda on my side."

"I only wish there was some way I could've filmed you today. I was really proud."

"Barney," she said softly, "almost every bull's-eye that I made was an idea of yours."

"Aha, Castellano, my stopwatch shows you have actually been free from low self-esteem for almost twelve hours—that must be a record, huh?"

She did not reply.

"Laura, for God's sake, *I* didn't write your application to NIH, *I* didn't write those papers that you're publishing. You may recall, *you* were the one that got the A in Pfeifer's course. When will you get it into your head that you're terrific?"

"Come on, Barn, don't be ridiculous. So far my greatest achievement in life is being five-foot-ten and blond."

"You know something, Castellano, they've got this new operation out in California that can reduce height. I think I'll treat you to five-foot-five for Christmas."

She laughed. "Goodnight, Barney."

"And one more thing."

"Yes?"

"You could always dye your hair a frumpy color."

It was a foregone conclusion that Laura's Fellowship would be renewed. To their credit the directors knew a national asset when they saw one. For Laura was moving in circles above theirs and meeting people socially whom *they* met only once yearly, when they pleaded poverty and begged for increased funding.

Meanwhile, Laura showed team spirit and genuinely lobbied for more NIH funding.

She was so euphoric that she did something totally unprecedented for her—she threw a party in her woefully underfurnished apartment.

Gifted though she was, Laura did not count cuisine among her many virtues. Here she relied totally upon the sage advice of Milton—of the Deli of the same name in the Silver Spring Shopping Center. On the afternoon of the festivities, he loaded his van with dips and sandwiches and cakes. Milton was even wise enough to ask if Laura had sufficient cutlery—which naturally she did not. So he brought her several dozen plastic forks and knives.

"Now you're set," Milt pronounced. "The only thing you have to do is make the punch, from which I know nothing—and greet the guests, from whom I also know nothing. Goodbye, good luck, and I'll be back for all the garbage in the morning."

"Thank you, Milt," said Laura. "Have I forgotten anything?"

"Yes," Milt answered. "In my humble opinion you have forgotten to get married. Goodnight."

It occurred to Laura as she was mixing enormous quantities of punch (her laboratory expertise made her adept at measurements) that in all the time she and Palmer were man and wife, they never had a single party. Was she ever really married?

Barney, who had of course been the first to be invited, had been a fount of praise. "This is a real step forward for you, Castellano."

Actually, this time even Barney did not notice the nuance. For in truth the party was not in honor of the real Laura, but rather the Public Image of Ms. Laura Castellano, M.D.

Barney had arrived from New York early the morning of the party, helped Laura set up, and—since he saw her growing tense—insisted that she jog with him.

"So who's coming tonight that I should be especially nice to?" he asked as they ran along.

"I want you to be nice to everyone, Barn, because frankly I think I've invited everybody. We may have a thousand people if they all show up."

"God, wouldn't that be something—a thousand doctors in a single room."

"Hey now," she cautioned, "the purpose of this affair is not to give you more material for analyzing the medical profession. It's so I can get to see what all my colleagues are like when they're dead drunk."

"Okay, that could be educational as well."

No one will ever know exactly how many people were milling in and out of Laura's apartment and on the lawn two floors below.

Milton's catering had envisaged fifty. Everything was gone in the first hour. Fortunately, Laura had presumed that every guest would be a lush. The punch—its vodka content growing more predominant as her supplies of juice and ginger ale ran out—flowed endlessly.

A little after nine, Florence (the power behind the pediatrics throne) came up to Laura and shouted above the din, "Laura, darling, everybody's here. You should feel flattered—even Dr. Rhodes has left his laboratory for this."

"You mean he's here? Paul Rhodes, the big enchilada of all the Institutes, is here in person?"

Laura had forgotten she'd been brash enough to drop an invitation at the Supreme Director's office. And he actually had come!

She scanned the faces in her apartment, unable to find his. Then she went out to the lawn where Rhodes was holding court. When he spied her, he called out, "Ah Laura, what a lovely party, do come join us."

God, she thought, in awe, he's tipsy. One of the greatest medical minds in the world and he might fall over on my front lawn.

Surrounding him was the equivalent of his round table. Shining knights, themselves subservient only to God and Rhodes (and not necessarily in that order), they were all of middle age—except for one man in his early thirties. And notwithstanding the warm weather, all wore ties and jackets. That is, all except the younger man—who was in tennis shorts.

Laura could not help looking at him. Who, she wondered, would dare confront Paul Rhodes in sweaty tennis gear—for he had clearly come straight from the court.

Their glances met, and Laura disliked her unknown guest at once. He was one of those attractive men, muscular, brown curly hair, whose attitude showed they knew they were attractive.

"Hello," he said in what he probably thought was a sexy baritone. "I've seen your picture in the papers, but I don't believe you've seen mine—at least not yet. I'm Marshall Jaffe."

"Hi, I'm Laura," she said unenthusiastically.

"Oh, please, we all know you, our hostess and the pin-up of the Institutes."

"Oh," said Laura dismissively, "do you work there, too?"

"In a menial capacity," Marshall replied.

"Just what is your capacity?"

"For love? It's endless," he replied.

Under normal circumstances she would have brushed him off like a mosquito. "Just what is it you *do,* Mr. Jaffe?"

"Well," Marshall answered slowly, "it's Dr. Jaffe, actually. In fact, to be precise it's Doctor-Doctor Jaffe—M.D., Ph.D. Are you impressed?"

"Why should I be? Almost everybody at this party's got a double doctorate. So what's your field-field, then?"

Marshall put his arm around the shoulder of Paul Rhodes, the Institutes' director, and announced, "Paul's just seduced me."

"I beg your pardon?"

"Well, up until last June, I was a microbiologist at Stanford. Now I'm a Senior Fellow, and that means I do just about whatever takes my fancy. Even try to build a better mousetrap. But I'd be really interested to know what you would like me to do."

There was no doubt about it—he was an egomaniac. But he was fascinating—the way a rattlesnake is fascinating. And, if Rhodes had made him a Senior Fellow, he'd have to have the goods. He'd have to be as brilliant as he said he was.

"Well, if you'll excuse me, Doctor-Doctor, I have got other Doctor-Doctors' glasses to refill."

"The name is Marshall. Don't forget it, Laura."

It won't be for lack of trying, she thought to herself.

FORTY-FOUR

"I'm not here, Harvey. Tell him I'm out to lunch."

"But it's only nine-thirty, Laura," her lab mate protested.

"I don't care, tell him I got hungry early. Only keep that balloon-head off my back."

Harvey transmitted Laura's message to the caller and hung up. As he returned to his lab station he casually inquired, "What's wrong with the guy, Laura? I mean, I saw him at the party and he seemed like a nice enough guy. And I guess you know what everybody says about him."

"And what's that?"

"Jaffe's Paul Rhodes' fair-haired boy. He's grooming him as his successor."

"But he's just a child," she said incredulously.

"Yeah," Harvey remarked, "that's what's so amazing. The guy is maybe thirty-three at most."

"That's amazing," said Laura, thinking to herself, He's younger than I am. And then aloud, "Especially since he's got the mind of an adolescent. By the way, what was his answer when you gave him my message?"

"He said he'd go over to the cafeteria and look for you."

Half an hour later Marshall Jaffe was standing next to her, holding a small white paper bag.

"Good morning, Laura," he said merrily.

She frowned. "What brings you here, Dr. Wonderful?"

"Well, it's obvious since the cafeteria was closed you didn't get the breakfast you wanted, so I sweet-talked George the chef out of two cups of coffee and some rolls."

"Thanks. I'll take one of the coffees," she replied.

"I only brought you one, the other is for me. It's pretty nice out—want to drink it on the steps?"

"Look, Marshall, I don't know about you, but I like to get some work done in the morning. So if you don't mind—"

"I don't mind, Laura. But you'll work a hell of a lot better with some carbohydrates in you, and you'll make up for lost time. Besides, I'd like to hear how your research is going."

Minutes later they were sitting outside in the hazy morning sun, having rolls and coffee.

"How come you *already* know so much about my research?" Laura asked.

"Well, I work with Paul and spend at least an hour every day discussing how things are going. I happened to see your application on his desk—"

"And you sneaked a look at it?"

Marshall was offended.

"No," he said with much less flippancy than usual, "I may be arrogant but I'm not the Watergate type. I don't nose around in other people's business. If you can credit this, Miss Holier-Than-Thou Castellano, Paul gave it to me to look over and see what I thought."

Aha, she said to herself, now he's trying the power game with me. I can screw you with the boss.

"And what was your opinion, Dr. Jaffe?"

"I think it's great. I mean, it's not that cosmically imaginative, but it's intelligent, pragmatic. And the proof is that you're getting good results."

Laura had not heard the second, complimentary part of his remark, for she had fixed upon the inference that her project was not all that original.

"Well," she said, a little defensively, "we're already making healthy babies out of what, even half a year ago, would have been very sick ones."

"I know, I know," Marshall protested. "I'm a father. I appreciate these things."

"Oh," she said, reluctant to confess—even in thought—that she was disappointed by his last remark.

"I'm married, Laura, in case you're wondering."

"I'm sure your wife appreciates how lucky she is. And of course, you're always right there with your brilliant bibliography if it should slip her mind."

"We don't discuss that sort of thing," he answered. His voice was strangely hollow. Then he explained simply and undramatically. "She's got MS."

"Oh," said Laura, chastened. "I'm sorry, Marshall."

"Yeah," he sighed, "I'm sorry, too. It's really worse for our two kids. I mean, Claire has long stretches of remission when she's absolutely fine. But then that damn disease attacks again and it's like their mommy's gone away. Fortunately we found an old-fashioned nanny and pressed her into service. Otherwise we'd all go nuts—"

"And so you can keep your tennis game up," Laura said—and was bewildered by her own sarcastic outburst.

His jaw tightened. "Hey, look," he said, "it's obvious you've lived a cozy, insulated life. But let me tell you, smashing a ball with a racket is my tranquilizer. Because with everything I'm carrying on my shoulders, if I couldn't sweat it out I'd probably be taking pills to freak it out. My kids both understand that I've just gotta have a safety valve to keep my head screwed on."

He lowered his voice and then said un-self-consciously, "And Claire knows that I date."

Laura did not know what to think. Liberated though she thought she was, she found the notion that Marshall "cheated" openly more than a little distasteful. And yet she had a curious admiration for his honesty.

He stood up. "Okay, Doctor, coffee break's over. Let's both go back and save the world from pestilence and athlete's foot."

"Yeah," Laura replied, still filled with conflicting feelings.

"See you, Marshall," she said blankly.

He paused and answered softly, "I would like that very much."

She could not concentrate all afternoon. As usual, she blamed herself for being callous and misjudging Marshall's brashness. And she hadn't even acted like a true professional and asked him what *his* research was. Good going, Castellano, half a dozen conversations more like this and you'll be a total creep.

Barney was almost ready to call up Fritz Baumann and ask for professional help.

Yet there was an irony to it all. In his valiant struggle to remain professionally aloof, he had succeeded too well. He had "suspended" his attention to the extent that Shari was aware of his emotional involvement but not of his romantic inclinations.

He thus had created the ideal analytic environment and hastened the day when this lovely bird who had come to him broken-winged would fly off.

She had rapidly regained her artistic self-confidence and had been chosen as understudy to Odette/Odile in *Swan Lake*, a definite step upward—albeit backstage.

Barney could not keep from thinking that Tchaikovsky's ballet was yet another tale of an impossible love that ends in tragedy. Although, he concluded, the lovers are united in the end—by leaving life on earth together.

Could that not also be a way for him and Shari? Could they both leave New York—and their professions—and go to some Arcadia and live forever after as two happy swans?

"Brice," he reported one day at the coffeemaker, "if you hear shrieks from my office, call the hospital, because I think I'm on the verge of cracking up."

"Still the same girl?" his colleague asked.

"Yeah. She's had to suspend therapy. The company's been touring on the West Coast. And now they're all going to Europe for the rest of the summer. Brice, what should I do?"

"Thank God I'm not your shrink—you couldn't afford me, anyway— but I'll give you a little seed you might plant inside your head and see if anything blossoms. . . ."

"Yes?"

"Are you sure you're not just cathecting on this girl?"

Barney was offended by this suggestion. "Why do you think so, Brice?"

"What matters is what *you* think, Barney."

At this moment both their intercoms were buzzed.

"Well," his office-mate said, smiling, "back to the salt mines."

"Did you say 'back to *assault minds*,' Brice?"

"No, I didn't, but it's valid either way."

Even as she walked into the office, Shari Lehmann somehow seemed transformed. She had called from the coast to book a single session en route to London.

"I feel wonderful, Dr. Livingston," she announced. "And I'll never know how to repay you. What you've given me is—how can I say it—a second birth."

So I'm her mother, Barney glumly thought.

"I guess I won't be seeing you after this week," she added with a smile.

"I know," he answered quietly, "your company is touring in Europe."

"Yes, but I'm not going."

Wait, Livingston, he thought, all is not lost. Perhaps she's leaving me-the-doctor so she can have a relationship with me-the-*man*.

"I never thought a thing like this could happen," she continued effervescently. "I mean, it's so unlike me. Up till now I've always been attracted to men like Leland, who would use me for a mop. But now, thanks to you, I've learned to know myself a little better and I'm sure I haven't made the same mistake again."

Barney waited. The news was either going to be very good or very, very bad. Either way he held on to his chair.

"Kenneth is a very special man."

"Who?" asked Barney.

"Oh, I guess I'm so excited I didn't start from the beginning. I'm in love. I could almost say for the first time. I mean that now I know that what I had with Leland sure as hell wasn't really love. Coincidentally, he's a doctor—professor of Neurology at Santa Barbara—Kenneth Glover. Have you heard of him?"

"Mmm," Barney answered.

"I know you're thinking that I'm acting hastily. But Doctor, Ken and I have spent at least part of every day with each other for the last six weeks. That may not seem a lot by psychiatric timetables—or whatever you use to gauge these things—but I honestly feel I know him. You'd like him. In a lot of ways, he reminds me of you."

And Barney asked himself, Why is she settling for margarine when she could have real butter? I mean, here I am, melting away.

There was a momentary pause.

"Doctor," Shari said, "would you just this once answer a specific question? Please. Please tell me if you think I'm doing the wrong thing."

Thank God for training, Barney thought, because I can just read out from the standard textbook farewell ceremony.

"If we've really accomplished something here," he said, "then you should be able to determine what's right for you by making contact with your inner feelings. After all, the purpose of our work was not to make you depend on me, but rather to make you independent. If you feel confident—"

"I do, I do," she quickly answered. "But I'm glad you're not ambivalent—" she stopped herself and said apologetically, "I didn't mean 'ambivalent.' I mean if you have doubts about my judgment—"

There were still a few more minutes left. But Barney rose and said, "I've always thought of you as someone basically mature, who only needed—shall we say—a little psychological first aid after a nasty crash."

He held out his hand.

"Good luck, Miss Lehmann."

"Doctor," Shari asked, "is it against the rules for me to kiss you?"

Before he could reply, it was too late. She had pecked him on the cheek.

And danced out of his life.

Barney's and Laura's love lives seemed like a seesaw. When she was up he was down, and vice versa.

"Down" was not the word for what he felt that evening. "Rock bottom" came close, "six feet under" might have been even more appropriate.

"Castellano, I think I've lost the will to go on," he said melodramatically. "I mean, without Shari, what is there to live for?"

"There's your book, for one thing," she suggested. "You could even use this heartrending experience as material."

"Really—how?"

"Well, you could talk about the perils of countertransference."

"No thanks, I'll leave that to your—excuse the pun—bosom buddy, Grete. How is the old girl, anyway?"

"Thriving in Houston from what I last heard. She's even assisted at her first transplant."

Barney instantly regretted his question, for the mention of Houston was an instant reminder of where Bennett *wasn't*. To think that a flake like Grete should be hopping merrily up the echelons two at a time, while his best friend was battling in the to-and-fro conflicting wind and rain in Cambridge.

For, from all he could gather, Bennett was not having a roaring social life.

("I'm sublimating, Barn," he had told him. "I'm using rage instead of amphetamines to keep me going through the night. In fact, I'm taking extra courses so I can get this damn thing over in two years instead of three. I hate law school because it really teaches you how to use 'facts' to convince people of your version of the truth—which may not really be the truth. In medicine, at least, a live man is alive and a corpse is dead. Up here they'd have a mock trial and let the jury decide.")

"Are you still there, Barney?" Laura asked.

Her voice snapped him from his reverie.

"Sorry, Castellano, I was just thinking of a patient."

He shifted gears and asked, "Is there anything cheerful we can talk about?"

"Well, first of all, I promise you by this time next month you'll have totally forgotten your beloved patient and be completely wild for some new madonna."

"That was interesting, what you just said," he commented. "Do you really think I go for the 'unreachable' madonna types?"

"You want the honest version, Barney? Or shall I wrap it in Styrofoam?"

"I can take it. You think I unconsciously go for women who are unavailable."

"Well, you've been pretty pissed off ever since Emily walked out, and I think you're scared of getting burned again."

Barney thought for a moment. Dammit, Castellano was right.

"Hey, listen, Laura, I don't like this. Suddenly you're reading me with psychic x-ray vision. That's supposed to be *my* job."

"Don't worry, Barn, I'll always give you plenty of material to criticize. Take Marshall Jaffe."

"Who the hell is he?"

And then she told him. Nine dollars and eighty-five cents worth.

To Barney's mind the whole thing sounded like a losing proposition.

"I don't care how you try to rationalize it—the guy's not available. Aren't you smart enough to leave the married ones alone?"

"Barn, do you know that in Washington the ratio of eligible men to eligible women is five cows to every bull?"

"Do *you* know that you're ten times better than the average 'cow'? If you only got your act together you could generate a damn stampede."

"But Barney, I *like* him. I can't help it. I didn't want to, but I really—"

"—feel sorry for him?"

She did not reply. For she had to acknowledge there was at least an element of that.

"Look, Castellano, I feel sorry for the guy, too. But I'm looking out for you and I don't see what's to gain if you get more involved."

"Barn, I'm over twenty-one. You don't have to look out for me."

"Castellano, if I don't, who will?"

"He's very attractive," she answered, almost as a non sequitur.

"I know, I know. I saw him at the party."

"In all that mob?"

"It's not hard to distinguish the only guy in short pants, Laura. Don't you find that a little creepy?"

"Well," she said, only half in jest, "he's got nice legs."

"So do I," Barney replied, "but I don't go to Fritz Baumann's house in my basketball pants."

"He's also one of the brightest guys I've ever met—"

"As he himself constantly tells you."

"Yeah, I'll grant he's somewhat enamored with himself. But that kind of balances the two of us."

"You mean like Mr. and Mrs. Jack Sprat—he's too *over*confident and you're too *under*confident?"

"Something like that."

"Have you forgotten that the Sprats were at least married? I'm sorry, Laura, but I really disapprove."

"But I like being with him, Barn. He's nice—in a funny kind of way. I mean, at least he's better than nothing."

"Okay, okay. Get your heart broken again. But you're walking up a 'down' escalator. Or, to use an appropriate tennis metaphor, I see the score as love nothing. So between games try and give a little thought to where you're going to be in, say, five years."

There was a pause. Had Barney finally won a volley?

"You know something," Laura said with wonderment, "I never had the slightest illusion it would last half that long."

But she knew well what he meant. The female biological clock was ticking away her fertility. She would soon not have to "worry" about getting pregnant.

Oh, cut the self-pity, Castellano, who the hell knows what can happen in five *weeks,* let alone five years.

Laura had at last found something resembling inner equilibrium.

She and Marshall had a stable—if slightly incomplete—relationship. They would eat dinner at her place one or two evenings a week (he was teaching her to cook), perhaps preceded by a game of tennis (which he was also teaching her). He took her out to theater or a ballgame as often as their schedules allowed. And she was satisfied. At least she did not think she could aspire to more.

Marshall had a passion to be "best" at everything. And when he made up his mind that he was going to be Number One at something, no force on earth could stop him.

But he wasn't in the science game just for the golden prizes. The thing he really cared about was seeing his ideas bear fruit. He wanted to break new ground in bio-engineering and produce results that he would be blessed for generations later.

And after having worked with Rhodes for eighteen months he felt that they were on the brink.

"This is it, Laura. This is going to be the year a lot of cancers bite the dust."

Doctors Rhodes and Jaffe and their junior staff at NIH were on the verge of concluding a five-year collaboration with Professor Toivo Karvonen in Helsinki and *his* junior staff at Meilahti University Central Hospital. They were well into the final test run of the method they had jointly developed to induce cell differentiation and deficiency in oncogenes.

"Can you believe it, Laura? We're on the five-yard line, goal to go."

He almost made her living room glow with the sparks of his enthusiasm.

"We'll get those malignant tumors by the genes. Isn't that fantastic!"

"I haven't got the words, Marsh. All I think of is the patients that I've lost that I could save in—how long till it hits the hospitals?"

"Three years, maybe two if we get lucky. Jesus, I can't wait to scream this to the whole world!"

Marshall lived and breathed his project.

"We can produce the synthetic substance at uncytotoxic levels, Laura—isn't that terrific?"

Laura's joy in their relationship was immeasurably enhanced by the fact that he could speak to her as a scientific peer. Perhaps he used the jargon to boast too much, but at least she understood it.

She accepted her somewhat amorphous status as "part-time wife." Marshall un-self-consciously escorted her to all the Institute functions. Still she could not help wondering how her lover spent the evenings he and Rhodes were in Helsinki, where, as everyone knows, the nights are very, very long.

But after all, he had told her categorically that what they had was all she could expect from him. And he had acknowledged that he was prepared for the day when she would tell him that she'd found a full-time husband. He would bow out gracefully.

Which only bound her more to him, for she had yet another thing she could admire—his generosity.

At one point he invited her to join him on a trip to Finland. ("It's so pure there—a hundred and eighty thousand lakes and none of them polluted.") Perhaps, he suggested, while the two big boys honed their data, they could steal a day or two and ski.

"I don't know how," she answered.

"I could teach you, Laura. I'm the best instructor you could ever have."

"Yeah. That's what my first husband said."

The conversation blended to another topic. Though Laura was intent on hiding her embarrassment at her reference to "my first husband," she knew what she had inadvertently revealed, and surely Marshall had noticed it.

And yet he never mentioned it.

Late one evening Marshall woke her with a telephone call. He was in a state of panic.

"Laura, I need help."

"What's the matter?"

"Scott, my eight-year-old, has got some kind of FUO. He's spiked a fever so damn high it's nearly scorched the mercury. Can you come over quick?"

She was awake enough to feel the shock.

"Marshall, do you realize what you're asking?"

"Laura, this is no time to play by the rule book. This is life and death. He needs an expert doctor fast."

"Then take him to the hospital," she answered, feeling torn and angry.

"Laura, you can get here faster than I can get him to the E.R.—and with all that bureaucratic bullshit he could die."

He broke off with his plea still hanging in midair.

"All right," she sighed, "I'll be right over."

"Jesus, thanks. You'll hurry, won't you? Do you know the way?"

"I know exactly where you live, Marsh," she said quietly.

The Nova rattled as she gunned it up to ninety-five on Route 15. And even as she sped she tried to put a brake on her emotions.

Listen, Laura, you're a pediatrician and this child is sick. Whatever you may feel about . . . his parents is irrelevant. It's an emergency.

She kept repeating it, a kind of self-hypnotic litany, so that she could function. So that she could breathe.

The Jaffes' home was in Silver Spring just off the Beltway. But the last eight hundred yards were on a dirt road, totally devoid of light. Despite this, Laura scarcely slowed her car.

She pulled to a sudden halt in front of the two-story white saltbox with a little lawn in front and a mailbox labeled THE JAFFES. It was the only dwelling that was fully lit.

She got out of the car and reached back for her bag. Marshall stood in silhouette at the front door.

"Jesus, thanks for getting here so quickly. I won't forget this, Laura. Really—"

She nodded wordlessly and walked inside.

Up on the landing a boy no more than five or six, in Sesame Street pajamas, was staring down at her with saucer eyes. "Hey, Dad," he cried in worried tones. "You said you'd called a doctor. Who is *she*?"

"This lady *is* a doctor, Donny," Marshall answered reassuringly. "Now you just tiptoe back to bed and let her see what's wrong with Scott."

Laura hurried up the stairs, trying her best to be invisible, and ran straight to the open bedroom door.

Marshall had already swathed the boy in cold towels.

She walked up to the bed and spoke softly to the feverish child.

"I'm Dr. Castellano, Scott. I know you're feeling very warm. But is there anything that hurts?"

The boy's gaze was unfocused as he slowly moved his head from side to side. Then Laura turned to Marshall.

"When was the last time you checked his temp?"

"Maybe five minutes. It was one-oh-six plus."

Laura felt the child's burning forehead. "I can believe it," she replied. "Go down to the kitchen and bring up lots of ice, stat. Do you have any rubbing alcohol?"

Marshall nodded. "In Claire's bathroom. I'll get it."

He quickly left the room, his normally tanned face drained of color.

She turned and took a good look at her patient. The boy looked so much like his father.

Laura checked Scott's lymph nodes—they were badly swollen—and put a stethoscope to his chest. She could hear nothing but an elevated heartbeat, so that pretty much ruled out a respiratory problem.

At his age Scott's fever might indicate endocarditis, an inflammation of the lining membrane of his heart—but that was just conjecture. What was important at this moment was to treat the symptoms, get the fever down.

"Excuse me, Doctor," came a female voice from the doorway. Laura turned and saw a matronly woman of indeterminate age in a tartan bathrobe. She had a screw-cap glass bottle in her hand.

"Dr. Jaffe said you need rubbing alcohol." She now held out the flask. Laura nodded and took two steps forward to accept it. Before she could say thank you, the woman spoke again.

"I'm Mrs. Henderson. Can I help in any way? Please, Doctor, we all feel so helpless."

"Well, we could use a lot of washcloths—"

"Yes, Doctor, right away."

The woman turned and disappeared. Almost simultaneously Marshall entered with a bucket full of ice. Young Donny trailed behind him holding a bowl that held a cube or two.

"Is this enough?" Marshall gasped.

"It'll have to do. Now quickly, fill the bathtub with cold water."

"What? Couldn't that cause shock? I mean, a cardiac arrest or—"

"Marshall," Laura snapped, "either you trust me or not. If you want to treat your own family, go right ahead. But don't you *dare* try second-guessing me."

Chastened, Marshall rushed to the children's bathroom to fill the tub. Then he raced back to help Laura strip Scott and carry him.

"Hey," squeaked Don, "what are you doing to my brother? He'll freeze in there!"

"Shut up, Don," his father barked. "We've gotta do exactly what this lady says."

Laura turned to the frightened boy and in a much gentler tone said, "You could really help us, Donny, if you brought in some ice."

But Mrs. Henderson was already there with the bucket.

"Thank you," Laura whispered. "Dr. Jaffe and I will put Scott in the water, and you and Donny can drop ice cubes all around."

She turned again to the younger boy and smiled, "Not on your brother's head."

Donny's fright was suddenly dispelled by giggles. The prospect of inserting ice in his brother's bath seemed amusing. Scott scarcely whimpered as they placed him in the freezing water. As he lay soaking, Laura checked him for clues that might be on the surface of his body.

"How much longer, Laura?" Marshall muttered anxiously.

Laura turned to Mrs. Henderson and said, "I'm sorry, I seem to have left my thermometer in Scott's bedroom. Could you . . ."

The woman disappeared and was back in an instant. Laura now monitored Scott's temperature. At last she ordered Marshall to pull the boy out, help dry him, and get him to bed.

"But Laura, you just saw, he's still got a fever."

"One-oh-two is low enough. Stop backseat driving, dammit."

Back in the young boy's room, Mrs. Henderson and Donny set about the task assigned to them by Laura—gently dabbing alcohol all over Scott

to get the fever down further. Laura and Marshall stood together at the
doorway.

"So what do you think it is?"

"I'll take some blood and have a complete workup done in the
morning. That'll tell us more than anything."

She looked at him and then commented, "You don't seem exactly
relieved."

"I'm worried, Laura. What about rheumatic fever?"

"I don't think so."

"Are you *sure?*"

"Is any doctor ever sure?" she asked him with exasperation. "Marshall, has it been so long since you've been in a hospital that you've
forgotten we're not omniscient?"

He lowered his head and scratched the back of his neck. "I'm sorry,
Laura, but if it were your own kid . . ." He stopped himself in midsentence.

"I know," she said softly. "In fact, doctors tend to be the most
hysterical parents I have to deal with. And you, Marshall, are no exception."

"Sorry, sorry. I just lost my head. I . . . I'm not trying to pin
you down, but can you tell me what you think?"

"At his age, probably CID or maybe Juvenile RA."

"Tissue inflammation—rheumatoid arthritis?"

"Ah, you still remember one or two things from Med School days.
But if it turns out to be RA, it's not that big a problem in a kid his age."

"Any other ideas?" he asked nervously.

"Hey, listen," Laura said with annoyance, "at this hour of the night
I'm not about to give a differential diagnosis. It's highly unlikely he's got
anything serious, like bacteremia. Just believe me, he's okay. Meanwhile,
give him two of these junior aspirins every four hours—if he can keep
them down."

"Just aspirin?" he asked, frowning.

"It's still the best drug we have, Marshall. If you want your child to
take a drug of last resort like corticosteroids, get another doctor. Which
reminds me, don't you have a pediatrician?"

"Sort of. But I wouldn't trust the guy with anything more serious
than poison ivy."

"Call me tomorrow at the office, and I'll give you the names of some
good ones." She turned to the others in the room and said, "Take it easy,
Scott, you're going to be fine. Mrs. Henderson and Donny, thanks for all
your help. Now it's time for everybody to go to bed."

She had almost made it to freedom.

But just as she was on the landing a door opened and a very pale, slender woman in a pink silk dressing gown leaned unsteadily against the wall and asked, her voice barely audible, "Will he be all right, Doctor? Will my boy get well?"

"He'll be fine," she answered. "Please don't worry, Mrs. Jaffe." She had turned and started down the stairs when the same weak voice called out, "Doctor?"

"Yes?"

"You're very kind to come here at this hour. Marshall and I are very grateful."

Laura nodded and continued down the stairs without another word.

She climbed back in her car, folded her arms across the steering wheel, and leaned her forehead on them.

"Jesus Christ," she muttered. "Why the hell do I stick my chin out like this?"

She could still hear the painful, wounding words, "If it were your own kid."

As she started the car and began driving down the road, an Armageddon of thoughts raged in her mind.

But she did not, as part of her wanted to, drive a hundred miles an hour off a bridge.

FORTY-FIVE

Barney tried to reason with her.

"Castellano, I've told you a hundred times, you're caught up in a very sick situation. Where's your confidence? Don't you think you deserve a full-time relationship?"

"He says he loves me, Barn," she protested weakly.

"I'm sure he does—in his own way. He probably regards you as the romantic equivalent of fast food. The real problem is that you don't love *yourself.* Why don't you talk to a shrink about it?"

"Like Andrew Himmerman?" she asked facetiously. "Then I could have my analysis and my social life in the same hour."

"Don't be snide," he objected, "Grete's given you a distorted vision of the guy."

"Now I know you've joined The Establishment," she retorted, "sticking up for another member of your club."

Barney longed to tell her about his meeting with Himmerman and the true version of the "seduction" of Grete. But he couldn't. It had been a professional confidence. So he closed the discussion by saying, "I'll get you a good name, Laura."

"Fine. Be sure he's blond. It takes one to understand one."

She hung up feeling satisfied she had won the debate. But was it really a debate? Wasn't her best friend only looking out for her best interests?

She suppressed an impulse to call him back. Instead, she phoned Marshall, who was working late in his lab.

He was happy to hear her voice. "I was really feeling low," he confessed. "Let's connect in half an hour."

There, Laura thought to herself, he needs me. He wants me. Ergo, he loves me. Isn't that all that really matters?

It had been a terrible day for Marshall. Not only had the department secretary called in sick with yet another of her psychosomatic illnesses ("I think she reads *The Merck Manual* in her spare time," Laura once joked), but he had also been summoned to Donny's school because his younger son had been "clowning around again."

And to aggravate his already bad humor, he had returned to the lab to find that the afternoon mail did not contain the urgently awaited proofs of the Rhodes-Karvonen article that would trumpet their breakthrough achievement to the scientific world.

And so, unable to concentrate, he drove to the tennis club, purchased an hour of the pro's time, and pounded the poor bastard to smithereens. But when he went home to have dinner with the boys, he was still incapable of suppressing his frustration.

Donny was right on target when he complained, "Daddy, it's no fun when you're angry all the time. Couldn't we just eat with Mrs. Henderson?"

Great, great. He was striking out on all fronts today. Claire was asleep when he went up to see her, and she seemed unlikely to wake till morning. And thus, feeling otherwise useless, he had returned to his lab. But there was no one else in microbiology, which was yet more dispiriting.

A little after ten his phone rang. It was Laura.

"Listen," he suggested, "let's meet in the parking lot and go for a drive."

She readily agreed.

Marshall went to the bathroom, washed his face, checked his hair in the mirror—and then started for the stairway. When he reached the landing he looked down the corridor. There were lights in the director's office. He decided to say goodnight to Rhodes. It might even win him some Brownie points for working late.

He knocked on the wooden frame of the glass-paneled door. There was no answer. He knocked again, and then tried the knob and found the door was open. He walked in hesitantly, calling softly, "Paul? Are you here? It's me—Marshall. Anybody home?"

He looked at the director's inner office. Every light was on and there were papers strewn across the desk. Rhodes must have just stepped out for a breath of air. He would wait a bit.

He could not resist the temptation to sit in the director's chair—which he was hoping to make his own in another year. Besides, even if Paul found him with his tennis sneakers up on his desk, Marshall knew his elder colleague had a sense of humor. Indeed, theirs had been almost a father-son relationship.

He sat on the throne and leaned back, thinking to himself, Hello, peons, this is your new director, King Jaffe, about to begin my thirty-year rule. Anyone who wishes may come kiss my Stanford graduation ring.

He savored the fantasy. What would come after that, he wondered? Perhaps a phone call from the White House—or the U.N.? Perhaps an invitation to appear before Congress. Rhodes had gotten lots of those.

I wonder what he's working on tonight? Temptation triumphed and he allowed himself to take a closer look.

And he was glad he did. For there atop Paul's desk were galley proofs from the *New England Journal of Medicine*—the ones that should have reached Marshall that day.

He picked up a sheet and tried to find the paragraph or two that he had written. God, he thought, my name is somewhere in this landmark article.

His passion now aroused, he rummaged through the galleys for the title page. It took him several minutes till he found it, face down on the desk. Somewhere after Rhodes and Karvonen (or Karvonen and Rhodes—he knew they were squabbling over this) his name would be inscribed, recording his modest assistance.

He leaned back in the chair and took a breath. The article was on page one of the journal. Its simple title belied its great importance. "The Use of Bio-Engineering in the Destruction of Oncogenes: A New Approach."

And there it was. Sandwiched in between Asher Isaacs and James P. Lowell: "Marshall Jaffe, M.D., Ph.D."

He gazed at the letters, savoring a moment of intoxicating self-congratulation.

Then he noticed something. Sirii Takalo's name was missing. And where was Jaako Fredricksen—with whom he'd spent many a long Finnish night getting smashed on *pöytäviina*? Shit, Jaako had been on the project longer than he had. Rumor had it that he was Karvonen's heir apparent—an honor he richly deserved, since his boss could never have charted the structure had not Jaako been his navigator.

In fact, if one judged by these galleys, Finland did not exist—at least in academic medicine. For even the name of Toivo Karvonen, founding father of the whole project, appeared *nowhere*.

At first Marshall simply could not accept the fact that Rhodes, a man he so respected, was capable of such gross professional misconduct. But there was no other explanation.

The sonovabitch was trying to steal the ball and run for a touchdown on his own.

Suddenly he heard footsteps. Paul was on his way back. Shake ass, Marshall, he thought. Put the galleys down and turn the title page back over. Get the hell as far as you can from the desk.

His tennis reflexes paid off. By the time Rhodes opened the office door, Marshall was standing at the wall, admiring the photographs of his boss with various immortals.

"Well, Marsh," the director said genially, "what brings you here so late?"

"I had a lousy day, Paul," he answered with a hoarseness in his voice.

"Want to sit and talk about it?"

"No, thanks. That's very kind—"

"It's all right, I've got nothing pressing. Is it Claire's condition?" he asked sympathetically.

"No, no. She's pretty stable at the moment. Uh—I don't know if you noticed, but I wasn't here all afternoon."

"Oh, come on, Marshall, we don't punch time clocks here. Was it something to do with the boys?"

Marshall nodded. "Yes. The principal says Donny's misbehaving. Thinks it's probably reaction to—you know—the situation." Marshall let his voice trail off. "I'm sorry, Paul, Laura's waiting for me in the parking lot right now. I'll see you in the morning."

"Good," the director said, smiling. "Go and relax a bit."

"You, too," Marshall answered, "and don't work too hard."

Laura was running her car heater at full blast to keep warm.

"Jaffe, I was going to give you another two minutes. What the hell took you so long?"

"Hey, Laura, listen," he said in a strange tone of voice, "I've got to talk to someone."

"Did you have anyone particular in mind?"

"Hey, this is serious. I really need your advice."

"Then I advise going to my place and opening up some Emerald Dry."

He shrugged and shook his head like a zombie. "Would you mind if I left my car here and drove with you?"

"Sure, Marsh, climb in and start talking."

Laura was so staggered that she had trouble concentrating on the road.

"Christ," she said, "maybe every doctor is something of an egomaniac at heart."

"I know I am," Marshall offered, "but God knows, I'm not a kleptomaniac. I mean, Toivo's research was fundamental to the project. He came with the oncogene practically deciphered—and they worked together on the antibody. Paul is not just screwing the guy's career, he's screwing up the poor bastard's life!"

"I agree," Laura commented. "The only question now is what you can do about it."

They rode on in silence until Marshall untangled a strand from his web of thoughts,

"You realize if I blow the whistle on Rhodes I'm as good as dead at NIH."

"I know," she said quietly.

"I mean, not just in Washington. He's so wired-in he could short-circuit me at every university in the country. He even goes on lecture tours to Australia every summer—which means I'll be guano there, too."

Laura held fire till they neared her apartment.

"Marsh, I'd be lying if I didn't tell you that this would be kamikaze heroism. But what Rhodes is doing reflects badly not only on the Institutes, but on every scientist in this country. You've got to stop him somehow."

"At the price of committing professional suicide? Of totally destroying my own chance for Stockholm some day? Laura, I've got two kids and a sick wife. Unemployment won't even pay for Mrs. Henderson."

She looked at him and demanded, "What exactly do you want me to say?"

"Laura," he said earnestly, "I respect your opinion more than anybody else's in the world. If you were in my place, what would you do?"

She answered quietly, "I think I'd blow the whistle on him, Marsh."

As they walked up the stairs to her apartment, he asked, "Laura, haven't you ever compromised to save your skin?"

"No, at least I don't think so."

"What about that dead baby in Toronto?"

"I raised hell with the chiefs of service," she answered proudly.

"But you didn't tell the mother, did you?"

Laura paused at the door. He was right. She had told the captain, but she hadn't rocked the boat. Nobody ever sued the hospital for that inexcusable error—and cover-up.

"You're right," she confessed. "Besides, you've got your family to think of. Why not simply call Toivo and let *him* decide what to do? After all, it's *his* problem."

Marshall checked his watch. "It's nearly midnight. That would be almost seven in the morning in Helsinki. He'll be in his lab in another hour."

They sat in the kitchen without talking, growing increasingly impatient as they watched the hands on the clock move toward 1 A.M.

At last it was time to call. Laura glanced at Marshall. He rose, took a deep breath to calm himself. And then he carefully dialed the fourteen digits.

"Hello, this is Marshall Jaffe in Washington. I'm—"

"Don't tell me," the Finn interrupted, "I can guess why you are calling. I'm angry as hell myself."

"What's that?" Marshall asked, somewhat confused.

"You're calling about the galleys, aren't you?"

"Uh—yes."

"Then you haven't got them either, eh? I was planning to call that pompous editor at Harvard and give him glory Hallelujah!"

"I wouldn't if I were you," Marshall cautioned nervously. "I mean, I've already contacted the guy and I'm—getting a set this afternoon."

"What caused the delay? Didn't they find this important enough? For heaven's sake, I could make one phone call to London and *The Lancet* would take it on my word alone."

"I know, Toivo, I know. But there's a little problem—"

"What are you talking about?

"Uh—actually, I've had a look at the galleys—at least the first page. . . ."

"Yes?"

Marshall gazed helplessly at Laura as if to say, Can I really go through with this? Then he steeled himself and blurted into the phone, "There are no Finns listed, Toivo."

"What—is this some kind of joke?"

"I sure as hell wish it was—but a few hours ago I got a look at the only extant copy of the galleys. There's no authorship credit for anybody in your Institute—including *you*."

There was another pause. This time because the eminent scientist in Meilahti Hospital was himself at a loss for words.

Professor Toivo Karvonen had been a scientist all his life, and as such, drew conclusions only from empirical data. And the statement he had just heard seemed unfounded—not to mention incredible.

"Marshall, I've known Paul for more than twenty years. He's such a brilliant fellow—why on earth would he try something so stupid?"

"For God's sake, Toivo, I'm putting my own head on the block. Do you think I'd be calling if I hadn't seen the proofs with my own eyes?"

Karvonen's reaction surprised Marshall.

"Dear me," he whispered like a disapproving parent discovering his child had misbehaved. Marshall had expected a cascade of epithets in a multitude of languages. But there was none. Just a soft and sincere expression of gratitude.

"Marshall, this was very brave of you. I know the risk you are taking. Is there something I can do for you in return?"

"Well," he responded, not at all in jest, "I may be asking you for a job. Anyway, I'm sorry I had to tell you this. What are you going to do?"

The Finn remained calm.

"Listen, I need a little time to work things out. It must be very late for you. Get some sleep and I'll ring you at a decent hour."

"Uh—not at the Institutes, Toivo. I think that would be a little dangerous."

"I agree. May I call you at home?"

Marshall looked at Laura.

"Actually, I'm staying with a friend. It would be better if you called her." Then he quickly added, "I mean, she's another doctor, a colleague at NIH—"

"No need to explain," Karvonen replied sympathetically, "I know about your situation. Now get some rest. *Hyvästi.*"

Marshall hung up and, arm around Laura's shoulders, walked into the living room. He sat down on the couch, leaned his head back, and mumbled, "Oh, Christ. You're looking at a soon-to-be-totally-blackballed scientist. Do you think your friend Milton would give me a job in his deli?"

"Let's take one step at a time," she replied and bent down over him to pull off his loafers.

"What the hell are you doing? Laura, I'm in panic on the verge of hyperventilation. You surely don't want to—"

"Hey, relax, Marshall. I just want you to get some sleep. You're going to have a rough day tomorrow."

She lifted his feet onto the couch.

"Laura," he said, already curling up, "it's going to be a rough day for me for the next thirty years." As he reached up to kiss her, he murmured, "God, Laura, I don't know what the hell I'd do without you."

You'd probably be better off, she said to herself, already having second thoughts about encouraging him to be a hero.

She looked down at him. He was fast asleep.

FORTY-SIX

When she awoke, Marshall was already pacing the living room floor.

"Are you okay?" she asked.

"Sure—apart from being freaked, frantic, and totally catatonic, I'm perfectly okay," he replied.

She put her arms around him. "Stay loose, Jaffe," she murmured. "Justice will triumph."

"Do you really believe that?"

"I believe in you," she replied, trying to camouflage her own anxiety.

At which point he was bolstered enough to act. "Listen, I've got to make a guest appearance at my own house and then spread myself around the Institute and make sure everybody sees my innocent face."

He then looked at her sheepishly and asked, "Do you mind waiting here in case Toivo calls?"

"What about showing *my* innocent face?"

"Don't sweat, Laura," he reassured her. "Nobody has the slightest idea that you know about this. You can call in sick or something. If you get any important news from Toivo, drive to my office and we'll take a walk."

"Marshall, I'm scared," she confessed.

"That's two of us. I'm already regretting my George Washington performance—I mean, it was Karvonen's cherry tree, anyway. If I can find a safe phone, I'll try and give you a ring."

He squeezed her shoulders affectionately, and started off. Then he stopped abruptly, turned, and said, "If I forgot to say I love you last night, I'm saying it now."

Then he was gone, now leaving Laura to pace back and forth like a worried father outside the delivery room.

Suddenly the phone rang.

"I've got really bad news, Laura." It was Marshall from a roadside phone booth. "Has he called back yet?"

"No."

"In that case, it's all over. Rhodes just announced a press conference—and party—for this afternoon. Anyway, if Toivo does phone, say we did the best we could."

Laura hung up distraught.

As she headed toward her balcony for some fresh air the phone rang again. She rushed to answer it.

"Yes?" she asked breathlessly.

"Hello," said a distant-sounding voice. "Karvonen here—do I have the right number?"

"Yes, Professor, this is—a colleague of Marshall's."

"Splendid. Please convey to him that everything has been taken care of."

"I don't understand, sir," Laura countered. "Marshall's just phoned me to say Rhodes has called a press conference for this afternoon."

"I know, I know," said the old man genially, "Paul and I already discussed it at great length by telephone." He then waited a split second and continued, "My own conference was an hour ago."

"What?"

"Yes. And please do tell your courageous friend Marshall that I was able to gather quite a high-powered press group and broke the news at noon Helsinki time. Which, as you may know, is only 5 A.M. in Washington. According to my secretary's memo, not only were the wire services present, but *The New York Times* and even Tass and the New China News Service sent their own correspondents."

"That's amazing—I still can't believe what I'm hearing," Laura responded with excitement. "But how did you ever manage to get all those people together in so short a time?"

"Miss—I am sorry, I don't know your name—"

"Laura Castellano, sir. Dr. Castellano, actually."

"Well, Doctor, you must be very new to the world of media medicine. Don't you know the one magic word that can attract every journalist on earth?"

"Free booze?" she joked weakly.

"No, my dear lady, *cancer.* It's the most potent drawing card on the entire planet."

For a moment Laura was taken aback by this unexpected cynicism. Marshall's description had led her to imagine the Finn as some sort of avuncular Santa Claus in a white lab coat. But she was learning. Learning fast.

"Uh, sir, does Dr. Rhodes know about this?"

"Of course," he replied. "I have been absolutely collegial and aboveboard. I called him at his home. I was sorry to have to wake him, but I think he was grateful to be told of my intentions. But then it was barely dawn in Washington and what else could he do but go along with it? Anyway, please give your gallant young man an affectionate embrace on my behalf. *Hyvästi.*"

At four that afternoon, over a hundred of the more distinguished Fellows—augmented by a huge platoon of reporters and photographers—crowded into the main reception room of the Institutes to hear their senior director—elegantly dressed in his pinstripe "public appearance suit"—proclaim (in this case re-echo) to the world the thaumaturgic properties of the Rhodes-Karvonen factor. All present then drank to the health of the two scientists—and to their global patient, Suffering Mankind.

His confidence bolstered by the excellent champagne, Marshall bounded up to the podium, kissed and congratulated Mrs. Rhodes, and then heartily shook his mentor's hand.

"This is a great day, Paul," he enthused, adding (without, he hoped, any perceptible irony), "for all of us."

"Thank you, Marshall," Rhodes replied cheerfully. And then said under his breath, "Could you possibly drop by my office at six o'clock?"

"Sure thing," Marshall responded cheerily and went off to look for Laura.

He found her surrounded by a group of reporters, all seeking her opinion on the new discovery. My God, he thought buoyantly, it sure is risky inviting Laura to a press conference for *anything.*

Rhodes was already waiting for him, leaning against the front of his mahogany desk. Marshall entered and took his usual seat.

The director merely stood in silence, glaring at him as if he were a butterfly fixed by a pin.

At last he spoke. One syllable.

"Why?"

"I don't understand, Paul—"

"Cut the crap, Jaffe. You had to be the one who told him. There was only one set of proofs and they were on my desk the other night. Incidentally, does Toivo have you on his payroll?"

Marshall did not dignify the insinuation with a reply.

Rhodes shook his head incredulously. "For the life of me, I can't imagine why an overambitious sonovabitch like you would have done what you did."

"To tell the truth, I'm not really sure myself," Marshall confessed. "Call it an aberration—a kind of spasm of integrity. I mean, I've worked on this project and I know how much Toivo's contributed."

Rhodes now affected a look of pained sympathy.

"I can't believe a fellow with your smarts wouldn't know how to play the game. When I was doing post-doc work at Tech my bosses published both my projects without even mentioning my name. It's like the wages of apprenticeship."

"Come on, Paul, you can hardly call Karvonen an apprentice. And he clearly has more scruples. Sorry if I've let you down by doing what was right. May I go now?"

"When I tell you, Jaffe," the director answered sharply. "I just don't want you to leave thinking you've accomplished something noble. Obviously, the article will be published with the names of all your bosom buddies in Helsinki." He then paused to savor his revelation: "I just thought you'd like to know that I've already got the patents."

"What?"

"Honor's only part of it, my boy. You can't just retire and rest on your laurels. It's much more comfortable to rest on your royalties. And let me tell you—my phone's been ringing off the hook just in the last three hours. Every major drug concern from Switzerland to Japan and back has already offered me deals that would turn those curly hairs of yours into electric wires."

Marshall shrugged his shoulders. Shit, he thought, Karvonen got screwed anyway. So much for my altruism. He looked at Rhodes.

"*Now* may I be excused, Herr Direktor?"

"Excused? My dear Marshall, by tomorrow you will be *expunged.* Go clear your office—that is, of items that belong to you. I've asked Captain Stevens of Security to help you separate what's yours and what's

Uncle Sam's. Because as of midnight, they won't even let you through the gate as a tourist. Goodnight."

It was only when he had turned to go that Marshall realized how hard he had been hit.

But there was more to come.

"Jaffe, I want to say that I'm sincerely sorry for your wife. You should have thought of—"

"Can it, Paul. Claire doesn't need your pity. She may have lost her health, but she still has her principles. So on behalf of all my family, I'd like to tell you to go straight to hell."

"And on behalf of Dr. Castellano, too, may I assume?"

Marshall was furious.

"Laura had nothing to do with this, Paul. You wouldn't punish her—?"

"Wouldn't I? By sheer coincidence I've discovered that she called in sick this morning. Since she looks more radiant than ever this evening, I think I can safely assume she was an accomplice in this treason. Unfortunately, at the moment she seems to be to this institution exactly what the Silver Lady is to a Rolls Royce. But be assured, I'll manage it."

Laura was waiting for him in the now-empty reception room. They sat side by side and spoke amid the clatter of the cleaning staff. She touched his shoulder gently.

"I know how you feel, Marsh, and I feel guilty for encouraging you to tell Toivo. I never believed Rhodes would go that far. But I swear you'll land on your feet."

"Thanks, kid," he said with a sad smile. "You wanna come help fill some boxes?"

She nodded and they set off for his office.

Captain Clyde Stevens, B.S., Howard, '62, sat calmly smoking as he watched the two of them ransack Marshall's office of everything that did not have to be rendered unto Caesar.

Every so often Marshall would shake a paper in front of his eyes. "This is a record of my tennis games against the Senior and Junior Fellows—and the cash I've won. Does this constitute top secrecy, sir?"

The captain, genuinely sad to see the young scientist depart, was baffled—and resented having been burdened with this unpleasant task. "Hell, Dr. Jaffe," he complained, "don't play around with me like this. I couldn't care less if you took all the toilet paper from the bathrooms."

"That's not a bad idea," said Laura, trying to relieve the tension with a little humor.

"Oh, no," said Marshall broadly, "we'd deprive the good Dr. Rhodes of the material he uses for his articles."

Captain Stevens did his best to suppress a smile.

When Marshall picked up his Rolodex, he thought for a moment of asking the Security officer to remove the phone numbers he thought should be classified. But then another notion struck him.

"Hey, Laura," he said, "this is my last chance to make a free call on the government's penny. I might as well prepare Karvonen for the shock."

She nodded. "Good idea."

He turned to Stevens and explained, "Captain, my word of honor. This call is official business."

The officer signaled his permission.

It was still very early morning in Helsinki, so Marshall had to wake up Karvonen at his home.

"Marshall, I assure you," the Finn jovially protested, "I was wide awake. I'm in my study now doing some calculations. I assume you're calling to report you're fired. But I hope you know you're more than welcome at my Institute."

Marshall shuddered. "I'm afraid I've got some really bad news, Toivo—Rhodes already filed for the patents three months ago. I guess we underestimated him."

Karvonen let out a burst of laughter.

"Toivo, are you okay?"

"I'm fine, my boy, I'm fine," he answered heartily. "*I* registered the patent *six* months ago. It takes a while, so Rhodes will not have heard that he's been beaten to it."

Marshall was struck dumb. And then he slowly began to boil.

"Toivo," he said, trying to rein his anger, "are you telling me that *you'd* already screwed Rhodes by the time I risked my neck to warn you that he was trying to screw you?"

"I am, my dear friend Marshall. But that does not make me any less grateful for the sacrifice you've made. Now at least you know the way the world spins. Dog eat dog. And scientist knife scientist. Please stay in touch. *Hyvästi.*"

It was a totally new experience for Laura.

Though it was a time of grieving, she had a curious sense of fulfillment by being able to share with Marshall his misfortune. She held him in her arms all night.

The next morning they woke early, had coffee, and then separated—she to the lab and he to his family.

After the friendly guard waved her through the gate, Laura parked and started walking across the campus. She glanced at Marshall's window. Even from a distance it looked empty, bare.

She spent an hour in the Neonatal ICU, which mercifully today contained just three sick preemies—whose aggregate weight was probably less than seven pounds, but who were being sustained by what seemed like seven *tons* of electronic machinery. She sometimes wondered if the babies did not feel overwhelmed by it all—as she was.

Back in the lab, she was unable to think of anything but Marshall.

The phone rang. It was Rhodes's personal secretary. Would it be convenient for Dr. Castellano to stop by at, say, four that afternoon?

Curiously, she was not upset. She convinced herself that it was probably some administrative matter like the pending renewal of her Fellowship.

She arrived three minutes early and the receptionist ushered her straight into the director's office.

"Good afternoon, Dr. Castellano," he said paternally. "Take a seat, will you?"

She could not help but notice that he had not called her Laura.

"I suppose you have some inkling of why I've asked you here, Dr. Castellano?"

"I assume it's something to do with my reapplication," she answered.

"In a way, yes."

Rhodes rubbed his brow as a kind of demonstration of concern.

"Dr. Castellano, I don't know how to tell you this. I mean, I've come—we've all come—to think of you as occupying a special place in our constellation."

"Don't beat around the bush," she replied as calmly as possible. "Just tell me what I've done wrong."

" 'Wrong?' " Rhodes replied, "I wouldn't exactly use that term. It's just that—well—we can't see ourselves renewing you for another three years."

"Oh."

"Nothing personal, of course. Just a case of too many qualified candidates."

"Of course."

"And as you know, it's common practice to inform Junior Fellows in the spring of their last year, so they can make other arrangements—you know, seek a post elsewhere. I'm sure Dain Oliver will have some suggestions. And you can count on this office to back you to the hilt. Besides, you've still got till the end of July. . . ."

Laura was at a loss for words, her mind felt battered by a relentless drumming at her temples. She needed time—perhaps only half a minute—to get her emotions under control. For she was determined not to surrender without a pitched battle.

Meanwhile, Rhodes wanted to twist the knife a little further.

"I'm terribly sorry to have to tell you this. We all like you very much. We'll miss you at parties."

By now she had pulled herself together sufficiently to be able to fight back.

"Paul, you've got no right to make this decision unilaterally. And I'm positive you haven't even spoken to Dain or anyone else in the field. I'm going to appeal this to the Board and I'm willing to bet they'll overrule you."

There was a sudden silence—which Laura interpreted as a point in her favor. Paul rose slowly.

"Dr. Castellano, let's lay all our cards on the table," he said in a tone like the slash of a stiletto. "You and I know what this is really about. Why don't we discuss the real issue?"

"Fine. A little straightforward truth would be refreshing."

The director looked at her and grinned. "You like Marshall Jaffe, don't you? I'd go so far as to say you like him a great deal. Am I correct?"

"I don't have to answer that."

"Of course you don't. You really care for him—and you wouldn't want to jeopardize his career, would you?"

"He's one of the most brilliant microbiologists in America. I don't have to worry about his career."

"Oh, *yes*, you do, Dr. Castellano," Rhodes responded condescendingly. "I don't care how smart that treacherous little weasel is, I still outrank him in the scientific community and I can close every door—and I mean *every* door—in this country. If I wanted, I could see to it that he couldn't even get a job teaching junior high school biology in Harlem."

"He was a full professor at Stanford," Laura retorted. "They even offered to double his salary when he was asked to come here. They'd be overjoyed to have him back."

"Oh, I suppose under normal circumstances you might be right. But Max Wingate, his former chairman, owes me one—a very *big* one. And as much as he likes Marshall, he wouldn't dare cross me."

"I think you're bluffing," she replied.

"Want me to call him right away? I'll put on the speaker phone so you can hear with your own ears while I blackball your lover with his home team. I promise you, Laura," he continued, now raising his voice, "one word from me and he'll be out in the professional cold forever."

There was a sudden silence.

At last she inquired softly, "What does this have to do with me?"

"Absolutely everything, Dr. Castellano," he replied with a tinge of savage delight. "You hold the fate of that worm Jaffe in those sweet little hands of yours. Because if I don't get your resignation, Marshall Jaffe dies."

"That's a bit melodramatic, isn't it?" Laura commented.

"I don't think so. You and I both know his career *is* his life. And I can take it away from him with one phone call. Now have I made my point?"

"I'll sleep on it," Laura answered disdainfully.

"I'm sorry, Laura. I want your answer now. Then, as far as I'm concerned, the two of you can go to sleep—or to hell."

Laura had never experienced such a brutal verbal assault. She looked fiercely at Rhodes and spat out, "You are one slimy bastard."

"I don't care what you think," he replied smugly, "just as long as a letter withdrawing your renewal application is on my desk in half an hour. And I don't mean thirty-one minutes."

Laura sat in her lab, desperating trying to numb herself into signing the document she had just painstakingly typed. Did she dare test Paul's threat?

The phone rang.

"Hi, Baby." It was Marshall.

"How's it going?" she asked, trying to sound cheerful.

"Well, you know me," he jested, "the cat with eight more lives. I think I'm gonna get my job back at Stanford. Max Wingate is calling a special meeting of the department. They're probably rubber-stamping me as we speak. So much for the Colossus of Rhodes."

Laura was petrified. She looked at her watch: ten minutes to five.

"Marsh, let's meet for dinner. I have something to finish in a hurry."

"Okay, sweetheart. What if we rendezvous around six at the Jefferson Memorial?"

"Why there, of all places?"

"I like to look at all those great words of Thomas J., carved on the huge marble tablets. It sort of soothes my soul when I feel really down."

I'll give you more comfort, she thought to herself. And then said aloud, "I'll be there, Marshall. Just stay loose."

He had been serious.

When Laura arrived in the great domed marble monument she found Marshall gazing up at Jefferson's eloquence. He kissed her.

"I can understand why you feel uplifted in this place. Are you okay?"

"Well, it's official," he announced joyfully. "I've got my job back at Stanford. They were really great about it."

"Oh," she said. And thought, At least Paul kept his part of the deal. "When are you going?"

"Well, Max says I can move back into my old lab whenever it's convenient. But I think we should wait till the kids finish the semester at school. I don't want to upset their lives even more—they've got enough to deal with."

"Well," she commented, "I guess that gives us both time to get used to it."

He gripped her firmly by the shoulders. "No, Laura—I want you to come to California with me."

She was astonished for a moment. And then confused. Could he possibly be willing to abandon his family for her?

"Are you sure?"

"Absolutely."

Laura was in such an ecstasy of hope she almost felt guilty. She asked for reassurance.

"As what?" she asked.

"What do you mean, 'as what?' There's no question—you'd be a full professor."

"I don't understand."

"I guarantee you—Stanford, Berkeley, San Francisco—they'd all fight to get you on their faculties. And trust me, I've got pull in California."

Then slowly it began to dawn on her. "Are you actually saying that—except for a jump in my academic rank—things between us would be just the same?"

"Absolutely. We'd be like a married couple."

"Only Claire would still be Mrs. Jaffe and I'd be like a second car."

"No—" he began to protest.

"That's what you're asking, isn't it? You want me to drop everything I've accomplished in Washington—to go and be your geisha girl."

"I thought you loved me, Laura."

"I thought so, too, Marsh. But since you're not a Mormon or a Moslem, you're not entitled to more than one wife—and I refuse to settle for only half a husband."

"Hey, for God's sake, Laura, can't you appreciate what a bind I'm in? My two kids are already screwed up. Can you imagine what it would do to their heads if I divorced their sick mother? I mean, I'm a bastard—but God knows I'm not *that* much of a bastard."

She did not know how to react. She wanted desperately to be "legitimized," yet in a way she could understand his quandary. And could even grudgingly respect his refusal to hurt his already-wounded family.

"I don't know, Marshall," she said, stalling for time.

And then he questioned *her* motives. "Or are you still too dazzled by the Washington limelight to exile yourself to the provincial vineyards of California?"

"I'm entitled to a career, dammit!" she retorted indignantly.

"How the hell would this compromise your career? Berkeley's not exactly the boondocks. In fact, if you've been keeping up with the academic scene, you should know most of its graduate departments now outrank Fair Harvard."

"It's not that," she protested, unwilling to concede that he was even partially right. And then she added softly, "Look, one of these mornings I'm going to wake up and suddenly discover I'm over the hill, and I just might want to have a baby before then. I mean, look at your hero's philosophy."

She pointed to the tall majestic panel engraved with Jefferson's famous description of man's inalienable rights to "Life, Liberty and the pursuit of Happiness."

He waited for a moment and said almost in a whisper, "Laura, you're asking too much. You're not being fair—"

"*Fair?* You're talking to me about fair?" She was so incensed that she nearly told him of the deal she had struck with Rhodes. But somehow it no longer seemed to matter.

"Laura, do you think I like the cards life has dealt me? Don't you think I would change things if I could? And can't you even meet me halfway?"

"You mean like Chicago?" she joked bitterly.

For a moment they just stood there looking into each other's eyes. The monument was empty and so quiet that their breathing seemed to echo in the dome.

"Well," she said wearily, "scientifically speaking, I'd say our relationship can best be described by the second law of thermodynamics—it's just about run out of energy. Otherwise stated, I can see now that you've got to stay with Claire. But I also know that *I've* got to stay away from *you*. Goodbye, Marshall."

She turned and started off. He called after her.

"Laura, please—are you sure we can't—"

Moments later she was out of earshot and kept walking down the many steps of the memorial into the darkening twilight.

And kept descending. To a depth of sadness she had never known before.

She was proud of herself.

Laura felt distraught, depressed, nearly suicidal. But she was nevertheless proud that she had not broken down in front of Marshall, for whose career she had just immolated her own. It took all her strength to keep from phoning Barney during office hours. She knew he usually got home around eight. She'd call a little later.

But suppose he had a date? If he got back at midnight he wouldn't want me to disturb him then, either, she thought. Shit, I'm going crazy.

At that very moment the phone rang.

"Castellano, what the hell's the matter with you?"

If ever she had doubted the existence of ESP, she was now a true believer.

"Hi, Barn," she said in a voice that could not help disguise the deadness of her soul.

"Hey, I'm not interrupting something, am I? I mean, I wouldn't want to cramp the style of that tennis-playing asshole. Has he made you boycott me or something? I mean, you haven't called in weeks. Is everything okay?"

"Fine, fine," she answered mechanically.

"Hey, kiddo, your enthusiasm sounds pretty underwhelming. What's up?"

"Nothing's up," she answered. And then, still unable to reveal her pain, she said obliquely, "You might say everything's down."

She paused for a moment and then asked, "It just occurred to me, are *you* alone?"

"Yes. At the moment, anyway. Ursula's coming a little later."

"Who's Ursula?"

"Oh, you should see her, Castellano. She's Holland's gift to cardiology—and my heart in particular. In fact, tonight's encounter might decide the gold medal in the Livingston Matrimonial Olympics."

"Then I'd better hang up," Laura said apologetically, her tone more leaden than ever.

"Aw, come on, Castellano, what's the problem?"

"Are you sitting down?" she asked.

"Why, is this going to shock me?"

"No, but it might take a while."

As Barney carried the phone over to an easy chair, he answered gently, "Laura, take all the time you need. I'm a professional listener, remember? Come on—spill."

At that moment her emotional dam cracked.

After nearly forty minutes he cut her off. "Hey look, Castellano, I've got to rush to the airport."

"Oh, sure," she responded apologetically, "you're meeting Ursula."

"Negative—she lives two blocks away. I want to catch the last shuttle to Washington."

"No, Barn—please don't. I'm okay. I really am."

"That's for *me* to judge. You just better be there at the other end to meet me. Meanwhile, do not drink. Do not take a pill. Do not even drive. Take a friendly taxi and be waiting for me. And wear a red rose so I can recognize you."

"What about your patients?" she asked in a semi-chiding tone.

"Hey, kiddo, don't you even know what day it is? Tomorrow's Saturday. The couch doesn't work weekends. So like it or lump it, I'm on my way."

Although subconsciously she had hoped for this, Laura protested weakly, "But what about Ursula?"

"No sweat. I'll explain it to her. She's used to my antics—she'll understand. You just be there," he commanded.

As Barney was stuffing clothes into an overnight case, Dr. Ursula de Groot let herself in.

"Were you planning to elope tonight?" she challenged.

"Listen, Urse, sit down for a second. I've got a short time to tell a long story."

He did his best to impress upon her the urgency of his mission of mercy. But somehow the flaxen-haired cardiologist was not convinced.

"I hate Laura," she said bitterly.

"Why?" Barney asked as he hastily snapped shut his valise.

"Isn't it obvious?" she replied, holding out her key to his apartment. "Here, you'd better take it back. I think Ms. Castellano needs it more than I do."

FORTY-SEVEN

Laura did not breathe for the next two hours. At least it felt that way. It was only the hope of seeing Barney that kept her minimally functioning.

She was waiting in the arrival lounge when he hurried in from the tarmac, jacket lapels pulled up to protect him from the cold wind.

His first glance at Laura made him ache. She looked sheet-white and so vulnerable, as if she had wept away all her energy.

"Hi, thanks for coming," he said, hugging her.

"Shouldn't that be my line?" she asked weakly.

"Okay, take it if you want it. But where are we having dinner?"

"At eleven at night?" she asked.

"I'll bet you haven't eaten yet, have you?"

She shook her head. "I wasn't hungry."

"Well, be anorexic on your own time. *I'm* starving, and I've gotta get some pasta in me fast or I'll die of starvation."

They were standing on the curb now. As a cab pulled forward and Laura climbed in, Barney asked the driver, "What's the best Italian joint between here and the Mason-Dixon line?"

"Well, I take a lot of people to Pasquale's in Georgetown."

"Then take us, too."

He got into the cab and they zoomed off.

*   *   *

"I am sorry, signore, but I do not see a reservation for Yehudi and Hepzibah Menuhin."

"Well, I'm very sorry," Barney retorted in his best imitation of artistic temperament. "Our impresario assured us that he'd made arrangements. Can't you manage even a small table in the back?"

"*Mi dispiace,* signore. Even if I could, you are both lacking the proper attire."

He did not for a minute think he was dealing with the great violinist and his sister. And in any case, Pasquale's had a sartorial as well as a gastronomic reputation to uphold.

"Listen, Captain," Barney said, "I want to tell you the truth. I'm a medical doctor and this woman is in carbohydrate shock. If we don't get some fettuccine into her fast she may die right here. And that certainly wouldn't be good for your business."

The captain, fed up with debating, was about to call Rocco, the barman-bouncer, when one of the elegant diners—a tall, gray-haired man whose attention had been caught by the animated *recitativo*—came to the rescue.

"Is there any problem here, Pasquale?" he asked, and quickly turned to greet Laura. "Nice to see you, Dr. Castellano."

"Nice to see *you,* Senator Otis. This is my friend, Dr. Barney Livingston."

"Hello, Doctor. Would you two care to join us for a drink?" the lawmaker asked hospitably.

"Actually," Laura replied, "we were about to leave. They don't seem to have a table for us."

The Senator frowned at Pasquale. "Are you quite sure, *padrone?* Dr. Castellano is a very important staff member at the NIH. She's probably been on an emergency call and was unable to change. I'm sure you can bend the rules just this once."

Not wishing to risk Congressional disapproval, Pasquale withdrew his veto and murmured, "Actually, we were holding a table for two but the clients appear to be late. Would you come this way, please?"

Laura smiled gratefully at Otis, who reiterated, "You're still welcome to join Amanda and me—even if it's just for coffee."

"Another time, Senator," Laura replied. "Dr. Livingston and I have to discuss an important case. But I'm very grateful for your help."

"Not at all, Laura. Any time I can be of assistance, just call my office."

As they were being led to their (excellently placed) booth, Barney glanced over at the Senator's table and commented, "Jeez, that guy has a beautiful daughter."

"She's not his daughter," Laura replied matter-of-factly.

"His wife?"

"Guess again, Livingston," she retorted.

"Wow! Is that one of the perks of being a U.S. Senator?"

Laura nodded affirmatively. "I told you the ratio of women to men in this city is five to one. So imagine the possibilities."

"Yeah," Barney answered, "that means every guy could have his own girls' basketball team."

After ordering fettuccine and a large, straw-bottomed *fiasco* of Chianti Ruffino, Barney got down to the serious business of his troubled friend.

He made her recount all the details of the Rhodes-Karvonen skullduggery—sometimes even jotting down notes, which he assured her would be useful for his work-in-progress on the mind of the physician. From there it was a short step—down—to Marshall Jaffe.

"I know this sounds sanctimonious, Castellano," he preached. "But as I've told you maybe a million times, one complete human being deserves another complete human being. Love isn't a part-time job."

"That's a good line," she responded. "You ought to use it in your book."

"I already have," he smiled. "But it bears repetition. When the hell are you going to believe that you're a terrific person who deserves a terrific marriage and terrific children?"

"I won't have any children. I don't believe in marriage. I don't even believe in love."

"Bullshit, Castellano! I don't believe you don't believe. You know, Hippocrates said—"

"Screw Hippocrates. He didn't have to live in Washington."

"Neither do you, for that matter. Have you thought about what you're going to do after July?"

She shook her head.

"I don't know. Every so often some med school writes to see if I'm interested in a job. Columbia P & S asked me to head a new neonatology program. Last time I heard, they still hadn't filled the slot."

"That's great," he exclaimed. "Then you'll be in New York."

"Yeah," she said glumly, "that's the drawback. It's the worst city in the world to be alone in."

"How can you say that, Castellano? I'm there, aren't I?"

"Yeah, sure. But you have Ursula to take care of. You don't need me around. It's just that the idea of starting over in a new place really scares me. And at the moment there are too many black clouds in my mind to think of next week, much less next year."

"I can imagine," he said softly. "You probably feel like walking straight into the sea—like Virginia Woolf. Am I right?"

"Pretty close. I feel like a wounded animal that ought to be taken to the vet and put to sleep."

"That's a pity. The world would lose a good doctor." He paused and said gently, "And I would lose my best friend."

At this she raised her head and gazed into his eyes.

"You'd never do that to me, would you, Castellano?"

She did not answer. But inwardly she acknowledged that he was still one of the few things worth living for.

"Honest to God, Laura, you've gotta learn to be happy—even if it means taking lessons at Berlitz or something. I mean, I don't know if *you* notice, but I can feel that fortieth birthday breathing down my neck. I mean, by now we're supposed to be middle-aged parents, worrying about the braces on our kids' teeth—and stuff like that. At the rate time is moving I feel like I'm in a crucial basketball game and playing so damn hard that when I finally look up at the clock I'll have only thirty seconds left. . . ."

She merely nodded.

They talked on until at last they were the only patrons in the restaurant. A cordon of waiters stood around them, emitting polite coughs.

"Seems to be a lot of bronchial problems among the personnel here, don't you think, Dr. Castellano?"

"Barney, you're smashed," she replied.

"So are you," he countered.

"Then why don't we leave?"

"Because I don't think I can stand up, that's why."

By some miracle they were able to pour themselves into a taxi and head for Bethesda.

"I hope you don't mind sleeping on the Castro," Laura said, her speech blurry but her mood lifted.

"Not at all," he replied, "I regard sleeping on a memento of the great Fidel as a sort of homage to Luis."

Half an hour later Laura unlocked her apartment door and asked, "Do you want some coffee, Barn?"

"Actually," he said apologetically, "I sobered up during the ride, and since I'm gonna have a headache anyway. . . ."

He did not need to finish the sentence. Laura merely smiled, went to the refrigerator, and withdrew a bottle—the one she had originally intended to share with Marshall.

They sat facing each other and continued to pour out their thoughts.

"Barney, something you said this evening bothers me—something about us both being unhappy."

"Yeah—what's so astonishing about that?"

"It wasn't news to me that I'm incapable of happiness—but I thought at least *you* were okay. I mean, you were analyzed and everything."

"Analysis makes you aware. It doesn't automatically make you stop acting in the way you've discovered to be self-destructive. No, Castellano, I've been thinking all tonight how ironic it is that we've both made it in the outside world and yet screwed up in our private lives. Was it maybe the fluoride in the Brooklyn water?"

They sat in silence.

Had they run out of conversation? No, Barney thought. The best thing about the two of us is that we've never been at a loss for things to say to each other.

After another moment, Laura said, "You know, Barn, I don't think a therapist could help me, anyway."

"Why not?"

"Because probably what's wrong with me is like a tumor that's inoperable. It's too metastasized through my self-esteem."

Then she confessed what she had long been pondering. "Maybe, deep down, somewhere, I really don't like men."

"You know that's not true," he responded.

"I mean in the sense of trust, Barn," she explained. "I've never really trusted any man."

"But you trust me."

"That's different," she responded quickly.

They were again silent for a moment.

And then Barney whispered, "Why?"

"Why what?"

"Why am I different from other men?"

She could not reply. She had never really thought about it.

No, of course she had.

Finally she said, "I don't know, Barn. I mean, for as far back as I can remember, you've always been the most important person in my life."

"You didn't answer my question, Laura. Why am I different from other men?"

She shrugged. "I guess because we've always been . . . such good friends."

He looked at her and then asked softly, "And that precludes every-thing else, huh?"

She was silent again, so he continued his catechism.

"Can you honestly say that you've never thought of us as . . . a real couple? I confess that I have. I mean, I've always chased those fantasies away because I didn't want to run the risk of losing the special thing we have. . . ."

Laura smiled self-consciously, then found the courage to admit, "Of course I've had those thoughts. I mean, I've spent my life explaining to the world why we were just friends and not, you know . . . lovers."

"That makes two of us. But Laura, I can't do that any more."

"What?"

He answered her with another question.

"Which of us do you think is the most afraid, Laura?"

The question came from left field, but the answer had always been central to her inner thoughts.

"Me," she answered. "I always thought you knew me too well—I mean all my secret faults—to like me that way."

"But I *do* like you in that way," he said. "I love you in every way, Laura."

Her head was lowered, and even without being able to see her face he knew she was crying.

"Hey, Castellano. Tell the truth. Have I just lost my best pal?"

She looked up at him, the tears on her cheeks contradicting the smile on her face.

"I hope so," she said softly. "Because I've always wished that you could . . . you know . . . love me as a woman." She paused, and then added, "The way I love you."

Barney stood up.

"I'm sober, Castellano. How do you feel?"

"I'm sober. I know what I'm saying."

There was no further conversation. Barney walked over and took Laura's hand. They started slowly to the other room.

And that night ended their platonic friendship.

FORTY-EIGHT

The next morning Barney and Laura found themselves experiencing a phenomenon that they had never known existed: an indescribable feeling of wholeness.

For here, if anywhere on earth, were a man and a woman who did not need priest or clerk to sanctify their union.

"How do you feel?" Barney asked.

"Happy, really happy."

That was the real miracle.

At first they kept their joy a secret, like a treasure that was richer still for being shared by only two. But by July Laura's Fellowship was over and to celebrate her moving to New York, they took fifteen minutes of a judge's time to make themselves "respectable."

As the couple walked arm in arm down the courthouse steps, Laura Castellano, M.D., newly appointed Professor of Neonatology at Columbia College of Physicians and Surgeons, confessed to Barney Livingston, M.D., Professor of Psychiatry at NYU Medical School, "Things have happened so fast that I never really had the time to tell you."

"What?"

"When I saw Luis last year in Mexico, he said something that really shook me up. I mean, it seemed so crazy."

"What? What?"

"It was just two words," she answered. "He leaned over and whispered, 'Marry Barney.' "

FORTY-NINE

Seth Lazarus feared that he was going mad.

Too frightened of the dreams now haunting him, he spent whole nights awake. His actions, like Macbeth's, had "murdered sleep."

It had been more than ten years since he had helped Mel Gatkowicz to die. And in the interim there had been three—no, four. At times he wasn't sure how many ghosts were lurking.

There was Mrs. Carson, then that teenage girl so cruelly injured in a car crash she could only blink her eyelids—and whose brain could only function well enough to let her feel the pain.

Then there was . . . who? Why did his memory betray him? Perhaps it was instinct in his psyche fighting to preserve his sanity. If it could just obliterate them *all*—a merciful amnesia to assuage his conscience.

Except for Howie, he had never acted merely on his own initiative. Had he intervened in every instance where he'd seen a life reduced to nothing but a mass of suffering, he would have helped—*how many others, Seth?*

For in every other case, he had been implored—by words and circumstances, external forces that would finally erode his will to let remorseless Nature take its course (and let *him* sleep).

There had always been distraught petitioners, anguished families in pain almost as great as that which racked their loved ones.

And even then, he always had made certain that the patient was aware and had consented to the termination of his life.

Though his faith was strong, Seth was aware that he was moving into that shadowy area claimed by both God and Satan as their eminent domain.

The Lord declared, "Thou shalt not kill." There was no Holy Book to justify Seth's belief that Man deserved the same respect as he himself gave to sorely wounded animals—a swift and painless death.

Judy saw how he was haunted, but what could she do? Was there a doctor in the world who could repair such an injured soul?

She saw catastrophe ahead. Either Seth would be caught—because, despite his promises to her, she knew that he would be unable to refuse the pleas of yet another tortured family—or he would simply break under the weight of his enormous burden.

He brooded in his study late at night.

One evening she went down to talk to him.

"What are you doing, Seth?" she asked.

"Nothing. Just reading the journals. I barely understand the stuff these days—genetic engineers are taking over from physicians. Pretty soon we'll all be put away just like an old Corvair."

"Corvairs were faulty, Seth, 'unsafe at any speed.' Are you implying that there's something wrong with you?"

He looked at her. "Judy—you and I both know it. I fall in the category of what the psychiatrists call an 'impaired physician.' "

He tossed her the publication he'd been looking at.

"Here, read for yourself."

The article was called "The Wounded Healer: Crises in the Lives of Practicing Physicians." It was by Barney Livingston, M.D.

"Didn't you go to school with him?"

Seth nodded.

"Yes. He was a good man. From that paper I gather that he's lately come to specialize in 'psycho' doctors. If you believe his statistics, it's almost an axiom: To care is to crack."

"And you have other pressures, too," she added.

"Yes," he said, "I—"

He paused in midsentence as if reconsidering what he was about to say. Or not say.

Judy walked over and put a comforting hand on his shoulder.

A voice suddenly emerged from the innermost recesses of his being. "Where does it end?"

She sat on the desk and faced him.

"Here. Right here and now. You'll take a leave of absence and we'll go someplace far away so you can heal."

"What about the kids?"

"We could go for a month and maybe ask your mother to take care of them."

"My mother, Judy? Maybe you're the one who's cracking up. May I remind you you're talking about a woman who on every January twelfth gets up, bakes a cake, and invites imaginary friends to come in and sing 'Happy Birthday, dear Howie.' "

The thought cast a heavy pall on both of them. For they knew that was where it all had started. When he'd "saved" his brother to release his parents—and himself—from living with his helpless, endless agony.

He should have learned his lesson then. It had not worked. To his mom, still crazed with grief, he was a living ghost. And her distraction surely was one reason for his father's early death.

"All right, Seth," Judy said sternly, "I'll make a deal with you. The kids get out of school on June eleventh. On the twelfth you'll take off your white coat, put your stethoscope away, and we'll travel till Labor Day."

"And the syringe," he added blankly. "We won't pack the syringe."

She held his face with both her hands and said, "That's over now, Seth. That's over as of this instant. Let someone else show mercy on them, Seth. You've done enough."

But Seth had already gone too far. The previous Saturday night, Nurse Millicent Cavanagh had seen him attend a patient in the Lakeshore V.A. Hospital (where he was now working one afternoon a week). The patient, Sergeant Clarence T. Englund, a paraplegic veteran of World War II, was, after nearly thirty years of hospitalization for his wounds, all too slowly dying of bone cancer.

It was Millie who, in her next routine check of vital signs, had found the patient dead. The next morning the official certificate listed cause of death as the sequelae of the patient's many maladies, which resulted in heart failure.

But in her mind it should have read "premeditated murder."

In the eighteen or so years that she had worked at the V.A. she'd grown fond of "Old Clarence T.," as everybody called him. What she perhaps admired most was his amazing courage to endure—and now and then even to smile through pain.

Indeed, the night before, though comatose from analgesics that dulled his mind but could not wholly ease the agony, he had said something so beautiful to her that she recalled it word for word. "When I get to paradise, Millie, and all this pain is over, I'll sit and wait for you and the two of us will live together for eternity."

And she also remembered him saying, "I'll be seeing Saint Peter very soon and I'll ask him to start looking for a special cloud for us."

Clarence died two days later. Loving him as she did, Millie was glad that his earthly suffering was over.

On the other hand, she had often heard him plead with doctors—in fact, with every new physician who would come to him—to put an end to his life.

And even as she mourned him, Millie could not keep from thinking that he had finally found a doctor who had helped fulfill his un-Christian wish for a sort of suicide.

Perhaps the impact of the death of Clarence Englund would not have been as great as it was had it not occurred just before an election year.

At Thanksgiving, which Millie always spent with her parents and two brothers, she was brooding. Her younger brother, Jack, took her aside to ask if anything was wrong.

She welcomed the opportunity to share the burden she'd been carrying—especially with Jack, who was a lawyer.

He was astounded by her story and—she could not fathom why—strangely excited.

"Millie, will you come and talk about this to the senior partner in my firm?"

She suddenly was hesitant. Her retirement was just a few years off and she did not want to rock the boat.

"Please, I don't want to get involved," she responded nervously.

"Hey, look, Sis, I guarantee your name will never come up—*ever*. Just tell Mr. Walters what you've just told me and that's the end of it. We'll take the ball and run from there."

"What do you mean, 'ball'?" she asked uneasily.

"It's nothing you have to worry about, Sis. And you'd be doing *me* a real big favor."

Edmund Walters, the senior partner in his firm, was Attorney General for the state of Illinois and made no secret of the fact that he harbored loftier political ambitions. One of the senatorial seats was coming up for grabs and Ed was seriously thinking of going for it—even though he knew the governor himself had eyes on it. Edmund had more money, but the governor had the significant advantage of his high visibility.

What Walters needed was a cause célèbre—a controversial case that would attract attention. Anything that could position him on center stage in limelight strong enough to get him on TV and make his name a household word.

And so the next Monday when young Cavanagh came down to see him at his office, Edmund Walters knew he had found the chariot to carry him to Washington.

"Thanks, Jack, I won't forget this. In fact, I'd like you to stay here and help me break the case."

"But, Mr. Walters, we don't have a case yet."

The attorney general then pointed straight at Jack and said, "Then you help me make it one."

They met again that afternoon at four o'clock. Jack already had some news that would enhance the attorney general's prospects.

A Veterans Administration Hospital is legally a federal government facility, and, according to Section 18 of the U.S. Code, that means that the FBI could be called in—to do the legwork in pursuing this allegedly homicidal doctor.

"That's good news, Jack," Walters said, grinning. "Let's get in touch with the Bureau."

"I already have," said Cavanagh with satisfaction. "He'll be glad to see you tomorrow morning—if eight o'clock isn't too early."

"No, that's absolutely fine. I don't have to tell you what the early bird always catches."

They met for breakfast at a run-down diner near the State House. Walters thought it best that the matter not attract the attention of the governor. Besides, *he* was attorney general, and this was by rights his case.

Even among the nondescript patrons of the diner, the FBI man looked exactly like an FBI man. That is to say, he looked like someone trying to look unobtrusive and nondescript. His name was J. P. Sullivan, officially assistant special agent-in-charge (ASAC). He was, as he himself put it, "a fighting Irishman."

Sullivan was morally outraged by what he heard. Not only was it a felony, it violated all the tenets of his personal convictions. No one should be able to make such judgments; they are in God's jurisdiction.

"You can count on the Bureau, Mr. Walters. As our late chief used to say, 'We always get our man.' "

Both of them realized they had no hard evidence against Dr. Lazarus for what he'd done to Clarence T. But this guy had doubtless struck before. The likelihood was that he'd strike again.

From that moment Sullivan would have Seth under around-the-clock surveillance. And would get some of the Bureau's new "egghead" computer agents to search the records of all hospitals in Cook County.

"That could take years," Walters complained. He needed some hard evidence right now if he had any hopes of making hay out of the trial.

"That's the point, sir," the agent answered. "The info that used to cost us so much time and shoe leather takes these characters just a few minutes. I think we can count on them to come up with some evidence."

"I can't impress upon you enough that time is of the essence," Walters urged. "I'll never get a wink of sleep until this 'Doctor Death' is put away."

"Hey," Sullivan said. "That has a catchy ring to it. 'Doctor Death'—I think that's what we'll call the case." He stood up. "Okay, sir, I'll get cracking."

The attorney general shook the hand of the agent-in-charge.

"I think for all our best interests, we should have our meetings here. Just leave a message at my office that you'd like to have a cup of coffee."

"Yes, sir," Sullivan replied, and slipped away.

Walters stood there for a moment, stoking the fires of his ambition.

He wanted "Doctor Death" to take the stand.

The information the FBI fed into the computers did not lead to anything conclusive. But it did confirm that when three fatalities from certain terminal diseases had occurred in University Hospital, Seth was known to have been somewhere on the premises.

Furthermore, when Seth was on vacation in the summer, none of these natural but coincidentally "merciful" sudden deaths occurred.

"He's our man," said Sullivan, tapping the manila envelope that lay upon the diner's laminated table.

"Can we call him in for questioning?" asked Walters eagerly.

"I wouldn't, sir. This evidence says something to you and me. But I don't think it's solid enough to pin the rap on him. I mean, it doesn't show him with a needle—or whatever his MO is. If we want an airtight case, we've gotta catch him in the act."

"Have your men been watching him?"

"Day and night," said Sullivan. "We've known every move he's made. We're tracing his previous history. We've even had a specialist from Washington get access to the files up in Pathology, to see if something turns up. So far, the autopsies all show natural deaths. So we've got nothing in our hands unless we catch him at it."

"What the hell's he waiting for? Isn't there anything you Bureau guys can do?"

"Well, yes and no. It might be very risky. . . ."

"What, man, what?" he demanded.

"We could set him up. You know, get someone who's got a relative in pain and who wants to die. That's the way it usually works."

"You mean, this isn't just an isolated incident? There are other places in the country where this sort of thing occurs?"

The agent nodded. "There're a lot of dirty doctors who play God, sir. Frankly, I wish I could string 'em all up. That's why I'm so hot to nail this bastard to the wall."

"Then why not try your plan?"

"But there's a big risk. We've had a case similar to this, and the defense managed to convince the jury that it was police entrapment, and the guy got off." To which he appended in a whisper: "And just between you and me, that's pretty much what it was."

"Sullivan, you just get your man, and I'll take care of those twelve men in the jury."

The agent shrugged. "Well, sir, my gut feeling is still that we should wait it out. This kind of sick human being can't help repeating his crime. But if you want us to 'inspire' him, I'll do my best."

The two men rose and shook hands.

"One thing, Mr. Walters," the agent continued.

"Yes?"

"I don't think we should see each other or communicate until . . . we've got the evidence."

The trap was now set for Dr. Seth Lazarus.

Special Agent Madeline Hanson, among the first females hired when the Bureau went co-ed in 1972, had used her talents as a onetime aspiring actress in the service of the Bureau many times. Of course, a lot of her assignments were "garden variety" seductions which, despite the danger involved, now bored her. At last she was presented with a challenge—and the promise of ascending yet another step in the hierarchy of the Bureau.

She spent three days in a hotel in midtown Chicago being tutored and drilled by medical experts and psychologists. The agents had already gone through the medical histories of the terminally ill at the Lakeshore V.A. Hospital and had found the most likely candidate who could unwittingly—or, more accurately, unconsciously—impersonate her husband.

Just reading the file of Captain Frank Campos made her cringe. He had stepped on a land mine in Vietnam, lost a leg and an arm, and had become legally blind and partially deaf. He had 80 percent hearing in one ear and none in the other. But his worst affliction was the shrapnel still welded to his spine. It was inoperable, and the pain unbearable, despite the Demerol and morphine and the other licensed analgesics, which had long since lost the power to give him much relief.

He had pleaded with the doctors for cocaine or heroin—both of which he had tried in Nam, and which he desperately believed could allay his suffering. But his doctors would not act illegally. And thus the wounded hero of America's most unheroic war was doomed to undiminishing agony.

Once, when they had brought him up to the roof to get some sunshine, Frank had summoned all the strength in his warped body and attempted to propel himself from his chair and over the roof railing. Only the alertness of a nurse saved him from death.

Also on the record was an incident recorded the previous Christmas Eve when Campos's younger brother Hector came to see him at the hospital with a .32 revolver in his pocket, determined to fulfill his brother's wish: for an end to his relentless pain.

Ironically, his hand was shaking so much that the two shots he had fired missed his brother's head by inches, and the orderlies subdued him so that he could not shoot again. He was not brought to trial, since a police psychiatrist determined that he was mentally incapable of knowing what he was doing. Instead, he was remanded to an institution for six months' observation.

"Christ," Madeline remarked, her stomach churning. "Are we at least going to let Doctor Death put this poor man out of his misery?"

"Of course not, 'Lainie. We don't sanction murder."

Agent Hanson grinned and said sarcastically: "Yeah, tell me all about it, guys."

Agent Sullivan directed that the little group go back to business.

"Well," he said after another hour. "Are you all set, Madeline? Do you think you've got the details of Captain Campos's life in your head?"

She frowned. "Guys, this just won't work. If this doctor's half as smart as you, then he'll never buy a 'grieving wife' act. I mean, the poor bastard's been in the hospital for eight years. Just where am I supposed to have been hiding? This bullshit you concocted about 'missing dog tags' wouldn't fool a dog."

Sullivan glowered. "Have you got a better idea?"

"No," she countered. "I'm just trying to be smart. You need someone who can really play the role of suffering relative. I mean, his brother has already tried to kill him. *He* could make a really convincing pitch to Doctor Death."

The psychologist added his weight to Madeline's argument.

"I think she's right, J. P. If we could somehow get to this guy's brother and convince *him* to ask Lazarus to put his brother out of pain, that would be foolproof."

"And," she continued, "the court could never call 'entrapment' on this, either."

Agent Sullivan was persuaded. "Hey, Madeline, you're some smart cookie. I mean, you could say you were a nurse—and that you know this doctor—"

"Now you're talking, sweetheart," she replied. "That sounds like something that'll really nail this Good Samaritan."

Seth finished his rounds at the V.A. Hospital and mentally ticked off another Thursday in his calendar: exactly three more months and he'd be liberated. He and Judy would take the kids cross country to see Yellowstone, Yosemite, and Disneyland. They would then be able to forget the hospital, the pain, and the ungodly burden.

As he was walking toward his car a small dark man came up to him. "Dr. Lazarus?"

His accent was slightly Hispanic.

"Yes."

"I am Hector Campos. My brother Francisco—they call him Frank—is a patient in this hospital."

"Not one of mine, I don't think," Seth replied.

"He's on a different floor from where you work. But I was waiting here to ask you to become his doctor."

"I'm sorry," Seth replied. "I'm afraid I only work here part-time, and I'm sure your brother's being well looked after."

"Please, Doctor," Hector begged. "For Jesus's sake, please just read his file."

And he unbuttoned his shirt and took out a manila folder, which he pushed into Seth's hands.

"Just why do you think *I* should read it, Mr. Campos?" Seth asked, and then looked up.

The man had vanished, leaving Seth holding the file. And terrified.

Seth tried to read the details without emotion. He was determined not to let his pity be aroused.

But there, recorded in Frank's history, was a brief—but explicit—

description of his brother's desperate attempt to end Frank's misery. And it was clear the boy was mad with grief.

Just then Judy entered his study in her dressing gown and sat down on his couch.

"I'm here, Seth," she said softly, "and I won't leave until you tell me. I know what you've got there in your hand—and I don't have to ask what you want to do. But if we say it's over and you keep on going, will we ever stop?"

"It's not 'we,' " he answered stoically, "this is my responsibility."

"I'm sorry, Seth," she countered, "I share your life, and I share all the guilt, too."

"*Feelings* of guilt," he corrected her.

"At least let's discuss it."

He gave her a brief account of Captain Campos's terrible mutilations.

"Oh God," she responded. "Why couldn't they have let him die on the field?" She then concluded with bitter irony, "I suppose that would have raised the U.S. body count. So now this poor guy's up there just ticking like a clock that doesn't know the time."

"I want to do it," Seth said quietly, "for both of them. It won't make my hands any bloodier than they are now."

"But Seth, it's much more dangerous in the V.A. hospital. You're there just one afternoon a week. If anyone suspected anything they could pinpoint that his death occurred while you were there."

"I've thought of that," he said. "I'll find some sort of 'problem' that'll make me have to come back after dinner. The place is really dead at night. It's not like our hospital, with all the visitors bustling in and out. It's a house haunted by the ghosts of people no one wants to see."

"Seth, no. You're . . . you're not yourself. You're not completely capable of—"

"You mean I'm crazy?" he interrupted, uncharacteristically raising his voice. "Sure I'm crazy. I've been killing since my brother Howie, since—"

"They were acts of mercy," she protested.

"Mercy," he muttered grimly. "I wonder if *I'll* ever get God's mercy for the things I've done."

They were silent for a moment. Then a minute, then a quarter of an hour. Gradually she noticed that he'd leaned back in his chair and was asleep. She shut the light and curled up on the couch to be near him.

The decision was clear-cut. He'd simply not tell Judy. He'd make some excuse to come there on a different day so he would never have to tell her. But first he'd have to see poor Captain Campos for himself.

At the end of his usual Thursday rounds he said goodbye and then, instead of taking the elevator down, walked up the stairs to the fifth floor. It was extremely difficult to find the wounded Marine. Everybody in this ward was mutilated, cut off from society because no one wished to have these horrors of Vietnam recalled to them.

Even in the days he worked up in Pathology, he'd never seen such awesome injuries, such macerations, such disfigurement, such sordid mockeries of human form.

At last he found him. He picked up the clipboard hanging from the bedpost and saw "Campos, Francisco R., Captain USMC."

The official record stated that he still could hear and had some vocal capability, so Seth inquired, "Captain Campos?"

"Uhnn?" the bandaged figure moaned.

"Can you understand me when I speak, Frank?"

This was answered with a groan he took to be affirmative.

"Are you in much pain, sir?"

This was answered by a tirade of anguished groans that needed no words.

"Captain, do you sometimes wish that you could end it all? I mean, that somehow all this would be ended and you'd die?"

A groan. In a tone that only could be described as a supplication.

"I understand," Seth answered softly. "I'll be back to see you very soon, sir."

And then before Seth could begin to walk away he heard an emanation from the mutilated man that seemed to say, Thank God, thank God.

While interviewing Frank, Seth noticed the tokens of family affection that sat upon the captain's little bedside table. A crucifix; some flowers from Hector.

What he did not see was the microphone that Agent Sullivan had installed there.

His drug of choice was morphine, so aptly named after the god of sleep. And undetectable.

Seth's strategy was exquisite and simple. He'd arrive just after dinner while the trays and dishes were still rattling—nearly two hours before the routine taking of the patients' vital signs.

Seth parked his car, donned his white coat, and with the full syringe held in his pocket, climbed the stairs to the fifth floor and walked unnoticed to the bed of Captain Campos. He seemed to be resting quietly and—happy sight for Seth—at peace.

Perhaps he could just do it now and Frank would never have to wake up again in pain. He'd already spoken to him, after all, he'd more or less got his consent.

Go on and do it, Seth, he told himself. Just draw the curtain around his bed, inject him, and go home.

But he had his protocol. His code of ethics.

"Captain Campos, can you hear me?" he began. "It's Dr. Lazarus. I'm here to help you end your pain. I'm here to help you sleep forever. If you agree, I'll give you just a small injection that will put an end to everything."

He paused for a response. There was none. He moved closer to the mutilated soldier. The man was not breathing. Jesus, he was *dead.* Seth was too stunned to move.

Suddenly the curtains shielding Captain Campos's bed were opened and Seth was confronted by a group of men, all dressed in the same funereal dark gray.

One of them showed his wallet and identified himself. "Sullivan— FBI. You are hereby arrested for the murder of this Marine."

FIFTY

"**F**BI NABS DOCTOR DEATH."

The shrieking headlines stirred up mass hysteria that circled Seth Lazarus like a whirlwind. Cynical journalists played upon a universal latent paranoia: *My physician holds the power of life and death in his hands. If for some reason he did not like me, he could kill me with impunity.*

The news that this malevolent Dr. Lazarus had acted out one of man's most horrific fantasies made Seth an object of anger. Of fear. Of loathing and resentment.

But, most of all, of curiosity.

For Judy every waking hour was a nightmare. It was impossible to send the children to school, for there were always photographers lying in wait. The whole world, it seemed to her, was talking about her husband—their father—and what he had done.

To the unsilent majority he was a monster. They were afraid that merely going into the hospital might expose them to someone like Seth. And many called Judy up and made obscene and terrifying threats.

Yet to others who dared not raise their voice in this emotional debate he was a brave, heroic man.

The case was being tried in every home across America. Husbands asked their wives, "If I were in excruciating pain, would you get a doctor like that to kill me?"

Still others wondered how many other Doctor Deaths were still lurking undiscovered. In fact, how many others besides Captain Campos had been murdered by the doctor from Chicago?

There was an avalanche of letters to editors of newspapers. The lines of demarcation were clear: "Right to Life versus Right to Death," in a kind of moral Superbowl.

For there were also those who went to church and prayed for Seth's salvation.

They were people like the Carson family, whose mother, thanks to him, had been delivered from her suffering. But all they could do was pray. For by coming forward in defense of Seth, they would merely add to the already weighty evidence against him as a murderer.

And, if truth be told, a few of the families were scared for their own skin. Would the doctor become vindictive—name names? And would that make them accessories?

The frenzy that whirled around Seth's family turned each day into a macabre circus, with Attorney General Walters as ringmaster. His profile was steadily growing more prominent. And he always found time to grant the press a few of his valuable minutes.

Nor was Agent Sullivan a man of reticence. Being an assistant special agent-in-charge—that is, a high official of the Bureau and no longer in the field—he could be photographed and interviewed. And he proved to have a rich imagination. But he was always careful to employ those verbal safety nets like "alleged," "presumed." Or else the worst of all—a slyly smiling, "I can't comment on that at this time," which seemed to answer the reporter's question without incriminating himself.

All of this was happening beyond the prison walls where the accused was now confined. For at the arraignment, the prosecutor had been so persuasive in the matter of keeping "so dangerous a criminal from threatening the public" that the judge had denied him bail.

From the moment of his arrest, Seth had been gripped by terror, and his feeling intensified with each new circumstance.

First of all, the FBI agents seemed to derive some perverse pleasure from tormenting "Doctor Death." Little things like pulling strenuously at his handcuffs, pushing him a little bit too hard into a car, and other such niceties.

But the worst pain of all was not physical: it was the humiliation. The police officials and FBI men mocked him constantly with phrases like, "Who's going to be your lawyer—Jack the Ripper?"

In fact, he didn't have a lawyer. There was this nice guy Murray, with whom he'd gone to high school, who had helped him with his tax forms and sued a man who'd crashed into his car. But it was clear to Murray that this case was far out of his depth. "Don't worry, Seth," he said. "I'll get you an excellent attorney. I mean, I'll even call my friends in New York to find out who the best trial lawyer is—"

Seth sat unmoving in his cell for hours on end, not knowing what to do. He longed for Judy's daily visit. She was his lifeline and his sanity.

"I've driven the kids to Naomi in Indianapolis," Judy reported. "She says not to worry and that she'll take care of them as long as necessary. I always told you my sister was a good kid."

He shook his head. "My God," he muttered, "what am I doing in this place? Why am I being persecuted? Don't these people have any compassion?"

No, Judy thought to herself, compassion is doled out inequitably in mankind. You had too much; they have too little.

"What's happening about the lawyer?" he asked.

"Murray's doing his best. He keeps saying we need someone who's strong enough to stand up to the A.G. in a courtroom—Walters is as sharp as hell and has political ambitions. Murray says we need a Perry Mason or Mark Sylbert."

"Sylbert? You mean the famous 'champion of lost causes?' Is my case so futile? Anyway, I don't think we can afford him."

"I don't care. I'll sell the house, Seth—anything to help you."

"Oh, please," he moaned, holding his head in his hands, "somebody please get me out of this place."

She took him in her arms. He was always thin but now he felt fragile—in body as well as soul. She made up her mind to go to Sylbert's office and remain there until the lawyer consented to see her.

It was the shortest siege in history.

The moment the receptionist indicated who had appeared unscheduled in their anteroom, Mr. Sylbert ordered that she be brought immediately to his office.

For the first time in a week Judy felt that she might have a friend in this angry, savage world.

As the secretary led her down the corridor, she said confidentially, "Please don't be upset by the sound of Mr. Sylbert's voice, he's just getting over an operation."

"What kind of operation?" Judy inquired.

"It's called a laryngectomy. It's—"

"I know," the former nurse replied, "that means they removed his vocal chords."

The secretary nodded. "He's been very brave about it. A speech therapist comes in every day to help him learn how to use the electronic device they've strapped to his throat so he can learn to talk again. He still sounds kind of—I don't know—spooky. But you'll get used to it."

Perhaps, Judy thought to herself, but will a jury?

Even though forewarned, Judy could not suppress a feeling of shock when she first heard the white-haired lawyer rasp with the help of his machine, "Hello, Mrs. Lazarus. Do sit down."

It was not merely the metallic sound of the small loudspeaker, it was the voice seeming to come from the bottom of a deep well.

"I trust my secretary has explained why I'm no longer with the Metropolitan Opera," he joked, though forcing each word out with difficulty.

"Anyway, I won't be doing much talking in court till I master this damn thing. But there are plenty of tough cookies in my office who can handle that job. I'm glad you've come to me. From everything I've read in the papers, certain special interest groups are anxious to turn your husband's case into a show trial. And that puts him in a very dangerous position."

Judy thought to herself, *He's going to take the case.* So what if he can't talk, the operation didn't take away his brains. And she then realized she had not asked the second most important question.

"Mr. Sylbert, Seth earns a good living, but we're not wealthy people."

The lawyer cut her off with a wave of his hand, and then said in those harsh, grating tones, "Don't worry about the fee, Mrs. Lazarus. This is one firm that cares about the law more than the honorarium. Besides, we have paying customers who subsidize our moral crusades. For example, we've just won a huge case against Eagle Pharmaceuticals because they failed to specify that taking Saranac for nausea during pregnancy could cause birth defects."

"Yes, I read about that," Judy remarked, "that was really a wonderful thing."

"Matter of fact, I think the colleague who helped argue that case is the perfect one to handle yours. He's brilliant. Got his law degree in two years. And he's been an expert witness in some important medical malpractice suits. Naturally, we'll prepare the case together. But let me get him in here so you won't have to tell the story twice."

He pressed his intercom and said, "Will you ask the doctor to join us, please?"

Judy was confused. "Did you say 'doctor' ?"

Sylbert nodded. "Yes, he's a doctor *and* a lawyer. I can't tell you how superb he was when he cross-examined Eagle's expert witnesses—he made them look like schoolboys who had just got their first chemistry set. In fact, right after he began to pulverize the opposition, Eagle threw up their hands and settled—*big*."

At this point Bennett Landsmann entered.

"Hello," he greeted Judy, and held out his hand. "I'm happy that you've come to us. Partly because I think the whole damn thing is just a political football, and partly because your husband was a Med School classmate."

"You do realize, Ben," Sylbert interposed jocularly, "that actually might be used against you."

Bennett smiled reassuringly.

"Mark, whenever I put my black face in front of a jury I know there's two and a half strikes against me. But I usually pull it out."

Then, turning to Judy, he said, "Mrs. Lazarus, can you tell us the whole story from beginning to end?"

After only twenty minutes, Bennett was ablaze with indignation. Still he was able to reassure Judy that there were many precedents on record in which "mercy killers" were exonerated by the jury when they were made to understand the special circumstances—usually a unanimous plea from the family to end a patient's suffering. Yet they still had to bear in mind that Walters was using this case as a springboard for himself, and it would be far from easy.

His first priority was getting Seth out of that cell and arguing for bail.

To both Lazaruses' great relief, Bennett pleaded successfully. And Seth was liberated—for the moment—on a hundred thousand dollars' bail, which Ben's firm arranged.

He advised Seth and Judy that for their own safety and peace of mind they would be better off staying anonymously in an out-of-the-way hotel.

They readily agreed.

"And feed him up," Bennett said to Judy, "it's obvious that prison food didn't agree with him."

Though still a little shaky from the trauma of his incarceration, Seth went up, took Bennett's arm, and said, "I'll never forget this, Ben. I mean, we barely knew each other in school and yet you're sticking your neck out for me."

"No," Bennett countered. "I'm doing this not just for you but for those patients you helped. God knows, *I* could reel off cases when surgeons I worked with found a really ugly cancer—in almost every organ of a patient's body—and would tell the anesthesiologist to let the guy 'sleep a little more deeply.' And they never woke him up to ask his consent, either."

"Would any of these guys testify?" Seth asked.

"No way," said Bennett, "they'd be putting their own heads in the noose. They're not *that* compassionate."

In fact, that was the nub of the problem: trying to get a doctor—or, with luck, three or four—who would testify that what Seth did was not a violation of ethics, because it was the doctor's primary task to keep his patient from suffering.

The trial was set for the first Monday in November. Bennett felt he would need all that time to scour the medical community for doctors brave enough to speak in Seth's defense.

Yet by midsummer he had not found a single expert witness. The surgeons—his friends in Boston and New Haven—either denied to him they'd ever done what *he* had *seen* them do, or simply refused to testify because of the unwritten law that doctors should not criticize their peers' behavior.

Hell, he thought with exasperation, I may actually have to take the stand myself.

With time running out, Mark Sylbert petitioned the court for a postponement.

Attorney General Walters also regarded the November date as inconvenient. For it meant the trial would come *after* elections and lack all the political momentum he was counting on. Thus he, in turn, had petitioned—for an *earlier* date.

This was, of course, outrageous and unjust. But Edmund Walters had not labored in the party wards for the last twenty years in vain. He had the right connections. He called in all his markers.

And the trial was advanced to the first week in *September*.

Bennett exploded. Sylbert fulminated. They both objected. But to no avail. The trial was drawing near and though they had the ammunition, they were totally lacking guns.

He voiced his frustration to Barney on the phone one evening in mid-August. That night he was determined to stay at his desk telephoning till every single physician on the East *and* West coasts had left his office.

"It's a goddamn disgrace," Barney said angrily, "I can't believe that so many doctors could be so self-serving when there's a human being's life at stake—especially one of their own."

"Well, Barn," said Bennett wearily, "if I could disclose to you the names of the distinguished healers in our nation who have refused to testify for us, your book would be a veritable Who's Who in American medicine."

"Has the other side got any heavy artillery?"

"Are you kidding?" Bennett exclaimed. "They've got a damn battallion champing at the bit to condemn euthanasia. Suddenly the medical profession has turned sanctimonious. And you'll never guess who their most eminent expert witness is—I mean, this'll freak you out—none other than Dean Courtney Holmes!"

"Holmes? You must be joking. Why would he go out of his way to testify against a former student?"

"Well, to his credit, I hear they had to subpoena him. There's just a chance he's not that keen to testify against Seth."

"Is there any way I can help?" asked Barney.

Bennett thought a moment and then said, "Actually, you could do one thing, Barn. The deceased's brother, Hector, has had some mental problems. Would you see him and go on record as to whether, in your expert opinion, he's competent to testify?"

"Sure, Ben, sure. But why do you want to call an unstable person as a witness?"

"Listen, Barn, " his old friend said. "Aren't you getting the picture? Nobody in his right mind would testify for this defense."

"That isn't funny, Landsmann."

"I can assure you, Barney, I'm not laughing. How soon can you fly out?"

"Next weekend okay?"

"Fine. I'll set up the interview and meet you at the airport. Bring Laura and we can have a mini-reunion. And hey, thanks for sticking your neck out."

"No, Ben, Seth's really the guy with his head on the block."

He hung up and turned to Laura.

"Well, Castellano, how does a weekend in the Windy City sound to you?"

"Great. But I can't go."

"Hey, come on, kiddo. Don't we have an exclusive contract with each other for the weekends?"

"I mean I can't fly, Barn."

"What is this—some new kind of phobia?"

"It's new, but it's not exactly a phobia. I'm pregnant."

FIFTY-ONE

"**H**ear ye, hear ye. The United States District Court for Northern Illinois is now in session. All rise for his Honor Justice Julius Novak."

A craggy-faced Mount Rushmore in black robes marched to the podium, sat down, and without ceremony looked at the opposing lawyers.

"All right. We're going to hear 'United States versus Lazarus.' Are counsel ready?"

The dense crowd, combined with the brutal Chicago heat pressing in from outside, had turned the courtroom—despite air-conditioning—into an oven.

Mark Sylbert rose with some difficulty and replied with a dignity that transcended the grating sound of his voice. "We are ready, Your Honor."

Although legal protocol required that an assistant U.S. attorney be the official prosecutor in a Federal case, Ed Walters had deftly maneuvered himself into the starring role, leaving the scholarly government representative, young Rodney Brooke, with but a single line of walk-on dialogue:

"Yes, Your Honor."

At which point Walters jumped to his feet, strode from behind his desk, and took center stage.

He turned toward the jury in a stance like that of an operatic tenor poised to overwhelm his audience with a magnificent aria.

"Your Honor, ladies and gentlemen of the jury, our evidence today will establish beyond any reasonable doubt that on March twelfth of this year, the accused, Dr. Seth Lazarus, M.D., did willfully, and with malice aforethought, murder U.S. Marine Captain Francisco Campos, a patient in the Lakeshore Veterans' Administration Hospital."

He then removed his glasses and let his gaze pan across the faces of the members of the jury.

"The case we are hearing today has significance far beyond the walls of this courtroom. It involves the most fundamental principles which make us a society of law.

"My colleagues for the defense, Messrs. Sylbert and Landsmann, may argue that what the defendant has done is a 'mercy killing.' But that is tantamount to a confession of guilt. For, with the obvious exceptions of self-defense or insanity, there is *no* code of law *anywhere* which sanctions any kind of killing—for malice *or* mercy.

"The prosecution is well aware that the accused has heretofore been regarded as a doctor of great wisdom and compassion. Nonetheless, with the help of various expert witnesses, we shall prove that he acted unlawfully in the murder of Captain Campos."

Judge Novak then asked if the defendant's attorneys had an opening statement.

Sylbert stood up and again in his rasping, metallic tones replied, "We have none, Your Honor. We are confident that the prosecution will not be able to prove beyond a reasonable doubt that the defendant is guilty."

Again in the spotlight, Walters called Special Agent John Patrick Sullivan to the stand. The FBI man sat down comfortably in what was for him a familiar seat.

Walters began the catechism.

"Agent Sullivan, can you tell us how your Bureau became involved in this case?"

"Well, sir, under Section Eighteen of the United States Criminal Code, any unlawful act that is committed on federal property comes within our jurisdiction. Dr. Lazarus's activities were brought to my attention through a nurse at the V.A. hospital who was suspicious about the sudden death of a patient—and worried that the perpetrator might strike again. Our Bureau therefore had the defendant followed day and night—and obtained a warrant to place a microphone by the decedent's bed."

"Why was that?" Walters asked.

"Because we had good reason to believe that Captain Campos would be his next victim."

"What led you to believe this?"

"We knew the captain's younger brother had tried to kill him last Christmas. The poor kid had an obsession with trying to find a way to end his brother's suffering." Sullivan quickly corrected himself. "Or at least what he assumed to be suffering."

"And what did you learn from the tape?"

"We heard Dr. Lazarus tell Captain Campos that he was going to kill him."

"How did Captain Campos react?"

"Obviously he was upset—but he was a complete cripple and had no way of communicating his fears to the other medical staff."

Bennett interrupted angrily.

"Objection—that tape will prove conclusively that the captain, however mutilated, was still sound of mind and had sufficient powers of communication."

Walters turned and addressed the defense lawyers directly.

"Are you willing to stipulate that tape into evidence as an authentic recording of what transpired?"

"Absolutely," Bennett replied.

The court once again stirred. After a cassette player was produced, Walters announced like a master of ceremonies:

"Your Honor, ladies and gentlemen of the jury, you will now hear a so-called 'conversation' between Captain Campos and the defendant, Dr. Lazarus."

With a flourish, the prosecutor pressed the "play" button.

The entire courtroom now heard Seth ask the wounded Marine if he could understand him, and the pitiful whimpers with which he was answered. Once again, when he asked the patient whether he was in pain, and wished to die, there was another series of groans. Finally they heard Seth say, "I'll be back to see you very soon."

Walters snapped off the machine and looked at the jury with undisguised satisfaction.

"Ladies and gentlemen, I leave it up to you to decide whether those tortured syllables, those meaningless and—dare I say, pathetic—animal sounds were consent—or expressions of a fear that he had no way of communicating to the outside world."

Seth covered his forehead as if in pain. A few rows behind, Barney placed his hand reassuringly on Judy's tightly clenched fist.

Bennett interrupted, "Objection, Your Honor. This is summation and should rightfully be kept until the end of the trial."

Novak nodded. "Sustained." And turning to Walters he ordered, "Go on to your next question, Mr. Prosecutor."

Walters turned back to the FBI official and asked, "Would you tell us what you did after you heard the defendant's offer—promise—to kill the captain?"

"Sure. We had two agents in the cellar to monitor the microphone, so as soon as we heard something incriminating, we could get right the hell up there."

He then added apologetically to the jury, "Excuse the profanity, but we were trying to save a life." And then turning back to Walters, he concluded, "I'm sorry to say the actual murder is also on the tape."

With another flourish, the attorney general once again pushed the button, and Seth was heard to say, "Captain Campos, can you hear me? It's Dr. Lazarus. I'm here to help you end your pain. I'm here to help you sleep forever. If you agree, I'll give you just a small injection that will put an end to everything."

Walters stopped the machine, and then asked his witness, "How did you and your men react to this?"

"We moved as fast as we could. But I'm afraid Dr. Lazarus acted too quick for us, and by the time we arrived at the scene he had already killed Captain Campos."

"Objection," Bennett called out. "The prosecution's terminology presumes guilt."

To which Judge Novak replied, "Sustained, Dr. Landsmann. I instruct the jury to ignore Agent Sullivan's last statements."

Unruffled, Walters courteously concluded, "Agent Sullivan, I commend you on your action in this case."

"Thank you, sir."

The FBI man began to push himself out of the witness chair, but then recalled that he had to be cross-examined.

"Agent Sullivan," Bennett began, "I would like you to interpret the last portion of the tape, and explain to us what you assumed happened."

"I do not assume, Mr. Landsmann," Sullivan responded with annoyance. "I *know*. I am a professional officer of the law."

"Excuse me, sir. You were not present. All the firsthand evidence we possess is your tape. Incidentally, did you edit it in any way?"

"I most certainly did not," the FBI man replied indignantly.

"Then may I ask you, sir, what the response of Captain Campos was to Dr. Lazarus's offer to give him an injection?"

Sullivan thought for a minute.

"Well, there doesn't seem to have been any. Maybe the guy was too drugged."

"Or maybe Captain Campos was already dead. Is that a possibility?" Bennett suggested.

"For God's sake, anything is *possible*," the agent replied with irritation. "I mean, you heard Lazarus say in his own words that he was there to help the captain die. What difference does it make?"

"I would think it made a great deal of difference. The defendant has already asserted in his pretrial deposition that he would never have continued his action if he had not received the rational consent of the patient. Do you agree?"

"Mr. Landsmann, I've been in this business a long time. And when a policeman walks in and finds a dead body and somebody standing above it with a smoking gun, it's pretty clear what has happened, wouldn't you think?"

"It's pretty clear what *you* think, Agent Sullivan." Bennett walked back to his seat and picked up a thin blue-bound document. "Agent Sullivan, have you read the autopsy report on Captain Campos that was stipulated into the evidence?"

"Yes, sir."

"Do you recall that it concluded that death was the result of a massive dose of cocaine hydrochloride?"

"Yes, sir."

"Did the FBI find a syringe or any other implement with which cocaine might have been administered that bore the defendant's fingerprints?"

Sullivan hesitated a moment. "That doesn't mean a thing. We found a full hypodermic on him with enough morphine to kill a horse."

"You have not answered my question, sir. We are not denying that Dr. Lazarus had a syringe of morphine—and I am certain the jury noted that you yourself indicated it was still completely full—but by what means do you surmise Dr. Lazarus introduced cocaine into the deceased's bloodstream? And how do you explain that no implement has been found?"

"He must have gotten rid of it."

"That is merely speculation on your part, is it not?"

Sullivan reluctantly nodded. "You might say."

Bennett looked at the jury as he casually dismissed the witness. "No further questions."

Sullivan scowled at Bennett and left the stand.

Before calling his next witness, Attorney General Walters picked up a large law book, opened it to a page he had bookmarked, and addressed the jury with an undisguisedly smug grin.

"I respectfully ask Judge Novak to instruct the jury on this state's penal code regarding the 'law of impossibility.' " He then handed the tome to Novak, who put on his reading glasses and complied with the prosecutor's request.

"Ladies and gentlemen of the jury, I instruct you as follows: 'It is recognized that a person can be guilty of attempt to murder an intended victim who is *already* dead, providing there is evidence from which it can be found that at the time of the attempt the defendant believed the victim to be alive.' "

Walters beamed at the jury. "I would say that is pretty unequivocal and relates directly—"

"Objection!" Sylbert rose. "The prosecution should not be permitted to comment on the law."

"Sustained," Novak ruled.

Walters merely gave a histrionic shrug of defeat that seemed to say to the jury, We all know he's guilty, we're just going through the motions.

Walters continued. "Since my colleagues on the defense have spoken of depositions, I would call the attention of all to the grand jury testimony of Hector Campos, who is on record as having attempted to kill his brother—in circumstances later adjudged as temporary insanity. Moreover, the deceased's brother admits having asked Dr. Lazarus to perform—and again I use this word with incredulity—a 'mercy killing.' So we have yet another piece of evidence that the defendant acted with intent."

He paused for an instant and announced, "The prosecution would now like to call Dr. Courtney Holmes."

Several of the doctors in the room, including one of the defense lawyers, watched awe-struck as their former Med School dean marched straight-backed to the witness stand, was sworn in, and waited for interrogation.

They listened as Holmes reeled off his impeccable credentials. He had been professor of Medicine at Harvard for thirty-five years, twelve of which he had spent as dean. And now, though an emeritus professor, he served on a number of national boards and congressional advisory councils.

Yet although Walters justified the witness's appearance by having him cite several of his publications that dealt with medical ethics, the defense could not imagine what light Holmes could possibly cast on the case before them.

"Dean Holmes, are you acquainted with the defendant?"

"I recall him as a brilliant student of the class of '62. I believe he graduated Number One."

"Is it not true," Walters inquired, "that in February of 1959, and again a year thereafter, there was a series of unexplained murders at the Medical School?"

Bennett was instantly on his feet.

"Objection, Your Honor. The prosecution is implying by omission that human beings were killed, when in fact—"

Walters interrupted him and addressed Bennett directly—and sarcastically.

"Ah, so you know about these murders, too, Counselor?"

Judge Novak banged his gavel. "Gentlemen, this is not a college debate. Will both Counsel approach the bench."

The two attorneys complied. Novak addressed them in whispers.

"What the hell are you trying to prove, Walters?"

"Your Honor, I am merely attempting to establish that the defendant has committed prior 'bad acts,' in order to show a consistent longstanding pattern of behavior."

"That's pretty vague," Bennett protested. "The defense objects."

The judge sighed. "I'll allow him to continue and then determine the admissibility of the evidence. You may proceed, Mr. Walters."

Bennett surrendered and returned to his seat, glancing dourly at Mark Sylbert.

Walters continued to interrogate the witness.

"Will you please describe these murders, Dean Holmes?"

The distinguished witness replied slowly. "Well, these were mysterious deaths of laboratory animals—dogs, to be specific—that occurred once in 1959 and again in 1960."

"And was the accused not a member of one of the surgery classes that was performing experiments on these animals?"

Bennett burst out.

"Objection—what do the deaths of those dogs have to do with the case of Dr. Lazarus?"

"I'm still withholding judgment, Dr. Landsmann, and I will rule when I have heard a little more."

"Dean Holmes, would you describe what happened to these dogs on the two occasions as 'mercy killings'?"

"I would say that was stretching it a bit."

"Let me rephrase my question, sir," said Walters, trying to hide a growing frustration with his own witness. "Would you say these killings were—from the victims' point of view—an alleviation of their pain?"

"Well, I suppose so."

Walters turned to the jury. "Ladies and gentlemen, I put it to you that, albeit by association, Dr. Lazarus was a student when both bizarre incidents unique in the history of the Harvard Medical School occurred, namely, the so-called 'mercy killing' of—how many dogs was it, Dean Holmes?"

"I can't recall."

Walters glanced at his notes. "Would it refresh your recollection if I told you there were nine killings in the first instance and six in the second? Was this mystery ever unraveled?"

Dean Holmes replied tonelessly, "No, it was not."

"And did this ever occur again in any subsequent year?"

"No, sir, it did not."

Walters turned to Bennett. "Your witness."

Bennett suddenly felt a curious diffidence. Although he had already confronted many formidable witnesses, he was now about to question one of his most respected teachers. It took enormous psychological effort to remind himself that he was no longer a pupil.

"Dean Holmes, sir, have you ever published your views on euthanasia or given specific lectures on the topic?"

"Yes, for example, in *Proceedings of the First International Conference on Medical Ethics,* and from time to time, in more abbreviated form, to members of the press."

"Well, sir, could you tell me specifically if you have publicly espoused or even now maintain any strong views either for or against what is commonly called 'mercy killing'?"

There was a sudden breathless hush. Holmes replied with quiet dignity. "When there is no hope of life and the suffering is beyond our ability to relieve, I have known situations in which doctors—even my own teachers, I should add—have 'hastened' the death of the patient."

All through the room, voices and tempers were raised. The judge gaveled furiously for order.

"Are you familiar with the ethical debate on this matter, Dean Holmes?"

"I believe so."

"As an expert, do you believe it is proper to consider the views of religious groups?"

"Yes."

"Are you perhaps aware of Pope Pius XII's view on this question?"

"I am."

"Will you tell the court what the Pontiff believed?"

"Well, I do know that in 1958 His Holiness was asked directly whether he thought a suffering patient should be given morphine or other painkillers that would ease his agony even if it would endanger his life."

"And he answered—?"

"Yes. I can give you the source. This view is also supported by the *Vatican Declaration on Euthanasia.*"

"Are you saying—in so many words—that the Pope believed in mercy killing?"

"Objection! Objection!" Walters bellowed. "The witness should not be allowed to speculate on what the Pope *might* have meant."

"Sustained," Novak ruled. "Unless Dr. Landsmann can produce it in print, the jury is instructed to ignore the words 'mercy killing' in association with the Pope's recorded opinion. Please proceed, Dr. Landsmann."

Bennett was sweating now. The surprising statement of a Pontiff not known for having any liberal views was one of his smoking guns. But his arsenal was not yet depleted.

"One final question, Dean Holmes. Theory aside—would you yourself ever 'help' a patient to die?"

There was a pause. The crowd strained to hear the distinguished physician's reply.

It was in a subdued tone: "I might."

Bennett's "No further questions" was lost in the loud murmurings of the audience that needed several strokes of the judge's gavel to subdue.

Walters rose.

"If Your Honor is going to admit that last line of questioning, then I would like to ask Dean Holmes if he is familiar with the declarations on this matter by Dr. Edwin London, Surgeon General of the United States?"

"I am. I can't remember the exact words, but . . ."

Walters reached for a document and declared:

"I am happy to refresh your memory. Dr. London is on record as having said, 'Only God can decide when life has no value. Once we embrace this ethic that man has the right to decide on who of his fellow men lives or dies, we are on the road to the concentration camps.'" He then looked at the judge and said, "No further questions."

The judge turned to Bennett. "Dr. Landsmann?"

"No, Your Honor."

"Any more witnesses, Mr. Walters?"

"No, sir. I would merely respectfully remind the jury that we have already submitted into evidence the autopsy report and that they have heard read to them the pretrial testimony of unavailable witnesses. The prosecution rests its case."

"All right. We'll recess for lunch and reconvene at 2 P.M."

By one-forty-five every seat was filled.

Bennett rose to begin his defense. He intended to barrage the jury with examples of cases in which so-called 'mercy killers' had been found innocent.

"The precedents are legion. For example, in 1961 the father who killed his horribly deformed—"

Edmund Walters did not have time to object.

Judge Novak was already pounding his gavel. "Inadmissible, Dr. Landsmann, inadmissible! I forbid you to proceed in this line of argument."

Bennett was now deprived of his most powerful argument. He looked helplessly at Mark Sylbert, who gave him a signal with his left hand.

Bennett now glanced at Barney, whose expression seemed to be shouting the words he had spoken after interviewing Hector Campos. ("The guy is very unstable, Ben. He's a walking time bomb.")

Yet Bennett reluctantly called the deceased's brother to the stand.

"Hector," Bennett asked gently, "were you aware of the extent of Frank's injuries? Did you know that he was blind, partially deaf, and couldn't move?"

"Yes."

"Were you aware that he was in pain?"

"Yes."

"How did you know that?"

"He told me, sir."

"In words?"

"Well, no, sir. He could just make noises—like the tape you play. I could easy tell when he mean no and when he mean yes. That is why, when I asked Frank if he want to die, I know he say yes."

"And what did you do about it?"

"I buy a gun. I try to shoot at him—but I miss." He was now holding back tears. "But I miss. ¡Ay! ¡Qué dolor! so terrible—I miss!" His head was in his hands and he was weeping.

Justice Novak leaned over and asked Bennett, "Would you like me to call a recess?"

"No, sir. He'll be all right."

The court watched for nearly a minute as the young man gradually regained control.

"Hector," Bennett continued gently, "can you tell us why you did it?"

"Frank was hurting so bad. He wanted so much that God please take him to Heaven."

Bennett looked at Walters. "Your witness, Mr. Attorney General." And as he walked back, he once again glanced at Barney, who was wiping his brow with relief.

Walters fairly bounded from his seat and eagerly told the jury, "I'll ask this man one question, one single question, and I'll be satisfied with his answer, be it yes or no.

"Mr. Campos, did you or did you not ask Dr. Lazarus to use his skills as a physician to kill your brother?"

Hector nodded.

"Please can you just say the *word*—yes or no."

"Yes," he replied. "I ask him."

With a histrionic wave to the jury, Walters proclaimed, "No further questions."

Bennett was already standing.

"Your Honor, I have some redirect. In fact, like my esteemed colleague, I have but a single question for the witness."

He paused, tried to comfort the young man with his eyes, and then asked softly, "Hector—yes or no—was it you who injected the cocaine?"

The witness was mute. Bennett tried to prod him gently. "Was it you, Hector?"

"I'll go to jail," he muttered, shaking his head from side to side.

He was a pathetic sight. Bennett wavered between sympathy for the young man's suffering and fear that he would now crack, and his testimony be nullified. He asked again quietly, "Please answer yes or no. An innocent man's life depends on it. Did you inject the cocaine that killed your brother?"

The young man hesitated again—this time for but an instant—and then said, "Yes. Francisco *begged* me to."

There was a stirring in the courtroom and Bennett addressed the judge.

"Your Honor, on the basis of this man's testimony, I move that the indictment be dismissed."

"Objection." Walters was in there before Judge Novak could even react. "I believe my young colleague has let a matter slip his mind. He perhaps forgot your instructions on the 'law of impossibility,' that in this state a man is guilty even if he *intends* to do a deed that has already been done for him. Therefore, the testimony of Hector Campos has no bearing on the case of Dr. Lazarus."

Judge Novak turned to Bennett. "Mr. Walters is correct. The issue of intent still validates the charges. Will you call your next witness, please."

Bennett paused for an instant, waiting for absolute quiet before saying, almost in a whisper, "The defense calls Dr. Seth Lazarus."

The rest of the courtroom was frozen as Seth, stoop-shouldered, pale, and nervous, slowly made his way to the witness stand.

"I am going to make this short and simple, Dr. Lazarus," Bennett said. "First, dealing with the prosecution's questions of intent, will you tell us whether or not you intended to end the life of Captain Campos."

"I did, sir."

"Can you tell the jury why?"

"Because he had no life. I mean no viable life. There is a difference between 'living' and a life. Being alive is just a biological phenomenon. Chimpanzees and bugs—even trees and bushes are 'living' things. But a life is more. It means biography as well as biology. I wanted to alleviate the suffering of someone who was no longer human. I believed Captain Campos deserved the same mercy society always accords a wounded animal."

Never in his wildest, most optimistic dreams had Edmund Walters imagined that the defense would call the accused to the stand. For the FBI had compiled a dossier on Seth that could keep him on trial for the rest of his natural life.

The prosecutor rushed to cross-examine.

"Dr. Lazarus, when you were in Medical School and in 1959 took a course called 'Surgical Procedures,' do you remember the incidents recounted by Dean Holmes, when the lab animals were slaughtered—or as you scientists put it, 'sacrificed'? Please answer yes or no."

Without hesitation, Seth replied, "I did it."

There was loud, agitated murmuring. Strong feelings had been aroused.

"I have just one more question," Walters announced. Then he fixed Seth with a riveting gaze.

"Dr. Lazarus, between the days when those lab animals perished and the Marine captain's murder, did you *ever* 'help' patients to die?"

"Objection," Bennett snapped. "This line of questioning is very prejudicial."

Novak reflected for a moment and then said, "Overruled."

The court was now as still as a tomb. Barney put an arm around Judy.

There was no reply from the witness stand. Then Walters cajoled:

"Dr. Lazarus, we are very anxiously awaiting a reply. Have you ever 'helped' another patient?"

Seth paused and with quiet anger answered, "Yes, Mr. Walters. *Out of mercy.*"

The prosecutor took off his glasses and declared, "No further questions."

Deadly silence filled the room as Seth returned to his seat.

A moment later, Bennett rose to offer the concluding plea.

He had always thought it unfair that the defense had to speak first and allow the prosecution the last word. Jurors, however well intentioned, were mere reeds in the wind—especially at this late hour of the day. They were more likely to be swayed by whatever impression they were left with at the end.

So he'd better be goddamn good.

"Your Honor, ladies and gentlemen of the jury. We have heard a lot of emotional words thrown back and forth in this courtroom. Indeed, the facts might almost have been lost in a smokescreen of moral and ethical questions that have nothing whatever to do with the case of Dr. Lazarus.

"I would have thought it sufficient that Hector Campos had confessed under oath to killing his brother before Dr. Lazarus arrived. I'll grant the prosecution's citation of the 'law of impossibility,' but I put it to you that mercy killing—or, as some of my fellow doctors prefer to call it, 'death with dignity'—has been practiced since time immemorial. Job in his wretchedness called out for death. And though it is true that God relieved his suffering, there is no other record of divine intervention in any cancer ward I know of.

"The defendant, Dr. Lazarus, has conceded that he intervened in cases where the patient had no hope of life, and was in desperate pain."

He paused for breath, and continued softly,

"In any case, Dr. Lazarus did not kill Captain Campos. For after his mutilating, agonizing, sense-depriving injuries in Vietnam, Captain Campos was not really alive. The defense rests."

Attorney General Walters had three silver bullets in his gun and he intended to fire them all.

He started with the AMA.

"Ladies and gentlemen of the jury, I should like to comply with the judge's wish that we restrict this argument to the accused, and so I'll merely mention in passing, as you heard at trial, the American Medical Association's 1973 policy statement entitled 'The Physician and the Dying Patient.' It declared, and I quote: 'The intentional termination of the life of one human being by another'—and here they even use the words 'mercy killing'—'is contrary to that which the medical profession stands for.' Unquote.

"But forget the AMA. You may recall the defense's attempt to rope in the Catholic Church by asking Dean Holmes about a single statement made by Pope Pius many years ago. But let us also bear in mind the words of Father O'Connor, the Catholic chaplain of the V.A. Hospital in which Captain Campos died—"

He raised his voice and read, " 'The Church is now and always has been against the taking of life in any circumstances.'

"Let me hasten to add that, as we heard at trial, Jewish theologians are no less emphatic on this matter. Maimonides—himself a doctor— wrote that 'a person who is dying should be regarded as a living person in all respects.' "

He paused, then added, "And we heard evidence that the *Koran* explicitly states that euthanasia, even if requested by the victim, is a sin, and those who perform it should be, and I quote, 'excluded from the heaven forever.'

"The defendant has admitted under oath that he has 'helped' people to die. Put another way, he has made a subjective decision as to who lives and who does not. Surely, this is only God's prerogative. Once upon a time the Nazis did this to six million people and the entire civilized world cried out for their punishment.

"Ladies and gentlemen of the jury, we know we are not gods. I pray you will not let us act like Nazis. The prosecution rests."

The hour was late. The judge earnestly instructed the jury to ignore the emotive pleas from both sides. To pay no heed to the defense's "philosophizing about life and death" nor the prosecution's invocation of the bizarre trinity of the AMA, the Catholic Church, and Hitler—none of whom was on trial in these proceedings. They were merely to decide whether Dr. Lazarus was guilty of murder or intent to murder and should therefore be punished.

Nobody slept that night. Nobody.

Though doubtful that a verdict would be rendered even by late afternoon, the principals were all present by the stroke of nine the next morning. Twenty minutes after twelve the jury entered.

The room seemed deprived of oxygen, as if those in it had inhaled all the available air.

Judge Novak took the bench.

"Ladies and gentlemen of the jury," he asked, "have you reached a verdict?"

The foreman, Arthur Zinn, a dentist by profession, rose and said, "We have, Your Honor. We find the defendant guilty—"

Bedlam erupted. Novak vigorously hammered his gavel and demanded order. The foreman obviously had not concluded his remarks. When some measure of calm had been restored, the justice once again inquired, "Yes, Dr. Zinn, you were saying . . ."

"As you ordered us, we based our guilty verdict on the letter of the law. But we have voted unanimously to ask you to impose the most lenient sentence you can."

The jury had shifted the onus completely to the magistrate. He could send Seth to prison for the rest of his days, or to his house for dinner that night.

"All right," Novak responded gruffly, glaring at the lawyers, "they've asked for leniency. I'll hear a plea of mitigation from both of you—*and make it brief.*"

Walters rose.

"I think it is pretty clear, Your Honor, that Captain Campos was far from the first one 'treated' by this so-called 'doctor.' So I think the defendant has the deaths of many people on his head."

"All right," said the judge impatiently. "How about you, Dr. Landsmann?"

"Your Honor, the defendant has a spotless record. We plead not only for his sake and that of his wife and family, but for the hundreds of sick people he has conscientiously treated all these years, that you make your sentence as merciful as possible."

"All right," said Novak once again, "adjourned until 3 P.M. today." He slammed his gavel and was gone.

It was twenty after four when the judge reappeared and took the bench.

"Will the defendant rise."

Seth stood up, leaning on the table before him, unsteady on his feet. It was clear from his eyes that Judge Novak was incensed. Seth's head began to spin.

"Dr. Lazarus," the judge began, "the jury has found you guilty. But I would like to add that the attorneys on both sides are also guilty of making this a question of philosophy, religion—and a lot of hokum. They have done you no great service.

"Despite this, one thing has come through to me. You are sincerely committed to alleviating human suffering. No human being should be tortured, whether by a Nazi—*or* a rule book. I therefore sentence you to three years—suspended.

"Ladies and gentleman, let's all take our consciences and go home."

FIFTY-TWO

The evening after the trial, Seth, Judy, Barney, and Bennett had a victory feast at Le Perroquet.

"I can't believe it," Seth kept murmuring to himself as Judy held him tightly, "I can't believe I'm going home tonight. It was like a bad dream."

"I'll wake you up," Judy said lovingly.

The Lazaruses were so anxious to get home and be alone that after the Baked Alaska they pleaded tiredness and went off, their arms around each other.

That left Bennett and Barney on their own—and half a magnum of champagne yet to consume.

"Landsmann, you were brilliant out there," Barney congratulated him.

"No, you're wrong," Bennett answered soberly (though getting drunk). "Every goddamn trial is like a roulette wheel. There's no way of picking the winning number in advance. It depends on the day, the mood of the jury, the attitude of the judge—and most of all, Lady Luck. I mean if medicine isn't an exact science, law is ten times more of a crapshoot."

"Are you trying to tell me you don't like it? I mean, your career's gone up like a skyrocket."

"Yeah," Bennett answered wryly, "that's probably the biggest reason I can't stand it. I sometimes hate myself for what I have to do—like rough up medical expert witnesses. You know, break them down, bedazzle them with facts that aren't always strictly relevant—even use my medical expertise to intimidate the poor, well-intentioned schmuck who's been roped in to perform the unthinkable—to tell the truth."

"You really miss the O.R., don't you?"

"Not really," Ben replied unconvincingly, and an instant later confessed, "Yeah, I do and it's not just the surgery, it's the satisfaction of—I don't know—healing. I mean, the law's just a profession to me—medicine was a calling."

He took another swallow of champagne and changed the subject.

"By the way, how's your book coming?"

"I'm pretty close to a first draft. What makes you suddenly think of that?"

"Just the fact that so goddamn few doctors were willing to testify on behalf of the so-called 'fraternity.' So much for the Hippocratic Oath."

"Don't worry, Ben, it'll all be there—the good, the bad—and even the ridiculous. But you have to understand—as I keep trying to—that doctors are just frail human beings. And no human being is immune from fear."

"C'mon, Barn, doctors may be a lot of things, but you couldn't call them human beings—they might sue for slander."

Barney laughed.

"You know something, Landsmann? You sound like a combination of a depressed lawyer *and* a disillusioned doctor. That's one for the record books."

Bennett watched the bubbles in his glass slowly evanesce.

In the silence that ensued, Barney realized for the first time how unhappy Bennett was.

Who are his friends—besides Laura and me? And sometimes I even think he holds *us* at arm's length. Why has he dated a million women and never latched on to just one?

"Ben, can I ask you a serious question?"

"At this hour of the night?" He smiled.

Barney hesitated for a moment and then, overcoming his diffidence, finally asked, "Why are you such an incredible loner?"

Bennett was not fazed. "You're the head doctor," he replied, "you tell *me*."

"I *can't,* that's why I'm asking. I can't bear to see my best friend so miserable. For chrissake, talk to me—I won't be judgmental. Where are the women in your life?"

Bennett once again stared into his glass.

"What woman could relate to me, Barn? To the Jews I'm a black, to the blacks I'm a Jew, to the whites I'm a black, to the soul brothers I'm a pecker. I live in a kind of no-man's-land. Where do I fit in?"

Barney was hesitant, wondering if after all this time, he dared make his best friend face the truth about himself.

"You know, Landsmann, they're not *all* that way."

"Who? What the hell are you talking about?"

"The subject was women, Doctor. And I was merely offering both a professional and a personal opinion that all women aren't like your mother."

"Hannah?"

"No, old buddy, I mean the woman who gave you life . . . and then walked out of it."

Bennett suddenly lost his temper, and shot back, "That's a lot of psychiatric bullshit, Livingston. I *don't*—"

Barney interrupted him. "Hey, I've heard you say you didn't give a damn about her a million times. But honest to God, Ben, you're lying—especially to yourself."

"Damn, you shrinks are all the same. What would you be without 'mothers'?"

"Exactly what *you* were without *yours*."

Barney paused for a moment to allow the mood to settle. "Listen," he said softly, "they're not all like Lorraine. They don't all disappear and leave you with a hole in your heart. . . ."

Both men looked at each other, neither knowing what to say next. Finally Bennett spoke.

"You know what hurts the most? That you could see it and *I* couldn't."

The wounded expression on his friend's face instantly filled Barney with remorse.

"Hey, I'm sorry, man. I stepped out of line."

Bennett shook his head. "No, Barn. That's what real friends are for." And then added, "Which is another thing you taught me."

Their silence was broken by Mark Sylbert's metallic voice. "Excuse me, Ben—"

Both men looked up, and from the ineffably sad expression on his black colleague's face, Sylbert came to an incorrect conclusion.

"Oh—I guess Barney's just told you. Ben, I'm sorry, I'm very, very sorry."

Bennett looked up, baffled. "Mark, what the hell are you talking about?"

"You mean, you haven't heard about your dad?"

Instinctively standing up, poised to respond to whatever was the emergency, he responded, "No—is anything wrong?"

"He's dead," Sylbert said, in the closest approximation of a whisper his machine could manage. "He died last night. An oncoming car jumped the rail and hit the driver's side. Your mother's not hurt badly—just in terrible shock. She was even able to speak to Herschel in the ambulance. And he made her promise—"

"Promise what?"

"That . . . she would keep whatever happened from you till the trial was over."

Sylbert now stood there helpless, not knowing what to say or do.

Barney rose and put his arms around his wounded friend.

"Come on, Ben," he said softly, "I'll go home with you."

FIFTY-THREE

"Oh Lord and King, who are full of compassion,
Receive, in Thy great loving kindness, the soul of
Herschel Landsmann, who has been gathered unto his people."

It was a searingly hot afternoon. Tears and perspiration mingled on the faces of the mourners at Herschel Landsmann's funeral.

There were nearly a hundred people, but most of the deceased's acquaintances and employees kept a respectful distance from the grave to allow Hannah, convulsed with sobs, and Bennett, on whose shoulders she was leaning, to bid farewell in privacy.

Herschel's brother, Steve, was also present but, characteristically, stood with his wife on the opposite side of the grave.

An unwitting referee, a clean-shaven rabbi in a skullcap, stood at the far end, almost breathless in the suffocating air.

"Herschel requested that there be no eulogy for him. . . ." He glanced uneasily at Steve, whose frown made it apparent that he had tried to countermand this final wish.

"However," the rabbi continued, "I am sure that he would not object to my reading a brief passage from the *Sayings of the Fathers*: 'When a man dies, neither silver nor gold accompany him—only righteousness and good deeds. For it is said, when you walk it shall lead you; when you lie down it shall watch over you; and when you wake it shall speak with you.'

"Herschel Landsmann has finished his days on earth. May his memory still live on in the hearts of those who loved him."

The rabbi looked to his right and to his left and declared softly, "It is time for the Mourner's Kaddish."

As Steve took a step closer to the grave, Bennett whispered, "Are you okay, Mom?"

Hannah nodded. "Yes, yes. Say Kaddish for him, Ben."

Despite her reassurances, Bennett was hesitant to let go of his mother. Barney hurried forward and put his arm around her.

Ben approached the grave and looked toward the rabbi for a signal to begin.

Just then he heard Steve say, "Come on, Bennett, this is carrying things too far. Let me pray for him."

Steve turned to the rabbi for support.

"I don't understand," the clergyman said.

Steve looked across the grave at Bennett. "You see, he doesn't know why you're there. You have no reason to—"

"Excuse me," the rabbi interrupted, and then, indicating Ben with a nod, responded, "but is this not Herschel Landsmann's son?"

Before Steve could begin to protest Bennett's legitimacy, Hannah cried out, "Leave him, Stefan, he's Herschel's boy. Herschel loved him with his life. *You* go away!"

Steve was stunned into chastened silence. He remained mute as Bennett asked, "May I begin?"

The rabbi held out his prayer book to Bennett.

"No, thank you, sir. I know it by heart."

Now, mustering all his self-control, he recited with full voice, *"Yisgadal ve yiskadash shmei raboh. . . ."*

In a sense Bennett's act of piety was a dual one. For nearly thirty years earlier, Herschel had stood at his natural father's grave and said the prayer for *him,* as surrogate for Bennett.

And in this hour of terrible sorrow, that act of love was once again performed.

FIFTY-FOUR

Professor Laura Castellano felt uneasy.

There she was, nearly forty years old and sitting in an obstetrician's waiting room alongside girls almost young enough to be her daughter. Barney had asked that she let him come along, but she refused. His excitement was already making her a nervous wreck at home.

Moreover, she was worried that Dr. Sidney Hastings ("the best, the absolute positive best," Barney's zealous research had concluded) would misconstrue the mad psychiatrist's passionate involvement with the welfare of his unborn child as meddling.

And if the truth be known, Hastings was not all that flattered to have been chosen, even by so distinguished a couple as Laura and Barney. For he knew physicians are notoriously nervous and difficult parents. And to deal with *two* might be beyond the pale of reason.

He was not wrong. For Laura, thanks to her specialty, was a complete and up-to-date catalogue of potential disasters in the uterus.

"Could it be a Trisomy-13, Doctor? How early can you detect spina bifida or Down's? How often will you want to scan?"

"Calm down, Laura. You're getting hysterical over nothing."

"It's not hysteria, Dr. Hastings. It's incontrovertible scientific fact that with every year over thirty-five, the chance of having a malformed baby grows dramatically. One in a thousand at forty, one in three hundred at forty-two, one in eighty at—"

"Laura, you don't have to tell me all the possibilities and you shouldn't worry about them, either—because it can't do either of us any good. Week after next we'll do an amniocentesis and we'll know."

"But is this guy Levine a good sonographer? Have you worked with him before? Are you sure he can direct your needle so there won't be any damage? Where did he train? What kind of hardware does he use? Could I arrange a meeting with him just to, you know—"

Hastings leaned on his desk and put his head in his hands.

"For Heaven's sake, Laura," he groaned melodramatically, "maybe I should let you and Barney handle this yourselves. After all, each of you is sleeping with a Second Opinion."

"Okay," Laura sighed. "I'll try to stop. But Barney made me swear to let him come here next time."

"Good. Give me an hour's warning so I can get out of town."

Laura rose slowly. She was not amused. Hastings could not possibly comprehend how much this baby meant to her and Barney. But as she reached the door, he called out in a soft and calming voice, "Laura, please don't sweat. I promise you that everything will be all right."

She gave a wan smile and said, "Now, you know and I know that no physician can make promises like that. So let's make a deal. You spare me the plastic platitudes and I'll spare you my husband."

"It's a deal," said Hastings, and he smiled with satisfaction and relief.

It was bad enough that Barney called him on the phone whenever he discovered an obscure—but hypothetically possible—anomaly described in passing by some obstetrician in the nineteenth century.

"Breathe, Laura, breathe!"

Barney was a tyrannical coach when it came to preparing his "star athlete" for natural childbirth.

"Don't forget . . . one-two," he would encourage her as he was supervising her leg lifts on the floor, "you'll want to get your figure back as soon as possible . . . three-four."

"You mean *you'll* want my figure back—"

"Yeah—that's 'cause we share everything," he'd smile. "Come on . . . three-four."

Laura's morning sickness was mild. This worried both of them, for nausea, though unpleasant, is a reassuring sign that all the hormones are coursing through the woman's body at a healthy pace.

"But listen, Laura," the poor, bedeviled Hastings protested, "there's no norm about this thing. Your pregnancy is progressing fine—you should be grateful you're not nauseated."

"No," she'd counter, "I'd be happier if I were throwing up my lunch."

Hastings increasingly gave silent thanks to God that human pregnancies were only forty weeks. (After all, he told himself, gestation in an elephant is nearly *two years*.)

Then suddenly they were at week sixteen. And at Dr. Levine's office for the amniocentesis, Barney dreaded the delicate procedure in which the doctor would insert an alarmingly long needle through the abdomen into the fetal sac to bring out a sample of the fluid surrounding the baby.

He knew that when analyzed by the laboratory the sample can reveal almost all possible deformities and abnormalities, but he also knew that the procedure is not without risk; it raises the chances of miscarriage by another percentage point. And adds yet another furrow to the brow of a forty-year-old pregnant woman—and her husband.

"How quickly will we know?" asked Barney—who had demanded to be present.

"I told you when you called yesterday," said Hastings. "I'm sorry to report that science didn't come up with any innovations overnight. Amnio results take two weeks. But since you're both doctors, I've arranged a special deal—"

Barney's eyes widened with hope. "Really?"

"Yes," said Hastings with a grin. "For you it'll be only fourteen days."

"It's bad news. There's a malformation—Trisomy-21—Down's syndrome."

"What makes you so sure, Laura?"

"I don't know, Barn, I just feel it. I mean, I don't feel it. Surely I should have felt some kicking or something by now."

"Maybe it's a night person and only does its acrobatics while you sleep."

"It couldn't—I never sleep."

But somehow a fortnight passed. And somehow Barney and Laura did not drown in the whirlpools of their own pessimism. At last, Sidney Hastings called at nine one evening.

"I'm sorry I'm so late in getting to you, Laura, but I've been in surgery. . . ."

The doctor suddenly heard sounds of a scuffle. Barney had snatched the phone from Laura's hands and burst out, "Sidney, just one word, is it okay or not? Please, just one word!"

There was hearty laughter from the other end of the wire as the obstetrician paternally reassured the agitated psychiatrist, "Everything's fine, Barney. And it's a he."

Two days later, Laura called Barney between patients and said tearfully, "Harry kicked me, Barn. I felt him kick."

"Was it the right foot or the left?"

"What difference does it make?"

"If he's going to be a lefty I'll have to revise my sports development plan."

Perhaps the most terrifying thing about the second trimester of a pregnancy is that nothing happens. That is, nothing seems to happen. The organs are all formed in miniature and now simply need time to grow. All of which gave Laura's fantasy the freedom to imagine every possible disaster.

Twenty weeks: A baby born this early would have zero chance of living. Twenty-five: If it came now the odds would be ten to one against viability and even less against normalcy.

It was only when they measured the baby by ultrasound at twenty-eight weeks that Laura breathed a sigh of relief. If he arrived at this point the chances for his viability—in the hands of a good neonatologist—were in their son's favor.

Somehow they calmed each other and—what with natural childbirth classes two evenings a week and "Coach Livingston's" strict daily regimen of exercises for muscle tone—they were able to retain the remnants of sanity.

Then at last, week forty. But nothing happened.

Hastings called them both into his office. Barney was uneasy, for this was the first time Hastings had actually taken the initiative and *asked* him along.

"Don't worry," he assured them. "More than ten percent of pregnancies go over forty weeks, especially with primiparas like yourself, Laura. I mean, it's still fairly unusual for women to wait till your age to have their first child."

A solemn look came over his face.

"Uh, I have a serious question to ask the two of you. . . ."

Barney's heart fell. Laura stopped breathing.

"This is in strict confidence, of course." He paused and then said, nearly at a whisper, "My marriage is in a little trouble. Matter of fact, you might say it's pretty close to being on the rocks."

What the hell could this possibly have to do with us? Laura wondered.

Hastings explained, "Louise and I have agreed to give it one more shot. A friend of ours has offered us his cabin on Lake Champlain. I think five or six days there might very well avert disaster."

He stopped and looked at them.

Barney sensed what he was about to say and was already resentful.

"I've seen a lot of pregnancies like this," Hastings continued, "and I feel certain Laura won't deliver during the period I'd be away. And besides, if she does go into labor there's a small airport nearby—I can hop on a private plane and be back in no time." His tone then turned parental. "Look, I know how important this baby is for both of you. And I'm completely devoted to you, personally as well as professionally. If you'd feel in any way insecure about my being out of town, say it and I just won't go."

There was a silence. Both Barney and Laura knew this was not a genuine request—it was a guilt trip. They were being emotionally blackmailed with the price of this guy's marriage.

"Listen, Sidney," Laura began, "I naturally want you to do the job. But if your backup team is good—"

"Laura, I promised you an all-star team and I've made complete arrangements. First of all, Armand Bercovici has just about the best hands of any obstetrician in the country. In all honesty, he's the only one I'd let near my own wife if she ever needed surgery. I've left him all your notes and he's totally familiar with your history. And instead of a nurse, you'll actually have our Senior Fellow in Ultrasonography himself—an absolutely brilliant Iranian kid named Reza Muhradi. He'll be there just to monitor the baby's state so Bercovici will be able to concentrate completely on Laura."

"That sounds great," Barney replied, his mind obsessively focused—as it had been for the past weeks—on the sight of their child being held upside down before them in the bright lights of the Operating Theater.

"Again," Hastings offered, "if you'd feel more secure with me around, I'll put off our trip. This baby's too important."

Barney and Laura looked at each other and saw nothing but doubt and hesitation in each other's eyes. They were caving in to Hasting's pressure. Finally Laura spoke.

"What the hell, your marriage is important, too, Sid. Go—I'll talk the baby into waiting for you to get back."

A look of enormous relief crossed Hastings's face.

*   *   *

"Shit, shit," Barney commented as they were driving home. "How could two doctors let themselves be conned into agreeing to a thing that we both know is a risk?"

"It's amazing—even doctors are afraid of other doctors. But actually, there may be a bright side to our cravenness. I know about Bercovici. He's twice as good as Hastings and, truthfully, I'd rather have *him* in the room if something went wrong. In fact, it might be lucky if our *niño* came while Sidney was away."

Barney nodded and then spoke to her swollen belly. "Hey, Harry," he called, "you've got just five days to come out, so let's start shaking ass."

The child turned out to be a prodigy—antenatally obedient. For less than twenty hours later, Laura was in labor.

"Oh, shit," said Barney suddenly in panic, "I'd better call Sidney. He'll have just enough time to fly back here."

"No," Laura disagreed, "he's probably still on the road up there. Help me time the next contraction and then call the hospital and have them get hold of Bercovici."

Barney ran for a stopwatch, clocked his athlete at eight minutes, then hastened to the telephone, so nervous that his fingers twice dialed the wrong number.

"No problem, Castellano," Barney reassured her. "Bercovici is already at the hospital operating on some woman's carcinoma. He should be out by noon. They said to wait until we break four minutes and come in. I think we ought to leave now."

"No, Barn, if they say it's too early we'll—"

Her reprimand was interrupted by a uterine contraction.

At twelve, Barney could wait no longer and he helped Laura to the car, carrying the suitcase they had packed three weeks before, and showed up at the Maternity Ward. Laura just made it to a couch, where she doubled up with increasingly severe contractions.

Barney asked for Dr. Bercovici and was told that he was still downstairs in surgery. He saw this as a good sign. The guy was obviously very careful.

A wheelchair was brought out and, though she protested, Laura finally allowed herself to be transported to one of the labor rooms.

It was a small cubicle, actually, with tubes hanging from the ceiling, an oxygen tank and a monitor to measure maternal and fetal heart rates. A huge mural on the wall showed a peaceful New England forest—no doubt to help the mothers gaze at something while they tried to breathe the labor pains away.

2 P.M. Still no Bercovici.

"What the hell's he doing?" Barney asked. "Removing every organ in the woman's body?"

"Shhh," Laura ordered. "Let's concentrate on concentrating. Worst comes to the worst, you'll do the delivery."

Her remark did not amuse her husband.

Three o'clock. A small, slender young man with jet-black hair came in and introduced himself as Dr. Muhradi, the Senior Fellow in fetal monitoring.

"Where the hell is Dr. Bercovici?" Barney demanded.

"He's still in surgery. I'm told that it is a very delicate procedure. But in any case, I'll be his understudy. Now I'll check your wife."

As he proceeded to examine Laura and check for cervical dilatation, Barney got the uncomfortable feeling that this kid was somehow taking over.

By now, Laura's contractions were so frequent and so painful that she was unable to concentrate on anything else.

"I'll ask one of the nurses to come and stay with Dr. Castellano while I take you to get a cup of coffee," Muhradi said to Barney. "It will calm you down."

Barney glanced at Laura, who had managed to understand this last exchange.

"Go on, Livingston," she said, forcing a smile, "you deserve a break from me."

Feeling ambivalence verging on guilt, Barney welcomed the opportunity to get a break from watching his beloved wife in pain. He and the young Iranian stood drinking coffee at the nurses' station, when a doctor who looked barely old enough to be an intern hurried up to Muhradi. "Reza," he said breathlessly, "I've got some trouble with a preemie in Room Five. I'm kind of scared I'm not controlling labor—"

The Iranian smiled and said, "I'll take a look." He put his arm around the younger doctor and went off to give advice.

Well, Barney thought, he must be pretty good if they run up to him like that with their problems. He went back to see Laura.

The interval between contractions had diminished slightly but they were lengthening and intensifying.

"Call Bercovici, Barn," she muttered, "I can't take much more of this."

"No need to worry, Dr. Castellano," came the voice of Muhradi, who had glided into the room. "I have spoken to the doctor and assured him that you are nowhere near full dilatation and he had time to take a breather. He was in surgery for seven hours."

Barney was growing increasingly anxious. "Don't you think it's time to give her something for the pain?"

"Oh, she will have an epidural just as you requested, so she can be conscious at the birth. But that will have to wait. Meanwhile I will consult the anesthesiologist about giving her something to ease the discomfort."

"Great," said Barney with relief, "that's great."

"Hey, tiger," Laura weakly called out, "have you eaten anything today?"

Barney came and took her hand. "I don't remember. All I know is that you haven't eaten anything since yesterday."

"I can't. You know that. But that doesn't mean that you should starve to death. Go down and get a—"

"No, Laura. I intend to stay right here and be a sort of medical Ralph Nader."

Just then Muhradi strode back into the room, his modest stature dwarfed by an enormous anesthesiologist, who began the tedious protocol.

"Hello there, my name's Dr. Ball. Is the little lady feeling some distress?"

Despite her discomfort, Laura could not help but think, Why does this pompous asshole have to be so supercilious?

But in her helplessness she merely answered politely, "Yes, if you've got something that can just dull this, but keep me awake."

"No problem, little lady. No sweat at all. I'll just give you a little shot and you'll be higher than a flag on the Fourth of July."

"She doesn't want to be high, Doctor," Barney interposed. "Just take the edge off her pain."

Unaware that Barney was himself a doctor, Ball merely answered patronizingly, "You let me handle this, my boy. I've helped more mothers than old Dr. Spock."

At which, with a speed and dexterity that belied his girth, he injected Laura with scopolamine. It made her dizzy almost instantly. The large man then nodded to the small man and said, "Call me when you're ready for the epidural," and padded out.

Barney sat down to hold Laura's hand, helping her to breathe. Her pillow was drenched with sweat.

A nurse came in, holding some papers on a clipboard, which she gave to Barney. "We need the husband's signature to give the analgesic and the epidural. Will you sign here, please, and on the second sheet as well?"

"Barney," Laura gasped, "this isn't right. These damn contractions shouldn't last so long. I mean, that's not normal."

Barney rushed outside to find Muhradi. He was in the waiting room, smoking a cigarette.

"Doctor," he called out, "her labor's getting out of hand."

"That's good," the young man answered with a tiny grin.

"What is?" Barney asked.

"I put a bit of oxytocin in her I.V. It stimulates the uterus. It will help things along."

"Well maybe it's helping just a bit too much. I mean you'd better come."

The Iranian snuffed out his cigarette and went toward the labor room.

From outside they could hear Laura shrieking hysterically.

"Get me that stupid doctor!"

Dr. Ball was among the interns and the nurses gathered around Laura's bed.

"The woman is hysterical," the anesthesiologist said angrily, "I think I'd better put her out."

"You do it, buster, and I'll put you out," Barney snapped, as he rushed to Laura.

She was gasping, "The monitor . . . the monitor."

"What's wrong, Laura? Tell me!"

"I made the nurse turn it around so I could see the printout. Isn't that moron Muhradi supposed to be some sort of expert? Why the hell didn't he have his eyes on that damn monitor?"

Her panic was increasing.

"It shows fetal distress—our baby's in trouble!"

"Now, just a minute," Muhradi interceded, "let's not all play doctor here. I am in charge of Mrs. Livingston."

"You are? Where the hell is Bercovici?" Barney demanded.

"To hell with Bercovici," Laura shouted hoarsely. "This printout shows the baby's heart is slowing. There's a problem. Somebody's got to do a caesar stat."

At this point, Muhradi took a good look at the monitor and realized that his patient was all too correct.

"All right," he ordered, "everybody out. And that means *everybody*."

He turned to a nurse. "Strap some oxygen to her face and take her to the O.R. stat. I'll scrub up."

Before anybody could move, Laura cried helplessly, "Barney, help me, help me."

He rushed up to her, "What—what do you want me to do?"

"Help me turn over. I'm so drugged I can't do it by myself. Help me get on my knees. It takes the pressure off the baby—helps it get blood."

"You heard her," Barney yelled to the nurses. "Help me turn her over, dammit, I'm a doctor too!"

Laura had gotten very heavy during pregnancy. It took all of Barney's strength—with the help of the single nurse who understood what he was doing—to turn Laura over so she could rest on her elbows and knees. The doors flew open and two other nurses rushed in to roll the bed to the delivery room.

"Barney, stay with me," she pleaded.

"Don't worry, Castellano, I'll be right there in a second."

He ran into the surgeon's dressing room. Muhradi, panic on his face, was putting on his greens.

"Where're the gowns?" snapped Barney.

"I'm sorry," the Iranian replied, "this is no time for husbands. She needs a Caesarian."

"And who the hell is competent to do one around here? The coffee boy? How many have *you* done? Fewer than me, I'll bet."

The young doctor lost his temper.

"Listen, Dr. Livingston, she's *my* patient and you will stay outside and wait or else I'll call Security and have you tied to a chair. Every minute that we spend arguing is taking time from your baby in distress. So sit down, shut up, and let me go."

Barney slammed the heel of his fist against one of the lockers.

You little prick, you're treating me as if it's *my* fault that you didn't read the fetal monitor. If Laura hadn't been a doctor, God knows how much longer you would have waited.

But he did not speak any of his thoughts aloud. For what little rational capacity he had left said, This guy's scared enough, don't shake him any more.

"I'm sorry I flew off the handle, Doctor. Go on and do the job. I know it'll be fine."

Muhradi did not reply. He merely turned and disappeared into the scrub room.

Barney sat outside the operating room doors, trying to eavesdrop. He heard just two things: Laura crying, "Where's my husband? Barney! Where's my hus ..." And after that the words of the anesthesiologist stating, "This'll shut you up."

Thereafter total silence.

He kept looking at his watch. A nurse approached—to comfort him, he thought. Instead she said, "I'm afraid you're blocking the operating room door, sir. You could cause an accident. I'll have to ask you to move."

"I'm a doctor," Barney retorted, "I should be in there."

"Well, clearly Dr. Muhradi didn't want you in there."

Barney went out into the empty, darkened lobby and, alone with his anguish, shouted out, "Fuck you, Dr. Hastings—is *this* what you call your all-star team?"

For he had scrutinized the operating personnel as they went in. Ball, Muhradi—and two interns who looked as if they were in long pants for the first time.

He looked at his watch. Thirty-five minutes. No normal C-section can—or should—take that long. Something had happened and it couldn't be anything good.

"Good news," called out a voice in the darkness. It was Muhradi.

Barney whirled around. "Quick, tell me."

"Everything is fine. You have a lovely, handsome son."

Barney nearly fainted with relief. The Iranian came up amicably, put his arm around Barney's shoulder, and asked, "What are you going to call him?"

"I don't remember," Barney muttered, then immediately gathered his wits and asked, "How's Laura?"

"She'll be asleep for some time in the recovery room. Dr. Ball had to administer a pretty hefty general."

I know, thought Barney, I could hear it through the door.

"I'm going to see Laura and the baby," Barney said. "Where are they?"

"In the recovery room," said Muhradi. And then he added uneasily, "That is, your wife's in there. The baby is upstairs."

"What do you mean, upstairs? He should be with his mother. She'll be frightened if she wakes up and he isn't there."

"Look," said Muhradi, in his best attempt at a paternal voice, "there was a little problem with the baby's breathing and we thought it best to put him in the ICU at least till morning. I am sure your wife will understand."

In an instant Barney was at her bedside. The women in the room were separated merely by a curtain and so the voices of the new mothers and their husbands—and their babies—were all audible.

Laura was comatose and fighting for lucidity so she could find out how bad the situation was. Because she knew that if her baby wasn't with her, he must be in trouble.

"Barney, Barney," she was muttering.

"I'm here, kiddo," he whispered. "And we've got our little Harry."

"Where's my baby, Barney? Is he dead?"

"No, Laura. Please believe me, Harry's fine. They just had a little problem with his breathing, so he's upstairs."

"That sounds bad, Barn. What were his Apgars?"

"I don't think they'll let me see the scores, Laura."

"You're a doctor, dammit," Laura moaned.

"Not tonight, it seems," he answered bitterly.

"Barney . . . everybody else has got her baby. Do you swear he isn't dead?"

"I swear."

"Go up and look. Make sure he really is alive. And *please* find out the numbers. I want to know how long it took to get him breathing."

He nodded. Both of them realized that when doctors withhold information, they are never suppressing good news. Neither of them had to admit they were afraid there was brain damage.

Too impatient to wait for the elevator, Barney sprinted up the stairs and down a long corridor to the Neonatal Intensive Care Unit.

"I'm sorry, you're not sterile, sir."

It was an officious nurse guarding the door. "You have to scrub and put on a gown to go inside."

"Okay, okay."

As Barney walked to the sink in the anteroom, he noticed Muhradi in whispered conversation with the ICU resident in charge.

Barney called out, "Take me to him, Doctor—take me to him now!"

Unruffled, Muhradi smiled. "Come right this way."

The young doctor led them down a row of tiny doll-like premature infants, their lives wholly dependent on technology. Finally they reached a baby boy, much bigger than the rest.

"Isn't he a beauty?" the Iranian said, smiling.

Barney stared at the infant in the isolette and felt half on the verge of tears. All he could utter was a muffled, "Hello, Harry, I'm your dad." And then he meekly asked the resident, "Can I touch him?"

"Sure, go on."

Barney caressed the chest of his young son. Then he took his hand, marveling at the perfection of those little fingers. But he couldn't help noticing there were traces—barely perceptible, but definitely there—of blue at the fingertips. He stood up and asked the resident, "Where are his Apgar numbers?"

"I don't know, sir. I was too busy assisting Dr. Ball with intubation."

"Well, if you two helped the baby, then Muhradi had to be the one who took the Apgars."

Barney once again locked the Iranian in his glance.

"Well, Doctor? What were his numbers for color, heart rate, respiration, reflex, and tone?"

Muhradi shrugged. "I don't recall the exact figures but I know they were on the low side at first."

"That's vague enough," Barney snarled. And persevered.

"And the score at five minutes? What was my son's Apgar at five?"

Muhradi hesitated. "Actually, we didn't do the second test till a little later."

"How much later?"

"Six or seven minutes."

"Cut this damn evasion, buddy. Obviously you mean seven. Or are you saying seven because you really mean *eight*? Come on—you know damn well we're talking about potential brain damage."

At this point the Neonatal resident interposed. "Your baby's fine, sir. He should be out of this ICU and back down with your wife in forty-eight hours."

Barney no longer suspected that something had gone wrong with the baby. He *knew* it. And the awesome thought occurred to him that something might also be wrong with Laura.

"Is there a phone around here?"

"Certainly, certainly. In the head nurse's office. You can call your family and tell them the good news."

Barney stared angrily.

"I'm not about to give anybody any 'good news' until I'm sure I really can. I want to call Dr. Hastings and tell him to get his ass right back."

"Oh, there's no need for you to do that," Muhradi said with a satisfied grin. "I have already done so. He is chartering a plane."

The "unsuccessful" patient—as the doctor construes one with whom *he* has not succeeded—is the loneliest person in the hospital.

No one visited Barney and Laura. Even the ladies who brought the food darted in and out so swiftly it was as though they believed that Laura's anger was contagious. For she was furious after her first reading of the fetal monitor printout.

Their son had obviously been in trouble for the better part of an hour, and Muhradi, alleged brilliant virtuoso at this wonderful new instrument, had not paid enough attention to notice it. For the simple reason that he had not been conscientious enough to look.

And they lacked the most important piece of information: How much time had *really* elapsed between the taking of the first and second Apgar scores?

For this would be the crucial determinant of how long the baby had been without oxygen. Had it been not seven minutes but rather nine—or maybe ten—the chances for the baby's viability would surely have been compromised. He might even be seriously brain-damaged.

Barney had of course reported the disturbing observation he had made—that there were still clear traces of blue on the baby's fingertips. This alone would cast doubt on the doctor's passing score for "color."

"I've gotta look at him," Laura insisted, "I've gotta check him out myself."

"Relax," said Barney. "You've just had major surgery. They promised I could take you up there this afternoon."

There was a knock at the door, followed by the cheery words:

"Good morning. Have you handed out the cigars yet?" It was Sidney Hastings.

Laura answered sternly, "Come in and close the door."

"I've been up to see the baby," Hastings went on, in an attempt to create a verbal smoke screen between them. "He looks like a real superstar. And with his mother's—"

Barney cut him off. "Don't waste your breath, Sidney. You know damn well that sooner or later Laura's gonna go upstairs and find out what's really going on. So why not have the decency to tell us the truth?"

"I don't know what you mean—"

"Come on, Sidney," Laura interrupted.

"How long did they really take to make him breathe?"

"I haven't had the chance to look at his report. . . ."

"You're lying," snapped Barney, "you've probably been studying it for an hour."

"Look, Livingston," Hastings replied, in calm but clearly angry tones. "I won't be talked to like that. I wasn't here, so I can't be held responsible for any screw-ups that might have occurred."

"Aha," said Laura, "so you do admit that somebody screwed up!"

"Excuse me, Laura, I know what a night it's been for you. But I still refuse to be treated like a criminal in the witness box."

Barney made a titanic effort to appear calm. "Sidney, please, all we want is the truth. We all know accidents can happen. Christ knows, we've all of us—at one time or other in our careers—been . . ."

He was about to say "negligent," but stopped himself. Laura finished his thought.

"Listen, we've all encountered misfortunes. And from my experience I've always found that patients take it best if they're told the truth, even if it's the 'sorry-we-screwed-up' truth."

And then she waited. The ball was in Dr. Hastings's court.

Uneasy at the silence, the older doctor spoke as if reading from notes.

"Dr. Muhradi and Dr. Ball are both men of probity. And if they wrote down that respiration was restored at seven minutes, I would take them at their word. Now if you insist on behaving in this way, I suggest you find another doctor." He turned and walked out.

"What a sonovabitch," Barney said.

Laura reached out and touched his shoulder.

"Barney, get me a wheelchair right now!"

They lowered the isolette so she could examine her son without having to stand. She checked his fingers and toes for color; she listened to his chest for what seemed like several minutes; she took a pin and scratched it on the bottom of his little feet.

Barney, watching all this, said to himself, Thank God. The kid's got some reflexes.

The final test was the most crucial. Would he suck? For if he was so damaged that he could not, then his chances of a normal life were absolutely nil.

She took him and put him to her breast. After a moment she looked up at Barney and wept with joy. "He's all right. He's going to be all right."

They left the hospital as soon as possible. All three of them.

"Well, Castellano," Barney said, trying to generate some joy. "We've had a lousy time. They've treated us more shabbily than anybody could imagine. But the bottom line is in your arms—weighing in at eight-point-two pounds. Harry Livingston, the future champion of the world."

But they knew better.

For they were both physicians. They knew that although their lovely

Harry would grow, smile, and frolic in the sandbox, it was still possible he might never have the mental prowess to write his own name. Only time would tell. Not even doctors held all the answers.

Meanwhile they would have to live in purgatory.

FIFTY-FIVE

Who could have predicted that the the failed Jesuit priest, who was socially self-conscious, insecure—and innocent—would ultimately become one of the most respected (and the richest) men in Hawaii?

But such was indeed the happy fate of Hank Dwyer, M.D.

Moreover, he not only did well, he did good. The number of people who blessed him, remembered him in their prayers, named their children after him, were legion.

And wisely he decided to remain unmarried in the future. While still, of course, remaining uncelibate.

Everything seemed to come to him as easily as a coconut from a palm tree—right into his hand, opened and ready to enjoy.

His wife, Cheryl, had not been blind to her husband's diminished affection. And from the time Hank had signed up for yet another tour of duty in Vietnam, she had sought priestly counsel. Indeed, since she faithfully attended mass at the Cathedral of the Holy Cross, the cardinal of Boston himself became her spiritual advisor.

His Eminence felt that a pure soul like Cheryl Dwyer should not be forced to live in limbo and would better raise her Catholic children if she could be free of Hank and marry someone worthy of her goodness. And though the Vatican does not countenance divorce, there still were other measures to alleviate the situation. Perhaps there could be a Church annulment of the marriage.

And thus Hank had not had to bestir himself; he had not missed a single Sunday on the beach at Maui. The papers simply came to him to sign, which he did expeditiously and unemotionally. Actually, the only thing he felt was gratitude for His Eminence's intervention.

On July twenty-sixth, 1978, a miracle occurred. In England a child named Louise Brown was born. It was an uncomplicated birth and she was normal in every possible way—except for one thing. She had been conceived not in her own mother's womb, but in a laboratory jar.

Because of tubal blockage in the baby's mother, the pioneering doctors Patrick Steptoe and Robert Edwards had introduced the father's sperm to the mother's egg inside a small glass dish. Only when the union had grown into a healthy blastocyst did they return it to its normal habitat, where it implanted happily in Mrs. Brown's womb—and nine months later emerged a healthy baby.

Procreation was one of the few things for which Hank could claim more than average competence, and it seemed only logical to him that if the prizewinning doctors would allow it, he should go to England and work (unpaid) as their assistant merely to acquire the necessary expertise.

The innovating scientists looked at his records. Hank's mediocre grades in Med School were more than counterbalanced by his medals for bravery in Southeast Asia.

Such a doctor merited a chance to learn the new technique and be one of the first to bring in vitro fertilization to America.

When Hank returned a full year later, word got out swiftly that he was setting up a clinic on the lines of those he'd seen in England. And, although he never sought publicity, the journalists went after him. Suddenly he was a household word in the fiftieth state.

In fact, when the governor of Hawaii was apprised of Hank's plans to establish a new institute, the likes of which even California had not yet established, he arranged for a low-cost state loan for Hank to expedite his project.

Unhappy West Coast women who longed for children quickly learned that IVF was at last being done at their doorstep. They flew in droves to "The Henry Dwyer Institute."

And yet even amid the lushness of Hawaii some vestiges of Hank's ascetic priestly days remained: he had a regimen and certain principles by which he lived unswervingly.

For instance, he would not eat red meat, knowing, doctor that he was, that it had lately been proved dangerous for the colon, and he did not want to do anything that would impair his longevity.

He only worked three days a week.

He only drank after five o'clock.

He never—without exception—dated any girl older than twenty-five.

When Barney Livingston's questionnaire had reached Hank's Hawaii office, he had been in England, studying the making of babies. And his secretary, thinking it was junk mail, did not send it on.

In one sense Hank was glad, for he thought Barney's queries were irrelevant to his own medical life.

How could he answer such a stupid document? "The tensions of the job"? "The strain of the commitment"? "Regrets"? These words meant nothing to him. So instead of filling out the form he simply wrote:

Dear Barney,

I am glad to hear from you. I guess we should have kept in touch while I was in Vietnam. But you know how things were out there and it was pretty hairy at the end.

First the sad news—for reasons of her own, Cheryl did not seem to appreciate my commitment and during my second tour of duty in Nam connived a way to get our marriage ended and still be declared a spinster so she could wed some other guy (and make him *miserable).*

I console myself that the girl of my dreams is still out there somewhere. Perhaps she will ride in on a surf board one of these days in a golden bikini. Don't think I haven't been looking.

The only classmate I have seen in person is Lance Mortimer, who came here on his first and second honeymoons. For some reason he decided to try Mexico for marriage number three.

Anyway, he's doing very well. As I don't have to tell you, anesthesia is a cushy number and Lance works something like four days a month. The rest of the time he devotes to projects he's developing for television. I hope you hear from him. I count him as one of the big successes of our class.

On another matter: Just the other day I came across Mind of a Champion *remaindered in my local bookstore for just two bucks. Let me tell you that's a real terrific book. You should be very proud. I wasn't here when it came out, so I don't know what kind of press it got, but it deserves to be a smash.*

You can be sure that when your book on doctors hits the stands I won't wait until it is sold at discount, I'll put in an order in advance. I hope you're good to me in it.

Look me up if fate should ever bring you to Hawaii. I own one or two small hotels and everything would naturally be on the house.

Best regards,
Hank

P.S. *I am enclosing a photocopy of the full page spread done by* the Honolulu Advertiser *when our thousandth baby was born. The picture kind of says it all: me in the center holding quads, surrounded by rows and rows of happy mothers hugging the offspring they always dreamed of.*

In a very real sense I feel like the father of them all.

FIFTY-SIX

"The infant with asphyxia at birth is at risk for a long-term . . . damage ranging from mental retardation, cerebral palsy, and seizure disorders to minimal brain damage, perceptual handicaps, and learning disorders. . . ."

"Disturbances of the Newborn"
The Merck Manual of Diagnosis and Therapy (14th ed.), p. 1759.

No child in history was more studied than little Harry Livingston.

He was also scrutinized, examined, analyzed, tested, and retested.

Since they both felt they would never know the truth about how long Harry was denied oxygen, Barney and Laura had to assume the worst. And their joy in him was tempered by a constant apprehension that the signs of brain impairment might reveal themselves. Today. Tomorrow. Next week.

On alternating months, Laura would take Harry to be examined by the chairman of Pediatrics at Columbia, or Barney would take him to the chief at Bellevue. (They never revealed their medical bigamy to either specialist.)

The doctors did not make light of their obsession. For the Livingstons had genuine cause for concern.

"We certainly won't be out of the woods until he's at least two."

This was the opinion of Professor Adam Parry of P & S, the most respected pediatrician in New York.

Laura quickly countered, "But that's of course if there's little damage. If not—"

"Yes," Parry conceded, "if it's something like cerebral palsy, we'll know soon enough."

"Jesus, Castellano, I wish you wouldn't be so nervous," Barney commented as they were coming back from their *n*th consultation. "The kid looks fine to me. I mean, I've kept up with my neurology. Why are we worrying so damn much?"

"You can deny it all you want, Barn. But you *know* about brain development—a third of the intercellular connections are formed *after* birth. The neural ridges are still developing in Harry's sweet little head, and some of the pathways might have been blocked while that Iranian asshole was romancing the nurses. Now, be honest—doesn't that make you nervous, too?"

"No," he replied matter-of-factly.

"Are you telling the truth?"

"No," he answered candidly. "But I figured I could be more supportive if I lied."

She looked at him with grateful affection.

"You're holding your breath, aren't you, Barn?"

"Yeah," he replied tersely. And after brooding for a moment he added, "It's murder, isn't it? That sonovabitch Muhradi handed us a bundle of joy—and a time bomb. If only he had told us the truth. I mean, however bad the truth was—but the *truth*—we could at least sleep at night. If I knew Harry would have to go to a special school or something, I wouldn't love him any less. . . ."

He did not need a word from Laura to know she agreed.

"So why the hell couldn't he be honest with us?"

"Maybe he was worried about a malpractice suit."

"He damn well should be—he was negligent as hell. If Harry turns out not to be okay, I'll go back and strangle the guy."

They rode on in silence. Laura stared blankly out of the taxi window and at last muttered, "He's one of those holier-than-thou types."

"What?"

"You know, the kind of doctor who thinks he's not answerable to anybody but God—and maybe not even then. He's not the first of that ilk that I've come across."

"Me, either."

"Are you going to write about them in your book?"

He nodded. "I've already outlined a chapter called 'Doctors Who Lie.' The only problem is I can't write it yet."

"How come?"

"Because I'm still too goddamn angry."

*   *   *

And so they continued watching, ever on the alert for the minutest irregularity, the tiniest sign of impairment. In short, the slightest hint that Harry was not *perfect*.

If nothing else, their offspring was perceptive. Through some as-yet-undiscovered baby sensory system, he seemed to know what his parents were thinking and tried to allay their fears at the earliest opportunity.

At six weeks old he smiled. They could both remember the precise circumstances. Estelle, on one of her frequent trips from Miami to dote on her grandchild, had brought Harry a multicolored "gym" to go across the top railings of his crib.

Laura shook the plastic blocks to illustrate that each was not only a different color but made a different sound.

The tinkle of the red one made him smile.

Thank God, they thought to themselves, one hurdle cleared.

The next big milestone would be when—or if—he would sit up. And Harry dutifully obliged by sitting up in his cot well before his seven-month deadline.

And then—wonder of wonders—just a week after his first birthday, he took five wobbly steps from Barney's easy chair to Laura's arms. The boy was indeed a champion!

All Barney could do was repeat again and again, "Thank God, Laura. Thank God, the kid's okay." And think to himself, *So far.*

And then one evening when they both were bathing him, Barney was struck by yet another fear. "I only hope we haven't freaked him out by letting him sense all our anxiety."

"I don't know, Barn," Laura said, lifting their cherubic treasure out of the water and placing him in the towel held out by his father. "We've got at least another year to wait. I mean, there's still time for all kinds of subtle cerebral abnormalities to manifest themselves."

"Thanks, Castellano, thanks a lot," he muttered.

"What for?"

Barney looked up from the table on which he was powdering Harry and replied, "You just gave me an incredible gift—another three hundred and sixty-five nights of worry."

Barney's first patient was at 7 A.M. But he got up at five-thirty to be sure of having a few quiet moments with his son. To indulge in the joy of changing his diapers, giving him his bottle, burping him—and all the mundane things he never dreamed would bring such ineffable pleasure.

While Harry sucked his breakfast, Barney would lecture him on current events, literature, philosophy, and sports. Not because he thought this would make his son grow up to be more intellectual, but just to talk to him and hear him gurgle in response.

And he hated like hell when the unsympathetic kitchen clock told him he'd have to put Harry down again.

Laura and Barney had a serious argument. She insisted that Harry's first spoken syllables (at eight and a half months) were "Da-da," and he stubbornly insisted they were "Dak-ta"—which indicated his already-chosen profession.

Being a fully psychoanalyzed psychoanalyst, Barney knew enough not to put pressure on his growing son. Which is why he bought a fireman's helmet *as well as* a doctor kit for Harry's second birthday.

That summer they moved to Connecticut. Although it meant long train rides for both of them (Laura had cut her hospital commitments to one day a week), it would give their cherished offspring the fresh air, the greenery, the trees that had been less abundant during their own childhoods.

Overcompensating for his scarcity during the week, Barney lavished attention on Harry during weekends. Yet the boy was already showing such precocious signs of good social interaction that he sometimes preferred the company of the two toddlers from next door—who had a sandbox. Indeed, from the way their son behaved, both Laura and Barney agreed that Harry was longing for a sibling and decided to comply.

It was, of course, a pleasure to attempt to start production. But when things did not go right for seven months, Laura went to see her gynecologist, who told her that she needed surgery that would make further children inconceivable.

Thus all they had, and ever would have, was their little Harry.

The night that Laura found out, she and Barney swore an oath to each other they would not make Harry a neurotic kid—overprotected, overwatched, and overburdened with the weight of their expectations.

Laura had found herself initiated into the world's largest secret society—motherhood.

The days went by without her knowing how she had spent them. And yet her memories were visible and tangible: the playdough coloring on her hands, a flower Harry presented to her, slightly scrunched from being carried in his little fist.

Once when they were walking (Harry toddling) by a pond, they stopped to feed the ducks.

"Mommy, why ducks not wear shoes?"

Laura, unprepared for esoterica like this, could only say, "Actually, I've never noticed that. Perhaps your daddy knows. We'll ask him when he comes home."

And at dinner, when Barney asked, "What did you guys do today?" she usually said "Nothing special." But what she really thought was, Everything was special, everything was *magic*, really.

In fact, something selfish in her kept repeating, Don't grow up, Harry—stay like this forever.

Laura felt a painful wrench the first day that she left her child at his playschool (for three hours). In fact, she sobbed long after Harry was happily playing Simon Says with his new friends. ("He's so young, Barn," she had said plaintively the night before, "he's just a *baby*.")

She had never before realized how totally involved she was in loving him and therefore—even for so short a time—missing him.

Though they had pledged not to hover and examine, they could not help but notice that as his third birthday neared, Harry was ever-so-slightly lethargic. And although his girth was increasing, he was not gaining weight.

One night when Laura was washing him, she called Barney into the bathroom.

"Feel this," she said solemnly, touching Harry's belly.

He placed his hand where hers had been ("Ow, Daddy, that hurts!") and knew exactly what was on her mind—enlargement of the liver and spleen—a condition that bears the daunting name of hepatosplenomegaly.

It was the nightmare they had lived through in their minds.

But *this* was not what they had feared. This had nothing whatsoever to do with brain development. This was something altogether different.

At six the next morning, after a night of tortured self-recrimination ("We should never have let him play out in the rain that day." "It's my fault, I put too many blankets on his bed."), Barney called Adam Parry.

"Bring him in for tests so we can see what's going on," the pediatrician ordered.

In twenty-four hours Harry Livingston's milieu changed from the sandbox to the hospital ward. There were definitely signs of pathologic process.

But what? The staff performed innumerable blood tests ("No more needles, *please*," Harry yowled)—and repeated those that did not satisfy Laura.

"These are all to make you well, darling," she said to try and mollify him.

"I don't like this place. I want to go home."

At which Barney, now a silent witness, found the strength to say, "We all want to go home."

The doctors found that because of his enlarged spleen, Harry had anemia and thrombocytopenia—a low supply of platelets in the blood. He was at risk for rupture of the spleen.

And now an endless stream of specialists marched to and from Harry's bedside. They were tall; they were short; they were fat; they were thin. Yet all had *one* thing in common: they left the ward shrugging their shoulders.

Laura and Dr. Parry wracked their brains for possible diagnoses. Were not the signs best explained by Gaucher's disease?

To which Parry replied, "They are, but you could also make a case of metachromatic leukodystrophy—and it's neither. Listen, Laura, you're a colleague, so I can be frank with you. I don't know what the hell he has. And I don't know how the hell to treat it. All I know is that it's progressing . . ."

Barney tried his best to keep up with his sickest patients, but spent every spare minute either with Harry or in the Med School library, researching childhood diseases.

Warren called each day and asked if there was something, *anything*, he or Bunny could do.

"Yeah," Barney answered. "And don't take this the wrong way, War—but please just leave us alone." And then he added, "And please don't tell Mom."

They both slept in the hospital, which is to say the hospital was where they didn't sleep. For how could they? Every hour seemed to mark further deterioration in their child's condition.

If they slept, Laura said grimly, they might miss a whole hour of Harry's life.

They sat up, sheaves of paper between them, and tried to find some common link in the various reports of all the different specialists who had examined Harry.

"There's got to be a clue," Barney insisted, "some common denominator."

Laura looked at him with desperate sadness in her eyes and said, "Face it, Barney. Even if we do find out, it'll probably be too late."

"No, Castellano, no," he responded with quiet anger. "You try to get some sleep. I'm going to use the hospital computer and see what I can get from our linkup with the National Library of Medicine. At this hour of the morning there's probably no one else waiting to use it."

He left and she lay down into a semiconsciousness that neither dulled her pain nor gave her rest.

Her next recollection was of an unshaven Barney standing over her bed, a computer printout in his hand.

"I know what it is," he said somberly.

"Are you sure?"

He nodded. "Three cheers for computer science. Now I know exactly what our son is gonna die of."

She sat up, reached for her glasses, and took the paper from him.

"I'll save you the trouble of reading it, Laura. It's called RSS—the 'Reeve-Strasburger Syndrome.' "

"I've never heard of it."

"It was first discovered in the late eighteen-nineties by some guys in London. It's a lipid storage disease that affects the myelin coating on all the nerves. I found an article in a Norwegian journal that explains its cause. Abnormal myelin is produced because of the lack of a single enzyme—aryl sulfatase B."

"You mean like multiple sclerosis?" she asked.

"No, that's related but a little different. MS results in *de*-myelination. But the abnormal myelin in RSS not only coats nerves, it also accumulates in places like the liver and spleen."

"Jesus, Barn, what you're saying makes sense. I'll call Parry at home."

"It can wait, Laura," Barney replied in a state beyond exhaustion, "there's no need to hurry for this one."

"Why? How is it treated? Did the machine give you any answers?"

He nodded. "Here, take your pick. Bone marrow transplant, liver transplant, antileukemic chemotherapy. A magnificent range of possibilities."

He paused, and as he felt his throat tightening, said, "None of them works. In fact, there's no record of anyone surviving past the age of four."

At this moment he suddenly snatched the papers from her hand.

"What the hell was that for?"

"There's no point in your reading about it. It's the ultimate bitch disease. None of the senses are untouched. Christ, did we hit the jackpot."

Laura crumpled, sobbing, into Barney's arms.

Adam Parry arrived a little before seven, studied Barney's notes, and, having more or less digested the various specialists' reports, confirmed that Harry was indeed suffering from RSS.

"Although," he confessed, "I don't know where the hell this leaves us."

Laura answered softly, "It leaves us with Harry for just a few more weeks."

"No, goddammit!" Barney snapped. "We're gonna find a way. We're gonna shake the trees for every kind of doctor or faith healer—we'll even go to Lourdes—I don't give a damn what. As long as Harry's breathing we're gonna keep on fighting. I'm going to my own office and make a few calls. Laura, you phone the guy you used to work for in Children's Hospital."

Before she could nod, he was out the door.

Laura returned to their cubbyhole and began telephoning. First the Harvard expert.

"RSS?" asked the astonished voice.

"Yes, Professor," Laura said softly.

"My God, I don't think I've ever seen an actual case. Listen—would it be okay if I came down to New York—?"

"Of course."

"And can I bring some of my residents? This is probably the only chance they'll ever get to see the disease."

Laura slammed down the phone. Then she called Dain Oliver at NIH. And asked him to check the records. Here she received not only consolation but some elucidation. After all, the NIH had data that hadn't yet been published.

"Laura, there's at least a theoretical way of approaching a possible cure."

I want more than theory, Dain, she thought inwardly, but forced herself to listen.

"An abnormal myelin results from the absence of just one enzyme."

"I know, I know," she said impatiently, "aryl sulfatase B."

"So the problem is clear. You have to get the missing enzyme back into his body. Now, as I see it, there are three possible ways."

"What?" she asked, now breathless.

"First you might try a transplant of histocompatible skin fibroblasts. Of course, you'll have to find a matched donor and that could take time."

"Has it ever worked?" Laura asked.

"It's never been tried," Dain answered.

Okay, Laura thought to herself, let's put *that* on hold. We may not have time to find a donor, much less perform the experiment.

"What are your other two ideas?"

"You might try the technique that's used to treat kids with osteogenic sarcoma."

"You mean, first the poison, then the antidote to kill the killer cells? It's too risky. What's the third alternative?"

"Well," her former boss said with a sudden awkwardness in his voice, "there are people at the Institutes working on creating a laboratory model of the enzyme."

"How close are they, Dain?" she asked urgently.

"It's in the pipeline," Dain replied apologetically. "We're talking years, maybe two, maybe three. What can I say, Laura?"

"Dain, you have records of what's happening in every lab everywhere. Has anyone made advances in this field?"

"Well, actually the West Coast has several groups trying to duplicate all kinds of enzymes—mostly private firms. In fact, there's one person who seems to have the jump on everybody. But he's very peculiar and I doubt if you could even get to talk to him."

"Just tell me who he is, Dain, please," Laura implored, thinking, If this guy's got an answer, I'll crawl on my hands and knees all the way to California.

"He's with a very high-powered little firm called Neobiotics—a professionally discredited genius named Peter Wyman, who—"

"I know him," Laura said, quickly cutting him off. "Give me his phone number and I'll do the rest. What's the name of that firm again?"

"Neobiotics. It's in Palo Alto."

"Thank you, Dain, I can't tell you how much I appreciate this."

He gave her the number. Then, with a helplessness that she could feel across the telephone wires, he said, "I wish there were more I could do, Laura. I'm so sorry for you."

"Thanks," she answered, barely audibly, and let the receiver slip from her hands onto its cradle.

An instant later she was dialing California.

But the receptionist said firmly, "I'm sorry, but Dr. Wyman's rules are that he is never to be disturbed when he's working in his lab."

"Tell him that it's Laura Castellano—and it's literally a matter of life and death."

Moments passed, and then a facetious voice.

"Well, well, how is Harvard Med School's answer to Marilyn Monroe?"

Laura was not about to waste precious time on verbal niceties. "I've got to see you, Peter. I've got to see you as soon as possible."

"That's very flattering," he said, laughing. "But I'm a married man. You should have declared your feelings sooner."

"Please," Laura beseeched, "we'll take the next plane to San Francisco."

"May I inquire who 'we' is?"

"My husband, Barney, myself, and our little boy. He's very sick, Peter. We need to see you right away."

"Why me? I'm a research scientist, Laura. I don't practice medicine."

"There's a special reason."

He sighed a weary sigh.

"All right," he replied grudgingly. "I suppose the least disruptive time would be in the late evening. Most of the lab staff are gone by then—it's when I do my most creative thinking. If you could drop by tomorrow evening after ten—"

"What about tonight?"

"Is it that urgent?"

"Yes, Peter. And if you'll only say the word, we can still catch the noon flight."

"Well, I must say," he replied in peacock tones, "this is making me extremely curious. Anyway, it will be nice seeing you again, Laura."

"Thanks, Peter. We'll—"

"I can't really say the same about that husband of yours, but if he comes with the package . . ."

"Goodbye, Peter, we've got to catch that plane."

While Laura got the necessary apparatus to keep Harry stable during the journey, Barney called the airport. Three hours later they were airborne to San Francisco.

They had told only Adam Parry where they were going.

"You do realize," he had warned sympathetically, "that you may be coming back with no more answers than you have now?"

"We realize *everything*," Barney had replied.

Harry was almost comatose from all his medication, and Barney and Laura took turns holding him in their laps. Not because there wasn't room for him on the middle seat, but because they needed to touch him—both for his sake and for their own.

So that if the worst occurred, they would at least have precious tactile memories. How it felt to press him to her breast. How it felt to hold him with an embrace so tight Barney was afraid he might be crushing him.

It was primal. Barney wanted to shield his son from everything bad. He kept murmuring to reassure all three of them, "Mommy and Daddy will never let you go. Never, never, never. We're here, Harry, we're here."

At the same time, Laura was obsessively thinking, If I could only take you back inside me, Harry. So I could *protect* you.

"What a sweet little boy," cooed a stewardess, "and so well-behaved. Is this his first flight?"

Laura nodded. "Yes." And, she thought, maybe his last.

At the airport they rented a car and drove immediately to the University Inn near the Stanford campus in Palo Alto.

Barney and Laura were exhausted from the journey, the time change, and most of all the tension. They fought to stay awake till the appointed hour with the imperious Wyman. (It would be 1 A.M. in their body time.) And they discussed strategy incessantly. Should Laura go alone? Should she go with Harry? Or should all three of them go? Would Peter react with revulsion at the sight of two Med School classmates he knew loathed him? Or would he show compassion for a grieving couple whose only child had days, perhaps hours to live?

Finally, Barney decided for them.

"We're all going together, Laura. I want that bastard to look into my eyes. And into yours. And at Harry—and see if there's a molecule of humanity in his granite soul."

They drove along El Camino Real to a surprisingly modest rectangular brick building, whose small illuminated sign read NEOBIOTICS, INC.

As soon as Barney pulled up at the gate, however, he realized where this corporation had spent its money. Two armed security men asked them both to step out and be frisked. They even made Laura unwind the blanket in which she was holding Harry.

After passing through a glass door, manned by another pair of sentries, they reached the reception desk, at which yet one more guard was seated.

They identified themselves and were told to wait.

They sat down, now cradling their sleeping child across both their laps. They checked the clock on the waiting room wall. It was seven minutes to ten. Barney and Laura exchanged weary glances of disbelief. Neither was really sure why they were here. It would probably turn out to be merely a West Coast blind alley.

And Harry chose this of all times to wake and, frightened by the strange surroundings, began to wail. Laura had just managed to calm him down when Peter Wyman appeared in his white lab coat.

"Well, hello, old friends," he said, sarcastically. "You're a long way from civilization. What brings the mountain to Mohammad?"

Laura said quietly, "This is Harry, our little boy, Peter."

"Oh," said their erstwhile classmate.

It was an awkward moment, and Barney asked uneasily, "Uh, can we go inside somewhere and talk?"

Peter glanced at his watch.

"I do hope this won't take too long."

Barney took hold of Harry, and lifted him as he stood up.

"Don't sweat, Peter. We won't waste your precious time."

They had a sense that he wanted them to see his office: his huge desk, his space-age telephone equipment, his numerous trophies on the wall. He wanted them to see that though in Harvard's myopic eyes he was an outcast, to the real world he was a giant. Indeed, growing taller by the minute.

"Okay," he said when he had seated himself in his massive leather chair. "What seems to be the problem?"

Barney had rehearsed his speech a million times during the flight. Now he blurted out the essential details. Their only hope for Harry would be an infusion of the purified enzyme.

"I agree," said Peter, looking interested for the first time. "That might very well do the trick. But, as you both know, the Food and Drug Administration sets up strict guidelines for the approval of a new drug for use in humans. I mean, they wouldn't want another Thalidomide episode, would they? And my synthetic ASB is only in 'the trial stages.' So it would be totally illegal for me to give it to you. I could go to jail."

"We wouldn't tell, Peter, I swear it," Barney said desperately.

Peter ignored him.

"Besides, we're only halfway through our animal trials. Now, wouldn't I be irresponsible—not to mention criminal—if I administered to your child a substance that hasn't got the *Good Housekeeping* Seal of Approval? I mean, we all realize it might work. I'm confident it would. But at this point, even I couldn't say how long it would work for." And then he added, "There's also the possibility that it could kill him."

At this point Laura broke down.

"Please, Peter, don't let him die without at least having a chance."

Barney stood up and demanded, "Listen, Wyman, you took the Hippocratic Oath with all of us. Forget the FDA. *Look at my dying son.* Are you just gonna let us walk out of here and take him to his grave?"

Slightly cowed by Barney's bluntness, Peter looked nervously at his watch.

Nobody moved.

Then Barney spoke again. "Did you understand what I just said, Peter?"

"I haven't practiced medicine for quite some time. And certainly not pediatrics. But your son looks very sick to me. Why don't you take him to Children's Hospital and get him into bed with an I.V.?"

"And then what?" Barney demanded.

"Then I'll call you at ten o'clock tomorrow night."

"No sooner?" Laura implored.

"I need some time to think about it," said Wyman dryly. "This is a pretty serious thing. Make sure one of my secretaries knows how to reach you."

They walked numbly out of his office, down the long corridors, through the glass door, past the guards, and out to their car. In silence.

Harry was asleep against his daddy's shoulder. Barney could feel the warmth of his son's cheek. He's got fever, Barney thought to himself.

"What do you think, Castellano?" His voice was hoarse from emotion.

"I think he's right in one sense, Barn. We ought to get Harry to the hospital. I think he would be safer there."

The Livingstons found human beings at San Francisco Children's Hospital. Caring people, who dispensed with all the red tape so they could get Harry into bed and on a drip as soon as possible.

Too worn out to move anywhere, Barney and Laura slept on mattresses in Harry's room. They woke early. The time change was still messing up their body clocks. And after seeing that their son's condition was stable, they started out to find the cafeteria so they could get some coffee. They had just reached the elevator when a nurse called to them from her station.

"Dr. Livingston—there's a phone call for you."

They both sprinted madly back.

"Who is it?" Barney asked the nurse.

"It's Dr. Goldstein, our head of Pediatrics. She says she knows you both."

"Goldstein?" Laura asked an equally puzzled Barney. "Does that mean anything to you?"

Barney shrugged and then picked up the phone.

"This is Dr. Livingston."

"Welcome to San Francisco," said a female voice with a special lilt he still remembered.

Suzie Hsiang.

"Suzie! Are *you* Dr. Goldstein?"

"By virtue of marriage to Dr. Mike Goldstein," she replied. "I saw your name on the overnight admissions list and I wanted to know if I could help."

"That's very kind," Barney replied, "but unless you discovered a cure for RSS last night, I don't think you can. Still, if you're free, we'd love you to have a cup of coffee with us in the cafeteria."

"I'll come down as soon as I've taken a look at your little boy."

Barney and Laura were toying with their scrambled eggs when Suzie came into the near-deserted cafeteria.

"He's a lovely child," she said warmly. And then more somberly, "But he is awfully sick. What brings you all the way out here?"

"It's a long story," Barney sighed.

Yet by now he was used to presenting the case with a minimum of words.

"But Wyman's got to help you," Suzie stated emphatically. "I mean, he must have some human feelings."

"Don't bet on it," Laura remarked. "He gives a pretty good imitation of a stone."

"So when is he letting you know?"

"At ten tonight."

"Why does he need so much time?"

"I don't know," Barney replied, "the workings of Peter's mind are beyond my capacity to understand."

"Why don't you come out to my parents' house before you go back to see him? You could have a real Cantonese dinner—and besides, I'd like you to meet my father."

They did not know what to say. On one hand, they wanted to be alone with Harry. On the other hand, they knew that any distraction from their chilling, persistent fear would be welcome.

"Let me give you the address. It's easy to find from here. I'm only sorry Mike is at a Nephrology congress in Texas. Anyway, if you want to, we're all at home by six o'clock."

They exchanged thanks, and Suzie excused herself to hurry back to her rounds.

They spent the day at Harry's bedside. Their only dialogue, "What time is it?" The answer always, "Just two minutes later than the last time you asked."

Late that afternoon they bundled up their little son—who had slept most of the day—and asked that he be discharged. For they had decided that if Wyman said no, they wanted to be alone with Harry—out of the hospital—when he died.

A little before six, they walked up the hill from Union Square and through the ornate green and white pagodalike gateway whose dragons seemed to be saying, Lay down your newfangled Western ideas, and come in to an older, wiser, Eastern world.

The main thoroughfare was lined with touristy trinket shops, offering China-in-a-packet to take home to the folks in South Dakota. But branching to the right and left were smaller streets such as Kearney and Washington, which were decorated to make the Chinese residents feel at home: lanternlike street lamps illuminated the sidewalks, which at intersections bore the names of the streets in both English and Chinese.

"Look, Harry," Barney said with manic, desperate enthusiasm, "isn't this great? Can you imagine how Marco Polo felt when he first saw stuff like this?"

Laura said nothing. And merely indulged Barney, whose rational mind knew that Harry was far too febrile to comprehend what he was saying. Still, Barney was desperately trying to cram as many years of life into him as he could.

Suzie's parents lived in a ground floor apartment on Jackson. A Chinese placard in the window announced, they presumed, that this was the office of a practitioner of Oriental medicine, whose origins antedated Hippocrates by at least two thousand years. Dr. Hsiang, his wife, Suzie, and Suzie's unmarried younger sister were seated, dressed in silken robes drinking tea. The elderly man rose when the visitors entered and said something in Cantonese.

Suzie translated: "Father welcomes you to our home and says he shares your sorrow about your son. He wonders perhaps if you would allow him to examine Harry?"

Barney and Laura looked at each other.

What the hell harm could it do? Laura thought to herself. He's a real doctor, after all. Just not *our* kind of doctor.

Barney nodded to the elderly man and said, "Thank you very much."

Dr. Hsiang beckoned them into another room, stacked floor to ceiling with boxes of herbs, each identified by Chinese characters. They put their feverish child on his examination table and each held a hand while the doctor slowly and painstakingly placed his fingers on various parts of Harry's arm.

Just the arm?

"He's taking twelve different pulses," Suzie explained. "That's our traditional way of diagnosis."

Dr. Hsiang then opened Harry's mouth and with a magnifying glass scrutinized his tongue. He said something in rapid Chinese to Suzie.

"Father says he can prepare a medicine for your son and would like your permission to perform some acupuncture."

"Will it hurt?" Barney asked.

"No," Susie explained, "not when my father does it."

Once again, Barney and Laura communicated merely by a glance— and agreed. Their eyes were saying to each other, We'll take any chance.

The procedure took nearly half an hour, with Doctor Hsiang concentrating his needles mostly on and around the little boy's ear. He then excused himself to go and prepare an herbal medicine.

"Is Harry able to drink?" Suzie asked.

"Yes," Laura answered, "thank God."

Harry was awake when they finally sat down to dinner. He looked saucer-eyed at the rich colors of what he no doubt imagined were the Hsiangs' party costumes. Pointing to the brocaded design on Mrs. Hsiang's *cheongsam,* he murmured, "Mommy, look at the birdies."

Mrs. Hsiang, perhaps understanding him, perhaps merely intuiting, smiled at the boy. Then Harry turned to Laura and inquired, "Why is everybody in pajamas?"

To which Barney replied, "That's probably because they're going to bed early. Not like you, champ, you get to stay up really late tonight."

To Laura's relief, he was taking liquids better. Not just the medicine that Dr. Hsiang had carefully mixed, for she could tell from his expression that it tasted awful. But he even sipped some of the soup.

When it was time to leave, the doctor gave them a small bottle of Harry's herbal medicine, to be given twice more that evening and again the next day. Laura thanked him politely.

It was only nine-thirty when they arrived at the motel, but there was a message awaiting them. "Please meet Dr. Wyman at ten tonight."

*   *   *

Naturally, they were there early, for they had construed this invitation as his acceptance of their plea.

And they were right. Although, even in generosity, Wyman remained incorrigible.

"Now I don't want any blubbering or thank-you's—especially since we don't know for sure what effect it will have. If you must know, I decided to do this because I believe you two will shut up about it."

He handed them a manila envelope. Barney could feel it contained several glass ampoules.

"Try giving him one ten-mil shot—and if he tolerates it, double the dosage two hours later. Then t.i.d. for another forty-eight hours. I've given you a supply of disposable syringes—on the house."

Laura nodded.

"I'd be grateful if you didn't inject the kid on company property. And let me know whatever happens—it could be vital in my research."

How does one say *thank-you* to this glacial bastard? Wyman solved that problem for them by looking at his watch and announcing, "I'd better go."

And yet he did not move. They could both sense that he was struggling to say something more.

At last Peter muttered, "I—uh—know how I'd feel if it was one of my own kids. I mean . . ."

Unable to complete his thought, Peter simply walked over and stroked Harry's cheek. Then, before his visitors could say another word, he swept out.

They drove back to the motel at breakneck speed, rushed to their room, placed Harry gently on the bed, and immediately closed the curtains.

Then they looked at one another helplessly.

"Do you want me to inject him?" Barney asked softly.

"I can do it," she replied numbly.

Barney then confessed, "Please, Castellano. I'm no good with needles. And I can't stick one into my own son."

Harry yelled as Laura injected an ampoule of the fluid into his buttock. And then he suddenly went quiet.

They were terrified. Had they killed him?

They stood like statues on either side of the bed, staring at their son.

After a few seconds that seemed like an eternity, Laura leaned over and put her fingers on Harry's wrist.

"He's got a pulse, Barn. It's as steady as before."

"Do you think the medicine conked him out?"

She shook her head. "We've all had a helluva two days. Imagine how tired he must be."

Then she gathered Harry in her arms and held him close.

Barney touched his son's forehead. "Still like the Sahara Desert," he commented. "How long's it been since you gave him the shot?"

"Four, maybe five minutes. Stay loose, Barn. Even if it *is* a miracle drug . . ."

The word "miracle" stuck in her throat. If there is a God, she thought, He doesn't owe me any favors.

"Laura," Barney said softly, "lie down—or at least *sit*."

"I'm too nervous," she replied, gently placing Harry on the bed.

"Would you like something from room service?" he offered.

"I'm not hungry—are you?"

"No, but it passes the time. And . . . it gives me something to *do*."

"There are some vending machines down the corridor—why not get something from there?"

He welcomed the assignment. "What can I bring you?"

"Nothing—anything. As long as it doesn't taste good."

He knew what she was saying: I abjure all earthly delights—even the sweetness of a candy bar—so that my abstinence might prove the final molecule of sacrifice needed to placate an angry divinity. He darted out of the room.

The long corridor was carpeted in what seemed like gray Astroturf. Racing down it gave Barney some physical release.

But he could not outrun his thoughts.

Oh, Christ, Harry, the dreams I had of the two of us jogging together along a leaf-strewn forest path. How we would talk, man to man. How I was gonna tell you all the stupid mistakes I made in my life—so you could learn from them. What can I teach you *now*?

At this moment all I want is for you to keep breathing. Something I can't teach you. Or do for you.

He walked slowly back to the room, carrying two drinks in paper cups.

Laura was seated now, staring at Harry's face, afraid to blink lest she miss the minutest hint of change.

"He hasn't moved," she announced like an automaton.

"Maybe it's just a deep sleep. Did you notice any REM eye movements?"

"No."

In other words, if he was sleeping, he wasn't dreaming.

Laura placed her Coke on the night table, and merely took out a piece of ice to suck. All the while, her eyes never left Harry. Perhaps her overwhelming feelings of love could somehow heal him.

"Can we talk?" Barney asked hesitantly.

Laura nodded. "What do you want to talk about?"

"Oh, you know, stuff. Like should he go to public school or prep school. Or you could talk about yourself."

"What could I possibly tell you that you don't already know?" she said, smiling wearily.

"You could speculate on what your life would have been if your folks hadn't emigrated to Brooklyn. . . ."

She looked at him and answered without words. Her eyes were saying, Without you I would have nothing to live for.

Which he believed with equal fervor.

But they both were wondering how—or if—they could survive the loss of Harry.

No, dammit. We don't have to face that yet. They could not even face the thought.

"Can I hold him a little, please?"

Somehow half an hour passed. Barney touched the sleeping boy's forehead. He looked up at Laura and said with perhaps self-induced optimism, "Castellano, I think his fever's down."

Laura felt Harry's face, looked at Barney, and said to herself, Wishful thinking. But she answered, "Maybe, Barn." And thought, Let him cherish his illusions if they keep him sane.

The sick boy continued to sleep while Laura and Barney breathed to the clock, waiting for a hundred and twenty minutes to pass, so that they could try the second dose.

This time the shot wakened Harry, and Laura wanted to take advantage of the moment to get some more liquid into him. But all they had at hand was Coke and Dr. Hsiang's potion. She opted for the herbal drink.

Though half-asleep and febrile, Harry had strong opinions. As Laura brought the medicine to his lips he shook his head and protested, "Yech, want appa juice."

"Tell you what, kiddo," Laura cajoled, "you drink some of this stuff, and I promise you'll have all the apple juice you want tomorrow."

At which point his thirst overcame his taste buds and Harry swallowed, grimacing.

"How do you feel?" Barney asked his son.

"I feel sleepy, Daddy," Harry replied.

"Well," Barney replied in his best imitation of happy-go-lucky. "Why not go to beddie-bye?" His voice dropped, "Sleep's good for you."

By the time they each had kissed him he was slumbering again.

Laura put him down, and they returned to their posts on either side of his bed to continue their watch.

By now they were too frightened even to speak to one another, and so Barney flicked on the radio, found a San Francisco all-talk station, and half-listened to a debate on the subject of topless restaurants. ("If they can have nude beaches, why can't women show their boobs anywhere they want? I mean, man, the law's got to be consistent.")

After fifteen minutes of silent brooding, Barney interrupted the broadcast colloquium and murmured, "Do you believe this, Castellano? Two qualified doctors are actually sitting in a motel in Loonyland with a dying child trying to believe that some egomaniac's snake oil is gonna save the kid's life. Do you think we're in our right minds?"

Laura shook her head. "I don't know," she confessed. "I honestly don't know." She paused for a moment and then, looking straight at Barney, added, "But if Harry dies I don't want to go on living—"

"Laura—"

"I mean it, Barney. And you won't be able to stop me."

He protested no further, knowing that he himself was not sure how he could live . . . without his son.

All the while they could hear Harry's breathing rise and fall as the radio host, still broadcasting, was questioning a caller from the so-called Church of Eros. Their situation was getting too serious. Barney rose and shut off the babble.

He looked at Harry and touched his forehead once again.

This time he was certain.

"Castellano, I swear to God, he's got *no* fever. Come on, feel."

But Laura did not have to feel; she could tell merely by the change in Harry's color that Barney was right. She quickly palpated his abdomen.

"Oh, good Christ," she said, "his spleen."

"What?" Barney asked in terror

"His spleen is less enlarged, Barn. *It's already less enlarged.* I think this damn thing is gonna work!"

They kept vigil through the night. This time not watching their son die but rather watching him return to life.

At seven-thirty in the morning, Laura startled Barney by saying, "I want to go to church."

Barney nodded. "I know just how you feel."

Laura put it into words. "Barn, I have to say *thank-you* to someone. And today for once I hope there is a God to hear me."

"You're right, let's all go."

They looked at their son, who was sitting up in bed.

"Mommy, I wanna go home," squealed little Harry. "My teddy misses me."

The Stanford University Chapel was a mere five-minute, tree-lined walk from the motel. At this early hour the huge cathedral-like building (belying its humble designation) was so empty and silent they could almost hear one another's hearts beating.

For the first time in her adult life, Laura knelt to pray—and did not know how to begin. But she bowed her head, that and hoped her thoughts would reach the proper destination.

Barney stood, holding Harry in his arms, and gazed at his son. The soft early light shining through the tall stained-glass windows played on his face, making it glow with a kind of magic aura.

And for a moment he could reflect calmly on the dark night of the soul—or was it night of wonder?—he and Laura and Harry had just experienced.

What *was* it, he asked himself. Wyman's enzyme? The Chinese potion? A doctor's touch? A parent's love?

He had spent most of his lifetime studying the art of medicine and realized now that he would never really understand its mysteries.

For medicine is an eternal quest for reasons—causes that explain effects.

Science cannot comprehend a miracle.

Laura stood up. "I'd like to hold him now," she whispered.

Barney returned Harry to his mother's arms. He embraced Laura and their son. And they walked out together into the morning sunshine.

ACKNOWLEDGMENTS

Though in the course of researching this book I walked hospital corridors with a name tag that legitimately identified me as "Dr. Segal," my degree is in comparative literature, not comparative anatomy. I therefore had to rely in great measure on many secondary sources as well as the medical knowledge of several experts who are not only good doctors but good friends.

They include Professor A. B. Ackerman M.D., of the New York University Medical School; Professor Alan Beer M.D., of the Chicago Medical School; Dennis Gath M.D., of Oxford University; Professor Norman Charles M.D., of NYU; the late William W. Heroy M.D., Chief of Surgery at the Huntington (N.Y.) Hospital; Dr. Geoffrey Leder of the Devonshire Hospital, London; Professor John Leventhal M.D., of Harvard Medical School; Alison Reeve M.D., of the National Institutes of Health; Rodney Rivers M.D., of St. Mary's Medical School, London; Professor Richard Selzer M.D., of Yale; and Professor Victor Strasburger M.D., of the University of New Mexico Medical School.

I am not personally acquainted with Professor Harry Jergesen M.D., of the University of California at San Francisco Medical School, but am grateful that he agreed to wield his scalpel on several crucial scenes.

These generous physicians—and some of their colleagues—read portions of the manuscript (and in the case of my oldest friend, Bernie

Ackerman and Strasburger, the entire book), offering valuable suggestions and pointing out errors of fact and procedure. What scientific mistakes remain result from my invocation of dramatic license or, more likely, my own ignorance.

There are an extraordinary number of books that chronicle the student experience at Harvard Medical School. Since they describe more or less the same events, the accounts are inevitably similar and differ only in their authors' perspectives. Charles LeBaron's stimulating *Gentle Vengeance* was the first of this genre I read and therefore drew upon most often, though I greatly admired Kenneth Klein's *Getting Better,* as well as Melvin Konner's recent *Becoming a Doctor.*

William Nolen's works, especially *The Making of a Surgeon*, were rich in detail and anecdote. I derived much information about the psychiatric *cursus honorum* from David Viscott's *The Making of a Psychiatrist.*

I am also indebted to books by Joseph Califano, David Hellerstein, David Hilfiker, Perri Klass, Elizabeth Morgan, William Nolen, Richard Selzer, and Victor Strasburger, as well as the writings of George E. Vaillant, Professor of Psychiatry at Harvard—particularly his probing and compassionate essay, "Why Doctors Fail to Care for Themselves," prompted by the publication in 1982 of the fact that six M.D.'s of the Harvard class of 1967, people in their late thirties, had already died, all but one from "maladaptive lifestyles." Vaillant's conclusion is chilling: "I fear that this is no more than one of the painful realities of life in an unbelievably demanding profession."

My principal medical reference sources have been *The Oxford Companion to Medicine, The Oxford Textbook of Medicine, The Atlas of General Surgery, The Merck Manual,* and, most often, *Taber's Cyclopedic Medical Dictionary.*

Many of the ethical issues argued at Seth's trial owe their substance to James Rachels's important book *The End of Life: Euthanasia and Morality.* Much of the chronology draws upon the bibliography in William Manchester's *The Glory & the Dream.*

Some of the medical scenes in this novel were based on descriptions by the aforementioned authors—who had already camouflaged the identities and personal details of their patients. Since I, in turn, altered their cases, the result might be called a "fictionalized fiction." There was no intent on my part to identify any physician, hospital, or patient.

There is one exception: the case of Mrs. Carson was drawn directly from Dr. Leon Schwartzenberg's exceptionally moving *Requiem pour la Vie.* I am grateful to the author for permitting me to use several pages of his book almost verbatim.

The law firm of Morgan, Lewis & Bockius, especially Carolyn Jaffe and James B. McKinney of the New York office, was extremely helpful with points of law and judicial procedure. Edie Lederer of the Associated Press provided valuable details of the last days of Saigon.

My thanks, as always, to Jeanne Bernkopf, the only editor who can perform major surgery without an anesthetic.

At various points in this novel, some doctors are treated with sarcasm and deprecation. But in the course of my research, I became increasingly aware that the gruesome deals of malpractice and venality are the sins of a minority whose cynical behavior gives them a higher profile. The medical profession contains far more saints than sinners.

I think Dr. Konner's words in *Becoming a Doctor* express the majority view: "... healing is possible—indeed, it is ubiquitous. It goes on in every creature every day. And among our privileges as the most sentient, most clever creatures on this planet is the ability, occasionally, to perform acts in aid of it. In a spiritual as well as in a technical sense—not just for the sake of healing but for the sake also of meaning—we would do well to take that privilege seriously."

—E.S.